RETURN TO FOREVER

To my good friend Katie)
May God Jesus &
All of The Holy
Angels Bless
you with Peace,
Love & Miracles!
Your Friend Bedy Life

RETURN TO FOREVER

MARK SALVATORE PITIFER

iUniverse, Inc.
New York Bloomington

Return To Forever

iUniverse books may be ordered through booksellers or by contacting:

iUniverse
1663 Liberty Drive
Bloomington, IN 47403
www.iuniverse.com
1-800-Authors (1-800-288-4677)

Because of the dynamic nature of the Internet, any Web addresses or links contained in this book may have changed since publication and may no longer be valid.

*All of the characters and events in this book are fictitious, and any resemblance to actual persons, living or dead, is purely coincidental.

* Edited by: Sharla Pitifer Toups (Poppa's Cloud Inc.)

* Note: The Cover Picture was painted by my son **NOAH PITFER** (8 years old) on 9-11-01, the day of the World Trade Center Bombings. This was also my mother's 63rd birthday. My sister Sharla who worked in the World Trade Center Plaza might have perished, had she not decided to surprise my mother with a birthday visit.

ISBN: 978-0-595-35100-8 (pbk)
ISBN: 978-0-595-67198-4 (cloth)
ISBN: 978-0-595-79802-5 (ebk)

Printed in the United States of America

iUniverse rev. date: 11/20/08

Christopher Cohan (My name is-topher), Lee, Luke & Sophia Lawson, Jeffery "Mellow" Jurjens, JoeyWickum (Never Give Up!), Benny Rozelle Jr., Christopher Mimms, Chris Hunter & Brittany Grady, Mike "Diko" D'Amico & Mary Lou Love, Ray Lerkins & Dan White, Samantha & Tom Meeks, Danielle Morin, Samantha Sargent, Andrew Bounds, Tarentha Johns (Don't Point at me, my momma aint dead!), Douglas & Sonya Crawley (Pitt for Mayor) Carabello, Alex & Tommy Villa, Justin "Full House" Stone, Michael "BUZO" V, Tonya, Michael 3 & 4, Lynn, and the entire Ruiz family, Mary & John Riccione, Eric Mason, Alyssa Bruno, Jake Hoffa, Joey Nucci, Amber Impson, Eric "Lyod Hill" Frederick, Nancy Modera. **Joey Iaconis Jr. (GHS #1 Fan)**, William Robert Cady (Is his name!), Crystal Bruzee (Remember your promise), Gisbert Hanft, **Robert "MVP" Andrews**, Jack Spellecy, Captain Peter Burke, Paul Stivers, Nick & Corey Roof, Daiquan Ellis, Stephen H. Bogart, Jimmy Alexander, Joel Welch Jr., Willie Rivera, & **Tremaine "RC-The Catch" Green**. I love ya man. FTG!

The families of: Romeo "Bandi" Liberio, Lacey "The Root" Mckoy, Ron Lawson, Kennedy Bucklin, Bruce Z. Curtis, Joe Lynch, Elvin Cruz, Michael & Tonya Ruiz (Your family is famous in Heaven!), Irene Greco, Janet & Bill Cole.

GHS Class of 1978-Mark Wilson, Penny 'Collier' Northrup, Jimmy Mallard, David Brind, Jerry Miller, Amy Dunham, Ivan Sanchez & John McFadden. **Also Mike Oyer, Dr. David & Judy Curtis, & Scott Bartucca**

-All of my students & athletes (Believe In Your Dreams!)

-ALWAYS REMEMBER HOW DEEPLY YOU ARE LOVED

<u>*MY PRAYER FOR YOU*</u>
As you go through this Great Game of Life:
May God's Angels guard your every step.
May His Holy Spirit and wisdom dwell in you, and
may His holy power flow through you, and keep you walking bravely
along the Path-of-Jesus, back to the land of our origin.
For we are the Lions Abijah!

EARLY ACCLAIM FOR RETURN TO FOREVER

"The author's very descriptive portrayal of the "afterlife" gives those of us with solid faith in the existence of God, the reassurance of a glorious eternity. However, as importantly, the novel provides for those struggling with their faith, a way to help, "read God's mind." It puts into words a prescription to live one's life, thus securing the glories of an unimaginable Heaven, which the author believes can await us all!"
-DR. STANTON TEPFER

"The time and effort that was put into this book was worth every word. Once you pick it up to read, you don't want to put it down. I wish this book was around while I was growing up. But, I'm glad its here now. This book can touch every soul, and help to bring love, peace, and harmony throughout the world."
-ANN MARIE PITIFER

"I can't thank you enough for writing this book. It continues to alter my perception in such a broad way. I needed this information in the way that our earth needs the sun & water. I was starving and I now feel nourished! Thank you, thank you, thank you!
-JOLENE STAMP & (BELLA)

"Mark Pitifer and his "unexpected prophet of faith, Nino Jones" accomplished what very few have, a way to bring all religions together while still showing the importance of believing in one another. Pitifer does the unimaginable, reminding us that faith is about <u>believing</u> even when the odds are against us. He also shows us that <u>Forever</u> is not just a lifetime … but an eternity.'
-MATTHEW ALLEN BLUE

"Without reliance on secret religious organizations or Da Vinci codes, Return to Forever conveys the simple story of the universality of God's love for all people, and truly presents Heaven as an attainable new beginning for even the least of us all. Mark Salvatore Pitifer's adaptation of earthly tribulations, overlaid with God's grace, transforms perceptions of Heaven being only for saints to a reality for everyday people seemingly trapped by the harsh realities of this world. While we live, there is hope. Return to Forever gives us that hope and, in so doing, perhaps a last chance at redemption and salvation."
-DR. TYRONE SCOTT

"Once you've read Return To Forever you'll wish you could return to it over and over again. It's like a visit with a good old friend that you wish didn't have to end. It educates, enlightens, instills hope and reinforces ones faith in humanity. It will move you to tears, make you laugh out loud and compel you to share it with everyone you know. It will frighten and comfort you all at once and it will change the way you look at everything and everyone. Return To Forever is a journey you will never forget."
-SHARI LYNN MINETTI

"Nino Jones, an elderly homeless man in New York City of the near future, is initiated into God-centered explanations of the cosmos and the meaning of life in a series of discussions with such figures as Pontius Pilate and Malcolm X. Jones is joined by the author himself in the construction of their all-encompassing Narrative, which comes to a climactic ending weaving all the book's themes ingeniously together. Jones is an Everyman for Spiritual America, and Mark Pitifer is his chronicler."
-MARVIN BRAM, Ph.D.

"When I got finished reading Return To Forever I went to church for the first time in 10 years, and I've been going ever since. Thanks a lot Pitt."
-KEVIN KORZENIEWSKI

"In Return To Forever Mark Salvatore Pitifer brings together scientific facts and Biblical truths, with a touch of fantasy to tell the World a beautiful story of hope, faith, and the love and power of one God, and all of his children. Mark answers the question W.W.J.W. (What would Jesus want?) To find your way to the P.O.J. (Path of Jesus) of course. Then you'll know that you will live on "Forever, in Forever!""
-SALLY ANN FRATTO

"Return to Forever points out the beauty that is inherent in all peoples and all religions. It illuminates God's most basic and important message carried to us by Moses, Mohammad, Krishna, Buddha, all the great prophets & holy messengers, and through Jesus Christ which is simply BE KIND. Follow a path of goodness and gentleness, and try your best not to hurt others in any way. When we reach Forever we will find that it was always more important that we did what was right, than that we were right!"
-MARY BAKOGIANNIS

"Return to Forever" is a heartfelt, entertaining adventure that delivers a powerful message to all. It will strengthen your faith and reassure you how important it is to follow a path of goodness, to be kind and selfless, and to enjoy and respect the special gift of life. It teaches us to be grateful for what we have, and to take the time to care and make a difference. Return To Forever is an interesting journey of faith that will lift your heart and make you realize how gifted and blessed we truly are. It will make you think about who you are, and our purpose here in the Great Game!
-DONNA & STEVE VISCO

"God creates a simple yet profound act of love which is intended to draw ("traxit") all creation back to the Creator along the Path of Jesus. Creatures for their part can shroud this path in mystery, or they can clarify this path in simplicity. Mark Salvatore Pitifer has accomplished the latter through the pilgrimage genre. Travel with Mark and Nino, meet some impact players in the "game of life," adjust your perspective to positive, and Return To Forever."
-FATHER MACK SPELLACY

"In his book Return To Forever, Mark Salvatore Pitifer has beautifully expressed what we in our hearts know to be true. That it does not matter by what name we call him, there is only one God."
-SHARON ZIMMERMAN & JOHNNY Z

"Reading <u>Return to Forever</u> provided me with not only a gratifying literary experience, but a true spiritual experience as well. Pitt crafts his characters and situations with care and creativity to deliver a compelling and delightful storyline. Through this story of Nino and Mark, Pitt shares with us his alluring insight on the beautiful Kingdom of Forever, the love and omnipotence of God, and what it means to walk the Path of Jesus.
-DR. RYAN GRAHAM

"Return To Forever is the most inspiring book that I have ever read. The research and the knowledge that you put into this book is just phenomenal, and I really found myself looking at my faith in a whole new perspective. I just can't tell you how much I enjoyed it. When I read about all of the different people that you met throughout your journey, I couldn't help but wonder and believe that maybe you really are a messenger from God. I love you honey. I laughed and I cried throughout the whole book. You really got to me buddy. I called your mother right after I finished and told her how much your book affected me. I felt that sadness that you felt about yourself, and that need to find yourself, and I'm so glad you did. Mark I just love you and I'm so proud to be one of the first people to read your book. It's just beautiful, and I will pass it on to everyone I know. I love you Mark. God Bless you."
-ROSE BRUNO FELICE (A phone message that I will never erase!)

I really liked your book Return To Forever, in fact I am just about to read it again! Your story has really helped me in many ways. It has opened my eyes to a lot of things that I did not see, like drugs. Even though I never used them, I now see that money was my drug. A drug that put me on a path that would ultimately lead to death and jail. So here I sit in this miserable cell, and all I can think about is poor Elvin Cruz and his family. I wish I would have read your book before the night that innocent child was killed. I was told that the gun was only going to be used to scare some people who had been shooting a pistol over their heads all night. Believe me coach no one was ever supposed to get hurt, or I wouldn't have got involved. However, I now see clearly that no matter what my intentions were, the path I was walking is not a good one. Nothing spiritually worthwhile was ever going to come from it... I will now do whatever I am able to help children learn from my mistakes. Maybe God put me in here for a reason. Maybe if I can do something to help kids, Elvin's death and my 23 years in prison will not be in vain. Return To Forever is a book that every kid should read, especially those children who are glamorizing the thug life. I will now help spread your message, and I will never forget you Pitt. You believed in me! Peace & Love.

-TREMAINE "RC-THE CATCH" GREEN

Reading Return to Forever has truly been a life changing experience. This incredible book is both a spiritual and educational guide for all who read it. You will laugh and sometimes cry. It will fill you with serenity and a genuine, kind feeling toward the world and all of the people you encounter in your lifetime. It gives hope and peace to the faithful, knowledge and guidance to those still searching, and faith to those who are without it. Once you complete this journey your eyes will be open...FOREVER!

-MIA PRINCIPIO CALABRESE

If you would like to write to me, please send your letter with a self addressed stamped envelope, and I will answer you as soon as I am able to. My address is: 33 Nagel Place, Geneva, New York 14456. You can also email me at mark@heaventown.net or mpitifer@rochester.rr.com

A NOTE FROM THE EDITOR

"The best and most beautiful things cannot be seen
they must be felt by the heart"
-Helen Keller

*"Greatness is not in where we stand, but in what direction we are moving.
We must sail sometimes with the wind and sometimes against it—But sail
we must, and not drift, nor lie at anchor."*
-Oliver Wendall Holmes

A religious studies class I took in college was called "Journeys and Stories." We read "Malcolm X" and "Black Elk Speaks," and discussed the great transformations each character made during their journeys.

Shortly after I graduated from William Smith College, my brother handed me his first draft of "Return To Forever". It was 800 pages of dialogue, full of spelling and grammar errors. I had no idea that by asking me to edit his story, my brother was sending me on my very own transforming journey.

The "college girl" who read his first draft was full of doubt. Fresh from the classrooms where science usually prevails over faith and women's rights are of the utmost importance, I had a hard time reading Mark's book without wondering how my peers and professors would react to his ideas.

That was 14 years ago....

As I read the second draft I was settling into life in New York City, my eyes already opened to a world much larger than Geneva, New York. The pages of the book came alive as I walked along the same streets Mark and Nino Jones toured. I could no longer pass a homeless man without wondering if he was a messenger from Heaven, or what circumstances landed him on the city sidewalk. As the third draft passed my desk, I was in a building three blocks away from the World Trade Center. The air in my building was tested daily, as was our faith in God. New chapters mentioned the recent tragedy, and I remember thinking that it was important that the book hadn't been completed before this monumental change took place in our world. Finally, as I awaited the birth of my first child, the final draft was in my hands. I was worried that I would be too preoccupied with my impending motherhood to focus on my brother's book. Instead, my condition made the story more interesting to me. Now directly responsible for a precious little life, I realized how important Mark's book was to our world and our children.

"Return To Forever" is a wonderful story about a great journey that we must all take. Parts of it may anger you and even more will inspire you. Mark captures the true beauty and angst of life on earth, and introduces us to his joyous idea of the world that awaits us.

Reading it is a journey worth taking.

Sharla Pitifer Toups
Geneva High School Class of 1988
& William Smith Class of 1992

"You may be disappointed if you fail, but you are doomed
if you don't try."
-Beverly Sills

TABLE OF CONTENTS

*** "Every person should try during the course of their life time to formulate a theory about who we are, where we come from, what the meaning of life is, and what happens when it's over … Read the holy books, look at the evidence provided by science, history, math, archeology etc. And then ask yourself: "What does it all mean?" As you can see there are 48 chapters in Return To Forever. That's one chapter for every year that I have been alive! I think you will enjoy what I have written, but I hope it will not prevent you from seeking out your own answers…. One last thing, in this world we live in, HOPE is what gives us the energy to persevere. Truly I tell you, all who believe in God and Heaven, will never be disappointed. So give yourself something to hope for. Because if you are wrong, and you die into nothingness, you'll never know. But what if you're right? … Now that seems to me like a good reason to hedge your bet. Entertain the possibilities of God & Heaven. All it costs to get in is a little extra love, kindness, mercy & compassion. And we all can afford that!"—MARK SALVATORE PITIFER

"All roads if we pursue them long enough and far enough, lead to
God! So be tolerant of all faiths, and nither dispise nor oppose what
thou dost not understand. For tolerance is a charity far greater than
faith or hope!'
-William Barclay & William Penn

"No eye has seen, nor ear has heard, no mind has conceived what
God has prepared for those who love him."
-1 Corinthians 2:9

ACKNOWLEDGEMENTS

The completion of this book has truly been a life long journey. And now that I have reached the top of this enormous mountain, I feel compelled to thank those of you who have helped me along the way. This section is truly a trip down memory lane. If I forgot anybody it's not because you aren't important to me, it's because my memory is fading. I believe that every positive person that God sends into our lives has an impact on the eventual adult we become.... First and foremost I must acknowledge God, Jesus The Messiah, The Holy Angels (especially the Guardian Angels assigned to my family), and the Holy saints and prophets of all the love based religions (Most especially Muhammad, Mary, Krishna, Buddha, Moses, Isaiah, & Paul.) Thank you for all you have done and continue to do for my family and the world.

Mom and dad, thank you for loving me, believing in me, and always making me feel special. I consider myself one of the luckiest children ever born, and I love you both more than you will ever know. Mommy, I built my life around you, and you have never let me down. Thanks for always having my back. Where still around ain't we, Ann?

Leigh, without your love, faith, and loyalty I could have never made this climb. You are my wife, my best friend, and my first and only love. I thank God for you every day. "My one in a million you." Never underestimate how important you are to me.

To my dear little lambs: Nina, Noah, and Markie, you make daddy's heart sing! You are God's most sacred gift to me, and the essence of all that I am. My unconditional love for you has opened my heart and mind to God's boundless love for us all. As you grow older always take care of each other and stick together as a family. Never forget that we are the Lions Abijah, and always remember how much your daddy and mommy love and enjoy you: All those days of playing Lion ("Who are you? What's your name? What kind of animal are you? Scar, Nimbo,

The Doctor & Mother Scar/Lolly), The Little Light, Nina, chasing Michael Jordan across the court at the Carrier Dome (Dota-Doto), **BIG-BOAT-NIGHT**, Frying Pan Pop-Corn, Upa-Da-Boom-Booma, Special Porridge & Making Pig Cookies, Sea Breeze, Special Rock Beach "Blue-a..Green-a), Slate Rock (Bike rides & our waterfall Jacuzzi), Chimney Bluffs (Grandma's Hill), Bus rides & Basketball games: Coach Lauer (clack-clack-clacking), Helping Julius Bryant (Thanks Julius!), The Trampoline (wrestling), Collecting Chestnuts, The Hammock, House Graffiti, Poppa's Bean-Beans, My Sally's Field (Mowing), Riding the golf cart, The Blinking-off Tower, The Canale's July 4th Clam Bake & fireworks, The King Rabbits House, Playing Hide and Go Seek (ABC base on me), All God's Children Shows & practices, The Big Fan & Sleeping in the Attic, Bed Time Stories **"On a cold night … In a black house … A dark wind … Mean old dog … Bad old cat … Markie Da-monster came … He scared away the dog, chased away the cat, and he saved them all!** (The Pipe, Sindoni, One legged Joe, & Poppa and the door) & Songs (God Bless My Baby Boys, Oh Bella Figlia, & Reach for the stars), The Tickling Spider & Horsey, Tommy The Whale, Timmy, Happy Bear & Penny The Penguin, The Whale Watch, Sledding, The Pink & Green (Rolling up & The Mummy), Noah: "My mind is telling me…." The Sprayground & The Jumping Tree, Jimmy's Beach, The Hall Hay Ride, & Bobby Hall's giant moon that we tried to catch, Kosem, Nala, Tigerlilly, Pinkyapplefritter, and Lolly Pop & her first play, Taughannock 'Vader' Falls, Sylvan "Peanut Butter" Beach, Naples (Cummings Nature Center, Poppa & Nala's Heaven Rocks, & Monica's Pies), Wixons Bee's & Ice Cream, All those early morning Boys & Girls Club Basketball Games & Breakfast at L & R's (A special over easy with Italian toast, hot peppers in the potatoes, extra toast and spicy hot sausage, with a side of hot sauce for Claw.) Texas Holdem with Nonni, Sonni & The Boys, Our New Years Eve Parties (Fried dough, & Dancing in the attic "Pollinate & Shake It Like A Salt-Shaker". Playing Trouble (1 Geta-man-out & I hate 2's), Climbing Bristol Mountain, Darian Lake Fright Night, Krista-Markie-Noah & Daddy golfing at Big Oak, Claws "John Daly" Swing, Sun Down Golf at Seneca Lake Country Club (Thank you Josh!), & SANDTRAP Pitifer & the tree cart! The Dudes Pool, Chuck & Mary's "ChinDah-E! & Kahhh", "Ha-Bee-Bay!" (Mary & George), Marine Land,

Going to see Shari and Sharla in New York City & New Jersey, St. Millers Tower, Albany—The Pool, Jeepers, Tokalimo (Nina hangs up), he first Kiss-Ricky Torres "Daddy on a scale of 1 to 10 it was a 20!). Markie & Alondra, Noah & Nicole (Hunter), Nina (one of the great ones!) gets a hug from Chazz Palminteri & Markie gets his card, Usher gets daddy's Autograph and book after Chicago Musical ("You wrote this book for me man?!"), Visiting Chirs & David in San Diego, Your first plane ride, Disney Land, Marine Land, Sleeping with the Lions, Hollywood & Johnny Depp, Spiderman's House (Demi Moore had to wait), Clint Eastwood & Leonardo DiCaprio's house, UCLA, Milan Tiff, Smoothies, & The Colonial Motel (Donna) and Jenkinson's Boardwalk at Point Pleasant Beach! Noah & Markies first movies "The Tandle Chronicles, Borat II, & The Dharma Initiative. Noah's staring roles as Romeo/Chomeo, and as the tree in the Final Dress Rehearsal. Also, Markie's famous LOST Party at the Wallworks. Nina sings and dances to Michael Jackson's song Shattered. Nina's starring roles in CATS, FIDDLER (Markie did the lights), and Kiss Me Kate! Nina & Allauna singing McCavity. Your famous sayings: Nina "I give the bad people rides. Isn't that good? & OoomeQuuume", "I can speak like a native listen hear, Uga-bugga-bugga-lugga" & "But you have heard of me." Noah "Mommy, I can't do the five.", Markie "I dip it." And last but not least, "I-YI-YA." Didn't we have the greatest adventures?! Chickadeemic, Choahnyoonicka,&Claw wwleeeelaawww-Linwood-Laaawww! **ALWAYS REMEMBER WHO YOU ARE! THE LIONS ABIJAH!** I know you guys are going to get mad at me for bringing this up, but since no one knows the hour of their earthly departure, I will say my goodbyes now while I am still able. Some day you will recognize the wisdom of it. So, farewell my little lambs. I will miss you terribly. My heart breaks to even think of it. But rest assured that I will never leave your side. Love one another as I have loved you. Be kind, merciful, generous, and courageous in all that you do, and this will make me smile. Take care of your mother in her old age, and always remember that I loved her more than you can ever imagine. If God sends you children some day enjoy them with every ounce of your soul. You must now become the Lion King, and through your play I will growl and laugh with your chickadees. I will look them in the eyes and say "What kind of animal are you?" You never know, one of them might be me! So there it is. In the life that we have shared, in the memories we have made, and in the words of Return To Forever, I will be with you always, now until the end of time. I love you,.I love you, I love you, **I-YI-Yah! Good Night!**

To my sisters Sally, Shari, and Sharla, each one of you in your own special way, through your love, support and undying faith, gave me hope. It is so important to me that you have always believed in my dreams. Thank you for surrounding me with your deep love and talent. You are my fountains of youth, and the foundation of my kingdom.

Sally you are the most like our father, and you bring us all much joy and laughter. You are kind, generous, entertaining, and the world's greatest Italian cook! Thanks for always watching my back. "Don't let-em get you sister, you're the one."

Shari, my spiritual soul mate and confidant. I love you and miss you very much, and I long for the days that we will no longer be apart. Thank you for nourishing my soul, and for bringing Rino, Luciano, and the Minetti family into our lives. Especially, Maria Pia & Luciano Minetti Sr., also Taso, Sonia, Stefano, & Oriana Sengos! What a beautiful family! It's 11:11 make a wish, and say a prayer for the Angels.

Sharla, what can I say? The smartest and brightest sister. Without you there would be no book. Thank you for being the world's best, most thorough, and slowest editor of all time! LOL. Also thank you for bringing the Toups family into our lives. **Robert**, thank you for taking care of my sister, for my beautiful nieces Nina and Annie, and for all of your used camera equipment! Welcome to my family.

Rocky Fratto (NABF WORLD CHAMPION & WBA #1 CONTENDER) you showed me that it is possible to climb to the top of the world from little old Geneva, New York. Thanks for always being there Rock. I love you my brother, and I am so very proud of all of your accomplishments. In my heart you will always be the World Champion. You have won the 16th Round! ... How many of your contemporaries can say that?! Also a special thank you to Ralph Sr., Connie, Anna, Gina, Geneva Granite, and all of the Fratto families. God bless you all.

Sonny Tandle, thank you for taking care of our mother and our home. You have my families love and respect, and you have earned the right to sit in our father's chair. Your are a wonderful father and grandfather. May God bless you and all of the Tandle Familes.

Beverly, Chris, David, Grandma Sue, Billy, Bee, Brian, Shannon ("I've got to get my flower some air."), **Madison, Sam, and Houston.** You have been a welcome addition to all of our lives, and we appreciate all that you do. Especially your kindness, generosity, and Grandma Sue's cooking!

Marco II, Ivy, & Marco III, Allison & Dave, You are loved and prayed for always.

Last, but certainly not least, my beautiful Sister-in-Law **Mamma Mia,** who inspired the 11th commandment … Thank you for bringing the wonderful **Calabrese family** into our lives (especially my loving, and generous brother **Mike.** What a blessing it is to have you in my life.), for counseling the counselor, and of course, the always HUUUGE Albany Disco parties & The Chocolate Martinis! I love you all more than you can ever imagine. Also special thanks to: Velma, **Gene Sr. (REFUSE TO FADE!),** Gene Jr., Kathy, Dave, Darcy, Nicole, Deanna, and Jeanie. I love and enjoy all of my Albany people! Albany is where my shade trees grow, and where my hair comes down! Thank you for bringing me joy!

My Nieces & Nephews: Ralphie, we have shared many big nights together. Especially the Forman fight! Thanks for inventing the "Fake Big Night, Fake Serious, the Fake Barber Syndrome, and for bringing Nick Massa & the Undertaker into our lives. You could be a very talented screen writer, or a real life Rocky Balboa. I'm a believer! **Mario, Via Abruzzi!** Thanks for all those nights at the canal museum buffet (The Banana Boat Back shaver's conference!), and for discovering the beautiful **Manna Schtreeka!** "I want your tears gypsy." Use your talents and live the dream Mario! The clock is ticking. Good luck at Syracuse Law School Via. **Frankie "Quarterback",** our two seasons together were wonderful, and I will never forget them. I hope that college is in your future plans. You can do it. Always remember the greatest shooting exhibition of all time! Especially who won! The NBA finals in Boston, Magic Johnson, & **The Rick Fox Story!** Never underestimate the power of the uncle! **Giana "Gi-Money", Mitchell "Stichell" & Sophia "Phi-pha"** "Whose that little bird?". I love you all very, very much. Always remember our summer days at your house, playing in your pool, Money's "Michael Jordan" Game, Texas holdem, Point Plesant, and sleeping in the cellar. **Little Nina,** Playing Lion with you, and eating Lion Pudding! I will always remember "The Madder of the Badder" Dance. The night before your little sister arrived. **Annie**, you were just born two days ago. However, your name alone already gives you a special place in my heart. **Luciano**, welcome to the family. You're a very nice boy, and I look forward to beating you up on a regular basis! **Angelina**, my little angel. I have seen you in my dreams. Dark curly hair, sparkly brown eyes, & rosy cheeks. If God does send you at this time, what a lucky little girl you will be! To all my nieces & nephews always remember how much your uncle loved & enjoyed you. Play forever with me in your heart!

Special Friends, Big Boat Regulars & Road Dogs: Brittany Valder, Brittany Nardozzi, Christopher "Bunny" now "Money Rabbit" Tapscott, Rosa "The Italian Moon" Gentile, Allauna Overstreet, Joey 'Joesepy" DiCampli, Jordan & Cory "Corrett my name is Corrett." Meyers, Joey Warner, Tony "Tonito" Chabrier, Krista (Hole-In-One)-Bethany "Betania" & Daniele Baroody, Jimmy (Jimmy Beach)-Kenny (Special K)—& Patrick "The General" Rissew, and Kaitlyn & Ethan Bakogiannis (The worlds prettiest kids!)

THE SPECIAL FAMILIES: Pitifer, Fratto, Toups, Calabrese, Minietti, **Pizzoferatto**, Sarratori, Principio, Sears, Simpson, Siclare, Tandle, Blue, Henderson, DeFazio, Riley, Natelli, Bellis, Tapscott, Mazzocchi, Fountain, Modera, Bakogiannis, Newland, Theobald, Warner, Spellecy, Pearson, Meyers, Thomas/Eldridge, DiNardi, Gringeri, Oxendine, Augustine, Tuxill/Thompson, Overstreet, DiCampli, Bekauri, Burrall, Herrick, Cole, Nardozzi, Valder, Massa, Riccione, Gentile, Oliver, Sculli, Laurenza, Tiballi, Smaldone, Wilson,Dean, Alvaro, Sanchez, Wenzel, and Reese. If I listed the individual names of all of those with whom I have a special relationship, I would have to right another book! May God's peace and blessings shine upon the families for all their love and support.

The Nagel Place Neighborhood Famlies: (Past and Present): Sbrocco, Teague, Driscoll, Tapscott, Sanchez, Millerd, Campbell, Capozzi, Belcher, Baroody, Rissew, Parish, LaRocca, Decaro, Hoskings, Curle, Heffernan, Wells, Bogart, Iredale, Evangalista, George, Mickleson, Johnson, Towndrow, Michaels, Sullivan, Soscia, Harling, Laurenza, Connell, Dewitt, and Corcoran.

Special thanks to **Aunt Lucille & Uncle Charlie Simpson** for encouraging me to write, your financial backing, and making me shoot for the top. God bless you both. Also **Dawn Bartholomew**, what a beautiful soul!

Thank you to my good friends **Uncle Richie, Aunt Eva Siclair** & your wonderful family (Paulie-bear, Monica, Chrissy, Julie, Jana & Richelle). You enriched my childhood by sharing your Angelo street paradise (The food, the fun, & the entertainment!) with me. There was always a spot at your table for me, and I love you all. God bless you and yours.

My childhood religious advisers and teachers: **David and Harriet Young** (Jehovah's Apostles) thank you for all those Thursday night religious discussions. The wisdom that you shared, along with your knowledge of the Bible, is the cornerstone of my faith. Gods' Peace …

Father Tomian Uss (You meant more to me than you could ever imagine.), Brother Benedict, Brother Gregory, Brother Cashmire, Brother Tim (Rudy Fusko & The Pipe), and all of the Priests, Brothers, and students from **St. Anthony's of Padua** (including **the Chamberlain Family (Especially Johnny)**, & **Witold "Poochie" Plucienkowski** (You were then and always will be my hero #22, Padua 1969! I am blessed to have a role model like you.), thank you for a childhood filled with faith, sports (My Gymnastic team 69 & 70), and delicious water! Also thanks for Long Island/Brooklyn accent, everyone I meet thinks I'm from down state! Also the Glen Springs Academy & **Fly Williams!** #1 in the Nation! Heaven is a playground.

St. Monsignor Gerald Krieg, thank you for sharing your love, holiness, and wisdom with my family. You are truly a saint. Behold, the Kingdom of Forever awaits you.

Rev, Jim Gerling, and Rev Nancy Birdsong, you two are cut from the same holy cloth. Thank you for always making us feel welcome at your church, for sharing your wisdom, and feeding my Geneva lambs. May God always bless your beautiful little church. You are loved.

Aloquin: John, Dale, Tom & Louise Oliver, & Charlie Rice.

Dr. Abul Kosem Muhamad Bayazid, thank you for your spiritual guidance, illuminating the Muslim path, and for introducing me to the beauty and holiness of the Sacred Qur'an.

Father Mac Spellecy, thanks for sharing your wisdom, and treating me like a son. An Irish Blessing to all of the Spellecys of Hornell: **May the sun rise to meet you. May the wind be always at your back. May the sun shine upon your face and rains fall soft upon your field. And until we meet again may God hold you in the hollow of his hand.**

Thank you to all of **my loyal GHS/DHS alumni who still come by the neighborhood**, Hankie Pearson, Thomas "Zipp" Mazzocchi, Niel Reese, Lenard "Legbah" & James "Mooshetti" Thomas, Welton Eldridge, Alton Sutton, Timmy Northrup, Marvin-Gene & Pop Sapp, Joe Sweeny, Tom "Red" Myers, Alton Sutton (The neck weight workouts!), Harold "The Swan" Flowers, JJ "Frazier" Smalldone, Tina Phillip, Jeff "Gook", Frankie, Joey, Mike, Tammy, Lori, Julie, Mary, & Beverly Alvaro, Mark Allen, Jackie Augustine, Al "Magic" Hudson, Steve Felice, Jeff Quartaro, Mike Bruno, Joey Iaconis, Gregory Jackson, Mike Bradley, David Marr, Vincent Ray (Nobody did it better!), Erving "May-May" Archibald (The Big Hit), Biddy-Bobby & Willie Spann, Alec Huff & Matt Fegley (2 on 2 full court! Pitt & Nitt never lossed a game!), Wilmer "The Standing Ovation" Alexander, Jimmy Alexander, Mike & Joey Woody-Mike Bonaventure (The Memorial Day Massacre!) Tyrone "Cogitate" Scott, Joe & Neil Augustine, James "Crunchy" Wells, Marc Melito, Gino Yannotti, Jesse "Ketchup" & James "GooGa" Truly, Lonny "The Gap Club" Spearman, Adrian "Tut. How many raisins?", James, & Rodney Lennon, Steve DeMatties, Marty Olmstead, Cynthia-Allan-Aaron-& Anthony Waye, Willie "The Juiceman" Houghton, Aaron Montaglione, Brian Ozog, Greg Brown, Corey Barnes, Eric Boynton, Homer & Sugar Mckoy, Baryy Hagadorn, **Tony "The Rum Cat" Angel**, Benji Torres, Tyrone-Reggie "Rasberry", Frank "Brother Ish" & Sam Collins, Rocco "Modykline" Iannapollo, & Pat Martin (Cowboys 73 & GHS 2006!).

My DeSales & YMCA Basketball Crew: Jimmy Natelli, Welton Eldridge, Billy & Timmy Tapscott-Bobby Taney-Bobby 'The left handed hook" Manion-David "Bird 9 in a row!" Iddings-John "The Hawk" Hawkins-Tim "Baby Jordan" Irelland-Charlie "I'll Make it." Evangelista-Mike Cemoni-Tony "MVP" Scaramuzzino YMCA Champions!)-Tim "Baby Jordan" Ireland-Q-Larry "Poison" Guererri-Greg Baker-Eddie Brinson-Scott Baroody-EJ Michales-Mike Rouland-Jesse McConnell White—& Steve

'Gus" Salone (You were one of the great ones!). Thank you my friends, I enjoyed all of the games. Especially the ones that I dropped the game winning shot in your eye!

Thank you to **Jimmy "Nitt" Natelli** (My little brother & Heavenly CPA). You mean more to me than you know. Thank you for my second childhood! Remember all those 500 pushup days? Especially the basketball, followed by the nectar at Kay's Corner Store. Never forget CRAZY COVE WALL, the chicken dogs, the punky ties, and washing his back! **Joe 'Joesepy" Natelli**, thanks for being my road-dog. I can always count on you. Never forget our times with Dr. Al, and Suzie of Notingham! LOL. Also a special thank you to **Mary Natelli** for your support and movie critiques, Vinny (Rocky IV & The Frat house Fight) and all the Natelli's. God bless you all.

To my agents: **Judge Tim "Beaver Tail" Buckley and** future **Judge Lesley Cohen Hickey**. Thank you for believing in me, and investing your personal time and energy. Also a special thank you to Josh Cohen for having me on your radio show, and to Joey for selling my book. The judge would be very proud!

Special thanks to all of my teachers, coaches, and instructors at Watkins Glen Elementary School, Geneva Middle and High Schools 78, Finger Lakes Community College 79, Hobart College 82, Brockport College 82 & 90, UCLA 86, and Fort Benning Georgia D92 Infantry Training/11-Charlie 1984. Each of you in your own little way had an impact on my book: Doris Quick, Ray Gagnon, Helen Maney, Mr. McDonald, Mrs. Loveland, Rick Wheeler, Mrs. Russell, Kathy Henderson, Carl Wenzel, Mike Canale, Wes Kubacki, D.K. Khoury, Coach Bogart, Diane "Pit" Guererri, Mrs. Hemmingway, Putt Moore (FLCC's first winning basketball season 78-79!), Lynn "Mrs. Woman" Broderick, Dr. Butch Cuony, Coach Dave Urick, Guy VanArsdale Sr., Dr. Debbie Demise, Dr. Wes Perkins, Dr. James Spates, Dr. Jack Levin, Bob Lee, Bob Marr, Vincent Scalise, Dr. George Appleton, Dr. Muyhi Shakoor, Dr. Jane Vogan, Dr. Gerry Donigian, Dr. Dave Kendall, Richie Blue, Jim Henderson, Dr. Marvin Bram, Joe Dan Tipps, Bob Paradiso, Don Peters, Professor McNally, Dr. Raymond Duell, Dr. Winston Hamilton, Dr. David Curtis, Dr. Robert Weinberg, Dr. Justin Martin, Dr. Gringeri, Drill Sgt. Dezy Scales, Sgt. Bob Rose, Sgt. David Hagg, Pvt. Joel

Taylor, Pvt. Andrew Perkins (The Blue Angel), Pvt. Willie Murray, Pvt. Jeff Greco, Jane Jones (FLCC-Tutor), Dr. Al Katz, Dr. Julius Bryant (Thanks for taking care of my boys!), My Hobart Laundry Bandits: Dr. Oscar Hosking & Dr. Abe Solomon, and my Kappa Sigma Brothers from Hobart college & around the world.

All of my colleagues at Waterloo School District, Geneva High School, & Monroe County Pre Trail Diversion. Especially those who helped me directly or indirectly with my book: **CAROL EMERSON** (Thanks for looking out for my soul), **PETER BURKE** (Barangus!), **Joe Sposato**, **MIKE FERRARA** (My Brother), **Bobbie Didsbury** (I wanna go back!), **Jackie Mull**, Mike Simon, Rich Byndas, Lori Miele Doron, **George "Slazinger" Dutton**, Jim Elkin, Jay Lauer, Steve "The Mojo" Marchitell (Thanks for the formula!), Mark "The Undertaker" Sutter, Matt "Daisy Duke's DJ" Tumbelekis, Aaron Backhaus, **Joan "Jazzy" Daeffler**, **ANN JOHNSON** (My Conscience), Diane Macaluso, Deb Doverspike, Karen "Valentine Room 222" Greco, Dave Pullen, Randy Grenier, Mickey & Karen Donnelly, Ermie "Flower" Wooster, Josh "Dr. Serious" & Julie Bailey, Wendy Doyle, Lisa Andino, Barb Christopher, Carol Wolf, Sally Covert, Marcia Hiserodt, Sandy Bohman, **Mary Parker Gagliano**, Terry Elias, Sandy Hopkins, Sharon Cudlin, Deb Trumble (Rocky Roads), Linda Arichiello (The Parrott), Mike Hunsigner, Carol Davis, Cathy Ross, Dave Whitcomb, Ray Torrey, Val Fish, Lola Morabito, Chuck Nightingale, Scott Reed, Ben Raymo, Laurie Finch, Rick Spalding, Katie "The Wall" Wright, Jada Bryant, Mike Crespo, John Butler, Tad Rounds, Babette McCulloch, Tracy Flach, Lynne Baker-Osserman (Thanks for the Piano!), **Susan Burgess**, Laurie "Guz" Guzewicz, Trisha Rogers, Patty Johnson, Kathleen Bremer, **Al Pace**, Leann Donnelly, Julia Ticconi, Emily Rittenberger, Joanne Corey, Heather Bonetti, Mike Cooper, Allison Panek, Amy Rogers, Stephanie Ferrara & John Riccione, Emily Rittenberg, & Jeff Panek **(The Noble Project!)**

Thank you to **My Readers:** Ann Pitifer, Mac Spellecy, Ann Johnson, Dr. Marvin Bram, Mary Bakogiannis, Shari Pitifer Minetti, Dr. Stanton Tepfer, Sally Pitifer Fratto, Sharon Zimmerman, Kevin Korzeniewski, Ryan Graham, Mathew Blue, Jolene Stamp, Donna Visco, Dr. Tyrone Scott, & Mia Principio Calabrese. Thank you for helping me polish my story. I couldn't have done it without you! Also a special thank you to Janet Cole, and Rosy Felice. Your kind words will never be forgotten!

*SPECIAL THANKS: to all of the authors listed on Nino's Book List and mentioned throughout the story. Your facts are the weapons I used to slay the red dragon.

Special thanks to **My Famous Inspirtations: Maurice White, Philip Bailey & Earth, Wind, & Fire** for the music, the faith, and the path. **Muhammad Ali** for the courage, the poetry, and the dance. "Forever, you will be the champion!" **Julius "Dr. J" Erving & Michael Jordan** for your artistry in perfecting the game I love! **Nadia Comaneci** (The Perfect 10!). **Rocy Marciano** (Undefeated Heavyweight Champion!), **James J. Braddock** (Cinderella Man), and **Tiger Woods** (U.S. Open 2008), **Andrew Loyd Weber** for Jesus Christ Superstar. Your musical turned me on to Jesus … **Sylvester "Sly" Stallone** (Rocky, Over The Top, & the character: **ROCKY BALBOA!**) for convincing me that fame is a trap, and that there truly is "No place like home." Special thanks to **Morgan Freeman, Louis Gossett Jr.** and last but not least **Will Smith (The Wild-Wild West!)** for giving Nino Jones his soul. **Chazz "C" Palminteri** (A Bronx Tale: the movie and Broadway play.) for the picture, and agreeing to play the part of Barabbas! Ok, I made that up. Thank you in advance to **Oprah Winfrey, Ron Howard** (Cinderella Man & Happy Days!), **Milan Tiff** (60 feet!), **Henry Winkler & Rob Reiner** (The Sure Thing & Happy Days!), **Mel Gibson** (The Passion & Braveheart), **Steven Spielberg** (Back To The Future & ET), **Spike Lee** (Do The Right Thing) & **Molly Ringwald** (How I learned to drive.) for services to be rendered. Also **Nadine Eid (UCLA/Paris). Kirk Frankland, Israel & The New Breed, Gym Class Heroes (Congratulations to Geneva's own Travis McKoy & Matt McGinley), Emanuel LeBlanc (GQ-Disco Nights!), Britney Spears (Stick to the POJ and you will never fall again!),** "Rejoice!", **Mariah Carey, Steven Posen** (11:11), **Danny Wegman, Usher Raymond IV** (Chicago), **David Foster, Jaime "Jackasso" Cabrera, Shalom "Sam" Kovnator** (The worlds greatest violinist!), **Mighty Mouse, Kimba The White Lion, Tarzan, Speed Racer & Bugs Bunny!**

My band ALL GOD'S CHILDREN: **Greg Passalaqua, Frankie Blanke, Hankie Peason, Al Roth, Ken Foster, Corey Boatwright, Diana Fountain, Sally Pitifer Fratto, Shari Lynn Pitifer, Sharla Pitifer Toups, Nina**

Pitifer, Noah Pitifer, Markie Pitifer, John Theobaldi, Chuck Bruzee, NickMazzocchi, and Alex Wallwork. Also the members of my former band M.S. Pitt & The Power: Jimmy Smith (Thank your for opening my eyes to the possibilities. Your one of the best musicians & producers on the planet!), Mario Sbrocco Jr., Bobby Greco (The Pudgies Pizza Hyphen & The 16th Round-Bell Note! You were the first one to believe in me, and I'll always love you for that.), Ki Ki Leon (Let's do some travlin.), Lee Fancett (Hollywood), Craig "Lefty" Carlson, Chuck Leo (Manhattan Solo), Rob Lee, and Vincent "Accelerando" Sarratori. Also Greg Bennett (Moon Dog Sound) & Ray Howard (The two best sound men in the world).

The old neighborhood: Thomas "Zipp" Mazzocchi (Kimber-Limber-Limberly! Coumon, I'll drill ya!, I can't breath ...) & Mark Wilson "Soooni", Marc Melito (Pushups, boxing, & Maryrose), Paulie Peters (The Weavers!), Chris ("The relished rump of a resurrected rhino & The Miami Motel!") & Jimmy Carroll, Harold Flowers, Frank Sindoni, Steve Nepolitano (The car!), Mike "Kip" Connell (Thanks for the use of your court!), Bobby, Mike, Diane, and especially Suzzie McLane, Steve "Gilly-Heon", Bob, Beal, and Amy Gilpatrick "Coumon Heon", Jimmy "Harry" Handlon "Hunnah-Hunnah-Ginny-Ginny" & Ellen, Peter "Peta-head, Brian, Brenda, & Bob Verdehem (also thanks for the court.), Al Gordan "I'll bat ya looney. I tell ya!", Sylvia "Tibby" & Andy Evangalista, Liz & Pat Cappozzi, Bobby-Bernie & Suzie Belcher, Jimmy & Mary Kelly Sullivan, John Fitzsimmons, Burt, Reb & Gary "Jasper" Phillips (Thank you for sharing the miracle story about your dad! He's a great soul! & singer!)

A special heartfelt thank you to Gino Yannotti and his family for helping me to have a wonderful childhood. For opening your home to me, and happily feeding the hungriest kid in town! Also Jimmy 'The Duke" Pedulla & family, The Luzzi family, including Uncle Dan Bennett, The Great Wife Search: Honorale Mention: Terry Luzzi, Patty Paris Notebaert, Lynn Luzzi, Maryrose Melito, Michele Dematties, Kathy Augustine, Barb McLellan, Lou Ann Gillotte, Bootsy of Canada, Mia Principio, Lori Mielie, Carol & Mary "Chunk" Roberti, Judy Bero, First Runner Up: Diana Fountain, & The Winner: Leigh "The Mongoose" Principio!. T.G.I! Actually I'm the winner.

All My Pollinators: Leigh Pitifer, Mia Calabrese, Mary Bakoganis, Kirsten Burrall, and especially my Triple Dippers: Doris Myers, Ci Ci Collins, and Carmen Sapp! Special Mention: Diana Fountain, Dee Dee "The Badger" Tuxcill, and Pam "Look if you want to." Greco. I must also give a special call out to the Billy Long dancers: Lesley Cohen Hickey, Nancy Long, and Jodi Sloane Taylor! Also my personal trainer: Tiffany Sculli Tiballi. I love the way you move! Peace.

Watkins Glen Crew: Ni-Ni the barber (2 Creams & 1 Sugar), Sandy (The liquor store), & Rocco the human flag. Also Mr.& Mrs. Teemly, Peter & Phylis, Tony Ferry, Danny Lewis, Johnny Angel, Laura, and The Knotty Pine Gang, especially Aunt Adelle, Ci Ci, Mary, Laura, Johnny Jr. Hedi, the Wollacks (Andy, Phylis, Eddie, Mike, & Ann), Todd-Steve-Adam & Cindy Henby, Chrissy (Post office & my first real kiss!)-Tina—& Andrew Stivers, Maureen Hannon, Mike Cook & family, Joe & Paul Dunbar, Ernie Engles, Sam & Dom Schimitz, Greg Paradiso & family, and Peter & Vera (The Motorcycle Hippies). **Ashley "Bingo" & John Herrington**

Mario Sbrocco Sr. "The Dude" and family (For your love, generosity, & pool!) **John Engles** for your wonderful youth ministry, and **Tommy "The Dragon" Huang** (#1 Chinese Chef).

Future Security Guards: Bill "The King" Hausner, Harry Bennett, Kip Goodman, Lewis McKoy (You been ducking me a long time sucker!), Tommy Dean, Erving May-May Archibald, and Biddy & Willie Spann, John Cleere, Lee Jr, Les, & Chief Marquart. **Senator Bryant Bailey.**

King Louie Ferrara of the "The Provalone Society & 5 Points!"

Steve McCheyne (My computer Doctor! Thanks for saving my book.) Also Mike Altman, Carl Lebate, & **William "Biddy" Spann** (Chartres Homes Entertainment Inc.) Scott "Superman" Perkins & Joel Welch Jr.

Neil Sjblom (The worlds best Photographer!) Thanks for everything Niel. God bless you and your family. **Art Mieggs**: First Base Line Sports.

Mr. Paul Bartucca (Viva Pualito! The Greatest Barber of all time!) Nancy & Scott. My new hair stylist **Luann "Gillotte" Grillone & Carol "Tucceri" Mazzoli.** Also Creator's Touch, and Prime Time Cuts: **Raul "Sofrito" Fuentes, Eddie Brinson, Skeet-Skeet-Skeet Sims,** and **Melissa Cardinale.** Special thanks to **Jolene Stamp** (Heaven's Brooke Massage). You are the world's best Masseuse and all around ambassador of kindness. Thank you for easing my weary mind! May God bless and protect you and Bella.

THE ZOOOOOMER GAME of Seneca Falls: **Sky Captain Matt "Zoomer" Ferrara Sr.** "That's a very unfriendly raise!", **Matt/Sonny** "All In" **Jr. & Sarah Ferrara. Paulie** "That was a good buy.", **Frank Jr.** "Was that your arm?", **& Joe Caratozzolo. Rich "The River" Ricci** (7 straight pots!), **Mike "Bundy", David, & Tony Ferrara, Dick "Scutt" Scibona, Uncle Harry Liddell, Pat Sinicropi & Ronnie Constable.** Also a special thank you to **Sam Ferrara** for his lucky cane tip. & last but not least, in one of the greatest poker upsets of all time, **The 2008 Champion: Mark "Pitt" Pitifer** No huckle Chuckles allowed! **Also, My poker mentor Andy Balduzzi.**

My Chartres Homes Families 1978-1992. (Especially Chris "Moses-the miracle" John, Singleton, Cure, Sapp, Waye, Robinson, Strong, Griffin, Brown, Rivera, Pesante, Archibald, Calapari, Myers, McCant, Carabello, Crawley, Golden, Mims, Bynum, Ray, Lennon, White, Jackson, Porter, Curle, Whitfield, Collins, Pearson, Coleman, Godfrey, Bogan, The "Hatchet Lady", Santiago, Sanchez, Fowler, Fryer, Vanalstien, Mallard, Frank, McClan, Collier, Spann, Cornacchia, Henderson, Woody, Allen, Alexander, Ford, Dean, Williams, West, Green, Miller, McKoy, Thomas, Eldridge, Brinson, Gramling, Phillip, Johnson, Wilson (Sunday School Shoes & Roller Skates!), **Northrup, Parish, Russ, The Cung-Wha-La-Madre Gang, Richardson, Harris, Whitley, Truly, Grarcia, and Torres.**

Radio Personalities: JOHN THOMAS (Thank you John. You were the first DJ to believe in us, and play our music on the radio! You'll always be #1 in my book. Also you kind words of encouragement mean a lot to me and my family.), **Josh Cohen** & The Greek, **Scott Spezzano** (Rochester's Finest! 98 PXY), **Mike Rusinko, Patty Blue, Doug Finch, Mary Sinicropi, Mike Smith, Mark Legotte,** and last but not least, **Jerry Sherwin** (The voice of the finger lakes).

<u>**GHS Football 2006 State Champions!**</u> (A 7 year View from the announcers booth): Melvin "The Cruz Missile" Cruz, Big Nick Martin,

B.O.B. Bobby Greco, Jeff "The wizard" Wise, Ronnie "Run Power!" Collins, Brian 'The Black Knight" Knecht, Kelvin "JADA" Cruz, Dom Mazzocchi, Alfonzo "Legend Killer" Whitfield, Marc "The Champion" Tapscott, Jerimiah "The Shake" Allen, Markie D'Amico, Jeff "The-Big-Mac-Special" McNamara, Pat "The King" Lyons, Little-Bobby Martin, Andy "The Destroyer" Tourella, Terrell "Wheatie-Wheat" Northrup, Matt "Moppy" Augustine, Cheagan "The Terminator" Wilson, The Warner Brothers: John & Jimmy, Brian "The F-Train" Fowler, & Tremaine RC "The Catch" Green. <u>My Booth Crew:</u> Dave D'Amico, Kevin Smith, & last but not least **NEVADA GREEN!** Also Dave Whitcomb, Carol Davis, & **Pat Martin 78 "This raggedy bunch of kids are going to win you the championship"** Cowboys 14, Packers 12! 1974 Jr. Football champions!" Pat Martin is the x-factor.

Pitt For President Campaign Managers: Taretha John's Douglas, Sonya Crawley Carabello, Dawnette Crawley, Elvie Johns, Aaron, Alan & Anthony Waye, Mike Strong, & Mike Phillip. "WE WANT PITT!.... WE WANT PITT! I love you guys. "Who wants the salt & vinegar? Me!"

RYAN PARRY and THE MIRACLE MILE. I will never forget the grit, determination and perseverance that you displayed during those four laps at Waterloo's Tom Coughlin Stadium. We should all be willing to get down on our knees and crawl towards those life goals that are truly important! I will always remember how your wonderful classmates ran behind you cheering every step of your final two laps. Thank you little brother. I love you. Ryan Parry for President 2037!

-May God, Jesus, and all of the Holy Angels bless you with a wonderful life. And may they guide and protect you always.

FOREWORD

A book as overflowing with passion for its themes and as rich in religious speculation as <u>Return to Forever</u> will be different books to different readers. Let me tell
you what book among these different books it is to me.

When I was a young teacher reading on the cultural history of Europe, I became
absorbed in the work of the great founding psychoanalysts. Sigmund Freud in
the James Strachey <u>Standard Edition</u> seemed the twentieth-century Homer, con-
structing over a lifetime the epic narrative of our time; and indeed Freud won no
Nobel Prize for medicine but the Goethe Prize for literature. But Freud's intention
from the beginning was to alleviate suffering. The psychoanalyst Melanie Klein,
who turned her attention specifically to young children, wrote an unusually
long account of a series of sessions with a patient. That case study, I thought,
replaced one narrative, held close by the child and causing him great suffering,
by another narrative, supplied in increments by her, that would relieve his suffering. Freud's and Klein's were "healing narratives."

The two narratives, one unfolded over volumes, the other inserted into the
privileged discourse of an actual analysis, were created by two individuals. Do
entire cultures create their own healing narratives? Carl Jung once remarked that a
young psychoanalyst might well thrive in a particular corner of Switzerland.

When asked about another part of the country, a devoutly Catholic area,
he said that there was no need for psychoanalysis there: Catholicism cured
psychological suffering. I will call a culture's healing narrative, as distinguished from a particular practitioner's, a capital-n Narrative.

The United States at the beginning of the twenty-first century possesses two Narratives. One is secular and centrally involves the European
Enlightenment carried over to the New World. The other is religious: it
is the Narrative of Christendom.

The United States is a very religious Christian country. It would be likely that the relationship between its two Narratives is that the Enlightenment Narrative be absorbed into the Christian Narrative. That is one of three possible relationships between the two Narratives. They can also be held separately; many scientists, for example, hold the two as parallel, non-intersecting world-views. Or the Christian Narrative can be absorbed into the Enlightenment Narrative. One of Freud's projects was to accomplish this.

The absorption of the secular Enlightenment Narrative into the Narrative of Christendom—the antithesis of Freud's project—is Mark Pitifer's project. His protagonist, Nino Jones, an elderly homeless man in New York City of the near future, is initiated into God-centered explanations of the cosmos and the meaning of life in a series of discussions with such figures as Pontius Pilate and Malcolm X. Jones is joined by the author himself in the construction of their all-encompassing Narrative, which comes to a climactic ending weaving all the book's themes ingeniously together. Jones is an Everyman for Spiritual America, and Mark Salvatore Pitifer is his chronicler.

Marvin Bram, Ph.D.

THE TAO-TE-CHING

-The Sage does not hoard and thereby bestows…
-The more he lives for others, the greater his life.
-The more he gives to others, the greater his abundance.
-Stay Peaceful….Do not have any violence in your mind,
No revenge, and absolutely no judgment.
-Live joyously with deep gratitude for all the Tao brings…
& you will always be FABULOUSLY WEALTHY!

-LAO-TZE/550 BC
(Dedicated to my friend & Noble Sage: DR. MARVIN BRAM)

NOTE FROM THE AUTHOR

"Every man's life is a fairy tale written by God's finger."
-Hans Christian Andersen

I was raised by a mother and father who were open-minded seekers of wisdom and truth. From as far back as I can remember they would invite people of many different walks and religions to sit in our living room every Thursday night, and share their faiths with one another. These discussions were always impassioned and sometimes even heated. As a very young child I was allowed to sit and speak at these gatherings. It was fascinating for me to hear these great minds try to answer life's most profound questions (Who are we? Where do we come from? Why are we here, and where do we go when this life is over?). Although I always left each discussion with more questions than answers, the process blessed me in many ways. I learned not to be threatened by people whose beliefs and appearances were different from my own. I began to see that hidden within every religion were some of the answers to the great mysteries of life. However, it also became clear to me that no "one" religion possessed all of the answers. I developed a love and appreciation for all of God's children, and their ways of worshiping and knowing our Heavenly father. It was in this climate that I grew up, and it was in this fertile garden of wisdom that the seeds of <u>Return To Forever</u> were planted.

The little boy has grown into a man, and the son is now a husband and a father of three beautiful children. A father who is trying to leave his family and this world something more than just a memory. My father died on June 13, 1992, and it was from this darkest period of my life that I decided to write this book. A novel that attempts to answer the questions that he and I had asked so many years ago. A story that reveals the land of our origin, illuminates the path that leads us home, and exposes the enemies who seek to possess our souls. Although this is a fictional book, I have tried diligently to base this novel on as much Scientific, Historical, Archeological, Mathematical, Religious, Meteor-ological, Psychological, Sociological, Anthropological, Literary, and Astrological factual evidence as I was able to obtain. Unfortunately, or maybe fortunately, the facts only take you just so far, the rest is purely imagination, speculation and inspiration. I do not consider myself a prophet, or a saint. I am just an ordinary person, who has been given an extraordinary gift. It is with the deepest humility and gratitude that I now share with you this wonderful story called…. Return To Forever.

"The whole course of human history may depend on a change of heart in one solitary and even humble individual—for it is in the solitary mind and soul of the individual that the battle between good and evil is waged and ultimately won or lost."
-M. Scott Peck

'One film will come upon the scene that will contain the fingerprints of creations at which time all humanity shall be enlightened."
-Ellie Crystal

PROLOGUE

▼

"Knoweth thou this, O Prince, that when ever the world declineth in virtue and righteousness; and vice and injustice mount the throne—then cometh I, the Lord, and revisit my world in visible form, and mingleth as a man with men, and by my influence and teachings do I destroy evil and injustice, and reestablish virtue and righteousness. Many art the times that I have thus appeared—-many art the times hereafter when I shall come again."
-KRISHNA/THE BHAGAVAD GITA (3,137 BC)

"Keep your head to the sky."
-Maurice White/Phil Bailey & Earth-Wind & Fire

Imagine how content you would feel if you could look back at your life and career with no regrets. How satisfying it would be for you to sincerely believe that you have made a positive impact on the world, the people, and the times in which you have lived. Barabbas the Zealot, was one such brave and noble soul. He lived during the days of Jesus, and was the leader of a patriotic militia called the Zealots. He stood up to the most powerful army in the world, with just a small band of men. He spent most his life trying to free his people from the bondage of Roman occupation. Biblical and historical record states that Barabbas was the person whom Pontias Pilate pardoned instead of Jesus. To most of the Jews of his era he was seen as a hero; a loyal, sovereign soul, who served his God and his people with all his heart, soul, mind, and strength. He may not have achieved all of his life's goals, but when he finally died he had left nothing on the battle field. He had fought the good fight, and he was confident that hero's paradise awaited him.

It was with this self-image that Barabbas, content with his accomplishments, passed over into the great beyond. Into the land of paradise referred to as Heaven in the holy books, but recognized as the Kingdom of Forever by its citizens. The servant had returned to bow before his king. However, he never imagined that this king would be none other than Jesus of Nazareth. When he saw who his King truly was, he threw himself down at the feet of Jesus and begged for mercy. To his surprise Jesus warmly consoled him, and as he allowed Barabbas to view his life's work, he stood by his side and placed his arm lovingly around his shoulders. He complemented him for his determination, commitment, bravery, and faith. And yet, as Barabbas continued to watch his life unfold before his eyes, all he could do was weep. The king's words although kind and forgiving, could not change the reality he was now faced with. He now saw clearly that he had spent his entire life fighting the wrong enemy. He had rejected the true messiah. He refused to become one of his Apostles. He even convinced others that Jesus was a false-messiah, and a friend of the Romans. As he watched the part of his life in which Pilate pardoned him, he turned his eyes away, for he could not bare to watch any further.

He was devastated by the reality of who he really was, and the depth of his infamy. Jesus told Barabbas that many souls experience this kind of pain when they get to truly look at their lives. He assured him that time spent in paradise would eventually ease his pain, and that very soon his soul would feel content again. As Barabbas gazed out at the tranquil beauty of the kingdom for the first time he thought to himself. "Paradise? What possible good is paradise for someone with history like mine? I don't care what the king says, He's just trying to make me feel good. I'm a disgrace, and he knows it! I'm nothing more than a criminal and a failure! I let down my God, and my people. I can not bare to spend my eternity with this terrible legacy. There's got to be a way to right these wrongs. There's just got to be…."

It was not unique for a soul to react as Barabbas did; this is a daily occurrence in Forever. Disillusioned souls faced with the reality of their lives often crumble emotionally when they stand before their king. However, what is uncommon, is that even after 2,000 years in Heaven, Barabbas is still discontent. His mind remains disturbed, and his vision remains as clear today as it was when he spoke the following words on his very first day in the

Kingdom of Forever. "I will now become a Heavenly Zealot, and I will find other similar souls who want to become patriots for the Kingdom of Forever. We will be holy warriors, whose sworn enemies are satan and his army of fallen angels. I don't care what the price is, even if I must forfeit my spot in paradise. I will do something during the course of my existence to truly help my people, and serve my God!"

"God has forethought for all things, and there exist Angels, divine and good spirits, who behold all that is done, and from whose caring observation there is no escape."
-PORPHYRY (Letter to Marcella)

"No ears have heard. No eyes have ever seen. Nor child's mind imagined all the Heaven will truly be. So much more than words, more than we could ever dream. Somewhere far above the stars, there's a Heaven for all who dream. There's a Heaven for you and me ..."
-Mark Salvatore Pitifer (From the song Heaven

CHAPTER 1

▼

"Man who has no imagination has no wings."
-Muhammad Ali

"Man Sabura Zafura: "Whoever endures, overcomes!"
-Muhyiddin Shakoor

"Whatever you can do, or dream you can, begin it. Boldness has genius, power, and magic in it."
-Goethe

The year is 2020 AD. Barabbas has successfully assembled a band of Heavenly Zealots who share his passion and vision. Over the past 2000 years he and his Zealots have been able to do much to help the earth bound souls that take part in the Great Game. However, these are but tiny battles won, and they do little to appease his shame. Satan and his army grow bigger and stronger every day, and yet Barabbas, as he always has, continues to think that his small group of Zealots can mortally wound this immensely superior opponent. For years Barabbas and the Zealots have been planning their ultimate attack, but they have been unable to find the proper earthbound soul to be their long awaited Prophet of Faith. They need the assistance of an earthbound soul to successfully implement their final battle plan. When the Heavenly Zealots were first assembled back in 70 AD there was no sense of urgency in regards to time. The Great Game seemed like it would go on for possibly 100,000 years or more. However, the rumor around the kingdom over the past 100 years is that The Hall of Souls is nearly empty. This means, that the Great Game of life is now in its final quarter. Nothing confirms this more than the increased amount of time the king has been spending with his subjects.

Jesus is usually too busy working on the New Jerusalem, helping troubled earthbound souls, or meeting with new arrivals, to spend time partying with his heavenly subjects. Oh, he will stop by Forever every once in awhile for short visits, but he never stays very long. However, in the last year or so he has been spending more and more time in the kingdom. In fact, our story begins with Jesus making an unexpected and extended visit to the Kingdom of Forever. Many souls, including Barabbas, suspect that this is a sign that the New Jerusalem truly is nearly complete. Jesus' presence and his overly festive mood are concrete proof that the Great Game is drawing to a close. This is very exciting news for everyone in the Kingdom of Forever, everyone that is, except Barabbas and the Heavenly Zealots. So while most of the citizens are busy celebrating with their king, Barabbas anxiously awaits the return of his most trusted friend, and fellow Zealot, Chebar. It is Chebar to whom Barabbas has given the immense responsibility of finding their long awaited Prophet of Faith.

Barabbas discontent looks out over the beauty of his Kingdom, "Ah! I could easily be distracted by the perfect peace which surrounds me. Everything is so much softer and more beautiful up here." Barabbas sighs heavily. "All my favorite souls are gathered. Why just the simple fragrance of the air fills my soul with the bliss." He breathes in deeply and thinks to himself. "It's another perfect day in Paradise.... The emeralds and opals which pave our streets are blinding me with their spectacular opulence, and when I close my eyes to them, my soul is flooded with the joy and love which radiates from every being in the Kingdom."

Barabbas scowls, "But where is Chebar? He must be on his way. It can't possibly take this long to find an earth bound soul with his feet firmly planted on the Path of Jesus, can it? He's got to find him. The signs are there if he will only open his mind."

The P.O.J.—Barabbas knows it is the only road that leads to an eternity in Forever. The P.O.J as it is refereed to, is the path of Love, mercy, and kindness. It is a path of walked by individual souls, not religions. Krishna, Moses, Isaiah, Mohammed, Buddha, Zoroaster, Confucius, Shankaracharya, and of course Jesus Christ himself followed it, and countless others. They each deeply cared for all people, in the same way as they loved and cared for themselves. It didn't matter who they called God or what religion they practiced. What mattered was that the goodness of God was within them, and His compassion, mercy and love shinned through them in all their words and actions. They taught others to live the same way, leading them all along The P.O.J— the only path that leads humans back to their place of their origin.

Barabbas finds it hard to believe that the path is so hard to find, and follow.

Barabbas huffs in dismay, and speaks to God, "Can this passage to paradise be so difficult to find in today's world? Will it be impossible for Chebar to find our Prophet of Faith?

Barabbas tries to picture what Chebar is doing, "I wonder whom he'll pick. Up Here, we are ageless and enjoy freedom from the physical prisons which our human bodies can become. Up here everyone is healthy, vibrant, talented and utterly fulfilled at all times. In Forever there are so many-many worthy candidates. But on earth this is not so. He must look beyond the devastating wear and tear that the Great Game can have on the human body. He must look into the eyes, which are the windows to the soul, and search their hearts and minds. Of the billions of people who now roam the earth, Chebar must choose one. One brave and noble soul who will suite our needs…. Oh how I wish I could be with him. Oh, how my soul aches for his successful return."

Barabbas continues to pace back and forth as his mind races with the details of his plan. It means the world to him to make it work. He feels especially indebted to Chebar and would love to see him praised by their King, and their God.

Barabbas filled with sadness, "It was me, after all who convinced Chebar that Jesus was a friend of the Romans," Barabbas chastised himself, as he frequently does. "It was my words which led poor Chebar from John the Baptist to life as a zealot. He was on his way to becoming a disciple of Jesus! Maybe even one of the twelve apostles." Barabbas sighs, "But, that was a long time ago. Now, I hope I have given him the chance to redeem himself." Barabbas continues to pace about, "He will indeed find our unexpected prophet of faith—He must!"

Time slowly ticks away and Barabbas grows increasingly pessimistic about the news Chebar will bring. The sounds of laughter mixed with music serve as an ever-present reminder that his time is running short. For the first time since he undertook this challenge, he is starting to feel a sense of urgency—not just for himself, but also for the humans who are still in the heat of the Great Game.

Just when Barabbas sits down and tries to take his mind off Chebar, his friend rounds the corner. Barabbas springs to his feet, runs to greet him.

Every bit of Barabbas' anxiety is apparent as he approaches Chebar. Barabbas scowls, "Where have you been? Do you realize what's happened while you've been away?"

Chebar anxious, "I know … I heard … But I haven't been off having a picnic, you know. That earth is really becoming a miserable place," says Chebar. He is ever subordinate to Barabbas, but nevertheless surprised by his anxiety. As Barabbas continues to pace back and forth, Chebar describes' whom he found on earth. "Well, he seems to fit every—I mean, he's better than any of the other ones I have ever found. It's just that—"

Barabbas raises his eyebrows with impatience, "Chebar! What? What is it? I don't have time for this. Quit beating around the bush!"

Chebar tries to keep his composure. "To be honest he just isn't the type of fellow that one would expect to be a prophet."

Barabbas runs his fingers through his hair, "I'm losing my patience, Chebar," Barabbas interjects. "Just give me the normal run down. I'll decide if he fits or not. Actually, your reservations about this guy have me feeling optimistic. It's when you think they are great that I know they have no shot!"

Chebar takes his friend's comments with a grain of salt. "All right, here it is. His name is Nino Jones."

The name alone leads Barabbas back to his pessimistic mood. "Nino Jones?" he questions.

"Yes," continues Chebar, "He is a 67 year old homeless Negro. He is a citizen of the United States of America, and a—"

Barabbas' eyes pop out, "An American! Chebar, how many times have I told you not to bring me Americans? Their crazy! Their hero's are all make believe. They are unpredictable, and notorious for not following orders. Why, have you any idea how many times I've-"

Chebar is obviously annoyed by Barabbas' ranting. "I don't know why I am surprised. I knew when I sent you that you were going to look exactly where I warned you not to go!" Chebar smiles sheepishly. "If you will allow me to continue? He is a citizen of the United States of America, and a resident of New York City."

Barabbas acts like he is going to choke Chebar, "New York City!"

Chebar remains unruffled, and continues, "He is an unemployed veteran of the Vietnam War, and lives under a deserted building inside a giant pipe of some kind. He has no family. He is liked by many people. He has some people that are friendly acquaintances, but nothing really too personal. No one even really knows where he lives. But, let me tell you, he has a good mind and is fairly well spoken-though he does swear quite a bit. His formal education ended with high school, and after he graduated, he volunteered to join the army. His military service brought him a Congressional Medal of Honor, but it also brought on a breakdown from which he has never recovered."

Barabbas is interested now. "What brought on this breakdown?"

Chebar frowns in dismay, "Oh, it's very sad. During the war, he accidentally killed a mother and her two children. When he returned to the United States, he just dropped out of society. He felt that he was a disgrace—that nothing he did in the war really helped anyone. As a penance for killing the mother and her children, he decided to deny himself almost all earthly pleasures.

Chebar excited, "You have to see this man, Barabbas. He is a servant to the pedestrians and the merchants of New York City. He does odd jobs for money, but he refuses to take handouts. He is pleasant and friendly to most people. However, he does have a temper, but in spite of that I think he's perfect for the job."

Barabbas nods in agreement. "He does seem to fit the type of person I am looking for. Does he practice a certain religion?"

Chebar shakes his head, "No, not really. He believes in God, and he believes that Jesus is the Messiah. He just doesn't really belong to any church or anything like that. He prays everyday and is an avid reader of the Bible and other holy books. He believes that what one does to others comes back to them during their lifetime. He has a very simple, and yet beautiful faith. As I said before, he is not able to forgive himself for taking innocent lives. Although he lives righteously and prays everyday, he doesn't believe he will ever be forgiven for what he has done. Sound like anyone you know?"

Barabbas sighs deeply and lets it all sink in. He knows Chebar is referring to his own guilt, and he is relieved that his friend has found someone who just might help him gain redemption. "Yes, Chebar, it appears that this Nino Jones character may be exactly who and what I have been searching for. However, his position in society is going may be a problem. When he comes back with our message, who will take him seriously? He's a homeless Vietnam veteran. Most people will probably just shrug him off like he's some kind of nut."

"I never thought of that," Chebar says. "But you are right. We have got to pair him up with a credible, "normal" member of society. Almost all of the great prophets needed assistance of one kind or another. Moses could never have pulled off what he did in Egypt without the help of Aaron."

Barabbas agrees, "You are right, Chebar. If Nino Jones is going to be a modern day "Moses," then he needs an "Aaron" to help him along the way," Barabbas says. "And I know just the right person for the job. Remember last June when we were talking to some of the new arrivals?"

"Last June?" questions Chebar.

"Yes, don't you remember? It was your idea. You said we should start looking for some new recruits from the modern age to help us as consultants when it came time to put our plan into action."

Chebar happily, "Yes, now I remember!"

"Do you remember that fellow who stayed and talked to us long after most of the others had left? He was quite an entertaining fellow. I remember him being very proud of his family—especially his only son. He described him as someone to whom God had given much wisdom. His name was Salvatore, but he called himself Sully."

Chebar smiles, "You mean Sully Pitifer. His real name is Salvatore."

"Yes, savior," remembers Barabbas.

Chebar chuckles, "I see him all the time. Sully is a good man." Chebar pulls out his soul Scan 2020 and searches through his files until he finds the one marked *Salvatore Eugene Pitifer, arrived 10:25 a.m., June 13, 2019.*

Barabbas smiles, "Yes I remember him being quite an entertaining fella. So what does it say about his son?"

"Ah yes, here it is. His son's name is Mark Salvatore."

Chebar scans the information sheet for information that he knows will interest Barabbas. "Mark has been a school guidance counselor and coach for three years. Always helping children in this world; he and his wife have none of their own."

Chebar silently searches for some more pertinent information. "Ah yes this is interesting. From the time he was about four or five years old, his father let him sit in on weekly meetings at which representatives of different religious denominations would present their theological philosophy regarding biblical and Qur'anic scripture. He recognizes that the five major religions [Christianity, Muslim, Hindu, Buddhism, and Judaism] are all stumbling over one thing—Jesus Christ. And listen to this."

Barabbas leans closer. "One of Mark's major life goals is to do something that will unite the three major religions. He recognizes the Devil and his demons as the enemy, but not mankind. He seems like he would make a pretty good Aaron. And he's got a respectable position in society."

Impressed so far, but somewhat impatient, Barabbas urges Chebar to tell him more about Mark.

Chebar eagerly searches, "Well, let me see. Yes, here it is. He is currently spending a lot of time writing original music. His relationship with his wife seems to be in jeopardy. The strains of trying to have a child and striving to succeed with his music have frustrated the couple to the point where he takes everything out on her, and she feels like he puts his goals and dreams in front of his commitment to her. Which it appears he does. Since his father's sickness and eventual death, Mark has been in an ever deepening depression that has blinded him to the needs of his wife and his marriage. It says here that his wife is considering divorce."

Barabbas concerned. "Why, what's the problem?"

Chebar reads on, "Typical issues of communication, selfishness, and so forth. This man who wants to do such great things for the world is ignoring the problems in his own home, but not for long."

Barabbas now worried. "What happens?"

Chebar sounds nervous. "It says here that on September 28, 2020—Yom Kippur—he will be faced with a critical test. And you'll never guess where! New York City! While on a trip to visit his sister for the weekend, he will be tempted by a demon. The demon will take on the form of a beautiful woman, and tempt him to commit adultery. If the Demon is successful, Mark will be infected with HIV—the virus that causes AIDS. His wife will leave him, he will lose his job, and, ultimately, he will consider taking his own life on 12/24/2020."

Barabbas is disgusted and angry. "Oh, such potential just thrown away like that. The power of such demons is sickening. He needs protection. Who is his Guardian Angel?"

Chebar beams, "Well—thank God himself! I can't believe it. It's Gideon! Another zealot under your command, Barabbas."

This news excites the two souls as they start putting their plan into action. "Chebar, contact Gideon immediately and tell him that I want him to spend some extra time on this Pitifer assignment. Gideon is one of the best and most successful Guardian Angels, but we can't take any chances. Are you following me, Chebar? Pay attention. Contact Pilate. Tell him to be ready at a moment's notice. We will be taking Nino Jones as soon as the proper conditions present themselves."

"But Barabbas, I am confused by your orders," answers Chebar. "I thought you said that we had to pair Jones with this Pitifer fellow first. Why should we take Jones before we are even sure we have Pitifer? If the people will just shrug Nino Jones off as some kind of crazy veteran, why should we waste our time?

"I understand your concern, Chebar, but remember that we are working with Americans. Who knows? They might just make this guy their next president!"

Chebar worried, "But what if they don't? Won't the plan be ruined?"

Barabbas confident, "Chebar, nothing will be ruined. First of all, it's worth taking the chance because, if by some stroke of luck the people do believe him, then we only have to work with one human instead of two. Chebar, if God himself has a hard time getting humans to obey him, doesn't it make you a little worried about the fact that in order for our plan to be successful we must have the complete and total cooperation of a human being? A human being named Nino Jones? From New York City? Every ounce of logic tells me not to trust this plan, Chebar, but every ounce of my soul tells me that we must! Do you realize that this may be the last mission we will ever get to execute?"

Chebar understands his friend. They have had this conversation many times over the last 2,000 years. This time, however, there is an even deeper sense of urgency. The risk is great, but if the plan is successful the reward will be even greater. Chebar also believes in the plan. He knows that if they can convince Nino Jones to risk spending eternity in the outer darkness they just might be successful. The plan gives Nino Jones an opportunity to be like no other prophet in that after seeing the glory of the paradise that awaits him, he must choose to risk it all in order to defeat Satan and save his people. If Nino is successful, this last mission will be the greatest of all. And, maybe, just maybe, the miracle that they've hoped for all these years will finally come to pass. They will enter into the New Jerusalem knowing that this time they fought until the end for the right reasons. The Great Game will be complete, and Barabbas and his army of zealots will have no more reason to mourn.

Chebar filled with joy and anticipation, "Barabbas, this could set us free."

Barabbas to is excited, but does not allow himself to smile, "Yes, Chebar. You have given back to me the words that I once used to strengthen you in your moment of doubt. Like Jesus Christ in the garden of Gethsemane, we all look to have God's bitter cup pass us by. That special thing that we know we must do—something we know we were born to do, and yet we are afraid to try because the fear of failure paralyzes us. It prevents us from taking the necessary risks. It causes us to take what we think is the "safe" road. Satan's famous route-of-doubt. We are plagued by Satan's poison, even here in Paradise.

Who am I, Chebar?"

"You are—"

Barabbas frowns, "I am Barabbas, the notorious Jewish revolutionary who fought against the Roman Empire. In those days I believed it would be better to die for what I believed than to live as a coward. I believed that I was doing what was best for my God and my people, and yet, how am I remembered? As a murderer! I, Barabbas, am known throughout history as the murderer who was set free so Jesus Christ could be crucified. The Jewish priests prevailed on Pontius Pilate to release me instead of the Son of God! I am a disgrace. My life is meaningless. I am the laughing stock of my enemies."

Chebar puts his hand on Barabbas' shoulder, "You couldn't know, Barabbas. You did no wrong in accepting your freedom. How could you have foreseen those consequences?"

Barabbas pats Chebar on the head, "You are a kind friend, Chebar, but you are forgetting the facts. Jesus himself asked me to help him and I turned him down cold. Then to add insult to injury, I convinced many people that he was a false Messiah. I convinced them that he was a friend of the Romans."

"Barabbas, just think what Nino Jones—"

"Yes," interjects Barabbas, a new sense of pride rising in his words. "Our history will be changed! The real enemy, Satan, will be defeated—more soundly and swiftly than he could ever imagine. Then, once and for all, our past will be forgotten. We will be remembered forever as heroes to our people, zealots for the true King, honorable son of the most high God, and sender of the final prophet. May God be with us …"

Chebar can't hold back his own pride. He joins Barabbas in the accolades. "We will be heroes forever! It won't matter if we win or lose. All they will remember is that we tried. That's all any hero can do!"

Barabbas faking annoyance "Enough, Chebar! You are always getting me sidetracked."

Chebar shocked but in good humor "Me? Who was the one on the soap-box? 'I am Barabbas, the Notorious Jewish—'"

"Chebar! Okay, you got me. Just listen. I want you to get to Pontius Pilate and tell him what I told you. Also, I want you to ask him to meet with you and me here tomorrow at 1900 hours sharp so we can discuss the details of the abduction. In the meantime, I am going to the Grand Cinema to look in on history's most improbable prophets: Mr. Nino Jones, and his soon-to-be sidekick, "the son of Sully." What did you say his name was? Mark … Pitifer, right?"

"That's right, sir. I'll see you tomorrow at 1900 hours—sharp!"

As his dear friend leaves him, Barabbas is once again amazed at Chebar's lighthearted attitude. "His enthusiasm has distracted me so that I almost forgot an important part of the plan!" he says out loud. "Chebar—wait. I need you to stop off at the Royal Playground and get me those little rascals, Markie and Noah. I have to stop off at the Royal Cinema, and then I will meet them at my place. Tell them to wait for me in the garden."

Chebar turns quickly, a giant smile on his face. "Finally making them Zealots? They will be so happy!"

"Yes. They will be happy—and I will lose my hair! No—I am giving them the chance to help us out a little bit. As you know everyone that takes part in the plan is going to be providing me with highlight sheets that I will put together in a note book for Mr. Jones to take with him. I'm going to have Noah and Markie help me with my piece of this book. I could do this myself, of course, but it'll make them feel important—you know, puff them up a little bit."

"Ah, Barabbas—for a rough, tough old Zealot, you've become quite a softhearted old bear over the years."

Barabbas, not being able to handle such an accusation, starts to chase after Chebar, faking agitation. "If I get my hands on you, Chebar, I'll show you how soft-hearted I am. Now go do what I said!"

"Okay, okay," Chebar laughs while keeping his distance, "don't get yourself in an uproar. I'll go get the kids at once, and I'll see you tomorrow at 1900 sharp. I'll be here with bells on."

"Never mind the bells, Chebar" Barabbas frowns, his seriousness returned. "Just be there."

As Chebar mocks a salute and exits with a smile, Barabbas is compelled to kneel and pray. "Please, my Heavenly Father, please help us to achieve our goal. Please help us to bring our lost brothers home."

"Nothing can bring you peace but yourself."
-Ralph Waldo Emerson

Authors Note: The names Allah, Jehovah, Yahweh, Elohim, and God are all used randomly throughout this book to respectfully represent the different names of our Heavenly Father. To minimize the possibility of confusion in this regard, I limited myself to the names of God provided by The Jewish, Catholic, and Muslim religions. However, I believe that God equally loves and acknowledges all of the wonderful names by which his many children call him.

CHAPTER 2

▼

"My religion is simple. My religion is kindness."
-Dalai Llama

**"I was hungry and you gave me food, I was a stranger and you welcomed
me, I was naked and you clothed me."**
-JESUS OF NAZARETH/Matthew 25:35

"My country is the world and my religion is to do good."
-Thomas Paine

It is a complicated process for one of Forever's souls to return to Earth,
even for a short visit. Barabbas used to use his connections on the Paradise
Border Patrol to gain access, but this is no longer necessary. Jesus himself
built the Grand Cinema in order to keep the souls of paradise from asking
endless questions about their loved ones who were still playing in the
Great Game.

Inside a domed structure about the size of Manhattan is a gigantic piece of
technology unlike anything ever imagined on Earth. This apparatus provides
up to the minute information on every living human being. The computer
has millions of different isolation booths, each with 40 x 40 circular screens.
Visitors are placed in suspended animation in the center of the room, and
can stay there comfortably for days, weeks—even years if they choose to.
Every image is 3 dimensional, and the viewer experiences each scene hands-
on; not only seeing every detail, but also tasting, hearing and feeling as well.
The viewer becomes one with the human, knowing all his thoughts and
committing all his actions.

Specific questions can be asked about upcoming obstacles a particular person might be facing. The viewer is given times, dates and circumstances of these events. Plans of Satanic attacks are also provided, as are the probable outcomes of these attacks.

Barabbas makes his way into the Grand Cinema, greeted along the way by many souls. Barabbas is harder on himself than most of the souls in Forever, as they no longer think of him in connection with the death of their King, but rather as a leader who will help them win the Great Game.

He gradually makes his way to booth #707, his favorite, and once inside the plush studio he takes his spot in the center of the room. "Nino Jones," he says.

The sudden plunge to the depths of New York City's littered streets feels to Barabbas like he is on his way to Hell. Strong September winds seem to sway the tall buildings, and the ugliness of the city shakes the very soul of Barabbas. "I thought this was the city that never sleeps," Barabbas says to himself, wandering through the streets of lower Manhattan in the early morning. Creatures of the night, most of NYC's inhabitants stay in their beds for the first few hours of every day.

Barabbas only catches a glimpse of the quiet streets before plunging even further—beneath the ground! The underground trains whooshing by take his breath away, and he wonders for a moment whether Nino Jones is a human being or an animal that lives in a cave. He steps onto the 3 train and takes it to Canal Street, where he will finally come face to face with his soon to be prophet.

September's gusty late summer winds rustled the New York City litter like blowing leaves on an autumn day. Nino Jones lives in a giant pipe below the deserted F.S. Tandle Radiator Factory. He found the pipe thirty years earlier while seeking temporary shelter from a terrible snowstorm, and has lived there ever since. A fire in 1981 once sealed Nino in the pipe for over a month. The building was eventually torn down and is now a parking lot for Bing Lou's Famous Chinese Restaurant. After the tragedy, Nino was so exhausted and dehydrated that he almost died. He managed to dig himself out of the pipe and onto the subway platform before collapsing. He woke up three days later in a public clinic, but the only home he had to return to after treatment was buried in the ashes of the Radiator Factory. When his strength returned, he dug his way back to the pipe, and made a permanent entrance from the Subway platform. It is well camouflaged and cannot be seen from the tracks. Nino is the only person in the world who knows the whereabouts of his pipe, and that is the way he likes it. He normally goes into the Canal Street subway station very late at night when it is deserted and makes his way down the tracks toward Wall Street. It's safer to go late at night, because the trains don't come through as frequently.

Barabbas watches this curious character as he boards the train. If each wrinkle on Nino's face is a result of a trial during his life, then Barabbas couldn't begin to imagine the burdens this man has endured. But there is something beautiful about his weathered skin—something soulful. Immediately, Barabbas feels a connection with this torn and tattered old man.

Unlike the other decrepit looking creatures on board, Nino doesn't carry a cup and ask for money from the passengers. In fact, Barabbas is shocked to see Nino refuse handouts.

The train moves quickly from Canal Street all the way up Broadway, to 125th Street. Nino takes this ride every morning, boarding the train at 5:00 am. He likes to start at the top and work his way back down Broadway, doing favors for his favorite citizens along the way. This is how he gets his money for food. He earns it. Nino Jones does not believe in taking charity.

Officially starting his day in Harlem is part of his disguise. He doesn't want the people who see him every day to know where he goes to sleep each night. When they ask, he always says he lives in Harlem.

Barabbas follows Nino on his walk back down Broadway, all the while amused by Nino's gentle way with everyone he meets. If there is any beauty to be found in the concrete jungle, it is the different shapes, sizes and colors of the people one runs into on the city's streets. Barabbas can hardly hold back a chuckle as Nino approaches one of his favorite souls, a stocky, round bellied old man with massive arms and a hearty laugh. His name is Doyle, but everyone calls him Shorty—for obvious reasons.

"Good morning, Nino," Doyle exclaims, excited to see his daily helper. "It's gonna be a beautiful day today!"

"If you say so, Shorty. If you say so. You're sure off to an early start today," Nino says. "What's the hurry?"

"Oh, it's me and my wife Bessie's anniversary, and I'm going to surprise her by coming home early and … well … you know—maybe do something nice." The short man's cheeks turn crimson red and Barabbas is warmed by his obvious love for his wife. Nino appears to know exactly where Shorty is coming from, and comes to his aid immediately.

"I know, Shorty. Sure I do. Say, how would you like some help unloading the rest of those flowers?"

"I'd love some help, Nino, but you'll have to take at least $20 or no deal!"

Though Barabbas isn't completely familiar with current U.S. currency, he knows from reading the signs in the storefronts that $20 can't possibly get you much in New York City. He is surprised to hear that Shorty has to convince Nino to accept this modest stipend.

"You're a hard man, Shorty," Nino says. "But who am I to argue?" The two friends share a chuckle, and their strong arms finish the job quickly. Doyle hands Nino two ten-dollar bills and thanks him for his help.

"You sure are a good, hard worker, Nino. Bessie would thank you too if she were here."

Much to Barabbas' surprise, Nino hands one of the bills back to Doyle. "Shorty," says Nino, "you're a real generous man, but I can't take all of this. Do me a favor. Tonight when you go out to eat, you and Bessie have a drink on Nino Jones. That will make me feel very happy." Barabbas watches Doyle's cheeks warm with a loving glow. He and Doyle are both choked up by the homeless man's generosity and sensitivity. Doyle swallows hard and reaches out to Nino with a strong handshake. "You know," he says, "last Sunday while me and Bessie were sitting in church, our priest Monsignor Kreig was reading from some part of the Bible and he told us that we should be friendly to strangers, because many people have entertained angels without even knowing it. You are an angel, aren't you? Only an angel would do such a generous thing. You gave me half of all the money you have in the world, just to make my anniversary a little sweeter. By cracky, wait until I tell Monsignor that I know a real live Angel, and his name is Nino Jones! Have a good day, Nino—and thanks a lot, pal." With a tip of his hat, Doyle hops into his pickup and putters away.

Barabbas makes a mental note of Doyle's exclamation. "It takes an angel to know an angel," he smiles to himself. Nino, in the meantime, is still laughing about Doyle's words. "An angel? An angel!? Yeah, that's what I am," he says out loud to himself, spreading his arms like wings. "That's why I wear this raggedy-ass overcoat—to hide my wings! Angel Nino Jones! If that isn't blasphemy, I don't know what is! Angel Nino Jones. That'll be the day, when God has some use for a bum like me."

Barabbas shakes his head at the irony as Nino continues to laugh at his own virtue. "If he only knew," Barabbas thinks to himself. "If he only knew."

Author's Note: YOU NEVER STAND ALONE!

"Rejoice in the Lord always, and overcome by his words. For you are a friend of Gods. He calls you friend!"

-Israel and The New Breed (Rejoice!)

"Everybody Has A September In Their Life... You Know The First Time You Hear God's Voice and Feel His Love...Ba-De-Ya, and God Was Just A Prayer Away"

-Kirk Franklin's Tribute to Earth Wind & Fire

CHAPTER 3

▼

"All journeys have secret destinations of which the traveler isunaware."
-Siddhartha Gautama BUDDHA (563 BC)

"What is God? He/She is an existence that absolutely lives for others."
-Sun Myung Moon

"The very bravest souls see the world through their own eyes. They feel it with their own hearts. They hear it with their own ears. They speak to it with their own mouths, and they solve its problems with their own minds ..."
-Mark Salvtore Pitifer

As Nino makes his way toward 72ndstreet and Broadway, he witnesses a well dressed man bump into and knock down a young woman who was walking out of Kay's Corner Store with two toddlers in tow, and her arms full of groceries. As the children cried and the groceries spilled onto the sidewalk, the man just kept walking. Nino is overtaken with anger and chases after the man, using words Barabbas rarely hears ...

Nino fumes with anger, "Hey!" Nino yells after the man. "Yeah, you. I'm talking to you, you little punkass motherfucker! You take your sorry ass back to that woman and apologize or I'm gonna kick the living shit out of you," he yelled.

While Barabbas had a hard time witnessing such violence between human beings, he appreciated what Nino was taking on, and secretly rooted for him. The pompous, well-dressed man turns on his heel and glares down his nose at the future prophet. "My chivalrous little man," he condescends, "I think it would be a good idea if you found some other way to make your wine money today. Now leave me alone before I call the police, you home-less little Broadway roach." He then turns his back to Nino and steps to the curb to hail a taxi.

Nino, outraged but saying nothing, steps closer to the man and reaches out with his left hand, grabbing the man's collar and squeezing it tightly around his neck. Barabbas gasps to himself as he watches the scene. Nino takes things a step further by taking his right hand and reaching up between the man's legs, taking a firm hold of his family jewels. He then walks the barely breathing man to the scene of the incident. Other men who had stopped to watch are wincing in pain, just imagining what Nino's grip must feel like. The man is sweating and walking on his tiptoes as they arrive at the store-front where the girl is still picking up her groceries. Finally, Nino speaks.

"Now, apologize," he says calmly.

There is no response from the man.

Nino tightens his grip, "I said apologize," Nino repeats, his voice rising slightly.

In total defeat and humiliation, the young man mutters out a lame apol-ogy. "I am very sorry for knocking you down. Please accept my apology," he says through his clenched teeth. Nino loosens his grip and the crowd explodes with laughter and applause. Barabbas even chuckles to himself. He can't help but notice that the same glow that he had witnessed on old Doyle's cheeks now decorates the waif-like face of the young woman Nino had assisted.

"Thank you so much," she says to Nino. "That was a very brave and noble thing you did. Most people in this city wouldn't have given it a second glance."

"Well ma'am," Nino replies, "what that man did to you was wrong. I have learned to walk away from a lot of things in my life, you have to if you're going to survive in this city, but when I see a man treating a woman disrespectfully I cannot turn away. I'd rather die."

The young woman is obviously moved by Nino's virtue. "There's only one other person in the world that I can think of who would do something like you did here today," she says, a far away look in her big brown eyes. "You remind me of my brother. He would have taken care of me like you just did … We were always real close." The woman's voice quieted, and Barabbas thinks she might be on the verge of tears. "I just don't get to see him that often now that I've moved to the city. He always took care of me. If anybody bothered me, my brother would be hot on his trail. It's comforting that in this cold-hearted city there's someone like my brother walking the streets."

"Well," Nino says softly, "Your brother sounds like a good man, a real good man. I thank you for the compliment. Maybe I'll get to", the young suit, who has returned to the scene with a police officer, interrupts Nino.

"There he is officer. There's that piece of Harlem trash that assaulted me. I demand that he be taken into custody at once!"

"Sergeant Hank Pearson here ma'am. What seems to be the problem?" The Sergeant appears familiar with Nino, and hesitant to believe the claims of the cocky yuppie that wants him arrested. "I'm not taking anybody anywhere until I hear exactly what happened."

The yuppie tries to tell his side of the story, accusing Nino of assaulting him for no reason whatsoever.

"Wait a minute," Hank says, suspecting a lie. "How did he assault you? I don't see any marks on you."

"He falsely accused me of knocking down this woman. He then grabbed me by the back of my collar and my testicles and walked me—no, no—dragged me to this store front and ordered me to apologize for something that I didn't even do."

The young woman can't hold her tongue any longer. "Something you didn't even do? Sergeant," she says, turning to Hank, "I was coming out of this store holding a bag of groceries, pushing this baby stroller and keeping an eye on the little girl when this guy bumped into me and knocked me to the ground. He turned to look at me with a stupid smirk on his face and didn't even say he was sorry. If anybody should be in trouble for what happened here, it should be this insensitive creep that brought you here. Not Nino."

Smugly, "Oh," the creep interjects, "This woman has obviously confused me with some other pedestrian. There are thousands of people in suits walking up and down Broadway. Now are you going to do something, or not?"

Hank sees through the young man's sleaziness and turns to him. "Yes, sir, I am going to do something," he says. "I am going to give you ten seconds to hail a cab and get your lying, pompous ass off my beat, or I'm going to haul you into my precinct for harassment, endangering the welfare of these children, and leaving the scene of an accident. I have begun counting, sir, and if you have the misfortune of still being here by the time I get to ten then I am going to deputize Mr. Nino here and have him walk you to my patrol car which is parked five blocks north of here. Do we understand each other, sir?"

Needing no further encouragement, the young man sprints across the street and jumps into a waiting cab without looking back. Sgt. Hank, Nino and the young woman join the crowd in laughter, and Barabbas finds himself even more impressed with his prophet-to-be. He has seen more than enough to convince him that Nino is the right man for the job, and as he gets ready to end his visit to NYC, he listens to the three strangers brought together by Nino's unsolicited kindness.

"Boy oh boy," Sgt. Hank says, still laughing, "I would have loved to see you walk that prima-donna down Broadway on the tips of his freshly polished shoes! Nice work, Deputy Nino."

"Nino Jones, sir. It's a pleasure to meet you Sergeant Hank."

"No, sir. The pleasure is all mine." The two men shake hands and the Sergeant turns to the young woman. "How about you, ma'am? Are you alright?"

"Yes, Sergeant. Thanks to Nino. It makes me feel good to know that you and Deputy Jones are walking the beat in my neighborhood. You take care."

Sergeant Hank tips his hat and leaves the young woman and Nino alone.

Shari continues, "You know, you look familiar to me. I am sure I've seen you before," she says.

Nino smiling, "Oh, I'm sure you have, ma'am. I do a lot of work around this part of town."

"Well, thanks again, Nino. My name is Shari. I hope I run into you from time to time." Shari surprises Nino with a long-needed hug. Barabbas smiles as he watches Nino walk away, a little happier and a lot prouder.

"There are those who give little of the much which they have—and they give it for recognition and their hidden desire makes their gifts unwhole-

some. And there are those who have little and give it all. These are the believers in life and the bounty of life, and their coffer is never empty."

-Kahill Gibran

CHAPTER 4

▼

"Hope is the companion of power and the mother of all success, for those of us who hope strongest have within us the gift of miracles."
-Sydney Bremer

"All men should strive to learn before they die what they are running from, and to, and why."
-James Thurber

"The great danger for family life, in the midst of any society whose idols are pleasure, comfort and independence, lies in the fact that people close their hearts and become selfi sh."
-Pope John Paul II

Back in the Grand Cinema, Barabbas looks at his watch and realizes that he is running out of time and still has to check in on the other half of his plan—Nino's "Aaron. He winces thinking that he also has to stop and find Noah before he goes home."

"Mark Salvatore Pitifer," Barabbas says out loud. He is once again transported, but this time he feels like he is floating rather than plunging. He lands soundly on a small, tree-lined street in upstate New York. The warm September sun is just setting over the serenity of Seneca Lake, and Nagel Place is filled with the laughter of several cherubic children. For a moment, it is unclear whether or not he has actually left paradise. A big red house in the middle of the street is surrounded with music from the many wind chimes that decorate its porch.

Suddenly, a man's voice booms over the peaceful chimes, distracting the very air of Nagel Place. Barabbas is saddened and startled by the disruption, and tries to focus on its source. In the back of the big red house, two grown men are involved in some sort of contest. "It looks like a basketball game of sorts," Barabbas thinks to himself. He recognizes basketball, because it is one of the most popular games played in Forever. Jesus himself is an excellent point guard. As an audience of children watch, the taller of the two men laughed hysterically at the shorter, muscular man's tirade. As the tirade grows louder and louder, the kids are all chiming in. "Take it easy, Pitt. You can still win, Pitt ..."

"Pitt," Barabbas says to himself. "Oh, my. That must be the son—of-Sully!" Barabbas bites his lip as he watches his "Aaron" act like a spoiled child.

"This is my court!" Pitt yells. "I'm supposed to get the rolls on my court! Not him! If you are going to continue to torture me like this, I wish you would just take me now and get it over with." As Pitt continues to yell, it becomes clear to Barabbas that this angry young man is actually yelling at God. What a disgrace! He watches as Pitt punts the ball high into the air into a neighbor's yard. One of the children goes to retrieve the ball but by the time he returns, Pitt has calmed down and the game is resumed. Surprisingly, Pitt takes the lead. His opponent, Billy, is now one point behind and Pitt needs one more basket to win. Apparently, Pitt rarely beats Billy, and the kids are all rooting for him.

Billy has the ball but misses his shot. Pitt gets the rebound and, known for his outside shot, fakes the jump shot and then drives to the basket. He throws up a wild left-hand reverse lay-up that just makes it over Billy's outstretched fingers, it banks softly off the backboard and lands in the hoop with a soft swish. Pitt throws his hands into the air in a double fisted victory "V" and hollers at the top of his lungs. Billy shakes his head and smiles in disbelief, as does Barabbas.

Pitt imitates the boxing champion, Muhammad Ali. "I am the greatest of all time! I'm the Nagel Place champion now, and I might never play you again. Then, if we ever get into an argument over who was the better basketball player, I'll just say, 'who won last time we played?' Go home and tell your wife Carol how you just got annihilated!" Pitt boasts.

"Don't worry, I might give you a rematch in a couple of years. Long live the king! I am the champion of the world! Take your father home, boys," Pitt says to Billy's sons Andrew, Kevin, Joey, and Christopher 'Bunny", "He's had a very, very hard day."

By this time, the residents of Nagel Place have gathered at this all too familiar scene. Pitt grew up on Nagel Place, and right before he married he bought the house next door to his childhood home. His mother now stands on her back porch, laughing at her son's antics. Billy, the other neighbors and children all join in the laughter, but Pitt's wife seems less than amused.

Leigh scowling, "Mark," she calls from the porch, her voice strained with impatience, "I told you it's time for dinner. It's going to get cold. If you don't come right now I'm going to eat without you."

Pitt annoyed, "Go ahead and eat!" Mark yells at his wife, losing some of his joy. "I didn't tell you to wait for me. Get off my back."

Barabbas grows uneasy as he witnesses Pitt's behavior toward his wife. Surely a future messenger of God wouldn't treat the love of his life with such disregard. Barabbas decides he must hang around longer, to figure out what problems exist in Mr. Pitifer's life and marriage. He has to figure out why a man who is apparently surrounded by so much love and support speaks in such angry tones to his loved ones.

"It would be nice to eat together once in a while, like a family should," Leigh says sadly, storming back through her kitchen door. Pitt's mother, Ann, can't stand to see her son act this way.

Ann speaking sadly, "Mark," she says, "you should go eat dinner with your wife. You know how easily she gets her feelings hurt. Plus, she's under a lot of pressure right now. Go in and be nice."

Pitt kisses his mother on the cheek and heads into his house. Barabbas breathes a sigh of relief as he follows him. Inside, Pitt gets a plate of macaroni and meatballs from the stove. He sits down next to his wife, but says nothing. They both sit in silence for most of the meal. Leigh is the first to speak.

Leigh holding back her tears, "How long can we go on like this?" she asks, her voice cracking with emotion. It's obvious that you are very unhappy. You are never in a good mood unless your buddy Jimmy comes over, or you're playing basketball. You treat other people nicely, but you treat me like a dog!" Her sadness is slowly replaced with anger, and she continues. "It's not my fault we can't have any children!" she yells through her tears. "And it's not my fault your father died. I miss him too, you know. You're not the only one who is feeling bad around here!"

"Every time we get into an argument, you bring up this shit." Mark retaliates. "I'm not blaming you for anything. You just don't know how to live and let live. You're always on my back about something stupid, or you've got your feelings hurt again. I'm not going to walk on eggshells when I'm around you, Leigh. I know I'm moody, but just because I am in a bad mood doesn't necessarily mean I am mad at you! If you care about me like you say you do, just leave me alone. If I'm miserable, then just let me be miserable. If you're the cause of my problem, I will let you know—so don't worry!"

"I'm your wife and you won't talk to me!" Leigh shoots back, her husband's words seeming to go in one ear and out the other. "It kills me to see you walk around here so frustrated. Why won't you talk to me? Why won't you let me try to help you? You are all I have, Mark, and I have given you everything I've got. But it's obviously not enough. It's never been enough. I've never been first in your life and you've always been first in mine. It's always been sports or music for you, and now you've got this book that you feel compelled to write. Maybe I wouldn't mind if these things made you happy, or if you would let me help you with them, but they don't and you won't! I can't take this any more. I really can't go on like this much longer!"

Barabbas can hardly stand the tension in the small, cozy kitchen. Leigh is obviously torn up from the inside out, and Mark doesn't seem to have a clue as to how to fix things. From what he's witnessed, Barabbas figures there is a great amount of love in this room, but that there are obstacles that are even greater. He finds himself praying for the two of them to find peace. As if in answer to his prayer, Pitt's voice turns warmer. Softened by the tears of his beloved, he tries to console her. As he gently strokes his wife's hair, he begins to speak. "I'm sorry, honey. I know I'm miserable a lot of the time. I've just always felt that I was supposed to do something special during my life, but nothing has worked out. I never got to the Olympics. No one has shown any serious interest in my music. Now, I talk about writing this book, but I still haven't done anything with it. I'm 33 years old and it's starting to hit me that my dreams might not come true."

Leigh raises her eyes to meet her husband's, and he continues with his own eyes filling with tears. "I always had this big idea that I was going to do something great. Something big for the world and for God. But I'm a failure. I'm a foolish dreamer who thought he was something special. I was going to be a big star—someone who was known and embraced by the world. I always envisioned myself one day walking into the grocery store where my father worked as a meat cutter for 35 years and saying, 'come on, Dad, you don't have to work here anymore.' But, Leigh, he was gone before I got to do that. Nothing has been the same since he died, Leigh. Everything that was special and important to me seems to be insignificant. Everything I ever did was to make him and my mother proud. When he died, it seemed like my childhood ended, and with it, my childhood dreams. It's kind of like I have become my father. I imagine he used to have dreams, but the man I knew had given up on his dreams.

My mother always believed in my dreams. She and I are two of a kind in that regard. It was her belief that fueled my imagination and made me strong and brave, but it was my father that gave me the never-ending drive. He gave me something to shoot for. I was determined to show him that dreams really could come true, but now it appears that it is I who has been taught a lesson. He always used to say, 'you tell me all about it, pal. We'll see how you deal with it when it's your turn.' Well, I guess it's my turn now, and it looks like my father was right. Now you're married to a dreamer whose dreams have lost their meaning. I hope it's just some passing phase that I'm going through. I pray it is. All I know is that I need to spend some time by myself. I need to be away from my job; away from the people that know me, and, honey, I need to be away from you."

A small sob sneaks out from Leigh's throat as she hears these words. Barabbas can almost feel the pain within the hearts of these two.

"Leigh," Mark continues, "I'm just going to spend a couple of weeks with my sister, Shari. I hope when I come back you'll see the man you married again. Can you understand why I have to go?"

Leigh crying, "I just don't understand how you can say you're a failure, Mark. You graduated in the bottom 10% of your high school class, but now you've completed your Certificate of Advanced Study in Counseling Psychology. You are almost a Ph.D.! You became a school counselor and a coach and you are surrounded by people of all ages who absolutely love you. I only wish I was such a failure."

Pitt sadly, "I am thankful to God for all of the blessings he has bestowed upon me and my family, Leigh. I really am. But in my mind and in my heart, I feel like a failure. Don't you understand that all my life up until now I have always felt like if I hung in there I would eventually get my big break? I believed in the words on my business cards: *Believe in God, Believe in Yourself, Never Give Up.* This is the first time in my life that I have ever felt like my dreams are dead. If they are dead, then who am I? What do I stand for? How does a dreamer find meaning in a life that holds no more meaningful dreams to chase after? Believe me, honey, I don't want to stay like this. That's why I've got to at least try spending time by myself. Who knows? Maybe that big city of dreams has one more left for me."

Barabbas is glad to hear this glimmer of hope in Mark's voice, and enjoys the knowledge that one of Pitt's dreams is about to come true. Once again, he is convinced that the right man for the job has been found. It is obvious to him that Mark has wisdom to share with the world. He stays a few minutes longer, hoping that Mark and Leigh will have a peaceful departure from each other.

"Just pray for me, honey." Mark says to his wife. "That's the most you can do for both of us. Just pray, Leigh."

"What about your job?" Leigh asks, worrying as usual. "How will you get time off? School starts next week."

Mark reassuring, "I talked with Mr. Ferrara and explained my situation to him. He said I could take up to three weeks. How am I going to be able to help all those children and parents solve problems when I can't even get a grip on my own?"

Leigh nods, finally understanding. "When will you go?" she says, softly.

"I'll leave this weekend, and then get back by the end of September. Don't worry, Leigh. The time will go by quickly, and hopefully when I come home things will be better."

"I just hope you don't decide you like being alone better than being with me." Leigh says, showing her insecurity. "You always say what a nag I am."

Mark now sees how his frustration has chipped away at his wife's self worth. "Take off your wedding band and look at the inscription, Leigh."

She does.

"Read it to me."

"It says, 'don't worry forever. Pitt 3-27-87.'" Leigh says, choking back tears.

"I said forever. I meant forever, and forever is why I'll return. I love you, Leigh. Don't ever forget that. I know sometimes it's hard for you to believe, but it's true. I want you to remember something else, too, and I mean this from the bottom of my heart. In this miserable world, Leigh, you are my favorite thing. My most loyal friend."

As Leigh and Mark finally embrace, Barabbas decides he has seen enough. He leaves the Grand Cinema, knowing that he has found the perfect pair for his plan. He remembers that Markie and Noah are waiting for him, and he hurries off to meet them. Barabbas laughs to himself as he realizes that even though he is stressed, he can't remove the smile from his face when he thinks of his two favorite souls.

"You were born together, and together you shall be forevermore. You shall be together when the white wings of death scatter your days. Aye, you shall be together even in the silent memory of God. But let there be spaces in your togetherness, and let the winds of the heavens dance between you. Love one another but make not a bond of love: Let it rather be a moving sea between the shores of your souls. Fill each other's cup but drink not from one cup. Give one another of your bread but eat not from the same loaf. Give your hearts, but not into each other's keeping. For only the hand of Life can contain your hearts. And stand together, yet not too near together: For the pillars of the temple stand apart, and the oak tree and the cypress grow not in each other's shadow. Sing and dance together and be joyous, but let each one of you be alone.
-Kahill Gibran (The Prophet)

"All things will gravitate to thee if you will let love enter thy own heart without compromise. <u>You never know someday the music may return.</u>"
-Paul Twitchell-ECKANKAR & <u>Mark Salvatore Pitifer</u>

*Dedicated to my friends: Jimmy Modera & Diana Fountain

CHAPTER 5

▼

"The great unborn Self is undecaying, immortal, undying, fearless, and infinite."
-Hinduism Brihadaranyaka Upanisad 4.4.25 (3,500 BC)

"If you believe you will receive whatever you ask for in prayer"
-JESUS OF NAZARETH/Matthew 21:22

"Beware that you do not look down upon a single one of these little children. For I tell you that in Heaven their Angels have constant access to my Father.
-JESUS OF NAZARETH/Matthew 18:10

Is there anything more life-affirming than a child's laughter? It bubbles over the flowery hedge of Barabbas' yard as he awaits his two little friends, Markie and Noah. These tiny souls have been anxious to be involved in the heavenly army, and Barabbas is thrilled to give them their assignments.

The laughter grows louder. Markie must be playing with Bella the Bumble Bee again. Bella's delicate wings tickle the little soul as she buzzes by him. Everything in Forever is animated. Even the plants can communicate.

"Hello little Markie, how are you doing, my man?" Markie responds with a giggle, always beaming when Barabbas addresses him as "my man."

"I'm good, Barabbas," says Markie, still giggling.

"Well, if that crazy bumble bee will leave you alone for a minute, you could come with me to find Noah so we can have a chat. Do you know where Noah is?"

"Oh, he's playing a game of Around the World with his friends Robbie and Shoobo. He'll be here when he's done."

Barabbas, unable to wipe a smile off of his face when he pictures the cherubic face of Noah, one of his favorite little souls. "Oh, that Noah. He likes playing basketball too much to ever become a real Zealot!" This comment makes Markie start to giggle all over again. His big brown eyes glisten with delight as Barabbas picks him up and places him on his lap.

"Guess what, Markie," Barabbas says, deciding not to wait for Noah to begin his instruction. "The Heavenly Zealots are working on a very important mission. Can you keep a secret?" Markie nods, his eyes growing even larger in anticipation. "Markie, only the bravest souls are being asked to take part in this mission, and you are one of them. I need you to help me prepare a man who will be called the Prophet of Faith. His name is Nino. He and his messenger are destined to help our brothers and sisters who are currently being attacked by Satan and his demons. Their mission is very dangerous, and your piece of the plan is extremely important."

Markie doesn't know whether to be excited or scared. "What do you want me to do, Barabbas?" He asks, staring right into the Zealot's eyes. "Whatever it is I'll do it. I won't be afraid. I'll be a brave Zealot, just like you."

"That's my boy," Barabbas laughs, giving Markie a giant hug. "Now, pay close attention. I want you to write down some information about Guardian Angels and demons that you think Nino might need to know on his mission."

Markie nervously, "But, how much should I write? What do you think he needs to know?"

"You're smarter than you think, Markie. Don't worry. I'll give you some ideas to get started, and then you can finish on your own."

Barabbas hands two hand woven sheets of paper and two sparkling gold pens to Markie. "I don't want to tell you too much, Markie, because it is important that most of this information comes from a young soul, so it is easier for Nino to understand. Do you know what I mean?"

"Yes," Markie answers. "I can do it. Don't you worry, Barabbas. I'll fix Nino up real good!"

Barabbas is happy to see that Markie is gaining some confidence. Markie may be a young soul, but he has always been a very smart.

Sitting with Markie's curious eyes so intensely focused on him, Barabbas realizes what a delightful satisfaction it must be to work with children on a daily basis. Their curiosity shines forth, begging you for information.

"Okay, Markie. Let's pretend that you're Nino, and I'm you. Write down whatever you think sounds important, okay?"

Markie nods.

"Okay. Here goes. Guardian Angels are assigned to follow the lives of earthbound souls from the day they are born. **While the earthbound souls are still children, their Angels have constant access to God. This is why the prayers of children are so powerful.** Their prayers are sincere, and their angels have our Father's ear."

Markie giggles, "That rhymes, Barabbas!"

"Yeah—dig it Markie! I'm a poet." Barabbas laughs in spite of himself, unable to contain his inner child when he is in Markie's company. "Your Guardian Angels will stay with you only as long as your faith in God remains. If you reject God, then you reject his spirit, and if God's spirit does not dwell in you, then the angels cannot stand by you. They will still love you, and visit you from time to time, but they will no longer be with you every moment of every day."

Markie struggles with his pen as he tries to capture everything Barabbas says. He looks up at Barabbas, eager to hear more. Barabbas continues, speaking slowly so that Markie can keep up.

As Markie settles in on his lap, Barabbas gives a detailed lesson on the duties of guardian angels. Barabbas tries to explain what a conscience is, and how the little voice in the back of your head is actually your guardian angel, working together with your parents, to guide your decisions and important choices.

"It is that unseen force, Markie, that causes you to feel guilt and shame for doing something that no one knows about except you. When you die, and you are able to see for the first time all that your angels have done for you behind the scenes to help keep you safe, you will be deeply humbled & grateful. You see, Satan and his demons are immortal forces of evil that attack you every waking hour that you live. The Guardian Angels can do nothing to directly stop these attacks. But they can try to manipulate the situation so that Satan doesn't have complete smooth sailing—like having a barking dog interrupt a house robbery. This gives the angel more time to speak to the person through their conscience. The more time the angel can buy, the more likely it is that he will be able to get the person to listen to his conscience and do the right thing.

Markie listens closely, those big eyes of his seem to grow wider and wider with every new piece of knowledge Barabbas imparts. Markie wonders, "Why are the citizens of Forever so excited to see the Guardian Angels, Barabbas?"

"Most of the citizens of Forever keep in close contact with their loved ones and help the angels decide how to best assist them during satanic attacks.

"When and why do the Guardian Angels get to come to Forever?" Markie asks,

"Guardian Angels are sometimes called to Forever for special meetings, or just for some rest and relaxation."

Markie worried, "But, Barabbas, what happens to the protected soul when his Guardian Angel is up here?"

Barabbas explains, "While they are gone, replacements are sent to fill in for them. Guardian Angels are never on vacation for more than seven days ET (Earth Time)."

Markie filled with questions, "I heard that Angels can appear to their guarded souls sometimes, is that true?"

Barabbas takes a deep breath, knowing this part might be hard for the young soul to understand. "Well, they can appear, but they can't reveal their identity. The Guardian Angel is constantly trying to steer us in the right direction. He is always trying to get us out of a situation before that which we most desire is exposed. Toward this end, the Guardian Angel can, under certain circumstances, appear to the person who is under his guard and speak to him directly. However, this can only be done once in a person's life, and never again, no matter how grave the circumstances. The Guardian Angels are taught to use this only if it seems clear that the human will possibly choose a path that could prevent her from returning to Heaven."

Markie perplexed, "But, Barabbas! Humans fall to temptations all the time. How do the Angels decide which is the right time to appear?"

"The Guardian Angel knows his assignment's weak points better than anyone else. For example, it might not be that hard to convince a normally righteous person not to rob something simply because he is currently in some sort of financial distress. However, other situations are more difficult."

Markie smiles, "Like when a child gives up chocolate for Lent, and then they walk by a candy store?"

Barabbas laughs at Markie's innocent mind—to think that eating a Hershey Bar would be reason for a Guardian Angel to appear. "A parent usually protects a child from such temptations, Markie, but as a person grows older, their Angel may have more influence than their mom or dad."

Markie nods, "Like if a man covets his neighbor's wife, like the commandment says not to do?"

Barabbas smiles, "You're a smart little soul Markie! Yes, it can be very difficult to make a married man walk away from the attention of a sensual woman."

"So if that happens, an Angel can appear and let the man know to stay away?"

Barrabas nods, "If the Angel chooses to physically manifest himself, he can at no time identify himself as an angel. Nor can he do anything physically to stop the attack."

"Then, what can the Angel do?" Markie asks, getting frustrated.

"He can take on any human appearance he chooses. He will generally come up with words and actions so significant to the individual that the individual will be positively affected for the rest of his life."

"They have to be tricky and smart! Boy oh boy, Guardian Angels sure have a pretty tough job, I'll say!"

"You're not kidding, Markie. I wouldn't want that responsibility."

Markie wipes his brow, "Me either. Is there anything more I should write about the Guardian Angels?"

Barabbas continues, hoping Markie will be able to simplify the complicated ways of guardian angels. It will be difficult for Nino Jones to comprehend how the angels disguise themselves and affect an individual's surroundings, gently guiding a soul's decision without interfering with free will. Markie pauses and a serious look covers his face.

"What are you thinking, Barabbas? Now you look scared!" Markie laughs nervously, growing a little frightened by the expression on Barabbas' face.

"I think we've covered the Guardian Angels, Markie, but now I have to tell you about the Demons."

Markie quivers.

Barabbas hugs Markie, "It's okay Markie. Don't be afraid, it won't take long."

Markie sucks in his stomach and tries to look brave. "Who? Me? I'm not afraid of any old demons!"

"Uh huh. Well, I think it's a little scary when you think of all the bad that is caused by them." Barabbas says, trying to make Markie feel better about his fears.

"They're real scary looking, too!" Markie exclaims.

Barabbas laughs and the tension is eased a bit. "You're not kidding. It even makes me a little afraid sometimes to look at them!"

Markie surprised, "Barabbas! You get scared?! I didn't think you would be afraid of anything. You're so brave! How can you be afraid and brave at the same time?"

Barabbas nods, "Markie, my good friend Mark Twain once wrote that 'courage is the resistance of fear. It is the mastery of fear. It is not the absence of fear.' Think of our King Jesus. Nobody who was ever born had to go through something as scary as he had to go through."

"Was Jesus afraid sometimes, too?" Markie asks.

Barabbas raises his eyebrows, "Sure he was! He was so afraid of being crucified that he sweated drops of blood in the Garden of Gethsemane. And maybe you can say something in your notes to Nino about this. Let him know that it is okay for him to feel afraid, but that in the end he must be brave. His faith in God will allow him to overcome any demon. In fact, if his faith is strong enough, he would be able to stand toe to toe with Satan and whip him the same way Jesus did."

Markies eyes grow big, "He really could?"

Barabbas nods, "Sure he could. Anyone with strong faith can. You have to remember something about Satan and his demons. They are nothing more than big, scary looking bullies. All they can do is threaten you, or try to scare you. They can tempt you and set traps for you, but they cannot kill you or hurt you in any way."

Shocked "No way, Barabbas! I have seen demons kill earthbounds before!" Markie shouts.

Barabbas remains patient "I misspoke, Markie. They can kill or hurt those souls who have rejected God and given their souls to Satan. You are right." Barabbas calms Markie with a pat on the shoulder and then explains himself a little further. "Once a soul has given himself to Satan, they can be taken any time Satan wants to take them. However, he usually lets them live a long time, because he can accomplish much evil through a person whom he totally possesses. That's why it seems like the miserable people live for a very long time. Satan, out of his own pride, arrogance and evil, keeps these enslaved souls around as long as their bodies will last so that he can squeeze every last drop of evil out of them. God, on the other hand, keeps the bad people around as long as he can in hopes that they will repent and change their ways. God loves us so much that even when we refuse to acknowledge him he never stops loving us or believing in us. So, even if we have separated ourselves from Allah by the way that we live, he still protects us from Satan and his demons. If God protects those who do not acknowledge him, it goes without saying that Satan and his demons have no power whatsoever to hurt the children of God."

"Isn't everyone a child of Jehovah?" Markie asks.

Barabbas clarifies, "Yes, but I'm talking specifically about the souls who try to live by God's rules. The Lions Abijah."

"The Lions Abijah?" Markie asks.

Barabbas continues, "**The Lions Abijah. The lions whose father is God. All people who treat other people the way they want to be treated, and who believe and trust in God. The Lions Abijah all walk the path of Jesus.**"

Markie concerned, "What if these people believe and trust in God, but they don't believe in Jesus? You know, like the Jews, the Muslims, or the Hindus?"

Barabbas chuckles at Markie's wit, "That's a good question, Markie. Jesus is a free gift for all who can accept him. Accepting Jesus as your savior does, indeed, give you extra protection and power over the forces of evil, and God hopes that all people will eventually realize that Jesus is the Messiah. However, God does not hold it against people who are born into other religions if they do not believe in Jesus exactly the way he would like them to. God understands the barriers that exist in the world. Jesus came into a hostile, evil world and gave us all a path that leads to Heaven. In the end, it will not matter what you called yourself, but whether or not you walked the path of Jesus."

Markie perplexed "But how can a Jew, Muslim, or a Hindu walk the path of Jesus?"

Barabbas calmly continues "Each person will be judged according to how they treated the people, creatures and planet they encountered during their lifetimes."

Markie excited, "But everyone knows that Jesus is the only sacrifice that Allah will accept to atone for sins. These people who have not asked God to forgive their sins in the name of Jesus will die with sin-stained souls, won't they Barabbas? Won't they be thrown into the Outer Darkness?"

Barabbas smiles proudly "You know your scriptures well, Markie, but it goes a little deeper than that. Remember what Jesus said, 'You can call me lord. You can do mighty miracles in my name, but what's most important is that you obey our father in Heaven.' The path of Jesus is ultimately what is most important. If you truly follow the path, then you will be merciful, forgiving and non-judgmental towards others. **So, even if you die with a sin-stained soul, if you were merciful to those who sinned against you, you will be shown mercy. You see Markie, Mercy triumphs over judgment, because mercy is the heart of the law!** This is why non-Christians gain admittance into the Kingdom of Forever. The contrary is also true. There will be those who call themselves Christians but are unmerciful, uncompassionate and judgmental toward others. These people, although they call on the name of Jesus, will not be admitted, because they walked not the path of our king."

"Whew," Markie gasps. "So, the path of Jesus is what's most important, and all who follow it will make it home. Right?"

Barabbas grins widely. "There is only one God, only one Kingdom of Forever, and only one path that leads us home." Barabbas looks down at his watch and realizes too much time has slipped by. "Oh, dear. Just a couple of more things and then I've go to get out of here. Jeepers creepers! Sometimes when I get talking, I go off on tangents worse than Chebar!" Markie and Barabbas both laugh out loud. Barabbas collects himself and focuses on his lessons once more. "Markie, let Nino know that there are two kinds of demons that he may encounter. The regular demon, on leave from the abyss, only has the power to gain control over portions of a soul's personality. He can torment you in many ways, but cannot physically manifest himself. However, Satan's Soldier Demons, much like the Guardian Angels, can take on any appearance they wish. They can also stay invisible if they choose. They have the same power as Angels to talk directly to your soul. This is why, sometimes for some unexplained reason, good and bad thoughts constantly race across your mind, even when it has nothing to do with what you're doing or thinking about. The attacks from Satan and his demons are usually carefully concealed from the victim. Temptations are like the crusts of bread that lead a bird towards a hunter's trap. The hunter seeks not what is in the best interest for the bird, nor does Satan seek what is in the best interest of the soul. Satan and his Soldier Demons insert evil thoughts and perverted desires into our minds. They make us fantasize about doing some evil thing until it becomes something for which we long. When the temptation reaches this stage, the human begins to develop a plan of action. If the soul has no knowledge of the Holy Scriptures and no relationship with God, then she will, inevitably, fall to temptation."

Markie worried, "How will Satan and his demons find out about Nino, Barabbas?"

Barabbas disgusted, "How does he find out about everything we try to do? His demons are everywhere. It's like setting a piece of pie out at a picnic. How long does it take for the flies to find it? We know that he will find out about it. It's just a matter of time before he chooses when and how to attack."

Markie worried, "How do you think Satan will attack Nino?"

Barabbas is troubled by the very thought of it. He rests his head in his hands and runs his fingers through his hair a few times, nervously. "He'll probably try to scare him, or convince him to give up. He may try to frame Nino for a crime. He could do anything, really. We just have to do our best to prepare Nino and hope that Satan underestimates our prophet of faith."

"Once a demon discovers Nino, will he stay with him wherever he goes? I mean, how do you run away from a demon?"

Barabbas frowns, "Well, Markie—you can't. You either frustrate them with your knowledge of the Holy Scriptures, or the demon gets sidetracked and he inadvertently loses you. Demons are not allowed to put any sort of homing device on humans. If they lose you, they have to find you on their own. However, this is usually not a hard thing for them to do."

Markie wonders, "Since there are so many of them wouldn't they all just help each other out?"

Barabbas scoffs, "Team work? In Satan's ranks? Ha! That's a laugh! It's every demon for himself. That's another weakness in our favor. There is no loyalty or trust amongst the demons. It's truly a house divided. The big difference between God's Angels and Satan's Demons is primarily who they serve, not how they serve. Angels are not afraid of Satan, because they know God is on their side and if God is with you, no one can stand against you. Angels also stick together with love and loyalty. Demons, on the other hand, are scared of God, Jesus and his Angels. They know that their time is limited and that soon their eternal torture begins. It is only for the sake of the Great Game that demons, including Satan, are given any power at all. They are a necessary part of God's plan."

Markie takes a giant breath and sighs with all his might as Barabbas finishes his lesson. Barabbas chuckles, aware that he has given the young soul an overwhelming amount of information.

"So, Markie, what will you tell Mr. Jones when you meet him?"

"Dear Mr. Jones," Markie begins, his voice a little shaky. "When you are a child, you have a special gift. An angel is sent from heaven, to give your soul a lift. Your guardian angel sends your prayers directly to God's ears, and stands beside you, night and day, to chase away your fears. Like a guard dog's bark or a nightlight's beam, your angel warns you of bad things. Angels hold your hands as you take your first steps and guide you along on their wings. When Satan sneaks up on your soul, trying to lead you astray, your guardian angel makes something happen that scares that ol' meany away! But, you can't see your guardian angel; you just must believe he is near. And your faith may start to weaken—year after year after year. But even an old man like you, Mr. Jones, has an angel guiding your ways. And if you hold on to a little faith, he will remain for all your days." Markie bows and Barabbas claps for him.

"Anything else?" Markie asks, hoping Barabbas will say yes.

"Well, Markie—I think that should cover it." Barabbas walks in front of Markie, who jumps to his feet and stands at attention, saluting Barabbas.

"Never mind the salute," Barabbas laughs. "Give me a hug, you jelly slug!"

Markie jumps into Barabbas' arms and gives him a big hug, saying "Give me a kiss, you jelly fish!" Barabbas kisses Markie on his cheek and sets him down with a pat on the head.

"You can leave this on my desk when it's finished. I'll see you later." Barabbas starts to leave. "And Markie, I and the rest of the Zealots really appreciate your help. They all told me to tell you thank you very much."

Markie can't hold back his broad smile. "Tell them they are very welcome!"

Barabbas waves goodbye and disappears beyond the garden walls. As Markie finishes writing his notes for Nino, a thought pops into his mind. Maybe this guy Nino, while he is down there doing his thing, could look around for some good mommy and daddy candidates. It didn't seem like an unreasonable request—not to Markie, anyway. So, at the very end of his notes about angels and demons, Markie left this little note:

Dear Nino,

My name is Markie. I am the little boy who helped write you these very important notes. I know you are going to have a lot to do down on earth, but if you can get some spare time, would you please help find a mommy and daddy for me and my good friends, Nina and Noah? We have been in the Royal Playground for such a long time now. We're starting to worry that we might have missed our chance to enter the Great Game. Oh, and if we do get a chance, we would like to be a family.

As he finishes his note, Markie kneels in the Garden, facing God's holy mountain in the recesses of the north. He closes his big brown eyes and prays, **"Thank you for the world so sweet. Thank you for the food we eat. Thank you for the birdies that sing. Thank you, God, for everything.** Please, God, help this man Nino. May his mission be a success, and may he find a family for my friends and me. Amen."

Author's Note: So many of us only go to God when we have a problem, or we want something. Think of a friend who only calls you when they need a favor. How does that make you feel? God wants, more than anything else, to have a relationship with you. In order for you to have a relationship with him you must speak to him. Live a life of prayer. Talk to God often and always. Ask for what ever you like, but remember sometimes the answer is no. God already knows what you need, so simply thank him for the blessings you do have. Reflect on your life on a daily basis. Ask to be forgiven and helped with your problem areas. If you forgive those who sin against you, God will forgive you; but if you refuse to forgive them, He will not forgive you. Trust him in all things, and try with all of your might not to be a fair weather friend.

"When you pray, don't be like the hypocrites who pretend piety by praying publicly on the street corners and in the synagogues where everyone can see them. Truly, that is all the reward they will ever get. But when you pray, go away by yourself, all alone, and shut the door behind you and pray to your Father secretly, and your Father, who knows your secrets will reward you."
-JESUS NAZARETH/Matthew 6:5-6

CHAPTER 6

▼

"Blessed are the peacemakers, for they will be called the sons of God"
-JESUS OF NAZARETH/Matthew 5:9

"The gift is good, which is given, at a due time and place, to a needful recipient who can do no service in return."
-KRISHNA/THE BHAGAVAD GITA (3,137 BC)

Much more than you have sown will grow in your garden
-Croation Proverb

Beyond the Garden walls, there lays the most spectacular play land filled with the youngest of Forever's souls. It is the Royal Playground, and like the wide-open eyes of its inhabitants, it is magical, awe-inspiring and pristine. It cannot be compared to anything known on earth, as it is completely unaltered by man. It is the purest of God's creations. Marshmallow clouds and rich chocolate seas, the fairies that dance in a young child's dreams—these are the magical sights that pull you into Forever's Royal Playground. As your soul returns to its sweetest childhood memory, you are instantly surrounded by the laughter of your first best friend.

The souls who play here have yet to experience a full lifetime on Earth. Long before their first at bat, they were pulled from the game. A rosy-cheeked cherub named Noah is playing homerun derby with a tiny golden brown bear named Timmy. Noah grins sheepishly as Barabbas approaches him.

"I'm sorry Barabbas," Noah apologizes, trying to win him over with a sweet smile. "I forgot about the important meeting."

"Oh, Nimbo," teases Barabbas, using his favorite nickname for Noah. "What am I going to do with you?"

"Barabbas, stop calling me Nimbo!"

"Okay, Noni. Choahnyonicka!" Barabbas chides, using yet another nickname.

"Barabbas!" By now, Noah cannot control his laughter. Just looking at this giant of a man makes him silly, and when Barabbas teases him, Noah is nothing more than a ball full of giggles.

Barabbas scoops up the little bundle of laughter and tries to settle him down. "Alright, Noah. It's time to get serious." Noah swallows hard and puts on a straight face, looking right into Barabbas' eyes. Barabbas continues. "As I told Markie, the other Zealots and I are planning a very important mission, and we really need your help."

"I knew someday I would be a Zealot just like you," Noah says cheerfully, not able to contain his excitement.

Barabbas hates to disappoint him. "Well, you're not going to be a Zealot just yet, Noah. Don't forget, you've got to go through the Great Game, first."

"I know," says Noah. "But, Barabbas, do you really think I still have a chance to get into the Great Game?" Noah's eyes are about to fill with tears as he says this, because he knows that every passing day means he has less time to join the Great Game.

The souls in the Royal Playground are different than other souls in Forever in that their original parents took their first chance in the Great Game away from them. The souls in the Royal Playground are victims of abortion, and they are different in the eyes of Heaven than the children who pass away for other reasons. Almost all earthly youth who die young are what we refer to in Forever as "old souls". These souls have reentered the Great Game of Life for a specific time and purpose, and most of these individuals have lived as many as two or three times! The souls in the Royal Playground, however, have never had their turn in the Great Game. It may seem strange that they would want to leave such a controlled paradise, to face the harsh uncertainties of life-on-Earth. But they are not unlike the human children in that they want a chance to make their Father proud. Noah knows that his time is running out, as the Great Game is coming to an end. Barabbas hates to see one of his favorite souls in so much distress. He tries his best to comfort the little one, hoping with all his heart that his words are true. "Oh, don't be sad Noah. You'll get your chance. Don't you worry little buddy. Why, the way things are going down on earth, they will probably need another Noah very soon!"

"Do you really think so?" asks Noah, finding his smile again.

"Of course, my boy. You have sunshine in your soul, and the world needs some more sunshine right now." Noah laces his chubby fingers between those on the big, strong hand of Barabbas, and the two walk to the edge of a spectacular waterfall that flows into an aqua green pool. Barabbas turns to Noah to tell him what he wants, but before he can get a word out, Noah dives headfirst into the pool.

"Noah!" shouts Barabbas, annoyed but still laughing. "I didn't come here to go swimming with you. Now get up here! I need your help with something real important!"

Noah comes up from the water with his usual sheepish grin—cute enough to warm even the coldest of hearts. He floats on his back and giggles at Barabbas. Barabbas can't stay serious any longer, and, doing a cannon ball dive into the pool he shouts, "I'll fix you, you little squirt!" He lands with a giant splash that sends Noah rolling across the water.

"You are an awful lot of fun, kid. When I get through with all this Zealot business, you and I are going to play and play!"

"Do you promise?" says Noah, an even bigger smile on his face this time.

"Yes, yes. I most certainly do promise."

"When can you come back? Tomorrow?"

"No, Noah. Not tomorrow, but pretty soon."

"But, why can't it be tomorrow?"

"Noah, we need you to go on an important mission for us. The quicker you get it done, the sooner my job will be finished, and then we can play."

"You should have said that sooner, Barabbas. Let's get to it!"

"That's my boy. Now, here's what you have to do. I need you to go to the Holy Temple., and once you get there—"

Noah interrupts, "Can I bring Timmy?" he says, referring to his friend the bear.

Barabbas raises one eyebrow, "Well, I know he is your friend but the two of you might get sidetracked and who knows where you'll end up. Noah, what I'm asking you to do is very important, so if you don't want to do it, and do it well, then you've got to tell me now."

Noah is suddenly serious. He doesn't want to lose the opportunity to help the Zealots. "No, Barabbas. I want to do it. You will see. I'll make you so proud!"

"Okay Noah," says Barabbas, trying to swallow his smile. "When you get to the temple, I want you to find your angel friend, Lolly." "Oh, I love Lolly. She is one of my favorite Angels."

"I know she is. Now listen: ask Lolly to take you to the Holy Archives and help you run a search on a man named Nino Jones. Tell Lolly you are getting the information for me. I need to find out who and where his mother and father are. Do you think you can do that for me?"

"No problem, Barabbas." Noah exclaims."I'll be back before you can say 'spit tobacco or I'll …'"

Barabbas fakes agitation "That's enough, Noah! If you screw this up I'll make you spit tobacco alright." Barabbas is amused by this mischievous spirit, but needs to get back to business. "As soon as Lolly gives you the information sheets, bring them right to my mansion. If I am not there, leave them on my desk—the one in my room that overlooks my flower garden. Okay? Any questions?"

"Well," says Noah, thinking hard to say something unnerving, "do you think I have time to finish that game of homerun derby I was playing with Timmy?"

"Noah!" shouts Barabbas. Before he can say another thing, Noah is off and running toward the Holy Temple. Barabbas just shakes his head and smiles to himself as he thinks of Noah running all the way to the temple. Most other souls would simply fly as fast as they could, but not Noah. He doesn't fly too often because he's afraid he'll miss something that's happening on the ground.

As Noah fumbles and stumbles toward the temple, Barabbas moves on to the next step in his mission—the Grand Cinema.

Author's Note: As a school counselor I see fewer and fewer children who have Noah and Markie's happy, carefree personalities. Our modern children have more money, things, freedom, and activities to fill their days, than any generation that has come before them. However, in many ways they are the saddest, most lonely, and spiritually malnourished children to ever exist. This country alone has nearly 2 million children on mood altering/behavior controlling narcotics. This fact alone is a travesty, and positive proof that our children are mentally are spiritually crumbling. Our self-centered, "Me-oriented" society has lost touch with all that is really important in life: The nuclear family, the extended family, ethnic traditions, moral responsibilities, and most importantly faith in God. The following quote is a portion of a letter to the editor that I wrote back in 1991. It is not my intention to fill you with guilt or make you feel that the situation is hopeless. However, our window of opportunity is slowly closing. The time to act is now! Awaken

"Our children are crying, but who can console them? They are like beautiful flowers sitting in a field on which the sun has turned its back. Withering away, they gradually pale and lose their color, which is their imagination and their faith, until eventually all that remains is an ugly weed, something that only knows how to take, and whose only concern is for itself."
-Mark Salvatore Pitifer

CHAPTER 7

▼

"What is faith? It is the confident assurance that what we hope for is going to happen. It is the evidence of things we cannot yet see."
-Hebrews 11:1

"There is at last produced that living faith, by which we find, within ourselves, as something that is true in our own experience, all that we have believed in hitherto merely with the confidence of a child."
-ECKARTSHAUSEN. (The cloud upon the Sanctuary)

"Imagination is the true magic carpet."
-Norman Vincent Peale

Forever is filled with custom made mansions, but while most are filled with music and laughter on a day-to-day basis, Barabbas now sits with his comrades in complete silence. The mood is serious and somber. There sits Barabbas, Chebar, Pontius Pilate (the Roman Procurator who gave the orders to have Jesus Christ flogged and crucified), Thomas (the doubting apostle), Caiaphas (the high priest who turned Jesus over to Pilate), and Malcolm X (a Muslim who lived most of his life as a black militant, teaching people to hate based on race and religion). Each person in the room had two things in common: an earthly past in which they had done things they were ashamed of, and the longing for the opportunity to help their God and their King one last time. They each wanted to right a wrong, so to speak. They are all convinced that if successful, their plan will bring glory to God and their King and brother, Jesus Christ. They feel that it will hasten the inevitable downfall of Satan, and most importantly, that it could possibly save millions of souls from spending an eternity in Hell. While Barabbas looked over his notes, Pilate and Caiaphas talk quietly.

"Well, Caiaphas my old friend," started Pilate, "the time has finally arrived. No matter what happens, our miserable legacy will be erased forever. No longer will we be looked at as the two notorious villains who put God's Christ to death. Forevermore, we will be seen as heroes in the peoples' eyes. Sons of God; brothers of Christ; and Zealots of Forever. If we can convince two earthbound souls to risk an eternity in the land of the outer darkness in order to save the souls of strangers, then we can finally do something to help defeat Satan, and his counterfeit kingdom."

"Yes, my friend" answers Caiaphas, "even if the risk was Hell itself, I would still be here tonight. The risk is great, but the reward outweighs the possible negative consequences. The pleasures of paradise make those things that we thought so special during our earthly lives seem so insignificant and unsatisfying. Now we know what true pleasures really consist of, and now we see how precious that short interval called life truly was. It is a shame that we had to die before we came to these understandings."

"The understanding that it is Satan and his fallen angels, not people, who are the real enemy. I would have liked to know that during my time on earth," says Pilate. "And the understanding that to do what is right in God's eyes is more important and satisfying than any earthly treasure—can you imagine how different life would have been? Most of the famous heroes in the kingdom of Forever were not famous by any standard during their earthly lives. They were just humble servants of God. People who chose Gods' will over their own, and who loved all of God's creation. It's funny that during all of these years here in paradise, the thing I do most is long to go back. To have an opportunity to do something that will be seen as significant in God's eyes; something that will be remembered for eternity by God himself, this is the only true treasure of the universe. Once it is obtained, no one can ever take it from you. What can compare to this type of everlasting glory and honor?"

Caiaphas feels his friend's excitement, and joins it with his own. "Yes, Pilate, I too have longed for this opportunity! This unexpected prophet, whoever he is, is going to give me what I have dreamed of all these years. It's like being born again! If I could, I would go into the heart of Israel myself, and proclaim to all of the multitudes, 'behold, Jesus of Nazareth, your King and Messiah. The stone that we rejected has become the honored corner stone in the kingdom to come.' Jesus of Nazareth was the Messiah that my people had waited for; for so long. When I was younger, I always believed that the Messiah would come during my lifetime. When he did, I rejected him."

"But Caiaphas, who could believe that our messiah would be the son of a poor carpenter?" asks Pilate, understanding his friend's regret.

"Yes, yes. We all expected another King David: a conquering hero to free us from our earthly bondage. Our pride and arrogance blinded us to the truth, and we fulfilled our destiny—which was to reject the Messiah so that the Gentiles could be liberated. One man died so that the whole world could be saved. The plan was so perfect, and all so clear to me now. The irony is that the nation that turned their Messiah over to the world to be tortured and condemned was, because of its actions, also turned over to the world to share a similar fate. One nation was condemned, outcast like a scapegoat, left to wander aimlessly throughout the wilderness, saddled with the sins of the people until it dies; or in the case of Jerusalem, until the world ends. I thought I was doing what was best for my people. I knew that if the unrest caused by Jesus continued that our existence as a nation would come to an end. I decided that it would be better for one man to die than for a whole nation to perish. I was the high priest of the chosen people, but like Ramses the Pharaoh, who fought with Moses, I was blind and I hardened my heart. Why? Because if you cut through all of my rationalizations to the heart and reasons for my actions, I was a coward. Not only a coward, but a faithless, jealous coward. Jesus has tried many times to console me. He has told me that these things had to happen the way they did for God's prophecies and purposes to be achieved. However, this doesn't take away the sting of my humiliation. Nothing will, and nothing can—except for the plan which brings us together on this greatest night of my life!"

"Ah, Caiaphas, I cannot hide from the sting of such truthful words," Pilate answers, holding his heavy head in his hands. "Although we have been in Paradise for over 1500 years, we have suffered much. Our histories are similar, and our infamy the same. But tonight, dear friend, we will share one more commonality. This night that you have called your greatest, I too shall call my greatest, because from this moment on I no longer feel like an out-cast, or a villain."

Finally freeing themselves from self-imposed prisons, the two men look at each other in silence as their hearts flood with emotion. Caiaphas is about to speak when Barabbas enters the room.

"Gentlemen," addresses Barabbas, "I, like you, have waited a long time for this evening to arrive. We have all weighed the risks involved and are totally committed to this plan or we wouldn't be here right now. However, please be advised if you have any reservations whatsoever, now is the time to pull out. As of 0600 hours tomorrow, the abduction will take place and the plan will begin."

The room is filled with a sudden restlessness. None of the others had realized that things would begin so soon. Malcolm X, one of the younger members of the heavenly Zealots, is the first to speak up.

Malcolm concerned, "Barabbas, I have the utmost respect for you. I believe in your capabilities as a leader, and I will follow whatever orders you give me. Just answer one question: are we starting tomorrow because it is the best possible time, or because we are almost out of time?"

Barabbas looking worried, "I'm afraid, Malcolm, that it is a little of both. However, I will not act impetuously, just for the sake of time. It appears that although time is a problem, our hard work has paid off, and things have fallen into place quite nicely. Chebar has successfully found the man who will be our prophet. His name is Nino Jones," Barabbas takes a deep breathe before continuing. "He is a homeless man from the United States of America-"

Barabbas is interrupted by gasps from around the room. No one can believe that his or her prophet can possibly be an American. Barabbas raises a hand to quiet his comrades and continues.

"He resides in New York City."

Again, the room is filled with shock and surprise.

"Gentlemen," Barabbas starts again, trying to keep things in control. "Believe me, I had the same reaction. However, I have checked him out thoroughly and he is almost exactly what we need. The only problem that Chebar and I see possibly happening is that the people may not take him seriously due to his position in society. Which, if you will stop and think about it, doesn't put him in bad company. Remember, 'Nothing good comes from Galilee. How could a carpenter from Nazareth be the Christ of God?' In any case, we have already located a suitable person to assist him. I was going to wait and see how our prophet does on his own, but I have decided that it will be better for everyone involved if we unite Mr. Jones and Mr. Pitifer as soon as possible. You see, Mr. Pitifer is an aspiring writer of both books and music, and if Nino Jones is going to be the unexpected prophet, Mark Salvatore Pitifer is going to be the unexpected apostle. Like St. Peter, was the rock upon which the church of Jesus Christ was built, so too will Mark Salvatore Pitifer be the rock upon which the All God's Children Movement is built."

"But, I thought you said using two humans—especially two American humans—would only complicate the situation," interjects Chebar. "And what is the All God's Children Movement?"

"Initially, Chebar, I did feel it would be a mistake to use two American humans to carry out our plan. After careful consideration, though, I have concluded that it is the only way to go. Remember, we can't be sure exactly how much time Nino will have, or how much of an impact he will make on his own. That is why it is important for him to have someone who believes in his story enough to write down everything he says. With this two person approach, at least we have a chance that the message and the movement will continue on, even after Jones is gone."

Barabbas lets this information sink in with his followers, making sure there are no objections so far.

Barabbas continues, "As for the All God's Children Movement, it is simply a name I came up with last night that I believe encompasses everything we stand for. It is the religious movement that attempts to unite Christians, Muslims, Jews, Hindus, Buddhists and Gentiles—all believers and nonbelievers. We will attempt to show these people how they are all stumbling over Jesus Christ, and how if they unite they will be able to save countless millions of souls from falling into the hands of Satan. We will especially try to give them an idea of what life is like in Forever, so that they may begin to set their hopes in Heaven. Why, it is even remotely possible that the team of Jones and Pitifer will be able to prevent the United States of America from becoming the next Babylon. Each of us will still get our individual opportunities to tell Jones what we think is most important. Our own personal blows to that snake and his fallen brood of vipers will help Mr. Jones in his mission. However, what is our ultimate goal? This is what I have personally struggled with for a long time now, and the All God's Children Movement is what I came up with. Are their any objections?"

"I can only speak for myself, but I think what you have done is given our plan more of a direction," states Thomas. Barabbas is pleased that the biggest doubter of his group is showing his support, and nods to let Thomas continue. "Each of us will still be able to individually effect the plan; however, the ultimate goal is now there to remind us of the direction that must be taken."

"Yes, yes," Chebar chimes in, unable to contain his excitement as he watches the plan unfold before him. "All in favor of the name and the goal raise your hands. Very good! So, let it be written that from this moment on, we are the founding fathers of the All God's Children Movement. We are the Sons of Jehovah, the living God, brothers of Jesus Christ the King, and mortal enemies of Satan and his fallen angels; we are the Heavenly Zealots: The Lions Abijah. The true Muslims of Jehovah walking the P.O.J."

The Zealots all applaud and embrace each other in joy and excitement as their mighty plan rolls into action. Together like never before, they feel a new strength and confidence in their mission. Barabbas emerges from the jubilant group, addressing them once more. "Leave it to Chebar to get us all sidetracked," he jokes with the crowd. "Now, if there are no other comments, I will continue. As I said earlier, Nino Jones is a homeless man, with no living relatives. No one even knows for sure where he lives. The beauty of that is that we can take his body without any worry of it being discovered." Barabbas continues to describe the abduction, explaining how they will fool the Heavenly Admissions Station by making sure Nino's death is a natural one. His death needs to occur in the midst of a larger catastrophe, so that those in Admissions and the Heavenly CPA, Natelli, will be going so crazy that they won't notice who takes Jones through the gates. The natural, catastrophic death will occur easily enough, Barabbas explains, because of a prophesized weather change.

"On Wednesday, September 16, the temperature will reach 130 degrees Fahrenheit. It will decline steadily until 5:45AM the following morning, at which point it will plummet from 75 degrees to negative 30 degrees within fifteen minutes. This deep freeze will last for two days. Many people will naturally die, which although tragic, will suit our needs. Another positive is that we will be able to keep Jones in Forever for at least two days before we have to start worrying about his body decomposing. You will all be happy to know that Chebar's nephew, Gideon, is Nino's Guardian Angel. On the night of the abduction, Pilate is going to relieve Gideon from his post by explaining that his uncle Chebar wishes to see him. Chebar will detain Gideon until Jones is dead. Now, as I told you before, even with Pilate as the substitute guardian angel for Jones, he still has to get by our Heavenly CPA, Jimmy Natelli. Pilate will be disguised as a woman. He will have to explain what circumstances led him to take the body before he was signaled. However, Natelli is sharp. He acts very tough on this type of mistake. I guarantee that he will check out Pilate's story on the earth photo scanner. If the story checks out, Jones and Pilate will be sent forward to the border of Paradise. As soon as Natelli is out of sight, Pilate will cross the border of Forever, and then there is no turning back with the plan. I have arranged it with my friends on the border patrol to give me entrance. I told them that on the morning of September 17 I will be disguised as a black man and Chebar will be a woman. I told them that we would be returning from an unauthorized reconnaissance mission. Listen up, gentlemen. This part is very important. It will take Natelli at least seven days to realize that St. Peter did not talk to everyone that he has sent to him."

"Excuse me Barabbas," Chebar interjects, unexpectedly. "But, you are assuming we will have seven days. We won't have seven days unless the abduction takes place at the very beginning of a seven-day cycle. That can't be. As it is, the abduction will take place on the 3rd day of the cycle. If we keep Jones with us until early Saturday morning, this means that he and Pitifer could have less than 48 hours together."

"Barabbas," shouts Pilate, "Less than 48 hours?!"

Caiaphas is also taken aback. "Maybe we should reconsider?" he asks, his confidence clearly shaken.

"Reconsider? Reconsider what?" Barabbas paces the floor as he tries to contain his emotion. "Gentleman, I am just as upset as you are by this realization, but I am afraid this may be our last chance. If Jones and Pitifer only have a short time together, that is going to have to be better than nothing at all. We are all just going to have to do a very, very good job, in a very short amount of time. I am confident that we have selected the right people for the job."

"But will they have time?" Pilate questions. "Is it really worth the risk?" The others nod in support of Pilate's questions.

"If you think about the essence of this plan, whom does the weight of it ultimately rest upon?" asks Barabbas.

"Well, Jones has to take the information from us and pass it to Pitifer, and then it's Pitifer's job to give it to the world through his music and writings," answers Malcolm X.

"That's right. As long as Jones can give Pitifer the foundation of the message, the rest will be up to Pitifer." As Barabbas makes his point clear, confidence returns to the others, and they are ready to put their plan into action. "It's all about faith, men. Our faith will defeat Satan and keep our plan in place. In light of the new circumstances, though, I will give you one more chance to reconsider. However, I am still committed to this mission in spite of the obstacles in front of us. It all comes down to faith, my brothers. It's all about faith.

"I say we stick with Barabbas!" shouts Chebar, the consummate Zealot cheerleader. "All in favor say I."

Surrounded once again by support and confidence, Barabbas turns to his followers with his final words. "Thank you, my brothers. Thank you for having faith. Let's pick up at the point in the plan where Natelli discovers that there has been an error. If I know Natelli, he will probably blame the mistake on St. Peter and his end of things. St. Peter will probably be asked to do a Heavenly audit, but this will all be done on the QT, since neither Natelli nor St. Peter will want the King to find out that a mistake has been made. Even after the mistake is discovered and a search for Jones is conducted, Natelli will never suspect that a soul has been abducted. This means there will never be a real sense of urgency from his point of view. His next step will be to figure out which guardian angel was responsible for carrying Jones across the border. Eventually, Natelli will see that I have become Nino's guardian, and he will understand for the first time that this is bigger than he ever imagined. He will swiftly notify the King and St. Peter. I will be pulled from my post immediately, and instantaneously with my removal, Jones will die. The official inquiry will begin, and except for Mark Pitifer, our part of the plan will be finished. The King and his father Allah (the Living God) will examine the effects of the plan. If it is determined that Satan was able to use our plan in any way to his advantage, we will be banished to the outer darkness for eternity. The only other souls to ever violate the doctrine of Forever were Satan and his army of fallen angels. However, our purpose is the antithesis of what his purpose was, and therefore I pray that God may look favorably upon our deeds and us."

After a moment or two of silence, Barabbas concludes his address. "Does everyone understand what is going to happen? Very good, my brothers. We will meet here tomorrow at 0700 hours to meet in person history's most unexpected prophet: Nino Jones—the Prophet of Faith."

Author's Note: As I see it there are two paths that lead to failure in The Great Game of Life. The more common of these two paths is that of the person who never tries. Their fear of failure keeps them trapped in the role of the spectator. The second most common path, and maybe the sadder of the two, is the person who tries, fails, and never tries again. My brother-in-law Rocky Fratto (former NABF Champion, and WBC #1 ranked contender) used to say: "Everybody in this business gets knocked down once in awhile, that's the nature of the sport. But, to get knocked down and stay down, when you could have gotten up, is worse than never trying at all."

> "One of the most common causes of failure is the habit of quitting when one is overtaken by temporary defeat. Before Success comes in any man's life he is sure to meet with much temporary defeat, and, perhaps, some failure. The power that signals success is the power of your mind. There are no limitations to the mind except those we acknowledge. Dreams come true when desire transforms into concrete action. Ask life for great gifts and you encourage life to deliver them to you. Every adversity carries with it the seeds of a greater benefit. Whatever the mind can conceive and believe, it can achieve."
>
> -Napoleon Hill

CHAPTER 8

▼

"Fourteen years ago I was taken up to Heaven for a visit. There I was standing in paradise, and I heard and saw things so astounding that they are beyond a man's power to describe or put into words!"
-Paul/Corinthians 12:2-5

And Jesus replied to the faithful criminal hanging beside him
"Today you will be with me in paradise. This is a solemn promise."
-JESUS OF NAZARETH/Luke 23:43

"On this night I sank deep into the sea of sleep, far beneath the waves of worldly concerns and the restless current of dreams. I awoke to behold a beauty that no earthly eyes have seen, nor ears have heard, nor child's mind imagined."
-Mark Salvatore Pitifer

Far away from Barabbas and his troops, Nino suffers in the city heat. He takes longer than usual to return to his home, knowing it will take quite a while for the pipe that serves as his shelter to cool down. He couldn't get over how hot it had been during the afternoon. The whole city was outraged and amazed by the heat, with temperatures reaching a high of 130 degrees Fahrenheit.

As he descended the old familiar stairs of the Canal Street subway station, Nino began to talk to himself. "Good Lord, you sure did shine your sun brightly on us today. 130 degrees! Man, I have never been so hot in my life! I don't even think it got this hot over in 'Nam."

Stepping into his pipe, the first thing Nino notices is his little friend Papino, the Italian rat. When Papino was a baby, he came into Nino's pipe one night and shared a plate of spaghetti with him. Ever since then, Papino stops by every day. Sometimes he even sleeps next to Nino in a little cigar box. Nino came to love Papino—the closest thing he's had to family in a long time.

"Well, if it isn't the mightiest mouse—er, rat—in all of Chinatown! Man, it must have been like an oven down here today. I could go for a nice cool glass of milk. How about you?" Papino perks up, as if he understands Nino's words. "Boy oh boy, this has been some strange-ass weather lately. Can't even tell what season it is anymore. 130 today, snow tomorrow!" Nino laughs to himself, scratching his head at the mystery of it all. "Come on, old friend. We'll have our cookies and milk. We'll say our prayers and then it's time for bed."

Nino switched on a small lamp that was placed on the center of an old orange crate. Nino had figured out a way to hook up an electrical outlet by using the subway's power. He had been an electrician's apprentice for a short time while he was in the army, and had the job long enough to learn the basics. He also had a small am-fm radio and a compact refrigerator he found on the street. Each night, it was the same routine. He would have a cold glass of milk and some cookies (usually Oreos). If Papino were there, he would pour him some milk in the lid of an old mayonnaise jar, and give him an Oreo on the side. He would then read a couple of chapters from the Bible. When he was ready to go to sleep, he would say his prayers, and then turn on his old radio. He tuned into 104.7, to the cool sounds of Maestro Corey Boatwright's all night jazz show out of Harlem.

"Dear God," Nino prayed. "Thank you and Jesus for everything. We love you. In the name of Jesus Christ, we ask you to forgive us for all of our sins." As Nino prayed, a childlike glow came over his face and innocence gleamed from his eyes. If not for the age in his voice, one would think it really was a child praying. "Now I lay me down to sleep. I pray the Lord my soul to keep. If I should die before I wake, I pray the Lord my soul to take. If I should live for other days, I pray, dear Lord, to guide my ways. God, bless Papino, Nino, the little children and everybody. Amen."

Nino turned off the radio and tucked in his little friend. It was just another ordinary night in the pipe. Ordinary, that is, until about 6:00 a.m.

"We never know how high we are till we are called to rise; and
then, if we are true to plan, our statues touch the skies. The heroism we
recite would be a daily thing, did not ourselves the cubits
warp for fear to be a king."
-Emily Dickenson

*For More on Heaven go to APPENDIX 777 on page 636

CHAPTER 9

▼

"Do not be afraid nor dismayed because of this great multitude, for the battle is not yours, but God's."
-2 Chronicles 20:15

"Courage is the resistance to fear. It is the mastery of fear. It is never the absence of fear."
-Mark Twain

"Maybe I can't win. Maybe the only thing I can do is just take everything he's got. But to beat me, he's going to have to kill me. And to kill me he's going to have to have the heart to stand in front of me, and to do that he's going to have to be willing to die himself … If that bell rings and I'm still standing I'll know for the first time in my life I weren't just another bum from the neighborhood."
-Sylvester Stallone (Rocky IV & Rocky I)

Nino checked the clock on his radio. He could barely pry open his eyes to see the tiny numbers. "5:57 a.m." he said to himself in disbelief. Never had he tossed and turned so much in one night. Just minutes earlier he had been sweating, and now the sweat had frozen to his body. Partially in shock, he reached for a blanket. As he attempted to grab it, he felt his body go limp. His ears were filled with buzzing and ringing, and he thought his whole body might be vibrating. The uncomfortable noise was followed almost instantaneously by the feeling that he was moving very rapidly through a long, dark tunnel. Suddenly, he found himself looking down on his own physical body. He could see himself, and Papino sleeping beside him. He could hear the radio announcer speaking about some sort of weather disaster that had occurred during the night. At first, Nino thought he was just dreaming. After a while, however, he realized this was no dream. He gradually became accustomed to his odd condition. He still had a "body", but one of a very different nature and with very different powers from the physical body he had left behind. Catching glimpses of friends and relatives who he knows have already died; he notices someone approaching him. It looks like a woman, but he can't tell for sure. Pilate leads Nino to Natelli, who asks him a question nonverbally, to make him evaluate his life. While Nino thinks over the question, Natelli briefly interrogates Pilate. Natelli is unable to spend as much time as he normally would, because the weather disaster had caused such an influx of souls. Natelli sends Pilate and Nino on to St. Peter without a second glance. Pilate indicates to Nino that they must move on. Far off in the distance, Nino can see a beautiful being of light. It is a loving warm spirit of a kind he has never encountered. The being of light seems to be standing as some sort of barrier or border. Tens of thousands of souls of all different races were walking with their escorts toward this being of light, and the closer he got the more wonderful Nino felt. When they reached what seemed to be the halfway point, suddenly, in the twinkling of an eye, Nino was standing in the presence of Barabbas and the rest of the Heavenly Zealots (the Lions Abijah). The sublime feeling was gone, and so was the dream-like state. He still felt a strange sense of peace as Barabbas began to speak to him.

Barabbas smiling, "Welcome, my friend. We have been waiting for you for a very long time."

Nino is confused and scared, not knowing where he is or who these people are. "Waiting for me? For what? Where the Hell am I?"

Chebar can hardly hold back his laughter at the irony of this question. "Oh, quite the contrary, my good man. The more appropriate question would be where in Heaven am I?"

"Okay, Mother fucker. Where in Heaven am I? And what the hell do you want with a homeless old man like me? I know what this is.

It's some kind of alien abduction. I read about this shit all the time. Never believed it though."

This language and the tone of Nino's voice unnerve Chebar. "Now, now, dear sir, you mustn't use language like that up here. If you are going to be a prophet then you are going to have to stop using your earthly profanity, and realize that-"

Before Chebar can finish his statement, Nino breaks out in mad laughter. "A prophet! A prophet? Ha! My dear sir, it is painfully obvious that you have me confused with someone else. But, if by chance you are not confused, and I am the person you are looking for, then it is becoming ever clearer to me that you are out of your fucking mind!"

"Barabbas," Chebar whispers to his leader, "I'm afraid that I have made a very serious mistake. This man is—why he is just absolutely-"

Nino responds, "Now you're talking. Just put my crazy, poor, black ass back on the planet earth where you found me, and everything will be cool. You don't even have to worry about me telling anyone, because even if I did, no one would believe me anyway. I am just a crazy, homeless veteran. I live in a pipe with my rat and my radio, and I just want to go home." Nino clicks his heels, saying, "There's no place like home". None of the elder Zealots understand the meaning of this bizarre action, but Malcolm is near tears with laughter as he remembers "The Wizard of Oz". He decides that he is closest in age to Mr. Jones, and maybe he should be the one to explain things to him.

Malcolm puts his arm around Nino, "Nino," he begins, still laughing, "Nino, we are not aliens. You are not in the Land of Oz, so clicking your heels together is not going to help you return home to Kansas to be reunited with your Auntie Em. We are Zealots—The Lions Abijah-and you are in the land of Forever. We have not brought you here to throw water on the wicked witch of the west. Our enemy is much more real, and much more insidious. Our enemy is none other than Satan himself. Our enemy is your enemy. The people in this room are risking an eternity in Paradise to help our earthbound brothers and sisters who are currently being attacked day and night by Satan and his army of evil. Millions of souls have already been damned to Hell. We haven't any time to waste, and therefore, you must cease with the joking. My name is Malcolm X. During my life I was a militant Muslim leader for the Nation of Islam. For most of my life, I taught people to hate because of race and religion. Standing next to me is Barabbas—the Roman Zealot whose life was spared in place of Jesus Christ. Beside him is Pontius Pilate, the Roman procurator who sentenced Jesus to death. Seated next to him is Caiaphas, the Jewish high priest who collaborated with the Scribes' and Pharisees to kill Jesus. And Chebar, a disciple of John the Baptist. He was asked by Jesus to become an apostle, but Barabbas convinced him that Jesus was the false Messiah and he became a Zealot instead. Over by the window is Thomas. That's right, the infamous doubting Thomas. The final member of our group, Mr. Jones, is you. Our seventh member. The unexpected prophet of faith."

Trying hard to take all of this information in, Nino is more comfortable keeping it as a joke. "Yeah, and I'm Nino Jones—the Easter Bunny."

Barabbas takes over, feeling the need to make things clear to Nino. "Nino, everything that Malcolm told you is true. Each of us, in our lives, did something that caused us to feel disgraced before our God and our people. We fought wars that we didn't believe in. We killed people for what we thought was the good of our nations. We recognized man as our earthly enemy instead of Satan. We thought we lived productive lives—lives that made our God and our people proud. In reality, we did the exact opposite. We disgraced our God. We hurt our people, and we helped our enemy. We know, Nino Jones, that you harbor these same feelings in your heart. You dropped out of society because you fought in a war you didn't believe in. You have never been able to forgive yourself for killing that mother and her two children."

The truth of these words stings Nino into belief. For the first time, he starts to understand the significance of everything that is being revealed to him. His comic attitude disappears and he turns a serious ear to Barabbas.

Barabbas continues, "You can't believe that God really has forgiven you, because you can't forgive yourself. Oh, I can assure you that if you ask God to forgive you in the name of Jesus Christ, all your sins will be forgiven. Jesus himself will even try to console you. But, the pain never goes away."

Nino is surprised by the regret in Barabbas' voice. "I thought there isn't supposed to be any suffering or pain in Heaven?"

"Remember Nino, as extraordinary as the Kingdom of Forever is, it is not our final Heaven. It is only when we enter the New Jerusalem—the new Kingdom of Forever—that complete perfection of both body and mind will be obtained."

Nino responds, "So, in Forever, we may still feel pain caused by regret over our earlier lives."

Barabbas continues, "Sometimes it's regret, and sometimes it's worrying over our loved ones who are still in the midst of the Great Game. I know what you're thinking—if everything is going to be cool when we get into the New Jerusalem, why take such a risk?"

Nino concerned, "Well, yeah—if the New Jerusalem will be void of all negative feelings and regret, then why are you doing this?"

Barabbas serious, "The end of the Great Game means the end of our opportunity to do something that will significantly help our God, our King, and our people. Even though we will feel content with our lives in the New Kingdom, it's not how I want to be remembered. I feel called to do this, Nino. It burns deep in my soul. I know for me that there is only one way that I will ever really feel complete, and that is to deliver a lethal blow to that snake, Satan, and all of his fallen angels. We chose you, Nino Jones, over all other people who have lived since the death and resurrection of Jesus Christ. We chose you to be the seventh member of the Heavenly Zealots. You are our final Lion Abijah. You are our unexpected prophet of faith who will deliver the message that will unite Christians, Muslims, Jews, Hindus, Buddhists and Gentiles from all over the world. If you are successful, then we will all be successful. We will be responsible for saving millions of souls from Hell, and we will be heroes for eternity. But you can't just go through the motions. You have to feel it in your heart. You are now standing on the threshold of immense greatness—the very pinnacle of immortal bravery. You may even be saving your own beloved United States of America from becoming the next Babylon. As I said before, every member of this group is risking an eternity in Paradise to try and save our people, and bring glory to our King and God. I have to be completely upfront with you, Nino. If you decide to take part in this operation, you will also risk spending all of eternity in the outer darkness.

Nino puzzled, "The outer darkness? Do you mean Hell?"

"No, Nino. The outer darkness is that place beyond the borders of the kingdom of Forever. The light of God does not shine there. It is a cold, dark, barren land in which there is much sadness. However, the outer darkness, with all its miseries, is still a million times better than Hell."

Nino perplexed, "If our sole purpose is to do good, and our message is meant to save souls and bring glory to God, how can we possibly fail?"

Barabbas responds, "Although our intentions are good, we are still doing this on our own. On earth, everything happens for a reason. Nothing happens by chance in terms of what God and Satan are trying to accomplish. It is all a part of their ultimate plan. What we are going to attempt may turn out to be a time-honored event, and God may be pleased. However, if Satan finds out what we are attempting to do, he will try and pervert our doctrine, and in turn use our plan to his benefit. If this happens, we will all be banned from Paradise forever."

An all-encompassing silence falls over the room as all of the Zealots reflect on the gravity of their plan. Barabbas sighs deeply, and continues. "Oh, and Nino, Satan will find out. It's just a question of how long it will take him. The risks are extremely high, Nino. No prophet who ever lived was faced with such a risk. What is the risk of death if upon dying you are sent to eternal paradise? What is it to suffer on earth even 100 years if at the end of your suffering your reward is eternal bliss? The difference between us and the prophets who came before us is that they knew for sure that they were doing God's will, and therefore no matter what happened to them during their lives, in the end they would receive their reward. We are not in such a position. It is possible that everything could be carried out exactly as we have planned it, and still our mission could fail. All that the other prophets had to do was deliver the message, not convince the people to accept it. They did not have to worry about whether or not Satan would successfully pervert their doctrines. If you are unable to get the All God's Children Movement started, then we have failed. If it gets started and then Satan is able to manipulate it to his advantage, then we have failed. I am not trying to belittle the prophets in any way. They were all great and brave men and women. All I am trying to do is get you to see exactly the magnitude of what we are about to undertake."

"If I say I'll do it, how many years do I have?"

Barabbas somber, "You will have, at the very most, two days."

Nino shocked, "Two days?! Nobody even knows me! I'm not Michael Jordan, or Muhammad Ali. I'm Nino Jones! I'm a homeless veteran who lives in a pipe with his pet rat, and you expect me to have the world listening to me and my message in two days?"

Barabbas optimistic, "You don't have to convince the world in two days, Nino. You just have to get the ball rolling. Over the next two days, you will be given a tour of the Kingdom of Forever by each one of our brothers. You will be given wisdom. You will see things and experience things that you will have to share with your messenger."

Nino growing angry, "Oh, I see, you only want to convince a total stranger that I am a prophet, and after he accepts it, it will move to the rest of the world. At least now I know it won't be as hard as I thought." Nino's sarcasm has momentarily returned. "Will I be given some type of super powers so I can do some miracles? If I do something like split the Atlantic Ocean and take a limo to London, that might give some credibility to my story."

"Nino, you will not be given the power to do any miracles. All miracles come from God. He gave the world his only son, and he's not willing to give any more than that. You will be a man with a message, and that's it."

Nino apologetic, "Barabbas, I'm no coward. At least, I never thought I was. I like the idea about spreading a message that will unite all Christians, Muslims, Jews, Hindus, Buddhists and everyone else. I'd love an opportunity to help defeat Satan. I just don't think I'm the type of guy you need. You guys should search a little bit longer—try to find someone who's a little more refined. Find someone who the people won't have such a hard time believing."

Barabbas angry, "We're all out of time, Nino. The new Heavenly Jerusalem is completed. The beginning of the great tribulation is at hand! The world and the Heavens will be shaken, until all that remains is that which is unshakable. You are our last and only chance. Everything hinges upon you. Who you are and who you represent mean a lot more than what you are, and where you came from. Jesus Christ was a carpenter from an obscure little village called Nazareth. He wasn't a particularly handsome man by any stretch of the imagination. As a matter of fact, if not for his words and his deeds, you would find nothing attractive about him whatsoever."

Nino emotionally torn, "I can't believe the spot that you have put me in. If I say no, then I am a coward, and the plan never gets tried. But, if I say yes, I'll be attempting something that I don't really believe I can do. You know the old saying, 'If you think you can't, then you can't.'"

Barabbas trying to remain optimistic, "Don't forget that you will have an earthly messenger or apostle to help you. You may only have two days to tell him what you know, but it will be his task to help you spread your message to the public, and to write your story after you die."

Nino nervous, "After I die?"

Barabbas remaining calm, "Yes. Nino, if you agree to take part in this plan, then you will stay alive until Natelli, our Heavenly CPA, finds out about the plan. Once he discovers that you are the one who is missing on the books, you will be summoned to the high court of Forever immediately. Your earthly life will end and you will be judged according to your deeds. There is one last thing that I feel compelled to tell you. We checked and found that your name is written in The Book of Life. That means that if you just continued living the way you have been, until you die, your citizenship in the Kingdom of Forever is secured. However, if you take part in this plan, your admittance into Heaven will be in jeopardy. As far as being scared of dying, you're dead right now. How does it feel?"

"I've never felt better," Nino says, shocked to learn of his own death.

Barabbas smiles knowingly, "When we are young children, it is easy to believe in Heaven as this wonderful place that we go to when we die. As we get older, though, the constant attacks from Satan cause our imagination to die. We become disheartened souls, who fear death and lack faith. Fear of dying is one of Satan's best weapons."

"Barabbas why do you all sound the same to me, like you're from the 21st century?"

"We do all live in the 21st Century. We just don't happen to live on the earth. Nino, as you will soon discover everything that happens on earth, happens up here first."

Nino excited, "Man oh man, I never would have guessed that's how things work. Hey Barabbas, tell me more about my messenger. How will I meet him?"

"His name is Mark Salvatore Pitifer, and he is 33 years old. He is a white male of Italian descent. He is a school counselor, and he is married with no children. We have a plan worked out of exactly how the two of you are going to meet. He is going to be in New York City this weekend, and if you join in with us, that's when the meeting will take place. We will help you convince him that your story is true, but a large part of the convincing is going to have to be done by you. I really don't have anything more to say to you about the plan. If you decide not to join us, you will be returned to your earthly body, and have no memory that any of this ever happened. You will be sent back to fulfill your destiny, whatever that may be. The task is most noble, but the risk is incomprehensibly high. I will give you some time to make your decision, Nino. We will return in about an hour."

Nino sat for a long time and thought of everything he had been told. The risks were great, but all of the great people he had ever read about became great only because they were brave enough to take a serious risk. His thoughts immediately turned to the young firefighter who helped him to his feet after the Twin Towers were attacked by terrorists back in 2001. He recalled his wonder as the young boy ran back into the burning tower just as it collapsed. He remembered thinking that the child was literally facing the fires of Hell to save people he didn't even know. That brave boy was never seen again, but his spirit has stayed with Nino ever since. Nino imagined his ascent into Heaven was like the firefighter's climb up the burning stairs of the South Tower. God's gold, which is the loyal sovereign soul, must be tested by fire. Nino makes up his mind to accept the challenge. He and his apostle would have a very difficult challenge, but if they were successful, they would be heroes forever. He sat in silence as he waited for the others to arrive, and as he sat there he thought he heard someone playing Elvis Presley music way off in the distance. It sounded like some type of festival was going on. He stood up and walked over to a large window, just as the Lions Abijah returned to the room.

Barabbas walks over to Nino, "Have you made your decision, Mr. Jones?"

Nino faking sadness, "It is with deep regret and serious reservation," begins Nino, ever the comedian, "that I must accept the offer to become Nino Jones, the prophet of faith."

Sighs of relief and burst of applause fill the air. Barabbas is so overcome that tears of joy stream down his cheeks.

"So let it be written" Barabbas announces in a broken, elated voice, "that on September 14th, 2020 at approximately 10:00 a.m. earth time, the royal order of the Lions Abijah has finally found its sacred seventh member. Nino

Jones, from this moment on you are a member of the Heavenly Zealots of the Kingdom of Forever. You are our long awaited seventh lion. We stand together, and we are committed to the downfall of Satan, the saving of souls, loyalty to the king, and honor to the one and only God."

All embraced their new member, but the celebration had to end quickly as their time was limited. Nino and each of the Zealots would be given an opportunity to spend some time together. He would be given the grand tour of Forever, and each Zealot would be his escort for some part of the tour.

"Hopefully, the time for real celebration will present itself again some day in the near future," Barabbas assures his troops. "Nino, you will be taken on a tour of Forever. You will see things and meet people that your escorts feel are important for your message. Feel free to ask any questions you want to, and don't worry about forgetting anything that you see or hear. From this point on, you will have full access to your total brain. Nothing revealed during this tour will be forgotten. I will speak to you privately before your tour begins, to give you a little more background information. Your first escort will be Zealot Chebar, followed by Thomas, Caiaphas, Pilate, Malcolm X, and then myself. You will not see this group again until we are summoned before the throne of God and our king on the day our plan is discovered. Any questions?"

Nino shakes his head.

"Then let the grand tour begin."

Author's Note: In the following chapter (10) all of the information provided by the Albert Einstein character throughout this chapter is scientific, historical, archeological, meteorological, mathematical, geological, anthropological, climatological, zoological, paleoanthropological, and astrological fact. The only exceptions to this statement are his explanations regarding the formation and purpose of Pluto and Haley's Comet.

CHAPTER 10

▼

"As you do not know the path of the wind, or how the body is formed in a mothers womb, so you cannot understand the work of God, the Maker of all things."
-Ecclesiastes 11:5

"From the very beginning you have been immortal children of life."
-Valentinus

"YOUR HEAVENLY FATHER WILL FORGIVE YOU IF YOU FORGIVE THOSE WHO SIN AGAINST YOU. BUT IF YOU REFUSE TO FORGIVE THEM, HE WILL NOT FORGIVE YOU. MERCY IS THE HEART OF THE LAW!"
-JESUS OF NAZARETH (Matthew 6:14 &15)

When they were left alone, Barabbas and Nino got right down to business. Nino had a lot of questions, beginning with the very beginning of time.

"Well," began Barabbas, "the plan seemed simple enough. You create a society in which souls have the freedom to choose between good and evil, and sit back and watch what happens.... However, as the elders and God began to map out their strategy, they discovered that the problem was very complex, and would take thousands of years to complete. The making of the earth was a spectacular event for the citizens of Forever to watch, because all of the other universes had been made prior to our individual creation dates."

"Other universes?" Nino exclaims, surprised one more time. "You mean there is more than one universe? But how can that be? I thought a universe encompasses everything."

Barabbas explains, "God's universe does encompass everything, but it exists on many different plains and dimensions. Your universe is all that you are capable of experiencing at this time. However, your entire universe is but a tiny drop in a sea of universes so vast that it is beyond the scope of human comprehension."

Nino shakes his head in disbelief. "Barabbas, no one is going to believe this shit. Pardon my French. But how do I explain that there is more than one universe?"

"I see your point, Nino." Barabbas answers, taking a moment to come up with a strategy. "Okay. Try this on them. First of all, the notion of a universe is a perception. Let's see if this explanation will work ... You have a very pregnant woman and her husband, back in the early 1600's. The ship they are sailing on sinks in during a storm. The husband dies in the wreck, but the woman hangs on to a piece of wood and lands on a very remote island. Shortly after she reaches the shore, she goes into labor and gives birth to a baby boy. However, the mother dies as the baby is being born. By the grace of God, a mother gorilla discovers the child and raises him."

Nino can't help but to chuckle. "What's the boy's name? Tarzan?"

"Good one, Nino. But here's my point. The boy's perception would come to be that the gorilla is his biological mother, that the island is the world, and the vast ocean an uncrossable space that must go on forever, with no end. Is the boy's perception correct?"

Nino responds, "Of course not. He is limited by what he knows."

"Exactly. Humans, from their vantage point, believe that their universe is boundless, because they are limited by what their knowledge can prove."

"So, there really are many universes."

"That's right."

"Are they all like ours?"

Barabbas amused, "Are you kidding me? God has created so many beautiful universes solely for the pleasure of his children. Your universe in many was is the ghetto of God's creation."

Nino faking offense, "Hey! I know something about ghettos, but the question is, why did he do it? I mean, why did he make a ghetto universe?"

Barabbas continues, "Shortly after God had announced that he was going to create a son, Satan asked Him if he would create a universe for him that would test his creative skills. He wanted God to give him a fixer-upper."

"You mean like buying an old farm house and fixing it up?"

Barabbas smiles, "Right. It was when Satan made this request that God felt a pang in the depth of his eternal heart. God new that Satan had been sneaking off to what is called a "sleeper-universe" for a long time."

"What's a sleeper-universe?" Nino asks.

"A sleeper-universe is a universe whose foundation has been creatively laid in terms of planets, stars, moons, and space, but one that God has yet to fully develop."

"I think I understand what you mean. But why does God make sleeper-universes."

"God is in many ways comparable to an artist. He's always making things. He creates many universes from scratch, and because he is so imaginative they all take on different sizes, dimensions, and possibilities. Some of these universes he just gets rid of and some he keeps to develop further at some later date."

Nino grasps the concept, "Kind of like an unfinished painting, or sculpture."

Barabbas pleased, "Exactly. Satan would go there to pretend that he was a god. So this request was no surprise to him. Satan was also certain that God would grant him his wish, and this was an important part of his strategy to defeat God."

"How did this help him?"

"Although God enjoys this behavior immensely, it takes a tremendous amount of energy, even for God, to make a new universe, and Satan knew this. His plan was to attack God at a time when his holy powers were diverted; and he was in a weakened state, this is why he thought he could win the war. However, God saw him coming a mile away."

Nino's interest in the story grows as Barabbas's tone becomes more serious. "I always wondered how Satan thought he was actually going to be able to defeat God. It never made sense to me ..." Nino thinks for a moment. "Barrabas, if God was onto him the whole time, why did he let the revolution happen?"

"God knew that when he decided to make a son, and henceforth a new form of creation, that a possible conflict would occur. So, although it appeared to Satan that God was granting his request, in actuality he was setting the stage for the Great Game of Life. As God appeared to be gathering his powers to create Satan's universe, the Devil signaled for the revolution to begin. However, when the fallen Angels realized that their surprise attack was no surprise, they quickly surrendered."

"So God was never really in jeopardy right?"

"No, Never. The revolution ended very abruptly in giant blast of celestial brilliance!"

Nino Surprised, "And the citizens of Forever witnessed this spectacular event?"

"They certainly did. You talk about your firework shows! There was an explosion of energy on that first day of creation that rocked the cosmos. I'll bet you the sound waves from that blast are still resonating somewhere in the black void you call space.

"You mean the Big Bang theory our scientists write about has some merit?"

"Yes, indeed it does. You have to understand one thing about science. As contradictory as this might sound, all science will eventually lead to God. Like the slow unveiling of a very large and very complex mosaic, you can make many educated guesses about what you think it is as you see more and more, but you cannot be certain until you see the whole picture. Until then, all you have are theories. Some of the world's scientific theories are right on target, and some are ridiculous nonsense. Everything that is revealed in the world of science and technology is revealed by God according to time-lines in conjunction with world events. For example, Jesus Christ and the other prophets came before the invention of TV, so that people would have faith. If those mighty miracles that were performed by Moses and Jesus were seen by everyone and digitally recorded, there would be no need for faith. Can you imagine people watching the parting of the Red Sea, or seeing Lazarus being raised from the dead four days after he was in the tomb? Can you imagine watching TV on a Friday afternoon and seeing Jesus get crucified on CNN, and then three days later he's back from the dead and giving a detailed account of his experience to Barbara Walters or Oprah Whifrey? You would have a large number of people believing for the wrong reasons."

Nino chuckles, "It sounds kind of funny to hear you describe it that way, but I see what you mean," Nino replies. "Barabbas, you said the citizens of Forever watched the creation of the earth?"

"You and I were both there, but that part of your memory has been suppressed until you officially reenter Forever. Once a soul crosses the point of no return, their minds are opened and they discover that they held within themselves the answers to all of life's mysteries."

Nino annoyed, "Then why are we wasting all of this time when all that need be done is have me cross the border?"

Barabbas responds, "There are two reasons: first of all, Natelli, our Heavenly accountant, would know immediately that something is wrong. However, more important than all of this is that your mission must carry with it an element of faith. All previous prophets were called personally by God or one of his representatives. They knew that if they followed their instructions, they would be rewarded and that God would protect them and give them all the time and help they would need to complete their mission. Angels surrounded them, and guarded their every step. You, on the other hand, will be cut off from all angels, except for me, and I will be able to do very little to help you. We have to play by rules in which Satan will not be able to cry foul. When Satan discovers the rules by which we are playing, he will be convinced that he will be able to not only foil our plan, but also use it to his advantage. This is a calculated part of our mission. We have so many factors working against us. The biggest of these is time. If you die naturally or if you are taken because our plan is uncovered, then it will probably mean that we have failed."

Worry and doubt returns to Nino as he listens to Barabbas. "That time factor is what has me worried more than anything else," he says.

"Remember, Nino, you must have faith. Fore if you are successful, you shall be called the prophet of faith forevermore. You are different from all other prophets because you will be out there on your own, and like no other prophet before you; you are risking your eternity for the sake of your God and your people. You are the underdog of underdogs. Your chances of success are slim, but they do exist. If you pull this off, our eternities will be glorious. Imagine being a hero for all eternity!"

Nino worried, "For the first time since I have come here, I am starting to feel afraid. I don't know if I can go through with it. The reality of what we are up against, and the penalty for failure has just struck me."

Barabbas feels Nino's concern, "Now you can understand why we will be saving my piece of the puzzle until last. All of us have felt this pain you are feeling, but all of us have overcome our fear. We believe in you, Nino Jones. Our eternities rest on your shoulders."

"Why do you believe in me?" Nino asks, not able to find the same faith in himself as the others have put in him. "Who am I that you should place your souls in my care? I have been a failure all of my life. Ask anybody who knows me, and they'll tell you. I'm that crazy veteran who lives in the subway tunnel. I'm that kid-killer from Vietnam." Nino can no longer hold back his fear and sorrow, and he breaks down in tears. "Don't you see? You've picked the wrong man."

Barabbas sympathetic but strong, "Nino, I was a patriot all of my life. I was the leader of a small group of brave men who believed that they could defeat the Roman Army. I looked for good, humble, brave men of faith. They had the faith and imagination of a child. They believed that they could pull off a miracle, and they were courageous until death. This is the Nino Jones that I see, and this is why I believe in you."

"Well, then, what are we waiting for? Let's get on with it," Nino says, composing himself and trying to make the mood a little lighter. "You were speaking of how it all began."

"As I said earlier, all of the citizens of Forever were there to see the creation of this new Universe. The display was beyond spectacular. However, we were soon to realize that concealed within this amazing creative event, was the incomprehensible evil of the Heavenly revolution. The creation of this universe and the earth was gradually veiled in sadness. For the first time in our existence as a people, we experienced emotional pain and fear. Satan and all of his followers were very magnificent souls, and even though the people knew that they were getting a just punishment for the crimes they had committed, they were still heavy hearted for their family members that had been led astray."

Nino pops his eyes open wide, shocked to hear Barabbas refer to Satan and his followers as "magnificent souls". Barabbas notices his response and addresses it immediately.

"I see that you are confused by my stating that Satan and his followers were wonderful souls."

"Well, yes—it's strange to hear Satan described in a positive way."

Barabbas continues, "Let me explain. Nino, Satan's name was Lucifer, which literally means the "shining one". He was the "cherub who covers". No one in all of Forever was closer to God than he was. The angels who followed him were also beautiful personalities. I know it's hard for you to envision, but the loss of these souls was devastating to everyone. Prior to their fall from grace, they were key players in the Kingdom of Forever. Do you remember how you felt when JFK and Martin got assassinated?"

"Yea, I had that "where do we go from here" feeling. I see what you mean. So, losing these guys must have really changed the way of life in Forever for a while."

"Oh, without question! We are still suffering from their loss. On that first Sabbath following the war, we began to see just how drastic the changes in Forever would be."

Nino's head is swimming with all the information. He feels the need to jump in and ask for further explanation of every detail. First and foremost, he addresses Barabbas's mention of the Sabbath.

"Barabbas, the Bible states that on the seventh day, God rested. So, do you have Sabbath days in Heaven? … How often?"

"Whenever God feels like having one. They actually are really astonishing displays of affection and admiration to God by his children. It's like a giant talent show for the glory of God. However, the Sabbath-of-sorrow is one that nobody in Forever likes to remember."

"The Sabbath-of-Sorrow? What happened?"

Barabbas's expression turns sad, "God sent his angels to gather the multitudes from every corner of Forever. We were assembled at the foot of the great mountain of the north—the holy mountain that is the throne of the living God and his son. All of the citizens had heard of the great revolution; however, no one was certain what the ramifications would be. Many of the citizens assumed that the earth would be where Satan and his fallen angels would be exiled for eternity. The average citizen did not think for a moment that the earth had anything do with their future. I still shudder when I think of the words that God himself uttered that day: "**My dear, dear children, I love you with all of my heart, soul, mind and strength. You were created in my image, and destined to live with me, as my sons and daughters, in Paradise, for all of eternity. However, as you know, something very terrible has happened. I knew that when I created you with your own free will that something like this could possibly happen. The problem that we are now faced with is how can we prevent such a thing from ever happening again? I have been meeting with Jesus and the 12 elders, and we have come up with a plan that will take thousands of years to be implemented. However, it will ensure that our eternities will be more glorious than anyone could ever imagine.**" I can still remember the dreadful silence that came over the crowd that morning. There were billions upon billions of souls, as far as our eyes could see. God went on to explain that we must all be tested, like gold is tested by fire. I swear to you, Nino, that the words that he imparted that day were incomprehensible. We were immortal beings who had lived our whole lives without worry, fear or the constraints of time. We lived like gods! There was no such thing as sickness, and the idea of death was preposterous. However, that's what we were faced with on this Sabbath of Sorrow. We were told that our lives in Forever would temporarily come to an end. Each citizen would, in his turn, have to leave our beloved kingdom and embark on an extraordinary journey. This would be what is called the First Death. Can you imagine the shock waves that this sent through the kingdom? People were devastated. Death had come to Forever. The unthinkable, the unutterable was suddenly thrust upon us without warning. Time now became relevant in a negative sense. Each soul's life was now limited to an undetermined number of years."

"Was a year 365 days?" Nino asks, once more needing clarification.

"Yes. Time was the same. In Forever, we have the four seasons, and each one is marvelous. There is nothing difficult or disenchanting about any season. As you can see and feel, autumn in Forever is a time of stunning beauty."

Nino smiles warmly "Boy, your not-a kidding."

"Oh, and speaking of time, every soul has a creation date." Nino interrupts again. "You mean, like a birthday?"

"Yes, but in Forever nobody is born. You have a creation day. You come forth from a cyclone of love that forms between two loving souls who decide to create a new life. God's Holy Spirit mixes with the creative powers that exist in the parent souls. The process is beautiful, painless and perfect in all ways."

"So, it's nothing like our births on earth."

"That's true in all regards except one. The joy and admiration that a mother and father feel when they hold their child for the first time is similar to what we feel in Forever. Only, in Forever, the feelings of love are a million times more intense."

"So, even in Forever there is such a thing as age?"

"Yes, you start out as infants, tiny and cuddly."

"I wonder why God still makes it so we have to grow at all. Why not just make us fully mature from the start?"

Barabbas laughing, "Because everyone in Forever, especially God, loves babies! What kind of Heaven would it be without the constant presence of babies, puppies, kittens, and cubs? In Forever, you will continue to grow and develop physically until the age of 21. Once you reach the age of the adulthood, you will never physically age any further. In Forever, your aging stops at the pinnacle of strength and beauty. The only difference that will continue is the amount of wisdom, knowledge, and skill that you accumulate over the years."

Nino smiles proudly, "So, even in Heaven, there is a reason to respect your elders."

"Yes, definitely." Barabbas raises an eyebrow at Nino and Nino salutes him, respectfully. But Nino still has more questions and wants to fit them all in before Barabbas departs.

"Barabbas, when death came to Forever, what happened?"

"The oldest of God's created souls were the first to have to face death. The result of dying in Forever would be a life on earth. The result of dying on earth would be a life in the Kingdom of Forever and eventual citizenship in the New Jerusalem for all souls who prove themselves worthy. For those who will be found unworthy, it will be banishment to the outer darkness, until the time that they must face the second death."

Nino confused, "But, why is it called the second death and not the third death? After all, they die in Forever, they die on earth, and then they die once again in Forever."

"Real death is being cut off from the light and love of God. So, what we call our birthday on earth is actually the date of a souls' first death. The day of our earthly departure is actually the date of our second birth, unless we are found unworthy—"

Nino tries to understand, "and then we die the second death?"

"Yes. The second death is incomprehensibly awful in that it means the souls will be cut off from the light and love of God forever. An eternity in Hell, where the fire is never quenched and the worm never dies, is the ultimate punishment. The stakes were high and the citizens were petrified. God went on to say that every soul, even his only son Jesus, would have to go through the test. Life in Forever would go on as usual for an undetermined amount of time while the stage was set, and then the holy plan would be worked out until completion."

"So, every soul was forced to take part in the Great Game?"

Barabbas clarifies, "No, not exactly, Nino. I misspoke. You were given a choice. You could stay and be a servant of God for all eternity, which would mean that you would no longer have free will, or you could choose to take part in the Great Game, which would allow you to live like Gods in a Paradise called Forever for all eternity, if you were victorious. I will speak to you more about this at the end of your tour."

"I still don't understand Satan's part in the plan, and how it was that he and his followers fell."

"God knew that in order for our faith to be tested, there would have to be certain elements about the earth—its origin, history, and inhabitants, that would create many mysteries. The first problem was the age of earth."

"The earth is billions of years old, right?"

"Yes and no. If you are talking about the age of the physical planet itself, then the answer is yes. You see, your planet and all of the planets in your solar system are merely pieces of a gigantic older planet, which was taken from the sleeper-universe, that I spoke about earlier, by the hand of God."

"I see—by using an ancient planet that already existed, you would have the history you needed."

Barabbas smiles at Nino's wit, "That's right. If God really made the earth and the rest of your universe from scratch at the beginning of the Great Game, your modern scientist would have been able to prove that the religious scholars of the world are correct in the estimations."

"And that is?"

"If you go back to the creation of the modern earth, the placement of Adam and Eve in the Garden of Eden, and the beginning of the Great Game, you are talking about less than ten thousand years ago."

Nino happily surprised, "Oh my God. It's all true? All that's been written about in the Torah, the Bible, the Qur'an and the BHAGAVAD GITA? It's all true?"

"I know exactly what you mean. I remember when I first began to have the mysteries revealed to me. The answers to all those big questions. I can remember thinking to myself, of course-how could I have been so blind?"

"How could we have doubted there was a God? There really is a loving creator, who really does have a plan for us all."

"Yes, you've said it well."

"So earth, in a way, is really Satan's planet?"

"As I said earlier, Satan used to go off to a remote part of the galaxy to a planet he created called Earthonte. It was equal in size to all of the planets in our solar system combined. It was here on this planet that Satan made his first attempts at becoming an almighty creator. He spent billions of years trying to refine his creative skills. It was here that he experienced the first pangs of jealousy. It was here that he gathered his fallen angels together to plan their attack."

"So, what happened to Earthonte? Did God get mad during the revolution, and smash it to pieces?"

"Yeah, in a way, I guess you could say that is what happened. As Satan and his fallen Angels mobilized for their surprise attack on Earthonte, the Arch Angel Michael and his legion of Holy Angels swiftly and decisively defeated the devil and his army. God was very sad over the betrayal of his angels, but also became extremely upset. However, even in his anger, he remained creative. While Satan and his fallen Angels were cast into the outer darkness, and the rest of forever looked on, God smashed the great planet into many pieces. It was out of these pieces that he shaped and molded the planets and moons of your solar system—along with our sun. God formed the planets, and placed them into their appropriate spots."

"And what about the rest of our universe, was that made from scratch? Or was that also part of an older creation?"

Barabbas smiles with pride. "Nino, you are a very sharp cookie. It's hard to put into terms that will be understandable to your scientists. But to put it simply, he tapped into a previously created universe, and kind of fused it into your current universe."

"You mean like the Panama Canal allows the Pacific Ocean to flow into the Atlantic Ocean?"

Smilling, and once again impressed with Nino's wit. "Yes, that's a good example. This is why everything seems so old. The sleeper—universe that housed earthonte is something like 18 billion years old."

"Unbelievable … So when everything was in place, what happened to the Devil and what was left of his planet?"

"He left all of Satan's creations just as he had found them. Then when everything was in place he went to the outer darkness, and there, grabbing Satan and his fallen angels, he cast them down to the planet now called earth."

"And I'm curious, Barabbas, how old was Earthonte?" "Approximately 18 billion years old."

Nino laughs out loud. "Ha! I knew you were going to say that. That's exactly when our scientists claim the big bang happened!"

Barabbas joins his laughter. "Eventually, they will get it right!"

"So, Satan and all of his followers were now on earth, right?"

"Yes, Satan and his army were about to be taught a lesson in humility, and they were forced to stand on the planet that he had created. Flung into the midst of his endless series of creative failures, for the first time in their existence, they were cut off from the love light of their creator. At first, their diabolic wails were remorseful. However, they soon turned into rage."

"What was the lesson they were being taught about their leader?"

"That the only beauty that existed in him, and in all of us, comes from the loving union that exists between us and our creator. Once a soul is separated from the loving spirit of God, there is nothing but darkness and emptiness of being. Nothing good or creative can come from a soul who is not in union with God. Satan's personal part of this lesson was that he was going to have that which he created in darkness exposed to all of the souls of Forever, including his fallen angels——exposed under a harsh and glaring whitish yellow light, one that hurts the eyes and burns the skin. Satan was so much less than God and this was going to be a lesson for him. Satan always believed that if given the opportunity, he could create a kingdom of such grandeur that it would rival Forever. He had convinced his fallen angels that this was true, but now they encircled him like hyenas around a wounded lion. They stung him with their words, and lashed out at him with their fists."

"So, now everyone would see that he was a fool."

"A fool yes, but more importantly, a liar."

"The father of all lies ..."

"The father of all lies, cast down from Heaven to be king of his own creation. As he fell toward the earth, his wings were torn off his body, and replaced with a tail. The hot glaring sun caused Satan's skin to turn dark red and his feet were so badly burned and bruised that they resembled hooves. His hair was wild and spiked by the strong wind into shapes that looked like horns. This once beautiful angel now looked like some sort of savage creature."

"So, the story of the red faced Devil with hooven feet, horns and a tail has some merit."

"All of the stories of the Torah, the Bible, the Qur'an, the BHAGAVAD GITA, and many other holy writings are true. They all have merit. You just have to study and make determinations as to what is meant in a symbolic way, and what is straightforward."

"Is Satan the father of science?"

"God is the father of science. Satan is the manipulator of science. God knew there would be a need for science in the Great Game. He knew that the latter day inhabitants would have people called scientists, and that many of them would be Atheists. They would be champions of the theories of evolution, and the big bang idea, never realizing that this process of evolution was first a series of bad ideas by Satan. His original kingdom lacked order. His animal creations were excessively large and stupid creatures. At first, he decided to have all of the creatures living in the ocean, but then he changed his mind and decided to switch some of the creatures to land for the sake of his humanly creation. His attempt at making a man and a woman never got further than what we know as a Neanderthal man, sort of half man, half ape. It was a very simple minded creature who lacked compassion and mercy."

"So, the dinosaurs and the cavemen; this was all Satan's doing?" "All of it. He tried to impress with size and strength. Simply put: a feeble attempt at creation by a wanna-be-God."

Nino is momentarily silenced by his disbelief. He takes a deep breath and finally exclaims, "It is all so remarkable, but so completely believable. I feel like I have awaken from a dream, and can finally see what's real and true … I can't wait to begin my tour!"

Authors Note: Remember that Satan's greatest accomplishment is to convince us that there is no Hell, and that he does not exist.

"I will give you all these splendid kingdoms and their glory, for they are mine to give to anyone I wish, if you will only get down on your knees and worship me." "We must worship God and him alone."
-Satan & Jesus (Luke 4:6&7)

CHAPTER 11

▼

"Science without religion is lame; religion without science is blind.
Never lose a holy curiosity"
-Albert Einstein

Science can purify religion from error and superstition. Religion can
purify science from idolatry and false absolutes.
-Pope John Paul II

"Question with boldness even the existence of God; because if
there be one, He must approve the homage of Reason rather than
that of blindfolded fear."
-Thomas Jefferson

"Your wish is my command. I shall not keep you another moment. I will see
you some time later tomorrow evening.... However, in Forever it is custom-
ary to begin all great undertakings with a toast, and for that we must visit
one of Heavens greatest wine makers."

Nino can't hold back his enthusiasm. "You mean Jesus?!"

Barabbas laughs. "No, but that's a pretty good guess! His name on earth
was Albert Einstein, but up here we just call him Al the wine maker. Let's go.
I've arranged for Chebar to meet us at Al's vineyard."

Barabbas takes Nino by the hand and they land in a magnificent vineyard.
A handsome young man with short jet-black hair approaches them, carrying
a bottle of wine and a few wine glasses.

"Barabbas! How are you, my brother?"

"Very good, Al, and you?"

Al speaks in an excited voice. "Oh, just fantastic. I feel sensational!" He pauses for a minute and turns to Nino. "And this must be Mr. Nino Jones. It is such a pleasure to meet you, sir!"

Al extends his free hand to Nino, who grabs it in both of his own hands. "I can't believe I'm shaking hands with Mr. Albert Einstein!" "Oh, Nino, call me Al." Nino nods, and continues to stare at Al with an odd look on his face.

"I know what you're thinking," Al says. "It's the hair, isn't it? Up here in Forever, there just aren't bad hair days. My whole life on Earth was one everlasting bad hair day!"

Nino laughs, "Well, a lot of people will be glad to know that. You really do look great, compared to the pictures I've seen—I mean-" Nino tries to remove his foot from his mouth, and Al lets him off the hook.

Al grinning, "It's okay, Nino. Don't feel bad. Don't you think I know what I looked like? But, if you had E=MC2 rolling around in your mind all the time, your hair would probably look like that, too!

Hoots of laughter fill the vineyard as the three gentlemen get to know each other. Nino finds being in Einstein's presence fills him with questions about science and the universe. He can't wait to ask Al all kinds of questions.

"Al, I still don't know how you ever came up with such a theory."

Barabbas agrees. "Yeah, neither do I. You know, Nino, Al flunked out of school twice! Who would ever believe that a kid who flunks out of school not once, but twice, would come up with one of the greatest discoveries of the modern era?"

Nino is stunned. "You flunked out of school twice?"

"Yes," answers Al. "And I wish I would have flunked out a third time and never gone back!"

"Aw, Al, don't be so hard on yourself," Barabbas says, consoling his friend. Nino doesn't understand.

"Why do you wish that, Al?"

Al sad and angry, "Because maybe then I would not have come up with my atrocious discovery. The discovery that I knew from its inception could be used to do great harm."

Nino tries to console Al, "But, it's not your fault that people misused your discovery. Besides, a lot of good came from it, too."

"That's nice of you to say, Nino, but it eases not my pain. Do you know what I make now?"

"Well, are you still practicing science?"

"Yes. The science of making wine!"

Barabbas can't contain his enthusiasm for Al's talent. "He's being modest, Nino. Al is the best wine maker in all of Forever!"

Al nervous, "Now, now Barabbas," Al says, blushing. "Don't forget that our king is also a wine maker."

Barabbas shoos the thought away with his hand. "Jesus would agree with me."

Al is redder than ever as he turns to Nino. "Don't listen to him, Nino. He's gone mad!"

Barabbas hands a glass to Nino. "Taste and see for yourself, Nino. Al, how about that toast?"

"Yes, yes. Nino, tell me what you think of my latest creation. He fills each of their classes to the brim, and Barabbas clears his throat.

"Nino, may God, Jesus and all of the Angels bless, protect and sanctify your holy mission."

The three touch glasses and taste a small bit of paradise. Barabbas is overwhelmed.

Barabbas swoons, "Oh, Al, this is your masterpiece. This is …"

Nino interjects. "This is the most delicious wine that I have ever tasted. Ripple & Wild Irish Rose will never taste the same to me again!"

Laughter abounds as the gentlemen empty their glasses. Al is quite touched by their praise. "Thank you, my brothers. It gives me such pleasure to make something that people can truly enjoy." Al's voice tapers off into sudden tears. Barabbas puts his arm around his friend's heaving shoulders.

Barabbas tries to cheer up Al, "Now, Al, the time for tears is over. You have a chance to be a part of something that will erase your past once and for all. You are now apart of the Lion's Abijah Network, and it is for this moment that you were born."

Al is warmed by Barabbas' words. He has great faith in his friend. Half smiling, "Yes, yes my good friend, you are right. Nino, sit with me for a while. Barabbas, how long do I have?"

"Chebar is supposed to be here in a little less than an hour, but if I know Chebar he will not be on time," Barabbas answers, shaking his head.

"Good. Nino I have some important things to tell you." "I'm all ears, Al. Speak away."

Al's tone grows serious again as he pulls Nino over to a soft opal bench in one corner of the vineyard. He looks deep into Nino's eyes as he speaks. "Nino, if I could go back again, do you know what I would be?"

Nino smiles. "A wine maker?"

"Yes, I would be a wine maker. But I don't think that would fulfill my scientific, inquisitive mind. No, if I could go back and do it all over again, I would focus on the great mysteries of the earth. I would explore the facts that were right there waiting to be discovered, and illuminated for the world."

Nino is a little bewildered. "What facts? What would you do? Cure cancer?"

Al shakes his head and takes his time answering. "No. I would cure atheism."

"How would you do that?" Nino asks.

Al enthusiastically, "Scientifically. I would objectively collect and analyze the factual evidence that is available to anyone with eyes to see and ears to hear. I would be an archeologist, paleontologist, astrologist, and a gynecologist."

"Gynecologist?"

Al laughs like a dirty old man. "I have to have some fun!" Nino laughing, "Al, you're too much."

"Nino, do you realize that Earth has, scattered throughout its fossils, archeological, and astrological records, all of the evidence needed to prove the existence of God?"

Nino raises his eyebrows, "Wouldn't it be ironic if science ended up making a case for God?" "Indeed it would, but that is exactly what we will do."

"But how, Al? I'm no scientist. Even if I remember everything you tell me, I won't be able to make a good argument. I don't have that kind of mind."

Al confident,"Nino, trust me. When I'm done with you, you will. I'm going to give you irrefutable scientific facts, and you are going to present them in layman terms. You'll be like a reporter doing a story, okay?"

"Okay. Alright. I'm willing to give it my all. I just don't want to disappoint anybody."

"Nobody who tries their hardest is ever a disappointment." "I like that."

"Nino, let's start with the Earth. Did Barabbas tell you of its origins?"

"Yes. He told me about Earthonte, and how it was Satan's planet."

"Good. Now I will tell you the rest of the story. When God smashed Earthonte and put the planets into their proper orbits, this was not done in any haphazard manner. Each planet was made a specific size, and given a specific orbit in relationship to earth and the sun."

"I read somewhere once that even the slightest change in the planets' alignment would cause a problem? Is that true?"

"Let me give you an example. Nino, what would you guess are the two smallest bodies in our solar system?"

"Probably Pluto and Neptune. No, no—it's got to be Pluto and the moon."

Al grining with a proud smirk, "That's exactly right! And you said you didn't have a scientific mind! Here's something that's going to surprise you, though. Did you know that when God first put the planets into place, there was no moon or Pluto?"

"No, I didn't know that."

"Let me give you a lesson in creation."

"Is this from the book of Genesis?

"Well, yes and no. This is kind of the story behind the story."

"But the book of Genesis is true, right?" Nino asks, concerned. "God did create the world in six days, and then rested on the seventh, right?"

"Well, as you already have discovered, God did not actually create the earth. He kind of remodeled it, agreed?"

"Yup. Okay, I got you man."

"First God smashed Earthonte and made the eight planets of our solar system."

Nino confused, "I thought there were nine planets in our solar system?"

"Don't forget, no Pluto in the beginning."

Nino embarrassed, "Oh, that's right. Sorry Al. Who do I think I am, correcting Albert Einstein?"

Al pats Nino on the shoulder, "As I was saying, Nino, he put Mercury, Venus, Mars, Jupiter, Saturn and Uranus into place."

"What about Earth?"

"God first placed Mars in Earth's spot in the solar system to see how the various free-flowing weather patterns might effect the planet. This is why some people think there used to be water and possibly even life on Mars."

Nino shocked, "Isn't that amazing?! Were there people?"

"No, just water and plants."

"So, God was kind of experimenting?"

"Exactly. He was doing a trial run, so to speak."

Nino puzzled, "But, if God knows everything, why would he have to do an experiment?"

Al explains, "Because, this was a new area even for God. Not only was he going to give every living creature free will, he was also going to let weather patterns become free flowing. In Forever, all weather is controlled. The climate is always pleasing and the seasons are never harsh."

"I see what you mean. So, what happened to Earth?"

"He placed the piece of Earthonte that would become Earth directly over the kingdom of Forever. It hung there, like a giant Christmas bulb for a long period of time. This was intended to humiliate Satan and his fallen angels, and it did. There was no place for them to hide from their shame. All of the citizens of Forever could see the crudeness of Satan's kingdom, along with Satan's feeble attempts at creating man, beast, and plant life. Satan and his fallen angels also had to look down at the beauty of Forever. This was in direct contrast to their horrid planet. Their pain was agonizing—especially Satan's."

Nino curious, "How did Satan react?"

Al winces at the thought of Satan's situation, "You can't imagine how humiliated Satan was. God would speak to Satan while all of the citizens were looking on. And whenever he did, he and his cohorts would all hide behind rocks like scared little children. Allah would say, **"Come out, Satan. Stand toe to toe with me. Show us, almighty god, your creative power. Let us see the**

splendor of your kingdom. Expose the might of he who dared to ascend up my holy mountain."

"Did Satan answer him?"

"At first he was too shaken and scared to speak. But, eventually, as his strength returned so did is pride. On one occasion he said, "Give me back all of my powers Allah, and watch how my kingdom will blossom even in the midst of your realm.""

"The audacity! How arrogant ... So, did God agree?"

"Yes, he did. He gave Satan all of his powers. In fact, he gave him more power than he ever had before."

"So, Satan got a second chance to create his kingdom?"

"Yes. Satan was free to create for a predetermined season, but this time, everyone was watching."

"Did the extra power help him?"

"Not really, Nino. He just made bigger and uglier creatures, and his best effort at humans was the Neanderthal Man."

"Did the citizens of Forever mock him?"

"No. They were broken-hearted for him."

Nino surprised, "Broken-hearted? After all of the crap he caused?!"

"Yes, it was like watching someone you care about embarrass themselves. We all loved Lucifer just as God did, and still does. It was a tragedy. But Satan, blinded now by his distorted view of the world and himself, just continued to grow progressively worse in spirit and purpose." "Then what happened?"

"Satan grew increasingly bitter and angry. He envisioned, as all narcissistic people do, that everyone was watching him and laughing at him. At one point in history, he got so enraged that he attempted to pull the earth farther away from Forever so that no one could see him. It took a tremendous amount of his power, but he was successful. It took him over 100 days to move the earth a thousand miles. He was so enraged at the thought of his humiliation; he thought nothing of how his move was going to effect his creation. He took for granted that Jehovah's protective spirit was, even in his anger, protecting Satan and Earthonte from the random chaos of space. God decided that he would give Satan one more painful example of what it means to separate yourself from God."

Nino looks worried, "What did God do?"

"He called back his protective spirit so that it no longer covered the planet of Earthonte. It was left bare and exposed, like a tree with no bark. The first thing that happened was that Satan's movement of the planet triggered a weather upheaval that caused much of Earthonte to be flooded. Only the highest mountains were showing. Satan tried to pull his planet back, but he was too tired. Then to make matters even worse as his creatures drowned, a giant asteroid crashed into Earthonte, and sent so much dust into the atmosphere that it completely blocked out what little sun was still reaching the doomed planet."

Nino awe struck, "So, an asteroid really did kill the dinosaurs, but it's a lot different than anyone could ever imagine. Unbelievable … What happened next?"

"The whole venture sent Earthonte into a deep freeze. Almost everything was destroyed. Every dinosaur died, including almost all of the other animals and Neanderthals. For every 20 thousand living things alive before the asteroid event, only 200 were alive afterward. Allah decided that this would also be the end of Satan's days as god on Earthonte. He had used up millions of years all in vain. Now, the stage was set for the beginning of God's creation on Earth.

"So God put Earthonte into its spot in our solar system, and named it Earth?"

Al smiles, "That's right. However, once Earthonte was moved from Forever's protective galaxy, it could no longer sustain any form of life other than the supernatural kind. It was, for the fallen angels and Satan, their first taste of what their final resting place would be like—barren and destitute."

"Only is sounds like this was a watery hell, instead of a fiery one … Is Earth as we know it Hell?"

"No, Nino, it just took on some of Hell's characteristics for a time."

"So, in the beginning, things on Earth were pretty bad."

"Yes, which brings me to the book of Genesis. On the first day, God took earth and placed it on it's axis in the spot that Mars had been keeping warm. He then moved all of the planets into their rightful spots. Then God said 'let there be light,' and the light of the sun shined for the first time on the frozen planet earth. As the ice melted, the earth was like a giant ocean with only a few of the highest mountains visible. The wind roared over the giant sea at over 500 miles an hour, and 800 foot tidal waves crashed over the peaks of Mount Everest and Mount Kilimanjaro."

"Day two?" Nino asks his new friend.

"Well, the true biblical translation is 'after a period of time'." "So, that's a day?"

Al continues, "Yes. So, after a period of time, Yahweh reached out his mighty hand and pulled a giant piece of molten rock out of the center of the earth. As Eve was made from the rib of Adam so that they could propagate the sons of man, so was the moon made from a piece of the earth, so that they could together set the stage for life."

"I understand. Okay, so the moon used to be a part of the Earth. But, won't the people say that if that is true, then where is the massive crater it should have left behind?"

"The crater it left is massive." Al continues.

Nino searches for the answer, "Well, where is it? The Grand Canyon? No, that's not even big enough!"

Al laughing, "You're right about that. The crater it left is called the Pacific Ocean."

"Oh my God!" Nino exclaims. "And our scientists will accept this as fact?"

"Yes, they will." Al assures him.

"But why is the moon necessary? What did it do?"

"Well, before the moon existed, the rotational wind of the earth would blow around 500 miles an hour. At this wind speed, no form of life would ever be able to exist. As the moon orbited the Earth, the drag caused by its gravity slowed down the earth's rotational wind, so that God could begin to create life on Earth. He started first with plants. Then he added fish, animals and finally, man."

Nino excited, "That's amazing! But, won't the scientists argue that it was not the hand of God, but rather a comet or an asteroid?"

Al impressed with Nino's wit, "That's a very good question, Nino. But here is my response. If a comet or asteroid were to hit the Earth hard enough to break off a chunk the size of a small planet, it is scientifically illogical to believe that this could happen without the whole Earth exploding. Here is another interesting point. If the moon wasn't the exact size that it is, and if it didn't orbit the earth just as it does, there would be no life at all on this planet we call earth."

"So, what you're saying is that the system is perfect, and any change in it would make life cease to exist."

Al emphatic, "Nino, if the moon wasn't the exact size that it is, orbiting the earth just as it does, nothing more complex than algae and single celled creatures would ever exist."

Nino curious, "Al, what are the scientific odds for something like the earth-moon set up that we have happening by random chance?"

Al answers without hesitation,"One in a trillion, trillion, trillion, trillion. Do you know what those odds are?"

"Would it would be like Britney Spears fighting Mike Tyson for the heavyweight boxing championship of the world, and winning?"

"Nino, even the odds of her knocking him out in the first round, are still infinitely greater than what we are measuring."

"So you are saying there is no way this happened by chance, right Al?"

"Well, we already know that it didn't. But we have to get them to see how ridiculous it is for them to hold on to the hope that it did happen by accident. My colleagues often have a bad habit of dismissing what they cannot explain to chance theories."

"Is there more?"

"Yes, there's much more. Well we know that crater where the moon was is the Pacific Ocean. But there are two other large oceans the Atlantic and the Indian. What do you think happened to make those giant craters?"

Nino shakes his head, truly mystified. "I have no idea. Another planet?"

"Not a bad guess. In fact, you're exactly right!

"I' ll be damned."

"Let's hope not!" Al laughs. "Nino, scientists know for a fact that the Pacific Ocean is where the moon once was. Here's something they don't know, and it's also a scientific fact. God also pulled out three more giant pieces of the Earth. One he made into the planet Pluto and the crater it left behind is the Atlantic Ocean. The other he made into Haley's Comet, and its crater is the Indian Ocean."

"Remarkable!" Nino exclaims. "Haley's Comet? Why would God need a comet?"

"It's like a giant clock. Every 75 years Haley's Comet comes by. Every 27 circuits is the beginning of a new age."

"So what about the third piece. What did he need that for?"

"The last piece was taken from a combination of the Artic Ocean and some of your larger seas. He turned that in to the tenth planet in your solar system."

Nino surprised, "A tenth planet?!"

"Yes it hasn't been discovered yet, but it soon will."

"And the purpose of this last planet is?" Nino asks.

"The truth is that God needed some big holes to hold all of the water that was on the earth.

"So the Continental Drift theory?" Nino questions.

Al responds, "An interesting explanation. It made a lot of sense, but was way off base. The key word for much of what is called science is the word theory. A theory, even though it is widely supported and accepted by the scientific community, is not necessarily correct! Scientists need to stop putting so much faith in theories, and start putting their faith in God. They can still do a lot of fascinating things scientifically and have faith at the same time. One does not have to mutually exclude the other."

"Well," Nino starts, his scientific appetite peaked. "Are we done, or do I get to hit them some more?"

"You get to hit them with more, my brother! It is called the Jupiter Effect. If Jupiter were not the exact size that it is, with its perfectly circular orbit, Earth would be too close to the sun to sustain life. We would be nothing more than a burnt piece of molten rock. If Jupiter were any larger we would be too far away from the sun. I'm telling you Nino, just a couple of hundred miles further away, and the earth would be a giant snow cone."

Nino smirks, "Seems like a lot of mysteriously perfect coincidences for a universe that was supposed to have randomly occurred."

Al smiles, "Perfection hits the nail right on the head. Your modern physicists know that in their hearts that there is a creator, but whether they will admit it or not, that is another question. They have seen God's creative forces up close. When you hear them talking about gravity, electromagnetism, the nuclear force, and so on, they can't explain the forces that sustain them, they simply call them constants. These constants were set into place for one purpose, the creation of life. These elements and forces had to be exactly as they are from the very beginning, or no life would be possible.!"

"So these forces didn't accidentally evolve because of the big bang and so forth, they were there from the beginning right?" Nino asks.

Al nods, "That's correct. They are just like God. They always have been, and they always will be. The ingredients of life were all there from the very first day of creation. It's a mathematical and scientific fact. They were not caused by some big explosion or nuclear reaction. Think about it simply for a moment. Would an explosion in a bakery create a cake?"

Nino laughing "Nope, you'd have to have a baker."

Al Laughing "Now you're talking."

"Hey Al, Give me some simple examples of how finely tuned these forces are."

"Nino, even the very slightest changes would cause cataclysmic problems. For instance, if the nuclear weak force was just the slightest bit weaker, all of the hydrogen in the universe would become helium."

Nino nervous, but smiling "I have no idea where you going with this one Al."

Al Smiling "Don't worry Nino, this is just a little simple chemistry. All I'm saying is that the elements that allow us to have water would not exist."

"No water, no life?"

"That's right, and speaking of water. Water is mysteriously different from all other molecules, in that, it is lighter in its solid form than it is in its liquid form."

"So is that why ice floats right?"

Al continues, "That's right, but here's the cool part. If ice did not float all of our oceans and lakes would freeze from the bottom up. The earth would be a giant ice ball. Even our miraculous sun wouldn't be able to save us."

Nino curious, "What's so special about our sun?"

"Good question. Our sun is called a yellow dwarf. If it were a larger star, it would put out too much radiation, and if it were even the slightest bit smaller, it would not emit enough heat. Our sun is also a rare form of yellow dwarf in that it does not emit what are called solar flares, which is what yellow dwarfs usually do. If our sun was a normal yellow dwarf, it would shoot these gigantic radioactive flares all the way to Saturn. We would be burnt to a crisp."

"What about the theories of life on other planets? You know, Martians, the man in the moon …"

"There is no other Earth-Moon system like ours. All other galaxies are what scientists call "gamma ray busters."

"What does that mean? Their stars are too big?"

Al nods, "Kind of. What this means is that from time to time these galaxies have radioactive explosions that are so immense that nothing much bigger than a cock roach would ever survive. People have always liked to think that there are other intelligent beings somewhere out there, but the truth is Nino, we're all alone."

"What about the theory of evolution and stuff like that? Do those theories hold any water?"

"I'll get to the theory of evolution in a minute. Let's go back to the creation for a moment. After God put the moon into orbit he was able to separate the day from the night. Once the land appeared, God let the earth burst forth with every sort of grass, and seed-bearing fruit trees, with seeds inside the fruit, so that these seeds could produce the kinds of plants and fruits they came from."

"What about the fish and animals?"

"God filled the oceans with fish, the air with birds, and the earth with creatures. God said 'let the earth be filled as Heaven is filled with every kind of animal." He even allowed some of Satan's creations to live on."

Nino surprised, "Really? Like what?"

"Oh, let me see." Al sighs before he starts his list of less desirable creatures. "The Crocodile, the mosquito, the fly, all reptiles, the rat, the roach, and most notably, the snake."

"Of course. So when did man step on to the scene?"

"After a time, or if you go by the Bible, on the sixth day, Allah said 'I will make a man, someone in my own image to be master of all life upon the earth, in the seas, and in the skies.'"

"Did God make Eve out of Adam's rib, just like the Bible says?" Al nods, "Yes, and it's a scientific fact that all women have one more rib than men."

Nino smiles, "That's pretty cool. What about the Garden of Eden? Is all that true?"

"Everything is true, Nino. The Garden of Eden was a little slice of Heaven here on Earth. It was filled with much of the beauty that you have experienced here in Forever. Adam and Eve were living a simple life of ease and pleasure."

"Where was Satan while all this was going on?"

"Well, God decided to let Satan have one last shot at creation. He was allowed to finish the last attempt he had started on Earthonte before the relocation. Satan had convinced God to give him one last chance. God agreed, but this time, there would be a price.

"What was the price?"

"God made Satan agree that if he gave him one last chance to complete his projects, that when his time was up, he would once again come freely under God's authority."

"What do you mean?"

"Satan would once again have to serve God. He would actually have a job to do. Haven't you ever read the book of Job?"

"Oh yeah, many times."

"In Job 1:6-22 it says that one day as the angels came to present themselves before God, Satan, the accuser came with them. **"Where have you come from?"** the Lord asks Satan.

And Satan replies "From patrolling the earth."

Then the lord asks Satan, **"Have you seen my servant Job? He is the finest man on all the earth-a good man who fears God and will have nothing to do with evil."**

"Why shouldn't he, when you pay him so well. You always protect him and his property. Look how rich he is. No wonder he worships you! Take away his riches, and he will curse you to your face.' There is more but this passage in Job gives you an idea of how Satan will help God purify the souls that will make up the New Jerusalem.

"So Satan gets to finish his final painting, so to speak?" Nino asks.

Al nods in agreement, "God explained to Satan that he would be given one more short period of time in which he would only be allowed to focus on humans. It was during this final period of creation that Satan finished what our scientists call the Cro-Magnon man. This creation was very strong, but still not very smart in comparison with humans. They could communicate in a more advanced form of language, because they had longer necks. They could actually speak in sentences. They made tools, and even established villages throughout Africa, Europe, and Asia."

"So what happened back in Eden?"

Al raises his eyebrows and shrugs, "The Bible account is factual. Satan tricked Eve into eating from the tree of knowledge, and Eve convinced Adam to eat from the same fruit."

"Was it really fruit?"

Al chuckles, "Yes, it was an apple."

"What happened when they ate it?"

Al explains, "Their brains were turned on to a higher level instantly. They suddenly understood the meaning of good and evil, and there was a price to pay for that."

"And that was?"

"No more free lunch. Everything would have to be worked for. Nothing would be easy, or given for free. The ground no longer easily gave forth fruits and vegetables. Life became a struggle. Stress was introduced to our human ancestors and shortly behind stress followed sickness."

Nino wonders, "Is stress the cause of all sickness?"

Al speaks with confidence, "Stress and anxiety are at the root of nearly all human mental and physical illnesses."

Nino agrees, "I believe that. I mean, look at me. I live in an old factory pipe, and I'm always exposed to the elements, but I'm hardly ever sick."

Al smiles, "That's because you have a strong faith in God, and you must have a world view that allows you to be content."

Nino smiles, "It's true. For the most part I am pretty much at ease with the circumstances and routine of my life."

Al pats Nino on his head, "There you have it. Oh, here's another one. Labor became terribly painful, and it is a scientific fact that labor grew more painful, because as the human brain became more well developed (the result of eating from the tree of good and evil). Human babies' heads got bigger, and consequently the births got more painful, just as God said they would."

Nino interjects, "The snake that seduced Eve was cursed with having to crawl on its belly. That is also a scientific fact, isn't it? I mean didn't snakes used to have legs?"

Al proudly, "Very good Dr. Jones! Yes, this is also true. Another very important thing that happened was that the weather patterns were no longer mild. Before the fall of Eden, the weather was always perfect. But from the first day that Yahweh cast them out of the Garden, things turned progressively sour. When God removed his protective shield from the Garden, the sun beat down on this oasis and turned it into a desert."

Nino has a revelation, "So the fiery sword that chased Adam and Eve out of the Garden of Eden was actually the sun?"

Al nods, "Can you imagine feeling the full force of the African sun for the first time? What else could it be described as, if not a fiery sword?"

"So, is that when the Great Game really began, Al?" Nino asks.

"Yes. God knew that Satan would eventually be able to seduce and manipulate Adam and Eve, just as he was able to con his fallen angels." "God wasn't really surprised by this, then?"

Al shakes his head, "No, not at all. The Garden of Eden was a social microcosm of what happened in Heaven, and what would continue to happen over and over again throughout the course of the Great Game. The message is simple. When you move away from God, you will suffer. Not because he is punishing you, but because of the life choices you have made."

Nino interjects, "Like when Satan moved Earthonte and caused the flood. That was his fault?"

Al nods, "Yes, but Satan, like all people who choose to move away from God, assumed that Jehovah was punishing him for his sins."

Nino responds, "But in reality they are simply reaping what they have sown."

Al smiles, "Poetic justice, and yet no matter how heinous the crime, our creator is never happy when we suffer. Even when our suffering is deserved, it makes him ache for us. How lucky we are to have such a loving soul for a father."

Nino scratches his head, "Al, what about the rest of the world? Did Adam and Eve really populate the whole world? I mean, that's a lot of procreating, man! Even if Adam did live to be nine hundred years old, the numbers don't add up, do they?"

Al chuckles, "Your suspicions are correct, Nino. The Adam and Eve from the Garden of Eden are the first parents of humankind, but they are not the father and mother of us all. They started the Jewish race, and nothing more."

Nino grins, "Isn't that something?! So, where do the rest of us come from?"

Al explains, "When Adam and Eve were expelled from the Garden, God created prototype Adams and Eves for every race of people that would inhabit the Earth throughout the Great Game."

"Did this happen before or after the great flood?" Nino asks.

"Before it. All throughout the Fertile Crescent of the Middle East, and around the world, the electric sparks of modern civilization began to ignite. As Adam and Eve's lineage began to grow and multiply, a number of problems occurred. First of all, some of the human women were so beautiful that God's angels had sex with them. This produced a race of super humans. They were giant, and had an intellect and strength that normal humans did not possess."

Nino shocked, "Angels had sex with humans?"

"It's in black and white in the book of Genesis, Nino."

Nino shakes his head, "I know, and I've read it before, but it just didn't register in my mind as a real event."

"I know what you mean. There was also the problem of the Cro-Magnon man—Satan's final creation."

"Why was that a problem?"

Al explains, "For a couple of reasons. First of all, God couldn't allow any of Satan's creation to live into the modern era—into a time of organized science—because it would be clear that there is no missing link. It would expose the theory of evolution as a hoax."

"Why wouldn't God want that to happen?"

"Because in a way, the theory of evolution helps God's cause."

Nino understands, "You mean, by adding mystery to it all? So it sort of helps to test our faith?"

"Yes, kind of like that. The other problem was that the Cro-Magnon man was bigger, stronger and more violent than God's creation. Although the humans were smarter, in those early years of human existence, might ruled right. This was one of the reasons God let the Angels have sex with some of the humans in the first place."

"Oh! I see. God wanted to give his children a little extra beef on the defensive line."

Al laughing, "That's right, Coach Nino! The straw that broke the camel's back was that his own creation became selfish and self-centered to the point where only a small number of people were actually following Yahweh's path of love. There was murder, adultery, corruption, war, lying, divorce, barbarianism and ..."

Nino shakes his head in disgust, "Sounds like modern times?"

"Same type of problems, Nino, just different times. The times may seem to change, but the human problems remain the same."

"So that's why God decided to end the world."

"He didn't end the world, Nino."

Nino indignant, "What? Now I know what the Bible says about this."

"He destroyed the whole world of those to whom the Old Testament was entrusted. He sent a monstrous flood to the land of the Fertile Crescent. It killed all of the Cro-Magnon men, the giant angel children, and all of Adam and Eve's descendents, except for Noah and his family."

"What about the rest of the world?"

"There was much flooding all over the world and many sinful people from all races died."

"Did God just make it flood in certain regions of the world?"

"God used the Earth's natural weather cycle to create the climatic conditions necessary to cause world-wide devastation."

"Why didn't he just kill the ones he wanted dead, and go on with the game from that point in time?"

"Because, Nino, God knew that eventually science would be able to prove the flood story, which would strengthen the biblical story of Noah. He also knew that he must manipulate the natural weather patterns to serve his purpose, because he wanted no evidence of supernatural involvement."

"And that would lead people to believe in God for reasons other than faith?" Nino questions.

"The opportunity to have faith must never be compromised to achieve another objective."

"Alright, so God made it rain for 40 days and 40 nights."

"Well, God removed his protective spirit, and allowed the Earth's natural weather conditions to operate on their own."

"What caused so much rain?"

"First of all, when God wants it to rain, you better believe it's going to rain. But, as always, there is a scientific explanation. At this point in time, the Earth was overflowing with large mammals. The great herds of cattle and other larger mammals like mammoths, cave bears, mastodons and buffalo all over the world were creating so much methane gas that it actually turned the Earth into a giant greenhouse. As the Earth grew hotter, the oceans' currents and jet streams changed as the Earth attempted to cool itself, and large amounts of rain fell all over the planet."

"Are you talking about global warming?"

"Yes, I am."

Nino perplexed, "But, I thought that was a modern problem caused by world wide industrialization and pollution."

"Your global warming is caused by the same types of trapped gasses increasing in your atmosphere that caused the biblical flood to occur. The difference is that the gasses are now man-made, caused by pollution. However, how global warming can and will effect weather patterns is theoretically the same."

"Will the eventual result of global warming be a flood?"

Al pauses and then answers, "Well, ironically, the end result of global warming is an ice age."

Nino's shocked, "An ice age? What does an ice age have to do with Noah?"

Al breaths in deep and collects his thoughts. "Here's the short explanation of what happened, and what could happen again."

Nino interrupts before Al can get started. "I thought God said he would never destroy the world with a flood again?"

Al nods, "He did. He won't. But global warming can still happen and cause a lot of suffering. I mean, look at the weather conditions which allowed your abduction."

"You mean the sudden drop in temperature? Is that the result of global warming?" Nino asks.

Al continues, "Yes, it's the Earth's way of trying to cool itself down. It gets to a certain temperature and then you get these macrobursts of subzero air that come rushing in from the stratosphere. These macrobursts are so sudden and powerful that they could actually freeze a large mammal almost instantly."

"Is that what happened to those mammoths they found frozen solid in Siberia?" Questions Nino.

Al smiling, "That's a perfect example. Some of the mammoths they found still had food in their mouths, and many of them still had undigested flowers still in their stomachs. This shows two things. It was probably summer when they died, and they had to be flash-frozen or the flowers would have eventually been dissolved by their stomach acids.

"How cold would it have to get for such a sudden freeze to occur?"

"I can tell you exactly. It went from 75 degrees Fahrenheit to minus 185 degrees Fahrenheit in a matter of seconds."

"Does this macroburst hit the entire planet?"

"No, usually they only touch down at sites in the Northern Hemisphere."

"So how does the flood come into play?"

"The Earth's temperature is only allowed to get just so hot, and then suddenly you will see crazy, unpredictable weather conditions all around the world."

Nino wonders, "Is that why the seasons seem to blend together? Is this what the biblical warning was referring to?"

"Yes. In some places summer would resemble winter, and in other places winter would become extremely cold and stormy. Places like Australia may not have any summer at all, and states like New York would be hit by extremely cold weather, while horrific blizzards shut down places like

Niagara Falls, Canada. You would see a miserable sting of cold fronts that would cause world wide flooding. There would also be devastating storms springing up all over the planet."

"I'm assuming that this must happen in the summer, right? Otherwise it would be snowing."

"Yes. It would be summer for the northern hemisphere." Nino clarifies, "You mean, the United States, Canada and Europe?"

"Yes. When winter finally did show up with its snow and frigid wind, the flood waters now frozen would cover these regions of the world in a thick sheet of ice."

"So there really was an ice age at the time of Noah's flood?"

"No, because the storms came during the summer, all of the ice would melt during the following summer. However, the melting ice would cause severe flooding all over the world."

"Is that why we have all of those 'Noah-like' flood stories from all over the world?"

"Yes. And now you know why."

As Nino tries to take it all in, Chebar approaches the pair. He is breathless, worried that he might be a little late. "Al, how's it going?" Al stands and goes to his friend. "Chebar my man, how are you?" Chebar smiles, "All is well, Al!"

"You see, Nino, everyone is a poet! Chebar, Nino's going to do a splendid job."

"Did you cover everything we talked about?" asks Chebar.

"Almost. I didn't get into the zodiac or the sphinx, but all other areas have been covered."

Chebar turns to Barabbas, who entered right on his heels. "Barabbas, can Al have a little more time?"

Barabbas frowns. "Chebar, that's up to you. The longer he stays with Al, the more he cuts into your time together."

"That's okay. This is important. Go ahead, Al. you've got a little more time."

"Thank you, Chebar. I won't let you down." Al turns to Barabbas. "Don't worry, Barabbas. I'll be quick."

"Be quick, but don't hurry."

Al laughs, shakes his head and turns back to his student. "Listen to him, Nino. A former Zealot quoting John Wooden." He turns and shakes hands with Barabbas. "Thank you, my friend. You won't regret it. Barabbas forces a half-smile, then turns and walks slowly away ...

Author's Note: Speaking of time, did you know that an average human life of 75 years adds up to 657,000 hours. A statistical and time analysis of the average American citizen breaks down as follows:

657,000	Hours = 75 years of life
-219,000	Hours = 8 hrs of sleep per day
438'000	Hours Remaining
-136,000	Hours = 5 hours of TV per day
301,125	Hours Remaining
-16,380	Hours = 7 hours of school per day for 12 to 16 years
284,745	Hours Remaining
-67,200	Hours = 8 hours of work per day
217,545	Hours Remaining
217,545	Hours divided by 8,760 (hours in one year) = 24.83 years remaining

That's what hour lives come down to give or take a few hundred hours here or there. It doesn't seem like much when you look at it from an hourly perspective does it? Even our physical bodies if taken apart one atom (Did you know that atoms are mindless particles that are not alive!) at a time would leave us with nothing more than a small mound of atomic dust. Atomic dust that has never been alive, but all of which was once that person called you. You see, it is the presence of the soul that gives life and animation to these mindless dead particles called atoms. And it is what we do with our few precious hours that gives our life meaning, purpose, and splendor! Squander not this wonderful experience called life, and hold precious the little time that you are given. Truly I tell you this opportunity will not come your way again. Awaken!

"Look carefully then how you walk ... Making the most of time!"
-Ephesians 5:15-16

"Surely if unintelligent nature were the creator or evolver she would continue the process. Since without intelligence nothing would arrive at fixed conditions. If Darwin was right, then evolution would be a fact today, and we would see about us fish becoming birds, and monkeys becoming men!"
-Pastor Charles Taze Ruzzell

CHAPTER 12

▼

God speaking to his ministering Angels who wanted to sing their
usual victory songs before the Holy One, as the Red Sea Crashed
upon and killed the Egyptian soldiers. "My children [the Egyptians] are
perishing in the waters of the sea, and you want to sing?!"
-Sanhedrin, 39a

He isn't really being slow about his promised return, even though
it sometimes seems that way. But he is waiting, for the good reason
that he is not willing that any should perish, and he is giving more
time for the sinners to repent.
-2 Peter 3:8-9

Al takes Nino by hid arm, and walks him to the end of the vineyard which overlooks a spectacular flame blue lake. The view is absolutely breathtaking. As Nino takes in the unearthly beauty of the water and landscape, Al continues. "You see Nino, scattered all over the world, various pieces of evidence are apparent to anyone with an open mind that the Earth truly is Satan's planet."

"Really? Even now? Like what?" asks Nino.

Al scratches his head, "Well, for example, the Egyptian Sphinx. Modern archeologists agree that it was constructed somewhere between 4,500 years ago, or about 2,500 B.C. The truth is that it was built about 10,000 years ago."

Nino is surprised, "Even before the flood of Noah? So, who built it?"

All points out the facts, "Let's look at the evidence. There is scientific, irrefutable evidence that the sphinx was eroded by water. However, Egypt was a desert since before the rise of the Pharaohs, so where does this water come from?"

"The flood?" Nino guesses.

Al smiles, "Yes. And there is more. All of the other sandstone structures that were definitely built by the pharaohs show no signs of water erosion. This proves that the Sphinx was built during a period long before Egypt and its Pharaoh's ruled the world. Another important point of interest is that during the construction of the great Sphinx, all of the humans who settled along the Nile River led very simple lives of hunting and gathering."

Nino puzzled, "So, how could they have created such a gigantic structure?"

Al nods his head, "How, indeed? The Sphinx is massive. It is nearly 10 stories high, and longer than one of your New York City blocks. If you were to assemble a team of the world's top engineers and stonemasons, and give them the finest tools and modern technology available, it would take them over 60 years to construct such a massive structure."

"So there's no way it was built by the early Egyptians."

Al roles his eyes, "Nino, these people had only simple tools to work with. They didn't live in a city that was controlled by a king or government. They lived in tiny little villages. There would have been no way to even mobilize them into a team of workers. They hunted with primitive stone weapons. They lived in simple grass huts, made pottery, and wove baskets and blankets. So you tell me, Nino, who made the Sphinx?"

"If they only had simple tools available, then it would have taken something with supernatural powers to create a structure so massive and unbelievably engineered."

"That's right. The truth is, your scientists have no idea who created the Sphinx or how it was accomplished. But you do, don't you, Dr. Jones?"

"Was it God, or the Angels?"

Al faking disappointment, "Dr. Jones, shame on you. Examine the evidence before your eyes." Nino blushes "What do you mean? I can't see the things you are talking about!"

"That's right, you can't, can you?"

"Al, I'm sorry. You've lost me."

"You can't see any of those types of structures, because there is nothing like that in Forever. Nino, look around you. Do you see anything massive, gigantic or out of place?

Nino looks around, "No, nothing."

"Nino, have you ever heard of Feng Shui. The ancient Chinese art of placement?"

"Yeah, it has something to do with Chi and all that right?" "Yes, that's' right. But do you know what Chi is?"

"A little bit, but not really."

"Chi is the vital energy that animates, connects, and moves all things through the cycle of life. The Chinese believe that everything is alive with Chi, everything is connected by Chi, and the Chi in everything is changing."

"This Chi sounds like their talking about the Holy Spirit of God." "They are."

Nino confused,"But how can that be? The Chinese are for the most part atheists, aren't they?"

"It's ironic isn't it? However, if you look read the writings of Kung Fu Zi…."

Nino laughs "Kung Fu Zi. That's not that "Pay attention weed hopper" guy is it?"

All laughs "No, no … that's' Confucious' real name.'

Nino wonders, "Is Confucianism a religion?"

Al explains, "No it is a philosophy of life. Between 550 and 600 BC their lived to famous Chinese teachers, Confucious the founder of Confucianism, and Lao Tze the founder of Taoism or (Daoism). Confucious lived during a time period in Chinese history that is very similar to what you are now going through in the United States. There was mass disorder, confusion, and degrading moral standards.

Nino nods, "You've got that right."

Al nods, "Confucious felt in his heart that his beloved Chinese society was going to crumble if changes where not made. He believed that the cure for society was to come up with a philosophy of life that stressed a sense of social order, and mutual respect. He believed that benevolence and human kindness should always be demonstrated to one another. He also believed in the importants of etiquette, love of family, respect of parents, righteousness, honesty, trustworthiness, and loyalty to the state. He strongly believed that proper etiquette should always be used, and that all people should strive to achieve perfect virtue. Lao Tze came along a little later, and he had the some concerns. He taught the Chinese term Tao, which means "The way".

Nino shakes his head, 'These guys sound an awful lot like Jesus."

Al smiles, "I know. The P.O. J. is universal. It always has been and always will be the way that leads to Heaven, and human tolerance, harmony, and honor … Anyway, Lao Tze believed that nature has a "way" in which it moves, and that people should first recognize it, and then passively accept it. He emphasized the link between people and nature. You must of heard of the Yin and Yang effect?"

Nino nods "Yeah, its something like how everything has to have an opposing force that allows our harmonius universe to exsist. Light-dark, Male-Female, Heavenly-earthly, and active & passive."

Al smiles proudly, "Very good Nino."

Nino wonders, "So what happened, did Confucious and Lao Tze save their country?"

Al nods, "Yes. But not only China, Japan as well. The social ethics and moral teachings of Confucius, were over time blended with Taoism and the Buhdists ideas of the after life each philosophy complimented the other."

Nino interrupts, "Is that what the Japanese religion of Shinto is, a blending of all three philosophies?"

Al explains, "Not exactly. But as you suggest they are related. It is very interesting to note that during the 6th and 5th century BCE came Conffucianism, Taoism, Buddhism, and Shintoism."

Nino's eyes pop, "The Buddha, Siddhartha Gautama, was also apart of that crew? Man, what a period of wisdom!. So Shinto is the final child of these wise parents?"

Al smiles, 'Shinto means "The Way of the Gods" it is similar in many ways to the Animistic and/or nature worship practiced by the native Indians of North America. Shintos, like the American Indians believe that everything in the universe has a spirit, and therefore should be respected and honored. Indians for example praise the spirit of a buffalo for giving its life to them, so that they might survive. Like the Indians, Shintos also believe that our ancestors are watching over us from the spirit world. This idea is what lead to what is called ancestor worship. Belieiveing that ones ancestors are actively involved in our lives, is truly apart of every religion to some extent."

Nino agrees, "Like for example, how catholics ask certain saints to help them?"

Al nods, "Exactly."

Nino impressed, "When I think of China, I always thought of a faithless land. But they aren't are they. They have been blessed in many ways.

Al agrees, "It's true. They were one of the first peoples to recognize the power and energy of God. They simply have a different concept of life, its source, and how things work. I don't want to get side tracked any further. So I'll give you one last jewel from China. The Chinese believe that Chi is attracted to harmony. The more one lives in harmony with all things the more Chi will be available."

"That makes sense. It's like the more you do God's will the more you receive his holy spirit."

Al smiling, "Exactly. There is an ancient Chinese proverb that goes like this: **"If there is light in the soul, then there is harmony in the home. If there is harmony in the home, then there is honor in the nation. If there is honor in the nation, then there is peace in the world." And I will add if there is peace in the world then God is with us."**

Nino smiles, "That is so beautiful, and so filled with wisdom. We really are all God's children aren't we?"

Al scowls, "It is the world and Satan who divides us and categorizes us. Not God."

"So this Feng Shui your were talking about has to do with the harmony of living." Nino asks.

Al looks out at the landscape, "Not just the living, but the harmony and placement of all things. This is what delights the spirit of God. And this is how you can tell if God is involved. Look around you Nino, is there anything as far as the eye can see that does not perfectly fit in with its surroundings?"

Nino gazes out at the splendor of Forever, "No there is nothing like that here. Everything flows together ... **Forever is a symphony of splendor.**"

Al points at Nino, "So, Dr. Jones, now that you have reexamined the evidence, who is the creator of the Sphinx?"

"It was Satan."

"Yes. Satan not only made the Sphinx, he also assisted in the making of the pyramids. And not only that, but there is also evidence of many other of Satan's creations. The general population does not hear about them."

"So almost everything that Satan made was ridiculously large and often unattractive?"

"Yes. You see, Nino, Satan suffered from God-envy. His creations, when compared to God's, are so hideous and unattractive, that in his attempt to impress, he made everything as massive as he could."

"It's like a dog that barks loud because he's scared."

"Kind of. You see, the creative force of Yahweh is love, and love unifies and compliments all things. The creative force of the Devil is self-centeredness, which divides and corrupts."

"I think I see what you mean.... Al, what are some of the other things Satan created?"

Al scratches his head, "Well, there is a sunken city in the Pacific Basin that archeologists call the ruins of Nan Madol. There are gigantic blocks of stone that weigh more than fifty thousand pounds. Local legend has it that these stones floated on clouds to the place which they now stand."

"How old is the city?"

"The ruins at Nan Madol are left over from Satan's days on Earthonte. Also, coincidentally, these blocks cannot be age-dated by any type of technology that is currently available. So, science will have to guess and come up with theories. Are you hearing me, Nino? Life in Micronesia doesn't begin until about 1500 B.C! So there is no way these simple people moved 50 ton blocks, and your scientists know this."

Nino raises his eyebrows, "That's remarkable."

Al waves his hand through the air, "Shoot, that's nothing! There is a place in Lebanon called the platform at Baalbeck. That could probably not even be built today. Nobody knows who built this massive structure."

"What was it for?" Nino asks.

"Satan was going to accept sacrifices and worship. Archeologists believe that it had something to do with sun worshipping, but they are wrong. The clue is in the name Baalbeck."

"Baal is one of the ancient names for the Devil, right?"

Al nods, "That's right, Nino. These stones that make up this alter are thought to be the heaviest objects ever moved by man or beast. But there is no way these simple people could have accomplished such a feat."

"How big were the stones?"

"Each stone weighs about 1,000 tons. They are each seventy feet long, fifteen feet high and ten feet across. To give you an idea, each stone weighs as much as about 1,500 mid-size cars."

Nino wonders, "Al how big are those stone heads on Easter Island?"

Al smirks, "Nino, most of those were about 15 feet high, and weighed about 14 tons. They are like tiny babies compared to the stones at Baalbeck."

"So they weren't made by the Satan?"

Al shakes his head, "No those were all made, and moved by humans. And it was pretty remarkable feet. But here is a fact your modern archeologist don't know. Easter Islands original name was Mata-Ki-Te-Rani. Which means "Eyes looking at Heaven." The heads were built for two reasons: As an offering to God, to let him know that the people on this island believed in him, and were constantly searching the Heavens and awaiting his return. And as a reminder to the people to keep their heads to the sky. Fore God will come at a moment least expected to take you home. And that's exactly what happened."

Nino raises his eyebrows, "Really?"

Al explains, "A gigantic asteroid passed so close to the earth that it caused a planet-wide crustal shift or displacement. This caused a series of unbelievable earth quakes and volcanoes, which in turn created a tidal wave that was nearly 5 miles high, and traveling at a speed of over 400 miles an hour. In a single moment every one on the island was killed."

Nino grimaces, "How, awful … Why would God let that happen to a people who spent so much of their time trying to please him?"

Al explains, "The Island's growing population had begun to outpace its capacity to renew itself ecologically. The trees were all gone. The animals had been killed off. The soil was depleted and crops would no longer grow. They had used up all of their natural resources, and had slipped into a terrible famine that was so bad; the inhabitants had even begun resorting to cannibalism!"

Nino understands, "So God in his mercy brought them home in a single moment. Just like they knew he would."

Al nods, "Whenever Jehovah gets a chance to successfully bring us back to Heaven, he does ..." Al shakes his head, "I'm getting side tracked, but it's all good. You just remember what I told you about Satan's creations, and expose the facts."

Nino shakes his head, "It's all so amazing, and it seems so apparent once you point it out. But why can't the scientists see the truth? How, or why do they remain blind to such huge facts?"

Al frowns, "Our scientists need to stop protecting their theories and/or beliefs, and start explaining facts. If only they would look at the obvious, they would come to the supernatural conclusion. Which is, yes, there is a God."

Nino clarifies, "So, many, or most, of the Earth's mysterious structures are the artwork of the Devil. The remains of ancient cities often have impressive stonework, but, who the builder is, and how old these monolithic structures are, no one will ever believe."

"You make them believe, Nino. Present the facts. I'm just giving you a piece of your story. When it all comes together, people will be saying ..."

Nino responds,"Now, how could a homeless veteran, who lives in a pipe, have come up with all this shit on his own?"

Al pats Nino on the back, "Exactly! Nino, as my piece of the Grand Tour draws to a close, I will use these final moments to speak to you about time."

"You mean, how much time I'll have?" Nino asks.

"No. I mean how much time the world has. I'm going to solve for you the mystery of the zodiac."

Nino raises his eyebrows, "Astrology? You mean there really is some validity to that stuff?"

"Yes, there is. The Zodiac is known in Forever as the Great Clock of Brahman."

Nino curious, "How does it work?"

"The sun moves along a circular path called the ecliptic." "The ecliptic?"

"Nino, you've heard of the names of the constellations, right—Aries, Pisces and so on?"

"Yeah, sure. You mean like your birth sign."

"Yes, that's right. Okay, now I want you to picture in your mind two clocks. One small clock and one very large clock. In place of numbers, I want you to picture the zodiac signs. Can you do that?"

"Yeah, sure—1:00 is the ram, 2:00 is the fish, etc."

"Yes, yes. Very good! Now, this clock doesn't have any hands. On this clock, we use the sun to tell us what time it is."

"So if the sun is over the Aries constellation, we know it's spring, right?"

Al smiles proudly, "Yes, outstanding! The vernal equinox marks the beginning of the sun's apparent 360 degree circular path across the Earth's sky. The whole trip takes 365 days, 5 hours, 48 minutes and 4.5 seconds."

"A normal year."

"Yes. Now, if you use the northern or pole star—Ursa Minor—as the sun moves in its apparent circular path across the Earth—"

Nino interjects, "I thought the Earth moves around the sun?"

Al remains unflustered, "It does, but that is not how it looks. As I was saying, if you use this northern star as a fixed point, you will see the twelve constellations move through this point at various times of the year. Approximately once every 29 days."

"That's a cool way to explain it. I never really understood how it worked."

"Okay. That is our small clock. This small clock is what determines your birth sign."

"Is there anything to a birth sign?"

"Yes and no. One similarity between the Christian, Muslim and Jewish faiths is the concept of free will. According to this belief, every human has the right to determine his or her own fate. It is Allah's will that each of us should choose a personal form of self-expression."

"So the movement of the planets doesn't really have anything to do with our behavior, because if it did, then how is our will truly free?"

"What a mind you have, Nino! And you are absolutely right! However, the whole truth is that people born under certain signs do have a tendency to have similar behavior patterns. There is something about the compatibility of certain signs. One thing is for certain, much can be learned from the self-knowledge one can gain from being forewarned and prepared to comprehend and learn from events that may happen."

Nino surprises himself, "You're not saying these things will definitely happen, but they often do, and maybe the learning that comes from examining the possibilities could lead to greater self-understanding? Did I just say that?"

"Isn't it something how easy it is to express yourself up here?" Nino smiles, "Unhindered communication is a sweet pleasure."

Al sighs, "To always be able to say what you mean, and to be clearly understood, makes all conversation so enjoyable."

Nino jokes, "It sure does! I haven't been bored once!"

Al laughs out loud. "Well, I'm glad to hear that. Uh-oh! I'm getting sidetracked. On to the big clock."

"Is this the Great Clock of Brahman?"

"In the big clock we will look at the sun's movements against the backdrop of the constellations. This is not looked at in terms of months or years. This clock is concerned with the passing of centuries and millenniums."

"I read something once about the Great Year."

"The Great Year is the amount of time it takes for the sun to pass through all of the constellations."

"How long does it take? One hundred years?"

"A Great Year is 25,920 years. This massive segment of time is divided into twelve processional ages of approximately 2,160 years each. That's how long it takes for the sun to go from one constellation to another."

"My goodness, that's a long time. What is the Great Clock of Brahman used for?"

"Hidden within the Zodiac are the secrets of all that was, all that is, and all that will be. It tells you approximately when everything began, and …"

Nino nervous, "When it will end? But I thought Jesus said even he didn't know when it will end."

"He didn't then, but he has a good idea now. These twelve processional ages are called prophetic ages. Your religious historians and astrologers will tell you that the Great Game began during the Age of Taurus, which is 4159 B.C. to 2001 B.C. However, they don't know the whole story. When God placed Earth into its current resting place in our solar system, it was during the Age of Leo—10652 B.C.—8486 B.C. Here's a riddle for you, Nino—how many years is a day in God's eyes?"

"1000 years is just a day to the Lord."

"Good! Now, if a prophetic age lasts approximately 2,160 years, how many days is that to the lord?"

Nino scratches his head, "Pretty close to two days."

"Yes. Now, how many days did it take God to make the Earth, including his day of rest?"

"Seven."

"And how many thousands of years is that?"

Nino pauses then answers, "Seven thousand."

"Correct! Now, if a prophetic age is around 2,160 years, that means that in seven thousand years, approximately 3.5 ages would have passed, right?"

"Uh—yeah—that adds up!"

"Okay. Here's what we have established. The three ages that would have passed in the 7 days of God would be as follows:

Age of Leo—10,652 B.C.—8486 B.C.

Age of Cancer 8486 B.C.—6319 B.C.

Age of Gemini 6319 B.C.—4159 B.C.

The creation of Eve, and hence the mother of all creation, occurred on the year 3761 B.C. during the age of Taurus which was 4159 B.C.—2001 B.C. You may also be interested to know that 3761 is the date the Jews believe was the beginning of the Great Game called life."

"So, they got it right."

"Yes, they did. In the year 3500 B.C., also during the Age of Taurus, God created the other Adams and Eves all over the world. During the Age of Aries, 2001—7 B.C., came all of the prophets of the Torah. During the Age of Pisces, 7 B.C.—2001 A.D., came Jesus the Messiah, all of the New

Testament prophets, Muhammad, and the unexpected prophet of faith, Mr. Nino Jones.

Nino worried, "Please don't mention me in the same sentence with those holy men. I am not worthy."

"Your recognition that you are not proves that you are. Nino, isn't it an interesting coincidence that Jesus came under the constellation of Pisces, the sign of the fish?"

"Yes, that is something. 'Come and I will make you fishers of the souls of men'."

"The Age of Aquarius will begin soon, and during this age, you will see the completion of the game."

"How do you know?"

"God's number is 7. It took him 7 days to set the stage for the Great Game on 3761 B.C. So, it should follow that the end of the 7th day of the Great Game—actually the 14th day overall—will come some time during the Age of Aquarius."

"I read somewhere that Nastradamus predicted that the world would come to an end during the year 3797 A.D. Do you think he's right?"

"Maybe, he was a pretty good predictor of future events."

Nino continues, "I remember back in 2012 everybody was worried about the Myan's prediction that the grand cycle of human evolution would culminate on December 21st, 2012 (winter solstice)."

Al explains, "Yes the Myan's where avid stargazers. They understood some of the mystical meanings of what modern astrologers call the great year, or the Precession of the Equinoxes. They correctly believed that this 26,000 year cycle had something to do with human spiritual and technological growth and development. They made this parallel based on the 260-day cycle of human gestation. Collectively they believed that humans would eventually mature into a new form of enlightened being. However, they felt that just as a mother and child go through the struggle and pain of labor, so to would our world society go through a difficult time."

Nino rubs his chin, "You mean these hard times that we are going through in the world, the wars, terrorism, severe weather, and terrible earthquakes, are the worlds labor pains."

Al nods, "Exactly. This moment on Earth, with all of its heightened energies, has never existed at any other time in history. The stage is set. The birth of a new era in human development and enlightenment is about to begin. You will go from a time of cataclysm to a time of enlightenment. From massive earth changes and physical destruction, to a world wide spiritual awakening to are inherent oneness. We will once again realize our spiritual essence, and the ego will go from being self-centered, to soul-centered."

Nino adds, "Soul-centered, I like that...." Nino thinks for a moment and then continues ... "Man it sounds like all those people who predicted the apocalypse were right on the money."

Al agrees, "Hey Nino, this stuff is nothing new, and it's not just the Christians who predicted these events. The Egyptians, The Essenes, The Aborigines, even your American Indians (The Cherokees, Apaches, Senecas, and Iroquis) were all keen to this star guided event. However, they have all failed to factor in one important element, and that's' why no one has completely figured out where and when all this is going to happen. You see Nino there is one thing that even the Zodiac couldn't have helped them predict."

"What's that?" Nino asks.

"The depth of Allah's mercy ... And, you, Nino Jones—the unexpected prophet of faith."

"You know, it's nice that you all have so much faith in me, but if it was me, I would have picked somebody else. Somebody smarter, somebody more ..."

Al brushes the air with his hand, "No! Nino, you are made as perfectly for this plan as the moon was made for the Earth. Yes, I see it clearly Nino Jones. All will go well. God's speed, I'll see you when you get back. You, the King and I will drink some wine."

Nino laughing, "Now you're talking! Thanks for everything, Al. And to think I never liked science much when I was in school!"

"It must have been the teacher!" Al laughs heartily as he embraces Nino. Chebar approaches, hoping that Al has completed his lesson in time.

Chebar smiles nervously, "Well my friend I hope you finished all that you wanted to."

Al winks at Nino, "Well I did want to speak to Nino a bit about the new technology of light discovery that will soon change the world."

Nino wonders, "What's that?"

Al explains, "Very soon all of the power that your world currently uses will become obsolete. Your scientists will soon discover how to use the light that comes directly from the sun. Energy will be free for the world, and will no longer pollute the planet. It will also lead to wonderful applications in the field of medicine, especially in the area of genetic engineering. You will be able to go into a hospital and have whole organs recreated in your body without surgery!"

Nino is stunned, "That's amazing! When is this going to happen?"

Al smiles and nods, "Soon, very soon."

Chebar worried looks up at the suns position in the sky, "Al should I tell Barabbas you need more time? I don't want Nino to miss any of your important topics, but my time is almost up."

Al smiles, "No, you take him Chebar. I've given him all he needs for now. He'll have to come back and visit me for the rest some other time. Have no fear Chebar, everything went perfectly. Just as Nino's mission will go, perfectly. Goodbye, my friends."

Nino, Chebar and Al all embrace each other, and Chebar and Nino continue their Grand Tour. As Nino and Chebar walk away, Al returns to his winemaking with a new smile on his face and a fresh outlook on the future of the Great Game. He truly enjoyed his time with the unexpected prophet of faith, and his new friend, Nino Jones.

"If humanity wishes to save itself from biospheric destruction it must return to living in natural time, and once again become unitied with the rest of nature."
-Pacal Votan (Myan Prophet)

CHAPTER 13

▼

*"Your children are not your children. They are the sons and daughters of life's longing
for itself. They come through you, but not from
you, and though they are with you, yet they belong not to you."*
-Kahil Gibran (1923 AD)

"Someday, after mastering the winds, the waves, the tides and
gravity, we shall harness for God the energies of love, and then, for
a second time in the history of the world, man will have discovered fire."
-Pierre Teilhard de Chardin

Nino immediately feels at ease with Chebar. This gentle little man has an
easier way about him than Barabbas, as if he's not capable of taking things
quite so seriously. Nino is reminded of his friend Shorty Miller, back in
NYC.

"Well, Nino," says Chebar, "What shall we talk about first?"

"Well Mr. Chebar, I think you're supposed to introduce me to a few important people."

Chebar blushing, "Please, call me Chebar. We are all friends in Forever.
Nino, most of the souls you are going to meet will assume that you are
a new arrival. You can ask them anything that you like, and they will be
happy to entertain you. In fact, they expect new arrivals to be inquisitive.
You will also meet souls who understand who you are and what your mission is about. They are silent partners, so to speak. They are concerned souls,
and believe in our plan, but they are not willing to risk eternity as we zealots
have. Any questions?"

"Is there anything I have to be careful not to say or ask?"

"Well, it goes without saying that you are not to discuss our plan with anyone. Even the souls that know about it don't need to know any details. This is for their own good. Finding out too much about the plan could make them look like accomplices. Other than that, you are free to ask whatever you like."

"Chebar, this might sound childish to you, but I was wondering one thing. Ever since I was a little boy and saw Peter Pan, I have always dreamed of going to Never Never Land. Now, I know this isn't Heaven, but when I think of Heaven I think of Never Never Land, and I was wondering … well.…"

"Can you fly?" Chebar chuckles at Nino's innocent expression. He puts his arm around Nino's shoulder and sings, "Think of a wonderful thought, any merry little thought …"

Nino joins in and the two grown men look like schoolboys as they recite the familiar tune.

"I can't believe you know that song, Chebar."

"Not only do I know that song Nino, but I was the one who came up with the idea for Peter Pan. We citizens of Forever are all Guardian Angels from time to time. One of the special gifts that goes along with being a Guardian Angel is that we can influence those humans to whom we are assigned. We don't give our special ideas out to just anybody. It takes a lot of careful consideration. What are the individual's strengths and weaknesses? Could this idea make the person famous or rich? Will the person be able to deal successfully with the temptations and the stress that go along with such a lifestyle? How many people will benefit from this idea? You see, Nino, even in the best of circumstances the risks of passing on an idea to a human are very high."

Nino is shocked, "Are you telling me that all of the great stories, music, inventions and discoveries come from Guardian Angels?"

"Oh, not all of them, but many of them. Have you ever been struck with an inspiration, out of nowhere?" Nino nods, slowly taking in this new information. "Well, that's the kind of thing I'm talking about.

You see, each soul has within him a faint memory of life in Forever. There are traces of the songs we used to sing, the games we used to play and the things we used to do. There is a tiny seed of hope that God places within each soul before it departs to determine its eternal destiny in the Great

Game. The more faith one puts in God, the more this tiny seed grows. The more this tiny seed grows, the more vast a human's imagination becomes. A child has no doubt in God. They believe that anything is possible. They think they can fly and they believe they will live forever. However, as they grow older and they are faced with the turmoil of life, their imagination starts to fade away. They start out by doubting themselves, and eventually, if Satan is successful, they will doubt that there is even a God. This is why Jesus said that all who come to God must come as little children. If you trust in God, He will trust in you. If you believe that God will make all of your dreams come true, then he will. The dilemma for us is that this imaginative way of thinking is discouraged by many of the educators and leaders of the world. For example, Satan's big propaganda push right now is the idea that there is no such thing as God or Heaven. Satan has the world believing that humans invented the ideas because they needed something to give their life meaning, that they needed some type of philosophy that would perpetuate the soul beyond the grave. You have got to remember some important things about Satan. He is always a liar. Nothing he ever says is the whole truth. His goal is to create a constant state of confusion in your mind. He knows, too, that if he can get enough people to believe a lie, the lie becomes the truth. The Devil, who's name even contains the word "evil", is a master at turning any of life's events to his advantage. His main objective is to implant a tiny seed of doubt. He knows how your imagination deteriorates with each passing year, and that your faith dies right along with it."

"Strong imagination sort of equals strong faith, then?" Nino asks.

"Exactly. In a believer, a seed of doubt cannot grow. Doubt is like a weed trying to push its way up through a solid rock foundation. It will never give up pushing, and it will find even the tiniest crack to overpower. When you are young, the foundation is strong and there are no weak spots. However, as one grows older the game of life wears them down like wind and rain can wear through rock. The small seed eventually pushes through the once impenetrable rock. The small seedling continues to grow. The bigger the seedling gets, the more damage it does to the rock. The seedling grows bigger and bigger until it becomes a large tree, whose roots have crushed the rock to powder. When the imagination is dead, all that remains is doubt and confusion. There is no longer a Heaven to march towards, and therefore there is no moral compass to give your life direction. You become like the metaphorical leaf blowing in the wind. You see, God is moved into action by the measure of a soul's faith in Him. The more faith you have in God, the more you will find that you can turn every circumstance of life into something positive."

Nino can't help but to question Chebar on this point. "But, Chebar, I have a lot of faith in God, or at least I think I do, and there are certain prayers of mine that have never been answered. Is this because I don't have enough faith when I pray?"

"Possibly, but sometimes when we ask God for things, the answer is simply no. God, like any good father or mother, knows what's best for his children, better than they do, so he obviously cannot comply with every request that we make. Just remember, Nino, God loves you more than you could ever imagine. He is absolutely just and fair in all of his dealings with his children."

"So, God always considers what's best for our soul before he grants a request."

"Not only your soul, but the soul of every person whose life you touch. Everything is connected. There is a ripple effect in all that we do. Everything that you do and say in this world influences every person that you encounter, so if you believe in God, it should be clearly seen in your words and deeds."

Nino concerned, "But, what about the people who say they're not sure if there is a God or not? They don't influence people one way or the other. How does God feel about them?"

Chebar emphatic, "First of all, you can never not have an influence. If a parent is undecided about whether or not there is a God, what kind of effect will this have on his child? Will the child have strong faith?"

"I see your point. When it comes to God, you can't take the politically correct stance, can you?" Nino is taken aback by the burst of laughter that Chebar responds with.

"Politically correct! What a joke! That's a nice way of saying that the person is too much of a coward to say what he really believes, or to take a stand one way or the other. Which brings to mind one more important saying of Jesus. "I wish you were either hot or cold, but since you are luke warm, I must still spit you out of my mouth." The Bottom line is that being lukewarm and/or politically correct is a sin whether you intend for it to be or not. You either believe in God or you don't. There is no sitting on the fence when it comes to faith. Sitting on the fence teaches others to sit on the fence, and it helps the Devil's cause. Especially if you are a parent of young children."

"I heard our politically correct president the other day say he is against abortion, but he is pro choice. How's he touching the world?"

"You speak of a man who is more worried about how other people judge him than how God looks upon him. If he really was against abortion, then he should do something about it. His words say he is for it and against it, but his actions help to perpetuate it."

"Chebar, I know this is a tangent, but I always wondered what happens to the children who get aborted. Being raised Catholic, I was taught that their souls go to a place called Limbo. Is there such a place."

"Well, I guess you could say that they are kind of in a state of limbo. They are not citizens of Forever, because they have not played in the Great Game and earned the right to be citizens. They also have done nothing to cause their banishment to the outer darkness or Hell. Remember this, Nino, the number of souls that must take part in the Great Game is finite, and when the final soul has been tested, the earth and the heavens surrounding the earth will be destroyed. This cannot happen until every soul created by God has been tested. Since 2,018, your government agencies have reported that there have been over 1 billion abortions worldwide. 500,000,000 of these were in the United States alone. The truth, of course, is much worse. Closer to 2 billion abortions have taken place in less than 50 years, and that number stretches to about 50 billion if you start counting from the beginning of the Great Game. Here's the thing. The body is the horse upon which the soul must ride while in exile on the planet earth. Each body and soul is unique. They have one chance in all eternity to come into existence as one. The mother and the father that have the child and the circumstances that will surround its life are all unique. God knows the problems of the world and the answers to your prayers come through the creation of new life. Souls aren't sent into life as haphazardly as most people think. Each soul is sent into the world at a particular place and time for a reason. The greatest gift from God is the gift of life. If that gift is appreciated, nurtured and loved, than many blessings will come upon that family and the world that soul touches. However, if that gift is not appreciated, nurtured or loved, then no blessing will come upon that family or the world that soul touches. That particular soul's existence will be miserable and it will cause misery in the lives that it touches. People who choose to have abortions are cheating themselves and the world out of something that is priceless. In your "modern society," nobody who was given a Picasso painting would rip it to shreds, or dump acid on it. I tell you, Nino Jones, that any person who has an abortion destroys something so much more valuable than a Picasso, that there are no words to describe the difference. Some souls are destined from the womb for greatness, but if the child is aborted the special gift is also aborted.

I know the perfect way to explain how huge this is to you. You said you wanted to fly, right?"

Nino slips,"You bet your ass I do!—I mean, yes, I would really like that."

"Alright then, follow me. Second star to the right and straight on until morning. Next stop, the Royal Playground of the Unwanted. Come on Nino, let's test those wings."

As they traveled towards the Royal Playground, the beauty of the Kingdom of Forever unfolded underneath them. Flying was different than Nino had expected. It was effortless. There was no resistance whatsoever. His eyesight was unbelievable and he could see souls picnicking on a mountainside hundreds of miles away. He and Chebar made a trip of a several thousand miles in what seemed to be 10 minutes. Before he knew it, Nino was back on solid ground again.

"Well, how did you like your trip, Nino?"

Nino is energized, "I can't find words to explain it! We traveled so many miles in such a short time, but nothing seemed rushed. The beauty just seemed to slowly role by. I could have been on a country road in my old red Rambler station wagon! How perfect everything is here!"

"You have just touched upon something else I want you to remember. When most People-of-the-Game think about Heaven or Paradise, they envision a never-ending church service. People are all dressed in white robes, playing harps and hanging out on clouds. It is no wonder that more people don't try harder to get here. That snake Satan has been promoting that vision for years. The truth is, as you are beginning to see, that everything that was good, rewarding and beautiful on earth also exists in Paradise. The only difference is that up here it is flawless. Everything is perfect, and better than we could have ever expected it would be. The sunsets and the landscapes are awesome. Our roads and mansions are built with gems more precious and beautiful than those you have on earth. Our God is a loving father and a mother all rolled into one astonishing being. When I was a boy my mother used to say, 'Chebar, if you're happy, then I am happy.' That's exactly how God feels about his children. When most People think about God, they envision a stern old man with a white beard sitting on a throne with a lightning bolt in his hand, telling everybody what they did wrong. That is absolutely the biggest lie that has ever been spread. Think of your mother or father—or the best friend you ever had. Remember how it felt to be around them. Remember how you could just feel how much they loved you? How you could look at them and start laughing about something without saying a word? This is what it is like to be in the company of our God and our King, Jesus. They are resplendent, giving souls who get their pleasure from your happiness. They realize what some folks have not learned in two or three lifetimes: that the giving and receiving of unconditional love is the most valuable treasure in all of creation. People try to find substitutes for it, but they never can. Nobody on earth is ever really happy; especially the people who believe that there is some earthly dream or possession that will bring the contentedness they long for. Only God can satisfy that need. Why, God himself, creator of all things, would be discontent if he did not have someone that he could love and be loved by. Yahweh made the heavens and our beautiful Kingdom of Forever. He could make anything that his omnipotent mind could imagine, but he couldn't make people love him. Love is such a powerful force that even God cannot command it. Love is what God longs for, what everyone longs for, and why we brought you here."

"Isn't it something how you can make somebody hate you, but you can't make them love you? It just has to happen, doesn't it my friend?"

"It is true that you can make people hate you, but you could never make God hate you. No matter what you do or say, no matter how many times you fall back into sin, he will always forgive you if you ask him to."

Nino clarifies "You have to ask God to forgive you in the name of Jesus Christ, right?"

"Yes, Nino, this is God's desire. Jesus Christ is the holy lion of the tribe of Judah, became the spotless Lamb of God that takes away the sins of the world. All people who come to God in the name of Jesus Christ will be forgiven if their repentance is sincere."

"So, Christianity is the true religion?"

Chebar startled, "Oh, I didn't say that! Christianity, like all of the other religions, is stumbling over Jesus. Jesus himself prophesied that this would happen. However, my time is too limited to answer that particular question. That is another zealot's area to cover. Have no fear, Nino, all of your questions will be answered. For now, we must move on. I have some interesting souls for you to meet."

Chebar led Nino along a fiery opal path that surrounds the Royal Playground. Nino noticed that all of the souls were young children. They could all talk and run, or even fly if they chose to. Nino was perplexed by their happiness and their ages.

"Chebar, you said some of these souls have been here a long time, then how come they all look so young? I thought all souls grew until the age of 21."

"All of the souls in Forever do mature until the age of 21. However, these souls have not played in the Great Game yet. The souls that have already successfully made it through the Great Game will appear to you to be their twenties. The souls who have not yet gone into the game will appear to be about age 4, to about 14 years old. All of the souls here in the Royal Playground are victims of abortion. Their earthly mothers, led to believe they weren't ready to receive such a gift, decided to terminate their pregnancies. Now the young souls must wait here until another set of parents can be found. When an abortion occurs, a human body is destroyed. However, the tragedy of an abortion is much greater than the loss of a human body. God can make a human body out of a stone if he chooses to. Remember when I told you that the greatest gift God can give you is the gift of life? Well, when a mother decides to have an abortion it's like one of the most painful things you can do to God. You have rejected his greatest gift. He gets hurt because he knows that the child he was sending you would, if you let it, bring a lot of real joy and meaning to your life. He is also sad for the world that condones this action, because the gift of a child is not only for the parent or parents that have it, but also for the neighborhood, the city, the state, the country, and sometimes the whole world that would benefit from the life of that one individual. Certain souls are destined from the womb to do great things in the world. Like any good parent, God punishes his children when they do wrong. He sometimes finds it necessary to use pain to teach a well needed lesson. However, these individuals who opt to have an abortion are punished not by Allah, but by their conscience. God loves all of his children dearly whether they walk the proper path of not. When an abortion occurs God feels as bad for the mother who has the abortion, as he does for child that dies. This is because he knows how greatly they will suffer. He sees clearly that they will always have emptiness in their lives, a pain in their heart that will never really go away. Societies who allow this type of activity, and do nothing to discourage it, will also suffer greatly. God knows what people and communities need, and he is always trying to help them in everyway that he is able. As you will discover on your tour, most of the answers to our prayers come in the form of new lives. Unfortunately, once a gift is rejected it could be many generations until it comes again. These special individuals that are aborted are purposely denied entry until some far off date. For example, do you see that boy over there riding the flying dolphin? His Heavenly name is Luciano Minetti. He was supposed to be born on January 1, 1975 in Pratola, Itlay. In October of 2,013, he was going to discover the cure for Cancer. Now the world may have to wait for another 50 to 100 years before he comes again. Do you see that beautiful girl, with the wild hair, sliding down the rainbow? Her Heavenly name is Caroline, but around the Royal Playground she's known as "The Lion."

Nino Laughing "Why, because her long wavy hair look like a lions mane?"

Chebar chuckles. "Exactly, Lion was supposed to be born on July 4, 1957. On January 25 in the year 2,008, she was going to become the first woman President of the United States. It is ironic that the Woman's Movement of the United States is the champion of abortion. They fight so vehemently to keep their right to abortions, they lose sight of what Elizabeth Cady Stanton's original organization stood for. Mrs. Stanton was the mother of seven children. She respected God and life, and she believed that all human beings are equal in God's eyes, as they are. She was so excited about the birth of Caroline, and so destroyed when her birth was aborted. She cannot bear the idea that her movement is in a large way responsible for the abortion of Caroline. When we get back to Forever, we'll go over to Elizabeth's house for some tea. She'll tell you some things you need to hear. She is a real fine soul, and hopefully your message will vindicate her from her sadness."

"So she knows about my mission?"

"Yes, she does. We decided that it would be necessary to include certain individuals like Elizabeth Cady Stanton, Martin Luther King, and several other historically significant souls. All of them understand the mission and support it. They are each excited about expressing their views one last time. They are also all a tad bit frustrated about what direction their specific areas of interest are heading. They will each have an important message for you, and you will be able to ask them anything you like. The main difference between them and us is that if the mission fails, the level of their involvement will not result in them being permanently banished from Forever."

Nino excited, "This is going to be fantastic. I can't wait to speak to these people."

"We could spend more time here, but I think you get the point. The purpose of my bringing you here was not so much to talk to these unwanted gifts, but to understand how terrible abortion is." "Chebar, when is the soul joined with the body?"

"The soul is joined with the body at conception. It is necessary for the soul and body to become one. All souls are housed in the brain of the human being. Your scientists are correct in their assumption that humans only use a small portion of their brain's total capacity. This is because the rest of the brain is taken up by the soul. The strange electrical activities that take place in the brain for the most part have to do with the presence of the immortal soul."

"So, these souls must really go through a lot of pain during an abortion?"

"I told one of my friends that you may be coming by to hear about her experience?" Chebar points out a young girl in the distance with curly red hair. Her name is Nina Bella Faccia. She was destined to be a Broadway star, and to bring joy and laughter to everyone she met.

Chebar concerned, "Nino, she is going to get very sad when she tells you about her experience. You are going to feel something that you have never felt before. You are going to experience to the tiniest degree the pain that God feels when one of his souls suffers and cries out to him. Whenever another soul shares itself with you, the experience is one that you will never forget. Two separate souls become one and you feel exactly what the other soul is feeling. In the land of Forever, you have what is called soul touching, and it is done exclusively for pleasure. You also have what is called soul sharing. This is where you become one with another soul in a way that allows you to experience any part of their memory that they wish to reveal to you. In Forever, most of the soul sharing is a pleasant experience, but here in the Royal Playground it is a different story. The experience can be horribly sad if the question asked brings up a painful memory. Come, I'll walk you to Nina."

Nino and Chebar walked along a crystal blue shoreline. Nina had left her book behind and was now riding on the back of a giant killer whale that she had lovingly named Tommy. The whale was jumping high into the air, and the little girl would laugh as his big belly splashed back into the sea. After a short time, Tommy brought the child to shore, and she hopped off of his back and climbed into a large purple flower. She pulled out another book and began to read. Nino sat down at the base of her flower. He recognized the book she was reading as one of Mark Twain's most recent novels, Paradise Found. Nina smiled brightly as she looked into Nino's eyes. Her hair was as fiery-red as the opal path, and her eyes as crystal blue as the water she just came from.

"Are you Chebar's friend?" she asked.

"I am. My name is Nino Jones."

"And my name is Nina ... Nina Bella Faccia. Chebar told me he might be bringing you by to see me."

"Very nice to meet you, Nina. Chebar is over there, skipping stones."

"Oh, yes. I see him." Nina waves with all her heart. "Hi, Chebar!" "Hi Nina! He's all yours for a while, but we don't have time for whale rides this time!"

Nina sticks out her bottom lip and pretends to pout,"Oh, alright, Chebar!" Nina looks at Nino and winks. "You're such a party pooper!"

"Yeah, shame on you, Chebar." Adds Nino. "I want to ride me a whale!"

Chebar laughs and returns to skipping stones. "Maybe next time Nino."

Nina's expression turns serious as she turns back to Nino. "Nino, I know why you are here, and I think you are a very good man to risk your eternity, for the sake of our God, our King and our people. I also know that you want to share my soul to experience the dreadful pain of my abortion. It will be a very terrible experience for both of us, but the good that might come from it is worth the anguish we will soon feel. I have two dreams, Nino Jones. One is that you will do something to help bring an end to abortions; and two is that someday I will be sent to two parents who will love and want me, as much as I love and want them. I know only the King can help me find parents, but you might be able to do something to stop abortion.

Are you ready Nino?"

Nino a little nervous, "I guess so."

Nina smiles but still seems sad, "Okay. Give me a great big hug and don't let go until I do. We will soon be together in my memory. It will be like being awake during a dream. We will be able to talk, see, hear and feel. We will be aware of our surroundings and of each other. Everything will seem like it is really happening." Nino and Nina hug each other and their souls are immediately intertwined. The initial feeling is a bliss that Nino could have never imagined. Even in his wildest dreams. The ecstasy that comes from touching another soul is indescribable in human terms. Nino stops holding his breath long enough to speak.

Nino flushed with emotion,"That was the most beautiful feeling I ever felt!"

Nina's smiles warmly, "No pleasure in the entire universe can be compared to the ecstasy that comes from touching another soul. Do you know why humans are drawn toward one another? It is because their souls long to touch each other in the same way that you and I have just touched each other. In the Kingdom of Forever, every soul touches every soul, and with each soul that you touch, the ecstasy is distinctly different and unique. Think of all the countless souls God has created, and yet, no two are 100 percent identical. We are all distinctly beautiful, like snow flakes."

Nino swoons at the thought of it, "How intriguing."

Nina sighs with happiness, "It truly is the best feature of paradise … Anyway, each human in the recesses of their memory, a faint flicker of life in Paradise. We long for the freedom to love and live as individuals. Satan uses this faint knowledge to his advantage. He entices us with the forbidden fruits of the world. He magnifies our desire for each other and leads us astray. The paradox is this: on earth as in Forever, the soul longs to touch every soul that it comes in contact with. However, on earth, this is not possible. Satan tries to convince us to keep on searching. He pushes the propaganda that to stay with one lover for lifetime is a foolish mistake. He puts messages out there that make faithful lovers feel like they are missing out on something. The truth, however, is that the only way to really get a tiny piece of what you long for is to unselfishly stay with one partner for life. These are the few humans whose souls really do get to touch. When two humans who really love each other are making love, at the very height of their loving closeness, their souls briefly touch. This is God's reward to those who choose a mate for life. There is one other thing I should mention. Those people who break their wedding vows to God and commit adultery can be forgiven if they sincerely ask God to forgive them. However, if the person they committed adultery with also happens to make it to Forever, they will never be allowed to touch souls with that particular soul until the new Jerusalem is complete."

"So, there are still some forms of suffering in Forever?"

"If they would only restrain themselves for that short interval called life, they will be able to drink their fill of each other for an eternity. Oh, dear. I am getting side tracked. I am sorry Nino, but I hardly ever get an opportunity to share this much information."

"Hey, its okay Nina. It's all good to know." Suddenly aware of his surroundings, Nino asks, "Is this the womb?"

"Yes. Doesn't it feel nice? … Do you know why it feels so nice? It is because my mother's soul and my soul are touching. Why do you think expectant mothers seem to glow? This is why there is always that little extra something a child feels for his mother? It is because their souls have touched."

Nino moved to tears, "Unbelievable. It is just simply unbelievable."

"You see, the soul arrives at conception. The mother's soul is united with her baby's soul from the moment the new life is concieved. It was a wondrous moment for me, one that I will always remember. When a soul descends from Forever, it is a scary thing. You really don't know what to expect. But when you get to your mother's womb, and you are able to touch the soul of your earth mother for the first time, you are not afraid anymore. You are perfectly content."

Nino curious, "So, if there is this perfect contentedness, and your souls are touching, why would your mother ever consider having an abortion?"

"The soul is an immortal being which is housed in a mortal body. The soul knows where it comes from and where it would like to return to, but the mind is not eternal and does not comprehend this. It is concerned with the immediate well being of the individual, and there in lies the age old conflict.

The mind works like a computer. It takes all of the information that has ever been placed into its memory and comes up with solutions to problems that arise. If parents who believed in God raised the person, and they have stayed close to Him throughout their lives, then most of the time the solutions that their mind comes up with will be in accordance to what Jehovah and their soul would want. However, when the religious foundation is not there, the solutions the mind comes up with will often cause the soul to be troubled. The saddened soul cries out along with the voice of their guardian angel, and thus you have a troubled conscience. Even if a person strongly believes, for example, that abortion is their right and what they are doing is ultimately best for them and for the unwanted child, the essence of their being knows that it is wrong. My mother, sadly, was not close enough to God. Oh, she was a nice person, and most people liked her, but her career was more important to her. She was also a young, unwed mother, who didn't have a loving relationship with my father. She was also driven by her beliefs. Politically, she felt that it was her right to choose to have an abortion if she wanted to. She believed that to choose motherhood over a career would be a big step down. Satan is responsible for this propaganda. He and his soldiers infiltrated the woman's movement. As always, they take something that starts off as honorable and turn it into something perverse."

Nino curious, "So, did you have any idea that you were going to be aborted?"

Nina's painfully remembers, "I knew something was wrong, but I had no idea what was coming. I could sense the tension between my mother's mind and my mother's soul. Also, my mother's soul and her guardian angel did not let me know what was going to happen. They did not want to scare me.… The day that I was aborted was like any other day. I was feeling pretty good, in fact. I was a couple days shy of 3 months old. I was real tiny, but I had all my parts. My heart had been beating since about a week after my mother found out she was pregnant. My brain, eyes, ears, mouth, kidneys, liver and umbilical cord were all formed and working. I could use my hands, and my fingerprints were already formed. I had the same feelings and emotions of a newborn baby, and I was aware of my surroundings.

Suddenly, I went from a state of absolute peace, tranquility and love into one of absolute terror, pain and rejection. The doctor inserted a sharp loop shaped knife into my mother and immediately I felt the fluid that I lived in drain away. I was choking and gagging hysterically, crying like very small babies do when they are hurt and scared. I kept hoping that everything would be all right. I kept thinking that my mother would do something to make the pain stop, but that's when I felt the excruciating pain of the knife for the first time. The first thing that happened was that my leg was cut off from just above the knee. I tried to squirm away from the knife, but there was nowhere to hide. My right arm was ripped away and then the knife cut through my tiny belly. It severed my umbilical cord. The last thing that I can remember is a sharp pain to my head. When I woke up, I was here at the Royal Playground. I was in the arms of my Guardian Angel, and the pain had finally stopped."

Nino's face was streaked with tears and he could hardly speak. Every second of Nina's experience shot through his body and soul, and he felt as though the curette used to perform the abortion was cutting through every inch of his body. "I have suffered through a lot of physical and mental pain in my lifetime, but I have never experienced anything as disturbing as what we just went through. I could understand the physical pain, and the mental anxiety and terror, but there was another pain. There was a pain that was worse and cut deeper than the mental and physical pain. What was that?"

Nina puts her arms around Nino's shoulders."That is what is called spiritual pain. As there is ecstasy when two souls are united, a pleasure that is indescribable, there is an equal pain that comes from tearing apart two souls which God has joined together. God is love. When two souls are united, the bonding force that holds them together is love. To be totally immersed with another soul is to stand in the light of God. This is the ultimate ecstasy for all God's creation. God longs for the day that all of his creation will stand in His light. God sends His most pleasurable form of love into the world, while His creation is in its most pure form. Nothing is more beautifully-precious than a life that is not yet defiled by the inequities of the world, and the spirit of evil. God is light, and Satan is darkness. God is the truth, and Satan is the lie. God's light of pure love shines on the unselfish of the world. Satan's darkness overshadows the selfish of the world. The reason why a child brings so much love to the parent is that for the first time in the parents' lives, all of the joy that they receive comes in what they give to their child. They forget about themselves, and they focus on the needs of another. True joy, love and happiness comes from what a person gives in this life, not in what they receive. It is during this early part of our lives that the souls of the parents and their child truly touch, and it is during this special period that the light of God bonds them together as a family. Happy are those who rejoice at God's gift of life, for His light will shine on them in all that they do. His name and His son's name will be written on their foreheads, and their homes, and their names will be written in the book of life. His rod and his stave will protect them. His holy power and wisdom will dwell in them, and his beloved Angels will guard their every step."

"Nina, Chebar said I would experience what God experiences. What did he mean by that?"

Nina explains, "As I invited you to share my ecstasy and my pain, so too, does God share in the pain and ecstasy of all of his creation. Early civilizations used to call God "All", because he was responsible for all things, and a part of all things. God is truly All-in-All. Today, you felt the pain and pleasure of one soul's experience. Can you imagine the pain and pleasure that God experiences every moment of every day? The fact is that the pain greatly outweighs the pleasure. If God's pleasure depends on the unselfish acts of his creation, then it follows that the more selfish a society becomes, the more pain God experiences. The mercy of God is incomprehensible. He refrains from ending the world each day because he can find souls that are leading righteous lives and leaving behind good fruit. Jesus once said that only God knows when the end of the world will take place. This is because only God knows how long his mercy will last. Rumor has it that God's mercy is reaching its end. This year alone, millions of abortions will be committed all over the world. Not to mention the other terrible cruelties that exist in your modern world. It is God's hope that has allowed His mercy to endure so long; but the biggest tragedy about abortion & cruelty is that it steals God's hope. It will be increasingly harder for him to remain merciful if the world continues to destroy his most precious gifts."

Nino stands proudly, "Nina, I will never forget what you taught me here today. I will do my best during my mission to help bring an end to abortion. It will make me feel very happy if I could do something special for you someday. I'd like to make you smile."

Nina smiles and her flaming blue eyes twinkle, "I love you, Nino!" shouted Nina, throwing her arms around the old man's neck. "Good luck. And may God bless and protect you."

Feeling as though he truly has an angel on his shoulder, Nino finds his way back to Chebar.

"Well, Nino, did you enjoy your visit at the Royal Playground?"

Nino disturbed, "I enjoyed the beauty of the playground and all the little souls who dwell in it, but I learned such disturbing things. Now, I just feel down. Not so much for myself, but for God, the world, and especially for little Nina. She touched my heart, man. She touched me like nothing ever touched me before in my life. When I left, she hugged me and told me that she loved me, and I could actually feel her love. She completely loved and accepted me, and I feel the same way about her. That kind of thing doesn't happen on Earth, man. It just doesn't happen."

Chebar smiling, "One of the coolest things about living in Forever is that you will feel that same way about everyone that you meet. Once you've touched someone's soul, you will remember them for eternity, and you will always deeply ... deeply love them. Unlike your Eathly lovemaking, soul touching has no restrictions. There is no guilt or jealousy involved in soul touching. Everybody does it with everyone they meet, and each experience is as unique as individual soul. Each time is impossible to duplicate, and every soul you meet is equally irresistible."

Nino excited, "Are you telling me that everyone in Forever is equally popular?"

"In regards to soul touching, yes. However, you will still have some souls that you are closer to than others. This will be because of common interests or experiences. There is no jealousy, though. Everyone is absolutely free to live the way they want to live."

"Is that faint memory of how things are in Forever that which we earth bound souls are searching and striving for in our day to day lives?"

Chebar pats Nino on the back, "Yes, Nino. That's it in a nutshell. Unfortunately, what the soul longs for and what the human body longs for are almost always at conflict. For example, the soul longs to touch another soul, but the body longs to have sex. Satan uses the body's natural sex drive and combines it with the soul's innate need to touch. He creates a maddening desire in earth bound souls and this leads many good people astray. Your goal in this regard is to get people to discipline themselves for the short duration of their earthly lives, so that they can eventually experience the real meaning of pleasure."

Nino wonders, "Once we all get to Forever, is that it? Will God make any new souls?"

"That's a good question. Creating a new soul isn't quite as easy as waving a magic wand. A new soul is the product of soul mates that have decided to become eternal parents."

"But, if you can have a uniquely magnificent experience with every soul that you touch, how will you know if you have found your true mate?"

Chebar smiles and sighs, "Ah, that is one of the most beautiful experiences you will ever have, my friend. When you touch souls with your true soul mate for the first time, you will hear a song, (your song.). When this happens, you will immediately be transported to the Island of the Fertile Moon, where God Himself will give you the power to unite and make a new, unique soul. From that moment on, every one or two thousand years your song will fill the heavenly airways and you will be re-transported to the Island to make another soul. This is why you always hear music in Forever. It is the songs of soul mates, sending them to the Island of the Fertile Moon."

My time with you is just about up, Nino. We will stop at Elizabeth Cady Stanton's for tea before we part ways. She has invited some of her friends over who will help you with your message."

"Who will be there?"

"I'd just be guessing, but I bet she's invited some people you've heard of before. Maybe Abe Lincoln will be there. She probably also invited Martin Luther King and Joe Lewis, those are some of her favorites."

"Man, I never thought I'd be sitting down to tea with such famous souls! Do they know about my mission?"

"Yes, but again, they are not as involved as the zealots. They face no risk of banishment.

Lets go my friend, "With those words, Chebar takes Nino's hand and they are on their way. Nino's mind swims as his body floats through the air. The possibility of eternal banishment to the outer darkness has taken on greater meaning with each moment in the beauty of Forever. He starts to doubt his decision, wondering why God's original plan shouldn't just be played out to see what happens. Nina comes into his mind—that beautiful, red headed angel. "I've got to do this,"he thinks to himself. "I've got to make that little girl smile."

Author's Note: Jesus said that the person who is greatest among us, must be the joyful servant of us all. And I humbly add that: Those of you who are loving parents, teachers, coaches, and caretakers of our children fill the highest, most noble, and holy of all the callings in the Great Game. Never underestimate the power that your words and deeds have upon the young ones placed in your care. Jesus warns that anyone who intentionally physically or spiritually harms a child will suffer consequences so severe, that they will have faired better if they had never been born. Try with all of your might not to lead any of these little ones astray. In all that you do, in all that you say, always illuminate the P.O.J

One hundred years from now, it will not matter what kind of car I drove, what kind of house I lived in, how much money I had, nor what my clothes looked like. But the world may be a little better, and the universe a little brighter, because I was important to a child.
-Author Unknown

(Steve Muzzi, Mac Spellecy, Louie Pasqua, Kathy & Lori Fuchs, and Tim & Michelle Hill (The Geneva Boxing Club), you may not have wrote this, but you live it. Thank you for all you do for children, and may God bless you always.)

CHAPTER 14

▼

"Nature never repeats herself, and the possibilities of one human soul will never be found in another."
-Elizabeth Cady Stanton

"This country cannot afford to be materially rich and spiritually poor."
-President John Fitzgerald Kennedy

"The radical of one century is the conservative of the next."
-Mark Twain

"Here we are!"

"This is Liz Stanton's house? I wouldn't think she could throw such a hopping party, Chebar!" Nino peeks through the windows, trying to figure out "who's who" among the distinguished guests. Just then, Liz Stanton comes bustling through the doorway.

Smiling and laughing, "Chebar, my dear friend! I thought you weren't going to show!" "Oh, come now Liz, you know I'd never miss one of your tea parties. Especially this one."

"Well, it's a good thing you showed up. Barabbas and the rest of your "merry men" arrived about an hour ago. The all seemed pretty anxious."

Chebar looks worried, "Oh, dear, our plans must have changed. Where are they?"

Liz chuckles, "Chebar, relax, nothing has changed. Barabbas just wanted me to tell you to keep track of your time. He knows how you can get sidetracked at times."

Chebar smirks, "Oh, he's a fine one to point a finger at me. The reason he gets so mad at me is because I am so much like him in that regard!"

Liz lauging again, "Chebar, you are absolutely right. You both act and quarrel just like a couple of brothers.... Well, why don't you go and help yourself to some refreshments, while I talk to your friend. But stay away from the wine, Chebar. Now is a time for clear thinking!" Liz says jokingly.

Chebar winks, "Okay, Liz, no wine for me! Nino, you listen well to what this soul has to say and I'll be back momentarily." With that, Chebar leaves Liz and Nino alone to talk. Liz hollers after him.

Liz raises her eye brows, "Chebar, aren't you forgetting something?"

Chebar embarrassed, "Oh, of course. Do forgive me, Liz. Mr. Nino Jones, I'd like you to meet Mrs. Elizabeth Cady Stanton."

"It is an honor to meet you, Mrs. Stanton."

"Oh, call me Liz. Nino, I can't begin to tell you how happy I am that you have decided to take on this mission. The stakes are indescribably high, but the good you will be able to do is worth the risk.

By risking your eternity for the greater glory of God, His Christ, and our people; you have an opportunity to save millions of souls from an eternity in Hell. Successful or not, you and your cohorts will be remembered for all eternity as some of the bravest and most noble souls to ever come into existence. It is I who am honored to stand in your presence, Mr. Jones."

Liz's words cut straight into Nino's heart. He no longer felt afraid, and his doubt had been removed quite abruptly. For the first time since this all began, he realized the force that drove the other members of the Lions Abijah. It was a power he had never felt before. A self-knowledge that his purpose and direction were pure and noble. It was a purpose that transcended his body and soul. He had practiced the Catholic religion all of his life, and he always tried to follow the commandments of God and His Christ, but he never knew what it felt like to submit to that unseen power of God. To choose to do His will over your own, no matter what the personal cost, means standing brave and unafraid against the forces of evil. It means learning to hate the deed and not the doer of the deed. It means becoming one with God. At this moment in time, Nino realizes, nothing will ever hurt him again. His pain over the past is miraculously gone.

With tears in his eyes, Nino manages to speak to Liz. "I don't know what else you have to tell me, Liz, but I will never forget the words that you just spoke to me. Is it possible that a person's whole existence can change because of a few spoken words?"

Liz serious, "The spoken words that come from a heart that is true, and a faith that is strong can move mountains. When I first started the Women's Movement most people thought I was crazy, especially the people I was trying to help the most. My doctrine went against the mainstream. It challenged the established order. I was like Christopher Columbus sailing perpendicular to the coast line. It had never been done before, and man was I scared."

"I can't imagine."

"However, contrary to what some people may believe, I was a very happily married wife and a mother of seven children. I can remember being very discouraged when I first started to speak out for the equal rights for women. We had it bad, Nino. Women couldn't vote. We couldn't go to college or own land. We could work, but we were grossly underpaid. I received many threats of violence against my family and me as I fought for my rights, and as I said, I was quite often terrified. I didn't realize it at the time, but I was being attacked by the Devil and his Demons. Whenever you do something that God is behind, you get the Devil's attention. He starts out by working on your fear, fear of death, injury, reputation, and so on, whatever might shake you up enough to make you quit. I was reading the Bible, hoping that God would strengthen me with his words, and he did."

"God asked me a question through the word of his son, Christ Jesus. **"Do you love this world more than the world that is to come? Do you fear man more than God? Do you care more about what the world thinks of you than what God thinks of you?"** We are all cowards, and Satan knows it. He keeps us scared and preoccupied with what people think, and not with what God thinks. He is called the great serpent, because his evil spirit attempts to twist and turn everything to his advantage. He is the prince of lies. He can take on any form. He can appear as the miserable beast that he actually is, an angel of light, or anything in between. He very rarely reveals his true form or his true intentions. But make no mistake he is diametrically opposed to our Father. God puts forth the truth and his intentions are always good and filled with mercy. Satan puts forth lies, and his intentions are always bad. He knows that his destiny is an eternity in Hell, and his goal is to bring as many souls with him as he can. His promises are all empty. He makes you think that the pleasures of this world will give you the peace and contentment that all humans long for. In the silent memory of every soul is the knowledge of who we are, and where we have come from. Our souls long to return to Paradise and stand once again in the light of God—the light of pure love. Nothing on earth can fill this need, or take away this unknown longing. The pure love that comes from children is the closest earthly reflection of who and what God our father is really like. Nothing in the entire universe can compare to pure unconditional love. Parents who are thankful for their children can experience this sort of love from their children for a short time on earth. It is only the very young children who see us as God sees us, and who love us as God loves us. Nino, you must save the children. You must revive the pride that goes along with being a mother and a father. You must make the women see that being a loving mother and wife is now, and always has been, the noblest call of any soul. Always remember **the hand that rocks the cradle rules the world**, but who is rocking our cradles, Nino? Why are so many cradles empty? You must expose the current women's movement for the fraud that it is. They do not represent the best interests for the majority of the women in this country, or the world. They have their own agenda, and it is not based upon love, mercy or compassion.

In the early 1970s, the movement became focused on a woman's right to abortion."

"And you are obviously antiabortion, right?"

"Nino, I am antiabortion when it comes to late term abortions, and abortions of convenience. However, it's not a black and white problem. There were abortion issues that needed to be addressed in my day, and there will be new problems that arise in the future. However, abortion should not be the center piece of the movement."

"So what do I tell them when they ask me what your stance on abortion is? Should women have the right to choose or not?"

Liz pauses and thinks for a moment, "The only just solution is that women must continue to have the right to choose. However, they must clearly understand the spiritual magnitude of making such a choice. **Having the law given right to do something terrible, does not excuse you from the personal responsibility of exercising such a right.**"

Nino puzzled "But if it is a terrible right, why wouldn't you want if banned all together?"

"Well, for example, I certainly would never want to see abortion laws put in place that would prevent a pregnant woman who was raped, or sexually abused from having the right to an abortion. That would be ridiculous, and cruel."

Nino nods in agreement. "I agree with you Liz. I can't imagine telling a woman who was raped that she has to give birth to her rapist's child! That she has to forever mix her DNA with some psychopaths. How awful would that be?"

"Exactly, her psychological scars would be magnified, and God wouldn't want that either. What upsets God are the people who are simply undisciplined. Those who miss use their right to choose. In your modern world you don't have to get pregnant if you don't want to. That's why it is a travesty that most abortions occur in your world, simply because people are living irresponsibly. They have no respect for the miracle of life."

"But without banning abortions all together, and making it a crime, how will we ever be able to raise their level of concern?"

"I have done some thinking on this matter Nino, and the solution can possibly be found in the rights of the father."

Nino is Surprised "The rights of the father? This is very ironic. Elizabeth Cady Stanton speaks out on equal rights for men!"

Laughing but serious "It is isn't it? Here is what I will propose to raise their level of concern. As I said women must continue to have the rights to govern their own bodies. However, the body of the unborn child that grows inside them is spiritually and scientifically, only half-theirs. I think the act of consensual intercourse between to adults should carry with it binding legal implications."

"Like what for example?"

"If a woman agrees to have consensual sex with a man, then she is also, by this act, entering into a legal contract with that man. A contract which states that if a pregnancy should occur, than the child (born or unborn) will belong equally to both parents."

Nino surprised, "That's an interesting concept, especially the part about the unborn child."

"This is how we will ultimately raise their level of concern. This contract will further state that if both parties do not agree that an abortion should take place, than an abortion can not be performed. This may cause some concern at first, and I haven't worked out all the kinks, but it will make women and men think more seriously about who they have sex with. It will make the act of sexual intercourse something to never be looked at casually again. Once this attitude about casual sex changes, you will see a big drop in the number of abortions world wide. You will also see a drop in divorce, the welfare rolls, and crime."

Nino ponders, "What about the women who say they were raped, or victims of sexual abuse and incest?"

Liz adamant, "Anyone accused of rape, and sexual abusers, will have no rights to any child that they father."

Nino smiles proudly, "I like it. You get to the real source of the problem, which is irresponsible sex. But, I can tell right now, many of our modern women will not like your idea about the father's rights of the unborn child. They're not gonna care about men's rights."

Liz retorts, "That's because they are selfish byproducts of a "me-oriented" society, and this modern woman's organization has capitalized on protecting their rights. This is how they keep the political spotlight on their movement. It is disgusting, and I am repulsed to think that people associate my name with organizations like N.O.W. This spiritually-anemic group of individuals who profess to have the best interests of all women in mind have nothing more than their own selfish interests at heart. They support women who believe what they believe, and they degrade the women and men who don't. My organization did not hate men. We did not resent being married to them or bearing and raising their children. Being married to a good man was seen as a blessing in my day, and any individual or group that attacks the institution of marriage works for the Devil. One of his primary objectives is to destroy the family! ... We just wanted to be respected intellectually and physically. We wanted the world to know that we are by no means inferior to men. But when we asked for equality, we didn't want to completely lose our roles as women. We disliked some of men's chauvinistic attitudes, but we also enjoyed their chivalry. We liked being treated differently in that regard. It is the modern Women's Movement that created the "macho man".

When I started the movement, I did not disrespect or dislike men. There was a limit to what we wanted, and once our goals were achieved, we would have been content. I would much rather sit in my porch swing with my husband, and watch the sun go down. Than to stay entrenched in a never ending battle."

Nino smiles "You really wanted the best of both worlds, right?"

"Yes, Nino. We wanted the same rights men had, but we wanted to stay true to our own responsibilities—not assume theirs. For example, we would not want to live in a society that drafted women into its armed forces. If a woman wanted to join the armed forces, she should have the right to, but she shouldn't be forced to. The women's movement of today goes to extremes only because it is not a movement anymore. It is a company. It is a vehicle for its leaders and their staff to make a living. These types of organizations create the very crises that they claim to fight against. They help to create a sick society by the doctrines that they preach and the laws they help get passed. It is a self-perpetuated self-interest. I know Martin Luther King, Jr. shares many of my thoughts on this. I hope you get a chance to talk with him.

If the women really want to fight for something that will help them and society, they should get the government to set up a system that would make it financially possible for a mother to stay home until her kids started school."

Nino concerned, "Wouldn't they just say, 'why doesn't the father stay at home?'?"

Liz irritated, "Oh, Nino, just tell them that the father should be allowed to stay home if he chooses to, but he shouldn't have to. We will draw a compromise on this issue. The young men have to go to war, and the young women have to raise the children."

Nino beaming with pride, "Liz, I can't tell you how happy it makes me to hear you say the things that you are saying. I think that most people believe as you do, but they are afraid to stand up to these organizations. I guarantee you that when I come forward with this doctrine, I will be portrayed as someone who is anti-women, and anti-women's rights."

"I am sure that is exactly what will happen. But you just have to be brave and stick to the truth. Remember, they think that they represent me and my movement, but you know you do. Remain confident, and don't let their character assassins or threats silence you on these important issues. As I said before, Satan's hard line of attack is aimed at the family. This is how he always operated. Satan's battle plan in Sodom and Gomorrah, was no different than how he's attacking the world today."

Nino Curious, "When were those cities destroyed?"

"Oh, I'd say about 1955 BC, almost 4,000 years ago."

"Wow, that's along time ago."

"Yes it is. Very old societies, but very current problems. The evil and eventual downfall that happened in Sodom and Gomorrah, also occurred in succession to all of the great world empires. Egypt, Assyria, Babylon, Persia, Greece and Rome all crumbled for the same reasons."

Nino worried, "And now, the same thing is happening in the United States of America isn't it?"

"Nino, have you ever read any of Marcus Aurelius's writings?"

"Yes, I love Aurelius. He was a very wise man. It's hard to believe he was a Roman, who lived before the time of Jesus."

"I know what you mean. He sounds a bit like Jesus doesn't he? He wrote this passage in his book called Meditations that hits the nail right on the head: **"Look back over the past, with its changing empires that rose and fell, and you can foresee the future too. Look back at any of the fallen empires and you will see people marrying, bringing up children, sick, dying, warring, feasting, trafficking, cultivating the ground, flattering, obstinately arrogant, suspecting, plotting, wishing for some to die, grumbling about the present, loving, heaping up treasure, desiring consulship, and kingly power. The life of these people no longer exists at all. These great ancient empires of the past, after all of their epoch battles and dramas soon fall and are resolved to the elements. This pattern is the same down to the last detail; for it cannot break step with the steady march of creation. For all things soon pass away and become mere tale. I say this of those who have shone in a wonderous way. For the rest, as soon as they have breathed out their breath, they are gone and no man speaks of them. To view the lives of men for forty years or forty thousand is therefore all one; for what more will there be for you to see?"**

Nino nods in understanding, "So it's the same old song, sung over and over again."

Liz frowns with disappointment, "I'm sad to say it's true, and unless something miraculous happens our dear United States of America is in line to be the next Babylon, spoke about in Revelation 18 of the Bible. The reason the words of the Bible and the Quran always seem timeless is because Satan's plan of attack for the most part has stayed the same over ten thousand years. Abraham Lincoln said that **"America will never be destroyed from the outside. If we falter and lose our freedoms, it will be because we destroyed ourselves."**

Nino enlightened, "That's kind of like what happens to ours souls if we don't take care of ourselves spiritually isn't it? These empires fall because the people who make them up fall spiritually."

Liz smiles at Nino's wisdom, "Exactly, look at your world history, Nino. All of the great empires that have ever exist eventually crumbled because of the breakdown of the family. As the family unit breaks down in a society, the individuals that make up that society become increasingly ambivalent towards one another, and more and more self-centered and selfish individuals. Mothers and fathers are betrayed by their very own children. There is no one who can be trusted. The Devil thrives on creating an individualistic, pleasure oriented society. Eventually you have a society in which there is no love or compassion. A country whose laws, morals and values eventually resemble those of Satan's more than God's. In a chain reaction, God falls, and then family falls, then neighborhood, city, state, etc ... God's boundless mercy will hold back his wrath even if there is only one righteous person left in an entire society." Liz pauses amoment and then resumes, "The great plague of the Twentieth and into the Twentyfirst Century is AIDS. This virus emerged as a representation of a sick and faithless world. A healthy human body is made up of billions of cells. This deadly virus like a cancer starts out by attacking one cell. The virus tricks the healthy cell into letting it enter. Once it has gained entrance it reveals its true identity and takes control of the cell. The cell cries out for help, but few of the other billions of cells respond because they are too busy tending to their own business. Even those who do pause for a moment to see what the problem is are convinced that there is no real problem and that the cell is just overreacting. The virus, like Satan, is very clever. When he is close to being exposed, he either hides or disguises himself as something good. The virus starts out by attacking the very weakest of cells, just like Satan starts out by attacking those who are weakest in faith. The individual that is being attacked is unaware of the attack, because the billions of healthy cells vastly outnumber the sick cells. Many years can pass without the individual fully understanding how sick he really is. Even when he starts to feel the effects of the illness, he denies it to himself. Eventually, the sick cells begin to outnumber the healthy cells, and now it is the sick cells that are the majority. The sick cells have now gained the upper hand. Their goal is to eventually gain control of the vital organs; just like Satan's goal is to eventually possess the leaders of the world. Once the vital organs have been seized, the end is not long in coming. The United States of America that you and I both love now stands at the threshold of destruction. In just two hundred and fifty short years, Satan has taken a country that was established on God loving morals, values and principles, and turned it into a secular/faithless society."

"What exactly do you mean when you say we have become a Secular society?" asks Nino.

"It simply means that our country has less and less room for religion or spiritualism in the public sector."

"Do you think it should be removed? I mean what's your stance on the separation of church and state?"

Liz emphatic, "Our founding leaders never intended for us to become a secular society. They all believed in God, and they knew that in order for a free society to survive, it must be made up of moral people, who had a deep respect for God and their fellow man. They included God in every part of their lives. Nino have you ever read what is on the Jefferson Memorial in Washington D.C.?"

"No, what's it say?"

"It says **"God, who gave us life, gave us liberty. And can the liberties of a nation be thought secure when we have removed their only firm basis. A conviction in the minds of the people that their liberties are a gift from God."** Does that sound like a quote from someone who would want God and religion removed from all public functions?"

"No mam.... No it doesn't."

"When our early leaders wrote the Constitution, the First Amendment was put in place to insure that the congress would never be allowed to establish a national religion. They also wanted to insure that all US citizens would always be free to practice any form of religion. As long as it espoused good will towards all people."

Nino responds, "It seems like they just wanted to make sure that all people were free to embrace whatever religion they wanted to."

"That's simply it. They also wanted to insure your right to refuse to believe, if that's what you chose to do."

"So even if you were an Atheist or an Agnostic, no one could mess with you, right?"

"Yes, everyone's rights were protected."

Nino clarifies, "So what they intended was that we would be free from the tyranny of religion, not free from the exposure to religion."

"Exactly, any who claims that his rights were violated because he had to listen to a prayer at football game, is misinterpreting the intent of the Amendment."

Nino nods in agreement, "That's right. Now if a child in a public school was forced to say a prayer, or made to feel bad for not believing, that is wrong.... It seems to me that instead of keeping God out of schools that they should teach a world religion course that covers all of the love based religions."

Liz agrees, "That's what should happen, but that's not the way our country is headed. Nino did you know that for the first time in this country's history, you have presidents who are pro-abortion. Remember what I said, Satan either conceals his identity, or makes himself appear as something good. Jesus Christ said that a tree is known by its fruit. My point is not that your president is the Devil, but that he endorses and supports policies that are the Devil's cause. You see, from the very beginning it is all about control. The Devil grabs those who are weak in faith, blinds them to the truth, convinces them that their causes are noble, and goes to war against God, Jesus, and the souls of Forever. You are either for God or you are against him. With God, there is no in between. Jesus said if you even think about committing a sin, then you are already guilty. Maybe your president didn't inhale, but he still broke the law!"

Nino laughs, "I hear you sister. I hear you."

Liz smiles but remains serious, "My point is not to turn you against your commander and chief, because if it weren't him, it would be someone else. Satan's power is getting stronger every day. The faithless are coming close to outnumbering the faithful. Many of our vital organs have already been infiltrated, but it is still not too late to stem the tide. The United States of America is still a Democratic country, but it won't always be. You need to cry out to the Christians, Muslims, Jews, Hindus and all peoples who believe in God. If all God's children will unite and speak as one voice, they can save this country and the world. They can deliver a lethal, unexpected blow to Satan, one from which he may never recover. This is the prophesied end of time, when Satan is supposed to reach his pinnacle and faith in God is at its lowest. What did Jesus say? **'When I return will I find anyone with faith?'** Can you imagine how pleased Jesus will be, and how crushed Satan will feel, to see that during his most devastating period, one of the greatest religious moments of all time will be established? We are all God's children, Nino, and it's time to rally the troops!"

Nino worried, "I'll do my best, Liz. I just hope people will listen. I wish I had you coming with me. You truly are a motivator."

"You don't need me, Nino. Your message is good. Be courageous and the people will listen. Speak your mind with passion and don't worry about who you offend. All you can do is share with people the truth that has been revealed to you. When you tell the truth, you are representing God. If people hear your truth and reject it, they are rejecting God. All people who are given an opportunity to hear your message of truth and reject it will be held accountable. Real riches are not gold, silver or diamonds, Nino. Real riches are the wisdom that comes from God. Every message is a precious jewel that you will shower the people with. I wish you the very best, Nino. You will be in my thoughts and prayers. May Allah, Jesus, the Angels, and all of the Heavenly bodies rally behind your mission."

"Thank you, Liz. I won't forget your words. I hope I see you again soon."

"Don't worry, Nino. You will. Here comes Chebar, licking his fingers and rushing you off, no doubt. I'm glad we had this time together, Nino."

Chebar hurries toward Nino and Liz. "Well, I hate to eat and run, Liz, but we really must be going. Thanks for the invite."

Liz smiles brightly, "Oh, you're quite welcome Chebar. You and Nino can stop by any time you're in the neighborhood."

Nino and Chebar wave goodbye and head out through the front gate. Chebar takes Nino's hand and they fly into a beautiful glen. A labyrinth of waterfalls, and tiny pools. Babbling brooks of crystal clear water flow over precious stones, amidst a backdrop of wild flowers and beautiful colored water lilies.

"Boy, this place is like walking into a beautiful painting … It kind of reminds me of a place called Watkins Glen, back home in upstate New York. I spent my summers there a couple of times as part of the Fresh Air Program. What a beautiful glen and a quaint little village. I used to live on 111 5th Street with the Bellis family. What a loving family they were. Jimmy, Joyce, and their children: Jimmy Jr., Vicky, Michelle, and Sandy, always made me feel real welcome." As Nino drifts off into this memory, Chebar watches his face glow with traces of childhood."

"That's a fine memory, Nino. I wish we had time to share even more, but I must leave you now. You must wait here in the glen for Thomas, who will be arriving any moment. I have to go back and work out some details with Barabbas, before he gives you your final part of the tour. I really enjoyed our time together, Nino. I think in the future you and I will be good friends."

"Yes, I'm sure we will. Thank you for everything, Chebar. You're a nice soul and your piece of the tour was really helpful."

"Thank you for saying so, Nino. I know you are going to do well. I can feel it."

"I hope you're right!"

"I hope I'm right too. After all I am the one who recommended you!"

Nino surprised, "You are the one who chose me for this assignment? Why me, out of all the other people in the world? I just don't understand."

Chebar reassures the Prophet of Faith, "Nino, I have spent nearly fifteen hundred years searching for our seventh lion. In you, I know I have found the unexpected Prophet of Faith. You are a humble, brave, loving, loyal and true servant of God. Your life's deeds show that you have always tried to walk the P.O.J. and I know you feel honored that we have chosen you to be our seventh lion. We are just as honored that you have agreed to join our noble group. Be brave, my brother, brave and confident in your abilities.

You have more talent and power than you know." Chebar hugs his new friend and takes to the sky, adding, "Farewell, my friend. May the spirit of our king, the Lion of the Tribe of Judah, guard your every step. Look there—Thomas approaches."

As Thomas approaches, Chebar disappears over the trees.

"If Your heart is in the right place, you will overcome all obstacles."
-Tom Coughlin (Super Bowl Champions NY Giants Head Coach)

"You did not recieve a spirit that makes you a slave again to fear, but you recieved the Spirit of sonship. And by him we cry, 'Abba, Father.' The Spirit himself testifies with our spirit that we are ALL GOD'S CHILDREN!"
St. Paul (Romans 8:15-16)

CHAPTER 15

▼

"I charge thee, fling away ambition; By that sin fell the Angels; how can man then, The image of his Maker, hope to win by it? Love thyself last!"
-William Shakespeare (Henry The Eighth)

"There is far more than one way to God, and He fulfils himself in many ways.... <u>Many are the roads by which God carries his own to Heaven!</u>"
-Alfred Tennyson & <u>Miguel de Cervantes</u>

Thomas extends his hand, "It is a pleasure to meet you, Nino. I have waited a long time for your arrival."

Nino shakes his had firmly, "No, sir—the pleasure is all mine ... To tell you the truth, it makes my heart rest a little easier to know that one of the twelve apostles is a part of our mission."

Thomas worried, "I hate to tell you this, Nino, but the fact that I am a part of your group may makes your job that much harder."

Nino concerned, "Why?"

Thomas puts into simple words, "Because Satan hates all of the apostles more than any other citizens of Forever. It will be a dream come true for him to have another chance at getting one of the King's chosen apostles to spend an eternity in Hell. The fact that I am a member of this group means that Satan will focus all of his power on defeating our mission. He will pull all of his demons from their normal assignments, which will make your task extremely difficult. However, the fact is that millions of souls have already been possessed by these demons."

Nino shocked, "Possessed? You mean like in that movie "The Exorcist"?"

Thomas chuckles and sighs, "Hollywood…. No Nino, Satan very rarely operates in that type of overt manner anymore. He doesn't want to be exposed. He knows that if people see him as real, they will also come to realize that God exists, and he doesn't want that to happen. When I say possessed, I mean people who are controlled by sin and blind to the truth. The demons in their lives work very hard at keeping them preoccupied with evil or trivial pursuits."

Nino looks worried, "So, when Satan finds out about our plan he is going to remove these demons from the people they usually follow around? What are the like, evil guardian angels or something?"

"Exactly, when he removes the demons from their normal assignments, these people will have an opportunity to see and hear the truth of our message unimpeded by the normal demonic distractions. If you are successful, these lost souls will turn to God and begin walking the Path of Jesus."

Nino curious, "So are we trying to make Christian converts out of these lost souls?"

Thomas makes clear, "I understand that when I say Jesus, you immediately think that I am also referring to the Christian religion. However, you must cease thinking of Jesus in terms of specific religions. Jesus is much larger, and his existence is much larger than any religion. Therefore, it is not our goal to convert people into one religion or another. When God looks down from Heaven he doesn't see Christians, Muslims, and Jews. He simply sees his children…. We are simply giving people who have no faith, a chance to experience the true Path of Jesus. We are putting something where there is nothing. This is not conversion, it is illumination. Once they embrace these truths, and change their behavior, they will finally be on the path the leads to Heaven."

Nino concerned, "What will happen when the demons return?"

"When these evil guardian angels return to possess these souls, they will find that their spiritual locks have been changed. They will be furious over the loss of their homes, and you will have saved millions of God's children."

"You mean if a person believes in God and walks the Path of Jesus, then there is no way a demon can possess them?"

Chebar smiles, "That's exactly right, and the deed is always more important than the word."

"You mean like a person who claims to be religious, but is really a cold hearted hypocrite?"

"Yes, if a person does not believe in God, or if they claim to believe in Him, and walk not the path of brotherly love, then they are easy to possess. It follows that if you don't believe in God, you can't possibly accept his Christ. As I'm sure you've already been told, many of God's true believers have many different views on how Jesus Christ fits into their religion. However, the most important factor is whether or not we obey our Father in Heaven. If we are true believers, then we will be trying to live the way that Jesus lived. As I said before, how we live is much more important than what religious name we call ourselves.

Anyway, if a person does not believe in God, they are an unprotected soul. Any demon or number of demons can come in and take complete control over the non-believer's life. In the old days, it was easy to recognize a person who was possessed. They would often act crazy and fall into seizures, foaming at the mouth and so forth. However, now-a-days Satan is very slick. He has become very covert in his operations. He is an expert at camouflaging his evilness and his existence. A soul possessed by one or more demons in today's society most often is seen as someone who is very successful in the material world. They have nice homes, cars, money, lovers, etc ... However, these people are completely blind and deaf to the truth that comes from God. Slaves to sin and all forms of vice and greed, they are completely at the mercy of the Devil. Many others who are possessed often get diagnosed as mentally ill. It's no coincidence that the founders of psychology and psychiatry were atheists."

Nino's curiosity is sparked by Thomas, and he is eager to learn more about the threat demons pose to the plan. "Explain to me a little more about the lives of these demons," he asks.

Thomas explains, "A demon is a soul who was seduced by Satan either in Forever during the great revolution, or it could be an earthly soul that died in a state of sin and evil. These souls are banished to the outer darkness to await judgment, and their sentence is either purgatory or banishment to the abyss. The outer darkness is an absolutely horrible place, but it is a paradise compared to even the first level of Hell. A demon is a soldier for the Devil himself. These demons have avoided banishment to the abyss by agreeing to help Satan in his cause. They realize that their time is short and that if Satan is defeated they will spend eternity in the worst level of Hell. Those lost souls who regret their mistakes and feel remorse will be sentenced to an upper level of Hell for eternity. All levels of Hell are atrociously dreadful, but for those who knowingly follow Satan and oppose God, their punishment will be an eternity in the most vile of all places. The lowest level of Hell hasn't even been created yet, but if the New Jerusalem is beyond description because of its beauty and splendor, so too is the lowest level of Hell beyond description because of its extreme ugliness.

The demons who become a part of the Devil's Army are under the command of Satan and his Fallen Angels from the heavenly revolution. They have a chain of command like any army would have. You have Satan as Commander-in-Chief. You have the second in command who is the Anti-Christ, and you have the Joint Chiefs of Staff who are the kings of the Antichrist. These souls have possessed the great tyrants of the ages, including Ramses, Hitler, Nero, Napoleon, Nebuchadnezzar, Caesar, Lenin, Stalin and Judas Iscariot."

Nino is stunned, "Unbelievable. It's just simply unbelievable."

"The common demon foot soldier suffers in a world without a body to house it and give it pleasure. Once it finds a person who is unprotected, it stays there until the person is a slave to sin. Then the demon goes out and hunts for another lost soul to possess. While the demon is gone, there is a chance that this soul could be saved, but usually they are such slaves to vice and greed and so puffed with pride that change becomes increasingly unlikely. The demons leave these souls and go on reconnaissance missions, always returning to the souls they left behind, usually after a short period of time. Sometimes, they even bring some other demons back to the soul. Demons are the most desperate sort of souls. They are terrified at the thought of being sent to the abyss, and they know that if they don't capture souls, Satan will send an unproductive demon to the abyss for a punishment. Needless to say, these punished demons return to earth with a vengeance, more hungry for souls than ever before. A demon would rather face anything than being sent into the abyss."

Nino chimes in, "Like when Jesus exorcised those demons from that guy, and the demons begged Jesus not to send them into the abyss, but to instead send them into the herd of swine?"

Thomas is taken back by Nino's reference to the Bible. "That's a perfect example. You'd think I would have thought of that," he answers.

Nino curious, "Why does the Bible say that when a demon leaves a body it goes out into dry places, until it finds a new person to possess? What does that mean?"

"The demon cannot stand the earth's climate. Having come from the abyss in which it is very hot, they are often driven to the desert, or some other warm, dry place. They stay out in the desert until they become acclimated to the earth. A demon coming from a body doesn't take as long to acclimate as a demon coming from the abyss. All demons also hate rain. When it hits them it is like water dropping on a hot frying pan."

"What about holy water?" Nino asks, his earthly naivety showing through.

"Nino, You watch too many movies, don't you?" Thomas laughs. "They really just hate water. Holy, or blessed, water is especially painful because it is water in which the spirit of God has passed through."

"Why don't they just stay in one body after they gain entrance?"

"As I said before, Satan would view this as unproductive. There is no unconditional love or loyalty with Satan. Satan doesn't entertain excuses. Once you a line yourself with him, you either give him what he wants, or they will be sent into the abyss. This is why they are always desparately looking for new souls."

Nino nods understandingly, "That makes sense.... Thomas I read somewhere in the Bible that demons often return to a body that they have previously possessed, and many times they bring other demons with them?"

Thomas continues, "The demon must always return to the previously possessed soul from time to time to make sure it remains enslaved to sin. As I said before, when a demon leaves a soul or is initially released from the bottomless pit, it must go out into the desert to acclimate itself. It then returns to society and goes out searching for a new soul to possess. If the demon is unsuccessful in its quest, it finds some other demons who are also unsuccessful, and they go back to one of the original souls to make things even worse. The demon must report to Satan on a regular basis. Satan's primary concern is how many new souls have been claimed. He also wants to know how many old sites are being maintained and how many souls have been 'lost' to God. The demon must be productive, or else. By bringing some other demons with him to a former host, at the very least the demon will be able to say that he made a soul more evil. This doesn't totally satisfy Satan, but it does appease him temporarily."

"You said Judas Iscariot. The apostle who betrayed Jesus, is one of Satan's top dogs?"

"Yes, and this to me is a great tragedy."

"Were you close to Judas?" Nino asks, intrigued. Shame dawns on Thomas' face.

"Yes, I was very close to him."

"Did you know he was going to betray Jesus?"

"No, no one knew that. None of us would have any reason to suspect such a thing. Oh, yah, Jesus and Judas would get into arguments from time to time, but for the most part, Judas seemed to be one of the apostles that Jesus talked to the most. You see, Judas was formally educated. He was very well spoken, and he was a very good writer. He also had a clear understanding of the political and religious systems that controlled Jerusalem."

"So Judas was a valuable part of your organization?" Nino asks, growing slightly confused.

"Oh, definitely. He was a very good friend everyone, and he did a lot to help us all."

Nino surprised, "That's not what I expected to hear. So, what happened then? If he was such a good pearson, why did he betray Jesus?"

"Personally, I don't think he ever intended to betray Jesus."

"What makes you say that?" Nino asks.

Thomas continues, "Nino, when Judas found out that the High Priests' real reason for wanting to question Jesus was so that they could set up a mock trial and ultimately have him put to death, he was crushed. He was so devastated that he took his own life."

Nino puzzled "So, what do you think happened? The facts don't unfold they way that I would have expected them to."

"I know what you mean … I think Judas sincerely believed that if Jesus had the opportunity to prove himself before the Sanhedrin, which was like the religious supreme court of Israel, that he would be able to win them over. He often tried to convince Jesus to do it, but Jesus would tell Judas that he was thinking as man thought, not as God. He would tell him to open his heart, and not his mind. I think that Judas was kind of forcing Jesus to do what he thought would be best for the situation. I think he felt that if Jesus had to defend himself before the Sanhedrin, that he would do exactly that. I don't think he ever imagined that Jesus would remain silent and not defend himself. Especially when he never missed an opportunity to speak out on any other occasion in which he was confronted by injustice or hypocrisy. Judas was stunned by his behavior. Jesus stood dumb, like a sheep before its shearers, and he opened not his mouth. Jesus went like the Lamb of God that he truly was, and was slaughtered by the High Priests of the Temple."

Nino confused, "But, hadn't Jesus spoken to you all about his impending death?"

"Yes, many times. I believe Judas really thought that he was doing something proactive, which would ultimately save Jesus from the death of which he spoke. Can you imagine how Judas felt when he found out the exact opposite?"

Nino is silent as he reflects on the sad thought of the mother and two children that he had once killed.

"Judas was no different from the rest of us in that we had trouble understanding how a dead Messiah could help anybody. All Jews expected a Messiah who would be like a new King David. We expected a mighty ruler who would deliver us from our enemy, Rome. It wasn't until Jesus met with us after his resurrection that it became clear why he had to die. Then we learned that the enemy he came to liberate us from was not Rome, but Satan."

"How did the other Apostles react toward Judas?"

Thomas ashamed, "We were all enraged. He tried to talk to us. He screamed to Peter that the only way the master could save himself was if he proved himself before the Sanhedrin. But, Peter swore at him and said that Judas would be responsible for the death of Jesus. Some of the other apostles and disciples spit in his face. He fled from the Garden, disgraced. He bravely ran to the Temple so that he could be with Jesus. He wanted to stand by him during the questioning. He demanded that the temple guards summons master Zeriah. This was the high priest that Judas helped bring Jesus into custiody. When the High Priest finally came, Judas grabbed him by his robe, and said that he wanted to be with Jesus during this meeting.... : Thomas' eyes fill with tears, "That is when he found out that there was no hearing, but a trial. Zeriah smugly told Judas that Jesus was accused of blasphemy. He then thanked Judas for all of his help and handed him a bag of silver coins. The temple guards and everyone else watching assumed the silver was a payoff. Which was the high priests intention. The story spread quickly that Judas had betrayed Jesus for thirty pieces of silver. Judas hung himself before I ever had the chance to speak to him again." Thomas breaks down into heavy sobs ...

Nino puts his arm around Thomas' shoulders, "I'm sorry Thomas. I now see Judas in a different light. It is awful that you lost such a good friend"

Thomas dries his eyes, "He really was a good, good man. Judas simply wanted Jesus to set up his earthly kingdom, and he was trying to accelerate the process. Judas' motives were not malicious in any way. He thought that if forced to, Jesus would prove his divinity to those who were plotting against him, and they would in turn accept him as the Messiah. His sin was that he did not trust God's plan or timing. He wanted everything to happen the way he thought it should happen, and when. However, even though his intentions were good, and he was thinking of what would be best for Jesus and the Jews, he is still morally responsible for betraying the Messiah. I'm not trying to make excuses for him. It just kills me to think of him working for Satan. It just tears up my heart."

Nino is saddened as he watches his new friend in tears once again, but he still needs to know some more about Judas and his fate. Quietly, he asks Thomas, "How did that come about. Did he go to hell because he killed himself?

Thomas raises his eyes to meet Nino's. "No, no. When a soul commits suicide it is left for an unspecified amount of time to wander through the outer darkness."

"Is that like Purgatory?"

"No, Purgatory is for souls who have completed the Great Game, but are still not worthy to enter into Paradise. Pilate will speak to you more on this matter. A soul who commits suicide is left in the outer darkness to ponder its future. It would not be just to reward someone who thought so little of life, with an eternity in Paradise. Suicide is also something that indicates little or no faith. The soul must decide if it is willing to try again, or become a lower class angel, life as a servant of God in Paradise, but no free will."

"So what did Judas decide?"

Thomas sighs, frustrated by the very thought of it. "Satan convinced Judas that he would be better off reigning in Hell than serving in a Heaven where he would be remembered for all time as the apostle who betrayed the Messiah. Satan also convinced him that the Great Game would go on for billions of years."

"So why didn't Judas back out of the deal when he found out Satan was lying?"

"In the outer darkness, there are two borders. One border leads to Forever, and the other leads to a very deep cavern which ultimately leads to the first level of Hell. Once you make a deal with Satan, and cross over to the Hell side of the Border, you can never return."

Nino perplexed, "Still, he isn't forced to help Satan, is he?"

"Satan told Judas that he either agrees to be one of his right hand souls, or he goes to the Abyss until the Day of Judgment comes. Judas, like any other soul, does not want to go to the Abyss. He rationalized that in a round about way he will still be helping God by being a part of that which tests the true character of the soul. It is all he has left to hang on to."

Nino curious, "How do you know all of these things about Judas, if no one can cross the Devil's cavern?"

"I have spent time with him through the Grand Cinema." Thomas pauses for a moment and realizes how much time has passed. "Oh dear Nino, I'm getting side tracked. I'm sorry Nino. I don't know how learning about Judas is going to help with your mission."

"Don't apologize, I found it all very interesting. It's funny, even before hearing your story about Judas, I always had a feeling that there was something more to that story. I just wish there was some way my mission could help him."

Thomas sadly, "I have prayed and prayed for my poor friend. I guess we just have to accept his miserable fate as a casualty of war. But, none the less, we had better move along with the rest of our piece of the tour. Our time together will end very shortly."

"Can you tell me a little more about the outer darkness and the abyss? They're not the same place right?" asks Nino.

"Definitely not, Nino. The outer darkness is indeed a gruesome place. It is like a barren waste land. But what makes it an unnervingly difficult place to spend time is that you can see the kingdom of Forever. You can smell the exquisite meals, and hear the laughter, all of which is very disturbing. The Abyss or the Bottomless Pit that you hear the demons refer to is the first level of Hell. The difference is that in all levels of Hell, you are tortured. The pain that comes from the outer darkness comes from understanding the reality of your eternal loss, and separation from the divine light of God, but there is no physical torture."

Nino questions, "So why not stay in the outer darkness? I just don't understand why someone would choose to go to any level of Hell."

"Satan convinces them that he still has a chance to be victorious. He also assures them that God, in his mercy, will never end the world, and that they are better off experiencing earthly pleasures forever, than to spend eternity in the outer darkness. Satan is the quintessential deceiver. Once he convinces the lost soul to swear his allegiance to him, he is doomed to spend eternity in the lowest level of Hell. It's the proverbial fine print he fails to mention."

"So, Satan, convinced that he will foil our plan, will leave millions of his possessed souls unprotected, and if we are successful we will really catch Satan with his pants down! His pride, and overconfidence once again will get the best of him!"

Thomas worried, "Or the best of us." Thomas says, bringing Nino down again. "Still doubting Thomas?" Nino jokes.

Thomas remains somber, "I'm sorry Nino. That's been my problem for eons. That is why I took on this mission. I believe that Jesus himself will end up being on our side. I want to prove to him, more than anyone else, that I believe and have faith in him, enough to stake my eternity on it."

Nino proudly, "You know, Thomas, any way this thing works out you will have achieved your goal. It takes a brave and faithful soul to do what you are doing. No one will ever be able to call you doubting Thomas again."

Thomas beams, "Thank you Nino, thank you, and God bless you for those kind words." Thomas gets up and gestures for Nino to follow him. He has one more special person for Nino to meet before he departs.

**"Look for and magnify the best that you find in
all people, disregard their worst attributes, and fill
them with hope in all ways that you are able."
Sully & Ann Pitifer**

"Who is this" They asked themselves, "that even the winds and the sea
obey him?"
-The Apostles & Disciples of Jesus Of Nazareth-(Matthew 8:27)

Author's Note: Dr. Wayne Dyer's book, Change Your Thoughts-Change Your Life, Living The Wisdom of The Tao, (Hay House, 2008), is a must read. It is ironic that a country that is considered atheistic, would produce a philosopher that has such a clear understanding of the Holy Spirit, and how all people should try to live. Dr. Wayne's interpretation of the 'Tao Te Ching' is a materpiece of holiness!

CHAPTER 16

▼

"A fool says in his heart, "There is no God."
-Psalms 14:1 (King David 1,100 BC)

*"He who consciously or unconsciously has chosen to ignore God is
an orphan in the Universe."*
-Emile Cailliet

"Look for and magnify the best that you find in people, disregard their
worst attributes, and fill them with hope in all ways that you are able."
-Sully & Ann Pitifer

Is there nothing you can embrace? Do you know more than everybody
else? And can you explain every mystery of nature? Why
would you be so definite in the fact that there is no God? It doesn't
make any sense.
-Bill O'Reilly

"Why are you using your ignorance to deny my providence? Where
were you when I laid the foundations of the earth? Do you know
how its dimensions were determined, and who did the surveying?
Do you know the laws of the universe, and how the Heavens influence the
Earth? What supports its foundations, and who laid its
cornerstone, as the morning stars sang together and all the Angles
shouted for joy?'
-The Lord God as quoted from The Book of Job 38:4-7, & 33

"Before our time together is over I want to introduce you to a very special soul."

"Is it someone famous?" Nino asks in anticipation.

"By earthly standards, no. But up here in Forever, Charles Elkin Blindstone III is a rare and precious stone."

Nino interested, "Why? What did he do?"

"Chuck was an Atheist who found the Path of Jesus."

"You mean he was an Atheist who became a Christian before he died?"

"No, this is even more remarkable. He lived his whole life as an Atheist."

"You mean he ..."

"Yes he even died an Atheist."

Nino is extremely confused by this information. "But how can an Atheist get into Heaven? It doesn't make sense!"

"It is very rare indeed for an Atheist to be admitted into the kingdom, but it does happen from time to time. It's comparable to the coming of your Haley's comet. It's rare; it's beautiful; and it always ignites a grand celebration."

Nino is noticeably troubled by this theory. "An Atheist in Heaven.... There's an Atheist in Heaven. That's remarkable. But-"

Thomas almost laughs at Nino's reaction. "I know, my brother. I was just as shocked as you are, until it was explained to me in a way that opened my eyes to its beauty. Have you ever read the scripture that states man's good deeds are as dirty rags to God?"

"Yeah sure, many times."

"What do you think is the meaning of this scripture?"

Nino thinks for a moment, "I always thought that it must have something to do with the motives behind our good deeds. It's like, am I doing this good deed because I feel compassion and mercy, or am I doing it because I know God and maybe other people are watching me?"

Thomas smiles, "Exactly. Many people who believe in God do good deeds out of obligation, hoping that some day they will be rewarded in Heaven."

"Or they are trying not to get punished for not doing what they know they should." Nino adds.

"Yes, so their motives are not pure, and therefore are seen as dirty rags by Jehovah. God gives out of genuine mercy, love, and compassion. He seeks no reward and fears no punishment. He gives as a mother or father gives to a child. He feels our needs and is moved into action. It is his hope that eventually all who follow the path will open their hearts to the needs of others, serving only because they love, and for no other reason."

Nino puzzled, "But, how can you not be mindful of God either rewarding you or punishing you? It's always on your mind, unless you don't believe there is a God.... Wait a minute ... Yes, I think I see now. The ath—"

Thomas interrupts Nino before he can finish his thought. "The Atheist who finds the Path of Jesus; he who has mercy, love, and compassion for his fellow mankind and who has no fear of punishment, ironically has the ability to perform some of the rarest and most beautiful acts of kindness and mercy imaginable."

Nino concerned, "If this is the case then why is it so rare for Atheists to get into Heaven?"

"What was it that Paul said? 'Why is it the good that I want to do I don't do, and the bad that I don't want to do I do?' If it is hard for those who believe in God to walk the Path of Jesus, how much harder is it for a nonbeliever?"

Nino's eyes get big, "VERY HARD."

Thomas continues, "The worst thing that can happen to a person is that they stop believing in God, or even worse, they spend their life trying to hurt God and his many religions. These people don't realize that in so doing they have aligned themselves with the Devil and his cause. Instead of thanking God for the good that comes their way, they thank themselves. They become full of pride. You must not under estimate one human's ability to influence another's. Many times the influence is unintentional. For example, a child learns to swear because she hears her father swear when he gets mad. Now, let's presume that when the father swears at his lawn mower for not starting, his goal is not to teach his daughter to swear when she gets mad. However, that is exactly what he is doing."

Nino nods his head and almost laughs at the obvious lesson. "I see your point, Thomas."

"You understand, then, that the same is true for the Atheists and the Agnostics. They influence other people, especially young people, by what they do and say in their lives. You're a student of the Bible aren't you? Remember when Jesus said "Woe to the person who leads any of these little ones astray," and "there will always be sin, but woe to the person who does the tempting." Remember this Nino Jones: you will be held accountable for every idle word that you speak and every deed that you do. Your words and deeds today, are a reflection of your soul's fate: either you will be justified by them, or condemned. Ignorance of the law is no excuse on earth or in Heaven. The bottom line is this: what did you stand for in your life? How did you touch the world? How did you influence those people you came in contact with in your life? Did you help God's cause or hurt it? Atheists have a tendency to promote atheism, and quite often take on political and social stances that help the cause of Satan.

Nino understands, "I see what you mean. Although the Atheist's circumstances may give him the opportunity to do great acts of goodness, the human condition and the stress of the Great Game make it highly unlikely that he will ever find the Path of Jesus. But when it happens-"

"Oh how brilliant the stone does shine!"

Nino and Thomas walk on to what, to Nino's surprise, looks like some sort of Heavenly golf course. Clearly, it is not just an ordinary golf course. The green grass on the fairway redefines the meaning of color. The trees that line it on both sides are sculpted into perfectly matched shapes, each one fitting with the next like pieces of a jigsaw puzzle. As Nino walks into the open area, Thomas pulls him back and they hear some one yell "Fore!" The ball just misses Nino, and a handsome dark haired young man comes running up apologetically.

"Speaking of rare stones," Thomas laughs as he introduces the young man. "This fine golfer is my friend, Chuck."

Chuck runs over and grabs Thomas in a hearty bear hug. "Thomas, you got here sooner than I expected."

Thomas laughs even harder as he points to the ball that almost knocked out Nino. "I guess so. Poor Nino might not have been able to finish his tour."

Chuck blushing with embarrassment turns his attention to the unexpected prophet. "Sorry about that my friend, but nobody is ever on the same hole up here."

Nino laughs. "That's alright! Think nothing of it. Besides, you'd think my guide would have taken better care of me!"

"That's right, blame it all on the Doubting Thomas! ... Chuck Blindstone, I'd like you to meet Nino Jones."

"It's an absolute pleasure, Nino. I've been so anxious to meet you!" "No sir, the pleasure is mine."

"Chuck," Thomas says, "why don't I let Nino walk the last two holes with you, and I'll meet you up at the clubhouse in about an hour or so."

"That's fine with me. How about it Nino? Are you up for a little golf?"

Nino chuckles, "Golf? I've never played anything except miniature golf, and I was bad at that. I'll just be your caddy."

"Don't need a caddy up here. You just stand over your shot and the perfect club pops right into your hand."

"You've gotta be kidding me?"

Chuck continues, "No! I'm serious! This is a golfer's dream world. There are no lost balls or slow people to play behind. There are also a lot more holes-in-one up here. Oh, and get this, do you know how on earth the grounds keepers change the pin placement from day to day?"

"You mean like moving the hole to a different spot on the green?"

"Yeah, that's right. Well, up here the Angels in charge of our heavenly golf courses change the entire hole!"

"You mean-"

"Everything about the hole is different. The length, the scenery, the traps. It's remarkably challenging. Here, I'll drop a ball for you, and you stand over it."

Chuck drops a ball, and as Nino stands over it, a club pops into his hand. Nino shakes his head as he gets in position. "I can't believe it." "Well, go ahead take a swing at it."

"But I'm not a golfer."

"Nino, you're in Heaven. Everybody is a golfer up here."

Nino eyes a shot he estimates is about 250 yards from the green. He takes a big full swing at the ball, and stares awestruck as the ball sails long and straight, dropping on the green and rolling 4 feet from the cup.

Nino stares at the ball in utter astonyshment. "I can't believe it. That felt great!"

Chuck can't help smiling at Forever's newest golfer. "Welcome to Heaven my brother, up here everything is great."

Nino and Chuck finish up the last two holes and walk out on the porch of the pristine club house overlooking an aquamarine colored lake. The view is stunning. Nino follows Chuck as he walks along a pristine trail carving its way through a lush forest. They walk for awhile in silence, just taking in the beauty. Finally, Nino speaks.

"Oh, my God. What beauty." He exclaims, no other words being needed to explain his feelings.

Chuck laughs knowingly, but then turns serious. "That's just what I said when I first arrived, except I was petrified. Can you imagine living your life as an Atheist and then finding out you had bet the wrong way?"

Nino winces at the thought of it, "That must have been a horrible real-ization. You must have thought you were going straight to Hell."

Chucks mind drifts back to the moment,"That's exactly what I thought was going to happen. The town that I lived in was hit by one of those killer tornados that started emerging in the early part of the 21st century. I had no warning or anything. I was in the middle of watching an old Jimmy Stewart movie called It's A Wonderful Life...."

Nino interrupts chuckling "320 Sycamore Street. I love that movie."

Chuck smiles, and continues "When all of a sudden I heard what sounded like a jet-powered freight train ripping through my house! The next thing I know, I'm being walked toward Saint Peter, and man, am I scared!"

"At least you got that far. They pulled me out before I got to Saint Peter. What happens once you get there?"

Chucks face is filled with wonder as he recalls the moment, "I didn't know that it was St. Peter at the time. I just knew that he was a being of light, something I had never seen before. He looked right into my soul, and

I could actually feel his wisdom and power. He didn't really speak to me in words, but I could hear his thoughts in my mind. He said something like "What have you done with this life you were given?" Then he shows me this panoramic view of my life."

"What like a highlight film?"

Smiling "Yes, It's like a montage of your life. The highs and the lows. The sky above me turned into this giant movie screen. When the film begins St. Peter kind of disappeared, but I could still feel his presence the whole time. He would make comments at different times, but nothing judgmental. He just kept stressing the importance of love. Even when I had to look at difficult moments of my life, I did not feel that any negative judgments were coming from him. I felt an overwhelming sense of unconditional love and acceptance flowing from him at all times. He simply seemed concerned with what I was learning. It was like he was giving me the ability to look at my life with omnipotent wisdom and knowledge."

Nino wonders, "When you looked at the hard times of your life did you ever feel shame or embarrassment?"

Chuck looks away, "Yes, I did. I was ashamed of a lot of things I had done. But it was my own soul that spoke out against me, and no one else. As a part of this review, you are given the ability to evaluate your life objectively. You have this uncompromising sense about what is right and wrong. Do you know how it says in the Bible that you will be held accountable for every idle word that you speak?"

Nino looks worried "I sure do."

"Well that's only part of the truth. Your very own soul holds you accountable for every word, every deed, and every thought." Nino is shocked, "Even your thoughts are revealed?!"

"Yes, everything is recorded, and there is no arguing or rationalizing your actions. They are what they are. Your life must stand or fall on its own merits."

"So what happens after the movie?"

"After that, you are taken to the temple and led to the great courtyard of judgment where you are addressed and by Jesus. The angels split us up into two groups. I can remember looking over at the other group and seeing this born-again Christian woman from my town who had repeatedly told me during my life that if I didn't accept Jesus as my savior and follow her religion, I would go to Hell. She was looking at me with this proud, smug "I told you so" look on her face. I can remember thinking that this woman was so judgmental of me. She always acted like she was better than me, like I was beneath her because of my beliefs. When I saw her looking at me from her group, it only confirmed what I already knew. I was certain that I was going to be sent to Hell, and I started to cry. Then, all of a sudden everything got real quiet. Then Jesus, in front of all of the multitudes of people, said **"Charles Elkin Blindstone III, why do you weep? Was I not hungry and you fed me, was I not thirsty and you gave me drink, was I not sick and you comforted me, was I not imprisoned and you visited me?"** "When, Jesus?" I said, "when did I do these things to you?" **"When you did it to these the least of my brethren, you did it to me. You may not have accepted me by word, but you walked my path: The path of love, mercy, and compassion. You and all of the souls in your group have proved yourselves worthy to enter a paradise prepared for you since the beginning of time."** Can you imagine how shocked I was, Nino? I had positioned myself at the back of the group, knowing that I was unworthy to be anywhere near his throne. Then he called for me to come to the front of the congregation. Saying **"Of all of the souls that enter here today, none shines brighter than the soul of Charles Elkin Blindstone III. Although in his life he was an Atheist who sought not reward, or feared not punishment for his actions, in his heart he found love, mercy, and compassion for all he encountered during the Great Game, and in so doing he brought joy and comfort to many needy souls, and glory to our Heavenly father."** Nino, I was stunned. At this the crowd roared an ovation beyond belief. The angels broke into a victory song, and Jesus, with me at his right hand, walked us into Forever."

Nino is almost knocked off balance by the magnificence of what he has heard. "That must have really been something. I don't think I can come up with the words to do it justice."

"Neither can I." Chuck says. "Believe me, you can't begin to imagine the impact. There truly are no words to explain the overwhelming feelings that soared through me at that moment."

Nino wonders, "Chuck, how do you think you found the Path of Jesus? I mean, that's a hard path to find and follow even for people who are really trying to do so."

"My father and mother were killed in a drive-by shooting when my mother was 8 months pregnant. The doctors were able to save me, and I was raised in a state run orphanage until I was old enough to go to college."

"I am also an orphan," Nino says, empathizing.

Chuck's eyes soften, "I know. I think God must have a special place in his heart for us orphans."

Nino smiles, "I hope you're right."

Chuck continues, "Anyway, in our orphanage there was a librarian named Arjunit." Chucks eyes well up with tears. "Arjunita was the closest thing to a mother that I ever had. If it wasn't for her influence, I don't think I would have ever found the Path of Jesus."

"Arjunita? What is that, Spanish? Nino asks. "She must have been a Christian."

"No. Believe it or not, she was born in Dhaka, Bangladesh." Nino curious, "Did she practice a religion?"

"Not really. She was something like an Agnostic. Her father practiced Buddhism, and her mother was a Hindu."

"That's an interesting combination," Nino grins.

"Yes, it is…. Arjunita's father was involved in the Bangladesh government, and she and her family lived a fairly privileged life for a portion of her childhood."

"Only a portion? What happened?" Nino asks.

"One day when Arjunita's mother had gone to surprise her husband with his favorite dish of curried chicken & rice for lunch, a military coup seized the government officers, and Arjunita's parents were both killed."

"Oh, how awful." Nino lowers his eyes, still uncertain of the impact he had on that young family during the Vietnam War. Chuck tries to keep him focused and puts a hand around his shoulders as they walk and talk.

Chuck continues, "Arjunita and her older brother, Abul, were sent to live at what she called a work camp, in a very impoverished section of Bangladesh. The conditions that they lived in were atrocious. They were used as slaves, working for more than twelve hours a day in a huge sneaker factory. They lived in stick huts with dirt floors. They had rags for blankets, and fifty or sixty kids were crammed into huts that were only built to hold about 10 people. They were cruelly punished for even the slightest infractions. They were often dehydrated, always poorly fed, and quite often ill. The average life expectancy for these work-camp-children was 14 to 16 years old!"

Nino saddened, "Those poor children. Those poor, poor little lambs. There's so much evil in the world. Most of us Americans have no clue how rotten some of the other people around the world have it." Chuck listens closely to all of Nino's reactions. He can tell Nino has also lived a hard life and seen much suffering. Nino is anxious to hear more about Arjunita. "So how was she able to come to the U.S.?"

"Arjunita's brother discovered a terrible secret. The girls of the camp where they lived were being forced to become prostitutes once they hit puberty. But here is the worst part. These prostitutes were instructed to let themselves get pregnant. Their babies were then allowed to live to a certain age, and then killed so that their organs could be sold around the world on the black market."

Nino is almost stunned into silence. He mouths the words "Oh my God" before he finally says them out loud. "Oh my God! That's just about the…. Those sick bastards … Those sick, sick bastards." Nino seethes with anger and pity.

"Arjunita and her brother escaped with the help of two Jehovah Witness missionaries named David and Harriett Young. Arjunita and Abul spent the rest of their childhoods in an English orphanage. Abul, who was 10 years older than his sister, went on to Oxford University, and received his Masters in Business. He then transferred to the U.S. to work on his PhD. He told Arjunita that when she graduated from high school he would send for her. However, that never happened."

"What went wrong?"

"Abul got mixed up with a woman who had a history of seducing Hindu men with temporary visas. She seemed to be the answer to his prayers. She was an American citizen. She was, he thought, a devout Hindu. She studied the Bhagavad-Gita. She cooked Indian food, and she appeared to be deeply in love with him. However, as it turned out, she was a con-artist. She had been married three other times before Abul, all to Hindu men with temporary visas."

"What does she do, murder them?"

"No. She gets them to marry her. She has a child or two, and then she tells the authorities that she is being abused mentally and physically. She gets an order of protection, and files for divorce. Ultimately, the husbands end up deported, and she ends up with the children, and all of their belongings. Abul was just another fly that flew into her evil spider web."

Nino perplexed,"With her history, you would think Abul could have mounted a good court case."

Chuck shakes his head in disgust, "I worked in the U.S. immigrations office for a few years when I got out of college, and I can tell you one thing. Foreigners with temporary visas have no chance winning a court case against an American citizen. His wife was given custody of their daughter. She got to keep the house, the money, and all of their combined possessions. When Abul was deported from the USA, he was sent back to, Bangladesh, penniless. At this time, his sister believes that he must have been murdered, for she never heard from him again. When Arjunita graduated from college she came to the USA to search for Abul's only daughter, Jewel Hara Bayazid, but she was never able to find her."

"How come? Doesn't she have the wife and child's name? You would think that with today's technology she should be able to track her down."

"It's not uncommon for people who run that type of con to change their names. It helps cover their tracks."

Nino shakes his head, "That's too bad."

Chuck nods, "Yup. Poor old Arjunita spent the rest of her life living in Chicago, and working as a librarian in our orphanage."

"So what did she do that helped you to find the path?"

"Yes, yes … the point of all this. Forgive me Nino, in Heaven we never make a long story short." Nino laughs, having already found this true with several of his guides. Chuck smiles and continues with his tale. "Arjunita taught me to care about the needs of others. She loved me like a mother would love a son. She taught me to think about even the most insignificant creatures on our planet, and to reflect on their little piece of life."

"Like what for example?"

Chuck scratches his head,"Like a housefly. The housefly is the garbage collector of the world. They have a horrendous job that nobody appreciates. In fact, the only time that someone notices them is usually when they are trying to kill them."

Nino laughs, "I never thought of anything positive about a fly before."

Chuck smiling, "Exactly! But that was sweetness of Arjunita. She could see the beauty in all things. She would say that if you look closely you can find some good in every living creature. Once you find this goodness you will be more inclined to be merciful and compassionate. Mercy and compassion, she would say, are the fuels that lead to random acts of kindness and charity. Kindness and charity are what makes life endurable."

Nino interested, "Was this part of the Buddhists or Hindu religious doctrine?"

"I now know that it is at the heart of all religions, but Arjunita never cloaked any of what she did in religion. She just embodied it. She lived it."

Nino puzzled, "Why do you think such a loving and sensitive person did not follow a religion? I mean, you said her father and mother believed, didn't you?"

"They believed, but don't forget she was only two years old when they died. She was not raised by anyone except her brother who practiced Hinduism. However, when he disappeared, she could no longer bring herself to follow a religion. Because of all of the evils she had experienced in her life, she could not believe that there was a personal God who listened to our prayers, or cared about our many ways of worship."

"So she's Agnostic, not Atheist." Nino thinks for a moment, and then turns back to Chuck. "Chuck to be honest with you I have always had a hard time distinguishing the difference between an Atheist and an Agnostic."

Chuck smiles, "I know what you mean. Ok, here's the difference. In your world earthbounds fall into three categories. Theists, people who believes in God. Atheist's, people who deny the existence of all gods, and Agnostics, people who are uncertain about the existence of God."

Nino frowns, "Is an Athiest someone who tries to prove that God doesn't exist?"

"Not always. We atheists are often portrayed as negative people. However, I think that you would be surprised to find that Atheists for the most part see the inherent good and intelligence in all people. I believed that I was responsible for my own actions. If I achieved something, or failed at a task it was because of my own merits, and nothing more. I truly belived that most people possessed a thoughtful caring nature or rational, that if lived could make the world one of peace, morality and joy."

Nino smiles "You're a good man Chuck?"

Chuck smiles, but then turns serious, "The problem is, as you suggested are the staunch Atheists that actively try to prove to people that there is no such thing as God. These people believe that man created god in his image. Which in some ways they have."

Nino nods, "You mean people like Charles Darwin?"

"Believe or not Nino, Darwin was not an atheist.'

Nino looks surprised "Really?"

Chuck explains, "That's right. A true Agnostic is someone who not only is undecided about the existence of God, but also believes that the existence or non existence of God is improvable, and therefore they neither believe nor disbelieve. Darwin, once was asked if he was an Atheist, and this was his response. "The mystery of the beginning of all things is insoluble by us; and this is why I think Agnostic would be the more correct description of my state of mind. The whole subject of God is beyond the scope of man's intellect." You know Nino, most scientists have a natural skepticism about everything. So the concept of an improvable God is hard for them to accept. This type of mind demands concrete empirical proof. And Proof makes it impossible to have faith. It is a dilemma, but I think even God understands the difficulty that these kind of scientific rational thinkers have grappling with the notion of a creator."

Nino shakes his head, "I have to give Darwin some props. I thought for sure he had to be an Atheist. You know it makes a lot more sense to me for someone to be Agnostic, rather than an athieist. Why not hang on to the possibility that there is a God and a place called Heaven. It's not like you will ever be disappointed. I mean obviously we know the truth. But if the Athiests where right, and all death brings is nothingness, they would never know anyway. It makes now sense not to hope for Heaven."

Chuck agrees, "Your right Nino, it doesn't" Chuck becomes aware of the time, 'Where was I going with all this?'

'You were explaining Arjunita's beliefs."

Chuck remembers, and continues, "Yes, of couse Arjunita. She disagreed with scientific theories that would try to reduce human beings into mere conglomerations of matter. She strongly believed that we all have a spiritual dimension which transcends our material existence."

"What were her views on the creation of the world? Was there a purpose, or a did everything just evolve according to the laws of nature?"

Chuck gives details, "Oh, she believed that the world was created for some purpose. But by whom or for what reason she was not sure. All she did know was that the world was filled with many miseries and that everyone was universally struggling with the same fears and problems. Arjunita would say that **"We are all veterans of the same war. Our enemies are not people, but the invisible forces of evil that alter our true nature. To kill or maim in the name of some religion, political belief, or insensitivity is to ultimately destroy your own people. The earth is our mother, and we are all brothers and sisters of the same womb. Grapes from the same vine."**

Nino smiles, "She sounds like a truly holy person. I wish I could meet her."

"Your wish is my command," Chuck says with a wink. Instantly, a beautiful woman with black flowing hair and deep green eyes approaches Nino and Chuck.

Chuck beaming greets Gita with a Hindu hello "Kem Cho, Gita"

Gita laughing tickles Chuck under his chin "Kem Cho Chucky!" and then turns to Nino. "It is a pleasure to meet you, Nino Jones."

Nino struggling with the Hindu greeting "Keeeem Chooo it's nice to meet you … ma'am. Boy, you have to be careful when you make wishes up here, don't you?"

Arjunita smiles softly. "This is the land where every wish is granted and every dream comes true. Oh, and Nino, please call me Gita. There are no formalities in Forever."

Nino smiles,"Ok, Gita. I like that … Gita. That's a cool name. That nickname doesn't have anything to do with that holy Hindu book called the Bhagavad-Gita does it?"

Gita is delighted. "Why yes, it does. Are you familiar with the song of God?"

"Yes I've read it. It's an inspiring book."

"Do you remember the character named Arjuna?"

"Yes! He was the one who tried to get Krishna to stop the war, right?"

"Good memory, Nino. I'm impressed. When I died and came to Forever, I discovered that I am a direct descendant of Arjuna. That's why my name is Ar-"

"Arjunita. Isn't that cool!"

"When I returned to Forever and discovered the depth of my Hindu origin, I decided to study not only Hindu, but all of the other eastern religions."

Nino confused, "No disrespect, but what is the purpose of studying a religion after you have already been admitted into Heaven?"

Gita explains, "Oh, that's quite alright. Returning to Forever does not mean the end of learning. In many ways, it is the beginning of true learning. In Forever you have the freedom and time to learn about anything you choose. You also have such a powerful brain that learning is as effortless and refreshing as drinking a cool glass of water on a hot day. There is one other reason that I have been studying all these years."

"Why is that?"

"Chuck wasn't completely honest with you Nino. I didn't just appear at your request. Chuck brought you to me. It is my job to share with you, in the time that I am allotted, the beauty of some of the eastern religions."

"So you are a part of the plan?"

"Yes, Nino, and I have, like the others, been waiting for you for a long time. Now, we better get started because Thomas will be here sooner than we expect."

Chuck takes this as his cue to exit. "I'll go back and tell Thomas that Nino is with you. I'll try to get him to golf nine holes with me to give you a little more time."

"Thanks, Chuck. That sounds like a good idea. Sit with me awhile Nino, and I'll share some of what I have learned. First of all, people must understand that every nation has its own messenger. God is the quintessential teacher. He instructs every child that he has, keeping in mind the level of their cultural development, their heritage, and their language so that his message will be clear to them. So, while there truly is only one God, the ways to know him are many."

Nino agrees, "It's true a good teacher would never use the same strategy with every student. She would have to find a way of teaching a lesson that the student could relate to. It's kind of like a bunch of different paths up the same mountain."

"Well said, Nino. That's exactly what I mean. Another problem I see is that each religion thinks that they are the "true" religion. The idea that God should reveal himself in only one way, or at only one time in history, or to only one country, to me would suggest a limitation upon his love and power."

"So you're saying that God, like the good teachers, wants to reach everybody, because he loves and cares about all of his children."

Gita smiles, "Yes. God has revealed his word in each period of history, and in many different cultures through chosen individuals called the *manifestations of God*. Abraham, Jesus, Mohammed, Krishna, Zorrastor, Moses, Buddha, Joseph Smith, and many many more. All of these noble souls were vessels that carried the spirit of Jehovah, and each prophet or manifestation of God, gave people divine truths to live by. These truths and principals that most religions provide are universally the same, but the messages as well as the messengers, have been reshaped and redesigned to speak to the hearts and meet the spiritual needs of all people in every period of history and in every cultural environment."

Nino irritated, "If only people could see the big picture, and look at things with an open mind. We could learn so much from each other if we weren't so ... so ... prejudice I guess is the word I'm searching for."

"Prejudice is a good word Nino. Allah Bahai said that-"

"Allah Ba-who?" Nino asks.

Gita giggles, "Allah Baha'i is the founder of the Baha'i religion. He said that **religious, political, and patriotic prejudices are the destroyers of human society.** He also warned that we must beware of prejudice for light is good in whatsoever lamp it is burning."

Nino smiles, "I like that."

"A rose is beautiful in whatsoever garden it may bloom, and a star has the same radiance whether it shines from the east or the west."

"I like this Allah Baha'i. You know I've heard of the Baha'i religion but I just assumed that it was some strange cult, so I never really looked into it."

"I'm curious Nino, why did you assume that it was a strange cult?" "Well for one thing, the name seems kind of strange to me, and I guess the fact that it is a relatively new religion made me skeptical."

Gita nods knowingly, "Your reaction is quite common. Most people are afraid and skeptical of anything new, but especially religions."

"It's funny too, because I really do consider myself an open-minded person when it comes to religion."

"Don't feel bad Nino. Your reaction is very normal."

"Tell me some more about this Baha'i religion. I mean, if you have time."

"Actually, the Baha'i religion is a very good eastern religion for you to become familiar with. Allah Baha'i wanted the Baha'i religion to encourage any adherent of any world religion to develop a greater understanding of that religion to which they belonged, and to acquire a clear comprehension of its purpose. **Men and women need to mature beyond the limits of the prejudices which surround them, so that they really can become one family under God.** All holy manifestations are exemplars of what all people can become. These religious leaders developed themselves spiritually to the extent that they now serve the further development of all people. Their lives have become examples to follow. They are the good shepherds, and what does a good shepherd do, Nino Jones?"

"He guides and protects his flock."

"Not a bad answer for a city boy!" Gita jokes. "Yes, they must guide and protect their flock, but before than can adequately do so, they must gather their flock. All divine manifestations, since the day of Adam, have striven to unite all of humanity. All prophets of God have been divine shepherds of humanity."

"That's an important point isn't it? God is a unifying spirit who brings his children together. He magnifies our similarities and draws us near to one another, while Satan magnifies our differences and pushes us further apart."

"Yes Nino. All throughout history God has turned scattered peoples into nations and wandering tribes into mighty empires. Through his prophets and his divine manifestations, he has tried to lay the foundation of the oneness of God, and summons us all to the table of universal peace. All of God's messengers are of the same loving, holy, all encompassing spirit. They all served the living God, promoted the same truths, founded similar institutions and reflected the same light."

Nino clarifies, "So, not only are all the Gods of the various religions just different names for the same one God, but all religions are just different facets of the same one religion."

Gita explains, "There is something to be learned from every religion. Precious morsels of wisdom, which will, if lived by, help us break through Satan's traps of race, color, creed, politics, and religion which he uses to separate and divide the children of God. Yahweh is the flaming holy spirit of love that longs to unify all of his creations. He has given a piece of his spirit to all of the love-based religions so that no matter how different the various religions seem on the surface, with their distinct rituals, doctrines, and symbols, they are nevertheless very much alike on a deep, underlying level."

"But there are some religions that are not from God, right? I mean, I don't want to validate all types of religions, do I?"

"That's a good point Nino, and you're right. Some of these psuedo-religions are not religions at all. Many scientific-minded people think that if a religion does not agree with the laws of science, or go along with the regulations of reason, it is nothing more than a bundle of superstitions. However, this is not true. The common thread that weaves through and identifies all of the truly Heaven sent religions is that they must promote brotherly love, compassion, tolerance, charity, and sincerity. These are the attributes which are most important."

"Well said, sister! I just hope I can remember how you said it."

"Don't worry, Nino. You will remember everything you hear on the grand tour."

"Gita, I read somewhere that Hindus believe that there are 330,000,000 Gods. Is this true? And if it is true, how can God be a part of this religion?"

"For the Hindu, these 330,000,000 Gods that you speak of are really different aspects of the one God or one reality."

"I don't understand," Nino admits. Gita patiently continues.

"It's like the unique perception that 330 million human beings might have of the one God."

"I see what you mean Gita. Is it true that the Hindu religion is the oldest of all religions?"

"Yes. Hinduism is the oldest of all of the living religions." "Don't the Hindus call God Brahman?"

"The fundamental teaching of the faith is that underlying all of the manifestations that are worshiped in the temples, festivals and sacred dances are each but an aspect of the one reality which they name Brahman. From this unified Godhead came the Hindu trinity: Brahman, the creator, Vishnu, the preserver and Shiva, the destroyer or transformer."

Nino raises his eyebrows, "Is that similar to the Christian trinity?"

"Yes, it is." Says Gita.

"Hindus don't go to a temple service, do they?" Nino asks.

Gita makes clear, "A Hindu temple represents the dwelling place of a particular aspect of the deity that has been chosen for worship. People come before the image in the temple and bring it gifts of flowers, water or coins. There is no formal service. The people just either pray or meditate."

"Where do the Yogis come in?"

"These are holy Hindu men that teach their listeners their path to liberation which is called Darshina. Jesus' Darshina (love God and love your neighbor as yourself.) was for people of all religions. The purpose of human existence is to learn through personal experience, to realize this relationship with the one reality or God, and his many manifestations, both human and environmental."

"What about reincarnation? Does that really happen?"

"The Hindus believe that spiritual salvation of the soul occurs when it obtains oneness with the ultimate reality of the universe **Brahman**. To achieve this goal, the soul must obtain liberation from the **samsara**, which is the endless cycle of birth, death, and rebirth. The soul which they call the **atman**, will be reincarnated and take on a new human or animal body time after time."

Nino winces, "How do animals come into the equation?"

Gita explains, "Hindus believe in something called **ahimsa**, which means that all life is sacred, and should not be harmed in any way. For this reason, most Hindus are vegetarians, because they do not wish to harm other living beings."

Nino "It sounds kind of extreme but I can relate.... So they just keep being reincarnated indefinitely?"

"It continues until all of the lessons that physical life has to teach have been learned. Hindus believe that **reincarnation**, is influenced by **karma** (How you treat others in this life and previous lives comes back to you materially and physically), and **dharma** (fulfilling one's duty in life). This cycle of reincarnation is repeated over and over again until one finally achieves **moksha**."

Nino surprised, "So are you telling me that this happens to all everyone?"

Gita explains, "As you will find out later on in your tour, this is not true for all souls. Hindus and Buddhists both believe that the sequence of death and rebirth continues until the soul is ready to move on to a state of existence that is very different from anything earthbound souls can imagine. I mean, just think about what you have experienced already in the short time you have been here. Could you have ever dreamed it would be so wonderful?"

"It is magnificent in all ways. I have never heard any words or seen any visions on earth that would have painted a picture of Forever's beauty."

Gita smiles, "One thing that both eastern and western religions do agree on is that there is an immortal part of every human called the soul, and its final destination, as you already can see, is remarkable."

Nino smiles, "Wonderfully remarkable, but so far beyond anything we are familiar with that our language could never adequately describe it, which makes me worry about my part of this plan."

"It's true, Nino. Some of the wonders of Forever will not be sufficiently explained by any form of human language. However, much of what you experience is simply a higher form of an earthly event. So keep it simple, and use the word wonderful a lot. It's the best word you have when you're talking about Heaven."

Nino laughs, "Yes, I keep thinking "wonder-full". I have read on more than one occasion that people who practice Yoga and meditation are able to experience moments of what they describe as "spiritual bliss". Is Yoga an exercise or a religion?"

"In a way, it is both. The word Yoga means union. Earlier you mentioned that you have read the Bhagavad-Gita. The Bhagavad-Gita is a devotional poem that teaches a path that leads to union with God. For the Hindu, the soul is considered a part of, or one with, God. So, if this is the case, then it follows that the ultimate goal is self knowledge. In order to know how we should live, we must first discover who we are. Yoga is a way to achieve self-knowledge."

"So, you're saying that if our soul is one with God, to discover who we really are is to actually unite with God."

"Exactly, Yoga is a physical, mental, and spiritual regiment that aims at healthiness and wholeness within ourselves. Those moments of spiritual bliss are actually moments of contact between ourselves, and the divine reality that is the source of all life. **To know the self, one must refrain from all evil, control the senses, quiet the mind, and practice meditation. Yoga is a path that leads to self knowledge.**"

"The path that leads to God."

"The more true self-knowledge you acquire, Nino, the stronger the union becomes between you and God. The stronger this union becomes the more your life's deeds mirror the God with whom you have united. Krishna, Hindus holy messenger, said that the secret to a successful life is to do ones duty without concern for its outcome."

Nino clarifies, "To do a thing because it is right, and not because we hope to get something out of it."

Gita nods in agreement. "Or hoping to avoid unpleasant consequences. Once you have reached such a level your karma will be very good."

"Karma means "what goes around comes around", right?"

Gita smiles, "Yes, the Hindus believe that the good that we do and the evil that we do will come back to us in another physical life, if not this one. **When we can act free from all preoccupation with ourselves, and out of concern only for what is appropriate and natural, our life's deeds will become a form of worship and sacrifice.**"

"And we will love our neighbors as ourselves. What a beautiful religion. Hinduism always seemed so mysterious to me, but after listening to you explain it, I can say that I to am a Hindu."

"You are Hindu, and a Christian, a Muslim, and a Jew. All of the love based religions are paths that, if followed, will help you to form a union with God. He is All in All. **All humans have a constant yearning for this union. It is this yearning for union with God, that left unrecognized for what it truly is, can leave us chasing an endless stream of meaningless pursuits.** All faiths are designed to transform our inward selves, so that we can achieve harmony with our divine source. Human divinity is at first hidden, but as we draw nearer to God, the divine attributes latent within the soul gradually come into view."

Nino smiles "God is constantly trying to express himself through us, but we won't let him, will we?"

"What you have said in one sentence is the key that unlocks the gates of Heaven. God, this awe-inspiring spirit of love, simply wants you to let him touch the world through your deeds."

As Gita acknowledges the brilliance of Nino's simple statement, Chuck comes walking up with Thomas at his side.

Thomas gives Gita a quick hug. "Well, Gita, you look more beautiful every time I see you."

"Oh, Tommy you're such a big flirt! How are you?"

"Well, aside from losing my shirt to Chuck on the golf course, all is well. I am sorry to say that Nino and I must be moving on."

"Oh, I wish I had some more time to spend with you Nino, but if you understand the Hindu religion which is the mother of all eastern religions, then you will understand its children."

Nino reaches out to Gita with both hands, then turns to Chuck with a pat on the back. "I really learned a lot from both of you. Thank you, Gita, for your all that you have given me, and thank you, Chuck. It has been very educational. I was hoping to hear about Buddha, though."

Gita nods, "Ok Nino, I'll give you the crash course. Buddha gave us his philosophy of the nature of human suffering and its relation to desire in what he called the **Four Noble Truths:**

1. **Life is full of pain and suffering.**
2. **Human desire causes this suffering.**
3. **By putting an end to desire, humans can end suffering.**
4. **Humans can end desire by following the Eightfold Path.**

He believed that the endless cycle of life through reincarnation could come to an end if humans could learn to overcome desire and ..."

Nino interjects, "Oh yeah, I've heard about this. This has to do with that wheel thing right?"

Gita Smiles "That's right. A wheel with eight spokes is symbolic of the **Eighfold Path** which make up the Buddhists path:

1. **Know that suffering is caused by desire.**
2. **Be selfless and love all life.**
3. **Do not lie, or speak without cause.**
4. **Do not kill, steal, or commit other unrighteous acts.**
5. **Do not do things which promote evil.**
6. **Take effort to promote righteousness.**
7. **Be aware of your physical actions, state of mind, and emotions.**
8. **Learn to meditate.**

Nino shrugs, "That seems to go right along with most of what Jesus taught."

Gita laughs, "Buddha is alot like Jesus, minus the pleasurable view of Heaven, the virgin birth, and the crucifixion. Buddha was the king of moderation who believed that if you could tame all of your urges, eventually you would be without need, and this needless state of being he called **Nirvana**. I personally think that he should have enjoyed wine and life a little bit more, and had some fun. Compared to Jesus, Buddha's eternal dream is kind of dullsville isn't it?"

Thomas is surprised by Gita's frankness. "Gita shame on you."

Gita giggling, "Just kidding, Thomas."

Thomas winks, "Let's go Nino, time to leave dullsville behind."

Gita and Chuck share a laugh as their friends depart. "Oh, thanks a lot!" Gita yells. "Goodbye Nino, bye Tommy ..."

"Goodbye," Nino waves. "And thanks again."

Thomas leads Nino back to the woodland trail that he and Chuck had walked along earlier. Our time together is over for now. Good luck my friend, I believe in you Nino, don't forget ... I believe ... I believe

Nino loses himself for a moment before realizing that it's time for him to move on. He looks to Thomas for direction. "So, Thomas where do I go from here?"

"Just stick to the P.O.J. and she'll find you. No matter where you go. Goodbye Nino."

Nino laughs at himself for doubting Doubting Thomas. "Thomas! How do I-"but before he finishes his thought, Thomas disappears overthe horizon. As Nino walks along he is soon in the presence of a beautiful woman. She is the most beautiful woman he has ever seen ...

Author's Note: I used to think that my Christian path was the only one that lead to Heaven. However, Dr. Abul Bayazid, Monsignor St. Gerard Krieg, and (most importantly) my wife Leigh Ann removed my spiritual blindness. These three Holy souls showed me through their words and deeds, that God lives in, and works through, all of the love-based religions. When Gandhi was asked the question "What is your religion?" his answer was simply ... "All". It was his response to this question that led to his eventual assassination. He was killed by people who could not believe that God could live in, and work through any religion other than their own. I implore you my brothers and sisters, please begin treating each other with love, compassion, and tolerance. Judge not, and remember that mercy, not sacrifice, is the heart of the law. The Holy Qur'an states that the greatest act of charity is to "Over look another person's faults." If we can truly put our differences aside, and unite as the holy children of God, then we can bring about the social and political changes needed to direct the United States, and the rest of the world, towards a more peaceful and holy path.

"I AM ALIKE FOR ALL. I KNOW NOT HATE, I KNOW NOT FAVOR." -KRISHNA/THE BHAGAVAD GITA (3,137 BC)

Author's Note #2: I hold Kahill Gibran in the highest esteem and consider him a holy prophet of God. He has greatly influenced my spiritual journey, and this is why you will see his writings periodically throughout the story.

JUDGE NOT, FOR WE ARE ALL GUILTY
It is when your spirit goes wandering upon the wind, that you, alone and unguarded, commit a wrong unto others and therefore

unto yourself. Oftentimes have I heard you speak of one who commits a
wrong as though he were not one of you, but a stranger unto
you and an intruder upon your world. But I say that even as the
holy and the righteous cannot rise beyond the highest which is in
each one of you, so the wicked and the weak cannot fall lower than
the lowest which is in you also. As a single leaf turns not yellow
but with the silent knowledge of the whole tree, so the wrong-doer
cannot do wrong without the hidden will of you all. Any of you
who would punish in the name of righteousness and lay the ax
unto the evil tree, let him see to its roots; And verily he will find
the roots of the good and the bad, the fruitful and the fruitless, all
entwined together in the silent heart of the earth. Only then shall
you know that the erect and the fallen are but one man standing in
twilight between the night of his pigmy-self and the day of his
god-self, And that the corner-stone of the temple is not higher than
the lowest stone in its foundation.
-Kahill Gibran (The Prophet)

"Every night God freest our spirits from the body, so that soul can commu-
nicate with soul. It is also true that wen a person sleeps ... He has gone to
visit his own."
-Jalalu'din Rumi-Kwang & Chandogya Upanishad

CHAPTER 17

▼

"Behold! The Angels said: 'O Mary! Allah hath chosen thee and purified thee—chosen thee above the women of all nations. Behold! The angels said: 'O Mary! Allah giveth thee glad tidings of a word from him; his name will be Messiah Jesus. The son of Mary, held in honor in this world and the Hereafter and of (the company of) those nearest to Allah. He shall speak to the people in childhood and in maturity. And he shall be (of the company) of the righteous.'"
-MUHAMMAD/THE HOLY QUR'AN Surah 3:42-46 (600 AD)

"Do not be frightened Mary, for God has decided to wonderfully bless you. Very soon you will become pregnant with a baby boy, and you are to name him Jesus. He shall be very great, and shall be called the Son of God, and his Kingdom shall never end!"
-Luke 1:30-33

"He is no better than we are. He's just a carpenter, Mary's boy, and a brother of James and Joseph, Judas and Simon. And his sisters live right here among us."
-Mark 6:3

It is no accident that mother and beauty are synonymous in our world. There is no beauty greater to us than the first face we lay eyes on. No one means more to our souls until we have children of our own. A mother's love radiates from every pore of her skin, every strand of hair on her head. A mother's kiss is the first to welcome us and the last to send us on our own journeys. A mother embraces us from many miles away, and we are safe at home in the memory of her arms. Nino's breath is taken away by the sensation of motherly love as his new tour guide approaches him.

She smiles warmly at her visitor. "Hello my son. My name is Mary, I am the mother of Jesus."

Overwhelmed, Nino falls to his knees. He cannot look at her. "It is such an honor to meet you, blessed mother."

Mary gently puts her hand on Nino's cheek and guides his face upward until his eyes meet hers. Lovingly, she speaks to Nino as if speaking to her own little boy. "Nino, I'm not someone to be worshiped. Only God deserves to be worshiped. So please call me Mary."

Nino slowly rises to his feet. Awkward in the presence of such beauty and grace, he can't keep the tears from his eyes. "I'm sorry Mary, you just don't know how much it means to me to be in your presence. I've prayed to you since I was a little boy. I have always envisioned you helping me in times of trouble. Was I wrong to pray to you?"

"Did praying to me help you?"

Nino thinks for a moment, "Yes, I found it very comforting to envision a Heavenly Mother who would intercede on my behalf, a mother who would come to me when I was feeling down."

"Did praying to me help you to feel closer to God and Jesus?" "Yes, it did."

Mary smiles, "Then you were not wrong to pray to me. Praying to me, or any of the other Saints and holy people, although it is not necessary, will never do you any harm. God is your father, and he understands the needs that I and my son, along with the other religious saints and prophets, fulfill. We are more approachable than God. There is something about us that is tangible, and therefore more comforting. Think about when you pray to me. What do you see in your mind's eye?"

Nino sighs, "I always see your face, or what I thought your face looked like?"

"What do you see when you pray to God?" Mary asks.

Nino hesitates. He's not sure how to put it into words. "I feel something in my heart, but I see nothing."

"You see what I mean? God understands that it is nearly impossible for the earth bound soul to comprehend who and what he really is. Once you have found God's path, all that is really important to him is that you stick to the path. If it takes praying to your ancestors like the far eastern peoples of the world, or praying to me and the saints like the Catholics to help you stick to the path, so be it. The truth is that we do our best to answer the prayers that come to us, but we are limited in ways that God is not. As long as you stay on God's path, he is happy. However, you must not confuse prayer with worship."

Nino nestles into Mary's presence as if settling into his mother's lap. He looks up at her with the curious eyes of a child. "You mean like making the person you are praying too equal to God, and worshiping them the same way that you worship God?"

Mary nods. "No one should be worshiped like this but God. It is also important that you never try to make any image that you feel is symbolic of God. It is an insult to God, and it could lead to people worshiping the idol they created. God is beyond the comprehension of the earth bound soul. Even I would have a difficult time describing to you what God actually looks like. I can tell you he's not an old man with a white beard," she laughs, gently.

"I guess he's a little more than that isn't he?"

"I wish I could bring you to him so that you could experience who and what our God really is."

Nino jumps up in anticipation. He would love to meet God! "Why can't you take me to him? Does it have something to do with our plan?"

"Oh no. When Jesus ascended into Heaven, God released his Holy Spirit into the whole world, and in a true sense God was once again accessible to his children. However, God will not fully reveal himself until the Great Game is complete and the Day of Judgment comes. When the judgment is complete, God will lead those who are victorious to the New Jerusalem, where he will dwell amongst his children for all eternity."

"But until then nobody can actually be in his presence?" Nino asks, settling down again with a little disappointment.

"No regular citizen of Forever can see him or be in his immediate presence. Only his Holy Angels, Jesus, me, and the other Heavenly saints and prophets. Everyone else must wait for that glorious day when we are reunited with our father in paradise. Actually living in paradise in the presence of God!" Mary exclaims. "It is an ecstasy that is beyond any dream or longing. Oh Nino, it will truly be Heaven."

"It all sounds so unimaginable, blessed mother. So beautiful." Nino is lost in the very thought of it for a moment. Mary does not grow impatient, though. She just smiles gently and waits for him to speak again. Finally, he comes around. "Mary, going back to worshiping and prayer."

"Yes?"

"What about saying the rosary, or all of the religions that worship Jesus as God?" Nino asks.

"The Holy Rosary is meant to be a form of meditation and reflection on the lives of me and my son. It is not intended to be a prayer to me. The rosary represents what I have done, and what I continue to do for all of my children. I want no one to worship me, and I will accept no worship. As far as those religions which worship Jesus, it was prophesized that this would happen, and if you think about it, it's understandable. **It is not unusual for great religious leaders, once they have died, to be made into Gods by their followers.** Once again, it is the perceived tangibility of Jesus that makes him easier to worship and pray to than God himself. No one understands this basic human need more than Allah. Jesus' instructions to us were to pray to our Heavenly Father in his name. Nowhere in the Bible does he instruct people to pray to him. However, God gave Jesus his spirit in overflowing proportion. So much so, that in seeing Jesus act, and in hearing him speak, you were seeing and hearing God. Jesus did nothing of his own accord. He did only what our father wanted him to do. He was the perfect reflection of God. Therefore, worshiping Jesus is still a compliment to Jehovah. Much like in saying the moonlight is beautiful; you are also complimenting the sun which gives the moon its radiance. God would prefer that you pray to him directly in the name of Jesus Christ. But you will not be punished for not doing so."

"So, the Christian religion should be truly monotheistic," Nino adds. "Why did it drift so far from what Jesus actually taught?"

"Do not forget where Christianity was raised. It was born in Israel, but it was raised and grew into an adult in pagan Rome and Greece. Consequently, many of their pagan views and beliefs were woven into the fabric of the Christianity. These are things that inevitably had to happen in order for the Christian movement to take root."

Nino worried, "Is God angry over this?"

"No, this is not the kind of stuff that upsets God. He knew that this would happen. He knew that everyone would stumble over Jesus. When Jesus said that he would become a stumbling block, he meant for all people. Everyone is stumbling over Jesus. The Jews have not accepted him as the messiah. The Muslims view him as a prophet and refuse to pray in his name, and the Christians have elevated his position to God almighty. All this means that no religion can say "we are right, and everybody else is wrong". The truth is that each religion has within it part of the truth. Once they are all brought together in Forever they will realize that had they united by virtue of their similarities and common origin instead of fighting over their differences and trying to be the "true religion," they could have really found the truth. Like the separate pieces of a mosaic! What may seem coarse and unappealing when viewed by itself is, when united with the other pieces of itself, truly beautiful. The more we can unite with all of God's children, the more loving the world and we become."

"Mary can you explain the trinity to me? I have always struggled with this," Nino admits.

Mary thinks for a moment, "I will use the example of the sun and the moon once again. Let's make the sun symbolic of God, and the moon symbolic of Jesus. The invisible rays of light that come from the sun will be symbolic of the Holy Spirit. The Holy Spirit of God shined onto Jesus, in much the same way as the sun's light shines onto the moon. In seeing the moon's light, you are seeing nothing but the pure reflection of the sun's light. In seeing Jesus, you are seeing the pure reflection of God. As the moonlight travels to the physically dark earth to illumine the fruitful plains, so too did Jesus' light illumine the spiritually dark souls of the world. There you have the trinity. All in all. God, the Holy Spirit, and the Messiah. All separate, but the same. Mysterious, but when analyzed, very simple. Everything that comes from God is simple. He wants you to understand. Satan, on the other hand, wants to make things complicated. He wants you to be confused. Confusion eventually leads to doubt, and doubt can eventually leads to faithlessness."

"The trinity really is easy to comprehend when you think of it that way." Nino exclaims.

"Mary, I know that prayers really work, because I have experienced the power of prayer in my own life. But how do they work? I mean, do you really hear every prayer that is said to you? There must be someone in the world right now who is praying to you? How can you be talking to me, and listening to them?"

"Nino," Mary smiles, "your little friend Papino. Does he have to ask you for what he needs, or do you give him what he needs out of understanding?"

Nino is startled, "Papino? How do you know about Papino?"

"I have spent time with you in your pipe before. But answer my question."

"I just know what he needs. I've been with him a long time, and I know what he likes. I know what's good for him."

Mary smiles warmly, "And I know what you need. I know what all of my children need, even more than they do themselves. I pray to God on behalf of all his children constantly, every day and every night. Jesus and I are constantly in the presence of God on behalf of all of the earth bound souls."

"So what you're saying is that you don't have to hear individual prayers, because you already are doing everything you can for each of us … So why are prayers important?"

Mary explains, "Prayers are important for a number of reasons. First and foremost, prayers are proof of faith in God. When a soul that has true faith prays, the essence of the prayer shines like a glowing cloud of light. As God looks down upon the world, he sees these prayers and it gives him hope. This is important because it is God's hope that holds back his wrath, and allows him to remain merciful and compassionate. The prayers of the faithful, along with their deeds, have without question extended the Great Game."

"Are individual prayers ever listened to?"

"Are you kidding? All of the time! As you suggested, I cannot listen to all of the prayers that come to me all at once. But God can! He is like a giant telephone switchboard, only there is no limit to the number of calls he can receive."

"So God hears every prayer."

"Every faithful prayer," Mary corrects. "If you do not have faith, your prayer does not reach God. For example, If you want to make a local call using a pay phone you have to pay a dollar. No dollar, no call, correct?"

Nino nods in agreement, "That's right."

Mary continues, "Also the farther away that you want to call, the more money it costs. With God, faith is the money you need to get your prayer through. No faith, no connection. The greater the miracle you are praying for, the more faith you must have. Another important thing to know about prayer is the importance of group prayer, when two or more people gather together to pray for a common, unselfish reason. These prayers receive special attention. The more people you get together, the larger and more luminous their prayer cloud becomes, and the more of God's Holy Spirit the prayer attracts."

"Jesus said whenever two or more of you gather together in my name, I will be there with you. Is that what you mean?"

Mary nods in agreement, "Any time groups of people gather together to pray, the spirit of Jesus is there with them."

"What if these people are Muslims or Jews?" Nino asks.

"The spirit of Jesus is the spirit of God. For those who believe it is Jesus to whom they are praying, it is Jesus. For those who believe it is Allah or Yahweh, the same is also true. Jesus works behind the scenes for all God's children, whether they believe in him or not. Jesus is always going to God with the prayers of the faithful, and more importantly the unfaithful. He is the high priest and Messiah for all people. It is his position in the universe whether people recognize this or not."

"Jesus said if a person had faith the size of a mustard seed that he could order a mountain to throw itself into the sea. Why is it so hard to have faith?"

Mary loves Nino's eager curiosity. She is a natural teacher, and she is proud of all the prior knowledge this particular pupil brings to class. She smiles upon Nino as she answers him. "When you are a child and you learn about God and Jesus, you have complete faith. A child believes that anything is possible, Santa Claus, the Easter Bunny, and so on. If your mother or father tells you something is true you believe them whole-heartedly. However, when you become an adult you begin to doubt. You begin to question everything. You begin to see that much of what you believed in as a child was foolishness and fairy tales. You begin to see that your parents are just ordinary people who have faults, and who don't really know it all. God understands how hard it is for the earthbound souls to hang onto their faith. He just hopes that as time goes by, your relationship with him eventually gets back to that of a parent and a child. Life on the planet Earth is hard. Every soul experiences mental, physical, and spiritual pain of different magnitudes and durations all throughout their life. Even though your faith is weak, the fact that you continue to believe in God proves that your faith, weak though it may be, is loyal. It is true. God is spiritually hurt by those souls who are fair-weather friends or believers. This type of soul does much harm in the physical, as well as the spiritual, world. Nino would you like to hear a story?

Nino smiles, "Yes, of course."

When I was a little girl one day some Roman soldiers came through our town and were very disrespectful to everyone they met. One of them pushed my mother out of his way, and she stumbled and fell. I can remember seeing the tears roll down my mothers face, and I got very angry. I ran to get tell my father what had happened and he could see that I was very upset. I was crying, and I asked my father "Abba, how come God lets our people get so badly mistreated? Why doesn't he do something? Why does he just sit and watch us as we go through life's struggles? My father took into his big strong hands, and he petted my head and said. "It is written that Jehovah is like a refiner and purifier of gold and silver. Your great great grandfather was a silversmith. I can remember watching him as a boy. He would take a piece of silver and hold it in the middle of the fire where the flames where the hottest. The heat of the flames would burn away all of the impurities. Not only did Grandpa have to sit there holding the silver, but he had to keep his eyes on the silver the entire time that it was in the fire. Fore he knew if he were to keep it in flames even a moment too long, the silver would be ruined. I know dear child that sometimes it seems as though you are all alone in the world. But you are never alone. God is always watching you very closely, for you are far more precious to him than gold or silver." Then I asked him this final question. "Yes, but daddy, how does God know when we have been purified enough? How many tears have to fall?" My father chuckled and he continued. "I asked your grandfather a similar question about his silver. "Grandfather, I said, how do you know when the silver is fully purified and refined? Oh, that's easy. **When I see my image in it, I know its purification is complete."**

Nino shakes his head and grins to himself, "That's a beautiful story Mary. That's what Jesus mean when he said our souls will be tested as gold is tested by fire, isn't it?"

Mary nods, "Yes, the Muslims call this *Augnee Pawreekhha,* **the fire-test for the soul. As life's trials and tribulations mount, the soul must do its best to remain faithful until the end.** Be assured that our loving father will never keep you in the Great Game any longer than he must. When life gets hard we must continue to walk the path of love. We must remain faithful in Jehovah and his promise of Heaven…. Remember what happens to the character Job, from the Bible."

Nino nods and scratches his head with understanding. His mother has made all the mysteries clear for him. "So the path that leads to Forever is to love God with all of our heart, soul, mind, and strength, to repent for our sins, and to love our neighbor as ourselves. The fire-test of the soul is that no matter what happens to us, we must never denounce or curse God, as Job's friends advised him to do. Through all things we must remain faithful and true."

Mary smiles proudly,"Yes, Nino. This is all that God hopes for. The book of Job is very important in that it shows how Satan operates. He attacks your faith, he causes your problems, and he hopes that in the end you will either reject God or believe that God has rejected you. All God wants is for you to remain faithful. Just stick to the path no matter what. All that Satan wants is for you to lose your faith and hope."

Nino clarifies, "Let me see if I have this right. If we stick to this path, although Satan may be able to hurt us mentally, and physically, he will never be able to hurt us spiritually. Correct?"

"That's right. He cannot harm your souls in any way. He may be able to scare you, or cause us to stumble along the way, but he cannot prevent you from returning home."

Nino encouraged, **"So the only power Satan has over us is that which we give him."**

Mary happy that Nino understands, "Exactly, the loyal soul that sticks to the path until the game is over, in Gods eyes, is the most precious thing in the entire universe. It is also the most powerful of all God's creation."

"The most powerful?" Nino asks.

Mary explains, "If you align yourself with God, nothing can harm you. Satan and his demons will flee at your command, and God and his angels will come at your request. If this is the case, whom should you ever fear? If God is with you then who can defeat you?"

"And what about you, and Jesus? How are you with us?"

"We are always in contact with your Guardian Angels. They ask us to intervene on your behalf, when you lack the faith needed to attract the sufficient amount of Holy Spirit. Remember when Jesus got upset with his apostles because they told him they were unable to cure the possessed man? They were able to perform some miracles, but not everything they attempted to do, because they did not have enough faith. Even though they had spiritual strength, they still needed Jesus to come to their aid.... Jesus and I visit you at crucial moments of your life, times of sickness, crisis, death, temptation, and times when your faith is low. Those who walk the path are never alone. I know it may seem like it at times, but at least one spiritual being is with you always. The more faith you have, the brighter your prayer cloud shines, and the more Holy Spirit you receive."

"Does God's Holy Spirit hear the prayers? How does it work?"

Mary makes clear, "God's Holy Spirit not only hears the prayers, but God himself sees your prayers. They float into the Heavens of the spiritual realm, and fill this holy void with an exotic beauty and fragrance."

Nino intrigued, "Beauty and fragrance?"

Mary continues,"Prayers are the true incense of God. This is why incense was burned in the original holy temple of the Jews. It is symbolic of how God actually experiences prayer. A prayer, like the smoke from incense, floats upward toward the Heavenly Temple of God. The fragrance of a prayer is sweet to God. If you could see what God sees as he looks down at the earth from his holy mountain in the recesses of northern Forever, you would see billions of beautiful multicolored shimmering little clouds of different shapes and sizes slowly drifting upward towards the true heavenly temple. It is truly a fascinating sight. The prayers of children instantaneously attract

God's Holy Spirit. All other prayers attract the Holy Spirit based on the amount of faith that the person or persons have that are saying them. As I said, the more faith you have, the more of the Holy Spirit you receive. In addition, you also have prayers that come from the Guardian Angels."

"Guardian Angels pray?" Nino asks.

"When Guardian Angels pray it is because a soul either has no faith, or because they have very little faith left. For example, a depressed soul may be thinking of taking his life. The Guardian Angel tries its best to help the soul. They speak to them on a spiritual level. They work together with other Guardian Angels to bring people into your life that will help you. They bring books, articles, movies, and so on that will help enlighten you, and give you hope. For those souls who are walking the path, there is no such thing as good luck. You are simply blessed. Sometimes your angels are unsuccessful and they feel they need me or my son to get involved. God handles all of the prayers of the faithful, and Jesus and I, along with a host of many other Heavenly Angels and saints, handle the prayers of the Guardian Angels. As always, we come to help those who lack faith."

Mary pauses thoughtfully for a moment, and then takes Nino's hand in one of hers. "I can remember one particular evening not so long ago when a faithfully beautiful prayer caught my eye, and brought me to an abandoned factory pipe. I came beside your mattress and held you in my arms and told you to have faith. I reminded you that God loves you, and that killing yourself would be a terrible waste of a lifetime."

Nino's jaw hits the floor as the night comes rushing back to him. "I remember feeling so bad that night. I was really going to go through with it. I actually believed that I was supposed to die jumping off the George Washington Bridge. I was so depressed and despondent. All of a sudden I felt a warm and comforting feeling come over me. A voice inside my head said "Live on Nino, live on. Believe and have faith in God. Believe in yourself, and never give up." It was that night that I decided to live until I die. I made vow to never consider the suicide option again."

Mary gently squeezes Nino's hand. "It makes me very happy to hear you say these things Nino. How ironic it is to me that a man who once thought so little of his life is now in a position to possibly save millions of souls."

"I know what you mean. When I think of it I get chills. Just imagine, if I had given up at that low point in my life." Nino gets lost in thought once more, and Mary waits patiently. Finally, he snaps back to the present, and his questions start up again.

"Mary, could you please explain a little more to me about God, and the Holy Spirit. I mean what is God?"

This seems a huge question, but Mary gives a simple answer. "God is spirit. He always existed, and he always will exist. He dwells in those souls who draw near to him. He is All In All. God is especially interested in the lives of little children because he knows that childhood is where the foundation of your spiritual faith is laid. God is able to send his holy spirit out from himself so that it can travel anywhere in the universe. Just like the sun is able to send its light. The stronger your faith, the more power you are given through the Holy Spirit. The bright clouds of prayer attract the spirit of God. The more faithful the prayer the brighter the prayer cloud, and the more holy spirit a situation or an individual receives. It is possible, as in the case of Jesus, that your earthly faith in God can become so strong that you no longer need any spiritual being to intercede for you. You will receive God's Holy Spirit in an overflowing portion. You will become one with God, and you will be able to act as God acts. God's will and your own will become one, and therefore every prayer is answered. The reason Angels and other holy beings have to intercede for you is because of your lack of faith. The stronger your faith the less we have to intercede. This is why a child's prayers go directly to God. Their faith is strong. In a child there exists no doubt."

"This is all so extraordinary. And at the same time it all makes perfect sense to me. The people will be happy to learn that we have so many kind and loving souls working for us behind the scenes, in the spiritual realm. Mary, speak to me a little more about our Guardian Angels. How does that whole system work?"

"Every soul that enters the Great Game is given their very own Guardian Angel. This Angel is their spiritual guardian and adviser. It is what you call a conscience."

"Like Jiminy Cricket?"

"Not quite," Mary laughs, "but kind of."

Nino wonders, "I always thought that a conscience was made up of memories from childhood. You know, things that we were taught growing up."

Mary puts into plain words, "These memories that you speak of, this collection of what is right and wrong that is taught to you by the significant people in your life and lessons that you learned from your own life experiences, definitely do guide your behavior. If you were raised by good parents who walked the path, then your conscience and your mind will work in unison. Your memories provide you with the facts as they are in your mind. Your conscience is the voice of your Guardian Angel warning you of impending spiritual, and sometimes physical, danger."

"Can our Guardian Angels keep bad things from happening to us, or stop us from making bad decisions?" Nino asks.

Mary saddened, "Unfortunately, the answer is no. They can make you feel uneasy by what they are telling your soul on an unconscious or spiritual level. They can also manipulate things physically in a way that will give you an opportunity to get out of a situation. But they cannot physically prevent you from doing something that they know will harm you. You are born with the right to free will, and nothing can interfere with that."

"Do our Guardian Angels stay with us all of our lives?"

"Your Angels stay with you until you are about 16 or 17 years old, the age of understanding. The Guardian Angels of children have constant and swift access to God, and woe to the person responsible for causing any of these little ones to lose faith. Once you become an adult you will retain your Guardian Angel, only if you choose to follow the path. This does not mean that you have to live a perfect life. All it means is that you recognize the path, and that you are trying your best to follow it. People who turn their backs on God, or who never do come to believe in him, are left unprotected. They become easy targets for the demonical attacks, and usually become enslaved to the vices and evil temptations of this world."

Nino saddened, "Mary, why do bad things happen to people, especially the children? Why do children get cancer, die in accidents, or become crippled? Why does God allow this to happen?"

Mary's heart aches, because she knows how these earthly events spiritually crush so many earth souls. "This is the hardest question to answer, but maybe you'll understand, Nino. There is a reason for everything. Reasons that earth bound souls trapped in a mortal body would have trouble dealing with. God is concerned with your spiritual growth and development. Old age is not counted by the number of years that you have lived, the number of gray hairs on your head, or the number of life times you have spent in purgatory."

Nino startled, "Purgatory? There really is a place called purgatory?"

Mary explains, "Purgatory is not a place. It is a soul that must live another life time to atone for unforgiving sins, and/or to reach a higher level of spiritual development. Remember the parable in the Bible in which Jesus says to make peace with your accuser before you get to the Judge, because if you are found guilty you will be placed in a debtor's cell until you have paid the adequate price for your crime?"

Nino nods understingly, and Mary continues.

"The earth sees a child, but this child's soul could be very old as far as the number of earth bound years it has lived. When a soul that is in purgatory has finally suffered enough and learned enough, they are taken from the Great Game."

Nino astonished, "You mean that all the children that die or are sick are souls that are in purgatory?"

"Not all of them, but quite a few."

"What about the bad things that happen to those who are not in Purgatory?"

Mary explains, "The goal of every soul is to return to Forever. No child is ever taken unless they are going to paradise. Children and innocent people get killed, injured, and seriously ill all of the time, but it is the living and the caretakers that truly suffer. The reality is that all suffering is the result of sin, and all of the sin in this world is caused by the Devil and his demons. They convince people to do bad, selfish things, and these evil deeds have a ripple effect that is often very far reaching …

However, God is the master of taking bad situations and turning them into something good on a spiritual level. God is always surveying the lives his children and all of his living creations. No one can die without His knowledge. Not even a sparrow can fall to the ground without Allah's awareness."

Nino somewhat irritated, "But if God sees what's happening, then why doesn't he intervene?"

Mary understanding Nino's frustration,"God always intervenes only the earth bound souls don't recognize it. Sometimes he decides to take a truly holy soul out of the Great Game, because he does not like what he sees coming in that soul's future. For example, how often in your New York City do you hear about innocent bystanders that get killed by a bullet that was intended for someone else?"

Nino shudders, "It happens several times a week in our city. Why just the other day a wonderful young man named Elvin Cruz was killed right in front of his house! His House! Think of the pain his poor mother and family must feel. How can anything good come from that Mary? How? ..." Nino thinks of the mother and children that he accidently killed, and his eyes well up with tears.

Mary feels Nino's pain, but does not address it specifically, "I know it's hard to envision, but here's an example of how it works. God sees a good and holy boy who is associating with souls who are troubled, and walk not the path. God in his infinite wisdom knows that if this child continues his associations with these troubled souls, that eventually he may become corrupt, and in the process possibly lose his place in paradise."

Nino tries to understand, "So God causes the child to get killed in order to save him?"

Mary describes the way it is, "God does not cause any child to die. The rules of free will that exist in the Great Game are never compromised for any reason. The opportunity to take the child presents itself, and God in some cases decides it would be best to bring the child home. The innocent one whose life appears to be taken by the stray bullet is actually rescued, and any damage that Satan would have been able to do to his soul is stopped.

Nino responds, "So rather than letting this spiritual destruction to occur, God snatches the child from the midst of inequity thus saving his soul, and possibly the souls of countless others." Nino becomes heated as he thinks about the scenario. "But, what about the family he leaves behind?"

Mary calmly, "The earthly struggle that they will face, although it will be difficult, is a small sacrifice when one is considering the eternity of an immortal soul. You must also realize that their suffering is not caused by

God, but by the sin that resulted in the death of their son. Nino, I cannot over stress the negative ripple effect of sin. It is so far reaching and damaging that it can actually effect many, many generations. Satan can take one sin and do an unbelievable amount of spiritual damage."

"You mean like if the murdered boy's family seeks revenge?"

Mary saddened, "Yes. Vengeance only leads to more vengeance. Thus the sins of the one are compounded, and magnified. Vengeance is a cycle that never ends. It is a poison that embitters the avenging soul, and does nothing but provide little bursts of percieved solace. The reality is that there is only one thing that the brokenhearted can do to compensate for the death of a loved one, and that is to be merciful to the person who took their life. Mercy and forgiveness are the only elixirs that will heal their soul."

Nino understands, "Vengeance is a terrible cycle. I've seen firsthand what it can do to people and to entire countries.".... Nino thinks for a moment and then continues. "Mary are there any other reasons God would take an innocent soul?"

Mary frowns, "You must get people to stop seeing physical death as a punishment, or something that is always bad. Remember Nino, God cannot have everybody who believes in him living to ripe old ages, or the unfaithful would begin to catch on. People would come to have faith in God for the wrong reasons. So this is another reason why bad things are sometimes allowed to happen to good people. Occasionally he simply takes the soul because the opportunity presents itself. When he makes such a decision, all of the soul's family and friends in Forever rejoice, because they know that the soul is now safe for eternity. The earthbound souls, in their grief, often curse God and say "how could he let this happen". They fail to see that it is Satan who causes all that is bad to happen in this world. For example, Satan sets into motion the factors which cause a child to get leukemia by urging a rich company owner to save himself millions of dollars by illegally dumping radioactive waste in a company owned land fill. Eventually the local water supply is polluted, and the children start to get cancer. The company owner has high priced lawyers who prove the dumping was accidental. The man gets off with a fine, and the people end up being mad, not at the man, or Satan, but with God."

"I'm trying to follow you, Mary, but why does it seem that the good often die young, and the miserable people seem to live to be very old?"

Mary nods in understanding, "I know it may sometimes appear that this is the way things work, but actually it is not the case. However, God in his mercy does allow the evil to live as long as he can bare it. He keeps hoping that they will change their ways."

"So when a young person dies we should be happy, because they have returned to Forever, and they are victorious."

Mary smiling but melancholy, "As strange as it might seem, and as sad as you will be at the loss of a child, yes. If you could see the big picture. The spiritual picture. Yes, you would be happy. Very, very happy."

"And those in Purgatory?"

"They keep on being recycled until their debt is paid, and their learning is complete. Remember, Purgatory is about learning and spiritual enlightenment, but it is also about punishment. If you end up in Purgatory you have to experience a certain amount of suffering to atone for the suffering you caused during your life. You really do reap what you sow. What goes around, really does come around."

Nino astonished, "You mean we can just keep living life after life, so that it really doesn't matter if we get it right the first time. We can relax in knowing that we will get another chance."

"You must remember one important fact. Jesus said nobody knows the day or the hour when God will end all things. And nobody does. It will come upon you suddenly, like a thief in the night."

"So what are you saying?"

Mary sighs. She has to make her message clear so Nino will get through to the people of earth. She chooses her words carefully. "If you live carelessly, thinking that you will get another chance to live a life, and the Great Game comes to a close, your soul will not be allowed to enter into Forever and celebrate in the great wedding feast of the Lamb. Only those whose robes are spotless will be allowed to remain at this spectacular celebration. Your robe, of course, is your soul. If you have not paid your debt, and learned all that you must learn, then your soul will not be spotless. You will be banished to the-"

Nino interrupts. "The outer darkness?"

"Yes, for eternity. Just like a basketball game. When that final buzzer sounds, your chance to score points is over. When time expires in the Great Game, and Jehovah sends his holy Angels to gather his children from the four corners of the world, the opportunity to improve the state of your soul is gone forever. Another important fact about Purgatory is that each time that you have to live another life, the situation that you are born into and your life circumstances, including your temptations, becomes more difficult. Most of the time a soul that has to be recycled is put back into the same family line from which they were born. Only now they are the sons and daughters of their children, or their children's children."

Nino sees the meaning of real Karma, "Man, you really do reap what you sow don't you?"

"Just remember Nino, God loves you. He wants you to be victorious. He'll forgive you for all of your transgressions, but ultimately he must be completely just. The soul that is sentenced to purgatory goes to a prison that it created by the words and deeds of its previous life. That's why the final state of the soul is often worse than what it started out as. You must emphasize the point that Purgatory is a tough sentence, and one that should be avoided at all costs. **You must live your life like it is your final opportunity to return to Forever. Live each day like it is the final day that you will be alive. The Muslims pray each prayer like it is the last prayer they will ever be allowed to make. This is very wise, because no one knows the hour at which they will be called.**"

Nino shaken, "Purgatory is not at all what I envisioned it to be. I always thought it was a place that you had to stay at for awhile, and then were allowed to go to Heaven. You know, kind of like summer school … I understand the part about having to stay until you have learned all that you are supposed to learn, but why must you stay longer than you need to? Doesn't that give Satan more opportunity to steal the soul back again?"

Mary explains, "The punishment side of Purgatory is similar to an earthly jail. For example, let's say a person murders someone and gets sentenced to 20 years in prison. Let's also assume that at first the person has no remorse for his crime. This criminal may eventually, through counseling and imprisonment, come to see that what he did was really wrong, and ask God and the people he hurt to forgive him. If he is genuinely contrite, he will be forgiven by Jehovah. However, this enlightenment does not mean that his sentence should now be cut from 20 years to, let's say, 10 years. The sin he committed caused pain and suffering in the world, and that pain must be atoned for by the individual who caused it. You reap what you sow. And you're right, having to stay in Purgatory until your sentence is up does give Satan more time to, as you said, steal your soul back. This is just one more reason not to want to go to Purgatory. It really magnifies the problems of the Great Game, and makes it that much harder to be victorious."

"I'm beginning to see what you mean. It's like there is the risk that an imprisoned criminal could actually become worse instead of better."

Mary very serious, "That's right. So remember Nino, Purgatory is just a step away from hell."

"I understand the reason for the punishment side. It's just scary to think about those who don't make it. I mean, at least they're trying. An eternity in the outer darkness or Hell just seems so harsh. What if the soul is merciful, won't it receive mercy?"

Mary enlightens Nino, "If the soul has learned to be merciful, and forgiving, then the soul has discovered the path. No soul that discovers the path will be banished to the outer darkness. Remember Nino, these souls in purgatory have not found the path. They have never learned to love or to care about others as much as they care about themselves. To a large degree, this is what will make Forever an eternal paradise. Every soul that you encounter will be truly loving. God knows that one corrupt soul can threaten the established order."

"You mean like one bad apple can spoil the whole bunch." Nino asks.

"Well, in a way. I mean, look at what Satan did. He didn't spoil the whole bunch, but look at the harm he caused, and continues to cause. It will hurt God to banish those souls to the outer darkness, but he is not willing to risk the chance of history repeating itself. It's like curing cancer. The surgeon must be sure to remove all traces of the cancer. He must irradiate and medicate the infected area to the point of over kill, because he knows that all it takes is one bad cell that slips away to start the process all over again."

"I never thought of it like that. Why risk the chance of infecting Forever with any form of negativity, no matter how tiny? ... What about the soul in

Purgatory that finds the path, but is unable to complete the necessary length of his sentence? You know, the punishment side."

"These souls will all be admitted into Forever. Finding the path is the most important part of Purgatory. Allah is supremely merciful and compassionate. All who can be saved will be saved. All souls that are in Purgatory have been given every benefit of the doubt. They have been helped by some of the most glorious souls and Angels in Heaven, including me and even Jesus himself. They have been given endless opportunities and countless second chances. So believe me Nino, as sad as it will be, those who are not victorious in the end will have had every opportunity to be successful. I know this might sound a little cold, but those who fail to find the path don't deserve to spend an eternity in paradise. By their life deeds, they have set the stage for many souls to fail. It becomes increasingly hard for souls born into these family trees to find the path. Family behavioral cycles are very hard break. It is a very sad situation."

Nino wonders, "Mary, let me ask you this. Let's say that a soul somehow does make it to Forever from one of these bad family trees. Is there anything they can do to help their relatives?"

Mary beams with happiness, "Oh yes, I am glad you reminded me. A soul who is victorious in the Great Game can choose to join the Heavenly Red Cross."

Nino can't help laughing. "You're kidding me, right? The red cross!"

Mary smiles. "Remember, much of what you have on earth has a Heavenly origin. Some souls volunteer to go back through the Great Game, as you said, to help their relatives. Some souls simply want to go back for additional learning, or for the greater good of all souls."

"Are these souls like Angels when they go back?"

"No. They are just like any other soul in the Great Game. They have no special powers, and no knowledge of Forever."

Nino worried, "Then aren't they taking a tremendous risk?"

"Well, first of all, their eternities are already secured and nothing they do can jeopardize that. Secondly, Satan and his demons recognize these souls by a special aura that can only be seen by spiritual beings, and they are not allowed to influence or possess them in any way. These souls are also given a Guardian Angel for the duration of their life. They will have wisdom and faith even if all those about them do not. Haven't you ever met someone and said to yourself, 'How did someone so good come from such a miserable family?'"

Nino chuckles. "Yes, lots of times. Hah, isn't that something. My-my-my. So hopefully this good person might be able to rub off on those around them. Kind of like that character Meat Head trying to change Archie, on that TV show All In The Family. I know you probably don't watch TV up here, but I know what you mean."

Mary laughs. "And I know what you mean. That is a good example."

"You watch TV?" Nino asks, surprised.

Mary smiles,"No, but my children do, now and at the hour of their death! So, I can't help but see bits and pieces of a lot of different shows and movies while I am spending time with them."

"Now and at the hour of our death? Mary, you made a joke!"

Mary gently laughs,"Why does that surprise you? Nino, we are all the same. All children of the same father. Some of us have just been called into greater roles of service than others during our earthly lives. You won't find anybody on your tour who doesn't have a good sense of humor, a taste for good food, and who doesn't enjoy soul touching. We are all the same Nino. Everybody who finds the path is unique, but very similar." Mary takes Nino's and leads him along a smooth emerald path into a tiny glen filled with beautiful wind sculpted waterfalls flowing over topaz and sapphire colored musical stones. The view is breathtaking, and the music is the most soothing that Nino has ever heard …

"The real religion of the world comes from women much more than from men-from mothers most of all, who carry the key of our souls in their bosoms."
-Oliver Wendell Holmes

CHAPTER 18

▼

"<u>I am Gabriel! I stand in the very presence of God. It was He who sent me to you with this good news. Therefore my words will certainly come true at the proper time. For every promise from Allah shall surely come true.</u>"
-Excerpts form The Book Of Luke 1:19-37 (The Holy Angel Gabriel's Speech Zacharias)

"Suddenly his face began to shine with glory, and his clothing became dazzling white, far more glorious than any earthly process could ever make it! Then Elijah and Moses appeared and began talking with Jesus.
-Mark 9:3-4

Nino is amazed, "Mary are those rocks actually making music."

Mary smiles, "Yes, in Heaven all interaction is filled with rhythm and music. Even the flowers say to the groove. The symphony that we are hearing is actually being created by the interaction that is taking place between the wind, the water, and the rocks. Doesn't it sound lovely?

Nino smiles and sighs, "Yes, it's so peaceful." Nino drifts off for a moment, and then wonders. "Mary, what about Jesus? Was he different as a child? I mean … Um, what I'm trying to say is, was the Great Game fixed for Jesus? I mean was he incapable of sinning?"

"I know a lot of people think that Jesus and I were above all sin. But, the truth is that we had to find the path just like any other souls. If Jesus was incapable of sinning or being tempted, then what did he overcome? How could he be an example to follow, if his human existence was altered in some way?"

Nino is relieved to hear Mary say what he believed, "I have always felt that way. In deifying Jesus they actually took away from all that he truly accomplished during his life."

"Exactly."

"Mary, can you tell me a little bit about your life with Jesus when he was young? You know, some of the stuff that's not in the Bible."

Mary pleased, "I'll be glad to Nino. I'll tell you what. I'm not sure how much time we have left, and I'm also not sure exactly what you want to know. So you just go ahead and ask me anything you like in the time we have left, and don't worry about embarrassing or offending me. Just ask whatever you like."

Nino grows a little nervous, not sure it will really be okay to ask everything he wants to know. He figures he should start at the beginning. "What was it like for you when you found out you were going to be the mother of the Messiah?"

Mary laughs, much to Nino's surprise. "Can you imagine the position I was in? I was engaged to be married, I went away to my aunt's, and came back with the story that the Angel Gabriel appeared to me and told me that I have been selected by God to be the mother of the Messiah, and that I am miraculously pregnant by the power of the holy spirit. What would you say to your fiancé if she came home with such a wild story?"

Nino laughs nervously, "I see what you mean. I would have had a hard time believing you, so Joseph must have been miserable. I guessing he didn't believe your story, did he?"

"How can you blame him for not believing me and being upset at first? Thank God that Joseph was a good man! Even before Gabriel told him it was true, all he was concerned about was my well being. It was really an unpleasant time in my life. I mean part of me was ecstatic that I was going to be the mother of the world's Savior, but the bigger part of me was very scared and unsure of how this was all going to unfold. Don't forget Nino, I was only a young girl."

"How old were you?"

"Sixteen years old."

Nino shocked, "Sixteen years old, my goodness, you were just a kid!"

Mary raises her eyebrows, "You're telling me! But like I said, thank God Joseph was a good man. He was a good husband and father to all my children."

Nino shakes his head, "So you really did have other children?"

Mary elucidates, "I was a mother like any other mother, and a wife like any other wife. God said that people for ever more would call me blessed, and they have. Unfortunately quite often when you are made into a saint, the people try to take away your human qualities, which is understandable, but at the same time disheartening, because it takes away from what Jesus and I truly went through. I had to learn what it was like to be a wife and mother, just as Jesus had to learn what it was like to be a father. Jesus had four brothers and two sisters. Joseph was much older than I was, and he died when Jesus was a little over fourteen years old. Jesus had become a decent carpenter by then, and being the oldest boy he had the responsibility of making money to feed his family. In a way, by being the oldest son of a Jewish widow, he also learned what it was like to be a husband. This was a necessary part of his training."

"So, Jesus was raised pretty much like any other Jewish boy?"

"Yes, in every way. He was a normal little boy in all ways except one."

Nino curious, "And what was that?"

"Jesus had wisdom beyond his years. He had a fantastic memory. He would remember word for word readings from the Torah. However, even more impressive was the opinions he formulated about these sacred writings. Even as a child, he spoke with authority about the words of Jehovah."

"Did you tell anyone else that Jesus was the Messiah, and how he was miraculously conceived?"

"No, I was instructed to let things unfold according to God's will. The only people that I spoke with about this were Joseph, my cousin Anna, the mother of John the Baptist, and our village Rabbi. I wasn't even allowed to talk to Jesus about who he was and how he was conceived."

"Why?"

"A big part of Jesus' mission was that he experience the fullness of life. If he was truly going to be a merciful and compassionate King and High Priest, then he would have to be able to completely relate to the human experience.

He had the same hopes, dreams, and fears that all little boys have. He went through all of the different stages of development, and gradually grew into a fine young man. His father taught him the trade of being a carpenter, and Jesus was a fine craftsman."

"What did Jesus look like? How was he built?"

"Jesus really wasn't a particularly handsome young man. Although I thought he was beautiful." Mary smiles. "He really looked nothing like the beautiful pictures that were painted of him, but he sure does now. The poor thing had his grandfather's nose. As far as his physique is concerned he was kind of wiry. He didn't have an exceptional build, but he was very, very strong. Like the Bible said, there was really nothing to attract you to him, except his words, and his personality. Jesus was always a warm and loving soul. A very sweet little boy."

"What about girls? I mean if he really was like any other boy, then he must have had some interest in girls." Nino pries, feeling a little more bold.

Mary remembers, "Jesus had a girlfriend in whom he showed some interest as a teenager. He had the same appreciation for females as any other teenage male. He had to experience the pull of human sexual attraction, so that he could learn how to overcome it. However, his time to spend pursuing girls was very limited, due to the fact that he was raising a family, and working long hours as a carpenter. To my knowledge, he only kissed one girl in his life. But it must have been some kiss, because it was a fond memory of his. One of which he spoke of even as an adult."

Nino grins, "It sounds like Jesus got a little taste of what it feels like to be in love."

"I think he did, but it was an innocent kind of love. Not the kind that exists today in your sexually permissive society. As Jesus got older he began to see how Satan used the sexual pull to destroy families, and to cause unwanted children to be brought into the world. We had many long talks about the difference between love and lust."

"Jesus said that just thinking about adultery is the same as doing it. I never agreed with this. Why should someone who only thinks about doing something be as guilty as the person who actually commits the sin?" Recalls Nino.

"What he actually said was "to look at a woman with lust in your heart is to have already committed adultery with her in your soul." Of all of the teachings that Jesus gave his followers, this one I am certain came from what he learned from his mother. Once you allow yourself to look lustfully upon a woman, the mind will soon begin to fantasize and dream. Once this happens the mind starts to move you to obtain the object of your desire. The human sexual need is the strongest of all desires. Why? Because it is tied in with intimacy, and confused with, and sometimes is, love. Making love to the point of orgasm is pleasing to both body and soul. At the height of a human sexual encounter the souls very briefly touch. The physical gratification united with the spiritual gratification makes this the most powerful force known to the earthbound soul. We are not unlike God, in that we are capable of loving everyone that we meet. In the recesses of our mind we have the memory of the way things used to be in paradise. We long to touch all souls, without restriction. However, this is not a part of Gods earthly plan."

Nino sighs as he remembers,"That soul touch is certainly the most gratifying pleasure I have ever experienced," Nino says. "It truly is much more satisfying than making love. It seemed to warm my total being. I don't really have the words to describe it. It was like I was totally surrounded or encapsulated in love. It was like love was light, and that light made every cell in my body have its own little orgasm, or lovegasm. It was just so wonderful!" Nino realizes he has gone off on a tangent. "Forgive me Mary if I'm offending you talking so freely about this. It's just-"

Mary unoffended, "It really is just like you have described it, Nino. The soul touch is the blessing that comes from the gift of pure love, a gift with no strings attached, or hidden agendas. A love so pure that it would not possess, nor would it be possessed. In Heaven, love is sufficient unto love. However, what is commonplace in Forever, is extremely rare for an earthbound soul. Very few souls that have ever played in the Great Game have reached a point of spiritual enlightenment at which they could purely love another soul. Jesus is the only soul I have ever known that could do it. It is very difficult for a man to love a woman or a woman to love a man in simply a friendly way. The physical sexual needs of both man and woman are always present at various levels, whether they are acknowledged or not. The man's needs are more constant than the woman's, but the woman's needs can equal or even surpass a man's needs during the time of ovulation. The more time you spend alone with a member of the opposite sex, either physically or mentally, the greater the odds are that you will lust. You have to stop the process before it ever starts. You have to try not to let yourself get into a position that makes mental or physical lust possible. Remember this Nino, and let it be known. Lust and sexual desire are two of Satan's greatest weapons. He has corrupted more souls with lust than any of his other artilery. You need only read about King Solomon, or King David to realize how even those who are close to God, and filled with wisdom, can fall to lust. You must also make it clear that the lust that comes from Satan is almost always increased in its evilness by adding to it the sin of adultery, and coveting. You can see the damage that is done by having multiple mates, or adulterous relationships. Children who come from these lustful unions often end up troubled, more often than not repeating the same evil vice when they grow into adults. The cycle of evil is very hard to break. This is why Jesus came to the conclusion that even to look at someone with lustful intentions was a sin. It's like a family that lives near a river with a strong current. The mother, fearing that one of her children may fall in and drown, teaches her children that to even look at the river will make something bad happen to them. Is it true? No. But the children are so scared that they won't even look at the river, much less put their foot into it. That is really all Jesus is after."

Nino, though intrigued by what he is hearing, is a little amused. "Well, I am kind of taken back at the direction that our conversation took. But I suppose that it is fitting that my mother should have a talk with me about the birds and the bees. I guess this kind of talk, if it comes from your mother, is never too late is it?"

The corners of Mary's mouth turn up in a smile at her son. "Oh Nino, you're such a character."

"Mary, how old was Jesus when he found out who he really was, and what he had to accomplish?"

"As Jesus continued to grow in his knowledge of the scriptures and his relationship with Yahweh, little by little he came to the realization that he may be the Messiah. He knew that he was from the royal line of David. I told him of how he was born in Bethlehem in a manger. How the holy men from the east brought him gifts because they said a large star had led them to him. I told Jesus that they said the star was a sign that Jesus was born to be someone special. A king. But I never told him who his father really was. That was not for me to do. It wasn't until after he was baptized by John the Baptist that God confirmed to him and John who he truly was. John saw the Holy Spirit descending upon Jesus in the form of a dove, and Jesus, for the first time, heard the voice of his father. Jehovah said, 'This is my beloved son, with whom I am well pleased.'"

"Then he went into the desert to be tempted for forty days?" Asks Nino. Mary clarifies, "Forty days just means a long time. During this period in the desert Jesus had his first face to face encounter with Satan. He also had his first face to face encounter with his own Guardian Angel and many other spiritual aids, prophets, and saints. It was during this time in the desert that the Archangel Michael revealed to Jesus all that must happen over the next three years. When Jesus left the desert his story pretty much unfolded the way it is described in the New Testament. He gathered his 12 apostles. He toured the region preaching his message of brotherly love and repentance of sin. He verbally attacked the religious leaders and exposed them as hypocrites. He performed many miracles. He was betrayed and rejected by his own people. He was turned over to the Romans who flogged him, humiliated him, crucified him, and then to everyone's surprise, he rose from the dead. The rest is history."

Nino shudders at the thought of it, "The crucifixion of your son must have been awful for you."

A veil of anguish covers Mary's face, "It was more horrible than I care to describe. Can you imagine the pain of a mother helplessly watching these people torture and kill her son; her baby?"

Nino thinks of the woman and two kids he killed in Vietnam. He is choked by grief, and can only begin to imagine what Mary must have felt as Jesus was taken from her. He hangs on her every word.

"It was horrific. However, in the midst of the crucifixion, when I felt as though I was about to collapse under an ocean of sadness and rage, I was suddenly filled with a feeling of peace and love. I no longer hated the Romans and the Jewish priests, nor was I sad for my son. My mind was opened, and I saw in a moment of clarity all that was unfolding in front of me as if it were a book that I had read a hundred times before. Everything happened just the way it was supposed to happen. Jesus' death on the cross was not a defeat, but a victory, a victory of such magnitude, that even to this day it is incomprehensible to those on earth and in Heaven. The Gates of Forever were once again open, and God's spirit was now free to roam the earth. **Oh death, where is your sting?** However, more than any of the other things that I have just described to you, was the knowledge of how much God really loves us all. Jesus said that it is rare for a man to give his life to save his friend. It is rarer still for someone to give their life to save someone whom they do not know, let alone an enemy. Can you imagine the pain that God our father went through at the crucifixion of Jesus? I was powerless to do anything to help Jesus, but God had the power to intervene. God could have stopped the suffering of Jesus, but he couldn't for our sake. Can you imagine the torture that God went through? Seeing his beloved son beaten, humiliated, mocked and ultimately killed? Seeing his child's anguish, hearing his cries for help; having the strength to stop it, but not being able to? The good of the many outweighs the good of the few, or the one. Can you imagine being in a position in which you had to allow one child to suffer and die, so that all of the rest of your children could be saved? It wasn't the fact that Jesus was going to die that bothered God. With God there is no death. It was the suffering that he had to watch Jesus endure. It was the same ocean of sadness and rage that I felt was going to cause me to collapse, that God was feeling. But his pain was much worse and a million times more intense than mine. **God so loved the world that he sent his only son. Can you possibly begin to understand the depth of Gods love? Can any of us comprehend such a love?"**

Nino is amazed at Mary's selfless compassion for God. "No," he manages to answer. "I cannot comprehend that kind of love. It is as boundless and vast as the endless space that surrounds the earth. It always was and it always will be there for all of God's children. Our father truly is an unimaginable, warm and loving soul. God so loved the world that he sent his own son. The significance of these words is something that I will meditate over from this day forward, throughout all of eternity."

"Yes Nino, you and I together-"

"Mary, back on earth there are many people who say you have appeared in a place called Majegore. Is it true? Do you make appearances on earth? Are you the Lady of Fatima?"

"Yes Nino, it is true. I appeared because it was prophesized that I would come."

Nino is surprised, "It was prophesized?"

"Yes, in the New Testament book of Revelations. I am the lady cloaked with the sun. I came to help defeat the red dragon, which is symbolic of atheism. My first appearance in Fatima was, in a way, merely to set the stage for Madgegoria. I, like my son, come to bring faith to the faithless. My appearance at Madgegoria is also a sign that the Great Game is coming to a close."

"Mary, if nobody knows when God is going to end the Great Game, what makes you, Barabbas and the other Zealots so sure that the Game is almost over?"

"In Heaven there are an infinite number of souls that will take part in the Great Game. Many souls are victorious the first time around, and some souls have been around for a long time. You have already reached the point in time when the last new soul has entered the Great Game. The great hall of souls from which all souls enter the Great Game is now empty. This is why everyone is speculating that the Great Game is coming to a close. That is why your message is so important."

Nino looks worried, "It makes me a little nervous to hear you say that. The reality of what I am being asked to do is starting to sink in. I just hope you all haven't made a big mistake in choosing me for such an important mission. You people don't even really know me. What makes you think a bum like me can be some sort of prophet?"

"Nino, everything that you have experienced in your life, both good and bad, happened for a reason."

Nino feels a little anger rising in him, which takes him by surprise. "For a reason? What reason?! I'm a nobody. A sinner. My life has amounted to nothing. The people who see me, see a homeless, crazy vet. I'm not prepared for this! How could I be?"

Mary holds Nino's face in her hands and speaks to him,"Nino, there is nobody in the whole world who is more prepared, or more perfect for this assignment than you. This is your destiny. You were born to become the unexpected prophet of faith, and I believe in you with all my heart and soul."

Nino perplexed, "How can you? No one has ever believed in me. I haven't done one worthwhile thing in my whole life. I'm a failure as a person."

Mary smiles upon Nino's pain. She knows her son better than he knows himself. "Your name is already written in the book of life which is absolute proof that you are anything but a failure. All those little things that you have done to help God's people, his creatures, and his planet throughout the course of your lifetime, is what makes your life a success in God's eyes. Allah does not use the world's standards to judge the success of a soul. What kind of job you have, how much money you've earned, how well known you are, or how many college degrees you have obtained mean nothing to Him. The less you have according to the world's standards, the more capable you are of giving in God's eyes. Remember the old woman who gave her last two coins to the poor?"

"I do."

Mary smiles proudly, "Nino Jones you really are a special soul. You must never forget that. The road you have to walk will not be an easy one. You will be attacked by Satan and his demons, but you must remain faithful in your mission. No matter how dark a situation may seem you must not lose hope. Believe in God, believe in yourself, and never give up! I am confident that you will be successful. The time has come for us to part are ways for now. I will be leaving you with Caiaphas at the Holy Temple. You will be in my prayers, and the Holy Spirit will be with you. So be brave and strong in spirit, body, and faith. Go now my son, and make your mother proud."

Mary pulls Nino into her arms and hugs him close, kissing his cheek. It is hard for Nino to let go of this sanctuary.

"I'll do my best, Mary. I mean, I'll do my best, Mom."

Nino smiles at his heavenly mother one more time, and in the twinkling of an eye he is in the presence of Caiaphas at the Heavenly Holy Temple.

A MESSAGE FROM MARY THE MOTHER OF JESUS

Author's Note 1: There is a Sign Of The Times that I would be remiss not to mention. Mary the Mother of Jesus has reportedly appeared in Guadalupe, Lourdes, Fatima, Zeitoun, Akita, Garabandal, Medjugorge, and many other places throughout the world. It has been prophesized that a woman cloaked with the sun will come to Earth to slay the Red Dragon (Atheism). Many people from various religions (especially Catholics) strongly believe in Mary, and they are convinced that she is actively working with her son Jesus to help all of God's children during these troubled times. I have to admit that I was skeptical about these apparitions at first. However, the more that I have read, the more I am convinced that miraculous events have occurred and continue to occur. For example, in Zeitoun, Egypt she appeared to a devout Muslim named, Farouk Mohammed Atwa. He was undergoing a series of operations for a case of gangrene. However, when he reported to the hospital the next day, he was certified completely healed. She then appeared two or three times a week to crowds of over 250,000 Christians, Muslims, Jews, and Athiests. In Fatima the sun danced, and in Medjugorge she appears and prays for the conversion of sinners. In every place that she has appeared she leaves in her wake an atmosphere of unity and peace, and many people who receive miraculous healings. Her message is simple: Pray unhurriedly, often and always, love generously, care deeply, be merciful, and speak kindly … There is a woman in Garabandal named Conchita who says that Mary has told her that there will be A Warning, A Sign, and A Miracle from God, which will happen very soon. I am using Conchita, because, what she reports is in line with what Mary has said in Fatima and Medjugorge.… Some time after a predicted Roman revolution in which the Pope has to take refuge in another land, the Warning will occur. She says that this warning will be something supernatural that will not be able to be explained by science. It will look like two stars crashing into one another, or a fire ball that crashes into our sun! Beware the sunrise, and do not look up at the sky, or venture outside, because if you do, you will not return. Prostrate yourself on the floor and pray for God's mercy. The noise will be defening, and the heat will be very intense, but nothing will fall to the earth. In this Cataclysm everything will be separated from the sky, which will appear to roll back like a scroll. It will turn as white as snow, and there will be fantastic colors—blues, purples, and so on. There will be a tremendous explosion. This force shall go within the very core of each human, and will cause them to understand their offenses against God. So great will be the impact, that we will feel like the elements have shaken the very foundation of our being. This reminds me of a verse in the book of Mark (Mark 13:24-25 "The sun will grow dim and the moon will not shine, the stars will fall, and the heavens will convulse. Then all mankind will see me, the Messiah coming in the clouds with great power and glory.") This warning will come directly from God, and will be visible throughout the entire world in whatever place anyone might be. It will be like a revelation of our sins and it will be experienced equally by believers, non-believers and people of every religion. This warning will be a correction of the conscience of the world, and it will encourage all of us to lead a life of prayer and self-sacrifice. We will see all of our sins and feel the pain they have caused. The most important thing will be to recognize our own sins and the bad consequences of them. This phenomenon will not cause physical damage, but it will horrify us because in one moment we will see our souls and all the harm we have done. We will feel all alone in the world as our conscience stands in the presence of God. We will also see the good we have not done, but could have. This last warning from God is intended to purify us to prepare us to see the miracle, and hopefully we may draw enough grace to change our lives toward God. In between the Warning and the Miracle, there is to be 3 days of complete darkness. The only things that will give light are candles that have been blessed. You are to stay inside and not open the doors or windows because demons will try to seduce you. They will call out to you in the voices of friends and loved ones, but open not your door! Thes demons can only enter your house if you let them! Close your eyes and your ears, and pray. After 3 days the world will see the miracle. A cross of light will break the darkness for the whole world to see, and a sign will remain in the pines at Garabandal until the end of time. If after the miracle mankind continues to sin, a chastisement will come that will be comparable to what happened to Sodom and Gomorrah only on a world wide scale. A great and terrible war that will chastise the entire world with horrors and atrocities beyond belief.... The secret of Fatima made known in 2000, portrayed an Angel touching the earth with a flaming sword. It is not my intention to scare you. I simply want you to be prepared when these prophecies come true.... Pray for us Mary now and at the hour of our death.

"Behold, a virgin shall conceive in the womb, and shall bring forth a son, and thou shalt call his name Emmanuel (God is with us)."
Isaiah 7:14 (760 BC)

The Fatima Prayer
My God, I believe in you. I adore you. My hope is in you, and I love you. I ask pardon for those who do not recognize you as they should, and I beg you to convert the poor sinners of the world and those in purgatory. Dear God, in the name of Christ Jesus, and by the power of his body and blood, his soul and his sanctity, and the holy depths of your divine mercy, I ask you to forgive my enemies, my family, me and all who try to do your Holy Will. Lead us all to Heaven, especially those most in need. Dear God, in the name of Christ Jesus, and by the power of his body and blood, his soul and his sanctity, I ask you to bless yourself in the name of Christ Jesus, God bless God....

Authors Note 2: In the following chapter (17) all of the information provided by the Caiaphas character regarding the Jewish religion, The Roman Scourging, The Roman Crucifixion, Jewish history, Roman history, the authenticity and accuracy of the Bible, and the Messiah probability estimations are historical, archeological, mathematic fact.

CHAPTER 19

▼

"The spirit of man is neither born, nor doth it die. Unborn, undying ancient, perpetual and eternal, it hath endured and will endure forever. The body may die; be slain; be destroyed completely but he
that hath occupied it remaineth unharmed."
-KRISHNA/THE BHAGAVAD GITA (3,137 BC)

Those who believe in the Qur'an, and those who follow the Jewish scriptures, and the Christians and the Sabians—any who believe in Allah and the Last Day, and work righteousness, shall have their reward.
-MUHAMMAD/THE HOLY QUR'AN (600 AD)

I DO NOT WANT YOUR SACRIFICES-I WANT YOUR LOVE; I DO NOT WANT YOUR OFFERINGS-I WANT YOU TO KNOW ME.
-HOSEA 6:6 (750 BC)

The holy temple in the kingdom of Forever is breathtakingly beautiful. Unlike any conceived on Earth, Forever's holy temple sprawls out over miles of territory. There is a separate entrance to a separate wing for each and every religious background, all coming together at one spectacular altar at the temple's center. Only the true citizens of Forever can behold the whole image of this altar. Like the tree of Knowledge, all answers are found here, and all religions are united.

It is here that Caiaphas likes to spend most of his time. He smiles at his visitor, not letting his inner melancholy show through.

"Well, Nino, have you benefited from your tour so far?"

Nino beams, "Yes, it has really been astounding."

"Your time in Forever draws to a close, my friend. After I have given you my piece of the tour, you will then spend some time with Pilate who will then return you to Barabbas. The Grand Tour will be complete, and you will then be given your final instructions."

"Well, it certainly has been enlightening." Nino pauses to take in his surroundings. "This temple sure is stunning. I can see why you like to spend time here."

Caiaphas becomes melancholy "I wish it was simply the outward beauty that drew me to this magnificent place. Unfortunately for me, it is a place where I come to relive a game that has already been played and lost. Every time I come here the same old memories roll over and over again in my mind. And I sit here like the proverbial Monday morning quarterback, wishing I could go back in time and play the game over again."

Nino pats Caiaphas on the shoulder, "It must be hard for you, my friend. I hope there is something that I will be able to do, to ease your pain."

"Thank you, Nino. I've waited for you for such a long time. Through you, I will be able to speak to my people one last time." "Your people? You mean, the Jews?"

"The Jews, yes, but not only the Jews. All of God's children: the Christians, the Muslims, the Hindus, The Buddhists and everyone who recognizes the existence of God. Even the Atheists, and the Agnostics. I just want one more chance to speak to them as a priest from Allah's holy temple."

Nino wonders, "What is the significance of the earthly Holy Temple? I mean, the temple that existed during your time as High Priest? I've never been able to grasp that whole sacrificial system. The slaughtering of lambs and bulls to atone for sins, what does it all mean?"

Caiaphas explains, "Well, Nino, the earthly temple is symbolic of Yahweh's Heavenly Temple. It is intended to someday be a house of prayer for all nations of the world. It is a reminder to all of God's earthbound children that He is real, and that His most holy, most merciful spirit is accessible to them. The Holy temple is not mere stone; it is the earthly house of God. When God gave Moses the Ten Commandments, he-"

Nino apologetic, "I'm sorry to interrupt you, Caiaphas, but please tell me, according to your understanding, what were the actual Ten Commandments?"

Caiaphas grins, "I know it gets confusing sometimes, with all the different interpretations, but I will give you the Ten Commandments as they were originally written by the hand of God." Caiaphas leads Nino to a corner of the temple, where two stone tablets are engraved with grand handwriting. Nino reads the commandments out loud.

The First Commandment: "Hear, Oh Israel, the Lord our God is one and you shall love him with all of your heart, soul, mind and strength." & **You shall love your neighbor as yourself!**

The Second Commandment: "You shalt make no graven image of him."

The Third Commandment: "Thou shalt not take the Lord's name in vain."

The Fourth Commandment: "Thou shalt keep the Sabbath day holy."

The Fifth Commandment: "Thou shalt honor thy mother and father."

The Sixth Commandment: "Thou shalt not murder."

The Seventh Commandment: "Thou shalt not commit adultery." **The Eighth Commandment:** "Thou shalt not steal."

The Ninth Commandment: "Thou shalt not bear false witness against thy neighbor."

The Tenth Commandment: "Thou shalt not covet thy neighbor's wife or his belongings."

"That's it, Nino. These are the original Ten Commandments as they were written on tablets of stone, by the power—the very finger—of God."

"These Ten Commandments were more than just laws to live by, right?"

"That is right, Nino. They represent the covenant that exists between God and his people, and if they are sincerely followed they teach you the 11th and most important commandment. Do you know what the final commandment is Nino Jones?"

Nino scratches his head. "Is it to love your neighbor as you love yourself?"

Caiaphas smiles proudly, "Well said my brother. This is indeed the 11th commandment. And Hidden within this simple phrase lies the power, majesty, and purpose of God and all of his creation. The new and everlasting covenant is the covenant of love. By loving all of God's peoples and creations we are actually letting God touch the world through our deeds. In allowing God to work through us, we are virtually returning his love back to him, which is the most precious act in the universe. The old covenant which was the Ten Commandments, has been replaced with the new covenant "Love your neighbor." As the Jews used to house the 10 commandments in the Ark of the Covenant, we must now carry the new covenant (God's love) in the heart of our souls."

Nino smiles. "Those are beautiful words Caiaphas. So what you're saying is that, from now on each individual person is a miniature Ark of the Covenant."

Caiaphas smiles with pride. "Yes that's exactly what I mean. That which once was symbolic has now taken its true form."

"Caiaphas, what was the Ark of the Covenant really like?"

"The Ark of the Covenant was a fancy carrying case that held the 10 commandments. It was kind of heavy so it had handles that would allow four or more people to carry it."

"Did it have a unique shape to it?"

"No not really. It was shaped like a rectangular box, and it was made out of acacia wood that was covered with pure gold. That's why it was so heavy. The lid of the Ark was made of solid gold, and was called the mercy seat. Two baby angels, called cherubim, with outstretched wings, surmounted the mercy seat."

"What was actually in the Arc?" Nino asks.

"Enclosed within the Ark are the stone tablets on which the Ten Commandments are written, Aaron's rod that budded, and a jar that contains some of the original manna which came from Heaven when the Jews were starving in the desert."

Nino wonders, "You speak as though the Ark of the Covenant still exists. Does it really still exist?"

"Yes, it does. It is being guarded by an ancient order of Ethiopian Jewish priests."

"Why is it being kept a secret?"

"It will be returned to the Jews when the Holy Temple is restored, and the sacrificial system is reestablished."

"I can't believe it still exists. How did these Ethiopian Jewish priests wind up with it?"

"The Queen of Sheba had a son, Melinick, whose father was King Solomon."

Nino laughing "That Solomon loved the ladies didn't he? Caiaphas chuckles as well … "So the Queen of Sheba actually had a son by Solomon?"

Caiaphas explains, "Yes his name was Melinick. Melinick was supposed to take a replica of the Ark with him back to Ethiopia, but he took the real thing. He was afraid that if Jerusalem was overthrown that the Holy Ark would be destroyed. It is a good thing he took the original Ark to, because in 587 BC, the Babylonians destroyed King Solomon's temple and everything in it. And so, for over 2,500 years this sacred sect of Ethiopian Jewish Priests has guarded it. There is a monastery in Ethiopia under which lies a series of seven large circular corridors that all intertwine. It's like a giant holy labyrinth. The Ark is hidden somewhere deep within the seventh circle of this sacred maze. It is guarded by an Ethiopian Jew, who is one of a long line of special priests. These holy guards are chosen at birth to spend their whole life guarding the Ark of the Covenant."

Nino is stunned, "Their whole life?"

"Yes. They never see the light of day, but they are not unhappy, because it is the only life they know, and it is truly a most sacred calling."

"Unbelievable. Un-be-livable! All of these biblical events really did happen, but our modern day thinkers are trying to convince everybody that they were nothing more than myths, or folklore. Boy, are they going to be surprised! … So, getting back to the original temple, was it simply a place that was built so people could come to pray and see the Ark?"

Caiaphas elucidates, "Oh, no, it was much more than that. God gave Moses the design of the first temple, as well as the design for the Ark. The original temple was made out of three tents. There was one large tent that the people would come in to pray. The second largest tent was called the Holy Place, which only the priests could enter. The smallest tent was called the Holy of Holies. This is where the Ark of the Covenant was housed. The

Holy of Holies could only be entered once a year by the High Priest on Yom Kippur, which is the Jewish holy day of atonement. The Holy of Holies was always located in the center of the Temple. In King Herod's Temple, there was also a separate section for the women, and for the Gentiles. This was the temple that Jesus experienced."

Nino curious,"What happens on Yom Kippur?"

"Yom Kippur is an annual solemn fast of the tenth day of the seventh month, reminding the Jewish people that the many daily, weekly and monthly sacrifices of the temple were insufficient to atone for their sins."

"So what did you have to do as the High Priest?"

"I would be dressed in a simple white robe, which is supposed to be symbolic of our souls. I would then enter the Holy of Holies. The first thing I would do was to burn incense—"

"Why incense?" Nino asks.

"Because it symbolizes the offering of prayer to God. The smoke from the incense, like the prayers of his people, rises to Heaven. The perfumed smoke is symbolic of how pleasing prayers are to God, especially prayers that ask for forgiveness. Next I would sprinkle blood on the mercy seat to atone for my sins and the transgressions of the priesthood. Blood from a sacrificial goat was also sprinkled on the mercy seat for the sake of the Jewish people. After this I would lay my hands on a second, living goat, confessing over it the sins of Israel. This "scapegoat" was sent out into the wilderness, symbolizing the carrying away of the peoples' sins."

"So, you would go to God on behalf of yourself, the priesthood and your people. I still don't see how the blood of animals atones for sins. Why would God want anything like that?"

"Remember, Nino, with God everything has a symbolic meaning. God told Moses that the spilling of innocent blood atones for sins. The blood of animals and all Jehovah's creation was seen as being the life source, created by God ... In order for a blood offering to be acceptable, the victim offering the blood must die in a violent way."

"Why did the death have to be violent?"

Caiaphas appreciates Nino's curiosity, "There had to be suffering involved in the death. This was symbolic of what would one day happen to the Messiah. An innocent life is lost, and its blood is used to wash away the sin and the spiritual pollution caused by human transgressions. What happened to the scapegoat was also symbolic preparation for what would happen to God's chosen people. The scapegoat would have no home to call its own, very little food and water, harsh living conditions, and would be constantly pursued by wild animals. This is how the ritual of sacrifice began. These rituals were not meant to be the permanent way of atonement. As I said, this was intended to set the stage for the coming of the Messiah, and the destiny of the Jewish Nation. Remember, God knows all things. He knew that one day He would have to send Jesus into the world, and he knew that God's Chosen People would reject Jesus. You cannot put new wine into old wine skins. The new wine will cause the old skins to burst and then both will be lost."

"Meaning?"

"Meaning that the new covenant and the new message would have to, for the most part, be accepted by and grow up in the Gentile nations of Rome, Greece and so on. If we had accepted Jesus as our Messiah in the old country, then a very small nation of people would come to have a Messiah. By rejecting Jesus, the Jews sent him out into the rest of the world, where others would have a chance to accept him. And the first will be the last …"

Nino encouraged, "You mean the Jews will one day recognize Jesus as their Messiah?"

"Yes, they will. The first people that Jesus came to will be the last people to accept him. **Some day they will see that not only did Jesus give the New Testament to the Gentiles, but he also gave the Torah to the entire world! Without the Old Testament there would be no New Testament. And without the Jews there would be no Jesus the Messiah.** It is all a part of God's exquisite master plan. As I said, by rejecting Jesus, he became the symbolic Lamb of God and the Messiah for the Gentiles. Our people became the symbolic scapegoat for the nations of the world. The sins of the world were symbolically confessed over us, and our people were driven out of our homes, and once more sent into the wilderness. Scattered like blowing leaves amongst the nations, scorned and rejected as the murderer of Jesus Christ. The Jews actually became burnt offerings in the furnaces of Hitler."

Nino is outraged, "Why would that be necessary?"

Caiaphas remains calm, "Sin is a barrier between human beings and God. It is also an offense to Him. Some act must be done that appeases or removes the wrath of God against the sin. Remember, God is our judge, but he is also our redeemer. We all have a personal relationship with God. Jesus' death was an act of washing away our sins. Your sins are forgiven, but when it comes to sin there is always a ripple effect. For example, you can sincerely ask God to forgive you for committing adultery, and you could be forgiven. The sin is blotted out of Allah's mind. However, your wife may still leave you, and your children may grow up to be unruly. The sin's residue still continues to cause pain in the world. Do you see what I mean?"

"I think I do. The new covenant started with a new day of atonement. That is what Easter became. From that day on, the old way of sacrifice was no longer needed. God provided a heavenly alternative. Jesus became the lamb of God who takes away the sins of all who ask forgiveness in his name. He is the soap that takes away the stain of sin from all our proverbial white robes, our souls. The Jewish people became the scapegoat, having the sins of the world confessed over them, and sent out into the wilderness. Their sufferings parallel the sufferings of Jesus. What Jesus was asked to suffer as an individual, the Jews were forced to suffer as a nation. So it is these poor Jewish people who have been tortured, murdered and alienated that eventually will remove the wrath of God against the sins that were confessed over them when Jesus died on the cross."

"Yes, Nino. Yes. And this system of things will remain until the Great Game is complete."

Nino shakes his head,"So much suffering for the poor Jews. Being selected as God's chosen people was a blessing, but it was also a curse wasn't it?. I can't imagine having to carry such a heavy burden. The Jewish people should be held in the highest esteem. What a noble nation of souls they truly are."

Caiaphas is happy that Nino sees the Jews as a people that should be held in high esteem. "I don't mean to sound like I'm tooting my own horn, but you're absolutely right. The Jews are suffering for the sake of the entire world, and it is important to note that they are not suffering because they are sinners, or because it is God's will."

Nino is reminded of a friend. "I had a friend named Neil Reesenstien who served with me in Vietnam. When he was nine years old he lost every living relative on both sides of his extended family in the Holocaust. The only family members to survive were his mother, father, and sister. He became so terribly depressed that he was suicidal. His parents sent him to a rabbi to help him deal with this catastrophe. However, the meeting did nothing to heal his wounds. In fact in many ways this meeting actually deepened his anguish."

"I think I know what you're going to say."

"He said he was standing in a room holding one of those little Jewish prayer books, when the rabbi came in and told him that his family members were all dead because it was "God's will." He got so outraged that he threw the prayer book at the Rabbi, and he never went back. His suffering was magnified, and his faith was ripped from his heart."

Sighing and sad. "Poor Neil. That is an awful thing for a little boy to hear under those circumstances, but that was the rabbinical way of looking at things in those days ... And sadly, even today many religious leaders continue to throw that phrase around, a phrase I'm afraid that often does more harm than good. Remember this important fact my brother, it is never, ever God's will that we suffer. For when we suffer he suffers. Like a loving mother he feels our pain, and his sacred heart breaks for us when we weep. Do me a favor Nino. If you ever see your friend Neil again, tell him that it was not God's will that he lost his family. God was not punishing them, nor did he intend that they be harmed in anyway. They suffered because there is evil, hatred, and prejudice in the world. And they died because God in his mercy could not stand to watch their suffering any longer. Remember Nino, evil can torture, and terrorize, but it can not kill. Not one sparrow dies, without the knowledge of God."

"So their death was God's will?"

"Their death was God's rescue, like a father pulling his drowning child from the undertow of a treacherous river. God reached into Hitler's demonic camps of terror, and returned millions of his children back to the land of their origin."

"So he saved them in the only way that he could?"

Caiaphas enlightens Nino, "Actually he saved them in the best way that he could. He seized the opportunity to save millions of souls from a Satanic regime. The Jews believed that even under those severe circumstances that

God would save them, and that's exactly what he did. Earthbound souls no matter how strong their faith see death as an end, and therefore it is cloaked in negativity. However, the citizens of Forever know that death is the beginning of our immortal lives in paradise. For every soul that is born into the Great Game there is worry and apprehension throughout the Kingdom. But for every soul that Returns to Forever, there is joy, and endless jubilation. Satan can never harm these souls again!"

"So God always takes something evil that the Devil is trying to do, and turns it into something wonderful."

Caiaphas smiles proudly, "That's our Father! During the Great Game of Life there will continue to be periods of abundant goodness and periods of terrible evil, however, the rules of free-will can never be compromised for any reason. That is a tough reality for the earthbound soul, but a vital one in terms of the eternal plan, and what it will ultimately accomplish."

Nino tries to grasp the essence of it all. "So the scapegoat that is selected, is not chosen because it is a "bad animal" in some way. The Jews simply play a holy role in God's grand scheme of things. They have been sent out into a wilderness to be slaughtered and tortured not because it is God's will, but because of the power and influence of evil. It's not that God is ambivalent to our suffering. It's just that he must live by the rules that he established, in a game that must be played, if the joy of real love is ever truly to be found…. Did those words just come out of me?"

Ciaphas smiles & laughs. "You understand well Nino Jones. The Jews, like Jesus the Messiah, are holy vessels of God's redemption. The Jewish people remain, and always have been, God's chosen people."

"Why did God need to have a chosen People?" Nino asks.

"He had to enter into the Great Game, and in order for him to do so he would need a nation to help him set the foundation for of his campaign against Satan and the powers of evil. He chose the Jews because they are the descendents of Gods first earthly children Adam and Eve. Their royal line is what makes them chosen, their unwavering faith in God is what makes the beloved to him, and when the day comes that they finally claim their Messiah, The final piece of Gods holy puzzle will be in place."

Nino nods in understanding, "I now see why everything had to unfold the way it did, but what was it that caused you and the other religious leaders to reject him? I would think you would have welcomed a man with such a message of peace."

Ciaphas shakes his head with disappointment, "Our religion had become a gigantic conglomeration of rules and regulations. As long as you did what the oral law said you should do, and completed the proper rituals, you were considered a good person. It didn't matter how you treated your neighbor, or what your inner feelings were. We believed that strictly following the law was what was most important. Our religion was no longer just a simple path leading to God. It had become a constraint on the people. The yoke of our religion was too heavy for most people to carry."

"What exactly is a yoke?" Asks Nino.

"A yoke is a heavy wooden harness that fits over the heads of oxen. The heavier the yoke, the greater the oxen's burden."

"What caused your religion to become so heavy?"

Ciaphas gives details, "Back in the days of Jesus you had 5 ruling parties. The most important of which are called the Scribes' and the Pharisees. The Scribes' job was to interpret the Ten Commandments and provide the Jewish people with rules and regulations to live by."

"That sounds like a good idea.... So what went wrong?"

"The Scribes' turned Jehovah's Ten Commandments into a winding river of absurd rules, regulations, and rituals. This river was called the Scribal or Oral Law. When the Scribal law was finally put into writing, it became an 800-page book called the Mishnah."

Nino startled, "Wow, from ten sentences to 800 pages! These guys had too much time on their hands."

"Nino, this was just the beginning. They also wrote commentaries on the Mishnah called the Talmuds. The Jerusalem Talmud is twelve volumes long, and the Babylonian Talmud consists of over sixty volumes of printed text! I am telling you these things only so you can see how overwhelming and complicated our simple laws had become."

"Can you give me an example of what the Scribes" thought process was?"

Ciaphas thinks for a moment, "Take the commandment about the Sabbath day, for instance. It sounds simple and straightforward, until you begin to break it down like the Scribes did. The Scribes' came to the conclusion that no one should be allowed to work on the Sabbath. They believed that all people should rest like God had rested on the seventh day."

"That makes sense to me."

"Yes, but gradually it grew into absurdity. Here is an example of how the Scribes would look at a religious question. If you must rest, then you cannot work. Work is then defined as anything that causes you to carry a burden. Burden is then defined, endlessly in the Mishnah...."

Nino smiles, "But I like the idea that you can't work on the Sabbath."

Ciaphas raises his eyebrows, "Sure at first glance it would seem like a good thing. But whenever you take any idea, even a good one, to extremes, its intrinsic goodness becomes lost. For example here are some of the ridiculous restrictions that we had to live by. On the Sabbath you can gather enough water for only one sip, or enough ink to write two letters of the alphabet! These rules that were intended to ease our burden actually did the exact opposite. We were enslaved by absurdity.'

"So what if you didn't follow these rules. What would happen?" Asks Nino.

Ciaphas' expression hardens, "You would be ridiculed, alienated, and sometimes even punished ... The Sabbath, which God made for the benefit of all humans, became the most difficult day of the week. It was awful."

"So how do the Pharisees fit into all this mess?" Nino asks.

"The Pharisees would attempt to live their lives according to the rules and regulations of the Scribal law."

"Were the Pharisees mean-spirited people?"

Ciaphas roles his eyes, "Some of them were. Some of them were also very arrogant. But, in support of the Pharisees, they really did believe that in devoting their lives to try and live by the Scribal law, they were living the way they felt God would want all people to live. They loved the disciplined style of life of the Scribal law, but they looked down on ordinary people who did not share their devotion. They became proud and vain. Vanity, as you have learned, is one of Satan's favorite traps."

"So, the Pharisees thought that to live by the letter of the law was to please God, and to fail to do so was to sin?"

"Yes Nino, the Scribes would constantly raise their level of expectation, and the Pharisees would do their best not to disappoint them. The Pharisees were supposed to be the peoples' role models, but it was nearly impossible for a common person to live up to their expectations. Instead of inspiring people to live holy lives, we became a reminder to them of how sinful most of them truly were. This sinful awareness motivated our people to constantly go to the temple to pray and make sacrificial offerings. **The truth is that God wants us to live as his children, not as his servants. He wants us to obey his will out of love, not out of obligation.**"

"What about the High Priests? Were they Pharisees?" Asks Nino.

"No. The High Priests were in charge of running the temple. We were the experts on the whole system of sacrifice. We knew what was needed for every kind of offering. We had temple guards who were there to help protect the grounds."

"Now, did you guys actually burn all that meat that came into the temple?"

Ciaphas chuckles, "Are you kidding? We mostly just burned the fat. We shared the rest of the meat amongst ourselves. Nobody on the planet, not even Augustus Caesar himself, ate as well as we did! An ordinary person would be lucky if he had meat once a month."

"So, you guys definitely had a problem with Jesus. He was going to take away your meal ticket."

Ciaphas embarrassed by the truth, "Well yes, but it went deeper than that. We had a serious difference of opinion. The Scribes and Pharisees could not stand Jesus because he refused to recognize their authority. They were used to being looked up to by the people, but Jesus treated them no different from anyone else. In fact Jesus held them in contempt, and he would actually scold them publicly. Which was unheard of. He pointed out how they held sacred the traditions and laws of man, but that they and the religion that they represented had become a hypocrisy. Jesus told us that God did not delight in the sacrificing of animals, or the burning of incense. Our legal mumbo jumbo had stripped away the mercy, love and compassion of the Ten Commandments."

"And the Sadducees?" Nino asks.

"The Sadducees were the nobles of the Jewish community. They were super rich, and therefore they were accepted by the Romans because of their money. They really had the best of both worlds."

"How were the Sadducees different from the other religious leaders?"

"They only followed the Ten Commandments. But they could care less about how the Scribes thought people should live. They also did not believe in life after death or angels. The truth is that the Scribes', Pharisees and the High Priests disliked the Sadducees."

"Why did the Sadducees want Jesus dead?" Wonders Nino.

"The Sadducees would be against anyone who might cause a problem with the Romans. The Sadducees knew that their position in society was very unstable, and they didn't want Jesus messing things up for them."

"And the High Priests?" Nino asks.

"Jesus' doctrine would have eliminated the need for us and our way of life. Not only would our, I'm ashamed to admit this, food supply diminish, but our whole way of life would come to an end. We decided to unite with the Scribes, the Pharisees, and the Sadducees to put an end to Jesus."

Nino perplexed, "Couldn't you tell by Jesus' words and deeds that he was the Messiah?"

Ciaphas remembers, "Quite the contrary! We were convinced by his words that he was not our long awaited Messiah. We all expected our Messiah to be like a new King David. We expected a mighty king and warrior who would free us from our earthly oppressors."

"What about his miracles? Why didn't they convince you?"

"His miracles reinforced the beliefs of those who believed in him. For those of us who were against him, we were forced to come to the conclusion that his power came from Satan. Jesus said many things which I liked very much, but he attacked the heart of our religion. If it weren't for the rigidity of our religion, we would never have survived all those long years. The truth is that when I weighed all of the evidence against him, I did not feel he was the Messiah. If he was not the Messiah, then he must be a false preacher. Throughout the history of our religion, many false messiahs had arisen. The Sadducees were the first to say that it was better for one man to die than for a whole nation to perish. We used the political connections that they had with the Romans to come up with a scheme to have Jesus convicted by Pontius Pilate."

"Why didn't you just kill him yourselves?" Asks Nino.

"For two reasons, number one, Jesus was a real superstar for the people. They believed in him, and we were afraid that if we were seen bringing him harm, the people would revolt against us. That is why we could not arrest him publicly. We had to take him under the cover of night. We also had no authority under our Roman occupation to put anyone to death."

"So then what happened? Is that when Judas betrayed him?"

Ciaphas' face drops in saddness, "Judas did not betray him. We betrayed Judas. Judas believed that Jesus was the Messiah. He was convinced that if Jesus could address the Sanhedrin, which was like a holy parliament, then he would convince us. Judas had the ear of many of the top Pharisees. He confided in them that he was trying to convince Jesus to present his case to the Sanhedrin, but that Jesus wanted no part of that. We convinced Judas that Jesus' life was in danger. We told him that the only way Jesus would have a chance to fulfill his true destiny was to allow himself to be questioned by the religious elders. So, Judas agreed to take us to him while he prayed in the Garden of Gethsemane. When Judas found out that we had lied to him, and that Jesus was actually on trial before the Sanhedrin for blasphemy, he went crazy. He stormed into the temple demanding to see one of the Pharisees, and he had to be restrained by the temple guards. The Pharisees tried to console Judas by giving him a payment for his help, but he went even more wild. The temple guards then threw him outside, hollering 'here's the one who betrayed your Jesus.' Judas dashed from the temple before the crowd outside could close in on him. They cursed his name, spit and threw stones at him. He realized in an instance the magnitude of what had happened, and he was overcome with grief. It was in this state that he decided to take his life. He ran to the outskirts of the city so panic stricken and distraught that he had forgotten that he still had the bag of silver coins clutched in his hand. The guards later found the bag of coins underneath the tree on which Judas hung himself. The story of Judas is one of the most tragic ever told, because we lost a truly good soul for all eternity."

Nino now understands the depth of Ciaphas' anguish. "Poor old Judas … Not only did he fail to save Jesus, but he gets labled a traitor and blamed for his death."

Ciaphas hangs his head. "I know, it's just awful."

"So what happened next? Was Jesus actually put on trial?"

Ciaphas looks disgusted,"Yes, but it wasn't much of a trial. I was the High Priest in charge, but the court would not come to order. Everyone was hurling insults and allegations at Jesus, but he refused to defend himself. Jesus simply said at one point, "What I have done, I have done openly. I have taught in your streets, and in your temple. I have been accessible to you throughout my entire ministry. So why do you ask me? Ask those who heard me; these are my witnesses." At this point, it was mayhem. The crowd was enraged by his insolence, and screamed for his head. Finally, I was able to get the crowd to be quiet enough so that I could ask one final question. I stood up in front of the entire congregation and asked "Jesus of Nazareth, In the name of the Eternal Holy One, are you the Messiah, the son of God?" Ciaphas pauses for a moment. His face grows pale at the memory of it.... He looked me right in the eyes. He had this unblinking steel blue stare that seemed to pierce my very soul ... And then he answered "I am." ... Well, this was more than we could take. It was the worst case of blasphemy that I had ever seen. I got so upset that I actually tore my robe in half."

"Is this when you sent him to Pilate?"

"Yes. We convinced Pilate that Jesus was guilty of treason. Because we knew the Romans would punish this crime by death. Pilate attempted to question Jesus, but Jesus refused to answer him, and Pilate got very upset. This is when he ordered that Jesus be flogged."

"Is this when Jesus received his 39 lashes?" Nino asks.

Ciaphas winces at the thought of it. "A Roman flogging was something that would make even the bravest soldier turn pale with fear. First of all, the number of lashes you received was almost always more than 39, and it was no ordinary whip. The soldiers who administered these Roman tortures were some of the most sadistic individuals who ever lived. They showed no signs of human compassion. Their whips were made by fastening long pieces of heavy braided leather thongs to a club-like piece of wood. Metal balls were woven into the braids, and tied to the ends of the strands of leather were thick, sharp, pieces of lead, iron and bone. As the whip would strike the backs soft tissue, these iron balls would cause deep bruises and contusions which would break open with the continual blows. The razor sharp pieces of bone and stone would effectively rip the skin to shreds. A Roman flogging would actually strip the skin right off the bone. A large area of their back would be so torn apart that you could actually see the person's vertebrae! The scourging would rip a bloody chasm through the shoulders, the back, the buttocks, and all the way down into the middle of the victim's hamstrings. As the beating continued, these dangerously deep incisions would actually tear into the underlying skeletal muscles and produce shreds of bleeding muscle and flesh. Their veins would be laid bare, and the muscles, bones, and nerves of the victim would be exposed to the air. Half way through the flogging they would stop for a moment making the person believe that his punishment was over. They would let the person lay there for about a minute, and then they would then take a bucket of salt water and throw it on the open wounds. The pain is beyond human words, and the screams of horror scar even the observers for life. They would then continue the pounding. They say the pain and torture is so bad that most people went insane, and no person that went through this torture was ever the same again. The scourging was so painful that it was actually a mind altering experience. The sadistically inhuman Roman soldiers who volunteered to administer the floggings were used to having men beg for mercy. However, Jesus opened not his mouth. Even when he was doused with the salt water! However his silence and bravery only enraged the soldiers all the more, and they increased the power and speed of their blows. When Jesus was done being flogged, the Roman guards mocked him. They punched him in the face, beat him over the head with clubs, and spit on him. They swore at him, and some even urinated on him. It was dreadfully appalling. The absolute worse form of disgrace. One of the guards took a stalk of thorns and made him a mock crown. Another guard cloaked him with a royally purple robe. When he was brought back in front of Pilate, he as a hideous site to behold. He was beaten so bad that he was almost unrecognizable. He looked so repulsive that I actually had to turn my head. Pilate looked at us and said "ecce homo" which meant behold the man. Pilate then turned to Jesus and he said, "So, do you still think that you are the king of the Jews?"

And Jesus answered saying "If my kingdom were of this world my followers would have fought on my behalf."

Pilate then countered, "You speak of a kingdom, so you must be a king! Are you a king?"

Jesus replied, "I am. I came into this world for one purpose, to bear witness to the truth."

Then Pilate asked him "and what is the truth?" Again Jesus was silent. Pilate was starting to get enraged. "Who are you?! He screamed. What are you? Speak to me! Don't you know I have the power to let you go, or to have you crucified?!"

Then Jesus looked him right in the eyes and said "you would have no power over me if it was not granted to you from our Father above." "How did Pilate respond?" Asked Nino.

Ciaphas continues, "Pilate was visibly taken aback. He was used to having people beg him to spare their lives. Here stood Jesus, beaten beyond recognition, unafraid. You could see that Pilate did not want to have Jesus crucified, but my group and I began to protest. Pilate was perplexed. We were actually standing before him pleading with him to kill another one of our Jewish brothers. Pilate did not see Jesus as a threat to Rome, and something deep inside his soul was telling him to let Jesus go. His wife even sent him a note telling him to "Let this innocent man go." This only confirmed what he already felt in his heart. Pilate was actually pale with fear, but nobody would have ever suspected that. Pilate continued to argue on Jesus' behalf, but we badgered him so long that he finally decided to enact an old Roman custom that, in honor of the Jewish Passover holiday, he would let the people decide to let one prisoner be sentenced to death and the other released. Pilate decided to let the people choose between Barabbas and Jesus. He thought for sure that the people would choose Jesus. However, he was shocked to hear what the people were saying."

Nino raises his eyebrows, "I am surprised, too. If Jesus was as popular as you said he was with the people, why didn't they come forward?"

"Don't forget who else was up there. Barabbas was the leader of the Zealots. The Zealots were convinced that Jesus was a friend of the Romans and a false messiah. They let it be known that they would beat down or even kill anybody they saw screaming to release Jesus."

"So, Jesus was sentenced to be crucified, and Barabbas was set free."

"Pilate released Barabbas, but he still did not want to crucify Jesus. He asked the crowd, "What would you have me do with your king?" The crowd was made up of mostly Scribes', Pharisees, Temple priests, zealots and Roman soldiers who yelled back, "We have no king but Caesar: Crucify him!" At first, Pilate argued with them on Jesus' behalf, but eventually he gave in. He washed his hands in front of the people, symbolically showing that he was not responsible for this innocent man's blood. Pilate said, "So let his blood be on your heads." And the crowd responded, "Yes, on ours and our children's." Then in closing, Pilate said 'so let it be written, that Jesus of Nazareth is found guilty of proclaiming himself King of the Jews, and sentenced to be crucified.' The crowd cheered. Barabbas wept tears of relief, and Jesus was led away to face the horror of horrors."

*Author's Note: I do not believe that what the Hebrews suffered in the Holocaust was in anyway God's will. The Holocaust is absolutely the most abhorrent event that has ever happened in the history of the world. However, I do believe that the Hebrew people suffered, and continue to suffer because they are God's chosen people. Their role in the Great Game is extremely important and deserving of honor, not ridicule. The Jewish people should be held in the highest esteem, and prayed for always.

CHAPTER 20

▼

"Prayer is the appeal of the soul to God ... <u>Not to pray is to be guilty of the incredible folly of ignoring the possibility of adding God to our resources</u>.... In prayer we give the perfect mind of God the opportunity to feed our mental & physical powers ... <u>If Prayer was necessary for Jesus, how much more must it be for us!</u>
-Dr. A.D. Belden & <u>William Barclay</u>

"The prayer of the humble, pierceth the clouds."
-Ecclesiasticus

"Is death by crucifixion the most horrible form of death?" Asks Nino.

Ciaphas makes clear"The pain is so utterly unbearable that there are literally no words to describe it. The Roman's had to invent the word excruciating, which means 'the pain that comes from the cross.'"

Nino surprised, "They actually had to come up with a new word?"

"That's right. There was nothing that described the intense anguish and suffering that came from that torturous form of death. Nino, it is absolutely the most horrific form of death you can ever imagine. What makes it so terrible primarily is that it is a slow death and you are conscious through the most excruciating pain that you could ever imagine. Jesus was already weakened from the flogging and beating. In fact, it was not uncommon for people to die from this kind of beating before they could be crucified."

"So Jesus was close to death before he was even put on the cross." "After the flogging, Jesus was in critical condition. He was probably in what your modern medicine would call hypovolemic shock."

"I've heard of that when I was in the war. Soldiers who lost large amounts of blood would slip into it." Recalls Nino.

"That's right. Losing all of that blood causes your blood pressure to drop. The victim's kidneys and other organs begin to shut down. They faint or collapse, and they are extremely thirsty."

"That sounds just like what Jesus was going through."

"It's really not hard to figure out. Any medical examiner could give you a good idea of the hows and the whys. Jesus was bleeding from his back, shoulders and buttocks. He hadn't slept in over 24 hours. He also hadn't had anything to eat or drink, and he was very dehydrated. His face and head were swollen with dark purple welts from the blows he had received. His eyes were nearly swollen shut and blood was dripping into them from the head lacerations caused by the crown of thorns. He was forced to carry the shoulder beam of his cross, which weighed over 115 pounds. As a part of his torture, the Romans made him walk the longest path possible. His death path would weave throughout the city so that as many people as possible could witness it. Jesus collapsed at least twice during his walk to Golgotha. The final time he fell, it looked like he had dropped dead. His face smashed into the road under the weight of the beam he carried, and for a moment he just lay there motionless. The soldiers whipped him and beat him with heavy wooden rods until he struggled to get back on his feet. An Ethiopian man risked his life and came out of the crowd to help Jesus carry his cross the rest of the way. His dry mouth and bloodied eyes were now filled with dirt. He was on the brink of physical exhaustion. To add to the torture, the final twohundred meters was up a very steep hill."

"Poor Jesus. He suffered all that and still some of his worst pain was yet to come!"

"Unfortunately, you're right. The Romans used what looked like giant railroad spikes that were seven inches long and tapered to a sharp point. They were driven through the person's wrists."

"I thought the Bible said they were put through his hands?"

"The wrist was considered part of the hand in their language. If the spikes had been driven through the hands, the skin would tear and the person's weight would cause them to fall from the cross. It's also important to note that the spike would crush the median nerve."

"The median nerve?" Asks Nino.

"Yes. It's the biggest nerve that runs out of the hand. You cannot imagine the pain crushing this nerve will cause."

Nino winces at the thought of it. "It must be dreadful."

Caiaphas' complexion pales. "Niño, there are no words on Earth or in Heaven that adequately describe the physical pain and the mental anguish that Jesus felt when the spikes were driven through his hands and feet."

Nino is taken back "I'm assuming the pain to the feet would be just as severe?"

"Yes. The largest nerves in the feet would also be crushed. After the feet are nailed, the body is then hoisted into place on the cross. This further tweaks the already crushed and severed nerves."

"So, hanging from the cross intensifies the pain even more?"

"Yes. Once they pull him into place, his arms would immediately be stretched six to eight inches in length, and both shoulders would be dislocated."

"Psalm 22, 'My bones are out of joint'." Recalls Nino.

Ciaphas smiles, "Yes. You know the great book well. I can still picture the moment that they hoisted him up on the cross. His breathing became very labored, and then for the first time he raised his head and looked at the crowd that had gathered about him. His face was so badly beaten he was scarcely recognizable. At one point, he seemed to look at the group of priests that I was standing near. I had an eerie feeling that he was looking right at me, and then he spoke. '**Father, forgive them, they know not what they do.**' I was stunned. Here was this man who suffered more than anyone I had ever seen in my life. He was dying because of our judgment against him, and what does he say? Not "God, damn them!" but, "Father, forgive them." "We were all staggered into silence. We couldn't even look at one another."

"That must have sent chills up your spine."

"Chills? You have no idea. The whole thing seemed surreal. When he asked Yahweh to forgive us…. Only the son of God could have uttered those words under those circumstances."

"So what happened next?"

Ciaphas contiunues, "Yes … once a person is in the hanging vertical position, crucifixion is nothing more than an agonizing slow death of asphyxiation."

"What causes that?" Nino asks.

"There is so much stress on the muscles and the diaphragm that it becomes very hard to take a breath. In fact, the chest is sort of stuck into a drawn in position, and in order to exhale, Jesus would have had to push up on his feet so the pressure on his muscles would ease long enough for him to let a breath out."

Nino tries to imagine, "And pushing up on feet that had spikes through them must have caused great pain."

Ciaphas winces at the thought of it. "Yes, excruciating pain. When he would push up, the nail would tear through the foot and squeeze the main nerve. It would also, eventually, rub against the bone of the leg, which would only add to the already intense pain. After managing to exhale, Jesus would relax down and take in another breath. Then again he would have to force himself back up to exhale, each time scraping his bloodied, exposed spine against the coarse wood of the cross."

Nino winces. "Oh, how awful."

"This cycle goes on until complete exhaustion takes over, and the person can no longer push himself up to breathe."

"So, Jesus died of suffocation?"

"Possibly, but more likely than not, it was cardiac arrest. As his breathing slowed down and he neared death, his heart would have been beating erratically."

"Jesus probably would have sensed the moment of his death."

"Probably so. I can still hear the words, 'Father, into your hands I commit my spirit. It is accomplished …' and then, he was gone."

"You know, there are still a lot of people who believe that Jesus didn't really die on the cross. How do I address those people? Who confirmed that Jesus was actually dead?"

Ciaphas cringes with disdain, "With the Sabbath and Passover coming, we wanted to get it over as soon as possible. Normally, the Romans would use a steel shaft to break the person's legs. This would prevent them from being able to push up and breath, and death by asphyxiation would happen in a matter of minutes."

"But the Messiah's legs remained unbroken?"

"Yes, and thus fulfilling yet another prophecy. When they came to break Jesus' legs, they could see he was already dead. However, just to make certain, a Roman soldier stabbed Jesus through his right side. The spear went through his lungs and directly into his heart."

"Did any of your priests confirm his death for themselves?"

"Yes. We were aware of his claims about rising from the dead, so we had our own doctors certify that he was dead. Also, Nino, you have to remember another important fact. These Romans were experts in killing people. They also had a huge incentive in making sure that everyone sentenced to be executed was definitely killed."

"What was the incentive?"

"If a prisoner somehow escaped or survived the cross, the soldier or soldiers responsible would be put to death."

"So there really is no way that Jesus survived the cross."

"No. No way. We wanted him dead. The Romans wanted him dead. Most importantly, God said he would be put to death just as he was. Believe me, Nino, Jesus died on that cross. The spear thrust through his heart settled the matter once and for all. There is no way that a Roman soldier was going to risk his life by allowing Jesus to survive. There is also no way that we would have allowed it to happen."

Ciaphas continues, "Actually, for a person to believe Jesus survived crucifixion takes almost as much faith and imagination as believing that he was raised from the dead. To actually believe that Jesus could unwrap himself from his death rags, roll away the rock from the tomb, get past the Roman soldiers, walk 10 miles on feet which had two inch holes in them, and with joints all out of place and his spine exposed … he had lost a huge amount of blood, was stabbed through the heart and lung with a spear! It's ridiculous. No one could survive that!"

Nino interjects, "And even if he did, how could a person in such a fallen pitiful condition inspire his followers to go out and proclaim the Lord is risen? They must have seen something miraculous."

Ciaphas nods in agreement, "No one could deny that something supernatural was occurring. From the moment he uttered his first words from the cross, I began to realize that this was no ordinary person. In my heart I knew we had killed an innocent man, a truly good man … The lamb of God."

Nino is enlightened. "The spilling of innocent blood atones for sins. Not the blood of animals, but the blood of God's only son. The lamb of God who takes away the sins of the world."

Ciaphas smiles, "Yes, you have said it well. The Lion of the Tribe of Judah. He is the only one who is worthy of all that God ever created to stand before the living God in the Heavenly holy of Holies. Jesus of Nazareth is the Messiah, High Priest, and King of all God's children. **Let every knee bow, and every tongue profess that Jesus is the son of God. He was a Jew, born into the royal line of David. He was a Muslim in that he submitted to God's will even unto the death. He was a Hindu in that he came back from the dead to live again. And he was a Christian in the life that he lived and the message he imparted.**"

"So, by Jesus shedding his own blood for the atonement of all of our sins, there is no longer a need to sacrifice animals."

"That's right. Jesus is the spotless Lamb of God. He that overcame the world, he went head to head with Satan, and he was victorious. Now all that is required by God is that when you ask forgiveness of your sins, you ask in the name of Jesus Christ."

"I have always asked God to forgive me in the name of Jesus Christ, but I never really mentally grasped the meaning behind it."

Ciaphas explains, "Jesus is the ultimate High Priest in that the blood that he offered was his own. And his sacrifice was once and for all time. It is not something that has to be repeated year after year. He experienced what we experienced. He knows our weak points. And he loves us anyway. We are so fortunate to have an advocate like that in Heaven."

Nino worried, "What about the Jews, the Muslims, the Hindus, and all the other non-Christian religions? How can their sins be forgiven?"

"Jesus is a free gift for all who can accept him. However, you will not be penalized for not accepting him. Remember what Jesus said, "You can call me lord, and you can even do mighty miracles in my name. But what is more important than anything else is that you obey our Father in Heaven.'"

Nino puzzled, "So, how will those who don't believe in Jesus have their sins forgiven?"

"All who are merciful to those who trespass against them will receive mercy. All who do not stand in negative judgment over the people they encounter during their lifetimes, will not be judged. In the end you will see that God's mercy triumphs over his judgment against you."

"So what is the gift, if it is not really needed?"Nino asks.

"Before Jesus came into the world, the Gates of Forever remained closed. All those who died remained in the outer darkness, waiting for the resurrection or purgatory. When Jesus died on the cross, and was resurrected, the Gates of Forever opened. For those who were already dead and waiting in the outer darkness, their judgment day was upon them. The Holy Temple in the kingdom of Forever was once again opened. Jesus entered into the Heavenly Holy of Holies, and was seated at the right hand of God. Each soul was brought before the throne of the living God, and instantaneously they viewed a panoramic movie of all the highs and lows of their lives. After the souls had been judged, some were admitted into paradise. Some were sent to the outer darkness to contemplate their futures."

"What is there to contemplate?" Asks Nino.

"The soul who had not followed the true path of God is not admitted into Paradise, and must decide if it wants to go to Purgatory or whether it wants to take itself out of the Great Game and become an Angelic servant."

"Mary talked to me quite a bit about Purgatory. It isn't anything like I thought it was."

"There is a little more you need to learn about Purgatory, but that will be given to you by Pilate. Our time is growing short, and I am getting somewhat sidetracked. The main point here is that Jesus opened the gates of Heaven forever."

"So ever since that very first Easter, the Gates of Forever were literally opened forever!"

"That's right. On the day that Jesus died, the curtain that separated the Holy Place of the Temple from the Holy of Holies was ripped right up the middle from top to bottom. This was a supernatural sign because this separating curtain was a heavily woven piece of material that was more than six inches thick! You would have a hard time cutting through it with a sharp knife or scissors, let alone trying to rip it with your bare hands. It was also over 30 feet tall and it was ripped as I said from the top to the bottom!"

Nino imagines, "That had to make you a little nervous."

Ciaphas raises his eyebrows, "Nervous? I was petrified."

"So did this mean that the Gates of Forever were now open?"

"Yes, but more importantly, our King and High Priest had entered into the Heavenly Holy of Holies, and was now seated at the right hand of our Father."

"And everyone who believes in Jesus gets admitted into Forever when they die, right?"

"Not exactly."

Nino is flabbergasted, "Not exactly?! What do you mean?"

Ciaphas smiles gently, "Do you remember the parable that Jesus used describing the Judgment of souls?"

"When he separates the souls into two groups, one of sheep and one of goats?"

"Yes ... Remember how he said to those on his right hand side, 'Come ye blessed of my Father, inherit the kingdom prepared for you from the foundation of the world. For I was hungry and you gave me food. I was thirsty and you gave me drink. I was a stranger and you took me in. I was naked and you clothed me. I was sick, and you visited me. I was in prison, and you came to me.' Then the righteous say, "When did we do all these things for you?' 'Truly I say to you, inasmuch as you have done it to these the least of my brethren, you likewise have done to me.' Then, turning to those on his left, he said, 'Depart from me, you cursed of my Father, into the everlasting fire, prepared for Satan and his angels. For I was hungry, and you gave me no food. I was thirsty, and you gave me no drink. I was a stranger, and you would not take me in. I was naked and you would not clothe me. Sick and in prison, and you would not visit me.' Then they answered, 'Lord, when did we refuse to do all these things for you? We believed in you. We did mighty miracles in your name.' Then the Lord said, **'When you refused to help these the least of my brethren you did it to me.'** And these shall go into everlasting punishment, but the righteous to everlasting light."

Nino is immediately reminded of his conversation with the Atheist he met earlier in the tour. "I spoke with a soul named Chuck who actually lived through this parable."

Caiaphas smiles, happy to hear that Nino's tour has gone as planned. "Yes, Thomas told me he was taking you to meet Chuck. That's quite a story isn't it? I'll bet you were surprised weren't you?"

Nino laughs,"You're not kidding! An Atheist in Heaven! People are going to think I'm nuts."

"They'll believe you, Nino. Just tell your story. But if you have already discussed this parable there's no need for me to go on about it."

"Oh, please, I would still like to hear what you have to say about what it means to you."

Ciaphas clarifies, "It is obvious that there are people among the righteous who are not Christians, because they are startled at what Jesus is saying to them. It is equally obvious that there are most certainly people who considered themselves "good Christians" among the unrighteous. Jesus said "**I am the way, the truth, and the light, no one comes to the Father except through the son.**" What he is simply saying is that this is how you have to conduct yourself during the Great Game if you want to be victorious. **This is the way that leads to God: You must love Him with all your heart, soul, mind and strength. You must love your neighbor and want for them that which you want for yourself, and you must live examined lives in which you introspectively repent for your sins. We should always be trying to become better people in all ways.** I know that others have explained this to you, but it is worth repeating. If you follow this path, it does not matter what you call yourself. This is the road that leads you home. This is the path of Jesus (The P.O.J.). It is the only passageway that will allow you and all people to return to Forever. This must be the foundation of your message."

Nino clarifies, "And if I follow this path, then I have accepted Jesus? If not by word, then by deed?"

"Yes. Remember how Jesus said, "Whosoever obeys our Father in Heaven is my mother, my sister and my brother.' The true children of the light will be called from all ends of the earth. On that great day you will see representatives of every nation, and every religious denomination, except Satanism."

"How should I advise people regarding religion?"

Ciaphas thinks for a moment then answers, "They must do what Jesus did. Jesus, even though he attempted to make some changes, practiced the Jewish religion that he was born into all his life."

"So, you are saying I should be a Jew?"

Ciaphas startled, "No! No. What I am saying is that you should try to practice the religion you were born into, but learn as much as you can about all of God's love based religions. For example, what is your religion?"

"I was born into the Catholic religion, but as I grew older I started having some disagreements with the church, so I just started doing my own thing. I mean, that's what you said it all comes down to anyway, isn't it?"

"You are correct, but you are missing an important fact. Each religion is important to God. If everyone starts practicing his or her own religion, eventually the organized church, synagogue, mosque, or temple will fall. As we grow in our faith, it is normal to feel closer to God. The priests and the church become less significant as our relationship with God grows stronger. However, what about the people who have not yet reached your level of faith? Who is going to lead them to God? Who is going to feed the poor? Who is going to set up missionaries all over the world spreading the good news written in the Bible, the Qur'an, and the other holy books?"

"I see. I see what you mean. The organized religions play a larger role than I first perceived. But some people are so negative about religions. What do I say to the people who say that almost all wars occur because of religious differences?"

"There will always be religious fanatics who start wars, and commit terrible crimes in the name of religion. This unfortunately will always be a reality in the Great Game. However, the opposite is also true. There are also a countless number of true believers who do a tremendous amount of good in the name of religion as well. Every church, mosque and temple does a lot of good for the community it serves. Every religion, much like every person, has strengths and weaknesses. We just have to be careful that we don't, how do you say it, throw the baby out with the bath water."

Nino nods in understanding, "I see what you mean. We should all support or belong to some religion, preferably the religion we were born into, like Jesus. But what if I am a Jew and I decide I believe that Jesus is the Messiah?"

"Then practice the Jewish religion, but now when you pray ask for forgiveness in the name of Jesus. Believe me when I tell you, Satan wants nothing more than for organized religion and the family to fail."

"Tell me about the resurrection. The Muslims say Jesus never really died, and the Jews say his followers came and took the body. What really happened?"

"Let's look at the facts, Nino. When Jesus was arrested in the Garden of Gethsemane, his apostles and disciples headed for the hills. They were scared to death. Peter, as prophesied, denied three times that he even knew Jesus."

"The Shepherd was struck, and the sheep were scattered." Recalls Nino.

"Yes. Very good. After Jesus was crucified, we asked Pilate to send some Roman Guards to watch over the tomb where Jesus was buried. Joseph of Arimathaea provided the burial site."

"Who was Joseph of Arimathaea?" Asks Nino.

"He was a Pharisee. He was rich and a member of the Sanhedrin, but most importantly, he was secretly a disciple of Jesus, and so was his good friend Nicodemus. Joseph provided the burial tomb, and Nicodemus embalmed the body of Jesus with spices, herbs and grave clothes."

"Grave clothes?" Nino asks.

"Yes, long cloth bandages that were wound round and round the body, much like a mummy. Jesus was given a king's burial." "Tell me about the tomb."

Ciaphas explains, "Our tombs were more like caves that contained shelves of rock. These sepulchers were closed with a large round boulder that was rolled between two graves to seal the entrance. The richer you were, the larger your burial place. The larger the tomb, the greater the stone that must cover the opening of the tomb. The stone that covered Jesus' tomb was so large that it took nearly 12 strong men to move it into place. It was so heavy that even some of the priests had to help the soldiers push it into place."

"So Jesus is wrapped up like a mummy and placed in a tomb sealed with this giant rock.... So then what happens?"

"Shortly before dawn on that first Easter morning, two glorious angels came and moved the rock, went into the tomb, and came out with Jesus."

"The roman guards and the chief priests witnessed this?"

Ciaphas remembers the scene,"The Roman guards and the priests were there together, but only the Romans were able to see what happened. The Pharisees and the temple priests were blind to the truth while Jesus was alive, so they were not allowed to witness his glorious resurrection, lest they repent and have faith for the wrong reasons. God caused them to remain asleep throughout the whole event. When Jesus disappeared with the two angels, the temple priests came out of their slumber to see the tomb was open, and to hear the babbling of the bewildered Roman guards. The priests refused to believe the Romans' story, and they bribed the guards to say that Jesus' disciples came and stole the body."

"Did most of the people believe this story? I mean, considering what you have just told me, did you believe the story?"

"I think we all tried to rationalize that the apostles were able to bribe the Roman guards into allowing them to take the body. After all, Jesus was seen as a friend of the Romans."

"He cured that Roman commander's servant, right?"

"Exactly. I mean, think about it. If you were in my spot, what would you rather believe? That there was an apostle-Roman conspiracy, or that we were responsible for killing the Messiah?"

"Ah, I see what you mean."

Ciaphas confesses, "However, the more I thought about it, the more it gnawed at me. I personally watched Jesus die on the cross. When it appeared that Jesus had died, just to make sure he was really dead, a Roman guard stuck a spear into his side, ripping into his abdomen, and piercing his vital organs. I stayed with the body. I watched him laid in the tomb. I watched as Nicodemus prepared the body for the burial. And I saw the Roman soldiers struggle to move the massive stone over the opening of the tomb. The more I thought about it, the more it became clear to me that something miraculous had happened. What really opened my eyes to the truth of the resurrection was the behavior of his apostles and his disciples."

"How so?" Nino asks.

"His followers, upon his arrest, were terrified. They were hopelessly disappointed men who were afraid they were going to suffer the same fate as their master. They had all fled the area. As far as we were concerned, this new cult had been destroyed. The weeks began to pass, and it seemed as though our lives had just about gotten back to normal. Then, suddenly, without warning, these scared little fishermen were back again, preaching openly in the temple. However, they were no longer timid little followers. They were impassioned, fearless preachers. Some of them were beaten, some of them were imprisoned, and some of them were even killed. Yet they refused to stop preaching. All they would have to do to protect themselves was stop spreading their new Christian doctrine, and we would have left them alone."

Nino excited, "Yes, the apostles' changed behavior is the key to this mystery. If Jesus didn't really die and come back from the dead, then there would be no Christian movement. It makes no sense that his apostles would risk their lives to preach a message that was based on a lie or an hallucination."

Ciaphas agrees, "That's right. It is not like your modern times in which they would get book deals or movie deals. There was no Oprah Winfrey show or CNN. There was no fame and fortune waiting for these men and women. There was no human reward or payoff for what they did. There was no beach house on the Mediterranean Sea waiting for them. By their course of action, they were guaranteed a life of hardship and poverty. They would go without food. They would sleep in the streets exposed to all kinds of weather. They were ridiculed and beaten. They all walked a path that they knew for certain would lead to imprisonment, torture, and death. In the beginning the Christian movement was based on nothing more than the faith of this tiny group of men and women."

Nino invigorated, "Nothing, but everything. Jesus Christ really did die on the cross and rise from the dead on that first Easter Sunday. You know, I always thought I had faith, and I did have faith, but I never really examined the facts. I think if the people would really take the time to examine the facts that we present to them, I think, yes, I see! Caiaphas, I see what must be done, and now I know it can be done. Caiaphas, this mission can work. The people will hear, and the people will believe!"

Caiaphas smiles. "We are all God's children Nino, and there really is a path that leads us home. The Bible, the Qur'an, The Bhagavad Gita and the Torah are the lands on which the path to Heaven is forged."

"Of course. How beautifully you put it. Thank you my friend ... Caiaphas before our time is through, can you speak to me about the authenticity of the Bible and the Qur'an? Are they historically and religiously accurate?"

"The answer to your question is yes."

Nino smiles, "I was hoping you'd say that. So many educated people think that these books are merely collections of myth, legend and superstition."

Ciaphas smirks, "That is because these so called "educated people" are too busy handing out homework instead of doing their own. First of all, let me tell you for the record that the Torah, the New Testament, The Bhagavad-Gita and the Qur'an are all equal in the eyes of God. This is because the origin of each of these books is divine. The Qur'an is to the Muslim religion what Jesus is to the Christian religion."

"Really? How so?"

"There in Surah 15 that states the "This book (The Holy Qur'an) has been revealed to lead the souls out of darkness into the light. To rescue them from the darkness of false worship into the light of unity." Couldn't those same words be used to describe the mission of Jesus.?"

Nino nods, "Yes they could."

Ciaphas continues, "The Qur'an offers a way of life that should be emulated, just as Jesus' life should be modeled by his followers. There is much I can tell you about all of the holy books, but for the sake of time, I will stick to the one you know best."

"I am most familiar with the New Testament."

"Jesus died in 33 A.D. Paul's conversion occurred sometime in 35 A.D., and he met the apostles sometime before 38 A.D. This means that the Christian statement of belief or Creed, was already in writing within five years of the death of Jesus."

"The Christian creed? What is that? I have never heard of it."

"It is, without a doubt, the most important doctrine of the Christian religion."

"Where is it in the Bible?"

"It is in Corinthians 15. Paul says, '**For what I received, I passed on to you as of first importance: that Christ died for our sins according to the scriptures, that he was buried, that he was raised on the third day according to the scriptures, and that he appeared to Peter, and then to the twelve. After that, he appeared to more than five hundred of the brothers at the same time, most of whom are still living, though some have fallen asleep. Then he appeared to James, and then to all the apostles.'**"

"Why is this creed so important?" Asks Nino.

Ciaphas explains, "For two reasons: first of all, Paul said if you take away the miracles and you take away the resurrection then you've got nothing to proclaim. Paul said that if Jesus wasn't raised from the dead, our faith is futile, useless, and empty. This early article of faith establishes the facts about Jesus' death, why he had to die, that he was resurrected, and who he appeared to all dating back to about two years after the events themselves."

"I understand the importance of the story, but why is the time element so important?"

"Nino, these so called scholars who attempt to discredit the Bible hypothesize that its facts are overlaid with mythological elements. However, anyone who studies historical literature will tell you that two years is nowhere near enough time for legends to have seeped into the Holy Scriptures."

"So, that's pretty good!"

Ciaphas chuckles, "Pretty good! Nino, you're a former soldier, right?"

"Yes."

"Well, have you ever studied about Alexander the Great?" "Sure, he was quite a fella."

"Want to take a guess how long Alexander had been dead before his biography was written?"

"Ten years?"

"It was written in 77 A.D. That's nearly 400 years after his death, and yet most people and even historians would not question its factuality or authenticity. That's not all. Buddha lived around 600 B.C., but his biography wasn't written until 200 A.D.!"

Nino wonders, "How about the other gospels? How old are they? And who are the people that wrote them?"

"I'll give them to you in the order that they were written. The book of Mark was written in the summer of 57 A.D., which is 24 years after the death of Jesus. Mark was a disciple of the apostle Peter."

"So Mark is the first of the synoptic gospels to be written? I always assumed it was Matthew."

"A lot of people think that. Matthew's gospel was written 21 years later during the summer of A.D. 78. However, Mathew is the earliest apostolic writing about Jesus. The book of Luke was written 2 years later in the Fall of 80 A.D. and he was a disciple of Paul. John was also an apostle, and he wrote the final synoptic gospel 12 years later during the winter of 92 A.D."

"And Paul's letters were written?" Nino asks.

"Paul's first letters appeared in the late 40s, and most of his letters were written during the 50s A.D."

"So let me see if I've added this up right. **Mark** was written **24** years **after the death of Jesus, Mathew 45** years, **Luke** was **47** years, and **John 59** years. So the most important **Christian writings were all completed within 60 years of Jesus' death.** That's not too shabby."

Ciaphas laughs, "Not too shabby, indeed. If you compare the New Testament text with that of any other ancient writing, it has survived in a purer form than any other great book. It is 99.9% correct. The same is true for the Torah, The Bhagavad-Gita, and the Qur'an. The writers of the New Testament, not to mention the Torah, The Bhagavad-Gita and the Qur'an, had such reverence and respect for the holy sayings in these books that all copies made after the original version are unbelievably exact. To these writers it would be a sin to add anything, or take anything away from the original story."

"What about the people who criticize the gospels for contradicting one another?" Asks Nino.

"Ironically, these differences which are commonly pointed out are actually proof that they are truly authentic."

Nino puzzled, "I don't understand what you mean."

Ciaphas makes clear, "If these stories had all been exactly the same, you could make the argument that they all either used the same source, or that they conspired among themselves to make sure everyone was singing the same song."

"So, if the gospels were too much alike, it would make you start to question whether or not you really did have 5 independent perspectives."

Ciaphas smiles, "Exactly. Whenever something remarkable happens, and you only have one source, or a small number of sources that are all saying the same thing, the odds are it is a hoax."

Nino nods, "I got ya! I can't wait to go back and argue with those chumps."

Ciaphas grins, "You know something else? Not only are there five different stories being told about the extraordinary life of Jesus, but if these early believers were actually trying to fabricate a sugar coated story, you would think that they would have gotten rid of a lot of the details that are either, embarrassing or contradictory."

Nino curious, "Like what?"

"Well, for example, you have Jesus in the Garden of Gethsemane asking God to let this cup pass from him, and then you have Jesus on the cross saying 'My God, my God, why hast thou forsaken me?' If you're trying to say that Jesus is God, then who is he talking to in the Garden and on the cross? Do you see what I mean?"

"So, if they didn't lie about the stuff that would have made their story less confusing, then why would they lie about anything that didn't really happen?"

"You got it! Here's another really embarrassing yet extremely important fact. Back in Jesus' time, a woman's word or opinion was meaningless and not of any value at all. A woman couldn't even testify in court.

"I hate to say this but if that was the mentality in those days, then you could understand how they could have been motivated to leave out the part where Jesus appears to Mary Magdalene, or change the character to a man to increase its validity. They must have been telling the truth."

Ciaphas agrees, "The absolute truth. The whole truth, and nothing but the truth. The fact that they kept these embarrassing discrepancies is positive, objective proof that what was written down was either witnessed by the writer, or something that was heard first hand."

"What about archaeology? How do the holy books stack up historically?"

"Nino there has never been, nor will there ever be an archaeological discovery that will discredit the Bible, or any of the other holy books. Another interesting fact is that in all of the later historical Jewish writings about Jesus, there is not even one writer who attempts to dispute that Jesus was the performer of astonishing miracles. These Jewish writers simply say that Jesus was a "sorcerer", or "a worker of magic." They simply questioned where his super natural power came from, thus acknowledging that he really did possess the power of God."

Nino surprised, "Are you telling me that not one contemporary Jewish writer tries to say that the miracles didn't happen? I find that remarkable."

"It is remarkable. You would think if they could have put him down as a phony they would have, right? What about the darkness at noon and the earthquake? Is there any cosmic or fossil record that confirms these events?"

"Yes. There was an author from Greece named Phlegon who wrote that in the fourth year of the 202nd Olympiad, that the sun was eclipsed during the sixth hour of the day. Nino, this translates to 33 A.D. 12:00 Noon!"

Nino gushes, "No kidding? Isn't that something?"

"He said it got so dark you could even see the stars and the constellations."

"What about the earthquake? Does he say anything about that?" "Yes, he said that at the same time of the eclipse there was a powerful earthquake that destroyed and overturned many things." "Unbelievable … Ciaphas, was there any Jewish prophecy about the Messiah that Jesus didn't fulfill?"

"No, not one. He fulfilled all 48 of the Messiah prophecies."

"I don't need to hear all 48, but what are some of the big ones?"

"Jeremiah said he would be a descendent of Abraham, and that he would be from the tribe of Judah, from the royal line of David; Isaiah said that a virgin would give birth to the messiah; Micah said he would be born in Bethlehem; the Psalms say that the Messiah will be betrayed, accused by false witnesses, and they even mention the manner of his death, pierced in the hands and feet—and this is before crucifixion was even invented! The Psalms also claim that he would be resurrected, that he would not decay but would ascend on high."

"Wow. What are the odds of one man fulfilling all of those prophecies? It's got to be off the charts."

Ciaphas smirks, "It is exactly one chance in about 20 zillion."

Nino's eyes pop out, "20 zillion! How big is that?"

Ciaphas continues, "It's so big a number that it is literally incomprehensible to the human mind. It is equal to the number of atoms that would exist in a trillion, trillion, trillion, trillion, trillion, trillion, trillion, trillion, billion suns the size of your own."

"Whoa … I guess Jesus is the man, isn't he?"

"Nino, if you just look at the odds of someone fulfilling only 5 of the prophecies, it would be one chance in 700 million billion. That number is millions of times greater than the total number of people who have ever walked upon the planet Earth. That many marbles would cover the state of New York to a depth of about 5 feet. If every marble was black, and we added one white marble, what would be the odds of a blind man finding the white marble?"

"I don't know, but there's probably a good chance that he may never find it."

"That's right, now what would be the odds of our blind man finding the white marble on his first selection?"

"One chance in a 700 million billion?" Nino guesses.

Ciaphas laughs, "You are sharp Nino. That would be comparable to how great the odds were stacked against one person coming along who fulfilled just five of the prophecies."

"That's just mind boggling when you think of it like that! Wow. With all that you have told me, how can people still doubt that Jesus is the Messiah, or that there is a God?"

"Remember what I told you earlier, Nino. It takes a lot more faith to hang onto Atheistic beliefs than it does to believe in God, Jesus and the prophets."

"That sure is ironic."

"It sure is. Nino, my brother, I'm afraid our time together has come to a close."

"Thank you so much for spending this time with me, Caiaphas. I learned more than you can imagine."

Caiaphas smiles, "Thank you for hearing me, Nino. I can't tell you what a pleasure it has been. Our time together may be over for now, but very soon we will be reunited at one of the greatest victory celebrations of all time. God be with you, Nino Jones.

"And with you, my brother."

As Caiaphas disappears over the horizon, Nino notices Pilate approaching him on some type of flying motorcycle.

"KTO NIE PAMIETA HISTORII SKAZANY JEST NA JEJ PONOWNE PRZEZYCIE" ("THE ONE WHO DOES NOT REMEMBER HISTORY IS BOUND TO LIVE THROUGH IT AGAIN.")
-George Santayana

"If we all lived by the Golden Rule (Do unto others as you would have them do unto you.) then there would be no Holocaust to remember, Nagasaki, Hiroshima, and Pearl Harbor would be vacation resorts, and Adolf Hitler would be unknown to the world.
World peace begins with, and relies on, the individual actions of us all."
-Mark Salvatore Pitifer

CHAPTER 21

▼

"And Satan will say 'It was Allah who gave you a promise of truth:
I too promised, but I failed in my promise to you. I had no authority over you
except to call you, but ye listened to me: then reproach
not me, but reproach your own souls.'"
-MUHAMMAD/THE HOLY QUR'AN 14:22 (600 AD)

"Hell has three gates: lust, anger, and greed."
-KRISHNA/THE BHAGAVAD GITA (3,137 BC)

"There will always be sin in the world, because that is the way things
must be for now. But woe to the person who does the tempting.
Especially those who cause any of these little children to lose their faith
in me; <u>and the faithless parents and educators who prevent and discour-</u>
<u>age their children and students from developing a relationship with</u>
<u>God</u>. It would be better for these souls to have never been born!"
-JESUS OF NAZARETH & <u>Mark Salvatore Pitifer</u> (33AD)

Pilate revs the engine of his Heavenly Harley. "Nino, hop on. We're going
cruising!"

Nino laughing, "No way, man. I'm not getting on that thing!"

"Come on, you'll love it. I might even let you drive."

"No thanks, I'll pass." Nino walks over and looks at the odd contrap-
tion. "What is this anyway? A UFO?"

"Sort of, come on, I made it myself."

Nino smirks "You made this?"

Pilate Laughing "Yeah, from scratch. Now hop on we don't have much time together." Nino hesitates a moment longer, and then hops on to the space cycle."

Nino grins, "I must be out of my mind, but, hey, I can't get killed, right?"

"Now you're talking! Nino it's funny that you would ask me if this is a UFO, because outer space and UFO's are two of the subjects I am supposed to speak to you about."

Nino stares into space with wonder in his eyes. "When I look up at night sky and see all those stars, it's almost scary to me. I mean where does it end?"

Pilate Chuckles. "It doesn't. It has been expanding since its birth nearly 14 billion years ago.

Nino amazed. Our universe is still growing?!

"Yes it is. It has slowed down quite a bit, but as we speak it continues to grow larger and larger day by day. You have to remember something Nino. Our universe was created by God. He has put something where there was once nothing, and science can prove this. There wasn't some larger void that was being filled by our expanding universe. In the time it would take you to make a fluffernutter sandwich God created our universe. Every last speck of atomic matter that would ever be produced from here to the beginning of time was made in less than 3 minutes! The only space that ever existed is the incomprehensible space that our universe creates as it spreads out across the cosmos."

"So how far is out? I mean, how many miles away is the edge of our universe?"

"About 500 trillion trillion miles away!"

Nino puzzled, "Give me an example of how far away that is."

Pilate tries to come up with a scale that Nino can grasp. "I don't want to teach an astrology class here, but here is the short of it. Human beings would have a very hard time trying to comprehend how large their universe actually is, and what a minuscule part are earth plays in terms of size … Ok, I'll give it a shot. If you took your fastest NASA spacecraft you would travel at about 35,000 miles an hour."

Nino impressed "That seems pretty fast to me."

"It does doesn't it? But here's the problem. Traveling at that speed will get you around the world in less than an hour. However, it would take you 10 years to get to Pluto, and another 10,000 years just to get to the end of our solar system.

Nino shocked. "Ten thousand years! And that's not even that far is it?

"Not when you take into consideration that the average distance between stars is nearly 20 million million miles.

Nino tries to grasp the concept, "So even if we could travel at the speed of light (172,000 miles per second) it would take a very long time to go from one star to the next, wouldn't it?"

"Nino there are 400 Billion stars in the Milky Way by it self, and the Milky Way is just one of over 170 billion other galaxies! Are you starting to get the picture? The average distance between these galaxies is 200 light years. Do you have any idea how far 200 light years is? It is an extraordinary distance that equals billions of miles. When you consider how truly vast outer space is, it is amazing how far away your modern astronomers can reach."

Nino nods in agreement, "It's true, I was reading an article the other day and it said that if someone were to flick their bic on the moon, they would be able to see the flame!"

Pilate is impressed, "It's really something; they can determine the size and probability of life on planets over millions of miles away. There truly isn't that much going on in the universe that escapes their far reaching gaze."

"So what's that say about extra terrestrial life?"

"I guess that is the moral of this space story. **Even if there were some other intelligent life form out there who could see us, they would be too far away to ever make contact.**"

Nino "So even if we we're really not all alone in the universe, for all intent and purpose we really are, aren't we?"

Smiling "Well not exactly."

Nino stupefied "Not exactly?!"

Pilate now smirking. "UFO's have been landing on your planet now for many thousands of years. You've heard the stories, crop circles, scared farmers, Stone hedges, abductions, and so on … Sure enough a lot of the stories are made up, but many of them are true."

Nino is blown away, "Man oh man! I always thought all that UFO stuff was just some big hoax. So there really are extraterrestrial beings out there in the universe. I would have never guessed you were gonna tell me some shit, excuse me, stuff like this! What are they? Little green men from Mars? All looking for a pay phone?"

Pilate snickers, "Good one, Nino. 'ET phone home.' That's a Spielberg classic, but you guys are way off track. I wish they were just little green men from Mars, flying around in flying saucers. If only it was that simple."

"Well, are you going to tell me who they are, and what their purpose is in the Great Game?"

"The drivers of these so called UFO's are none other than Satan and his fallen angels."

Nino is taken aback, "Satan and his Fallen Angels? But why?"

Pilate explains, "In the end of times when the Great Game is drawing to a close, the Fallen Angels will reveal themselves as extraterrestrial beings. They will arrive in their UFOs and claim to be the ancient astronauts that visited your planet. They will provide answers to all of the great mysteries of life, both religious and scientific. They will support all of the modern day scientific theories that run contrary to what is written in the sacred books. Religions will come to be seen as mythological legends that were written by primitive, less sophisticated humans to help explain the mysteries that existed in their life. They will also claim that they appeared to many early civilizations, and that it was these appearances that are the source of all the God and Angel legends. They were seen as gods because they came from the heavens with great light and noise. They had powerful weapons, and they would destroy any person or army of persons who opposed them. They will provide a false, but very believable history of how things came to be. They will possess supernatural powers, and they will do mighty miracles. They will cure the plagues of the earth, and provide solutions for the problems that exist in the world. They will appear to be angels of light and messengers of peace. They will claim to have traveled to Earth from a planet billions of light years away called Heaven, but this will be a lie. They will explain that this planet of theirs is a place where souls can live forever. They will describe Heaven as a dazzling paradise. They will say that no person has ever died. The souls of earth have just continued to live life after life. The purpose they will say was to gain spiritual enlightenment, while they awaited the return of the mother ship, that will take them home to Heaven, the land of their origin. However, all souls that board this mother ship will be lost to Satan."

Nino is disgusted, "How diabolical! How insidious! How can God let this happen? You can see how the people will be tricked. It is all going to be so believable. So apparently wonderful, how can he let this happen?"

Pilate continues, "Satan has argued that in the same way that God allowed his saints and prophets to do mighty miracles to gain followers, he must also allow Satan to use these same powers, for a similar purpose, to gain followers. The game must be fair in all ways. The difference is that God united his mighty power with truth. Satan will unite this power with lies. What else can we expect from the father of lies?"

"Where is the place that the demons will bring these souls that board the mother ship?"

"They will be brought to Satan's command center which is located somewhere in your very own solar system."

Nino is shocked, "In our solar system?"

"That's right. Would you care to guess which planet he uses? Just think for a moment about the planets in your solar system. Where is Satan hiding? I'll give you a hint. Hidden is the key word."

Nino scratches his forehead as he thinks,"Where is that old Serpent hiding? Hidden is the key word. Of course, it's Saturn!"

Pilate is impressed with Nino's wit. "Well done, Nino. Good show! There are some other symbols that give it away as well. Saturn stands for Satan's-turn. Satan's turn to use miraculous powers and put on a show for the whole world to see. The halo, the symbol of holiness that encircles the head of a Holy soul, is present, but it's in a fallen, lowered position. This is symbolic of Satan and his demons' fallen spiritual state. The gases that hide in the planet are symbolic of the evil and confusion that Satan and his demons spread throughout the world. Satan hides his true identity, but how clever is his disguise? The more you learn about Satan, the more ridiculous and childish he appears. Once he is truly exposed to the souls, they will be perplexed at how easy they were deceived."

"So, if Saturn is Satan's command post, is my goal to have the United States nuke Saturn?"

Pilate frowns, "No ... my dear, no. If only it were that easy. You cannot destroy Satan with weapons of mass destruction. Satan can only be defeated by the power of the Holy Spirit. Faith in God, and love for one another are the only ways by which humans can defeat, and ultimately destroy this evil being. Furthermore, no earthly probe or telescope will ever be able to reveal Satan's whereabouts. He exists on a spiritual plane. In a dimension that humans cannot perceive. He will reveal himself only when he chooses to. So, to go out searching for his command post would be fruitless. What you must do is prepare people for Satan's grand finale. You have got to do what that little dog Toto did to the Wizard of Oz, expose these extraterrestrial frauds for who and what they really are. Pull back the curtain, so that nobody will be going for any balloon rides with that snake. The mother ship will be exposed for what it truly is. A one way ride on the space shuttle to Hell."

"Is Saturn Hell?"

"Saturn is one of the most horrible places that you could ever imagine. However, when you compare Saturn to Hell, it will appear to be a tropical paradise."

Nino looks worried, "Is Hell really that bad?"

Pilate grimaces, "Nino, there is only one way for you to understand what Hell is like."

"How? Wait a minute. Why are you speeding up, Pilate? I hope we're not going where I think we are?"

Pilate grins, "Hang on, Nino! You are about to go on one Hell of a ride!"

With that, they were soon traveling at the speed of light on the real Highway to Hell. There is no wind or friction when traveling at any speed in Forever. Although they were traveling at 172,000 miles per second, there was nothing physically uncomfortable about the ride. Nino could still take in all of the beautiful countryside of Forever, in much the same way as he could if he were moving slowly down a calm stream in a canoe. In no time at all they had reached the end of the beautiful Kingdom of Forever. The beautiful countryside that seemed to glow with a warm, unearthly light was now behind them, and what lay in front of them was the cold gray ocean of emptiness called the Outer Darkness.

They traveled down into a deep, dark ravine that seemed to be a barrier between Forever and the Outer Darkness. The ravine was very steep and vast. It appeared to be many miles across. Its floor was covered with razor-sharp black diamond stalagmites that would cut you to shreds with even the slightest contact.

"Is this Hell?"

"No, this is what is referred to as the Outer Darkness. Look up there, behind you. Doesn't the Kingdom of Forever look beautiful? Please, Nino, describe to me what you see."

Nino almost couldn't look directly at the glow which shone from Forever. He struggled for the words which would do it justice. "It's incredible. Like a magnificent, beautiful city built upon a hill or a high plateau. The climate is always perfect and unchanging. There is absolutely nothing that is unpleasant in any way. Everything about the atmosphere is pleasing to the senses. The streets are paved with gold, silver, and platinum, the sidewalks are made of precious stones. All of the homes are beautiful mansions, each unique with splendid secret gardens, natural occurring fountains, and babbling brooks. There are scenic trails decorated with lovely foliage. There are brilliant multicolored fish in the waters. The fruits and flowers on the trees and bushes are absolutely flawless. All forms of vegetation generate their own special light, while continually bearing fruit. A new flavor and color for every season. The leaves of the trees are spectacularly colored. The wonderful smells of the land seem to constantly flow past your senses, carried on a warm breeze that always blows, ever so gently. The lakes and streams are sapphire and turquoise blue, and the sands that surround them are pure white, with smooth fiery opals and precious stones scattered throughout. The mountains to the recesses of the north are solid diamond crystals which capture the light of God and reflect it back in a fabulous rainbow. And the souls, so many uniquely beautiful souls, as far as the eye can see. Every soul has a special beauty that carries across the miles. They have a unique scent that pleases your nose from worlds away. You can actually capture the essence of each soul, just by gazing upon them. It's just. Oh Pilate, how will I ever be able to find the words to adequately describe the perfection, the beauty, and splendor of Forever?"

Pilate smiles, "I think you'll do just fine, Nino. Now look at the Outer Darkness. Describe what you see there."

"The cold gray climate is rising up from it. There are great gusts of dark wind that seem to carry unexpectedly frigid air that chills you to the bone. The streets are made of rocks and mud. The houses are flatly colored and they all look the same. They are placed very close together, with raggedy yards filled with thorns and weeds. There is absolutely nothing appealing. The souls look care worn and miserable. They gaze at the beautiful Kingdom of Forever, so far away yet so stunning. The souls weep and grind their teeth in frustration, thinking about what might have been. Oh, the pain they must feel. To be close enough to see the light of God, to gaze upon the beauty of his kingdom, to hear the sounds of eternal happiness and to smell the beautiful aromas, only to be reminded that they may never dwell in that splendor."

Nino stops talking for a moment, his mind seems to be wondering. "Pilate, have you ever heard of Alcatraz Prison?"

"Yes, it's on an island near San Francisco right?"

"Yeah, that's right. My friend Korzy, from the bowery was talking one day about the time he spent in Alcatraz. He said that it was a terrible prison. The guards were cruel, many of the inmates acted like animals, and the food was awful. But do you know what he said the worst part about doing time there was?"

Interested in where Nino was going with this story "No, what was it?"

"Seeing the beautiful city of San Francisco across the bay, and the Golden Gate Bridge with all the free people coming and going as the pleased. He said it was torture. He said the worst day of the year was New Years Eve, because the harbor would be filled with boats of people. It was like a giant floating New Years Eve party. He said you could hear music, and laughter. You could even smell the food cooking. You know like barbecued ribs, and steaks. The sights and sounds of paradise actually seemed to settle over the prison like a thick fog…. I'm sorry Pilate, I didn't mean to ramble on."

Smiling proudly. "You weren't rambling. You are right on track. Your friend Korzy's tale is a perfect analogy of how the souls of the Outer Darkness suffer mentally. Let's get back to your description, what's your first impression of the souls you see here in the Outer Darkness?"

"Each soul is imprisoned in a fleshy, earthly type of body that has aches, pains and sickness but does not die or grow old. The souls in the Outer Darkness are collectively homely and unappealing to look upon. They each have their own unique, vulgar smell. They must work at difficult but mundane jobs. They must try to bring forth food from an inhospitable terrain. Their lakes and rivers are polluted with sewage, and carry a foul stench. The animals and birds are wild, mean-tempered and foul in their mannerisms. Everywhere you turn, as far as the eye can see, there is nothing but despair and mourning. This is truly an atrocious place."

Pilate nods in agreement, "Atrocious indeed, but pleasurable compared to any level of Hell. At least in the Outer Darkness, you can still reflect on your life. You can read, you can talk to other souls. But they are unable to touch other souls like you can in Forever. There are also no sexual relationships, because there is no sex drive in these souls. There is no need to propagate the species. Nor does the blue moon rise over the outer darkness. As your years go by in the Outer Darkness, most souls are able to come to that 'I'll make the most of it' frame of mind. Eventually, your thought process changes from dwelling on what you are missing in paradise, to being thankful that you are not in Hell."

Nino is now scared,"Pilate, please, if Hell is as bad as you say it is, I can take your word for it. I really don't want to see it."

"I understand, Nino, but it is a necessary part of your tour. I'm sorry my friend, but we must move on. Don't worry, Nino. We won't stay any longer than necessary."

They traveled across the Outer Darkness until they came to an even darker ocean of land. As they approached the end of the Outer Darkness, they stood on the edge of a great abyss. Unlike the ravine that separated the Outer Darkness from the Kingdom of Forever, you could not see the end of this vast black hole. It appeared bottomless.

"This is the Great Abyss. The bottomless pit. It is what separates the Outer Darkness from the hideous kingdom called Hell."

"Aren't there different levels of Hell? Like in Dante's Inferno?" Asks Nino.

"Kind of, but in reality, Hell is Hell. Dante's book was good reading, and a splendid work of art, but his Hell does not begin to describe how atrocious the actual place really is. As you will soon see, there is nothing poetic about Hell. There is nothing inspiring. There is no reflective thought or learning taking place. You will not find even one repentant heart. There is nothing to hope for. Hell is nothing but torture, agony and the endless sounds of suffering souls. Hell is complete and absolute hopelessness. It is, well, come, it is time for you to tell me what it is."

As they plunged into the gloomy darkness of the abyss, Nino heard in the distance the sound of what he thought were the waves of a roaring ocean tide crashing against the shore. However, as they continued to travel, the roar became louder and more distinct. It was an ocean, an ocean of souls set adrift on a sea of sulfur and molten lava. Pilate parked his space cycle on a high bluff that looked out over the kingdom of Hell.

Pilate has to look away, "This is as far as we go, Nino. This is Hell."

Nino trembling, "Boy oh boy, when Jesus said it would be better to gouge out your eye or cut off your hand than to go to Hell, he wasn't joking was he?"

Pilate replies grimly, "No, he wasn't. This is truly a place to be feared. Please Nino, describe to me your experience of Hell. What do you see? How does it make you feel?"

"I can't explain the evil I feel. It is a diabolical presence that has me petrified to the point that I feel like I'm going to collapse. As we plunge into the abyss, I can feel the heaviness of the air around me. Something about the air reminds me of Vietnam. Deeper into the abyss, I hear a roar of what I think are the waves of a mighty ocean. It was not the roar of its surf, but rather, the endless wailings of what must be billions of tortured souls all struggling to keep a float on this stormy sea. This ocean appears to be a turbulent sea of fire. Flames and smoke spew forth from a sea of molten lava. The smoke smells of sulfur, and it burns my eyes and skin even from here, in much the same way as the tear gas in Vietnam. As we approach the shore of this abhorrent sea, I am hit with another smell that is so obnoxious and putrid that it nearly causes me to collapse again. It is the smell of rotting, burned, human flesh. The souls of Hell appear to be imprisoned in bodies that are about to die, though they are incapable of doing so. They are hungry but cannot eat, they are thirsty but cannot drink. They are tired but cannot sleep. Although they do not eat or drink, they still urinate, have bowel movements and vomit. This only adds to the stench of Hell's sea and shore. This sea is furthermore filled with some kind of large eels or snakes that eat the flesh and make their homes in the bodies and skulls of these tortured souls. There are also wicked miniature sharks with razor-sharp fins that slice open anything they brush up against, and their jagged spear-like teeth are used to rip the limbs from the sorrowful souls. The souls feverishly try to keep afloat because to be submerged means that the reverse undertow will pull them to shore. The souls caught in the undertow are washed up onto the shore with such great force the skin is ripped from their bodies. The souls are doused with a salty hot rain that constantly falls upon the shores of Hell. This salt water causes excruciating pain when it comes into contact with the souls' open sores. The shores are filled with terribly ferocious lizards with heads like wolves and teeth like alligators. These miserable beasts partially eat all who come upon their shores. Also roaming the jagged coral beach are giant stinging scorpions that constantly and unmercifully sting the shore-bound souls. Every spider's excruciatingly painful sting turns into a cancerous tumor which throbs painfully and bursts through the skin like a giant red globe. These tumors are pecked at and eaten by miserable leather winged vultures of Hell. These are truly the most hideous looking birds I have ever seen. These vultures eat the tumors and then take what's left of the soul's body and fly it back out over the toxic sea of fire. As soon as the body hits the sea, it is completely restored, and the process starts all over again. There is also an area just beyond the horizon of the shoreline in which there are hundreds of thousands of shallow pits or holes. Standing in these pits are a countless number of souls that are endlessly tortured by sadistic demons. Although I stand here in its midst and attempt to describe what I see, Hell is a horror that is beyond my comprehension. My heart is so overwhelmed that I know not what I feel other than that which I felt when I first stood at the mouth of the abyss. I am petrified with terror, and at the same time repulsed. I feel very sorry for those who are sentenced to this awful place and yet I heard no cry for mercy. I only hear shrieks of pain …

Please, Pilate, take me from this place. I have seen enough. I cannot bear to stay here one more moment."

They traveled back up through the abyss and across the Outer Darkness. They paused for a moment to take in one last glimpse of how beautiful the Kingdom of Forever looks as they gazed up from the darkness below. As beautiful as it was, Nino felt compelled to turn from it and take one last look over the Outer Darkness.

"What is it, Nino?"

"As I look out over the Outer Darkness and all its misery, and then think of Hell and its atrocious suffering, I realize that I forgot to ask a very important question. How does a soul end up in …"

Pilate finishes Nino's question, "Hell instead of the Outer Darkness?"

"Yes."

Pilate explains, "The Outer Darkness is for all souls who ultimately die in a state of sin. Their soul, like a glistening white robe, is stained by the life or lives that they have lived. I know that Mary and Caiaphas have already spoken to you about Purgatory, but I have one final chapter on the matter. A soul that is sentenced to Purgatory must wait for a suitable entry into the Great Game. It goes without saying that they will be at the back of a very long line of souls who are also waiting to re-enter the Game."

"How long do you have to wait before you can get back in?" Asks Nino.

"Anywhere from 11 months to one hundred years, depending on the number of abortions that occur, along with the natural infant deaths."

"I see what you mean. No baby, no entry point. Why do some souls get to reenter so quickly?"

"Reentry also has to do with each soul's individual situation. So for example, if you die and then a year later your daughter gets pregnant you could reenter the game very quickly."

"I see what you mean. So it's really just a matter of killing time in a miserable place until your entry point comes along, right?"

Pilate grows serious, "That's right. However, the problem is more serious than you can imagine."

Nino senses Pilates mood, "What do you mean? Don't some souls just have to wait a little longer to get back into the Great Game?"

"Every soul that is not admitted into Forever upon completion of his life is banished to the Outer Darkness to contemplate their future. When you finally reach the front of the line ..."

Ninos interrupts, "You don't actually wait in line right?"

"No, you simply dwell in the Outer Darkness until you are summoned to the Gof."

"What is the Gof?"

Pilate continues, "It is the great hall of souls. It is a place from which all departing souls are escorted to their mother's womb by their Guardian Angels. Anyway, the soul that is banished to the Outer Darkness can still be tempted by demons. They are seduced into serving Satan, and convinced that they are not ever going to be successful. The souls that have been recycled many times are especially vulnerable. Their Earthly circumstances just keep getting more difficult, and they begin to doubt themselves. The demons tell them that God in his mercy will never end the Great Game. So, rather than enduring what will be this endless cycle of pain, they are convinced that it is better to reign in Hell than to suffer in the Outer Darkness for an eternity. However, the demons don't reveal the reality of Hell which you just witnessed."

Nino perplexed, "Why don't the souls just decide to become Heavenly servants?"

"Didn't Mary tell you? Once you go through the Great Game three times, you no longer have the option of becoming a Heavenly servant." "Three strikes and you're out, huh? Don't tell me ..."

Pilate grins, "That's right, that's where your baseball rule came from. Anyway, the soul entering Purgatory after that third time starts to get a little nervous. Each failure makes the next game that much more difficult. With each new life, the probability of success diminishes. They begin to lose faith in themselves and ultimately, God. These souls are particularly vulnerable because of the suffering they have to endure. They also have no help from Angels or the Holy Spirit. These lost souls become soldiers in Satan's Army. They are free to walk the earth as Demons and they gain earthly pleasures through the humans they possess. By uniting themselves with Satan they have committed the ultimate sin. They know, without a doubt, that God exists, and still they go against him. This is the same as the original sin that Satan and his Fallen Angels committed. It is the sin unto death. The unforgivable sin. To clearly understand that God exists, and to consciously turn your back on him and side with Satan is the worst sin imaginable. As long as the Great Game continues, the demons will be allowed to tempt the souls that are in the Outer Darkness. Once the Great Game is complete, the tempting of these banished souls will come to an end."

"So that is how a soul ends up in Hell?" Nino asks.

"Yes, along with the billions of original fallen angels. These are the souls that will occupy Hell for an eternity."

"And the souls that ultimately end up in the Outer Darkness?"

"Failures, or losers of the Great Game end up in the Outer Darkness. However, they are winners in the sense that they were able to keep from being lured into the greater tortures of Hell."

Nino frowns, "It seems like they should get some credit or reward for doing that."

Pilate's expression brightens for a moment. "They will. Once every seven years after the Great Game is complete, Jehovah will shine his holy light on them for seven days. During these seven days, the citizens of Forever will be allowed to cross the great ravine and bring gifts and food to their suffering brothers and sisters. There will be great feasts and entertainment. There will be music, and much laughing and singing. Jesus came up with this idea. He felt that although they had died the second death, they still deserved some credit for overcoming the demons of the Outer Darkness."

"The Second Death?" Asks Nino.

"The Second Death is a spiritual death in which your opportunity to spend eternity in Forever is over. Woe to those who die the second death. There will be much weeping, wailing and gnashing of teeth. These aren't my words."

"I know."

"Well, enough of the fire and brimstone part of the tour. We must hurry along. There is someone I want you to meet."

Pilate snaps his fingers and within the blink of an eye, Pilate gets rid of his space cycle and they are soon walking along the shore line of a magnificent ocean, toward a spectacular palace that overlooks the sea.

"Let's walk for awhile, Nino. I need to take in a different perspective."

"Me to." Nino notices the mansion for the first time. "Wow, that sure is some spread. Who lives there?" "A soul named Solomon."

Nino's eyes grow wide, "King Solomon?!"

Pilate grins, "The one and only. I thought it would be good for you to speak to him for a little while before I take you to Malcolm."

"I would be honored to speak to him."

"And he, you."

"When we were in the Outer Darkness, you said something that has me puzzled."

"Regarding what?"

"The immortal soul that is housed in its new body, you said that there are no sexual relations because there is no sex drive, no need to propagate the species."

"That's right."

"Well, if this is true, then why do I see what looks to be beautiful men and women everywhere I turn. Are the souls of Forever male and female? Or what?"

Pilate smiles, "Souls are who they are. On earth, you enter into the Great Game as either a male or a female. This was designed to propagate the species in a way that would allow people to still have faith. God couldn't just have babies appearing out of the blue, because people would begin to catch on."

"I see what you mean."

"The immortal souls that appear female to you in Forever simply have qualities and characteristics which you associate with traditional female roles on earth. The same is true of those who appear to be male."

"So, if there really are no females, why do I see so many beautiful women?"

"They are genderless. There is no sexual distinction. However, each soul is able to mold and shape its body so that it is an absolute representation of how it would like to be seen on that particular day. A body that will allow it to absolutely express itself. Also, once you choose a certain look or body type, you are not bound to it. You can change it whenever you like. Remember, Nino, there are no laws in Forever. There are no roles to shackle your creativity. You are absolutely free to express yourself and nothing is frowned upon. Everything is exciting and always changing."

Nino is perplexed by the thought of it. "How can people remember who anyone is if they are always changing what they look like?"

"It is in the soul's eyes. Remember how Jesus said the eye is the window to the soul? Well, in Forever, all you need to do is make eye contact with someone, and if you have ever met, you will remember them immediately. Haven't you ever run into an old acquaintance on earth and recognized them because of something in their eyes?"

Nino understands, "Yes, many times. The face might change, but it's something in the eyes that triggers the memory. Yup, I know exactly what you mean. Isn't that something! ... Pilate, I'm still a little confused about something, though."

"What is it?" Pilate asks.

"Now, here we are walking along this beach, and excuse me if I'm out of line Pilate, but I see many beautiful souls that look like women to me. I mean, they have breasts and vaginas for God's sake! What are the purposes of these? ... And the male looking souls have ... you know, male parts! Real long ones, too! Even the white guys!"

Pilate laughs "Nino, I'm surprised that you would believe such propaganda."

Nino laughing, "I'm just kidding ya. But, seriously, if there is no sexual drive and you have no need to go to the bathroom, what are their private parts for?"

Pilate smiles and sighs at the thought of it, "In one word, pleasure. The souls of Forever are in new bodies to be sure, but there is still a physical element to these bodies, and since that is the case, you can give and receive pleasure through the manipulation of these body parts. However, this pleasure is not like earthly sexual pleasure that comes from need. This is a Heavenly pleasure that comes for wanting to share and express your unconditional, needless love in a physical way."

"I thought that was what the soul touch did?"

"The soul touch is a spiritual ecstasy that starts in the soul and reverberates throughout the body. The soulgasm ..."

Nino raises his eyebrows, "Soulgasm?"

"The soulgasms start in the body and reverberate throughout the soul. It is just another sweet little ecstasy of paradise."

"So, the souls of Forever can have sex?"

"They have soulgasms."

"Yeah, but how does one have a soulgasm?"

Pilate laughs, "However one wants to!"

"Huh?"

Pilate explains, "In a way, lovemaking in Forever will be similar to what you experience on Earth in terms of all the different ways the pleasurable parts fit together. However, in terms of the pleasure you give and receive, the satisfaction you obtain, there is no comparison."

Nino is curious, "Does everybody have the same attitude about making love as they do about soul touching?"

"Yes. The lovemaking experience is different with every soul. It is uniquely beautiful in sight, sound, smell, taste, motion and so on. Everyone you meet will want to make love with you, but there is one distinction between this and soul touching. In Forever, while soul touching happens anytime of the day or night, lovemaking only happens during the evening hours while the moonlight is shining. Our Heavenly Father is the quintessential romantic."

"So, you can only make love during the evening under the moonlight?"

Pilate makes clear, "It's not that you can't make love during the daylight hours; it is just that you don't feel like it until after you eat dinner and see the moonlight. There is something about the heavenly moon's light that puts you into a romantic mood. In Forever, the moonlight actually physically arouses all of your souls romantic passions. The light that shines forth from our Heavenly blue moon is literally absorbed into the body, and the souls that are making love actually take on a certain glow. As the souls make love, the moonlight flows from one soul to the other, causing an endless stream of soulgasms that gradually build in intensity and ecstasy. The soulgasms roll through the body like waves on a giant ocean crashing into the shore. One after another, each wave of love slowly rises to its pinnacle and then gently subsides, perfectly timed to the desires of the souls that are making love. As one wave fades away, another slowly begins to rise. It truly is a fabulous experience. I wish you were going to be here long enough to try it out."

Nino gushes, "It all sounds pretty steamy to me. Barabbas probably knew if I tried that I might not want to go back to earth and finish my job!"

Pilate chuckles, "You are probably right, my friend!"

"So, that's why earth bound souls connect romance to the moon?"

"That's right, Nino. Everything on earth has its origin in Forever. The faint memory of what once was and what will someday be again lingers on."

"Pilate, I just thought of something. If a soul can form its body however it wants to, does that mean that I could have female characteristics or male characteristics whenever I felt like it?"

"Yes, and what's pleasurable about that is that it changes each experience for you. For example, you may have made love to a certain soul when she appeared female and you male; and then you meet again in opposite roles. Your experience will be uniquely and quite remarkably different!"

Nino somewhat embarrassed to broach the subject, "I just thought of something else, but I'm almost afraid to ask. What about homosexuality? Does that exist in Forever?"

"Well, first of all, there is no way for homosexuality to exist when it comes to souls. In Forever, you can make love with every other soul, whether it appears male or female, but when you unite, you each take on a more gender-specific role. God designed the male and female bodies to fit together like puzzle pieces, so these characteristics are bestowed upon the two loving souls, no matter what gender they may desire to be."

Nino a little rattled, "Man, I don't care what you say, it still sounds messed up to me."

Pilate reassures Nino, "Not in Paradise, it isn't! In Forever, it is just one more way to have a unique lovemaking experience. Remember in Forever its all about expressing your love spiritually and physically. There is nothing dirty, perverse, or possessive. There are no sexually transmitted diseases, laws or stereotypes. No discrimination of any kind exists in Forever. Unlike earth, in Forever anything goes. In Forever, you must cease to think of things in terms of male and female. Souls are just free to use whatever pleasurable pieces they desire."

"So, homosexuality is like the moonlight, huh? A faint memory of what once was?"

"What do you mean?" Asks Pilate.

"I mean, that faint memory of how things are in Forever moves them to express their love in a way that best coincides with who they are on the inside, not what they appear on the outside."

Pilate clarifies, "Free will and sexual desire, along with the faint memory of Forever, will inevitably set the stage for a sexually permissive society. People, both hetero and homo sexual can easily become bored with the sex that occurs in a monogamous relationship. The development of bisexuality is what comes from the factors you have described. The need to always be moving on to something new, something exotic or novel, this is what the soul remembers and longs for. You also have Satan in the background, peddling his forbidden fruit nonsense, and this trips up a lot of good people. If you break human sexuality down, it's biochemically the same as eating large amounts of chocolate. The body just wants a physical release. The soul is what creates the fantasies. True homosexuality on the other hand, is genetically induced. This does not mean that homosexuality is what God intended for humans. It is just that some individuals are born with a certain genetic make up which gives them a sexual desire for the same sex. This genetic abnormality causes the person to behave in a certain way. A homosexual's attraction to the same sex is the same as a heterosexual's attraction to the opposite sex. Therefore, how can they be considered sinners when that which drives them is genetically induced? The human sexual drive is a force of nature that is hard to control. It is harder still to satisfy."

Nino is confused, "But, I was taught that God considers homosexuality a terrible sin."

Pilate makes clear, "He did at one time. But now he accepts it as one of the conditions that can occur when a soul is given free will and born with a certain genetic make-up. That is why Jesus never spoke of homosexuality being a sin. A homosexual who is following the path of Jesus will get into Heaven as easily as a heterosexual who is following that same trail. It would not be fair for God to expect that a homosexually born person to deny his or her genetically programmed sexual impulses. It is the militant homosexuals that promote immoral, perverted sexually permissive lifestyles whom God has

a problem with. People who 'become' homosexuals to make political state-
ments, or simply to defy the laws of their states, countries, or organized religion are the ones who upset Allah. The sex sins of the homosexuals are the
same as the sex sins of the heterosexuals. The behavior that is looked down
on is immoral permissive behavior."

Nino is perplexed, "But what truly is immoral sexual behavior? Isn't it
up to the individual to decide what is good for themselves? I mean there are
lots of strange sexual practices, and attitudes about sex. What one person
considers vulgar of promiscuous, another person may view as absolutely
normal and inline with their sexual identity."

Pilate explains, "One of the greatest gifts that Jehovah has given us is the
ability to make love to one another. This act is sacred for two reasons; the
possibility of creating a new life usually exists, and when two people make
love their souls briefly become one. No matter what your sexual preference
or attitude is. When you live in away that cheapen's this wonderful experience, it's like throwing mud on the Mona Lisa. Remember this Nino, you
should only make love to someone that you are truly deeply in love with ...
And true love is something that is very hard to find. Therefore, people who
have sex with whomever they can just to satisfy their own selfish needs, and
people who lie and manipulate others in order to control or seduce other
people are the true sexual siners in God's eyes. For they have taken what is
precious, and thrown it before the swine."

Nino is surprised, "I'm beginning to see the world so much differently.
When one truly sees all the elements at play in the Great Game of Life it
is impossible to have a harsh world view. Some of the things you said, I
would have never believed it, but it all makes sense to me now...." Nino
pauses for a moment and scratches his head. "All but one thing ... You said
at first that homosexuality was a sin, but as time went by, God learned that
it was something that was bound to occur. I thought God knew everything?
How come he didn't see this coming?"

"You have to remember something, Nino. When we were souls in Forever,
before the Great Game began, we were all living in Paradise with God. Our
will, was his will, because we lived in his kingdom, and their was no outside influence to contend with. However, when he placed our immortal
souls into human bodies that could be tempted by Satan into doing things

that ran contrary to Yahweh's will, He was in unfamiliar territory. God, the all powerful, omnipotent and omniscient, can create anything imaginable, but he cannot make someone love him. Man was given free will and laws to live by, in the hopes that he would eventually come to love God. Yahweh had no experience with how to deal with a being who had free will living under these adverse human conditions. In many areas he was learning as he went along, and he made mistakes along the way like any new parent does."

"New parent?" Asks Nino.

Pilate clarifies, "In his making of mankind, he was like a new parent. There was nothing to prepare him for what he created. He was used to hanging out with Heavenly beings and Angels who did whatever he asked them to. Nine out of ten times, a parent's expectations are too high, and the parent is too severe with their first born child. The truth is, God was way too hard on his first children, the Jews. The later children that came along definitely had it easier in a lot of ways. Just consider the message of Jesus, as compared to the message of Moses. God was much more patient and merciful. He was much more willing to show his loving compassionate side."

Nino tries to make sense of it all. "So, the God of the Old Testament really is the same God. He just kind of mellowed out through understanding, like any other parent?"

Pilate smiles and continues, "He simply realized that a soul placed in a human body with a free will means that some things were out of his control. No matter how miserable he became, or how hard he chastised and tried to discipline his children, he could not control their actions. Ultimately, they had to make up their own minds about what they were going to do. God found that he could share his wisdom, but he couldn't make the people follow it. That was up to each individual. He also came to the realization that the hard line he was using to try and scare them into submitting to his will was not producing the loving relationship that he wanted to have with his children. He wanted them to respect him and live as he directed them to live. But ultimately, he wanted be loved. That's who and what our father in Heaven really is. He came to the realization that any parent would come to. That helpless, hopeful longing that your child will turn out good exists in all of us. The realization that although children come through you, they are unique individuals who ultimately must make their own decisions. You can try to force them into a mold, and you definitely need a firm hand to spank their behinds from time to time. But when they get to be young adults, you realize all you can do is give them advice, not make them follow it. God, like all parents, also had to deal with outside influences. It's pretty easy to control your children when they're little and spend the majority of their time with their parents. However, when your children go off to school, that sets the stage for a whole new batch of problems."

Nino clarifies, "So when God set us loose on the earth one of the biggest differences was the influence of Satan and people who were immoral and/or had no faith."

Pilate shakes his head in agreement, "That's right. And as time went by, God's perspective changed, and his disposition softened. He really has experienced much of what all good parents go through, and ultimately he wants what all good parents desire: a child who will love him and be a good person. A good parent's best attribute is to never give up on their child, to keep on hoping until the bitter end."

Nino understands, "I see what you mean. Even when your kid turns out bad, you just keep hoping that some day she will see the light and do the right thing...."

Pilate explains, "Exactly. I mean if you need further proof of how God looks past our short comings, simply peruse some of the evidence provided in the Bible. Abraham was too old. Isaac was a day dreamer. Jacob was a liar. Leah was ugly. Joseph was abused. Moses murdered an Egyptian guard and had a stuttering problem. Gideon was afraid. Samson had long hair and was a womanizer. Rahab was a prostitute. David had an affair and was a murderer. Elijah was suicidal. Isaiah sometimes preached naked. Jonah ran from God. Job went bankrupt, and Peter denied Jesus three times. I could go on, but you get the point. God's love for us, and his faith in our potential is what guides him and inspires most of the decisions that he makes."

Nino nods, "So like any loving mother or father, God simply want what's best for his children. He believes in us, and he assists us in every way that he is able ... It sounds like our Heavenly Father truly is a selfless servant of his children."

Pilate nods, "Nino, it is just as simple as that. And I can add nothing more to what you have so eloquently stated."

"The greatest human achievement is selflessness."
-Siddhartha Gautama: The Buddha 550 BC

CHAPTER 22

▼

"Whoever wishes to be great will be your servant, and amongst you, whoever wishes to be first will be the slave of all. For the Son of Man did not come to be served but to serve, and to give his life as a ransom for many."
-JESUS OF NAZARETH (Mark 10:43-45) (57 AD)

"Nothing great or meaningful ever appears fully developed. Even the great Michael Jordan had to walk before he could run, and run before he could fly!. Just as tiny drops of water can eventually, over time, wear a whole through the toughest granite. So to can the cumulative effect of our consistent efforts to spread kindness and mercy, change this world. Never be discouraged by the harvest of single day!"
-Mark Salvatore Pitifer (Banzi The Bravest Little Badger)

They walked on to the front porch of Solomon's house, and he was resting in a hammock that seemed to be made out of weaved clouds. Pilate crept up and gave the hammock a giant spin. Everyone in Forever is a practical joker, and nobody ever takes things the wrong way.

Solomon is startled but still laughing, "Pilate, you rascal! I should have known better than to take a nap knowing that you were on your way here!" Solomon grabs Pilate and smiles, "How are you, my friend?"

Pilate is grinning from ear to ear. "Very good, Solly, and you?"

Solly takes a deep breath, "Well, I was doing just fine until you showed up!"

Pilate turns towards Nino, "King Solomon, this is …"

Solomon cuts off Pilate and grabs Nino's hand. "Nino Jones. It is a pleasure to meet you."

"Thank you, King Solomon. I can't tell you what an honor it is to meet you."

"Oh, come now, Nino, no formalities here. You can call me Solly. After all, there is only one king in Forever! I am officially retired from royalty, thank God! … Nino we better get going. Since I'm only a retired king now, I only get to spend a short time with you. I don't rank as high as Pilate, and the other Zealots!"

Pilate grins sheepishly, "Oh, come on Solly, you can have as much time with Nino as you need."

Solly knows this to be the truth, "I really don't need much time to say what I have to say. I simply want to speak with you briefly about the plague that is currently ravishing your world. Especially your United States. I think there is something you can do to help bring it to an end."

Nino perplexed, "What can I do to stop AIDS?"

Solly chuckles, "I'm not talking about AIDS Nino. I am talking about adultery. As I'm sure you have read my father, King David, committed a terrible sin because he fell in love with the wife of one of his friends."

For Solly's sake Nino tries to down play David's offense, "But that's a common scenario isn't it? The crimes of adultery and murder are not usually committed by strangers, but by the people that we know. We covet what we see, and in so doing end up hurting the very people that we claim to love the most. If you truly look at the deed of adultery, how could you ever feel good about making love to someone else's spouse? I mean, I understand how these things happen. Two people become familiar and comfortable with one another. The relationship goes from friendly to flirtatious. This sets the stage for mild intimacies, which if left unchecked could lead to adulterous behavior."

Solly smiling "Nino, it sounds like you've had some experience in this area."

Nino blushing "I wish. Just kidding … I read a lot of romantic novels."

Solly laughing "Nino you're too much."

Nino, laughing, but turning serious again. "Hey, I just know how people are. Everyone wants to feel young and alive again, even if it's only for a moment. Heck, I think God even understands this sort of spiritual and emotional stumbling. But, the worst kind of people in my mind, are those to seek to possess. Those who intentionally destroy what God has joined together for their own selfish pleasure.... That's just so thoughtless, and cruel.... It's ... It's evil isn't it?"

Solly agrees "It's true, and that's what makes what my father did all the more heinous. He had his lover's husband placed on the front lines of the battle field hoping that he would be killed. He purposely placed his friend in harms way, so that he could be with his wife! This is the epitome of coveting thy neighbors wife. My father was a good and wise man Nino. But Satan was able to use passion and lust to make him behave as if he was selfish and cruel."

Nino feels bad, "I know. It's a sad story. I've read it many times. It's hard to believe that someone that was so close to God could fall like that."

Solomon continues, "Then you must have read my story as well. You would have thought that I might have learned from my father's mistakes, but I didn't. I spent my whole life trying to live by God's laws. I was known as the wisest of kings, but for all my wisdom, in spite of all my writings and warnings to my own sons, what happens to me? I was seduced by Satan near the end of my Earthly days, and I committed the worst type of adultery."

Nino confused, "I didn't think you committed adultery. I thought you were allowed to have more than one wife."

Solly explains, "What I did was worse than physically cheating on a wife. I worshipped a false God. I was so swept away with my feelings for a particular woman that I betrayed Allah. I left my God to worship a false one. This is one of the most offensive kinds of adultery."

"I never thought of what you did in those terms, but I see what you mean. That had to be awful when you finally realized what you had done?"

Solly winces at the memory of it. "Oh, Nino, it was horrible! I cried and begged God to forgive me. How I wished I could take it all back like it never happened. But I couldn't. It is a permanent part of my past and although God has forgiven me, the memory of it still causes me pain."

"I understand, Solly. Your pain is similar to most of the members of the group I represent. I hope I will be able to ease your pain in some way through my mission."

Solly smiles confidently, "I am certain that you will. First of all, you must stress the importance of marriage. Marriage is not for everyone, but for those who decide to marry, they must stay married."

"Is divorce a sin?"

"No matter what the circumstances are there is an element of sin in every divorce. A divorce that is the result of a totally selfish act, is looked at in a different light than lets say one that ends because of repeated abuse. The sin is further magnified when children are involved, because it almost always sets the stage for future divorces in the generations to follow."

Solly and Nino walked down to the shore and sat on chairs made out of a beautiful wood that was shaped by the winds, and made smooth by the waters of the sea. Solly continued to speak of the sacrament of marriage.

"Marriage is the most sacred pact that a soul can enter into. It is sacred because first and foremost, it involves making a vow to God." Nino remembers, "Jesus warns us not to make vows to God."

Solly nods in agreement, "He warned us because he knew that a vow that is made to God cannot be broken. In a soul's life, any sin that you are appropriately contrite about can be forgiven. However, a vow that is made to God must be kept. To break this vow means that no matter how good you live the rest of your life, you will still have a price to pay."

"Like what?"

"Possibly, purgatory or some lesser punishment. It all depends on the individual circumstances."

"So if you commit adultery you are definitely going to suffer in some way?"

Solly nods in agreement, "That's right, but if you are able to find your way back to the P.O.J. after committing adultery, God will forgive a truly contrite heart. However, there is a special penalty that goes along with those who commit adultery. If you are married and you have an affair with someone else, even if you stay married, your price is that you will not be allowed to touch your lover's soul in the Forever, until the Great Game is complete. Originally God was going to make the punishment for eternity, but that would have led to sadness being in the New Jerusalem. Jesus prevailed upon him to shorten the sentence."

"So now the souls are simply restricted until the New Jerusalem is complete." Asks Nino.

"Yes, assuming you both make it to Forever."

"True."

Solly concerned, "Also, don't forget this is still a terribly difficult punishment, one that could last for hundreds, even thousands of years."

"What about an unmarried person who commits adultery with a married person?"

"Their penalty is the same."

"Well, that's a tough sentence, but a fair one … Hey, hold on a second, what about a person whose wife or husband leaves them for another lover?"

Solly clarifies, "The person responsible for causing the marriage to end is the person God holds primarily responsible for breaking the vow. However, the other party is still held partially responsible. The only exception to this rule is in situations in which one of the people is an Agnostic or an Atheist. You are not forced to stay in a marriage with someone who does not accept and support your faith."

Nino, somewhat agitated "But shouldn't they have known up front that the person was an unbeliever?"

"They should have, and most of the time they do. However, what often happens is that the believer, filled with love, feels that they will be able to convert their prospective spouse. Unfortunately this is very rarely successful."

Nino tries to think of some other scenarios. "Ok, umm … What about if a spouse becomes abusive, or a drunk? What if you really do fall out of love with the person, and you are always fighting? Is that type of family good for children to be raised in?"

"No, it's not, but let's think about something for a moment. Are people forced to get married?" Questions Solly.

Nino chuckles, "Maybe in some countries, but not in mine."

"So, most people come on their own free will, and say to God that they will love and cherish this person in good times and bad, sickness and health, etc … This means that you are saying, 'God, no matter what happens or how bad things get, I will stay married until death ends the marriage.' The laws of your country and others in the world make it easy to get out of a marriage, but the laws of Allah make it impossible. When you leave your wife or husband, because you have fallen in love with someone else, you commit adultery. This also causes the estranged spouse to commit adultery."

Nino confused, "I thought you said only the person responsible for the marriage ending is guilty of breaking the vow?"

"This is true, but the other person is still partially responsible for the pain that comes from a failed marriage."

"How?" Nino asks.

"For choosing a poor mate, for not taking the time to really get to know the person they married; for not really considering the vows they were taking, and the spiritual impact and responsibility of marriage."

Nino agitated, "How can a person be held responsible for marrying someone who turns out to be an unfaithful or abusive idiot?"

"Here is how the mistakes are made. It is in pointing these out that I hope you can stem the tide of marriage in your country, and around the world."

Nino clarifies, "You mean divorce, don't you?"

"No, I mean marriage. If people would really stop and consider the spiritual and social ramifications of what it truly means to get married, you would have a lot less people rushing into it for the wrong reasons."

"Is God anti-marriage?" Asks Nino.

Solly shakes his head, "Of course not. He's just anti-bad marriage. It is bad marriages that take place for the wrong reasons that lead to divorce. Divorce may be the final outcome, but it is not the essence of the problem."

… Solly leads walks Nino into his dinning room where a beautiful meal has been prepared …

"Never let old age and diminishing skills keep you away from the sports and activities that you once loved. Refuse to fade away. As you grow older, play the games of your youth, not for competitive reasons, but simply for the feel of the game. Free yourself from the yoke of worrying about how far, how fast, or how many. I was an Olympian Triple Jumper, the first person ever to jump over 57 feet at sea level. I no longer compete for medals, now I merely jump for the joy of jumping. And each time I do, it is like dipping myself in the fountain of youth. In dancing through these movements from my past, I am forever young!"
-Milan Tiff (UCLA 1986: <u>Traveling Light)</u>

CHAPTER 23

▼

"The wisdom that comes from Heaven is first of all pure and full of
quiet gentleness. Then it is peace-loving and courteous. It allows
discussion and is willing to yield to others: it is full of mercy and
good deeds. It is wholehearted, straightforward and sincere. And
those who are peacemakers will plant seeds of peace and reap a
harvest of goodness."
-James 3:17-18

"I'm talking to that man in the mirror. I'm asking him to change his
ways. And no message could be made any clearer. If you want to make
the world a better place, take a look at yourself and make a change!"
-Michael Jackson (Man In The Mirror)

Solly holds out both hands and says "Dinner is served."

Nino smiles and jokes, "I was wondering if you guys were ever gonna feed
me up here."

Solly chuckles, "Why were you hungry?"

Nino perplexed, "You know come to think of it I wasn't. That is until I saw
this spread, and now I feel hungrier than a starving wolf!"

Solly smiles, "I know isn't it wonderful. Up here we never eat because we
have to. We simply eat because we enjoy eating. The nicest part about it is that
you will only feel hungry when you smell or see food that looks appealing to
you. Its' fantastic, and the food. Well, it goes with out saying, is out of this
world!" Solly and Nino break into laughter.

They finish their lunch, and walk down to the sea shore. As Nino looks out
over the topaz sea, Solomon begins to speak. "Nino, I am about to give you
my final book of wisdom to be shared with the world. This third book of

proverbs is intended to influence teenagers and young adults of your day and time. Are you ready my scribe?"

Nino bows, "Yes, I am honored sir." Nino sits next to Solly and gives him his full attention. As Solly begins to speak, the tone of his voice changes, as does the expression on his face ...

THE PROVERBS BOOK III

"Vows Made to God,"

'Set your desire upon my words; love them and you will have instruction. Wisdom is glorious and never fades away. It is better than strength! She is seen by those who love her, and found by those who seek her. Wisdom is an infinite treasure and all who use her become friends of God."
-The Book of Wisdom 6 & 7:12-14 (King Solomon)

Making a vow to God and keeping it will bring forth many blessings on earth and in Heaven.

Making a vow to God and not keeping it will bring forth many problems on earth and in Heaven.

Breaking a vow to God will almost always land you in purgatory ... And if the Great Game ends before you get to re-enter or are able to find the path, you will spend your eternity in the Outer Darkness.

"Does the person who tries to save the marriage usually end up in Purgatory as well?"

"No, Nino, but they have to suffer more than they normally would during the course of their life for the poor decision they made. They may also not be allowed to touch the soul of whomever they go with after their divorce."

"That doesn't seem like a fair way to treat someone who really did try to save their marriage."

"Remember, Nino, things are not always what they seem. For example, the spouse who does the cheating may at first glance appear to be the selfish partner in the marriage. However, if the situation is examined a little more closely, we often find that many of these people who see themselves as innocent victims were also selfish and indifferent to the needs of their spouse. As I'm sure you will be told time and again, selfishness is the foundation of all sin. A selfish act is a loveless act. Believe me, Nino, God takes no delight in handing out punishments. When God makes a judgment, it is based on what a person's own soul says about them. When a soul receives their sentence from God, they never argue. All they do is say 'I'm sorry, Father.'"

"I understand. It makes sense to me when you put it that way. So, what's next, my king?"

Solly fakes agitation, "Hey, cool it with the king stuff! There's only one King up here."

Nino smiling "Alright, alright. What's next, Solly?"

Solomon rubs his chin and looks up to the sky, as if he's waiting for inspiration. He instructs Nino to title the next section

"Dating and Premarital Sex."

"Time is sort of a river of passing events, and strong is its current; no sooner is a thing brought to sight than it is swept by and another takes its place, and this too will be swept away."
-Marcus Aurelius

You should not go steady with any one person, or allow a relationship to get too serious until you become an adult. Remember, very few people ever end up marrying their high school sweethearts.

Nino smiles, "It's true. When your young you think that your in love so many different times. But when you look back on that segment of your life as an adult it seems so silly. These kid now a days enter into serious relationships way to young. It's almost like our society pressures you into living old before your time."

Solly agrees, "You're right. A person should never allow themselves to be pressured into having sex of any kind. If a person really cares for you and is unselfish, they will be willing to wait until you are ready. Likewise, never pressure another into having sex with you."

Nino nods in agreement, "Adults can't even handle sexual relationships. Let alone teenagers! These young kids should be kissing and holding hands, not having sexual intercourse.' I tell them **if you stick to just kissing, no one will ever be able to take advantage of you!"**

Sexual intercourse is the most intimate form of lovemaking and should not occur preferably until one is married, or over the age of 21."

"What about kids that have already had sex. What is your advice to them?" Nino asks.

'If a person has already lost their virginity, then they should make a decision to go back to being a virgin. Making this decision and sticking to it will gain back your honor and self respect in your eyes and in God's eyes. It will also take a huge emotional weight off your shoulders."

Nino sighs, "It seems like so many of our young women have "Daddy issues".

Solly confused, "Daddy issues?".

Nino laughs, "Forgive me Solly for using my modern jargon. All it means is that many of our young women have a poor sense of self-worth due to poor relationships with their fathers. They are starved for male attention and approval. There is this giant void that they try to fill, only the truth is that nothing can replace that which they long fore. They often use sex as a tool to make the object of their affection stay with them."

Solly nods in understanding. "Ah yes. Modern jargon, but an age old problem. You should never use sex as away to feel good about yourself, or to try to get someone to stay with you. This approach very seldom works, and even if you are successful, what have you actually gained? For example, a man who is only staying around because you are giving him everything a wife would give him is not worth keeping. These kind of guys are a dime a dozen, and as soon as something better comes along, you are history. You've heard the old saying "why buy the cow when the milk is so cheap?"

Nino laughing." Oh, yes I've heard that one before. So, are you saying that our teenagers and our young adults should deny themselves sexual gratification of any kind?"

Solly explains, "Many people are able to deny themselves that which their body craves by redirecting their sexual drive and energy in another direction, such as sports, music, art or education. Some are able to redirect this energy into spirituality."

"Like people who are into Yoga, meditation, and stuff like that." Nino asks.

Solly smiles, "Exactly, Yoga is a wonderful example. However, for those who are not totally able to fight this urge, there are alternatives, which if used in moderation, will adequately satisfy their sexual needs."

Nino raises his eyebrows, "Alternatives?"

Solly clarifies, "Boys and girls should learn the art of masturbation so that they can satisfy their own needs until they are married."

Nino laughing "Solly you heard the old saying: "Don't play with your dick or your glasses will be real thick! Won't that make ya go blind?"

Solly laughing "No that's an old wives' tale. I mean, look at you—you can still see!"

Nino laughing hard. "Solly, that's low!"

"The sexual pinnacle of middle school age children ages 12-15 should not exceed the kiss. The sexual pinnacle of high school age children ages 16-18 should not exceed being touched. The sexual pinnacle of college or the legal pre-marriage adult phase of life ages 21 and over should not exceed oral pleasure."

Nino clarifies. "Solly when you say pinnacle, your not suggesting that this should be a common occurrence on a normal date are you? I mean because in my opinion there is a relaxed attitude about oral sex, and I don't want to promote it any more than it already is in our Pop culture."

"Absolutely Nino, what I mean by pinnacle is that this should be that "something special" that happens during that particular period of development."

"So for each period that you describe the norm for that period should be the pinnacle of the previous period. Right?"

Solly Smiling. "You are a sharp one Nino Jones. The pinnacle of the previous period, becomes the norm of the following one.... Now where was I. Ah yes, The sexual pinnacle of a married couple should be what-ever they want it to be, for the marriage bed is undefiled. There it is Nino. Conservatives of all religious faiths will still be unhappy, but it is a map that can be followed."

Nino worried,"You know, our modern day youth are going to think I'm nuts when I lay this on them."

Solly reassuring, "Some might. Others will be grateful, even if they don't come right out and tell you. It might seem strange, but kids although they will test your boundaries, really do want you to set limits for them. Children are perceptive, too. They can tell if your heart's in the right place. Just let them see that you really care. Convince them that if they listen to you, they will be better off in the long run. Don't force it on them. Present it to them in a caring and unobtrusive manner."

Nino trying to understand,"Like saying, "Hey, I'm not trying to tell you how to live your life. All I know is that if you follow this path there will be no loss of self respect, no unwanted pregnancies, no sexually transmitted diseases, and a lot more to look forward to'."

Solly smiles with pride. "That's right, Nino. Just like that. You won't have any shameful memories or regrets. It will also prevent bad marriages. You won't have people getting married because they got pregnant. You won't have, and this is very common, a woman feeling she must marry the person she loses her virginity to. Many young women have missed out on their youth by deciding to have sex at an early age. It is a fact that most of those relationships usually end right after high school, or result in a marriage that is unfulfilling and destined to fail." Solly thinks for a moment and then continues. "The years of puberty and adolescence should be the years that you learn the art of self-pleasure. By refraining from having premarital sex, you will be forced for the most part to satisfy your own sexual needs. The teenage years should be a time of sexual self-exploration. If you can develop an understanding of how your body works and how to please it, you will always be moderately content in this world, at least, as far as sexual satisfaction is concerned. You will never truly be able to let your mate know how to truly please you, unless you can learn how to please yourself!"

Nino chukles and shakes his head. "Like I said before, so much for the blindness theory!"

Solly somewhat embarrassed "I know it probably is surprising that I am speaking to you about subjects such as these. But the human sexual drive is a powerful source of control and manipulation that is exploited by Satan. You can't just go and tell these teenagers to abstain from sex, without giving them something in its place. You have to give them an alternative plan that is sensible as well as satisfying. Which brings me to my next topic area:

Love and Sex

"For fascination of vanity obscures good things, and roving desire perverts the innocent mind. Do not take comfort in ill-gotten gains for there will be of no profit on the day of calamity and judgment."
-The Book of Wisdom (King Solomon) 3:12

"In a sexually permissive society, the good feeling that comes from the intimacy of sex is often mistaken for love. It is rarely love, and nearly always lust…. Love is never there in the beginning. There is lust, longing, novelty, hope and passion. This is the fertlile period of life in which the seads of love are planted. However, love is not like planting a seasonal fruit. Love is a process that takes a lifetime to achieve. It is ironic, but true, that true love is rarely present at a wedding ceremony but nearly always present at a funeral as a spouse says goodbye to their life-long mate."

Nino interjects, "So if you say you love someone, than you will always love them. But if you tell someone "I don't love you anymore, than the truth is that you never did love them to begin with."

Solly Smiles, "That's exactly right. Love is something that grows with time. It is a life-long process. It is not something that you can fall in and out of. If a couple truly achieves a loving relationship, it will last forever and nothing can destroy it.

However, if what brought a couple together is physical attraction, and what is keeping them together is a good sex life, nothing will be able to save this relationship when it falls into hard times. This type of relationship is doomed, as its foundation is built on sand."

"I guess there is no such thing as love at first sight, then, is there?" Asks Nino.

Solly looks sad, "I'm afraid your right Nino. Lust at first sight is closer to the truth. Physical attraction, chemistry and personality will definitely draw two people together, but it will not keep them together. There is even such a thing as soul mates. This happens when you run into a soul that you were very close to in Heaven before the Great Game began, or a soul that you were close to in a previous lifetime." Nino is surprised, "Is it rare to find a soul mate?"

Solly puts into plain words, "Yes, it is very rare. But it does occasionally happen. However, even if you feel that you have found your soul mate, you will still serve yourself well by sticking to the rules and guidelines I am giving you. Therefore, beware and tread carefully along the path of new romances. No matter how charming the person seems, it is easy to be swept away on a wave of passion, as I myself can attest.... Good judgment and common sense are often abandoned, and you end up giving a stranger all that you have, both body and soul. These relationships are intense due to novelty, intrigue, passion and sexual lust. However, by the time the romantic flame cools, you could already be married. You wake up one morning after a few years of marriage to discover that your sex life has become routine, and you realize that your relationship lacks substance. It is the spiritual and personal connection that gives a couple the strength they need to remain married. Now, let's move on to

Sexuality and Illness

"Look not upon a promiscuous woman lest you fall into her snares. Gaze not upon a young girl lest her beauty be a stumbling block to you. Do not frequent the company of dancers, or give yourself to harlots lest you parish by the force of their charms."
-Ecclesiasticus 9:3-11

"God did not intend for lovemaking to be as it is in Forever. The human immune system cannot handle intimate sexual relationships with more than one person at a time. It will be overloaded, and the body will be laid waste by many different types of sicknesses and diseases. Married people often find that they are the sickest during their first year of marriage. This is because the two immune systems are becoming one. Multiple sex partners lead to multiple health problems at any age."

Nino agrees, "Especially in modern times. There are actually thousands of sexually transmitted diseases. Many of them stay with you for life. And if you hit the AIDS lotto, your days are numbered." Nino pauses for a moment. "Solly why do you think God let there be so many sicknesses and diseases on the planet Earth?"

Solly with a look of disgust, "Satan is the creator of all of those plagues. He gets you to do that which will make you vulnerable. He causes you to get sick and then he hopes you get mad at God."

"That's what he is Nino. Always speaking with a forked tongue, and twisting things to his advantage ... Ok, onto the next category."

Love and Marriage

"God of my fathers and Lord of mercy, who has made all things by your word, and by your wisdom has appointed human beings to have dominion over the creatures that you have made, to rule the world in equity and justice, and render judgment with an upright heart, give me the wisdom that sits by your throne,
and the strength to sustain my marriage."
-The Book of Wisdom 9:1-4 (King Solomon & M.S.Pitifer)

"If you believe in God, you should try not to allow a serious relationship to develop with a person who is not a believer. It is also advisable to try and choose a mate who shares your common faith."

"Why is that?" Questions Nino.

Solly explains, "Satan will use any weakness or difference in a couple to bring them down. If your belief in God is very strong and your mate's is not, It's like having a house with two doors. One door that is solid steel with a thick dead bolt lock and another made out of thin cardboard. You will not be safe from thieves. Satan will attack the weak side of the relationship, and the marriage will fail. The more differences you have in terms of race, creed, color, religion and so on, the more likely it is that your marriage will not last. Satan will use your differences to pull you apart."

Nino raises his eyebrows, "So, are you saying interracial marriages are no good?"

Solly clarifies, "No, all I am doing is giving a warning that anything that adds extra stress to a marriage is something that should be avoided if you can. There are millions of potential mates in the world. When it comes to making a decision to marry, just don't settle for anything less than exactly what you want."

Nino remembers, "One of my foster mothers, a black woman named Miss Mary Parker, used to say "Nino, marry your own kind." She wasn't prejudice against white girls or anything like that. Although, she did get mad when black guys would only go out with white girls. She'd say "These fools think that white girls are somehow better than black girls! Why can't they see the beauty of the African woman?" Boy she'd get mad sometimes." Nino chuckles thinking about her. "She also felt that if you marry someone with different race, faith, traditions and customs, that your family heritage would eventually crumble. I argued that blending two such diversely different peoples would make an even stronger bond, but she wouldn't change her position. She said marriage will magnify your differences, not dissolve them."

Solly impressed, "It sounds like Mary Parker was a very wise woman. And she is absolutely right. For every one interracial or interfaith marriage that works out, a hundred fail."

"What's more important, faith or race when it comes to picking a mate?" Nino asks.

Solly answers without hesitation. "Faith is the most important component. Marriage is the most intimate communion that two souls can enter into. A common faith will allow a spiritual harmony to develop, and this will accentuate the physical link that already exists. If two people love each other, their outlook on the highest meanings of life should be the same. So it goes without saying that your spiritual beliefs will more profoundly affect your lives than differences of birth, race, language, or your position in society."

"That makes sense to me. So a common faith is the key to a good marriage."

Solly nods, "Yes, however, it must still be noted that these less significant differences that I mentioned, can still cause your family's culture and traditions to get watered down over time, and will also cause marital problems along the way."

Nino somewhat irritated. "Why does everything have to be so darn complicated and difficult down here? It makes me sick sometimes. If people like each other or love each other, why can't that just be enough to make a marriage last?"

Solly understands his frustration, "I know what you mean. But you see Nino, marriage is hard work in the very best of circumstances. Why, even if you were to move in with your very best friend, eventually you would get to the point where you can't stand the way she eats her corn flakes. Such is the nature of the immortal soul trapped in the mortal body and asked to live a life of monogamy. As I said before first and foremost you should look for someone who shares your faith. Then look for someone you really get along with, someone who knows your good side as well as your bad side. Find a person who appreciates your sense of humor and who genuinely cares about your opinion. If someone wants you to change the essence of who you are and what you stand for, or if you think you are going to change who they are, get out of the relationship as soon as possible! It's just not going to work. Write this down in bold capital letters. **MARRIAGE DOESN'T DEMINISH YOUR DIFFERENCES, IT MAGNIFIES THEM!**"

"So, relationships really are hard for all humans, and since this is the case, all the more reason to take your time and choose the best possible mate."

Solly smiles and nods, "That's right. It may be okay when searching for your first house to buy a fixer upper. But when you are searching for a lifelong mate, like I said before, settle for nothing less than exactly what you want. If you cannot find a suitable mate, then don't get married."

Nino worried, "That is going to be hard for some people to swallow. What about women who want to have children? They know that their biological clock is ticking. You know for some of these people, time is a factor."

Solly remains firm, "Never let the time factor cause you to lower your standards. Always keep in mind that adults who have reached a marriageable age have already developed their personality and their religious foundation. If you think that marriage is going to somehow change all those things that you don't like about your prospective mate, and somehow make you closer than you are, you are sadly mistaken. The personality traits, characteristics and idiosyncrasies of an adult human are very deeply rooted. Even the most highly motivated people working with the best psychotherapists have a hard time permanently changing their personality traits and behaviors once they have become adults. You must ask yourself this question, "If my mate is not going to change, if this is as good as it is going to get, do I really want to spend the rest of my life with this person?" You must also remember that it takes a very long time to truly get to know someone. The courting human, especially the male, is particularly shrewd at concealing his true identity."

Nino wonders, "How long are you suggesting that people stay together before they start thinking along the lines of marriage?"

"You should date for no less than four or five years before you consider marriage as a future possibility."

Nino startled, "Four or five years?!"

Solly continues, "I think it takes at least that long to get to know someone with whom you have no previous history."

"I see, so if you knew the person as a friend, or you have some common history, maybe the engagement could be shorter."

Solly explains, "Maybe, but when it comes to engagements it's still better to error on the side of "too long" rather than "too short". The bottom line is that you have to stay with a person long enough to really begin to see all of their many facets. You have to have some real good arguments, see how the person acts once they start to get comfortable in the relationship. Stick around long enough for the person to lower their defenses and begin to show their true colors. If people would do this, you would see a lot less divorces."

"What if I want to get married and have a family, and I see that old clock ticking. I think to myself, "Well, she isn't exactly what I'm looking for, but she loves me and she'll probably make a good wife."

Solly continues, "As I said before, this is never a good reason to get married. **If Mr. or Mrs. Right comes along after your child bearing years, it is better to be married to someone with whom you have a lot in common both spiritually and socially, rather than to be in a bad marriage with children.** Women especially get this scene in their minds about marriage. It is like a story that has to be told, pictures that have to be painted, and songs that have to be sung. Marriage is this major motion picture, and they are the directors. A young woman grows up dreaming of the pageantry of marriage. She pictures herself in a lovely wedding gown, walking down the aisle beside her father, so on and so on.… Unfortunately, life does not always go according to script, and that's when we get into trouble. We try to make things happen like we imagined they sould, and force destiny's hand. This is the cause of a lot of bad marriages. People rushing off to the alter before they really know that other person."

Nino nods in agreement, "Bad movies and bad marriages seem to happen for similar reasons."

Solly agrees, "Absolutely, poor preparation, poor casting, and not enough time. However, some unions are good ones. These unions may bring children into the world, and these new souls are the hope of the future. Children are sent by God himself into our lives and they carry within them the answers to our prayers. Our little ones need to be raised by a mother and father who love them unconditionally. They need parents who are not afraid to discipline them and a mother and father who value their marriage and take their vows seriously. A mother and father need to prove by their actions that they have found the path of love that leads to Forever. The fruit never falls far from the tree, and this should always be on your mind if you are a parent. Your children are always watching, listening and learning. What you do is always more powerful than what you say. So, guard your words and deeds, especially you who are parents, and remember that you will be held accountable for every idle word you speak."

Nino shivers, "That is a scripture that has always made me nervous."

"Speaking of being nervous, children need to be a little nervous sometimes."

"What do you mean?" Nino asks.

"When a child does something that they know is wrong, sparing the rod will most definitely yield a spoiled child."

Nino nods, "I agree. A good spanking never hurt anyone ... But Solly, in today's world people are afraid to spank their children. They are afraid they will get turned in for child abuse."

"Well, they are just going to have to get unafraid. Look Nino, I know that there are a lot of sick people in your world who do a lot of atrocious things to children. However, you have got to discipline your own children when they are young or they will become unruly, disrespectful teenagers and adults."

"What are the parents supposed to do?"

"I'm not an advocate for beating a child into submission. I am an advocate for a firm hand, consistent discipline, and seeing things through. When a child gets old enough so that they understand the difference between yes and no, the time for swift, consistent and sometimes stern discipline has arrived. These young children are at what is called the concrete stage of their development."

"Concrete stage?" Questions Nino.

"All this means is that the majority of their learning takes place on a physical rather than verbal plane."

"Huh? I'm confused."

Solly understands, "I'm sorry, Nino. Let me make it simpler for you. Young children have not gained enough control over their brains to be spoken to in sentences that are directive or thought provoking. Infants and toddlers are forced to learn by what they experience in the environment around them. The child is by nature a very curious little creature. Children have more in common with a puppy or a kitten than an adult human when it comes to how they must learn about the world. They learn by experiences and not by words. For example, you could talk to a little child about not touching a hot stove. But what good is that really going to do for the child? Considering that the child knows maybe six words: yes, no, doggy, kitty, momma, dada, and so on … To tell the child not to touch the stove because it is hot means absolutely nothing to the child. It will not prevent the behavior from occurring. However, if that child touches the stove when it is hot, and his fingers feel the burning pain, his brain will immediately learn that this big white box should be avoided at all times. The pain caused learning to take place."

"I think I see what you mean."

Solly continues, "Taking these same principles to the next level, if you tell your child to do something and they say "no", they should be immediately stung. **The fleshy-cooley was made for two purposes in this world—to draw attention to the shaker, and to make you pay attention to your maker.**"

Nino laughs outloud, "I like that!"

Solly chuckles, "Your children will learn that when you say no, and they don't listen, they will get stung. At an early age, what you have done is give your child respect for your authority. The majority of your time should be spent loving, playing, and taking care of your child. This will build a foundation of love and trust. If you begin to discipline your children at an early age, they will also have a healthy amount of fear and respect for you. This means that when they do enter those difficult teenage years, you won't have to physically beat them, or bail them out of jail."

"So, parents have to go back to spanking their children?" Questions Nino.

Solly clarifies, "Parents should an array of punishments that they choose from. Like a good baseball picture, you must have more than one pitch, or you get knocked out of the box? The more pitches you have the more effective you are."

Nino laughs, "You watch baseball?"

Solly smiles proudly, 'Yup, ever since the 69 Mets! The truly were amazing! And what a pitching staff."

Nino agrees, "Your not kidding, Tom Seaver & Jerry Koozman were awesome!"

Solly laughing, "Don't forget Tommy Agee.… Let me make one last point regarding corporal punishment. The secret of physical punishment can be learned from watching the honey bee."

"The honey bee?" Nino asks.

Solly nods, "The tiny honey bee must do much of its collecting of pollen from clover flowers that grow to be no more than two or three inches tall. This means that on the planet earth, the bee's job is made precarious by the presence of all of these giant creatures called humans walking around. The honey bees have learned that if they sting the humans when they are little, they will remember that sting for the rest of their lives. And even when they grow larger and less sensitive to pain, they will still give this little tiny bee its due respect. The memory of the sting is actually much worse in the human's mind than what an actual sting would feel like to them as an adult. If the bee waited until we were adults to give us our first sting, the results would not be as effective. The honey bees wisely discipline us in our youth, and we always have respect for them. The bee does not have to beat you or increase the power of its sting as the years go by. It simply has to be consistent, prudent, and fair in its stingings. The honey bee, like a good parent, simply says, "follow my rules, and you won't get stung." I say again, spare the rod and you will most definitely spoil the child."

"It really doesn't sound like it's that hard to be a good disciplinari an."

"It's not. The hard part is just being consistent. That means that, no matter when your rules are broken, you take the time to discipline your child. It's easy to discipline your child when you are in a bad mood. However, if you are in a bad mood, take a moment of pause and ask yourself if the child is really doing something that deserves a pun ishment, or are you just taking your frustrations out on them. If you are in a good mood or on your way to a party or some function, don't allow yourself to tolerate bad behavior. The more consistent you are, the more effective you will be. Consistency is the key. And no one is more consistent than the honey bee.... Well my friend I have time to discuss one more topic. Name the last section Divorce.

DIVORCE

"A faithful friend is a strong defense and whoever has found one has found a treasure. Nothing can be compared to a faithful friend and no weight of gold and silver is able to unbalance the goodness of her fidelity. So never forsake an old friend for the new one will not compare to her. A faithful friend is the substance of life and immortality, and all who fear the Lord will find one. Do not say, "I have sinned and what harm has befallen me?" For the Most High is a patient rewarder. This is why a self-centered soul, in time, destroys its owner. Let the wife or husband of your youth be your delight!"
-Ecclesiasticus 6:14-16 & M.S.Pitifer

"When two people get married the going will inevitably get tough, even in the best of relationships. However, your generation went from having the seven year itch, to taking the seven year ditch."

Nino laughs "That's a good one Solly."

"Adolescence is a difficult period of life. The person kind of loses himself for awhile, and then at the end of the cycle, rediscovers a new and hopefully improved version of their former self. In marriages, when couples hit their late thirties & and early forties, this is usually accompanied by a period of crisis."

Nino smirks, "You mean a mid-life crisis?"

"Yes, and everybody goes through it. It is a very difficult period of life. I call this stage of life the 2nd adolescence. Once again these individuals are confused about who they are. Their parents and other significant role models are growing older and dying. Their bodies are aging. Most of the dreams that they always believed would someday come true have wilted away. Their children are growing older and less dependent. Their mortality seems more apparent than at any other point in their lives, and if matters weren't bad enough their sex drive seems to be stuck in neutral!"

Nino is bent over laughing, "Solly you kill me."

Solly remains serious "It's a scary period of transition because we are desperately trying to hold on to our youth, while at the same time reinvent our lives. We are forced to deal with feelings or attractions that we did not consciously try to bring about. Our mind is in panic mode and on a subconscious level it is desperately trying to come up with solutions to alter our midlife realities. These new longings will bring conflicts and vulnerablity into a marriage. You will say and do things to each other that you will later regret. Much like a teenager who tells their parents "I hate you!", and then later hangs their head in shame. Bad language, silence, lack of appreciation and diminished intimacy all stack up to douse the flame of marriage like a bucket of ice water."

Nino shakes his head in disappointment, "That's it Solly. They hit that low point, and they just cash in their chips, and walk away. They truly think that their marriage is dead."

Solly excited, "Yes, but this is their big mistake. It is not dead, it's in a love coma."

Nino interjects, "Only then love is stuck on the outside trying to get in right?"

Solly smiles, "Yes! Exactly, the marriage is like Walt Disney's "Sleeping Beauty" waiting for the kiss of true love to awaken it from its slumber.'

Nino hoping, "Is it is really as simple as that?"

Solly scratches his head, "Their problem is two fold. For the fist part of the problem the answer is yes. It is as simple as a kiss. If this couple rediscovers the joy's of kissing they will gradually rekindle their romantic fire. The other part of the problem is that they have to discover positive ways to fill the now recognized voids in their lives. They must make new dreams and new goals to work towards … Tell them to hang in there during these hard times and remain committed to their marriage. God completely understands the sufferings that can occur in a marriage, and he knows how terrible things can get. Therefore God has made a promise to all those who make the self sacrifices necessary to save a troubled marriage. They will be greatly rewarded in this life and the next, and their cup will overflow with joy!"

"Excuse me, Solly, but don't you think a big part of the problem is that many of these couples when they get married they have in the back of their minds that if things don't work out they can always leave."

Solly nods in agreement, "That's true. Once you begin thinking about leaving, your marriage is already half over. Then if you start going outside of your marriage for love, comfort, and intimacy, you have sentenced your marriage to death. You must remain committed to your spouse and Allah will help you weather the storm. As I said if you continue to let your mate, the wife or husband of your youth be the source of your delight, God will bless you in ways that you cannot even fathom."

"So, if they hang in there, things will actually become better than ever?"

"Yes, definitely. Once again the marriage will blossom and produce fruits of a new kind. Also, Nino, speak to them about children. Having children does much to solidify an already strong and mature marriage, but it tears down one that is immature. The added pressure is too much to bear. When you first get married, don't be in a hurry to have children. This is a time of bonding for a husband and a wife. The time spent as solely man and wife, is the foundation upon which the marriage is built. It is a time of freedom. The freedom to come and go as you please as a couple, and the freedom to be there completely for your mate. The decision to have children changes a marriage forever. Some of those changes are very wonderful, but they require a tremendous amout of physical and emotional energy."

Nino comments, "One of the problems that I see with our modern society is that people are waiting longer to get married. Then quite often they are in a hurry to have children, because they feel their time is running out."

Solly agrees, "A short engagement, lack of a common faith, and rushing to have children, are the common ingredients of a failed marriage.... If you are thinking of having children, first try getting a puppy."

Nino is surprised, "A puppy!"

Solly clarifies, "The puppy will give you a little taste of what is to come. Sharing of responsibilities, sleep deprivation, values clarification, discipline techniques, travel arrangements, and so on."

"I got ya. Make your mistakes on a dog, not a kid, right?"

Solly laughs and slaps Nino the the back, "That's right; when you find out how hard it is to bring up a puppy, you may realize that maybe you better not have any children right away. Remember, you can always give a dog away, but when you become a parent, that's for the rest of your life."

"You kind of make it sound like becoming a parent is a bad thing."

"For those who truly understand the significance and the challenge of being a parent, each child is a new blessing. For those who do not, each child simply adds to their torment. Parenting is not for the faint hearted, the selfish or the cruel. If you are a mother, you have to try not to forget about being a wife, lest your husband becomes your son. If you are a father, you have to remember that you are still a husband, lest your wife becomes your daughter or even worse, your mother."

Nino tries to understand, "Please explain what you mean."

Solly makes clear, "The maternal drive is so powerful in women that, if left unchecked it takes over every part of their life. The motherly side of their being grows so strong that it actually overshadows the wifely/sexual side of their being. She begins to treat everyone as her children. All of the people and creatures in her life get everything they need, except for the husband, who slowly begins to realize that he has slipped to a level equal to or below the household dog."

Nino is laughing."Solly, you kill me!"

"This is serious stuff, Nino. The husband's relationship begins to go from lover and partner, to child and subordinate. This sets the stage for future marital problems if the woman doesn't rediscover her female sexual side."

"But if the woman keeps having children, this situation could continue for a long time."

Solly agrees, "That's right. Seven years could go by in the twinkling of an eye, and before you know it, the man is out there searching for someone to make him feel like a man again. Also, about this time the children stop needing so much attention and the woman will start to rediscover her female sexual side, only to find that her husband may not respond, because he now sees her as a mother. He no longer sees her as someone who is sexually appealing or exciting. This leaves the woman hurt and searching for someone who will look at her and treat her the way her husband used to. Now, factor in money problems, health problems, car troubles, home repairs, lack of communication and onset of puberty, little league baseball, soccer, basketball, football, dance lessons, piano lessons, report cards, teacher conferences, orthodontist bills, lost retainers, the aging body, mental fatigue, the old age and death of their own parents, and the walls start closing in on them. Their only chance to make it is to rekindle their romantic flame and become partners again. However, by this time they have become so estranged and frustrated that they either can't stand each other, or they feel nothing. The only option they can think of is to start over, to get out. They actually believe that they don't love each other anymore. However, the truth is, that love, if it ever did truly exist, at some level is eternal. Love may get occasionally buried by the problems, concerns temptations, and new relationships that occur inthis world, but it never really goes away. It just lies there patiently waiting to be rediscovered, or rekindled."

"So, what is the answer?" Nino asks.

"Understanding, commitment, patience, adaptability and improvisation are key ingredients in the relationship. The understanding that hard times will inevitably come to every marriage, but if you remain committed and learn to be patient, the good times will eventually return. The ability to adapt to all different types of ever-changing situations and circumstances and the courage to improvise are extremely important. That is to say, do whatever is necessary to overcome the temptations that will be used against you by Satan, and the demands that will be placed upon you by your own mind and body."

Nino sighs, "I imagine that this is all easier said than done."

Solly also sighs, "You're right. It is hard to keep a marriage together, but it's not impossible, not by any stretch of the imagination. If the young people follow all the advice I have given them, then they will have all that is necessary to successfully make it through the hard times. If they refrain from having premarital sex, then they will truly learn the art of self love dur ing their teenage years. If they have learned to delay gratification and to get along with less than what their body and mind demand, they will be able to overcome the most difficult of Satan's temptations. If they are truly wise and prudent in the selection of their mate, if they have a common faith, and an equal commitment to each other, then their marriage will truly endure until death and only by death will they part."

Nino smiles proudly, "Solly, you may be retired, but you are still one wise king. I just hope they'll listen."

Solly appreciates Nino's compliments, "Thank you, Nino. I hope my words are able to help build strong, lasting, and loving relationships. I hope they help stop the adultery that exists in your modern world."

"Excuse me if I am ignorant Solomon, but how does adultery fit in to what you have just said?"

"Nino, don't you understand that every time you do something that helps the cause of Satan, you are committing adultery? When I became king, I made a vow to God that I would be faithful to him, and him alone. When I fell into lust with a non-believer, I worshipped a pagan god and greatly hurt our Heavenly Father. To do what Satan wants you to do is to worship him. You are either for God and against Satan, or you are for Satan and against God. In life, it is your actions that mean more than your words. To disregard your vows to God and do what the world says is okay to do, is to reject God and accept Satan. You also end up teaching your children and your children's children that this way of life is acceptable. Like I said, I hope there will be fewer marriages."

"So, is all sin considered adultery?"

"Yes, all sin is a form of adultery, but to break a vow to God is the worst kind of adultery. It is the worst kind of sin." Solly is distracted by the appearance of Pilate.

Pilate walks over to Nino, "Well, Nino, what did you think of Old King Solomon?"

Solly jokes, "Hey Pilate, what do you mean by 'Old'?"

Nino laughs, "I think he's great, Pilate. I'd feel much better if he were going in my place."

Solly understands, "Now, now Nino—you are going to do just fine. I think the boys have made a perfect selection. You have my confidence and my blessings. As a former king of Yahweh's chosen people, and by the powers vested in me, I consecrate you a holy knight of Allah. Sir Nino Jones, the Prophet of Faith. Now, go my son, and make us all proud."

Solomon reaches out to Nino and hugs him like he would hug a son. Nino is sincerely touched by this affection.

Nino is filled with emotion, "Thank you, Solly. I am more honored more than I can describe."

Pilate chimes in, "Sir Nino Jones.... I like how that sounds. Hey, Solly, how come you never knighted me?"

Solly jokes, "Knight a Roman? Unthinkable!"

"Solly, that's, how do you say it, Nino?"

Nino grins, "That's cold, Solly, real cold!"

Pilate laughs, "Yeah, Solly! That's cold ..." Pilate grabs Solly in a head-lock and then releases him. "Thanks for taking the time to meet with Nino, my brother. We really appreciate it."

Solly smiles"Don't be silly. It is my pleasure. I only wish you could stay longer."

Pilate nods, "I know, but I've got to get him over to Malcolm. I don't want to go over my allotted time. You know what Barabbass' temper is like."

Solly winces at the thought of it, "I know exactly what you mean. Hey, Nino, make sure you come back and visit me some time when this is all over. I will love to hear all about your adventure."

Nino give him a thumbs-up. "Solly, you can count on it!"

"Come on, Nino, we've got to get going. Goodbye Solly. Hope to see you again soon."

"Goodbye Pilate. Goodbye, Sir Nino. And good luck!"

"Goodbye, Solly. And thanks again."

Pilate grabs Nino's hand, and they are immediately transported to the sidelines of a beautiful outdoor basketball court. The souls that are playing move with a grace and rhythm of pure fluent motion.

"What are we doing here, Pilate?"

"You see that soul shooting the ball?"

"Yes."

"That's Malcolm X."

Nino is startled, "That's really Malcolm X?"

"Yes, the one and only!"

Nino is amazed, "Wow! He's awesome!"

Pilate agrees, "Nino, in Forever we're all awesome. Up here, everybody's got game."

Nino remembers his youth, "Boy, I used to love to play basketball when I was young."

"Want to get in the game for awhile?"

Nino sighs, "Are you kidding? I'm way too old to play with those guys. Not to mention that my knees are shot."

Pilate grins, "Nino, in Forever, nobody is old and worn out. I mean, nobody, not even you, has bad knees."

Pilate calls out to Malcolm, telling him that someone wants to join the game.

"Cool, Pilate. Send him in. He can take the Goat's place, since he's shooting too much anyway."

Nino is stunned, "The Goat? That's the Goat? I remember watching the Goat play ball in Harlem when he was younger. Man, he was the best I've ever seen. Pilate, are you crazy? I'm not going in for the Goat. It sure would be a dream come true, but I'll end up looking like a fool."

Pilate reassures his new friend, "Nino, Forever is the land where dreams come true. You don't have bad knees anymore, no physical limitations whatsoever. When you step onto that court, you will be able to do everything that you ever dreamed of doing on a basketball court. Now just go out there and let it flow. I'll watch you for a little while, and then I'll have to go."

"You're leaving?"

"Yeah, there are some other parts of the plan I have to help Barabbas iron out."

Nino looks worried, "Everything's okay, isn't it?"

"Yes, of course, Nino. Don't worry. I know you are going to be successful. Now get out there on that court and show me what you've got! I'll see you at the victory celebration when this is all over. Farewell, Sir Nino, and God's speed." Pilate gives Nino a military salute. Nino smiles back at him with a melancholy smile.

"Farewell, Pilate, and thanks for everything."

Malcom hollers over to Nino, "Hey man, are you joining the game, or what?"

"Pilate, are you sure I can hang with these guys?" Asks Nino.

Pilate hollers, "Take 'em to the hole, Nino. Those bums can't hang with you. You know why Malcolm really changed his last name to X?"

"Why?"

Pilate laughing at his own joke, "Because he had such a weak game that it was the only way he could get an X after his name in the score book."

Malcom hollers back, "Hey Mr. Jones, don't believe a word that joker says about me! I could always play the greatest game ever invented. He's just talking trash because I spanked him last time he brought his old rusty behind out on here. Get out of here, Pilate, you bum!"

Pilate retorts, "That's not the way I remember that game, Malcolm. But, hey, in Forever the last game is not as important as the next game. Nino, that's my last little tidbit for you. In Forever, there will always be another day and another game. Now, go whip those bums for both of us!"

Malcolm laughs, "Just like a Roman, always talking about whipping someone! Come on, Nino, let's play a quick one before we have to split."

Nino and Malcolm wave goodbye to Pilate. He smiles, gives them a thumbs up sign, and disappears over the horizon.

Author's Note: I sometimes hope that God and Satan truly do have a common goal when it comes to the testing of our souls. In the movie Charlie And The Chocolate Factory Willy Wonka and Slugworth appeared to be arch rivals who were contemptibly working towards the others demise. However, at the end of the movie we discover that they were working together in different ways to discover each child's true character. This is a much nicer way to view the God-Satan relationship, and I'm sure it makes most of us feel better to do so. However, when you consider the following passage it's hard to believe that such partnership is possible: In Mark 9:43-49 Jesus says "If your hand does wrong cut if off. Better to live forever with one hand than to be thrown into the unquenchable fires of Hell with two! If your foot carries you toward evil, cut it off! Better to belame and live forever than to have two feet that carry you to Hell. And if your eye is sinful, gouge it out. Better to enter the Kingdom of God half

blind than have two eyes and see the fires of Hell, where the worm never dies, the fire never goes out, and all soulsvare salted with fire." Whenever Jesus describes what it will be like in Heaven, he often uses the example of the wedding feast. Because in his days and times nothing compared to the food, wine, and fun of a wedding. Jesus tries to do the same thing in his warnings about Hell. In his times as well as ours, nothing would be more miserable than to lose a limb or an eye. It's not that anyone will ever have to be blind or lame in Heaven. However, his point is that if eternal lameness or blindness was the price, it would still be a far better sentence than going to Hell. Awaken my people; Hell and Satan are as real as Heaven and God.

"God did not create laws for the purpose of control and punishment. He simply wants to prevent us from behaving in ways that will cause pain and suffering in our lives and those of our fellow humans. He labors for our freedom, not our captivity. He desires our love, not our worship."

-MARK SALVATORE PITIFER

CHAPTER 24

▼

Those who are The Companions of the Right Hand (The righteous dead) will dwell in beautiful oases in which no thorn can be found. Spectacular flowering fruit trees will line the pathways, providing shade long-extended. The crystal waters will flow constantly, and fruit will no longer be limited by season or production. There will always be an apple to be picked, or a lime to be squeezed. We will sit on Thrones of dignity, raised high. We will eat and drink all that we desire. We will also receive the companionship of beautiful souls with big lustrous eyes. These companions are Allah's special creations intended to add to the pleasures of the society of Heaven. They will be of virginal purity, grace, and beauty, inspiring and inspired by love. They will not possess, nor will they be possessed. They will also never grow old or have their beauty diminish in any way, because the factors of time and age have been eliminated. Thus every person among the righteous will have the Bliss of Heaven, and The Peace of Allah.
MUHAMMAD/THE HOLY QUR'AN: Surah 56:18 (Excerpts & Interpretations added by Mark Salvatore Pitifer)

The sun is still very high in the sky as the basketball game that Nino takes part in draws to a close. Nino and Malcolm's team is up 16 to 15 and they had the ball. In Forever, all pickup games are played to fifteen, and you must win by 2. A crowd of about ten or twelve thousand souls gathered to watch the game, and their roars of approval grow louder and louder as the game winds down. Nino is absolutely beaming as he bounds up and down the court with a grace and effortlessness that he had never experienced at any time in his life. His new body has what seems to be boundless energy. He has unbelievable speed, strength and agility that can be summoned at will. Any offensive move or defensive play that he can imagine is possible. Every element of the game is graceful. There are no hard fouls or injuries. The competition level is more intense than anything he has ever experienced. However, there is nothing stressful or uncomfortable about the overall experience. The Heavenly sun shines brightly and yet there is no sweating or exhaustion. Everything is absolutely perfect. There is a lot of trash talking going on, but it is all good natured. Everyone in Forever has such a keen and timely sense of humor. There is a mutual admiration that you can sense among the athletes, a camaraderie that seems to transcend the whole notion of winning and losing. This is not to say that each athlete isn't very competitive, and very much wanting to win. It just seemed to Nino that the bigger part of their enjoyment came simply from playing the game that they loved, the way they always envisioned it could and should be played. The whole scene is like one of those endless summer days from your youth. One in which you have so much fun, you never want it to end. On earth, even during our grandest times, there is always something in the back of our mind that knew it was all just a fleeting moment. A feeling that not only would this moment end, but the feelings would be hard to recapture. Nino was starting to understand the joy of Forever. In the midst of this grand game was the knowledge that not only was the moment not fleeting, but that it could be recaptured and replayed over and over, with different outcomes, from now and throughout all eternity. Malcolm is closely guarded as he crosses over the half court line. As he approaches the top of the key he fakes a hard left hand move, and drives to the basket with his right hand. As he becomes air born, he is challenged by two defensive players. Nino is filling the lane on the left side of the court. The duel defensive pressure that Malcolm is under causes him to be a little hard with his shot off the glass, but Nino catches the ball mid air and slams down a ferocious dunk over the other team's center for the winning shot. The crowd is going absolutely wild. Everyone is standing and cheering. All of the players are patting Nino on the back and giving him five. The feeling is absolutely exhilarating. Nino feels like he has just won the NCAA Championship. The ecstasy he feels is indescribable.

"Nino, my man! That was a heck of a great shot!"

Nino is beaming, "Oh, Malcolm, what an experience! This is basketball the way it was meant to be played! If this was all I could do for an eternity, I would be happy and content forever!"

Malcolm smiles, "My brother, if this little pickup game does it for you, let me tell you, you ain't seen nothing yet!"

"What do you mean?"

"In Forever, you have teams that represent various regions of the Kingdom. Anybody who wants to play can play. The fun part is that you will be playing with the souls who are most special to you. You play with your very best friends."

"Are there different cities in Forever?" Asks Nino.

Malcolm explains, "Many of these communities are bigger than earthly cities, but they feel like neighborhoods because everyone knows each other! Every community is distinct, but all a part of the same Kingdom. Remember, Nino, you are only seeing a very small part of the Kingdom of Forever. The vastness of this Kingdom covers the land mass of a million billion earths. It is boundless and ever growing. The Kingdom of Forever is always expanding."

"That's incredible.... So, how does it work? Do we choose where we live?"

Malcolm makes clear, "As you can see in Forever, there are many mansions. These are unimaginably beautiful homes that are built in a way that is perfectly tailored to what you would like. Your home will also be placed in a neighborhood that is surrounded by the most special souls in your life."

Nino smiles, "It sounds wonderful."

Malcolm sighs with happiness, "Nino, it truly is an amazing existence. Can you imagine your own beautiful mansion, perfectly constructed, and landscaped to be all that you ever imagined, set into a neighborhood that contains the most special souls that you have ever encountered? Just think for a moment how nice it would be to know that your good friends and family members will always be right near by. They will always be glad to see you. They will never be sick or tired. It is so comforting."

"So, nobody decides to move?" Nino asks.

"Hey, you can do whatever you want to in Forever. Think about it, though, why would you ever want to move? You'll be placed in a paradise setting that is tailor-made for you. In Heaven, you don't move, you go traveling!"

Nino is excited, "You mean, like taking vacations?"

Malcolm smiles at the thought of it. "Exactly. The only difference is that in Forever if you go to visit someone who is on vacation, the moment you ring their doorbell you are immediately transported to wherever they are. And everybody is always glad to see you, no matter where they are, or what they are doing.

"So theres no such thing as showing up at a bad time?"

"Nino that is impossible up here, because everybody wants you to be around. Forever is like one big endless celebration. The vacations are awesome because everything always works out perfectly. The accommodations, the food, the entertainment, the romance, the scenery—you get the picture? Oh, and Nino, the games against the different regions are awesome. We play in arenas that hold millions of souls. The atmosphere is unbelievable. The fans want their teams to win, but they also have such an appreciation for the game that they applaud for everyone. The ovations you hear and feel when you hit a shot, or make a steal are mind boggling." Malcolm points to his arm. "Look I get goose pimples just thinking about it … The best part is that win or lose, the host team throws these fantastic post-game parties that go on for days. Nino, I can't wait for you to get up here and experience it for yourself."

Nino gushes with excitement, "I can't either! I guess I'll finally get to feel what it's like to be rich and famous like Michael Jordan."

Malcolm waves his hand and smirks, "Earthly fame is nothing, compared to the riches of Forever. On earth, the famous are adored by strangers. Fair-weather fanatics who are living vicariously through celebrities do not compare to the adoring and always growing numbers of souls who love you unconditionally for who you truly are. And although they have an appreciation for and an interest in what you do, they are never fair weather. Forever is the land in which true love and loyalty abounds. Every new soul you touch loves you unconditionally and completely, forever."

Nino beams with excitement, "You mean, it's like your fame just keeps getting greater and greater. The more you do, the more souls you meet, the more well known you become?"

Malcolm smiles at Nino's excitement, "Athletes, singers, actors, artists, cooks, writers and so on. Forever has these types of souls just like on earth. The big difference is that no one is jealous of anyone else's accomplishments. There is the knowledge that you can achieve any goal you desire. It is really all about self-expression, and how you choose to spend your time."

"And what's time in Forever?" Nino adds.

"Insignificant. There is no urgency in Forever, there is no such thing as desperation, deadlines or any other time constraints. You will have enough time and energy to live out all of your dreams as many times as you like. The power of the living God flows through your body like a powerful river of love and energy. Your mind is set free, and your imagination is opened to dreams the earthbound soul could never fathom. In Forever, you become one with our creator and therefore you are a creator with ultimate power. The universe and all that you dare to dream is laid at your feet, a gift from your father, a God who takes delight in the cre tions and talents of his children. His joy comes from watching his children share their talents, hearing them laugh and wathching them play. We truly have a very softhearted … Loving father."

"Malcolm, is your section of the tour to teach me the joy of true sport and true fame?" Nino asks.

"Yes, but not only this. I have to speak to you about the Muslim religion and its true purpose. I also have a friend that I want you to meet, and that's where we are going now."

Malcolm leads Nino around the bend, where a well built man with curly jet black hair approaches them.

"Great Game, Malcolm. That was one fantastic finish!"

Malcolm happy to see his buddy, "Sully, my man! You always stop by to watch a game or two. I wish you would play with us once in a while, instead of chasing Marylin Monroe all over the Kingdom."

Sully laughs and grins sheepishly, "I'll play sometime. I promise. But for right now I just like to sit and watch. It reminds me of my son … Is this who I think it is?"

"It sure is! Nino Jones, I'd like you to meet one of my favorite souls, Mr. Sully Pitifer. Sully is the father of your soon to be messenger."

"Very pleased to meet you, Sully."

Sully smiles, "Hey, pal—that was some shot you hit to win that game. FANTASTIC!"

Nino shakes his head at the memory of it, "Thanks a lot, Sully. It's been a long time since someone has complemented me on my basketball skills. I've heard a lot about your son, Mark. I'm really looking forward to working with him. I just hope I can convince him that I'm not just some New York City nut case!"

"I hope and pray that he will believe in you, Nino. He's got a lot of talent. He worked hard all of his life trying to make me and my wife proud of him. He always believed that he was born to do something great in his life. He used to tell me that one day he was going to come into the A&P where I worked as a meat cutter and tell me that I didn't have to work anymore. He said he was going to pick me up in a limousine and ..." Sully gets tears in his eyes.... He loved me very much, and when I died, he sort of lost his motivation and his purpose in life. Oh, don't get me wrong. He loves his mother more than anything in the world. She always believed in him, but with me he felt he had to prove himself. I didn't realize until I died how much influence I had over him."

Nino is moved by Sully's love for his son, "I can relate, Sully. Believe me, I can ... He sounds like such a nice boy. I just hope he will listen to me ... and believe."

Sully confident, "He will listen, and here is your ace in the hole. When I was diagnosed with lung cancer, Markie tried to keep me optimistic, I knew that he was afraid for me, and terribly heartbroken, but he tried to keep a stiff upper lip. Two days before I died, I was sitting at the kitchen table and he came to me and hugged me and told me that he loved me. I felt his large shoulders heaving as he began to cry. It was the first and only time he cried in front of me since he found out I was going to die. He kneeled down next to me and put his head in my lap and cried and cried. My heart was breaking. I rubbed his head and his cheeks, and patted him on the back like I used to when he was a little boy. I told him that I loved him too. I told him that he was the father now, and that he should take care of his mother and sisters. I told him to go easy on his wife, Leigh, because she had a hard life. My very last words to him were 'Be a good boy Markie, I just want you to be a good boy.' If he doesn't believe your story about being the final prophet, then you tell him about our conversation and that should be all of the convincing that you need."

Nino is choked up, "Thank you, Sully. Thank you so much. I will keep your ace in the hole and I will only use it if I absolutely have to."

Malcolm agrees, "That is a good idea. Because, in order for God to really embrace what we are trying to accomplish, there must be a large element of faith."

Sully also sees the logic, "I see what you mean Malcolm. Nino saying words to Mark that only his father would know is kind of like providing some absolute proof. Yes, by all means, only use what I gave you if all else fails."

Malcoom shakes his head, "That's right, Nino. We don't want that snake Satan to cry foul. But, hey, if all else fails at least you know you are carrying the convincer if you need it."

"I understand exactly what you mean and I won't use this information unless there is nothing else I can do to make Markie believe."

"Well, I better let you be on your way. I know you are going to do well, Nino. If you have already thoroughly convinced him and you get an opportunity before you are called back, would you please do me a favor?"

"Anything, Sully. You just name it."

Sully chuckles, "Would you give him a hug for me, and tell him that I said to be brave, to be a good boy, and that I want some grandchildren! Goodbye, Nino. And God bless you, Pal. I'll see you around, Malcolm."

Malcolm waves, "Goodnight, Sully. Take it light dolomite!"

"Goodbye, Sully. You have my word." Nino promises.

"Hey Nino, when you get down there and things get rough, don't be afraid to hit the shot at the buzzer." … With these final words, Sully wandered back to the court to watch the next game. However, Nino was puzzled by his parting words, and he turned to Malcolm for a clue."

Nino confused, "Shot at the buzzer? What does he mean by that?"

"I think he means … don't be afraid to hit the shot at the buzzer." Nino fakes agitation, "Oh, thanks a lot, Dr. X. You're a real big help!…. So, who is this guy you are taking me to meet? Have I heard of him?"

Malcolm points "Oh I think you have. Look over there, off in the distance. Do you see the mansion that is built on top of that mountain over looking the valley?"

"Yes, who lives there?"

Malcolm smiles proudly, "A famous American who dared to climb up to the mountain to peer over the top into a future in which men were judged by the content of their character, and not by the color of their skin."

Nino is stunned, "Oh, my—Dr. Martin Luther King, Jr.?"

"Good guess, Nino! Come on, he should be expecting us. He's probably out in his garden playing with his feathered friends. He loves birds."

Malcolm and Nino walk up a sculpted path that leads to Martin's beautiful mountaintop mansion. They travel through a maze of picture perfect trails and eventually step into Martin's garden. Malcolm is perplexed, "This is odd. He knew we were coming but I don't see him anywhere. We better go ring his doorbell. I think I might know where he's at."

Malcolm leads Nino back to the front of the mansion and rings the door chimes. Immediately, they are transported at a speed beyond that which light can travel. They land in the back of a New York City taxi cab.

Traveling east on 125th street in Harlem, a black man with a heavy Jamaican accent is driving the cab and blowing his horn at a delivery van that is blocking his way. A big burly white man with wild looking hair comes storming toward the cab holding a crow bar. Nino cringes in the back seat with Malcolm. The white man shouts angrily at the taxi driver.

"Hey, asshole! My fucking van is broken down here. How would you like me to take that horn and stick it up your ass?"

Martin calmly answers, "Sorry, my brother." The driver answers in the calmest of voices. "I didn't think that you might have been broken down. But why so angry? Can't possibly be just from my horn blowing?"

"Nah, it isn't you mister. The fuckin' cop said he called Danny's Garage and they would be right over, but that was half an hour ago. I just called Dave Service Center, but their Mechanic Brian is sick, and Dave can't leave the shop. I can't get a fucking break today!"

Martin smiles gently, "Let me take a look see. Is she turning over at all?"

"Ye-yeah. The bastards turning over, but it's like she ain't getting no gas. It was running fine all morning, and I ran in to make a delivery and she just quit on me…. You some kind of mechanic or something?"

"No, but I know my way around an engine mon. You get behind the wheel and when I tell you, you turn that baby over. Okay, mon, okay … crank it mon."

As if by magic, the engine hesitates for only a moment and then turns over and purrs like a kitten. The white stranger stares in disbelief at the cab driver.

"Gee whiz, pal. Thanks a lot. I'm really sorry about the way I came at you. Do you want me to throw you a bone? I mean, can I give you some money for your help?"

"Oh, no mon. It's not necessary. But there is something you can do for me."

"Sure, whatever ya need."

"Control that temper of yours, son, before it burns you up. And follow the path of peace. That's the road home."

"What are you? A minister or something?"

"No mon, just little old Martin the taxi driver."

"Okay, Martin. You got my fucking word. I mean you got it 'Mon'. Thanks again."

"Cheerio my good mon. Peace." Martin returns to his cab and checks on his passengers in the back seat. "Where to boys? Heaven-town?"

"Heaventown? Martin, you are one crazy rascal. I should have known I'd find you here."

"Hey, I save more souls in this cab than I ever did in a church." "Martin, I'd like to introduce you to—"

"Nino Jones. It is a pleasure to meet you, my brother."

Nino grabs Martin's hand with both of his. He wants to fall to his knees before this peaceful, loving soul. "Martin, Dr. Martin Luther King, Jr., I can't tell you what an honor it is to meet you, sir."

"Nino, my dear little brother, the pleasure is all mine. When Malcolm asked if I would like to be a part of your tour, I felt honored. Now, throughout the ages I will be associated with one of the greatest prophets of all time. Nino Jones."

Nino honored but concerned, "I don't understand why you guys have so much faith in me. I mean, I am happy that you do, but …"

Martin adamant, "But nothing! Just the fact that they could find an earthbound soul at this late stage of the game who is brave enough to attempt what you are trying to achieve is going to bring great joy to God and Jesus. The fact that you are willing to risk your already secured eternity in paradise in order to help save souls and defeat Satan gives me goose bumps. You are truly one of the bravest souls I have ever encountered."

"I will never forget the words you have just said to me. And even if I fail and must spend an eternity in the Outer Darkness, the memory of your words will ease my burden."

"Martin, is Dottie Eldridge-Williams' Chicken and Rib Hut still open?" Asks Malcolm.

Martin Smiles, "Of course, and nobody can cook 'em like Dottie! She cooks the best sweet potato pie on the planet! I'll drop you off at her place, and I'll take Nino for a quick spin while you eat."

Maclom give Martin a thumps-up, "Now that sounds like a plan. Hey, Martin, speaking of easing burdens, how about spotting me a twenty? I'll send you over some bean pies later in the week."

Martin chuckles, "You know what you can do with your bean pies, mon!" Martin is laughing. "You see, Nino—once a hustler, always a hustler."

Martin tosses Malcolm a twenty and sends him on his way. Malcolm turns back to the cab.

Malcolm laughs, "Ooh, Martin, that was cold! But those ribs are gonna be right on time. Nino, the only reason I'm trusting you in Martin's cab is because you are already dead. Otherwise it would be way too risky. You still better buckle up!"

Martin fakes agitation, "Get your ass away from my cab, Malcolm! Criticize my driving, will ya?"

"Just drop him off at Frankie Sindoni's pool hall when you're done."

Martin raises his eye brows, "The pool hall?"

Malcolm is all smiles, "Hey, a rib and wing plate only cost $10.50, which gives me about $9.50 to gamble with!"

"Check him out Nino. He's going to try and beat the best 9 ball player in the city. Good luck my brother. Hey, say hi to Frankie for me, and tell him I said his jump shots flat!"

Malcolm laughing, "Will do."

As they drive down Broadway, Nino can't take his eyes off Martin. Martin is also intrigued with his passenger.

"Nino, I agreed to be a part of your tour for one simple reason. I don't like what is happening politically in this country. More person ally, I don't like the direction my civil rights movment has taken."

"Why? What went wrong?" Nino asks.

Martin shakes his head with disappointment, "I simply wanted equal rights for all people. I wanted a society in which people were judged by the content of their character, and not by the color of their skin. I wanted our minority children to have an opportunity to get a college education and pursue the American dream. My dream was to bring an end to all types of discrimination in our country, and I wanted it so desperately and believed in it so strongly that I was prepared to die for it. When I first returned to Forever and looked back on my life, I was content. The country and my movement seemed to be moving in the right direction. But now when I look out at the world, or when I am driving these cabs through the inner cities of this country, I am starting to think that in many ways I died in vain."

Nino feels bad to see his hero doubing himself, "What is it that has got you so down hearted? You accomplished most of what you had set out to accomplish. Your dreams are now a reality!"

Martin explains, "That is exactly why I am troubled. I had always said to myself that once I was able to achieve my goals I would go back to Alabama and get on with my normal life. I would go fishing, have a garden, sit on the porch with my wife and drink lemonade as we watched those beautiful Alabama sunsets. I know now that I was probably naive, but no one wants to embark on a journey or fight a battle that they feel will be endless. I believed that during the course of my lifetime I would achieve the goals that I had set for myself and our movement, and that would be that."

"So, what prevented things from working out?" Asks Nino.

Martin continues, "After I died, the cilvil rights movement I started gradually became a business; a business that consisted of thousands of employees, and one that has made most of its bosses rich and powerful, both politically and socially. These people did not see the movement as I saw it. As I said nobody wants to undertake a journey that has no end, but that doesn't seem to be their mind set."

"But won't there always be issues of prejudice and racial equality that will need to be addressed." Asks Nino.

"Yes, but not to the extent they existed before we had equal rights. Nino, don't get me wrong, I'm not saying that these new leaders are malicious or people with poor character. I just think that life goes by, and all of a sudden you realize that if this movement doesn't continue to be important to your people and the country, then your way of making a living will come to an end."

Nino understands, "I think I see what you mean. For them to acknowledge that they have achieved most of your goals, would mean that there would be a diminished need for their services. The political attention, dinner parties and fund raisers would come to an end. The newspaper articles, television shows, and cheering crowds would dissolve.... I see...."

Martin continues, "They went from wanting equal rights to wanting special rights...." Martin's voice has an angry tone, "I never wanted to be treated differently because I was black. I just wanted the same chances that everyone else had. Nothing more, and nothing less. The Affirmative Action program has good intentions, but it is a program that rewards based on the color of peoples skin, and not on the content of their character!"

Nino cringes, "It's true, you would have never stood for that. I see it now ... But should they get rid of these programs all together? I mean it has done some good, hasn't it?"

Martin thinks for a moment, "This is true. However, they should only reward minority people for reasons of academic merit or financial need. If they reward for any other reason, then the program is hypocritical, and we have become what we have despised.... Don't temper my words on this Nino. Our people have got to awaken to the truth!" Martin looks out over the city, and speaks in a majestic powerful voice that gives Nino goose bumps. "**A movement that asks for special rights for any minority is insulting because it** implies that we need more than just a level playing field in order to be successful. It says that if we are not given special rights, then we will continue to struggle because we are inferior in some way. This very type of thinking is what I died trying to overcome."

Nino looks at Martin with pride and admiration, "I never thought of it along those lines, but you are absolutely right. Anyone who supports programs that treat African Americans as a group of people who need more than just a level playing field, no matter how good and honest their intentions might be, are exhibiting one of the worst types of prejudice. Their sincere beliefs prove that they see black people and minorities as inferior to the Caucasian races."

Martin smiling and excited, "Yes, Nino. You tell my people that I died trying to level the playing field and nothing more. I believed that God created all men and women equal.… When the Unitied States Government finally gave us our equal rights, they also robbed our ambition by implementing an over-generous welfare system. It is time for our people to refuse special treatment of any kind. We must recognize it for what it truly is, an insult! No matter how nicely it is packaged, or how financially or socially profitable this federal gift may be, it must be refused. In my opinion all special rights programs should be banned, on the grounds that they are socially and morally unethical. The brainchildren of well intended, blind guides."

Nino wipes imagined sweat from his brow, "Are you saying that people who believe that minorities need special treatment, and who develop special rights programs, are racists?"

Martin scratches his chin, "Racists, prejudice … yes, but not necessarily malicious, or even aware of their prejudices. The bottom line is that all minorities must refuse to be treated as people with special needs. These kinds of programs are politically designed to keep minorities dependent upon the government in one way or another. They also cause tension between the races. Worst of all, they keep our people from recognizing their true potential. Even those who should be proud of their accomplishments have this cloud of doubt in their mind. This tiny voice that says 'Did I really get this position because I studied hard and was the best qualified applicant, or did I simply get hired because the company needed another minority?' It is a sad state of affairs, but not a hopeless one. The solution is really a simple one."

"The solution?"

Martin makes clear, "Well, Nino, one of the problems is that there are some minority people who look for racism in everything. They could be going 50 miles per hour in a 30 mile an hour zone, but if they get a ticket for speeding, it is because they are black. If they get fired from their job for repeated tardiness, it is not because the are habitually late, it's because they're black. This kind of over sensitivity to racism is what I believe creates prejudice and perpetuates racism in your modern society. All people of color must try to go the other way. Take racism out of everything. If somebody calls you lazy, maybe you are! Maybe that is just one person's opinion, but it probably has nothing to do with the color of your skin."

Nino worried, "But, what if you get unjustly fired from a job and you think it's because of racism. What should the person do? Just let it go?"

"Racism and prejudice are very hard to prove, especially in the work place. When you take a job, make sure you work hard and ask for periodic, written evaluations. Make your boss put in writing any specific complaints about your work performance, and then keep a daily journal of how you have tried to make changes. Racist or not, it will be hard for a boss to fire an employee who has a good work record. And if your hard work is unappreciated, then go and find a new job. Why would you want to work for someone who doesn't appreciate the best you have to offer?"

Nino nods in agreement, "That seems like good advice.… Is that it?"

Martin smiles broadly, "No you tell my people that the prophet of faith has my full support, and if they listen to him they will be able to overcome once again."

Nino concerned, "Martin, please don't put all this on me. I'm not the charismatic preacher you were, and besides, they are not going to like what I have to say."

Martin nods, "Nino, a lot of people didn't like what I had to say at first, but I knew that God was with me and that eventually what was truthful and righteous would prevail.… You are also forgetting something very important. A missing fact of which I am very proud."

"Whats that?" Nino asks.

Martin speaks with pride, "The fact that our great Prophet of Faith, who has been selected by some of the noblest souls to ever exist, is an African American named Nino Jones.… I can't find the words to express how proud that makes me feel…." Martin pauses for a moment and then he begins to speak in that powerful voice he used during his Mountain Top speech. **"Nino you must tell our people to get back into the sweet and powerful words of our Lord and savior Jesus Christ. We must go back to living holy lives. We must stop having illegitimate children. We must marry and stay married. We must raise our children in two parent homes. We must learn the value of education and our young people must learn that, in order to truly be free, one must be educated! The more educated you get, the freer you are. To drop out of school and go on welfare is worse than being a slave! Going on welfare is being a slave to the system. You don't have cotton to pick or fields to plow. Just remain uneducated and dependent on handout programs. Keep having those babies out of wedlock, and they will follow right in your footsteps! Keep on selling dope to one another and killing each other, and your masters, the government, will never have to whip you. The chains that our people are shackled with now are more insidious and more restricting than those used by the slave ship captains and southern plantation owners. Fore these new chains shackle the human spirit! The government may have forged these irons that we wear, they may have delivered them to our doorsteps, but it is we as a people who decided to lock ourselves to them. We must remove these chains of self-imposed oppression and once again live as free sons and daughters of the living God. People who are God-fearing, proud of their heritage, and capable of achieving any goal. This is what our people were meant to be.** This is my new dream, and Nino Jones is going to deliver my message with no less charisma than the doctor himself. Your ride is over, my friend. Go now and be brave. I know the mountain top looks high to you, and I know you are afraid you will fall, but you have already been to the top and you have seen the other side. Now you must lead all people to where you have already been. Goodbye, my brother. I'll see you soon. Oh, and, no charge Mon." Martin give Nino one last brilliant smile, and drives away.

"Those who kill in the name of religion are destroyers of their own people, and follow not the path of Allah. For the Earth is but one mother and mankind her children. Regard each other not as strangers, but as brothers and sisters from the same womb. When All God's Children are one day reunited in the kingdom of Forever you will see representatives form every nation and every religion. We are all equal in our Fathers eyes, save whosoever is more merciful and compassionate; this soul is nearer to God. For love is the only path that leads to Heaven!

                              -Mark Salvatore Pitifer

CHAPTER 25

▼
———————————————

"Intolerance is a sign both of arrogance and ignorance, for it is an indication that man believes that there is no truth beyond that which he sees."
-William Barclay (The Mind of Jesus)

"From this day forward I will speak ill of no man, and all the good I know of everyman."
-Dr. Joseph Bova ... or Ben Franklin

"Be kind for everyone you meet is fighting a hard battle."
-Plato (347 BC)

Nino grabs martins hand with with both of his, "Thank you Martin. Thank you so much. I won't let you down. Take care, Mon."

Martin's taxi pulls away from the curb and disappears into the endless stream of New York traffic. As Nino watches the cab disappear, he is suddenly struck by an unexpected feeling. Although he is standing on a busy street back in NYC, he no longer feels like this is his home. In fact, he feels like a stranger in a strange land. Everything seems dirty and grimy. The air is thick with exhaust and the buildings and storefronts appear cluttered and unattractive. For a moment, it reminds Nino of the Outer Darkness, and in that moment he is struck with a chilling fear. This really is Satan's kingdom, and what would it profit a man to gain the whole world, if in the process he loses his soul? Nino now understands that nothing on earth compares to the power, beauty, and splendor of Heaven. As Malcolm approaches Nino, he sees that something is troubling his new friend.

Malcolm concerned, "Nino, what's wrong? Didn't things go well with Martin?"

Nino looks preoccupied, "No, No.... things went fine with Martin. He is quite a fella. It's just that after he left, a feeling came over me that I didn't expect."

Malcom understands, "I know what you are going to say. It no longer feels comforting to be back home, does it?"

Nino is stunned, "How did you know?"

Malcolm rubs his cheeks with both hands, "I can remember the first time I came back. It was like everything was just dirty, dingy, and unappealing. The fact is that once you have seen the Kingdom of Forever, the sweet land of our origin where God's love shines continually through all he surveys, you will never view the earth in the same way again. Even its most beautiful aspects will seem mundane compared to our eternal paradise."

Nino grows melancholy, "It's kind of sad in a way. But you wanna know something? I am no longer afraid to die.... All I feel now is that I want to make it home, and I want to bring as many souls with me as I can. I want to pull back the curtain and expose Satan. The people have got to know the truth, and I will do whatever it takes to achieve our goals. I may not make it back to paradise, but with every last ounce of my life's energy, I am going to ensure that those who come after me will have a clear road home."

Malcolm is proud, "Why Nino Jones, you are starting to sound like a prophet!"

Nino feels a growning inner strength, "I would have never believed this could happen, but I'm starting to feel like a prophet!"

Malcolm inspires his new friend, "This is your destiny, Nino. It is what you were born to do. Everything that has happened to you in your life was meant to prepare you for this moment in time. I mean, look at my life. I was nothing more than a street hustler and con man. If someone would have told me back when I was sixteen years old that I would become all that Malcolm X became, I would have never believed them. But it was the culmination of all of my experiences during the first half of my life that set the stage for the final show. It's like each moment of your life is a piece of a puzzle. Most of these puzzle pieces looked at separately don't look like anything special early on in a person's life, a hodge-podge of stumblings, fumblings and fortune, both good and bad. These experiences combine to create the adult human being. We struggle to put the pieces together in ways that make sense to us, and little by little we are able to finish different sections of the puzzle. However, there is no final form. It is ever-changing. The fluctuations will become less extreme as time goes by, but the human personality can always be affected by life's events. So, the possibility of change always exists. I guess in a way it's good that we don't know for sure what our future holds in store for us. Knowing our destiny might prevent us from living a complete life. We would focus just on the end result and miss the most important parts of life. We … Oh, my sweet Lord! Nino, I can't be going off on these philosophical tangents! I've got some important things to tell you before our time is up!"

Nino disagrees, "What are you talking about? This is good stuff! I'm learning a lot listening to you. Preach preacher!"

Malcolm chuckles, "Thanks, Nino, but I only have so much time with you and there are some more important things I have to discuss with you. Take my hand. We've got to get back to Forever."

Nino takes Malcolm's hand and in a twinkling of an eye, they are back in Forever. The sun hangs low on the horizon, and soon the blue moon will rise in the east, painting the skies with romance and love.

Malcolm sighs as he looks at the heavenly sky,"You see, the blue moon will rise soon. When it does, your tour will be over and your earthly mission will begin."

Nino disappointed, "I guess I'll have to wait until the next time around to feel the blue moon's romantic magic?"

Malcolm chuckles, "You'll be better off, believe me. Barabbas was afraid that if you, by some strange twist of fate, were to run into your soul mate, you would be conflicted. It is important that you are focused when you return to earth. A romantic encounter with your soul mate, or any soul for that matter, would be so incredible that you would not be able to think of anything else! You'd be worse than a heroine junkie needing a fix. The memory would replay itself over and over in your mind like a vivid dream."

Nino gushes with excitement, "Is it really that amazing an experience?"

Malcolm glows with happiness, "Nino, my man, just the memory of the encounter would be a million times greater than any earthly pleasure you could ever imagine. You're just going to have to trust me on this, man. We need you battle ready and undistracted. This is why we decided that you must leave Forever before the blue moon completely rises."

"It's the old 'women weaken legs' theory, right?" Jokes Nino.

Malcolm laughs, "Earthly love making compared to soul-to-soul love is like comparing a single rain drop to all the water in the oceans. Once you have made love under the light of the blue moon of Forever, your entire perception of reality and what you desire out of life will be permanently changed. You will be like a feather floating along on a gentle breeze, and you will never touch the ground again."

Nino and Malcolm walk along a beautiful glen. A tapestry of wild flowers, babbling brooks and waterfalls. The light of the moon reflects off of the precious stones that are sprinkled throughout out the glen and theses swirling cascades of light overwhelm Nino with God's awesome wonder.

Nino sighs, and then breathes in deeply. "Oh, Malcolm, this truly is paradise. Everything is just so perfect. If only the people could see what I have seen. If only they could feel the way I feel right now. If only ... Genisteeceino."

"You'll have to convince them Nino. A book must be written. A movie must be made. And songs must be sung."

"But how am I going to do all that?" Asks Nino, worried again.

Malcolm clarifies, "Don't forget, the task will not be yours alone. Your job is to deliver this final message. However, it will be your apostle's job to do the rest. He has the talent necessary to get the job done. Once you deliver the message, he will understand for the first time in his life who he is, and what he was born to do."

Nino concerned, "But what if he doesn't believe me?"

Malcolm reassures Nino, "Oh, he'll believe you. He has always felt that he was born to do something special for God in his life. Your words will touch his heart and your story will confirm his beliefs. Have no fear, little brother. All will go well.... All will go well."

Nino once again notices the view, "Boy, the sunsets up here are really beautiful. And they seem to linger for just the right amount of time."

Malcolm looks and nods in agreement, "In Forever, there are no fleeting moments. There is the perfect amount of time for everything. On earth, God occasionally lets you see little pieces of Heaven, little reminders of what once was and is to come again. If only they would submit to God's will. If only the earth bound souls would become Muslims. They would...."

Nino startled cuts of Malcom, "Muslims? Are you telling me that the Muslim religion is the true religion?"

Malcolm explains, "There is no true religion. However, if current trends continue, Islam will become the most popular world religion sometime in the mid-21st century."

Nino shocked, "That's unbelievable. How many Christians are their in the world today?

"At this moment in time Christianity is the largest religion in the world. It is currently followed by about 33% of all people. Islam is followed by about 21%."

Nino shakes his head in disbelief, "Man, who would have ever guessed that the Islam would be the biggest religion. I don't think I could ever be a Muslim."

Malcom laughs, "Sure you could, and you wouldn't even have to change your religion."

Nino confused, "How can you be a Muslim without changing your religion?!"

Malcolm explains, "To be a Muslim means to submit to the will of God. Abraham was the first Muslim in that he agreed to sacrifice his beloved son Isaac. Jesus was also a true Muslim. He submitted to the will of God unto his death, and he gave all Muslims the path that leads back to paradise."

Nino is shocked, "You are calling Jesus a Muslim?! I can't believe it!"

Malcolms voice softens, "Jesus was, and is a Muslim to this very day. Remember what I told you. To be a Muslim is to submit to the will of God. Only a true Muslim can walk the P.O.J. Your life is your religion upon which you will be judged. Jesus said that we must love God, and love our neighbor as ourselves."

"But, how do we prove to God that we love him?" Questions Nino.

Malcolm continues, "By submitting to his will. It is in our submission to Jehovah that we prove our love. God does not desire a forced kind of love. Nor does he desire the kind of psuedo-love that is enjoyed by your earthly celebrities, you know, people loving you for what you are and not for who you truly are. This is not real love. God is simply in search of pure love, because that's what he is. True unconditional love is the greatest treasure in all the universe. There is nothing more valuable. Love is the most precious aspect of existence, because is not something that can be created or forged. Even our omnipotent creator can not command it. Love is free flowing and cannot be harnessed of forced in any way. God the father of love has sent his spirit out into the universe in search of Himself. He, has found, in his search for love, that if you treat others the same way that you want to be treated, your chances of finding pure love are most favorable. This is the doctrine by which Allah rules the universe. It is his supreme will that we treat all people with kindness. Kindness is the true religion. Fore God knows that if you can learn to live kindly on the planet earth, where people are fickle and not always grateful, then you will truly be eternally happy when you return to Forever. The only kingdom in the entire universe in which pure love is found in everyone and everything. All in All."

Nino clarifies, "So, to be on the path to Heaven, one must first love God. If we love God then we will submit to his will. If we submit to his will, then we will love our neighbor as we love ourselves."

Malcolm continues, "There is only one path that leads to Heaven, and it was given to us by Jesus, the king of all true Muslims. Satan has used our human pride to divide the religions and pollute their doctrines. It does not matter what you call yourself or what religion you follow. If you have found the true path, and your religion helps you stay on that path, then it is a religion that serves you well."

"So, all the different religions, religious doctrines, dogmas and traditions don't really matter much in the infinite scheme of things. What matters is that we follow Jesus' simple path of kindness, mercy, charity, and self-reflection back to Forever."

Malcolm smiles proudly, "That's right. Jesus is the Messiah, High Priest, and King for all peoples and all religions, whether they accept him or not. All religions are stumbling over Jesus. The Jews rejected him as the Messiah. The Christians exalted him to the position of God, and the Muslims demoted him to the position of simply a prophet. All religions should accept him as their Messiah, follow his example, and ask forgiveness in his name."

"And this will make their religions complete?" Asks Nino.

Malcolm explains, "Yes, however their lives will not be complete unless they find the path. When I discovered the Nation of Islam and became Malcolm X, I was extremely religious. However, I did not find the path until my life was almost over. In fact, once I found the path I was never the same again."

"What happened? How did you finally find the path?"

Malcolm grows somber, "In the United States, the Muslim religion was primarily a black man's religion. Many members of The Nation of Islam, although they followed the teachings of the Qur'an, were not walkers of the path. In fact, many were about as anti-white as the KKK was anti-black. I didn't realize it at the time, but I had become that which I hated most in the world, a racist."

Nino wonders, "How did you feel about what Martin Luther King, Jr. was trying to do?"

Malcolm makes clear, "I respected what he was trying to accomplish, but I didn't go along with his passive resistance approach. Remember Nino, I was a street fighter filled with hate. To me, white people were devils, and their religions were false and oppressive. Their pictures of a white Jesus, and a white God spoke not to me heart … Martin believed in the white man's religion. He supported and believed in the same doctrines as my enemies, so this was another major point of difference. The ironic thing is that in looking back, Martin was more of a true Muslim than I was. He wanted the path to become a reality for all people. He wanted the United States Government to support the path. He truly was a great man of God."

"So what happened that opened your eyes to the truth?" Nino asks.

"At least once in every Muslim's life, they should complete their pilgrimage, and visit the most holy city of Mecca. It was during this visit that I realized the beauty of the true Muslim religion. There I was in the most holy of all mosques, and it struck me. I saw people of all different nationalities and colors all congregating together and praying to Allah. It was then that I saw clearly how the ugly seed of racism had corrupted many followers of Nation of Islam. When I returned, I began to have disagreements with Elijah Muhammad."

"Elijah Muhammad?"

Malcolm explains, "He was the leader of the Nation of Islam at the time. We considered him a very holy man. To us, he was a prophet. I believed in what he professed so strongly that at one time I said that anyone who ever speaks against the prophet should be put to death. I would have never imagined that, in so saying these words, I had sentenced myself to death."

Nino startled, "Is that why you were murdered?"

Malcolm shakes his head at the irony of it, "Yes. I no longer supported the Nation of Islam, and it caused a rift in the organization. Half of the people sided with me, and half sided with Elijah Muhammad. It was better for one man to die than for the Nation of Islam to be left in such a state of disarray."

Nino raises his eyebrows, "It's kind of like why the Pharisees had Jesus killed."

"Satan has been responsible for the deaths of all people who have defended the path. Starting with the death of Abel, Satan has destroyed anyone who exposed his evil, his lies, and his need for war and destruction."

Nino confused, "I thought Satan couldn't kill anyone?"

Malcolm makes clear, "He can't, but he or his demons can seduce other souls into trying to murder or to spread lies."

Nino worried, "So, are you saying that ultimately everyone who exposes Satan have their lives ruined?"

Malcolm calms his friend, "If you are a defender of the path. God will not allow you to be taken until it is determined your work is over. Remember, once you get Satan's attention, not only will he try to turn others against you, but his evil spirit will also press on you to make decisions that will ruin your own life…. You see, as long as you stick to the path, Satan cannot harm one hair on your head. As long as your faith remains strong, Satan is powerless against you. However, Satan is very clever in his attacks. He strikes at our faith first. He tries to plant that little seed of doubt or rebellion in our minds. All he needs is the tiniest crack in our faith. That moment of doubt, fear, or bodily weakness is all he needs to get his snowball rolling. He will try to scare you. If your faith weakens and you veer from the path, he can cause you to have money problems, family problems, health problems and so on. He will try to silence you because of your fear for your own life. He will try to seduce you. He will even turn people against you. However, if you continue to treat others the way you want to be treated, even if they do and say harmful things to you, ultimately your good will prevail."

"How do you prevail?" Questions Nino.

Malcolm explains, "You either are left to continue your work because your faith has grown so strong that Satan now flees from you at your command, or your work is completed and God pulls you victoriously from the Great Game of Life."

Nino tries to put it into his own words, "So, it truly is Satan who makes all bad things happen in this world. He tries to steal our faith with empty threats and temptations. But, if we remain faithful and don't get mad or blame God for our problems in life, God will, as he did in the case of Jesus, turn our tragedies into triumphs, our losses into riches, and our dreams into realities."

Malcolm beams with pride, "You truly were born to be the final prophet. I have not told you anything that you didn't already know. I am only revealing to you that which is buried in the recesses of your mind. As far as Satan is concerned you will get his attention right away, and he will come at you more directly than he would another earth bound soul because he knows you already understand how the Great Game works...." Malcolm tries to relieve Nino's anxiety, "Still and all, he won't want to risk exposure, so he will operate covertly but swiftly. You just stick to the path, be brave, and arm yourself with these commands I will give you. **Believe in God. Believe in yourself. Never give up!** Be brave and faithful in all that you do no matter how grave a situation looks, and God will never abandon you."

Nino gaining confidence, "I will Malcolm. You have my word of honor. I will fight the hard fight, and we will be victorious!"

Malcolm smiles, "Anshallah. This means "if God wills". As Muslims, we always say Anshallah. This keeps us humble, and submissive to God's will."

Nino tries out his new word, "Anshallah, I like that. I think I've heard that before. What is that special thought that goes along with Muslim prayer? Do you know what I mean?"

Malcolm thinks for a moment, "You mean the thought that every prayer we say is to be considered the last prayer we will ever speak."

Nino smiles, "Yes, I really like that mentality. I try to take that attitude a step further and use it in all of life's situations. You know, like, live each day like it will be my last day alive. Play each game like it will be my last game. Speak to my friends and loved ones like it will be my final encounter with them."

"Nino, my brother, you truly are a Muslim."

"Malcolm, just now I had the strangest feeling that you said these words to me before. Right here, under these circumstances."

"You just had what's called a "de ja vu"? I don't want to get side tracked, but do you know why people have I experiences?"

Nino shrugs his shoulders, "No idea."

Malcolm enlightens, "While you wait in your mother's womb to be born, you are in a sort of dream state in which your mind plays and replays thousands of probabilities and outcomes. From this experience, you will develop an internal compass so to speak. It is where our intuition comes from. Deep in the recesses of our mind, we know when we are making a bad decision. It either doesn't feel right, or feels like it is good or "meant to be"."

Nino smiles, "So, in a way, this could be a positive sign that it was my destiny, and that if I stick to the path, God will turn our plan into something good."

Malcolm also smiles, "Anshallah."

"Right, right … Anshallah. So many little mysteries up here. But it's all cool. Man, is it cool!"

"Nino, the time has come for me to return you to Barabbas. However, I do have one more area to cover with you so we will walk over to where he is. Actually, let's float over. That will be more enjoyable for both of us."

"Float? Are we going in the water?" Asks Nino.

"Nope, just touch my hand."

Nino lays his hand on Malcolm's, and soon they are floating over the countryside on a gentle breeze that caresses them as they sail along.

Nino sinks into the moment, "This is peaceful man. It feels so relaxing. But how do you know where the wind will carry you?"

Malcolm winks, "The breeze simply knows where I want to go."

"This place is the bomb!"

"The bomb?"

Nino teases Malcolm, "It means it is awesome. Like a bomb. Get it? I know you old timers don't understand what's hip anymore."

Malcolm fakes agitation and laughs, "Say what? I used to be the King of Hip! Don't make me have to get rough with you!"

Nino continues the joke, "Okay, okay. I won't pick on you for being old and unhip anymore. It's not your fault. I mean, if I was to become old and out of the loop, I wouldn't want someone making fun of me!"

Malcolm playfully puts Nino in a headlock and then lets him go. As Nino rubs his neck he once again sips in the splendor of his surroundings.... Malcolm grows serious again.

"Nino, the last thing I need to speak to you about is Satanism." "You mean, worshipping the Devil?" Asks Nino.

"In a way, but not exactly. Nino, do you remember what you were like when you were fourteen or fifteen years old?"

Nino scratches his head, "A little, I guess so. Why do you ask?"

Malcolm explains, "The teenage years are a difficult time for most kids. Even children who come from good homes run into trouble during this dangerous time of development. They crave independence but they still need guidance and regulations."

"I agree with you, but what's this got to do with Satanism?" Asks Nino.

Malcolm frowns, "There are a growing number of children out there in the world who have not been properly raised. For example, children who come from broken homes have a very difficult time adjusting. Their parents left one another to reenter the dating game, and in doing so, returned to a quasi-adolescent period of development."

Nino nods in agreement, "So, what you have is kind of like children raising children?"

Maclolm nods in agreement, "Exactly. The parents don't have time for their children because they are busy trying to put their lives back together. They are working, dating, and trying to take care of their children. It's not really that they are malicious, but what they are trying to do is impossible."

Nino can relate, "A lot of the kids I see interacting with their parents on the street seem spoiled, disrespectful and demanding. Instead of the parents raising these children, it seems like they just try to keep them under control by buying them whatever they want and letting them live however they choose. These kids have no boundaries. It's like they might as well be on their own."

Malcolm shakes his head, "That's one type of neglected child. Oh, they have all the food, clothes, and material goods they will ever need. But they don't feel loved or cared about. This type of child could even develop in a home in which there are two parents who are married to each other, but have careers that keep them too busy and out of the home the majority of the time. The other type of neglected children are the ones who are not taken care of in anyway, whatsoever. They live in very chaotic homes. They are often poor, hungry, ignorant, ignored and desperate. The house holds they live in are unstructured. There are no predictable routines, or time honored family traditions. These homes are often overcrowded, noisy, and constantly in a state of crisis. Many of these children are amoral in that their conscience was never properly formed. The very worst of these children are uncivilized, and animalistic. They will kill a child to steal his coat, and not give it a second thought. They come up in a world of survival of the fittest. They are as egocentric, selfish and uncaring as the parents or parent who brought them into the world."

"I read an article the other day in LINK magazine that stated how some divorces are necessary to get out of an abusive or violent situation. but that nearly 80% of all divorces happen for lessor reasons."

Malcolm shakes his head, "It's true. Bickering is a normal part of marriage. Spouses who are constantly arguing, but who act civilized when it comes to their children, should think twice about splitting up the family. I mean if you look at the big picture there's nothing better waiting for you anyway. People who divorce for these normal marital problems end up complicating their lives and the lives of their children so much, that when the dust finally settles, this carefree period of life called 'Childhood" has been laid waste. Leaving spiritual and psychological voids that can neve be filled."

Nino still confused, "I agree with you 100 percent, but I still don't see what all this has to do with Satanism."

Malcolm explains, "There is a Muslim mystic who once wrote "Oh, thou that has no place in any place art appearing in every place within this wheeling world." Allah, who is responsible for manifesting all forms, can certainly focus in on a particular form. In other words God's nature may manifest in any way and fill any image—be it a burning bush, a cloud, or a glorified person. Unfortunately Satan also has many of the same powers on earth that God has."

Nino is still not puzzled, "So, if Satanism is your religion—"

Malcom cuts of Nino, "Satanism is not a religion. It is a way of life!…. As you have already learned God does not care about what religion you practice. When Jehovah looks down from Heaven he does not see Christians, Muslims, or Jews. He does not see race, creed or color. He simply sees his children, some who are following his holy path, and those who are following the path of Satan. Many of these people would not consider themselves Satanists, but they are still doing Satan's work by preparing a path for those who come after them to follow. A path that leads to the Outer Darkness, Purgatory, and ultimately Hell."

"Okay, but what about the Atheists who make it to Heaven?" Asks Nino.

Malcom nods, "As you already know there are some exceptions to the rule. However, more often than not these Atheists who are parents end up producing children who have a variety of problems as they move along in the Great Game. These spiritually neglected children are easy prey for the Beast. Most of them have never had parents who loved them unconditionally, so the idea of an invisible God that loves them is uncomprehensible. They grow into adults who are either Atheists or Agnostics. They go through life not caring about their neighbor, but constantly thinking of what is best for themselves. Oh, they may appear like decent, law abiding citizens who really do care about their neighbors, but underneath the surface they are souls who do not know how to truly love. They have no hope for the future, because they do not believe in God or Heaven. They are depressed and often desperate souls because they have nothing to make them feel good except for earthly possessions and earthly pleasures. What a miserable existence they must lead! Can you imagine how they feel as they begin to see the signs of age on their bodies? How troubled they must feel to know that their time here is running out? They have nothing to look forward to but old age, and the sufferings that go along with it. I truly feel sorry for these people. They, like all Satanists, have put their hopes on material worldly possessions instead of God and his children. They have nobody in their lives who loves them unconditionally, or who will be with them during times of adversity. Their relationships very rarely last because they don't know how to truly love."

Nino is troubled, "What a sad existence.… What can I do for these children to free them from the path of Satan, and lead them to the Path of Jesus?"

Malcolm smiles, "First of all, you have to get them to believe that Heaven is a real place. You have to get our children so interested in the Kingdom of Forever, that they begin to long for its coming. It's kind of like good advertising. If you make a place sound good enough, eventually people are going to start to want to know how to get there. Encourage our little ones to expand their imagination, and meditate on all of the endless possibilities of Heaven. Remember what Willy Wonka said **"We are the music makers, and we are the dreamers of dreams!"** Once you have their interest in Heaven, you must then show them the path that will lead them home. It is important not to try and scare the children into believing, because this approach ultimately helps Satan's cause. He wants children to either not believe in God at all, or to picture him as this giant, mean man with a white beard, who is waiting for them to sin so he can punish them and send them to Hell. Remember this, Nino, all paths lead to the throne of God."

"Do all Muslims believe this?" Nino asks.

Malcolm shrugs his shoulders, "If they don't, then they should. When I returned from my life changing pilgrimage to Mecca, I still called myself Malcolm X, but in my heart I was now Alairaphoon, which means that I now had openness to every religious belief. **The Muslim prophet Muhammad, peace be upon him, wanted to promote an understanding and brotherhood among people of all races, nationalities, and religions.… No founder of any love-based religion ever taught religious prejudice. Prejudice is now and always has been the devils child! Prejudice leads to war and enslavement. But Allah's children are born free. God hopes that every person will eventually find a religion that nurtures their soul. However, in their zeal and devotedness, they should not deny this same right to others."**

Nino curious, "What about the Muslim extremists who blew up the World Trade Centers? These guys must have been very devout Muslims in order to sacrifice their lives, and yet they did this unholy act."

Malcolm shakes his head in dismay, "Extreme is the key word here Nino. There are religious fanatics in every religion, but they do not represent the true essence of their faith. These poor misguided souls are casualties of a spiritual war, and should be pitied as such. They are desperate and depressed individuals who are so filled with displaced anger that they can no longer see the true path of their respective religions. They are manipulated and brainwashed from a very early age. The sad thing is that they truly believe that they are doing God's work. But 'vengeance is mine' sayeth the Lord, and even if the person or people you kill are evil, who are we to judge and punish? Anyone who kills in the name of religion is nowhere near the path of Jesus.

"Malcolm what does the Qur'an say about acts of War?" Nino asks.

"Surah 2:section 24 of the Holy Qur'an clearly states that **"War is permissible for self-defense, and only to restore peace and freedom for the worship of Allah."**

"So, as long as you are free to practice your religion, and no one is attacking you, than there are no holy-grounds for committing a terrorist act, especially murder."

Malcolm smiles, "Exactly. The true Muslim religion is intended to be tolerant of all peoples and all religions. Surah 2: section 8 says **"Those who believe in the Qur'an, and those who follow the Jewish scriptures, and the Christians and the Sabians, any who believe in Allah and the last day, and work righteousness, will have their reward.** You see Nino, God truly has no favorites, he passionately loves all of his children."

Nino's eyes twinkle, "The Qur'an truly is a holy book."

Malcolm smiles, "Yes, it is, and like all holy books it is a blessing for all times, and all peoples. **I believe the Qur'an is a book of divine quidance and direction for all mankind. It was given to Muhammad by the Angel Gabriel. I consider it a direct revelation from God, and equal in all ways to the Torah and The Bible."**

Nino beams with pride, "God truly is the father of peace and love.... I wonder sometimes, will the world really someday beat their swords into plowshares and their spears into pruning-hooks? I long for the day when the nations no longer fight with each other anymore, and all wars will end. Why can't we all just believe in one God and one Messiah? Why can't all people see that Jesus is the Qur'an, and the Qur'an is Jesus? In that both are divine gifts intended to bring peace and love into the world."

Malcolm is taken back. "Nino, you truly are the Prophet of Faith. As you said, the Qur'an, like Jesus, is a book revealed by Jehovah to lead people out of the darkness of false worship and war, into light of unity and peace. The path of the Muslim, the Christian, the Jew, the Hindu, the Buddhist and all of the love based religions may appear to be very different from one another, but each one leads to the same holy destination. For all those who have found Jehovah's path of righteousness, Jesus will be there at the end of their journey to welcome them into eternal paradise. He will hug them, and his heart will be filled with joy."

"What about the people who don't walk the path? Who is their to greet them? Satan?" Nino asks.

"No, remember what I told you. All holy paths lead to the same place. Jesus will also be there at the end of the journey of those who have walked the self-centered, uncompassionate path of evil. He will hug them, and try to console them. But there is no consolation for the soul that is confronted with its own guilt. Jesus will have tears in his eyes and pain in his heart as he tells them why they cannot enter the kingdom. Jehovah takes no delight whatsoever in the condemnation of his unworthy children. No matter how evil the soul, or how heinous its earthly crimes, Allah never stops loving them. It is not His will that even one soul be lost to Satan. You can not imagine how are loving father suffers Nino. It's heartbreaking to see, and unfathomable to comprehend how and why Allah cares for us so deeply. The children must know without a doubt who they are and where they must return! We are all God's children, and we must return to the land of our origin. We are strangers in a strange land, a land where the forces of good and evil battle for the right to our souls. You must enlighten them Nino! **It is not that God stopped caring about us, it's that we stopped caring about God!** We keep telling Him to get out of our schools. Get out of our courts. Get out of our government, and to get out of our lives." We keep pushing him away, and all he does is keep coming back for more. He's like a fighter who keeps getting knocked down, but refuses to give up. How much more rejection can our poor father take?!"…. Malcolm gets tears in his eyes. "How can we expect Allah to give us His Love, Blessings, Peace, and Protection, if we keep demanding that he leave us alone!"

Nino puts his arm around Malcoms shoulders. "You know the other day I heard this guy Ben Stien from CBS news giving a commentary that you would have liked. He is a Jewish guy and he was saying how he thinks that people who believe in God are sick and tired of being pushed around. He asked where this concept came from that America is explicitly an atheist country. He said it is not in the constitution, and he's tired of it being pushed down everyones throats. Madeleine Murray O'Hare complained she didn't want prayer in our schools and we said OK. Then someone said you better not read the Bible in school, and we said OK. Dr. Benjamin Spock said we shouldn't spank our children when they misbehave because their young personalities would be warped and we would damage their self-esteem. But he is an expert so we said OK. I can't really remember the whole speech but it was a good one."

Malcolm agrees, "You know your teachers, leaders, and parents keep wondering why our children seem to have no conscience, and why they don't know right from wrong, and why it doesn't bother some of them to kill strangers, their classmates, or even themselves. We take God out of everything and look to these so called experts. What a travesty! The blind leading the blind. Did you know that Dr. Spocks son killed himself? **You see our secular cures and theories don't cut it Nino. That's because there is no replacement for Gods moral foundation, laws and wisdom. There is no replacement for a loving mother and father, and a childhood filled with awe and wonder. There is no human remedy for that.**" Malcolm looks to the sky, then back at his friend…. "It appears our time together has come to a close, my brother. May God, Jesus and all of the Angels and Heavenly servants bless and protect you as you prepare to take down the morning star."

Nino smiling with confidence, "You can count on it, my friend. We will be successful! … Anshallah."

Malcolm smiles proudly, "Anshallah, Nino, Anshallah. Bismallah raheem."

"What's that mean?"

"It means go kick that devils ass!"

The breeze gently places Nino back at the mansion where Nino's tour began. As he walks through the beautiful flowing gardens, Barabbas is pacing back and forth like an expectant father.

Five Pillars of Islam

1. **Confession of Faith:** The belief that "there is no God but Allah, and Mohammed is His prophet."

2. **Prayer:** Muslims must pray five times per day, facing towards Mecca.

3. **Charity:** Muslims must give alms to the poor, and support the local Mosque by donating a portion of their income.

4. **Fasting:** During the **Ramadan**, the ninth month of the Muslim calendar, all Muslims must fast during daylight hours, except the very young or sick.

5. **Pilgrimage:** If possible financially, each Muslim must make a **hajj**, or holy pilgrimage, to the city of Mecca.

CHAPTER 26

▼

"How you are fallen from Heaven, Oh Lucifer, son of the morning! How you are cut down to the ground-mighty though you were against the nations of the world. For you said to yourself, "I will ascend to Heaven and rule the angels. I will take the highest throne. I will preside on the Mount of Assembly far away in the recesses of the north. I will climb to the highest heavens and be like the Most High." But instead, you will be brought down to the pit of hell, down to its lowest depths. Everyone there will stare at you and ask, "Can this be the one who shook the earth and the kingdoms of the world? Can this be the one who destroyed the world and made it into a shambles, demolished its great cities, and had no mercy on his prisoners?"
-ISAIAH 14:12-14 (760 BC)

"Hear, O Israel, the Lord our God is one Lord!"
-Deuteronomy 6:4 (680 BC)

"Well, Nino, did you enjoy your tour?" Barabbas asks.

Nino has a Heavenly glow about him, "Yes, Barabbas, more than anything I have ever experienced or imagined. I see things in a new and blinding light. For the first time in my life, I am absolutely sure that I am doing the right thing. I believe in our mission. I understand the possible ramifications for my actions, but if our small group must be sacrificed so that millions of souls can be saved, then so be it. I am not afraid anymore. I will go back to earth and tell the truth as it has been revealed to me. All those who deserve to be Citizens of Forever once again, will heed to what I say."

Barabbas is proud and pleased, "The spirit of God is with you, Nino Jones. For only the spirit of God can inspire us to think of the well being of others more than we think of ourselves. You remind me of our King, Jesus. He did not have to do what he did. Nobody forced him to do it. He chose to do the will of God. What God wanted and what people needed were more important than what he wanted and what he needed. Those who stand out as special in the eyes of God are those who serve others. Most of the truly great men and women who have ever lived are not world famous people. Kings and queens, presidents, professional athletes and movie stars are not the real heroes in God's world. His heroes are the simple, loving souls who choose to do His will over their own, and in so doing become one with God. One heart, one soul, one mind serving one king and one God. These are the souls who will be selected to help the king govern in the new kingdom of Forever. You have come a long way in a short time my friend, and now I must give you the final piece of this eternal puzzle."

Barabbas and Nino walk to the edge of a great canyon looking over the heavenly garden of Eden. The view is breathtakingly indescribable. They sit down on a giant tear-shaped emerald, and look out over the valley of a thousand waterfalls. As Nino soaks up the view, Barabbas begins to speak.

Barabbas somber, "Nino, there is nothing in the heavens and on earth that has not been created or allowed to be created by Elohim (the only God that matters). Before the earth was ever created, we lived together in the Kingdom of Forever. All souls that ever lived, and those yet to be born, were once all alive at the same time in Heaven. As you can see, prior to our earthly existence we had a glorious life. Everything was copasetic. God dwelt among his people. Every knee bowed and every tongue professed that there was only one God. Blessed is Allah, most generous, most merciful. It was truly paradise in all ways … That is of course until the great revolution."

Nino is startled, "You mean, there really was an actual war in heaven? I don't understand. If God dwelt among his people, and everything was cool, why would there be a revolution?"

Barabbas explains, "God had created many great and powerful Angels to help him run the kingdom. However his most marvelous creation was called the Morning Star."

"Satan?"

Barabbas nods, "That's right. Satan was an awesome sight, and you might be surprised to know that he was loved by everyone who knew him. He was

God's favorite creation, and his power was second only to God's. Satan was the first of all God's creation to have free will. He was given great authority by God to run the kingdom of Forever and lead the angels."

Nino curious, "Did all of the citizens of Forever start out as angels?"

Barabbas shakes his head, "The souls that made up Forever were similar to angels, but we did not have quite the same power as angels. When God created the souls of Forever, we were created not like the angels who were made to be God's servants, but like his children. We were given free will to live in paradise as we chose. We grew up in the presence of Yahweh, and our spirits were one. There was no evil force to corrupt us, or pull us away from God's will. All God wanted from us was that we enjoy his paradise, and that's all we did for millions of years."

"What went wrong?" Nino asks.

Barabbas remembers, "God decided that he would choose a citizen of Forever and create a new type of soul…. The announcement sent shock waves of joy throughout the kingdom."

Nino puzzled, "Why was this such a big deal if God made everybody and everything?"

Barabbas smiles at Nino's wit, "Before the creation of man, God had always made everything by himself. This time however, he would create a soul by uniting with another soul in the same way that the angels were allowed to create new souls. This creation would be different from God's other creations in that he would be called his son, and the soul he selected to help him create this new life would be highly exalted for all time."

"Why do you think he decided to enter into this type of partnership?" Nino asks.

"God knew he was cared for by his creations, but he wanted to feel the love of a child, and the attachment and mutual admiration of a spouse. Most of the kingdom rejoiced over the announcement. The soul that God selected to be the mother of his son was known throughout the kingdom of Forever as one of its most loving characters. No one could ever quite put a finger on it, but there was always something special about Mary."

Nino is shocked, "You mean, this is the same Mary who is the mother of Jesus?" Nino rubs his head with both hands and tries to think. "Is everything that happens on earth simply a reflection of what already happened? Is our life and this earth nothing more than a stage and scenery on which we act out scenes from a life which was already lived?"

Barabbas smiling, and once again impressed with Nino's mind. "You are starting to understand, but you are not entirely correct. As you have stated, many of the things that happen on earth are simply reenacting scenes from a life that we have already lived in Forever. The birth of Jesus, and Satan trying to kill the child all happened before. The temple that Solomon built is almost identical to our Heavenly temple. However, much of what we are seeing is not part of any script. When God first came up with the idea of earth and what he hoped to accomplish through its creation, he did not envision that so many souls would have such a hard time returning to Forever. The immortal soul, given free will and then temporarily imprisoned in a body with physical, mental, and emotional needs, sets it on a very precarious path. God commands that you deny your body and mind much of what they naturally crave, and the Devil constantly dangles these forbidden fruits in front of you—the soul is willing, but the body is weak."

"So why did Satan ultimately turn against God? … Was it simply out of jealously?" Asks Nino.

Barabbas makes clear, "Satan was simply focusing on Allah's son and his descendents, and how these children would gradually cause him to be less significant in the Heavenly scheme of things. The angels were created by God alone to be his servants. They have always lived an excellent life, and they had a great relationship with their creator. But for God, there was something missing. Our omnipotent all powerful father found that he could make anything that his wonderful mind could imagine, except one thing. He could not make someone love him. In order for there to be true love, all souls must have a free will to decide for themselves. That's why love is the most precious piece of existence."

Nino perplexed, "But how could you not love God?"

Barabbas nods in agreement, "Exactly, how could you not love God? This was in fact the essence of his problem."

"What do you mean?" Nino asks.

"It's similar to the dilemma commonly faced by your movie stars and professional athletes. They always have to wonder "Does this person love me for who I really am? Or because of what I am, or how much money I have?

If all your needs are met, and there is no adversity to suffer through. What does love under these conditions prove?"

"Ok, I see what you mean. He had to create these new souls, the earth, and free will to set a stage on which true love would finally come forth."

"That's right. God would create a son, and he and his son would become one in body and soul. Jehovah knew that his son would eventually provide a path that would allow all souls of Forever to also become his sons and daughters by proving their love was true in the Great Game. Allah knew how Satan was going to react. Because of his exalted position in the kingdom, Satan had grown proud. He began on occasion to be critical of God to some of his most trusted associates. He began to fantasize about how he would run things if he were God. Satan was so magnificently created that he began to look at himself as equal to God. Satan made the mistake of speaking some of these thoughts in front of Michael, the Arch Angel. You see, Satan was kind of throwing out feelers to see if he could create a following for himself. At first it was just an ego thing. He didn't intend to form an army. The mistake that Satan made was that he thought he had Michael's confidence, but he did not. Michael secretly met with God and told him of the things that Satan had been saying. Although God knew that Satan would betray him, he was still very troubled upon hearing the news. It was shortly after this conversation that God decided to expose Satan. He informed Michael to gather two legions of his most trusted angels to be on standby for an attack by Satan. God told Michael that he was going to have a son and that Satan was going to try to kill the child. In so doing, he would be exposed for what he truly was, a traitor. From the time God announced he was going to have a son, Satan began plotting the revolution. He knew that Jesus would be placed above his position, and he could not tolerate the thought of it. Sibling rivalry had come to Heaven, and Satan's pride was devouring him. He managed to convince a legion of angels to follow him. He told them how the son was only the beginning, the first of what would eventually become a new race of souls. Souls who he envisioned would eventually rank above them in God's order of things. He convinced these Angels that God had just been using them all along. He told them that they would become the new creations slaves for all eternity, and this made many of the angels get very angry. Michael the Arch Angel openly acted as if he was upset so that

Satan would believe he was on his side. The devil's pride had perverted his judgment, and his contempt made him forget who and what he was actually trying to dethrone. The plan was in place. Satan would destroy the child and his mother. While God was in a state of mourning, and physically weakened from making the new universe, Satan and his armies would ascend the holy mountain, kill our weakened Heavenly Father, and proclaim himself God most high. He would place himself upon the throne in the Holy of Holies, and reign there for all eternity. Well, as you can already guess, Satan was soundly defeated. Allah, Mary, and Jesus were unharmed, and he and his army of fallen angels were banished to the Outer Darkness to await their punishment. God had always wanted a society in which the souls were not puppets but had their own free will. However, God new that happened with Satan and his fallen angels could, under certain circumstances reoccur. To ensure that this never happened again, God decided that all citizens must be tested as gold is tested with fire. God met with his twelve elders to come up with a plan of action."

"So, this is when God decided to make the human race?" Asks Nino.

"That's right. The immortal soul would be temporarily housed in a mortal body. The first father of all humans was the Biblical Adam, and the mother was Eve. They were placed in an earthly Garden of Eden. An earthly paradise whose beauty rivaled Heavens."

Nino wonders, "This Garden of Eden sounds like it was a miniature copy of Forever."

Barabbas smiles, "That's exactly what it was. God was accessible to Adam and Eve, and everything was wonderful. However, at a specified time, God released Satan from his bondage, and the Great Game began. I'm sure you've know the story. Satan entered the garden and deceived Adam and Eve, just like he had deceived his fallen angels in Forever. Once Adam and Eve had eaten the forbidden fruit, they now saw things the way that God saw them. They now had the knowledge of good and evil, and from that moment on, these new immortal souls were set free. Also, on the very day that Adam and Eve were expelled from the Garden of Eden, different Adams and Eves representing every race and nation were created all around the world. These Adam and Eve prototypes were set free all around the world. The souls of Forever would now be tested as gold is tested by fire."

"But, free will is the key, right?" Asks Nino.

Barabbas nods in agreement, "Yes. In the Great Game of life, neither God nor Satan is allowed to force anyone to behave in a certain way. You are placed in a mortal body that has needs, and this makes you discontent. Like the restless tide always searching for something, our souls are constantly pulled by the powers of good and evil. What your soul actually longs for is to be back in Forever, standing in the loving light of our father. God, in his own way, with the help of his chosen angels, shows you pieces of himself in the world around you. He sends messengers and prophets to spread his word. He wants the souls to have faith without seeing. Satan, in his own way, with his fallen Angels, tries to cover up the existence of God and himself. God is all about unity, love and freedom. Satan is all about division, hate and enslavement. God's narrow road of rules leads eventually to freedom. Satan's broad road of no rules or anarchy, leads eventually to imprisonment. It is the irony of all ironies."

"So, all human beings are descendents of this new race of souls?" Asks Nino.

"The majority of us are."

Nino is shocked, "The majority?"

Barabbas explains, "Before God started the Great Game, he decided to give the angels the opportunity to become one of his adopted children. Any Angel who decided to take part in the Great Game and successfully returned to Forever is no longer considered a part of the race of Angels. They became one of God's actual children. Because they have learned to love."

Nino is perplexed, "I'm flabbergasted that not all of the angels wanted to be a part of the Great Game."

Barabbas understands Nino's reaction, "Many of the angels were very content with their position in God's kingdom. Don't forget that many of the souls who take part in the Great Game are not successful. In simply choosing to take part in the Great Game, you are risking where you will spend your eternity. All of the people whom you encounter during your lifetime are very brave souls. The angels who chose to stay and serve God will not have free will. They will exist simply to serve God and his children. The angels who make this decision are highly esteemed in Forever. They make up the true priesthood, and they are looked down on by no one. Their choice to give up their free will in order to be servants to God is as noble as deciding to take part in the Great Game."

"Why won't they be able to have free will? Is it because of the revolution?" Asks Nino.

Barabbas nods, "Yes. In God's new kingdom all chance of conflict is removed. The angels will be magnificent souls, but they will have no pride. They will blissfully serve their Lord and his children, and they will think nothing of themselves."

Nino worried, "What's to prevent one of the children of Yahweh from becoming jealous like Satan?"

"There will be no sibling rivalry in the new Jerusalem. Each of us is unique in our Father's eyes, and we know this without a doubt. Our relationship with our Heavenly father is a million times more special than that of the very best earthly parent-child relationship. We are loved completely and unconditionally by our father and all of our brothers and sisters. There is nothing to covet or envy because you can create or do anything that you can imagine. Nothing will be required of you other than that you spend your eternity in paradise doing whatever pleases you. In Forever everyone, and especially your father, is able to enjoy all the things that bring you joy. You will be a god in an endless, boundless, magnificent, ever expanding universe for all eternity, and the tree will be known by and delight in his fruit."

Nino sighs, "It sounds like a fairy tale, like it's too good to be true."

Barabbas also sighs, "It's that somewhere over the rainbow, Nino. It's the Land of Oz. Only the wicked witches have all been removed, and we are all wizards."

Nino wonders, "Did all God's children have a choice in whether we took part in the Great Game?"

"Yes. We were given free will from the very beginning. However, no son or daughter of Allah would ever choose not to go."

"Why?" Nino asks.

Barabbas smiles proudly,"It is because of who we are, and who our father is. We are brave because we are sons and daughters of Jehovah, most merciful and compassionate. We are all very loving souls who care as much for our brothers and sisters as we do for ourselves. Quite often we go into the Great

Game to help those who have gone before us, as much as we go there to help ourselves."

"Now, how does that family thing really work? Are we all really brothers and sisters?" Asks Nino.

Barabbas smiles at the thought of it. "Yes, we really are. And that family gets larger every day!"

Nino's eyes get big, "No kidding?"

Barabbas Chuckles, "Yes. In Forever, any two souls can decide to create a baby soul whenever they feel like it."

"What about incest, and retarded children?" Nino asks.

Barabbas smirks, "That is only the way things work on earth. In Forever, there is no such animal."

"So, on earth we really are all God's children?"

"Yes, and this fact must be an important part of your message. Every person whom you meet in your life is someone who you were very close to in the Kingdom of Forever. You must learn to overlook a person's physical characteristics, their annoying idiosyncrasies, or any crimes they have committed in order to see the precious soul that dwells within. This is your dear, dear brother or sister, and you may be the one person left in the world who can save them. If you had a son of a daughter and someone was trying to kidnap them you would fight with every once of your strength to save them. However, Satan is trying to do something a billion times worse. He is trying to take your dearly beloved from you forever. If the devil can get you to stop loving them, by manipulating them to behave badly, then ultimately you will be helping Satan destroy members of your very own family!"

Nino is shocked, "You mean, it is possible that in my life some of the people whom I couldn't stand were actually very dear loved ones of mine?"

"Nino, not only is it possible, it is true in every situation."

They walked a little further in silence and then Barabbas continued.

"Our time together has come to a close my friend. There is much more that I would like to tell you, and I know that there are probably many mysteries that you would like answers to, but believe me, you have already been given all that you will need to spread your message."

Nino sad that his tour is over, but confident,"I now feel in my heart that I am ready. I had my doubts early on, but I now feel prepared."

Barabbas moves closer to Nino, "So, what will it be? Your message?"

Barabbas looks directly at Nino, expecting to see a nervous old man, but instead encountering an enlightened soul. Knowledge and devotion are apparent in the very expression on Nino's face, and even before he opens his mouth to speak, Barabbas is aware that the tour has worked its magic, and Nino knows the message he has to spread.

Nino smiles and nods with absolute assurance as he begins to speak. "My message is that God exists, and that he is the Father of us all: Christians, Muslims, Jews, Hindus, Buhdists, Atheists, and Agnostics. We are all brave souls who chose to take part in the Great Game of life. We preexisted the world in a heavenly paradise called the Kingdom of Forever. Our goal is to return to Forever, and there is only one path that leads us there. When Jesus Christ of Nazareth said 'I am the way, the truth and the light. Nobody comes to the Father except through the Son', he was not saying this as a representative of the Christian religion, nor was he endorsing one religion over another. He was simply saying here is the path that leads to God our father. There is no other path that leads to Heaven than this: Love God with all your heart, soul, mind and strength. You can only show God that you love him by Submitting to his will, and that is to love your neighbor as yourself. We must live examined-introspective lives. We must pray often, and ask forgiveness for our sins in the name of Christ Jesus, the Messiah of the world, and King in the land of Forever. There may be some of you who can not except Jesus in his full capacity as Messiah, however, you must still follow his path. We must love all of the people that we encounter during the course of our lifetime, because they truly are our brothers and sisters. God is love, mercy, unity and compassion. Satan is hate, pride, unmerciful and divisive. All paths lead to the judgment throne of God. When you arrive at the throne of glory it will not matter what you called yourself while you were here on earth, but how you treated the people, creatures and the planet that you encountered during the course of your lifetime. All of us who are merciful will attain mercy. Mercy not sacrifice is the heart of Gods law, and the tree will be known by its fruit."

Barabbas beams with pride, "Very good, Nino. You have outlined the path clearly and concisely. Try not to touch on political issues; this will immediately stop large groups of people from listening to you. Your main goal must be to get people to entertain the possibility of God and Heaven. Focus your strength on letting them know how miraculously wonderful the Kingdom of Forever truly is. Remember the Soul Touch!" Barabbas jokes.

Nino laughs and nods in agreement. "I got ya. They will be more willing to follow the P.O.J if they have a better idea of where it is leading them."

Barabbas smiling, "Exactly. Well, Nino Jones, prophet of faith, the time has come to depart. When you open your eyes, you will be sitting in front of a store called "Wings" at the corner of 77[th]and Broadway, and the time will be about 12:00 midnight. You will be reading a Bible, and you will see your messenger, Mark Salvatore Pitifer, on his way to, and returning home from, the China Club. Wait until he is on his way home to speak to him. Any other questions?"

Nino has a stiff upper lip "No sir. Tell everyone I will do my very best."

Barabbas grins, "Okay. Now close your eyes and click your heels together three times, saying "there's no place like home, there's no place like home."

Nino fakes agitation, "Get your ass out of here!" Nino laughs as he opens his eyes and sees Barabbas cracking up.

Barabbas waves goodbye, "Good luck my friend."

Tears fill Barabbas' eyes as Nino disappears, and he falls to his Knees to say on final prayer. In the twinkling of an eye, Nino is sitting in front of a store front on Broadway. The city seems colder than usual. A dark wind chills his bones, and for the first time in his life, he feels like he is a long, long way from home.

Author's Note: God bless the risk takers of the world. They are the true livers of life. For planted inside these brave souls, are the seeds of heroism, greatness and adventure.

"If you can make one heap of all your winnings and risk it on one turn of pitch-and-toss, and lose, and start again at your beginnings and never breathe a word about your loss; If you can force your heart and nerve and sinew to serve your turn long after they are gone, and so hold on when there is nothing in you except the will

which says to them: Hold on! If you can talk with crowds and keep
your virtue, or walk with kings-nor lose the common touch, if neither foes
nor loving friends can hurt you, if all men count on you,
but none too much; If you can fill the unforgiving minute with
sixty seconds' worth of distance run, yours is the Earth and everything
that's in it, and—which is more-you'll be a man my son."
-Rudyard Kipling

CHAPTER 27

▼

"Let brotherly love continue and be not forgetful to entertain strangers: For in doing so, many have entertained angels unknowingly."
-Hebrews: 13:1-2

This might be the moment. The Red Sea might just part. Sometimes miracles do happen, and sometimes hearts find hearts.
-Muhyiddin Shakoor

"Nowadays you have to go to Heaven to meet an Angel."
-Andrew & Phyllis Wolak (Polish Proverb)

It was an unseasonably cold, windy night for the middle of September, in New York City. Mark Salvatore Pitifer was standing in his sister Shari's 37th floor apartment staring down at one of the most famous ways in all the world, the corner of 86th and Broadway to be exact. As he looked out over the city of lights, he couldn't help but think that the city seemed darker than normal, like a rose that had lost its luster. The city lights seemed somewhat cold and uninviting on this particular evening. It was like someone was trying to tell him to stay home for the night. He was about to take his leather coat off and do just that, when his sister Shari came into the room …

"You're not going out, are you?" Shari asked.

"As a matter of fact, I was just on my way down to the China Club."

Shari shook her head at her older, seemingly wiser brother. She couldn't imagine why anyone would want to spend time at an over-priced, over-crowded cave full of strobe lights and loud music. But Mark liked it for precisely those things. He could go there and be anonymous, maybe even run into a few movie stars.

"Why don't you just stay up with me tonight? I'll fix you a nice glass of tea, and we'll talk," Shari gently pleaded with her brother.

Mark scowls in agitation, "Shari, I really don't feel like talking. I do that for a living! I came to New York because I just wanted to disappear. I don't want to talk about my problems. I don't even want to hear anybody else talking about their problems. I'm burnt out, and I really need some time to myself." Mark softens his voice. "It's not that I don't miss you and want to spend time with you Shari, I do, but I just really need some time alone. You should know by now that New York City is a great place to be when you want to disappear. Ten million strangers seem a lot more inviting than a town full of friends right now."

Shari is concerned, "But you're worrying me, Mark, you're worrying everyone who cares about you. You are important to so many people. You are always there to offer help and support to anyone who needs it. Now it's your turn to reach out for help, and all you do is push people away. Your sisters, your mother—your poor wife—you push all of us away! It doesn't make you less of a man if you admit you're hurting, Mark." Shari could feel her voice breaking as she tried to stand up to her brother. "You know, for as giving as you are, you're showing a pretty selfish side right now by keeping all this to yourself."

Mark is angry now. "I didn't come here to talk about you, Mom, or especially Leigh. You didn't listen to one word I said! If you did, you would realize that I just want to be left alone!" Mark slammed the door behind him, ignoring Shari's calls. It was 1:00 a.m. and Broadway was alive with people. Mark walked toward Times Square, caught in the rhythm of 1,000 footsteps. He paused only for a moment on 77th Street to give some money to an old homeless man who was reading the Bible under the storefront display lights. However, when he reached for his money he discovered that his pockets were empty, so he headed to the ATM in Rudolfo Garcia's famous Mexican restaurant, and then onward to the China Club.

A small crowd stood behind the velvet ropes at the Club. The doorman quickly looked Mark up and down and nodded for him to pass. Mark had heard that they sometimes enforced a dress code, so he was alittle anxious whenever he went into the club. Inside, wall to wall people blended into one giant mass on the dance floor. Like the city outside, the China Club seemed darker than usual tonight. Mark was nervous about this until he realized he was still wearing his sunglasses. He smiled when he thought of Shari's description of the China Club—an expensive cave. She was right. The people looked like stalagmites clinging to each other and the walls around them. He laughed when he thought of himself standing there in his black pants, black shirt and dark glasses. Not only was he anonymous, he was incognito. Wondering whether the other guests thought he was stoned or some sort of cop, he approached the bar for a Corona with lime. Never much of a drinker, he ordered this particular beverage more for the memory than for any numbing effects it might have. One sip and he was back on the moonlit campus of UCLA with a French girl named Nadine. They shared Coronas, stories and the moon, nothing more. It was one of the more romantic evenings he could remember. Some times missed kisses make for more provocative memories than some actual encounters, Mark thought to himself. He wove his way through the gyrating bodies on the dance floor, dizzy from the sea of perfumes and colognes. His tour down memory lane was interrupted by a New York beauty with jet black hair and a thick Brooklyn accent.

"Hey, you a cop or something?"

"Nope."

"Then what's with the dark glasses, huh?"

Mark looks at his glasses and chuckles, "I thought it was kind of dark in here. I forgot I had them on, they're prescription."

The girl giggles, "Oh … So, what's your name, Cop?"

"Mark. Mark Stallone." Mark teases.

"Any relation to Sylvestor Stall.…"

Mark laughing finishes her thought, "Nope, no relation to Sly. Just trying to kid you a little. My real name is Mark Pitifer. What about you?"

"Madonna, no relation." She jokes.

"Come on!" Mark laughed. "What's your real name?"

"Well, you promise not to laugh?"

"I promise."

"My name is Bella Coolina. I'm from Brooklyn."

Mark had to swallow his laughter. The name wasn't as funny as the fact she thought she had to announce where she was from. "Your name definitely fits you. I kind of already guessed the Brooklyn part."

Bella fakes agitation, "Hey, no laughing! You promised...." Bella moves closer and grabs Marks arm and whispers in his ear ... "Is it true what they say about Italians?"

Mark grins, "What do they say about Italians?"

Bella laughs, "Come on you know what they say."

Mark laughing, "No, what do they say?"

Bella continues to laugh, "That all Italians are hung like stallions."

Mark holds his side with laughter, "It's true, but that's not my most charming attribute."

Bella intrigued raises her eyebrows, "Then what is?"

Mark chuckles, "My lips baby."

Bella lets out a devilish laugh and playfully slaps Mark's arm, "You're nasty."

Mark fakes surprise, "I'm nasty?!"

Bella puts her arm through Marks and leads him towards the dance floor.... "So, Cop, you wanna dance, or what?"

Mark smiles, "Who could say no to a Bella Coolina from Brooklyn?"

Mark could feel his strong moral fiber unraveling in Bella's company. No matter how wise he was for a young man, he enjoyed the company of women. Just like his father, the prettier the girl, the more he wanted to be around her. Also like his father, he would never cheat on his wife. He just liked to push the limits sometimes. He liked to see how close he could dance to the proverbial fire without getting burned. The Corona, the music, and Bella Coolina continued to intoxicate Mark's body and mind throughout the night. Around 4:00 a.m., David Sandborn's "A Tear for Crystal" faded out and the soft reflected lights from the disco ball spun a cocoon of tiny white diamonds around Mark and Bella. The throngs of people and time itself seemed frozen. Dark curls and green eyes mesmerized Mark as they moved closer to his face, about to devour him with a kiss. Just then a drunk knocks into the DJ's booth, and the music comes to a screeching halt. The people groaned and rushed for one last drink before the bar closed. Mark took a deep breath, realizing he'd been "saved" by the bell.

Mark tries to make his exit, "Well, Bella Coolina, looks like this show is coming to a close. I really had a nice time."

Bella tugs playfully at his sleave, "Where are you going when you leave here?"

"Just back to my sister's place."

"Would you like to come back to my apartment? I only live a couple of blocks away on 69th Street. I'll make you some breakfast and then some dessert!" She flips her hair and walks sassily away.

She laughs and winks slyly. "I'm gonna go to the little girls' room, and then we can leave."

Mark stood with his back to the wall as the DJ for some reason picked up the pace again, and turned on those wild strobe lights. It was the final song of the evening, and as the music played, Mark's mind began to swim. He knew he should go back to Shari's apartment. But what if he did go back to Bella's for a little while? How much could he do and not feel guilty? Could he have a little fun? A little sip of passion? And still not be committing adultery? What he once saw as black and white issues were now very gray. As he mulled all this around in his mind, a tall blond haired man came up and stood very close to him. Mark thought this was strange because the club was almost empty, and there was no reason for this guy to be crowding in on him. Their shoulders were actually touching, and Mark moved slightly away from the gentleman without saying anything. Before he knew it, the guy was bumping into him once again. Not wanting to make anything of it, Mark attempted to start a conversation.

"How ya doin?" Mark asked, but the tall gentleman just stared out at the crowd, bobbing his head to the music … Mark raised his voice above the music and asked again, "How are you doing?"

The tall man turned and looked deeply into Mark's eyes, and then said, "Is your heart empty?"

Mark is startled by what he thought he heard, "Pardon me? What did you say?"

"Is your heart empty?"

Mark immediately thought of Leigh, his family, his work, and his music. It was like he saw in an instant a panoramic view of his life. "No, it's not."

The tall man is frowning, and somewhat agitated, "Then what are you doing here?!"

The man walked away before Mark could explain himself, and he stood there for a moment in stunned silence. His heart was pounding, and for some unknown reason he felt afraid. What could have prompted a total stranger to speak those words? Even more remarkable was the timing and the effect this stranger's question had upon Mark. He rushed to find this strange man in the now empty club, but he was nowhere to be found. It was like he had disappeared into thin air. Mark ran up to the entrance and looked up and down Broadway, which suddenly seemed deserted, cold and even darker than before. Nothing but the rustling of leaves mixed with swirling cyclones of street litter could be heard. Mark suddenly felt all alone, and scared. He was no longer thinking about Bella Coolina, as he started to run north, up Broadway toward his sister's apartment. He ran for about two or three blocks before slowing back down to a brisk walk. He noticed the same homeless man he had seen earlier, still sitting in front of the storefront, and to his surprise, still reading the Bible. He felt in his pocket for some spare change, and slowly approached the man.

Mark smiled to himself as he handed two carefully folded one dollar bills into the man's cup, thinking to himself that he needed all the good karma he could get. "Here you go, pal. Have a good night."

Nino smiling, "Thank you very much, and God bless you."

Mark smiles, "Same to you pal." Mark lingers for a moment. "Boy oh boy, you've been reading for a long time, haven't you."

Nino chuckles, "Yeah, I guess I have. I really love reading the Bible."

"I really like reading the Bible myself." Mark replies.

"Really? What's your favorite part?" Nino asks.

Mark scratches his head in thought, "Oh, I don't know. I guess I like the New Testament the best. The simple words of Jesus mean a lot to me. I also especially like the apocalyptic passages."

Nino raises his eyebrows, "Really? Why is that?"

"I guess because I think we may be living in the end of times. I like to try and figure out where I fit in individually, and where we fit in as a country." Talking about the Bible starts to calm Mark down a bit, and he catches his breath. The old man seems eager to carry on a conversation.

"You mean, like Revelation 18?" Nino asks.

Mark is intrigued by the old mans knowledge, "That's exactly what I mean. To me, this passage is clearly talking about the United States of America."

Nino agrees, "You know, I think you are right. However, I don't think that chapter was written especially for the United States. I mean, look at all the great empires that have risen and fallen before us. This chapter could be applied to any of them."

Mark nods in agreement, "I agree. You know, I think what happens is that these empires become evil. They drift away from the teachings of God and what's morally good until eventually they are controlled by the spirit of evil."

"You mean the spirit of Satan?" the old man asks.

"Of course. I mean, if you look at ancient Babylon, and many of the other fallen empires of ancient times, you can see the same pattern of their rise to power and their fall into oblivion."

Nino enjoying the conversation, "Your right. Ancient Babylon may have been physically destroyed, but the spirit that destroyed it simply focused its energy somewhere else."

Mark's expression turns sad, "I know. The times may seem to change, the endless cycles rearrange, but there's no progress. You see, it's all been done before and in our lives we're just one more to face the big test."

Nino shakes his head in agreement, "The United States is simply just the latest world empire?" Mark is intrigued, but not at all surprised by the old man's wisdom. Some of the smartest folks he knows are those he encountered on street corners or at bus stops. He settles next to his new friend, waiting to hear more.

Nino is also encouraged by Marks insightfulness "This world has made many technological advancements since ancient Babylon, but spiritually our world continues to remain the same." Nino pauses for a moment, and then asks Pitt a direct question. "Don't you wish you could do something to break the cycle?"

"What do you mean?" Pitt asks.

Nino clarifies, "What I mean is, don't you wish you could do something more than just develop a keen understanding of what's happening in the world in a spiritual sense? Haven't you ever wished you could do something to bring Satan down?"

Mark frowns, "I used to think I was born to do something special for God and the world," Mark says with a sigh. It's always difficult for him to admit this, because he is now certain it will never be. "I used to even think I was born to be some sort of prophet, but the longer I live, I see that I am no different than anyone else."

Nino wonders, "What are your favorite Old Testament books?"

"I guess the books of Genesis and Isaiah." Pitt replies.

Nino smiles, "It's funny that you would pick out two of the greatest prophets of the Old Testament, Moses and Isiah." Nino thinks for a moment and than asks. "Do you think there will be any more prophets?"

Pitt shakes his head, "Yeah, probably. The book of Revelations talks about the coming of two strong prophets who stop the rain, and do various miracles."

Nino wonders, "Do you think that any prophets will come to the United States?"

"I wish one would, but I don't really think so."

Nino's expression turns serious, "What if I said to you that today your wish has come true?" Mark stares at the old man, no longer sure of his sanity. Maybe this guy's just another crazy bum. He stands again, and asks the man for clarification.

Mark frowns, "What do you mean, my wish has come true?"

Nino continues, "Not only your wish, but everything you've envisioned about yourself and your destiny in this world."

Pitt growing agitated, "What are you talking about?"

"My name is Nino Jones. I am the unexpected Prophet of Faith, and you are to be my messenger."

Pitt laughs, and starts to walk away, "It's nice to meet you, Nino. I'm really not laughing at you. Honestly, I really hope you are a prophet, but I'm afraid you're gonna have to find someone else to be your messenger."

Nino angry, "There is no other messenger! You are my only chance!"

Mark has sympathy for the old man, "I'm sorry, Nino, I wish I could believe you. It's been nice talking to you. Take care brother." Mark quickly starts away from the old homeless man before he has to listen to any more of what he can only think is insanity … Then suddenly, the old man calls out to him.

"Is your heart empty?" Nino asks.

Stopped dead in his tracks, Mark turns slowly toward Nino and walks back to him in a trance.

"Your name is Mark Salvatore Pitifer, but your friends call you Pitt."

Pitt's face goes pale, and he does not respond. His heart is pounding, and he is filled with fear.

Nino continues, "Ten minutes ago an angel said those same words to you to get you to leave that house of ill repute. Now I have said them to you to get you to stay, and to prove that I am what I say I am. I am Nino Jones. The Prophet of Faith, and you are my holy messenger."

Pitt grows angry with disbelief "You're a liar! You're screwy that's what you are! How do you know my name! … Pitt paces back and forth and tries to put all the pieces of this puzzling night together … "I see what's going on here. This is some sort of set up. Of course, you're probably all working together. Bella, the tall blonde guy, this is just some sort of New York City scam."

Nino is grinning, "I know what you must be thinking. But Pitt, you gave Bella Coolina a fake name. So how could I know your real name?"

Angry again "Now it's just stuff like that. How do you know that?! What do you have some kind of surveillance devices?"

Nino smiles gently, "I know everything about you. I've seen you grow up from a little boy. I know all about your hopes, your dreams."

Pitt grows more angry, "Bullshit, you don't know anything about me!"

Nino smiles gently and touches Pitts shoulder "Pitt I had the same reaction. I was madder than a hornet when they came to me."

Pitt grows calmer "When who came to you?"

"Barabbas and his new heavenly zealots, called the Lions Abijah." Pitts mind is spinning, "Barabbas? And the new What?"

Nino can relate, "I know it sounds crazy, but Barabbas …"

Pitt smirks, "Barabbas? The Jewish zealot who Pilate realeased instead of Jesus?"

Nino smiles, "That's the guy. Only now he's a Heavenly Zealot."

"A Heavenly Zealot." Pitt asks.

"That's right. He's got a band of souls who are trying to pull off one of the greatest spiritual victories of all time. During these end times while the devil's strength is at is pinnacle, we are going to deliver Satan a blow from which he may never recover. Remember what Buster Douglas did to Mike Tyson?'

Pitt Smiles, "Yeah, I couldn't believe it. What an upset, and he was never the same again."

"That's right, and that's exactly what were hoping will happen to Lucifer. We are going to derail Satan's train of spiritual destruction, and he's never going to know what hit him. You see Pitt, the United States, in many ways, is just another world empire. However, it is different in that it is the first world empire to be established on the words of Jesus Christ of Nazareth. If Satan is able to bring this nation down, it will be his greatest victory, and he knows that. You and I are the representatives of a group of very brave and noble souls. All of these individuals have already secured their places in Heaven and the new Jerusalem, and yet they are risking an eternity in the outer darkness to pursue their cause."

"The outer darkness?" Pitt asks.

Nino explains, "There is a place of paradise called Forever. It is the land of our origin, and every person you see in the world was once a citizen of This kingdom. When you die, you are either sent to Forever to wait for the completion of the Great Game of Life and the New Jerusalem, or you are sent to the outer darkness to await the possibility of Purgatory and/or Hell."

Pitt worried, "Will those who are sent to the outer darkness all end up in Hell?"

Nino makes clear, "No, some will spend their eternity's right there in the outer darkness, others will go through Purgatory. However, those who actually have wisdom, and chose to align themselves with Satan, will be sent to Hell for eternity. Those who set their hopes upon God and the possibility of Heaven will receive what they believed in. Those who have no faith in God, and only wish to obtain earthly gain, will obtain the Outer Darkness or Hell."

Pitt confused, "Why would God banish Barabbas and the others to the outer darkness for trying to do something good?"

Nino tries to explain, "I don't really know all of the details, but here is what I think it all comes down to. These Heavenly zealots have already had their chance to play in the Great Game. If they try to execute this self-imposed plan and Satan is in some way able to use it to his advantage, instead of doing something good, they will have inadvertently lead to thousands and possibly millions of souls being lost. It is an incomprehensibly danger-ous game we are going to play, and there is tremendous risk involved, not only for them—but for us as well."

Pitt looks worried, "What is our risk?"

Nino very serious, "Our risk is the same as theirs."

"You mean, if we fail, we will be banished to the Outer Darkness forever?"

Nino sadly shakes his head, "That is correct. I also must be completely honest with you Pitt. If you were to stay on your present course, your position in Forever is secured."

Pitt is puzzled, "How can that be? I am a sinner. If it hadn't been for your so called angel tonight, who knows what I might have done?"

Nino nods, "I do. I saw the whole thing. You would have committed adultery, contracted the AIDS virus, and your life would have ended in disgrace."

Pitt can't believe what he is hearing, "Oh, my God."

Nino continues, "However, your position would have still been secured because of your belief in Jesus Christ, and a well timed intervention by your guardian angel."

Pitt is surprised,"That was my guardian Angel?"

Nino smiles, "Yes it was, and from what I have been told, you have one of the very best guardian Angels there is. In fact there is no better guardian Angel in all of Heaven!"

Pitt is amazed, "I wonder why? Who am I that I should be assigned such a great guardian Angel?"

Nino raises his eye brows, "Who indeed. Are you starting to get the pic-ture yet? Seems to me that someone is really concerned about your spiritual and physical well being."

Pitt wonders, "I'm afraid to think of it. But how could my position be secured if I would have screwed my life up to the point that I died in disgrace?"

Nino makes clear, "All those who ask forgiveness in the name of Jesus are forgiven. It is a free gift from God, you do nothing to earn it."

"What about the harm that would come to the other people in my life for committing such a sin? Shouldn't there be a punishment for such a sin?" Pitt asks.

Nino continues, "Oh, but there is. Even though you go to Forever, you will have to watch and feel the pain caused by your sins. The ripple effect of one sin can affect many generations of people, just like the good deeds that we do can affect many generations. Our leader, Barabbas, for example, thought that he had lived a good life. He thought he did what was best for God and his people. However, when he died, he learned that the majority of what he accomplished during his life, simply helped the cause of Satan. He can not except his infamy, and the fact that he was deceived and used by Satan. This is why he is now willing to risk an eternity in the Outer Darkness."

"I always thought that the Outer Darkness was just another name for Hell?"

Nino cringes at the thought of Hell, "No, the Outer Darkness is the land beyond the borders of Forever, from which you can see both the Glory of Forever, and the atrocious entrance of Hell. Compared to Hell the Outer Darkness is a paradise."

Pitt is temporaily relieved, "Well, thank God for that."

Nino continues, "However, the Outer Darkness when compared to Forever, is more wretched than any place that you can imagine. A ghetto cock roach has a better existence."

"Thanks for the graphics."

Nino chuckles, "Hey, I'm just telling you like it is. Barabbas knows that the price of failure will be extremely painful. The risk is great, and if we are going to be a part of his plan, we must share the same risk."

Pitt is worried, but he finds everything he hears both remarkable and unbelievable. He pauses momentarily to take it all in, but before he can process one thought, another quickly pops into his mind. "I thought Heaven would be a place where there is no more pain and suffering of any kind? What kind of crap is that?!" Pitt is steaming, "We suffer down here, so that we can go up there and go through it all again!"

Nino is patient with all of Mark's questions. He had just as many himself, and he understands why Pitt is upset, "Mark, the kingdom of Forever, as glorious as it is, still has elements of sadness caused by the regrets each soul has over missed opportunities. They are also aware of the current sufferings of earth bound relatives and friends. As long as the Great Game continues, there will continue to be an element of remorse in Forever. However, when the Great Game is complete and the New Jerusalem is finished, pain, sadness, and all suffering will no longer exist in any form."

Pitt's expression changes to that of a little boy, "Nino, is Forever really a wonderful place?" Mark asks, gaining faith in the old man.

Nino sighs as he thinks of its beauty, "Pitt, I cannot find the words to express its physical and spiritual beauty. All I can say is that it is the answer to all of your longings. All of your hopes and dreams will come true in ways that you could never have imagined. Not even in your wildest dreams!"

Pitt tries to imagine such a place, "Oh, to live in such a land. I can't wait to see it with my own eyes." Pitt's mind wanders about the glories of Heaven, but then he remembers the consequences if their mission fails and he is worried again, "Tell me about our mission? What are we supposed to do?"

Nino explains, "I have to tell you all that I have learned about Forever in the short period of time that I have, and you have to tell my story to the world. If people can start to believe in Heaven, then maybe they will start trying harder to get there."

"What do I have to do? Write a book?" Pitt asks.

Nino nods in agreement, "A book, songs, a movie—tell the story to whoever will listen. Tell your children and they will pass the story on to their children and on, and on, the ripple effect, understand?"

"What are we going to do? How are we going to add validity to the story? Do you have any miraculous powers?" Asks Pitt.

Nino shakes his head, "Nope. You are just gonna spend time with me until I have to go."

"So how much time do we have?"

Nino braces for Pitt's reaction, "A couple of days, a week. Maybe a month. That's it."

Pitt can't believe his ears, "A couple of days? A week? Maybe a month? Nino, we are risking an eternity here!"

Nino shares Pitt's concern and sentiments, "That's what I mean when I say we better get started right away."

Pitt yawns, "Can't we at least start tomorrow? I need some sleep."

"We may not have tomorrow."

"Well, what do we do?" Asks Pitt.

"Let's go for a walk."

Pitt is perplexed, "A walk?"

Nino smiles, "Yeah, I've got to go and check on Papino."

"Papino?"

"Yeah, it's my pet rat."

Pitt chukles to himself, "Your pet rat? We're going to check on your pet rat? Shouldn't I get a pad and pencil or something? Shouldn't I be writing stuff down?"

"How should I know? You are the messenger. I'm just the damn prophet."

Mark's temper flares. "You are just the damn prophet!? I'm a messenger with no message, no paper, not even a pen to write with! We're on our way to visit a rat named Papino, while our eternal fate hangs in the balance!" Mark's voice raises and he realizes that he is scared half to death. If all this is true, it's the greatest adventure of his life. If this is just a crazy man with a pet rat, it could be the end of his life. He takes a few seconds to assess Nino one more time, and thinks back on their conversation. As he does he feels warmness in the heart of his soul. Pitt realizes that he believes all that he has heard, and that he knows in the deepest part of his being that he must follow this self-proclaimed prophet of faith. He smiles at Nino. "Alright, let go see this rat?"

Nino is relieved that he has won Mark over. The plan is in motion.

As they begin to walk, Pitt wonders where they are headed. "So where is this house of yours?"

"I live in an old factory pipe just south off the Canal Street Subway plat form."

Pitt is laughing to himself, but he wants to cry, "An old Pipe? This is just—I must be out of my". Nino continues walking and he has a smile a mile wide on his weathered face. Pitt notices that Nino is leaving him behind and hollers. "Hey! Nino, wait up!"

Nino and Pitt walk south on Broadway toward 72nd street and take the subway to Canal Street. As they get off the train the first rays of the red sun are just beginning to filter through the maze of skyscrapers.

<u>Author's Note:</u> I am ashamed to say this, but the incident described in the China Club with Bella Coolina, and the Angel, was a real life event that happened to me in October, of 1990. To this day I am certain that the tall man who spoke those poignant and timely words to me must have been an Angel. What do you think?

"Beware the beast called the Midlife Crisis. It will damage your marriage as surely as smoking cigarettes will ruin your lungs. It will stir the youthful part of your brain, and fill you with renewed vigor and excitement. You will be tempted to develop new relationships, and you will begin to confuse passion with love. However, do not be fooled by this temporary solace. This is a dangerous condition that you must recognize, and destroy. Lust is like a cobra that seeks to poison your marriage. So remember, there is no making friends with a cobra! You can avoid it, or you can kill it, but you can never play with it, or it will kill you (Your marriage). Stay with the spouse of your youth, and let them be your delight!"
-Mark Salvatore Pitifer

Author's Note: After 23 years as a counselor and 20 years of marriage I have come to the conclusion that there are no happy marriages. There are only marriages in which happy moments occur. The harder you work at it, the more happy moments you receive. The same is true for all aspects of life.

CHAPTER 28

▼

"The secret of rising above rather than being defeated by our handicaps, of being victors instead of victims of circumstances, is to be found not in rebellion—but in adapting and making the most of situations that confront us."
-Paul S. McElroy

"There will be no transgression which will not be set right, no displeasure which will not be forgiven, no anger that will not be pacified. There can be nothing that shall not be known, and no loss of anything beloved that shall not be regained."
-Welsh Triads

Nino feeds Papino and shows Pitt around his pipe. He then hands Pitt a blue spiral notebook and tells him about his out-of-body trip to Forever. He explains in detail the mission, the souls involved so far, the penalty if they fail, the reward if they succeed, and how Satan and his demons will try to stop them. When they finally emerge from Nino's subterranean dwelling, it is just about 6:00 a.m. The city is no longer quiet, and Canal Street is like a beehive. They come up from the subway station on the corner of Canal Street and Varick. Looking south, they stop to admire the giant Freedom tower that looms over the southern tip of the island.

Pitt Marvels at the tower, "That Freedom tower is awesome, 1,776 feet high!"

Nino prophesizes, "I tell you, there shall not be left one stone upon another that shall not be torn down."

Pitt is shocked, "Are you kidding me? What happens? Please don't tell me there's more terrorism. What is it another plane?"

They sit for a moment on a bench in a tattered little park across from the subway station. Memories of the death and destruction in 2001 envelop them in silence. Years later, most Americans haven't forgotten where they were on September 11, 2001. The day the massive twin towers fell to the ground. As they stare up at the restructured Manhattan skyline, Nino explains himself.

Nino looks up at the Giant buildings, "Not just the tower, but the whole city is destined to fall."

Pitt worried, "What is there? A nuclear explosion or something?"

Nino makes clear, "No, the whole city is built on a fault line. A giant earthquake is going to swallow up the city, just like it did to the lost city of Atlantis."

Pitt is surprised, "So, that's not just some legend, after all?"

Nino continues, "You see, that's part of the problem. All that legend nonsense. Do you know that all of what the great prophets wrote about in the Bible, the Torah, the Qur'an, and the BHAGAVAD GITA are true stories?"

"Noah, Moses, Muhammad, Krishna, Buddha, Sampson ..."

Nino cuts Pitt off, "All of them, and many, many others that you have never even heard of.... You see, even you don't believe completely, do you? But I'll bet you believe in George Washington don't you, but you have never seen him have you? All we have is painted pictures and the written words of historians. Why is it that people will believe anything they read in a history textbook or hear on the news, but when it comes to the Bible there is that moment of pause?"

Pitt ashamed, "I always believed that most of the Bible is true, but I figured some of the stuff was exaggerated, or made up."

Nino nods, "I used to think the same way, but I was wrong. Those miraculous lives and events really all happened pretty much the way the holy books report. One of the things you have to do is shed light on this point. Satan is the pusher of the legend/mythology propaganda. He wants us to believe that a simpler form of people who lived in obscure times had to develop the idea of God to give meaning to their lives. He would like us to believe that our ancestors made up these fantastic stories and characters to simply give credence, and provide proof for their God theory. Satan especially doesn't want people to think he is real. He loves the fact that in the twentieth century he has been cartoonized. He has been systematically de-vilified by our modern society, ultimately becoming nothing more than a mascot used by sports teams. Satan's greatest achievement to date is to convince the world that he doesn't exist! Creations most dangerous enemy is seen by many as nothing more than a fictitious character, created by people who lacked our modern day level of intelligence."

"Are we smarter than our ancestors?" Asks Pitt.

Nino shakes his head, "No. Not at all. In many ways, their minds were keener than ours are, because they had to use more of their complete brains than we have to. They didn't have computers to think for them, or TV's to spin their minds in all different directions. We are simply more technologically advanced than they were. You see, humans like to think, 'man, look how smart we are. We developed this or we cured that.' But these are all gifts from God. Well timed discoveries that come along when God feels the time is right. For example, can you imagine what would have happened if one of Attila the Huns people had developed the atomic bomb?"

Pitt raises his eye brows, "Thank God Hitler's people didn't invent it."

Nino agrees, "Thank God is right! If Hitler had the bomb, the whole world could have ended way back then, but it was not meant to be. The irony is that Hitler expelled or exterminated the very people who could have given them the bomb, but that's really not important. All you need to remember is that while we all have control of the individual choices that we make in our lives, God is in complete control of how the world stage is set."

"For example?" Asks Pitt.

Nino thinks for a moment, "He controls the times and tides, the prophecies, the duration of the Great Game, the rulers of the world and the rise and fall of various empires, natural changes in the earth and weather, sickness, disease, cures, and what the new toy trend will be."

Pitt understands, "I see what you mean now. God sets the stage, and how people respond determines how that particular scene plays out."

Nino smiles, "Well put. That's it. If people keep their faith in God and stick to the path shown to us by Jesus, they can positively resolve any situation. No matter how severe the crisis is, natural or manmade, those who remain faithful to God will emerge victorious. Every scene has the potential for a happy ending. It's up to the people to bring it about. One of the most painful lessons that souls must learn when they are allowed to look back on their lives is that they had the ability, if they had chosen wisely, to turn every situation that they encountered in their lives into something positive."

Pitt smiles to himself, "I always was good at that. I could always take the reality of the situation and somehow turn it to my advantage," Mark acknowledges, a little proud of himself.

Nino chuckles, "That's good to know. I'm pretty sure we're both going to need that type of mindset as we spend our time together."

Pitt worried, "Why, what do you think is going to happen?"

Nino explains, "I don't want to scare you, but Barabbas told me that we should be prepared for attacks from Satan and his Demons."

"What did he say they would do?" Asks Pitt.

"I asked him and all he could tell me was to not waste any time, and be prepared for anything. So, I guess we had better keep moving."

"So, now what do we do? Where do we go? What's your plan?" Mark feels a slight panic attack coming on. Nino quickly jumps into action.

Nino becomes energized, "We walk to the George Washington Bridge."

Pitt is startled, "The George Washington Bridge? That's gotta be about twenty miles away!"

Nino rubs his stubble, "No, actually it's just about ten miles. Listen, I don't know how much time we have together. I also don't know how or when Satan is going to start his attack. All I do know is that when I was in the army, we would set our goals according to the ground that we covered in a single day. In the Vietnam war, you never knew where or when the fight was going to start. So, it was ludicrous to plan for a particular battle at a town twenty or thirty kilometers north of our current location, so we would just start walking north. We were always looking, and ready for the enemy. At the same time, we would try to enjoy the scenery. That is what you and I are going to do today."

Pitt perplexed, "That's it? That's your plan? We just walk though New York City to the George Washington Bridge?"

Nino smirks, "This city has more good and evil going on than any other place in the world. I am an old man, I need stimulation to stir up my memory. I also said that someday I am going to march my ass out of the city, and never come back. I have always dreamed of doing what we are setting out to do. I take one last walk through the greatest city in the world. I smell the smells, taste the tastes, hear the sounds, look at the people, and then take one last endearing gaze from the middle of the George Washington Bridge."

Pitt looks worried, "I hope you are not thinking what I think you are thinking."

Nino grins, "Don't worry, counselor, there will be no need for any crisis intervention on this trip. You are perceptive, though. I'll give you that. Jumping off after that last look used to be part of the plan. My faith wouldn't allow me to go through with it, but boy oh boy, it was a struggle. Nope— if we make it to the GWB I'm just gonna keep walking west. I always did want to see California. And you, you better just call your sister to come and get you. I don't want you walking back through Harlem all by yourself."

Pitt looks panicked, "Oh no! My sister! She probably thinks I've been murdered or something. I've got to get to a phone." Pitt ran to the nearest phone booth but had given all of his change away. He reached into his pocket for his wallet, and his heart sank. His wallet, with his ID, credit cards and money, was missing. "Nino, you got a quarter?"

"I only got those two dollars you gave me last night. What's wrong?" Nino asks. "Don't you have one of those fancy calling cards?"

Pitt angry, "I don't have anything! I've been pick-pocketed!"

"Well, you better make a collect call."

"Yeah, good idea." Mark places the call and Shari screams "Yes" to the operator upon hearing the request.

Shari's voice is Horace and she sounds tired, "Mark?! Thank God! Where are you? Do you have any idea how worried I've been?"

Pitt is apologetic, "I'm sorry Shari. I've had so much happen to me in the last seven hours that I can't begin to explain it to you right now. You didn't call the police, or Leigh, did you?"

Shari starts to get agitated, "No, I didn't call Leigh. I tried to call the police, but you hadn't been missing long enough for them to do anything about it. What's happened to you? Are you alright? Why are you calling me collect?"

"I either lost my wallet or had it stolen." He explains.

"Where are you?"

"I am on Canal Street. Down in Chinatown."

"Walk up to Mulberry Street in Little Italy, and I'll meet you at Pittinaro's Pizzeria. You know where it is... on the corner of Mulberry and Hester. Teddy Jr. told me to tell you next time you're in town to stop by and see his father's Heisman Trophy. He and Scott decided to keep it in the restaurant from now on. You can eat some of Carol and Marlene's delicious food, and flirt with Pam while you wait. I'll be there in about half an hour."

"Shari, hang on a second." Mark covers the phone and calls out to his companion. "Nino, should I have my sister come and meet us?"

Nino frowns, "No, we'll stop at her apartment on our way uptown. Tell her we'll call her when we get closer to her end of the city. Probably sometime after noon."

"But we don't have any money."

Nino smiles, "Don't worry—I've got a plan."

"Shari, I'll meet you at your house sometime after noon. I'll call you when I get closer to your end of town. Call the Finger Lakes Credit Union and tell them to cancel my credit card."

Shari is getting upset, "Mark, what is going on? Who were you talking to? When will you get here?"

Pitt continues, "I can't talk anymore right now. I really don't know when I'll be there, but it will probably be right around noon. So, please wait for my call before you go anywhere. I'll fill you in on everything when I see you. I'm sorry I had you so worried. I love you."

Shari is crying, "You're not in any kind of trouble, are you?"

Pitt tries to calm his sister, "No, so don't worry. I'll let you know everything just as soon as I see you."

Shari remains upset, "Mark, write down my cell phone number in case I've gone to the store when you get here."

Mark sighs with anxiety, "Okay. Thanks, Shari. I'll see you soon." "Are you sure nothing is wrong?" Shari asks in desperation.

Pitt smiles as if trying to convince himself, "Don't worry. Everything is just fine. I love you Shari."

Mark hangs up the phone before letting Shari's voice get to him any further, and Nino is anxious to move on.

"What did she say?" Nino asks.

"She's very worried, but she's cool. She'll be alright.... So, what's your big money plan?"

"Follow me."

They walk into one of the tiny storefronts that sells lotto and Quick Draw numbers.

"You have Quick Draw, right?" Nino asks the clerk.

"Quick Draw? That's your plan?" Mark has to wonder if he's being had. He decides to go along with Nino's plan though.

Nino grins, "Yeah, some numbers just popped into my mind. This might be my first miracle. Get one of those tickets and put down 1-1-3." Pitt is annoyed, "Didn't you ever play this before? You can't play 1-1-3." "What are you talking about?" says Nino.

Pitt stays calm, "You can play 1 & 13. If you hit, you get 10 to 1 odds. But you can't play 113."

"Alright then, put two dollars on 1 & 13."

Pitt fakes sarcasm and laughs, "Are you sure you want to risk the whole two dollars on one roll?"

Nino shakes his head and purses his lips, "Oh ye of little faith. Go on now and play my numbers."

The numbers come on the final two drops of the ball. Nino is so proud, he struts like a peacock around the tiny convenience store like a kid who just sank the winning basket. He put one hand on his hip and with the other he gives every passerby a high five. Pitt, meanwhile, collects the winnings.

Nino is beaming with pride, "Well, non-believer, how much did I win?" Nino laughs.

Pitt can't believe it, "Twenty bucks! We're rich!"

Nino jokes, "What do you mean, we're rich? The way I see it, I've got twenty dollars. You're still penniless! Here's a couple of dollars. Go buy yourself some wine."

Pitt is hurt, "Hey, that's not fair! That two dollars I gave you was from the heart!"

Nino chuckles, "I know, I know. But be honest, isn't that what you were thinking?"

"Maybe. Yeah—probably wine or food."

Nino wonders, "Was it really from the heart? Or were you giving out of obligation?"

Pitt somewhat annoyed, "Obligation to whom? You? I didn't even know who you were!"

Nino detects Pitts anger, "Hey, don't get mad, Pitt. I am giving you your first lesson. My point is that a lot of people give because they think it is something that they should do. They do it out of obligation to God, and not because they are moved by their own heart to do so."

Pitt nods in understanding, "I see what you mean. So, we should all try to open our hearts more and more."

Nino makes clear, "God appreciates the good that we try to do. But his ultimate hope for us is that we learn to genuinely love all our fellow human beings, so that our good deeds really do come from the heart, and not the mind."

"You mean, if I could really begin to see all people in the same way that I see myself, or my family members, the motive for my actions will go from wanting recognition by God or the public, to simply acting in a loving way because I really do care? Like doing the right thing simply because you feel it in your heart."

Nino smiles, "Yes. When you see a neighbor or a stranger in need of assistance you should say to yourself, 'if that was me, what would I need? If that was my mother, my father, my sister or my brother, how would I want them to be treated?'"

Pitt speculates, "If I could really adopt that way of thinking, I wouldn't even wait to be asked for money or a favor. I would just do what I felt was needed. My love for my brother would move me into action."

Nino is happy that Pitt understands, "Yes, and one last point on this subject. In being kind to strangers, many people unknowingly have entertained angels."

"Shouldn't I stop and write some of this stuff down so that I don't forget it?" Pitt asks.

Nino unconcerned, "I was assured that you, like I, will have a clear memory of everything that is revealed to you. Now, let's go get a quick bite to eat before we continue our journey."

"That sounds good to me. I'm starving." Says Pitt.

Nino winks, "Oh, yeah, you better hang on to this ticket and remember this number 113. I think this was my big miracle."

"Second only to the parting of the Red Sea!" Mark jokes.

Nino fakes agitation, "Okay, smart ass. No breakfast for you! You get to watch me eat the best frittata's in Little Italy at Mama Mia's famous Cheznia Cafe."

"Come on, I take it back." Pitt pleads, his stomach rumbling in anticipation of breakfast.

"No, no. Nope. Too late. You dissed me for the last time."

Nino puts Pitt in a headlock and walks him east on Canal Street and into the heart of Chinatown.

__Author's Note:__ As a part of the research for this book I walked from Canal Street to the George Washington Bridge. As I took this ten mile walk I passed by a storefront church that had a sign in the window which asked the following question: "Is New York City the next Babylon?" Whenever I read chapter 18 in the book of Revelations, it is hard for me not to entertain the possibility that Manhattan or America is the next Babylon. For those of you who are unfamiliar with that text. I am providing you with my rendition of Revelation 18.

__REVELATION 18 (MY RENDTION)__

I saw an Angel come down from Heaven, having great power, and
the Earth was lightened with his glory. And he cried in a mighty
voice, saying, "The United States ofAmerica, is fallen, is fallen. It
has become the home of Satan and his demons-for all the nations
have drunk the wine of her excessive immorality. The merchants of
the world have all gotten rich through the abundance of her wealth."
I heard a voice form Heaven, saying, "Come out of her my children,
that you be not partakers of her sins, and that you receive not of her
plagues which will begin very soon. Her sins are piled up as high as

Heaven, and God has seen her iniquities. Therefore shall her disasters come in one day (in a single hour!)-death and mourning and famine. She will be utterly burned by fire, never to rise again. All the world leaders, who took part in her immoral acts and enjoyed her favors, will mourn for her as they see the smoke rising from her charred remains. They will stand far off, tremblingwith fear and crying out, "Alas, America, that mighty country! In one moment her judgment fell." The merchants of the Earth will weep and mourn for her, because there is no one left to buy their goods. She was their biggest and best customer. She bought and sold everything imaginable, even the souls of people. "All the fancy things you loved so much are gone. The dainty luxuries and splendor that you prized so much will never be yours again." The merchants will cry out "America was so beautiful-like a woman dressed in the finest clothes and jewelry. In one moment all the wealth in the country is gone!" And all the shipowners and captains on the Atlantic and Pacific Oceans will stand along way off crying "Where in all the world is there another country such as this? Poor-poor America, she made us all rich from her great wealth, and now in a single hour all she has is gone." Then a mighty Angel picked up a boulder shaped like a millstone and threw it into the ocean and shouted, "The United States of America, the great country, shall be thrown away as I have thrown away this stone, and she shall disappear forever. Never again will the sound of music be there-no more pianos, saxophones, and trumpets. No industry of any kind will ever again exist there, and there will be no milling of steele, or wheat. Dark, dark will be her nights; not even a lamp in a window will ever be seen again. No more joyous wedding bells and happy voices of the bridegrooms and brides. Her businessmen were known all around the world and she deceived all nations with her sorceries. The spirit that brought down America, is the same evil spirit that brought down Babylon and all the great empires that followed. This evil spirit is also responsible for the blood of all the martyred prophets and the saints. God bless, and please save America! Pray often and always. Awaken! The kingdom of Heaven is at hand!

"Preach the Gospel always. And if necessary use words."
-St. Francis of Assisi (For Reverend Nancy Birdsong)

"I the Lord of snow and rain. I have borne my peolple's pain. I have wept for love of them. They turn away.... I the Lord of sea and sky, I have heard my people cry. All who dwell in deepest sin, my hand will save. I will break their hearts of stone, give them hearts of love alone. I will speak my words to them. Whom shall I send? Here I am Lord. Is it I, Lord? I have heard you calling in the night. I will go Lord, if you lead me. I will hold your people in my heart."
-Presbyterian Hymn 525: Here I Am Lord (Daniel l. Schutte)

CHAPTER 29

▼

"Each one should use whatever gift he has received to serve others,
faithfully administering God's grace in its various forms."
-1 Peter 4:10

"Be always at war with your vices, at peace with your neighbors, and let
each new year find you a better man."
-Ben Franklin

"The characteristic of Tao is gentleness."
-Lao Tse (570 BC)

The pair continues walking east on Canal Street, through Chinatown
and into Little Italy.

"Keep your eyes open my boy, because over the next ten miles you are
going to see the whole world," Nino tells his companion. "What do
you mean?" Pitt asks.

Nino explains, "I guarantee you that during this walk you will pass by a
representative of every nation in the entire world. We will be walking for
blocks at a time where you won't hear a word of English spoken. It will be
like you are in a foreign land."

Pitt smiling, "My eyes are open, but aren't we kind of walking away
from the GWB?"

Nino raises his eyebrows, "Hey, you've got a pretty good sense of direction for a country boy!"

Pitt grins, "It's all a part of that good old military training they gave me
down in Fort Benning, Georgia."

"I'll be damned!" Nino exclaims. "You're a military man?" Pitt puffs out his chest, "Delta 92 Infantry, baby!"

Nino is tickled pink, "You've got to be shittin' me! What was your M.O.S?"

"11-Charlie. I was a mortar man." Says Pitt.

Nino teases Pitt and pretends that he is unimpressed, "Mortar man, shit, how long were you in the Army?"

"Oh, well, I wasn't in the army. I was in the National Guard." Nino is laughing, "National Guard! The National Guard. You were a no-go."

Pitt takes the busting in stride, "Yeah, yeah, yeah. You regular Army grunts always did think you were so much better. Truth is, you guys were just pissed off, because you knew that our obligation was easier than yours."

Nino agrees, "Actually, you are probably right ... So tell me something, why did an educated fella like yourself sign up for sixteen weeks of torture down at Harmony Church? Those high Georgia pines? The dusty red clay roads, and those frigid December mornings."

Pitt is surprised, "Sounds like you and I sniffed some of the same dirt? Is that where you were stationed?"

Nino shakes his head, "I was there for basic training, only I stayed a little longer. I had to earn one of those little green berets."

Pitt's eyes widen, "You were special forces? My father-in-Law Marco Principio was a Green Beret. He was a Major at Fort Bragg, North Carolina back in the seventies."

Nino's mind drifts back in time for a moment, "That name rings a bell somewhere.... Didn't his son Marco Jr. start that chain of restaurants called the Quesadilla King?

Pitt surprised "Yeah that's my brother-in-Law. They took his mother Ivy's recipe, and combined it with his sister Allison's business savvy, and turned it into a gold mine."

Nino smiles, "Yeah I remember him now. We used to tease him. We would say "Your son is the Quesadilla King and you're the Case-of-the-ass king. Maro had a good sense of humor. He was a cool cat."

Pitt laughs, "Case of the ass. I haven't heard that term in a long time. It's a small world though isn't it?

Nino continues. "Yeah, it sure is." Nino's mind drifts back to his days as a Green Beret. "Anyway a long time ago, I was a bad ass man! I would have given Shaft a run for his money.... Now look at me. I have a hard time just walking from place to place."

"You still look pretty good to me ... for a decrepit old man, that is!" Pitt teases.

Nino fakes agitation, "Decrepit old man! Why you ..."

Nino lunges toward Pitt trying to jab him, but he slides quickly out of the way. Nino stops and grabs his lower back and tries to straighten himself back up.

Nino laughs and grimaces at the same time, "I guess I am old. I thought I had one last good aggressive lunge in me, but I was mistaken! Go on, youngster, finish your story. How'd you end up in Georgia?"

Pitt continues, "It was close to the end of June and I had just finished Graduate school. I had no job, and I wasn't really in a hurry to find one. That is, until the mail came one day and told me that I would have to star making monthly payments on my college loan. The same day that letter came, a National Guard recruiter called and told me about this sweet deal they had that would pay off a big chunk of my college loan. Next thing I know, I'm in a sea of green. I also felt like if I was going to counsel kids about careers, I should have a little bit of an idea what the military was all about. It was actually one of the best things I ever did."

"Why's that?" Nino asks.

Mark smiles, "It's just that no matter how early I have to get up, or how tired I am during a day I know that there's some poor joker down there in Georgia who has been up a lot longer than me. He's either crowded into a cattle car, or an APC, and he's thinking to himself, 'What the hell am I doing here?' It just made the rest of my life like gravy, and I didn't even have to go to war or kill nobody."

Nino looks away. His eyes fill up with tears. Pitt immediately realizes he said something wrong. "I'm sorry Nino. What did I say? I didn't mean to upset you."

Nino tries to hold in his emotions, "It's alright. It's not your fault."

"You saw some hard time didn't ya?" Pitt asks.

Nino lets out a sob before speaking through tears. "Hard time? It's been a hell that I have never been able to put out of my mind. I saw people lose arms and legs, and sustain all types of debilitating physical injuries. But I'd switch places with any one of them in a heartbeat rather than lose what I have lost."

Pitt feels for Nino, "Why? What happened?"

Nino remembers, "There was a tragic accident. Something so terrible it caused me to have a piece of my soul amputated. Once you lose a piece of your soul you never get it back …" Nino stares off towards the east, allowing his mind to travel back to the scene of the crime. Then he continues to speak…. "There was one stretch of time when it seemed like, for a month straight, not a day would pass that I didn't lose a friend. I swear, Pitt, I really thought I was going to lose my mind. We were getting ambushed everywhere we turned by an enemy that had no face. Like Sun Su said in his book <u>The Art Of War</u> **"The most dangerous army has no form."** We were all scared, frustrated, and enraged. We were sleep deprived and run down. There were many times I just wanted to lay down and die."

Pitt tries to empathize, "It all sounds so horrible, like a bad dream."

Nino sighs, "Oh if only it was just a bad dream. How I wish I could …" Nino begins to cry, but pulls himself back together. Pitt tries to comfort him but Nino pulls away. Suddenly, Nino's tone changes from sad to enraged. His face contortes as he yells out, "That war, man! That miserable, motherfucking war! My whole life has been ruined because of it."

Pitt tries to help, "Nino, you've just gotta let it go man. What good does it do to carry those malignant memories around with you?"

Nino sighs, "I've tried Pitt. God knows I've tried to put it behind me. But it just keeps coming back. It's always the same scene over and over again." Nino's mind drifts back in time … "It was about 5:00 in the evening. We were on a reconnaissance mission and I was on the point. We were walking back through a village in which we had earlier been ambushed. It was like walking through a ghost town. There was no sign of life anywhere. It was raining very hard and the wind was really blowing. It was a real eerie scene, and everybody was very tense and wired tight. Suddenly, there was a loud crash to my left. I turned and opened fire in the direction of the crash. What I didn't realize was that a young mother and her two children had been hiding from us behind a pile of garbage cans. One of them must have stumbled into the cans and caused them to fall. We tried our best to save them, but the children were killed instantly. The mother held on for only a few minutes, but I can still hear her sorrowful cry as she realized that her children were dead and that she was dying. I can still see her trying to pull her children to her breast. I can still …" Nino's words turn into sobs. His shoulders heave heavily and he holds his face in his hands. Again, he is able to compose himself. He reaches into his pocket and pulls out a handkerchief to dry his eyes. Then he continues. "Sometimes when I run the event through my mind I think I can almost slow the images down enough to keep myself from pulling the trigger. Oh, what I wouldn't give for an opportunity to right that old wrong. I just hope God can forgive me, and those children and their mother, that's what I have struggled with for more than half of my life."

"God will forgive you, and you will right that old wrong." Mark says, somehow sure of his proclamation.

Nino is surprised at Mark's confidence. "How?!"

Pitt speaks with confidence, "By successfully completing your mission, and knocking the king of this world and starter of all wars on his char-broiled ass!"

Nino chuckles and wipes more tears from his eyes. "You got a way about you, Pitt. Maybe things wouldn't have been so bad if I had you by my side in 'Nam. Anyway, enough of this army talk. Let's go get us some breakfast."

They walk past the tiny store fronts that line Canal Street, one after another. These merchants sell everything from perfume to parachutes, and every price is negotiable.

Pitt waves to his friend Ritu Parvin on the corner of Canal and Broadway.

Nino surprised, "How do you know Ritu?"

Pitt smiles, "Ritu always gives me the best price on perfume."

Nino chuckles, "Yeah, her family are all really nice people."

As they continue walking Pitt can't help but be impressed with Nino's people skills.

Pitt is impressed with all the people Nino knows. He even knows how to greet them in Chinese and Arabic. All the stores in Chinatown are run by either Chinese or Arabic people. They turn left onto Mulberry street and the language suddenly turns to Italian. The smells are familiar to Pitt and he thinks about all those meals cooked by his mother and grandmother. His sister, Sally, is also a great cook, and even his wife Leigh was becoming quite a little chef. He laughs to himself remembering when Leigh made gnocchi for the first time.

"What's so funny?" Nino asks.

Pitt chuckles to himself, "I was just thinking of my wife, Leigh. One time she invited me over to her house for homemade gnocchi. Do you know what gnocchi are?"

Nino smirks, "Of course."

Pitt continues, "She was so proud of herself. She served me this huge plate of them." Pitt is lauging, "Nino, these things were like lead, but I couldn't embarrass her so I ate them all. Man, was I dying. To make matters worse, the sauce she made was what I call a garden sauce. It was nasty. But she makes a great sauce now. Once you master the sauce, you are on your way to becoming a great Italian cook!"

Nino agrees, "No question about it, sauce is the foundation of all great Italian meals."

They walk by Jimmy Legott's famous club 86 on the corner of Mulberry and Hester. Pitt had eaten there on more than one occasion, and he enjoyed their food.

Pitt grabs Nino's arm, "Nino, this is a nice restaurant. They make a great sauce."

Nino nods, "Yeah, Jimmy's Sauce and giblets are famous around this neighborhood, and he cooks the best chicken in the city! ... Speaking of great food, you just reminded me of lunch."

Pitt laughs, "Nino, we didn't even have breakfast yet!"

Nino grins, "Come with me, rookie."

They walk into a deli called the Italian Food Center on the corner of Grand and Mulberry.

Nino holds the door for Pitt, "In my humble opinion, this is the best Italian deli in the city."

Pitt takes a deep whiff of the aroma, "It smells delicious. Just like grandma Pitifer's cellar."

Nino walks up to a pretty Italian girl who was working behind the counter named Gianna.

Nino smiles, "Good morning Bella Faccia."

Gianna smiles back, "Good morning, Nino. The usual?"

Nino shakes his head, "You better double it today, Gi-money. I've got a guest.' He puts his arm around Pitt's shoulder. Pitt, this is my commada, Gianna Moni."

Gianna extends her hand, "Pleased to meet you Pitt."

Pitt smiles, "No the pleasures mine"

"So, you gonna spend the day with Nino?" Gianna asks.

Pitt sounds excited, "Yeah. I think we're going to take a little walk around, and he's going to show me the sights."

Gianna sighs in disappointment, "Gee, that sounds like fun. I wish I could go with you guys, but I gotta work behind this stinkin' counter until 5."

Nino reassures her, "Well, maybe the next time, Gi. Hopefully, this won't be my last walk through the old city."

Nino's mind wanders for a moment. He hadn't really thought about it, but this would be his last time seeing all of his friends for a long time. For a moment, his expression changes. Gianna notices Nino's worried expression, "God forbid, Nino. Don'tcha say such things. You gotta lotta walkin' left to do. Whatsa matta? You look funny to me. Don'tcha feel so good today?"

Nino forces a smile, "Oh, I'm okay Gi-money. I just seem to have a lot on my mind today."

Gianna concerned, "That's not like you. Whatsa matta? Somebody give ya the maloik?"

"Maybe this guy did!" He grabs Pitt playfully. "Did you give me the maloik, you son-of-a-gun?"

Pitt tenses for a punch that doesn't materialize.

Gianna smiling, "That's the Nino I know! Smile-smile. No faccia brute! Okay, here ya go Nino, two pieces of bruschetta, and two prusutti, fresh mozzarella and roasted pepper mini subs. Anything else?"

Nino tips his cap, "No mam, that'll be just fine. You take care Gi-money. I'll see you around little sister."

"Ciao, Bello, Ciao Pitt."

Pitt smiles and waves, "Ciao, Gi-money. Nice meeting you."

"I hope you enjoy your lunch!" Gianna says.

Pitt confident, "I know we will."

"Alright," Nino says, turning his attention back to Mark. "Now we go to Mama Mia's. And then we—oops, one more thing."

"What?"

"We gotta stop and get our dessert for after our breakfast." "Dessert, for after breakfast?" Pitt laughs.

Nino explains, "In New York City, just like in the Kingdom of Forever, you have to have dessert after every meal, especially on this walk!"

They turn left on Grand Street and north onto Center Street, following it to Cleveland Place. On the corner of Cleveland and Kenmare, there sits a quaint little shop called Eileen's Cheese Cake. Nino smiles, "This little shop is in many ways like the kingdom of Heaven, a hidden treasure."

"The Kingdom of Heaven?" Pitt chuckles.

Nino walks up to the door and points inside, "Tell me the truth. If you just looked at this place is there anything that would make you want to go in?"

Pitt shakes his head, "No, not really. It's so tiny, I probably wouldn't even notice it unless I accidentally stumbled upon it."

Nino beams, "Exactly. This little unsuspecting bakery has the best cheesecake in the city. And I love cheesecake."

Standing behind the counter is a tiny Italian man named Tony Scarmazino. He comes from behind the cash register and gives Nino a big hug, for a little man, that is.

Tony laughing, "Nino! Where in the hell have you been? You haven't come by the last couple of days? I was starting to get worried?"

Nino tries to catch his breath, "I was a little under the weather that's all. I feel better now."

Tony smiles, "That's good. Hey, who's your friend?"

Nino puts his hands on Tony and Pitts shoulders, "Tony Scarmazino, I'd like you to meet Mark Pitifer."

"Nice to meet you, Mark. Hey, you wanna try a piece of the best cheesecake in New York? It's on me. Please try it. Believe me, it tastes fantastic, like a gift from God, delicious, just wait and see."

Tony hands Pitt a miniature strawberry cheese cake. Pitt takes a bite and a big smile comes across his face, "Nino wasn't lying. This is the best cheesecake I've ever had. It's absolutely delicious."

"See, see. I told you, didn't I? See, Nino, he loves it! Just like you. He's just like you, Nino. The only thing sweeter than my cheese cake is my left handed hook shot."

Nino Laughing "You got that right. Hey. Tony, why don't you give us two of the miniature strawberry pies to go."

"Sure. My pleasure. It's my pleasure. But stick around for a little while and visit. I'll make us some nice espresso."

Nino almost sits down but changes his mind, "I'd like to Tony, but I promised Mark a tour of the city, and he's only going to be here for a short time. But, even though time is short, I still had to show him the greatest cheesecake baker in the city."

Tony beams with pride, "Yes, yes. Bravo, Nino! Vivala, Nino! God bless you and your friend. Here, take them no charge. I insist. Arrevaderce, my friends. I have to go. The buzzer she's a ringing."

"Ciao, Tony. Thanks a lot."

"See ya, Tony. Nice meeting' ya."

Pitt and Nino exit the little cake shop, and eat another of the sweet desserts. Pitt pauses and studies Nino for a moment.

Pitt shakes his head in wonder, "Nino, you're a rich man."

"What do you mean?" Nino asks.

Pitt smiling, "Everybody who knows you loves you!"

Nino raises his eyebrows, "I never thought about it, but maybe I am rich in that sense.... Come on, let's go get our breakfast."

They take a left on Spring Street and head toward Broadway.

Nino looks up at the signs, "Once we get on Broadway, we'll follow it all the way up to 178th Street. That is where we will say goodbye."

Pitt frowns, "Why does that have to be where we go our separate ways? Why can't you just stay with me until you are taken up?"

Nino makes clear, "First of all, that is what I was instructed to do. And furthermore you cannot be allowed to see me disappear, because that will mean that you had proof positive that my story is true. Remember, in order for our plan to be successful, it must be built on faith."

The two continue walking north on Broadway toward Mama Mia's. As they pass by a giant Victoria's Secret store on the corner of Prince and

Broadway, Nino catches Pitt taking a long stare at the beautiful picture of Victoria's angels.

Nino Laughing "Look at you. You're supposed to be my messenger, and your mind is off in Victoria Ville!"

Pitt grins sheepishly "I'm not in Victoria Ville, … I'm in Tyra Banks Ville!" Pitt and Nino laugh.

Pitt now has Nino looking at Tyra, "mmm-mmm-mmm, Lord-lord-lord you sure took your time making her. Boy I love me some Trya Banks. She is the epitome of Red-bone beauty."

Pitt gives Nino five." "She's always been my favorite. She's beautiful on the outside and the inside, and that's hard to find.… But I promise it won't happen again. From now on I'll be completely focused."

Nino smirks, "Yes it will, but you'll never guess why. The models of Victoria's Secret are beautiful, and Tyra is quite possibly the most beautiful woman in the world. However, she pales in comparison to the souls that I saw in Heaven. The citizens of the Kingdom of Forever are beautiful beyond words. In the recesses of your mind, your soul remembers this beauty and longs for it. In Heaven, there is no marriage. All souls are free for eternity. Endless encounters on sultry moonlit nights, romantic and fulfilling beyond words, await us in Forever."

Pitt relishes the thought of it, "So, you're saying everyone is absolutely beautiful and we are free to be with whoever we want? There's no jealousy or possessiveness?"

Nino explains, "The soul, once released from this prison which is our mortal body, will no longer wish to possess, nor will it be possessed. Like Kahill Gibran says "Love is sufficient unto love." In Forever, love abounds. It flows through and encompasses everything. You have no needs, only an endless stream of dreams that will all eventually all come true. However, what is commonplace in Forever cannot be obtained on earth. The needs for beauty, freedom and romance in Heaven are no longer needs. They are realities, and enjoyed as one might enjoy delicious water from a spring that will never run dry. Free from the fear of thirst you are now able to drink the water simply for the sheer pleasure of the taste and sensation of drinking."

Pitt smiles and sighs, "That's music to my ears Nino." Pitt's mind wanders for a moment, and then he continues. "So, in Forever, all our longings will be fulfilled, but what happens if we attempt to fulfill our longings during the Great Game?"

Nino cuts Pitt off. "Then you will stumble, and eventually fall. If you try to go after all that your body and mind long for on earth, you will become selfish, and in our selfishness we will cause pain to others. In causing pain to others, you will have left the path that leads to Heaven, which altimately destroys your soul."

"Because we became selfish?" Pitt asks.

Nino nods, "That's right. There is no selfishness on the path that leads us home. Believe me when I tell you, you must stay on the P.O.J., cause there ain't no other way."

"The P.O.J.?" Pitt asks.

"The Path of Jesus. P-O-J. Get it?"

Pitt smiles, "Yeah. That's cool."

Nino continues, "Pitt, selfishness is at the core of all sin. Take the act of adultery for example. Adultery is a sin simply because it is an absolutely selfish act. How can you make love to another man's wife, and maintain that you are treating them in the same way that you would want to be treated? You know damn well you wouldn't want another man trying to seduce your wife. So, you better not do it to someone else. You see what I mean? Satan takes our passions and our longings and gets us to behave very selfishly. Like I said, selfishness or self-centeredness are the foundations upon which all sin is built."

Pitt looks disappointed, "I have always tried to stay close to God and Jesus. Why is it that I lust so often?"

Nino puts his hand on Pitt's shoulder, "The closer you get to God, the more holy spirit you receive. This increases the love you have inside you for all of God's creations. Satan takes your love and passion for all, and ties it into your biological need for sex and intamacy. It is your biological need coupled with your subconscious memory about who you really are and where you come from that moves you to want to be with all of these different women. You must recognize how Satan is manipulating you, and fight against the pull of lust. Set your hopes on Heaven and all that Heaven can be and this will control your behavior. It is a fact that whatever you desire will control your behavior. Learn to capture the essence of the woman. Recognize that you will always have a sexual attraction for the opposite sex, but do not make sex your ultimate desire, and it will gradually lose its power over you. The truth is that what we truly long for is to touch the other person's soul."

Pitt curious, "What do you mean, touch the other person's soul?"

Nino explains, "In Forever, we are able to touch each others souls unencumbered by our mortal bodies. On earth, the body is the house of the soul. When we touch each other, our souls feel good because of proximity. When we kiss or make love, our bodies become more open to one another. The souls are still prevented from touching, but at the height of love making the souls sometimes briefly brush against each other depending on the depth of the love involved. Believe me Pitt, it is not the biological release that we long for, it is the need to touch another soul. The biological need merely attracts us more to the opposite sex. This is a shame, because think of all the time we spend, especially in our youth, trying to get someone to kiss us or make love to us. And much of the time we don't even really like them that much! It's all physical. Once you are married, it is even more important than any other time in your life to put your sexual needs in check. Let the wife of your youth be your delight. Let her, and her alone, satisfy your sexual needs. Instead of seeking out physical beauty, become a seeker of souls. See the beauty that dwells in all people and let that, and that alone, calm your roaring sea of passion."

Pitt clarifies, "I think what you are saying is that I should learn to appreciate the essence of all souls, and try not to be led around by my biological compass. Following that might lead me right past the best cheesecake in the city."

Nino sets Pitt straight, "Mark, from what I know about you and your life, back home in Geneva on 33 Nagel Place is the best cheesecake in the city. Don't you ever forget it."

Pitt sadly, "You're right, Nino. I know you are. I just have to show my wife more often that I really do love her."

Nino shakes his head in agreement, "There is only one way to show a woman that you truly love her, and it's not by sending her flowers or taking her to a fancy restaurant."

Pitt playfully agitated, "Well, what is it then? And what makes you such an expert on women? You're a bachelor for God's sake! What do you really know about marriage?"

Nino tries not to let Pitt see that he has hurt his feelings, "I was engaged to be married when I was twenty years old. I had just returned from my first tour of Vietnam, I was doing some advanced training at Fort Benning, when I met the love of my life. Her name was Diana Taylor. Her brother Joel went through basic training with me and he introduced us. She was a fine, old fashioned southern belle. She lived in a little town called Sumner, Georgia. I engaged her the night before I left for my second tour. It was a full harvest moon, and there seemed to be more stars in the sky than I have ever seen in my life. I knelt down on my knees and I asked her to be my wife. She cried when I asked her. She wanted to elope that night and go with me, she begged me to take her with me. But I told her that she would be safer there in Sumner, and that I would return for her when my tour was over.

Those were the best ninety days of my life, my romantic autumn in Georgia."

Nino's mind wandered and as he remembered those sweet romantic days, tears quickly gathered in the corners of his eyes.

Pitt feels bad, "I'm sorry, Nino. I shouldn't have questioned you like that."

Nino wipes his eyes, "It's alright man. Hey, how could you know?"

"Well, what happened? Why didn't you ever go back?" Asks Pitt.

Nino's mind seems far away, "I couldn't ever go back to her after what happened with that mother and her children, I had no joy left in my heart. I wasn't the same man who proposed to Dee, and it wouldn't have been fair to her. A piece of my soul and been amputated, and there is no prosthetic for that. I figured she would just assume that I died, and even if she tried to find me, she wouldn't have been able to. I left no trail." Nino's head drops for a moment, and he clears his throat, trying to swallow the memories. "Well, enough sad talk for now."

Pitt put his arm around Nino and held him close for a moment. He looked at his new friend with a warm, caring smile.

Pitt smiles,"Yeah, you said it."

Nino and Pitt continue walking up the street.

Nino excited, "Hey Pitt you see this little toy shop?"

Pitt laughs to himself, "The Angelo Street Toy Shop?"

Nino grins, "My buddy Gino Yannotti runs this place. But it doesn't look like he's here today, because his convertible would be parked out front." Nino walks over to a little table that is set up in front of the store. "Pitt, look at this thing. What do you call these things?"

Pitt comes over to take a closer look. Nino is looking at a clear globe that shoots pinkish purple colored electric bolts wherever he touches it. Pitt laughs, "Oh yeah, I love these things. I think their called Plasma Balls, or nebulizers, something like that."

Nino watches Pitt put his and on the Plasma Ball, "Remember when Jesus said "And you will see the son of man seated at the right hand of the power of God."

Pitt nods, "Yeah."

Nino continues, "This is sort of a reasonable facsimile of the power of God. In that no matter how many places you touch this globe it will send energy to the point of your body that is touching it. God's Holy Spirit flows out into the world in the same way. Whenever a soul reaches out to him in prayer or thought, his Spirit is sent to them immediately. When you go to Forever you can actually see Jehovah's spirit shooting out into the world, and since his powers are boundless no person who calls on him is ever ignored or overlooked."

Pitt chuckles, "You know I have always been intrigued by these nebula plasma balls, and now I know why."

Pitt notices that Nino looks a little tired, "Nino let's sit down for a second. I've got something in my shoe.

Nino points to a bench infront of the St. Anthony of Padua food pantry, and he and Pitt sit down.

"Jehovah will sit as a refiner and purifier of silver."
-Malachi 3:3

CHAPTER 30

▼

"We have been taught that in the annihilation of the family, the ancient virtue of the family is destroyed. And in the destruction of the virtue and traditions of a people, vice and impiety overwhelms the whole nation."
-KRISHNA/THE BHAGAVAD GITA (3,137 BC)

"Don't expect God's protection in places beyond God's dominion. When you are good, bad things can still happen. And if you are bad, you can still get lucky."
-Barabara Kingsolver (The Poisonwood Bible)

"Most humans have a hard time dealing with too much reality."
-T.S. Elliot & Mac Spellecy

Nino picks up a tiny pamphlet called Tomian's Tidbits. It is put out monthly by a Franciscan priest named Father Tomian Uss. Nino is familiar with it and he starts to read. Hey Pitt listen to this. "It says here that if you woke up this morning in good health, you have more luck than the one million people who will die every week.... If you have never experienced the horror of war, the solitude of prison, the pain of torture, were not close to death from starvation, then you are better off than the 500,000 million people world wide who have. If you can go to your place of worship without fear that someone will assault or kill you, then you are luckier than 3 billion people! And if you have a full refrigerator, clothes on your back, a roof over your head, and a place to sleep, than you are wealthier than 75% of the worlds population, and if your parents are alive and still married you are truly a rare individual."

Pitt raises his eyebrows, "Man that's some good stuff to know. I guess we have a lot to be thankful for in this country."

Nino nods and continues to read. "Hears a good one Pitt. Did you ever hear the story of **St. Augustines Apples**?

Pitt shakes his head, "No, I haven't"

Nino continues, "St. Augustine is probably one of the most down to earth saints to have ever lived. He once wrote that out of all of the sins he has ever committed, and he committed a lot. The worst thing he ever did was to steal apples."

Pitt smirks, "Stealing apples? What's so bad about that?

Nino explains, "Augustine said that there had been times in his life that he had stolen because he was poor and hungry, but he didn't necessarily believe that this was a sin. However, on this particular occasion he and his friends stole these apples just for the sake of stealing, they didn't even eat the apples. They just through them away. He said in hindsight this was his worse sin, because he did something he knew was wrong, and he didn't need to do it. The opportunity was there, and he couldn't walk away from it."

Pitt nod's understandingly, "It's kind of like me with that girl the other night at the China Club. I really didn't need to be fratrinizing with that woman. I wasn't sex starved or longing for intimacy. My heart wasn't empty, and yet there I stood. Just like Augustine, getting ready to take something that I didn't even need. He's right that is the worse kind of sin."

Nino chuckles and lightens the mood, "Well … You were almost like Augustine…." Nino laughs, "But I do believe you was probably gonna eat your apples." Nino slaps his leg and laughs at his own joke.

Pitt laughs and grabs Nino "You nasty joker…. Your probably right though…. Those were some sweet apples."

Nino continues to digress, "Probably right? Who you shittin? You would have made a pie out of your apples!" Nino and Pitt break into hysterics …

The laughter eventually fades out, and the two sit in silence for a few moments while Pitt pretends to look for something in his shoe. He puts his sneaker on and turns back to Nino. However, before he starts talking Nino notices a friend of his walking by with a dejected look on his face, and calls out to him."

Nino concerned, but smiling. "Corey Whidbee. What's the matter my man. You walked past me like I was a plate of leftovers or something."

Corey Forces a smile, "Oh, I'm sorry Nino. My mind is a million miles away today."

Nino worried, "Why, what's wrong. You should be walking on clouds. You just graduated from college, and you started you own business. What could have you so blue?"

Corey gets tears in his eyes, "Walking on clouds? … I'm a failure. My business just went belly up last week, and I lost all the money my family and friends invested in me … I'm a loser."

Pitt recognizing a counseling moment chimes in, "Excuse my man, but you're looking at this all wrong.'

Nino introduces Pitt, "Corey this is my good friend Pitt. He's a counselor."

Corey shakes Pitts Hand, "Nice to meet you Pitt."

Pitt continues, "Same here. Like I was saying, taking a calculated risk like starting a business and failing doesn't' make you a loser. Albert Einstein is arguably one of the world's smartest men, and yet he flunked out of school twice."

Nino chuckles, "But not the third time."

Pitt grins, "That's right. In this world it is the people who try and fail that are the true livers of life. If you would have kept your idea on a shelf and never tried it out, then you would have truly been a loser."

Corey eyes brighten a little, "I never thought about it like that, but what about my family and friends who invested in me? They believed in me and I gave them nothing in return."

Pitt continues, "That's not true. You gave them all that you had and it didn't workout this time. So what? If you continue to believe in yourself, and persevere eventually it will workout. Sometimes a battle must be fought more than once in order to be won."

Corey smiles, "Winston Churchill."

Pitt nods, "Exactly. You just keep on plugging little brother, and eventually the world will know your name."

Corey beams, "Do you really think so?"

Pitt serious, but smiling. "Absolutely, you've got that divine spark. I can see it in your eyes."

Corey sincerely, "Pitt, you just changed my life. I was walking around her thinking about jumping off a building, and now I'm thinking about building an empire. Thank you. Thank you so much." Corey glances at his watch. "I'm sorry fellas, but I've got to split. Thanks again."

Nino smiles proudly, and he and Pitt say their goodbyes to Corey.

Nino very impressed, "Well done counselor. You've got mad skills son."

Pitt grins sheepishly, "Thanks man. I wish all my sessions went that well."

Nino puts his arm around Pitt's shoulders, "**One by one my brother, you can save the world.** You were born to be a counselor. God has given you the seeds of hope. Plant well my brother."

Pitt curious, "Nino, how do you know so much about my life? Who told you about me?"

A large grin takes over Nino's weathered face. "I was able to watch you grow up from a little boy. It was like a highlight film of your life. It was awesome."

"Do they have highlight films on all of us?" Pitt asks.

Nino smiles, "Each one of us is the writer and director of our own movies. You know how Jesus said you will be held accountable for every idle word that you speak?"

Pitt looks worried, "It's all true isn't it?"

Nino shakes his head in agreement, "Yup, our words and our deeds stay with us forever. They either acquit us or convict us, and there's no arguing about the sentence."

"But I thought if we accept Jesus as our savior then we are saved?" Questions Pitt.

Nino makes clear, "If you accept Jesus as your savior then your life's words and deeds will be filled with mercy, love, and compassion, and even if you fall short of perfection, God will forgive you for your trespasses because you forgave those who trespassed against you. Jesus can only be your savior if you let God into your heart, and follow his path."

Pitt nods in understanding, "I see your point. What good is faith without deeds?"

"Exactly."

Pitt smiles, "Ok, now that you have proven your expertise, speak to me a little more about my wife. How can I show Leigh that I love her?" Pitt asks.

Nino responds, "Make her number one in your life, spend you. Talk to her. Enjoy her. Love her, and in your giving you will receive. You have always been a dreamer and a climber, but in so doing you have become selfish and self-centered. You forget that although her dreams may not be as lofty as yours are, they are still dreams, and no less significant than yours. The only difference is—"

Pitt looks ashamed, "Is that I have the power to make her dreams come true, and I haven't. She doesn't ask for much, but she stands behind me in all that I do. I see what you mean now, Nino. Sending flowers, buying candy, or going out for an occasional night on the town are meaningless to a woman whose husband has no time for her. It's like giving a stick of gum to a starving person."

Nino agrees, "That's right. The burst of sweetness momentarily takes your mind off the bigger problem. And the real sad thing is that you have the means to give so much more than the gum."

Pitt frowns, "What a fool I've been, Nino, a selfish, self-absorbed chump. How can I expect that God is going to help my dreams come true, when I refuse to help the person who loves me most in this world?"

Nino smiles, "Yes, now you have it. Love and you will be loved. Help your wife's dreams to come true, and then God will help you. But don't be surprised if your dreams change during the process of it all."

Pitt somewhat agitated, "What do you mean, my dreams will change? I have wanted to be famous all of my life. I have always believed that the world would one day know my name."

Nino continues, "What is fame, but the adoration of strangers. Why are you so willing to spend a lifetime trying to win the attention of the world? You will get your name up in lights only at the expense of neglecting those who really love you just the way that you are, as Jehovah does. Worldly fame and fortune means nothing to God. If you seek fame and fortune, then seek to be famous in Heaven."

"How do you earn Heavenly fame?" Pitt asks.

Nino explains "By walking the P.O.J. and loving everything that comes your way."

"That's it?" Pitt asks.

Nino clarifies, "Pitt, in Forever, everybody is famous. As we speak, you are already known by millions of souls, and the number will grow with each passing moment of eternity. Imagine meeting someone for the first time, and then in one twinkling moment, you know them completely, and permanently."

Pitt surprised, "Permanently? You mean no one is ever forgotten."

Nino nods, "That's right. In Forever, we have complete control of our minds and our bodies. We are in no way encumbered, and we are loved completely by everyone and everything we meet. Even the trees and flowers will know your name. In Heaven, all things are animated, and everything has a personality. You can talk to a bumble bee. You can tell a flower how nice it smells. You can ride a whale to the bottom of the ocean, or ride on an eagle's back into the outer stratosphere."

"And all these people, creatures and things will be my friends?" Asks Pitt.

Nino smiles warmly, "Yes, but friends in a way you rarely experience on earth. In Forever, every soul, creature, or plant will know you and love you completely. You will have an intimate loving relationship with all that you encounter, but you will be possessed by no one, and bound by no laws. You will be absolutely free to live a life of love for all eternity. True unconditional love is freedom. I was only there for a short time, and all I can think about is going back. This earth, and these familiar streets that I am walking on now feel alien to me. Now that I have seen the land of my origin, nothing can compare to the Kingdom of Forever. It is so awe-inspiring, Pitt. It is unlimited love. The light of Allah flows through all things. He is All in All. The sights, the sounds, the beautiful fragrances—there is nothing unpleasant. It's just so peaceful. I wish I could show you. I really do."

Pitt tries to soak it all in, "It sounds like I always dreamed it would be. I never bought into the white robes and harps description of Heaven. Who wants to sit around on clouds for an enternity!"

Nino laughs "You carack me up."

Nino and Pitt walk by a corner store with all sorts of fresh fruit and flowers for sale. Nino points to the fruit.

Nino sighs at the memory of it, "Pitt, wait until you see and taste the fruit and vegetables in Forever."

"I love fruit."

"Oh, it's just so completely delicious. I mean, it looks amazing, then it explodes with a flavor even more amazing. Actually, everything you eat in Heaven tastes fantastic. Even the texture of the food, and how it feels in your mouth is perfect. I stopped at this one pig roast, and the meat was perfectly seasoned and so juicy. It just about melted right in my mouth."

Pitt confused, "Nino, you said there is no death, dying or pain in Forever, right?"

Nino nods, "Yup. That's right."

"Well, what about the dead pig at the pig roast?" Pitt asks.

Nino explains, "Oh, I got ya. In Forever, there are all kinds of animals, fish, and creatures of the sea that are eaten just like here on earth. However, there is no such thing as death or pain. The fish and animals live enjoyable lives. They eat only the finest foods in a pollution free environment, and when they have reached physical maturity, they simply transfer their soul to another body."

Pitt remembers, "It's like Kahil Gibran said in his book, The Prophet, "A little while, a moment of rest upon the wind, and another woman bears me.""

Nino agrees, "Yes, just like that. The souls of the animals can even decide to be different types of animals if they choose. You know another aspect you will love is that in Heaven every animal has its own special purr when you pet it, and every baby giggles and coos when it looks into you eyes. It's really a funny place, man. Forever, in a lot of ways, is like an animated Disney flick. It's like a fantasy land where anything is possible, and everything is alive."

Nino slaps a mosquito from his neck.

Nino frowns, "Except mosquitoes. There are no bad bugs living in Heaven. Butterflies, beetles and bees are scattered about, but no mosquitoes. And they are all beautiful and a lot of fun to play with. This one bee I spoke to had a real nice personality. And you should have heard her sing!"

Pitt is shocked, "You spoke to a bee? A singing bee?!"

Nino chuckles, "I know. I know it sounds crazy. But that's the way it is. I also ate lunch with a lion, and he cooked the food."

Pitt chuckles, "Get out of here!"

Nino laughs,"I ain't shittin' ya! That lion could cook, too, almost as good as Mama Mia!"

They continued walking north and Pitt followed, assuming their next stop would be Momma Mia's, but Nino stopped in front of Bartucca's Barber Shop.

Nino points at the little shop, "Come on Pitt, let me introduce you to my good friend and the greatest barber in the world."

Pitt shakes his head, "Don't tell me you're stopping to get a hair cut?"

Nino laughs. "No I'm just stopping to see my main man one last time." Nino burst into the barber shop with his normal vibrant happiness. "Viva Pualito."

Pauly beams, "Nino my cumpari, how have you been?"

Nino puts his arm around Paulies big shoulders, "I can't kick Paulie. How about you?"

Paulie is still grining, "Everything's good…. So whose-a your handsome friend?"

"Paulie Bartucca, I'd like you to meet Mr. Mark Pitifer, but you can call him Pitt."

Pitt sticks out his hand, "It's a pleasure to meet you, Paulie."

"No sir, the pleasure is all mine." As Paulie speaks to Pitt, Nino talks to his friends who also happen to be in the barber shop—Tyrone "Ronnie" Scott, a 6'9 former Boston College basketball standout, and Christ The King High School coaching legend Richie Blue. Tyrone speaks up loud enough for Pitt to hear.

Tyrone fakes agitation, "What's the matter, we're not good enough to be introduced to your friend?"

Nino winks at Pitt. "Well I'm not gonna introduce him to just any old joker."

Richie and Ronnie laugh. "Pitt, these are my good friends Ronnie Scott and Richie Blue." Pitt shakes hands with Richie and Ronnie.

"Nice to meet you fellas. Coach Blue, I read an article recently in ESPN magazine that your son Matthew is one of the top players in Italy?"

Coach Blue smiles, "Yeah, my boy is making his daddy proud. This summer he started **The Elite Shooting Camp** in Framingham

Massachusetts, just outside of Boston. The camp is doing so well that next year he is going to run one in LA and New York.... As far as his basketball career, we're hoping he gets picked up by the Knicks next season. Their new owner Joe Augustine just hired my good friend Neil McVain as his head coach, so he should get a fair shot."

Pitt smiles, "That would be awesome! He really is a great player. I remember one time when he was playing for Rutgers that he dropped 47 points on Syracuse."

Coach Blue beaming, "Yeah that was quite a game."

Pitt responds "He is one of the quickest players I've ever seen. Can you imagine him, Vinny Ray, Glen Hudson, Abe Hara, Leonard Thomas, Gregory Jackson, Adrian "Tut" Lennon, Johnny Chamberlain, and Jimmy "Boom-Boom" Panek all on the same team?! That's like the dream team all over again!"

Coach Blue nods in agreement, and Pitt turns his attention to Ronnie "Didn't you play ball for Boston College a couple of years back?" asks Pitt

Ronnie looks proud, "Why yes I did. It's nice to be remembered."

Pitt continues, "Wasn't Carl Wenzel coaching that team? He went to college in Rochester. I saw him play when I was a kid. He and his teammate Sonny Wilson were dead-eye shooters."

Ronnie nods, "Yup old Carl could light it up. He was a great coach, and a good friend. I remember Sonny too. He would show up at practice once in awhile with his son Mark, and they would put on a shooting clinic."

Pitt smiles, "I remember when you hit those two free throws to send your team into the sweet sixteen. And your defense was phenomenal! In my opinion you were the Big East Defensive Player of the year."

Ronnie blushes "Thanks Pitt. Like I said sure is nice to be remembered. Well did you hear that Nino? Your man Pitt here has shown himself to know quite a bit about the great game of basketball."

Nino laughs "You think anybody who remembers anything about you is an expert. But I must agree with Pitt. Ronnie was an exceptional player. I just wish I could have run into him in my youth. I would have taken his narrow butt to the hole so many times he would have retired in high school."

Ronnie smirks, "In your dreams Nino."

Coach Blue speaks up. "I would have taken you on my team any time Nino."

Nino grins, "Pitt, now that's the voice of the most knowledgeable basketball mind in the city."

Everyone laughs, and Paulie joins back in the conversation. "So what are you guys up to today. Did you come in for a nice hair cut?"

Nino declines the invitation, "No, not today Paulie. Pitt is only here for a short time, and I am giving him the grand tour of the city."

Paulie smiles, "Well, Pitt, you picked a good guide. Nobody knows this city like-a Nino. Come on Nino, let me give you a quick trim. It's on the house."

Ronnie interjects, "Hey, how come he gets one on the house?" Paulie laughs, "Because I like him better than you."

Ronnie laughs, "Oooh, Paulie that's cold."

Paulie winks at Ronnie, "Come on Nino, just a quick one. A five minute trim. Pitt can talk politics and basketball while he waits."

Pitt speaks to coach Blue. "So Richie, how many years did you coach?

Richie scratches his head, "33 seasons, Pitt."

Pitt is impressed, "Man that's a long time. I've only been coaching about 10 seasons."

Richie interested, "What level do you coach?"

"High school, boy's JVs and assistant varsity."

"Do you like coaching?" Asks Richie.

Pitt smiles, "Yeah."

"What do you like best about it?"

Pitt thinks for a moment, "I like the excitement and the energy level of the high school game. I like how in most gyms the fans are right on top of you, but most of all I like the life-long friends that I have made."

Richie nods,"That's what I like the best too. Ronnie and I have been friends since he was a little boy."

Ronnie joins the conversation, "Coach Blue took me under his wing, after my father was killed. I was one of 7 boys and I could have easily gone the wrong way in this miserable city. Coach got me involved in basketball and the rest is history."

Pitt speaks to coach Blue. "Coach, what did you dislike the most about coaching?"

"I guess the thing I hated the most was the fickleness of the fans. You know, it's like, if you win everybody loves you and thinks you're a great coach, but if you lose, they turn on you very quickly. The second guessing and bad mouthing that goes on really is disheartening."

Pitt frowns, "I know, I could never understand booing your own team. Is that supposed to motiving? It's like the fans think that they want to win more than the players and the coaches do. It's ridiculous."

Coach Blue agrees, "It sure is, but it happens everywhere. These "boo-er's", quite often are the frustrated experts of the world. Former athletes that sit around and tell whoever will listen to them why the team lost, and who is to blame. They sit up in the stands with no pressure on them whatsoever, and wait for the team or coach to falter in some way."

Pitt chimes in "And they are always working from the position of hind-sight, so to the casual observer they appear to be wise and knowledgeable. They make people think that they could be the saviors of the program, if only someone would listen to them."

Blue smiles "However, if you follow these people long enough, you'll discover that they are apart of the problem, not apart of the cure. They are all about self-glorification, and nothing more. If you win it's because you're doing what they think you should do, and if you lose, well you know how it is …"

Pitt nods, "I know what you're saying. My experience has been when I have really good teams, there wasn't much coaching to be done. In fact, some of my teams were so good that I think you could have sat an alley cat on the bench and the outcome, 9 out of 10 times, would have been the same."

Richie and Ronnie are laughing. "Nino your friend is all right. Pitt you're absolutely right. Some of my greatest coaching efforts were with teams that didn't have good records at all. I would be working my tail off to try and get to 500, but the fans would be calling for my head on a platter."

Pitt smiles, "There's no unconditional love in coaching is there coach?"

Richie frowns, "No there's not…. Well except for my wife and kids. They were loyal fans."

Ronnie speaks up "That's not fair, coach. I was a loyal fan."

Coach Blue chuckles, "That's only because we won it all, and I would occasionally feed you."

Paulie jumps back into the conversation. "I'm not trying to take anything away from the importance of a good coach. But, I don't think they can do as much as people think they can. It's kind of like making a good spaghetti sauce, you put in all of the ingredients and then you let it cook. If you don't have the right ingredients you won't have a good sauce. Also, you must be careful not to undercook-a the sauce, for then it is too runny."

Nino joins in "This would be a team that is not well conditioned and prepared for the season."

Paulie smiles, "Yes, yes bravo, this is what I mean. And you must also be careful not to over cook-a the sauce. If this happens the sauce will be too thick and could even burn."

Pitt clarifies, "You mean like over coaching or over training."

Paulie smiles, "Exactly Pitt! If the ingredients are all there and you don't over or under cook the sauce, it should come out just right."

"I like your analogy Paulie," Coach Blue says. "What do you think Pitt? Should we book him for a coach's conference?"

"Absolutely." Says Pitt.

"Thank you. Thank you my friends." Paulie bows to his audience. Tyrone fakes annoyance, "Hey enough of this sports talk. Let's talk politics."

Nino steps up from the barber chair as Paulie brushes off the hairs from his coat. Paulie shows Nino the hair cut from the back and the front with a medium size mirror.

Nino smiles proudly, "Viva Paulito, just like a text book. You're an artist, not a barber."

Paulie is beaming, "Grazie Nino, tuti grazie."

Nino looks over at Ronnie who is now glancing at the newspaper. "You know, for as much as you like talking about politics, I would think you would take a run at the senate. Shoot, Barack Obama ain't got nothing on you. In fact, I think you would make a much better senator than you ever did a basketball player!"

Ronnie laughs. "You see how it works in here Pitt. A compliment is always followed by a slam."

Pitt laughs and joins in. "So is this a Democratic or Republican barber shop?"

Ronnie responds feigning indigence. "Pitt this is a Kantian Barber Shop."

Pitt laughs, "What do you mean?"

Ronnie grins, "I could explain it for you Pitt, but I'm gonna let Nino break it down for you, that is if he can."

Nino laughs, "Ok, smart ass, any time you want to see who knows more about philosophy, you just let me know."

Ronnie winks at Pitt. "Ok, then what did I mean Dr. Jones, when I said we were a Kantian barber shop?"

Nino feigns annoyance. "Well Immanuel Kant believed that most people are too afraid to formulate their own opinions, and they let other people do their thinking for them."

Pitt responds. "Like people who belong to political parties, and blindly vote the party line every time. That seems so ignorant. So ..."

Ronnie chimes in. "It's not just political parties. Any organization or label can be controlling. It's like when people ask me if I'm a conservative, or a liberal, and I tell them I'm both. I embrace both liberal and conservative values. Hey, when it comes to children and old people most of the time I'm liberal. But when it comes to crime, I'm usually conservative. It's just that ..."

Nino interrupts, "Hey are you guys going to let me finish or what?" Ronnie smiling, "Oh I'm sorry Nino, by all means continue."

Nino winks at the crowd and smiles. "As I was saying, Kant felt that people should be brave, and "think for themselves." Our opinions should form free from the influence or guidance of others. So what you were saying Ronnie, is that we men who sit in this barber shop are brave souls, who look at every situation free from partisan influence, and tell you exactly what we think."

Ronnie is glowing with pride and laughing. "Nino you bad motherf"

Nino cuts him off laughing himself. "Ronnie, Pitt's a religious man; he's not used to that type of language."

Pitt laughs. "Yeah, right Nino. I probably swear worse than the both of you."

Nino turns serious for a moment. "Ronnie, what do you think about us going to Korea? This guy could be the next Hitler if we don't do something soon."

Pitt joins in, "We thought Hussein's regime was bad, but this guy is a hundred times worse."

Ronnie retorts, "First of all, this guy is worse in some ways than Hussein, but he is no Hitler by any means. Although he is a proven danger to his people and possibly the world, his atrocities are incidental to the military intervention currently under way. His crimes against the human person, though horrifying, do not come close to the regime in Germany in World War II.

"But Ronnie," says Nino, "You can't just sit back and do nothing. We are one of the only countries in the world that stands up to bullies."

Ronnie annoyed, "But who is the bully, the dictator that is ruthless to his own countrymen, or the super power who tries to dominate the world through intimidation, utilizing tactics of "might makes right."

Coach Blue chimes in, "Ronnie does have a point Nino. This approach ultimately failed throughout the last century. I think if we go in we will win, and some good will come from that. However, we are also setting a precedent that any country can decide a certain nation or leader is a danger, and unilaterally move to assassinate its leaders, lay waste to an entire country, and install a government it finds favorable."

Ronnie nods in agreement, "That's right coach, and this is what we used to accuse the former Soviet Union of doing.… I am afraid that eventually the European Union, Russia, and China will forge an alliance, if not formally, then operationally, to contain the USA. I don't think we're ever going to be invaded again. We're just going to be left out of the loop."

Nino responds, "You have a keen mind Ronnie, but there truly is no absolutely correct response. To do nothing means that people will be tortured and killed, and yet to go to war for political reasons also means that innocent lives will be lost. I don't like war any more than you do, believe me, but to sit back and do nothing?"

Ronnie clarifies, "I'm not saying that we should do nothing. But I believe it is the responsibility of the people to choose their leaders and to replace them by the means they determine necessary. And this can include relying on the assistance of outside powers. The problem with this present scenario is that you have an external source making the determination for the oppressed people, and whenever this occurs you will always have unintended consequences. We do not need "Pax Romana" (peace of the Romans). We need universal Peace."

"I agree, but only God can give us that." Nino glances at the clock. "Pitt, we've got to split. Gentleman as always it's been a pleasure."

Ronnie interjects, "Where are you running off to? We're just getting started."

Nino really would like to stay, "I'm sorry fellas. Pitt and I are on a tight schedule today."

Paulie turns to Pitt, "Listen, next time-a you-a in town you come by for a hair cut, and we talk some more politics. We might not solve-a the world's problems from-a my little barber shop, but we come up with a lot of good-a ideas, right Nino?"

Nino salutes his friends, "That's right Pualito, take care my friends."

Pitt also says his goodbyes. "Next time I'm in town I'll stop in for a hair cut. I promise."

Pauly clasps his hands together and bows slightly, "Yes, yes please do."

"Nice meeting you coach, and Senator Scott, you got my vote." Richie and Tyrone speak at the same time, "Thanks Pitt. Take care."

As they open the door to leave, a pizza delivery man named Peter Forbes, a struggling, but talented musician, was just walking up to the door. As he approaches, Pitt holds the door open for him.

"Thanks a lot pal." Nino recognizes his friend Peter and introduces him to Pitt.

Nino smiles, "Peter my main man."

Peter grabs his friend in a bear hug, "Nino Jones, the coolest of the cool."

Nino pats Peter on the shoulder, "You still working CAM'S Pizzeria over on Exchange Street?"

Peter Gushes with excitement, "You know it brother. Its the best pizza in the city, and the Crisanti family are the nicest people in the world. Especially Sam, he's been like a father to me." Peter moves a little closer to Nino and whispers, "I also have a little crush on his niece Laura. She's an old fashion Italian girl."

Nino smiles, "Oh yeah the speech pathologist. She's a real gem, and pretty to. Just like her uncle!" Nino smiles remembering his genersosity, "Sam has given me a lot of free pizza over the years. He's got a real big heart, and he's always helping someone out. Give Sam and Rita my best will you, and slap his brother Boone in the neck for me!"

Peter laughing, "You got it boss."

Nino points to Pitt, "Peter, this is my friend Pitt."

Pitt extends his hand. "Nice to meet you Peter."

Peter grins, "Same here, any friend of Nino's is a friend of mine. Hey, Pitt what did you think of the barbershop gang."

Pitt chuckles, "That's my type of group. The conversation is fantastic."

Peter agrees, "You're not kidding. Their all opinionated, but intelligent. And they look at the issues from all sides. There's no political bias in this barbershop"

Peter's mind wonders for a moment, and then he continues to speak.

"You know what? If I ever make it big I'm going to produce a news show right from this barber shop. The people will love it."

Nino laughs and Pitt responds "Your right, that's a great idea, and the barber shop setting is perfect. That's how news should be. You present expert analysis on the pros and cons, and let the people decide for themselves."

Peter smiles and gives Pitt a high-five "You got it Pitt!"

Nino smiles and puts his arm around Peter. "You still playing with Frankie "The Loop" Blancke, and Greg Passalaqua?"

"You know it my brother. I gotta have my rhythm section tight!" "Give them my best when you see them again." Says Nino.

"Oh definitely. You should see. We're getting big Nino. We're ready to really step it up to the next level. Remember Corey Boatwright and Diana Fountain from my band AGC?

"I remember Corey, sure. Diana … Diana.…"

"They used to be in that band called Mother Freedom with the Jimmy and Randy Richmond."

"Oh yeah man. I remember her now. Long dark hair, very pretty, very Italian right? Yes, I remember her. That Diana can sing her butt off."

Peter chuckles, "Ha-Ha you bet your neck she can. You know what else I did. I got Kenny Foster playing the sax, and I got Al Roth …"

Nino raises his eyebrows, "The violinist from Brooklyn?"

Peter grows more excited, "Yeah we also picked up Rick Catanise on bass. He used to play with Groove Tree. You might of heard of him. He is a great engineer, and a fabulous producer! We also snagged Jimmy Smith who is probably, not to brag, one of the best all around musicians in the whole city. Prince aint got nothing on Reverend James Smith!"

Nino remembers, "Jimmy Smith, yeah I remember him. I thought he was playing with Wilmer Alexander and the Dukes?"

Peter nods, "He used to, but they split up."

Nino sighs, "Awe, that's to bad. What happened to their front man Bobby Greco? He was a great performer. He used to crack me up. Old Hyphen. I used to run into him at Pudgies Pizza all the time. He was a real funny cat."

Peter explains, "When the Dukes split up he opened Irene's Jazz & Coffee house. It's on the upper Westside on West 72nd street, near the Dallas Barbeque. It's named after his mother. It's a real cool place. It's the best coffee in town. Dana's Time Out is providing the food, and with his connections he'll get some of the best jazz artists in the city.… I am gonna miss seeing him with the Dukes though."

Nino frowns, "Yeah that's to bad. I always loved hearing Wilmer sing his song Give Me One More Chance."

Peter's excitement continues, "Yeah that's a classic. Oh and guess what? We even got Greg Bennett & Moon Dog doing our sound for us. You know that man has connections Nino, and he said there's a possibility that he can get us some time in Ray Howard's new Recording studio located in the new freedom tower. Isn't that awesome!?"

Nino raises his eyebrows, "You're not kidding. Ray Howard, now that's moving up. I can't wait to hear you guys.… Hey Peter, Pitt is a song writer too."

"Really? You got any CDs out?" Peter asks.

Pitt looking somewhat dejected, "No, but I've been recording some of my own stuff. You know how it is. It's my dollar and a dream."

Pitt brightens up. "I know you've must have heard of **Travis McKoy** and Matt McGinley's band **GYM CLASS HEROES**. They just released that monster hit **COOKIE JAR**. Well thy're from my home town, and if they can make it from little old Geneva, New York, so can I... Who knows, maybe he will be able to hook me up in some way? He is a friend of mine."

Peter laughs, "Hey just keep on dreaming my brother. That's the most important thing. I know sometimes you think it's all for nothing, but you gotta fight those negative voices. I wake up every day and I think this will be the day Hollywood finally calls. It makes this pizza delivery job tolerable. Sure, there are days when I get a little down. Those recording studio thanks-but-no thanks form letters are a little depressing.... But I just keep on pushing."

"Don't worry, Peter."says Nino. "You're a great musician, and some day the world is going to know your name."

Peter beams, "I hope you're right my brother. Well fellas, I gotta keep moving or the pizzas will get cold. Hey Pitt, if you ever need a guitar player look me up."

He gives Pitt his card.

"Thanks, I sure will." Says Pitt.

Peter reaches into his pocket and hands two tickets to Nino and Pitt, "Hey, if you guys want'em I got two free tickets to the Alex Wallwork concert at Point Pleasant tonight. It's right across for Jekinson's Pavilion on the boardwalk. You can hang out at the Tiki Bar afterwards, and then stay over night at the Driftwood Inn. It should be a great time."

Pitt gets excited, "That sounds awesome. I wish we could go. I love that song **JERSEY SHORE**. It was just voted MTV's #1 summer hit."

Nino tugs at Pitt's sleave, "Maybe next time Peter, Pitt and I've got to much happening tonight."

Peter puts the tickets back in his pocket, "Hey at least I tried. You take care, guys." Nino and Pitt wave good bye as Peter continues on his way.

Pitt shakes his head "This city has more talented people waiting on tables and delivering food than any place else in the world!"

Nino nods in agreement. As they walked by a New York City fountain a man dressed like he was from the cast of Jesus Christ Superstar was pacing back and forth. He was preaching to passersby, and telling them that he was John The Baptist. Indeed he looked the part. His clothes were made of camel's hair. He wore a leather belt and sandals. However, his food was not locusts and wild honey. He was eating a Quizno's sub, and drinking a Mountain Dew. As Nino and Pitt pass by he asks them if they would like to be baptized in his fountain.

Nino smiles and politely says "No thanks, but you keep up the good work."

Pitt also declines and snickers to himself. "No thanks brother, maybe some other time."

The Baptist somberly responds "You are like many of the people who pass me by. You think to yourselves that I am crazy. But I am not. I am John The Baptist. I have returned to complete my holy circle of visitations to the earth. I appeared in the 16th century BC as the prophet Elijah, during the time of Jesus as John The Baptist, and now lastly during These End Times I am once again the Baptist heralding the coming of our king!"

Nino responds "I wish we had more time to talk to you John, but we really do have to keep moving. Good luck to you though. Maybe we'll see you again sometime."

Pitt also waves good bye, and the two continue on their way. As they do The Baptist begins to preach again to all who will listen.

The Baptist speaks with passion, **"Repent! For the king of the world is coming soon! I baptize with water those who repent of their sins; but when the Messiah returns he will baptize you with the Holy Spirit and fire. Woe to those who scorn their brothers, and follow not the path of love. Very soon, at an hour least expected, you will see Jesus assend from Heaven in power and great glory. The whole world will see his sign, and he will gather his holy family from the four corners of Heaven and earth. Blessed are those who are prepared for his return."**

Nino stops for a moment and looks back at The Baptist. Nino wondering, "Hey Pitt, do you think that guy is crazy?"

Pitt purses his lips and thinks, "Yeah, probably so. I mean he did seem to have some knowledge of the scriptures, but Elijah. I don't think so."

Nino presses the issue, "But, isn't there a remote possibility that he is telling the truth?"

Pitt uninterested, "Yeah, I guess there is, but I still think he's crazy."

Nino won't let it go, "I understand why you believe as you do, and you're probably right. However, my point is that when the real John The Baptist lived, who would have believed that he was Elijah back from the great beyond?"

Pitt starts to realize where Nino is coming from, "I see what you're saying. I guess it's just hard to believe in that stuff, because there are so many people who truly are insane. How do you differentiate between a real prophet and a nut case?"

"How did you do it? Why is he crazy and I'm not?" Nino asks.

Pitt explains, "You knew about the situation at the China Club. You recited the Angels words back to me."

Nino looks somewhat hurt, "And if I didn't give you that proof, what would you have done?"

Pitt looks down at his shoes "I would have kept on walking."

Nino smiles and puts his arm around Pitt's shoulders. "I would have to if I were in your place. However the message to remember is that some of these people that at first glance appear insane, really aren't crazy at all."

Pitt imagines the possibilities, "So some of these people probably really are prophets aren't they?'

Nino agrees, "Probably a small number, but many of them are simply people who see and hear on a deeper mental/spiritual dimension."

Pitt nods in understanding, "So some of these people who see visions and hear voices are really telling the truth, but their truth is so different from what normal people experience, that we reject them as insane."

Nino smiling "Well said counselor. That's exactly how it was explained to me."

Pitt wonders, "What about psychics, are some of them legitimate?"

"Yeah, probably so."

"I have a friend named Mary Beth Lynch who gave me a tarot card reading last month. I don't really believe in that kind of stuff, but I was interested in what she was going to say."

"So how did it go?" Asks Nino.

Pitt remembers the experience, "Well, I was all set to rip it to shreds in my mind. But to be honest with you I liked what she had to say. She told me that I was going to work on a project, and that God was going to bless it. She said it is going to help a lot of souls."

Nino raises his eyebrows, "She sounds like she is the real thing to me."

Pitt concerned, "I hope so ... Hey Nino, did anyone speak to you about psychics in Heaven? Because, a lot of people use them down here."

Nino gives details, "Yes, I'm glad you brought this up. Positive minded psychics and astrologers who have a hopeful/helpful slant on life can have a good influence on certain people's lives. However, people who are negative and/or anybody who attempts to speak to the dead can do much damage in a persons life."

"How so?" Asks Pitt.

Nino continues, "First of all Jesus warned us not to try and communicate with the dead. If it wasn't something that could be done then Jesus wouldn't of had to warn us about it. He worries about this sort of behavior because he knows that demons will sometimes pose as our loved ones, and if this happens there is no way that the psychic or their clients will be able to know the difference."

Pitt concerned, "So the danger is that you could unknowingly be letting a demon manipulate you."

"Exactly. Demons love it when people try to communicate with the other side. It gives them an extra way to try and control your mind. The demons, like the Angels, can read your mind. So they will say the things that you want to hear, and describe the memories that you are searching for. They know your hopes and dreams and they will stop at nothing to gain possession of your soul. They are the ultimate seducers. This is why you should never, ever try and communicate with the dead."

Pitt clarifies, "It sounds like no matter how noble your cause, how astute your psychic, or how deeply you miss your loved one, speaking with the other side has the ingredients of spiritual disaster."

"Your absolutely right. And here is the bottom line. These people who get into occult practices, and customs, are opening the door for demons and Satan himself to possess their souls. Its very dangerous stuff, and should be avoided as much as possible.... Ok enough of this demon talk. I'm hungry, lets go get something to eat."

Pitt laughing "Hey, I was just thinking that. Are you a psychic or something?"

Nino laughing "That's right, and my tarot cards say you ain't gonna get as much to eat as I do."

The two new friends break into laughter ... They walk a little further up through SOHO, past the NYU campus, and finally to Mama Mia's restaurant on the corner of East 8th Street and Broadway.

THE CHRISTIAN P.O.J.
DO UNTO OTHERS AS YOU WOULD HAVE THEM DO UNTO YOU.

"This is the greatest commandment: "Hear, O Israel! The Lord our God is the one and only God. And you must love him with all of your heart, soul, mind and strength. The second commandment is no less great: You must love your neighbor as yourself. No other commandments are greater than these."

"The Bible is an inexhaustible fountain of all truths. The existence of the Bible is the greatest blessing which humanity ever experienced."
-Immanuel Kant (German Philosopher)

CHAPTER 31

▼

"Thus says the Lord God, 'You had the seal of perfection, full of wisdom and full of beauty. You were in Eden, the garden of God. You were anointed the cherub who covers; and I placed you there. You were on the holy mountain of God; you walked in the midst of the stones of fire. You were blameless in your ways from the day you were created, until unrighteousness was found in you."
-Ezekiel 28:15 (525 BC)

"The saddest thing in life is wasted talent!'
Lorenzo & Chazz "C" Palminteri (A Bronx Tale: Sonny)

"An unrecognized enemy is the most dangerous kind."
-Mark Salvatore Pitifer

If you were looking through the yellow pages for an attorney, the CSL Law Firm of Christian, Schrouder, and Li (pronounced lie), would appear no different from the thousands of attorney ads that are listed in the Manhattan phone book. In fact, even if you were to walk right past the high rise that houses the CSL law offices on 776 West 76th Street, there is nothing that would arouse your curiosity. No one would ever suspect that on the 77th floor of the Brimerstone Building Satan and his most powerful demons ceaselessly plan and carry out attacks against the Children of God. CSL, inconspicuous as it may be, is the most powerful law firm in the world. And yet, no case is too small for the CSL firm. As unimaginable as it may sound, financial gain is understandably not their primary objective. The attorneys at CSL strive on oppressing the innocent and the poor, and in exonerating the guilty and the rich. This is what gives them their pleasure.

Like vampires in search of blood, the attorneys at CSL are always looking for a guilty person to set free. Satan chose the profession of lawyer because it gets him involved in everything imaginable. However, the CSL is more than just an evil law firm, it is an army of demons. The CSL attorneys are the soldiers of Satan. They are Satan's highest ranking officers, those whom the holy books identify as the rulers of darkness, the wicked spirits who dwell in high places, or in this case, the 77th floor.

It is a little after 11:00 a.m. A special meeting had been called for all of the CSL head honchos, by Satan himself. Judas Iscariot, a former apostle of Jesus and one of CS L's highest ranking officers, is seated next to Adolf Hitler. One of Hitler's crew members had earlier that morning discovered that a covert operation from the Kingdom of Forever was currently underway in Manhattan.

Satan is seated at his desk with his feet up and his hands folded behind his head. "It has been brought to my attention that some form of attack is being mounted as we speak, by two earthbounds. And it appears that Barabbas and his band of heavenly zealots are directly involved."

"Barabbas and the Zealots!" The excited officers exclaim.

Satan remains unexcited, "It also appears that they have come in unauthorized, which as you know, means that if we can derail their offensive in some way, and use it to our advantage …"

Hitler chimes in, "Bye-bye paradise!"

Satan hisses with pleasure, "That's right! Their souls will be mine! Can you imagine the pain we will be able to cause in Forever? I can just see that pathetic king of theirs crying to his daddy over the loss of his friends. But big old, all powerful daddy that he is, won't be able to do a damn thing to help his little boy. Gentlemen, this is going to be like Cavalry all over again, Jehovah's little boy will be crying and hurt, and there will be nothing he can do except cry right along with him. Such a pathetic being. What a ridiculous waste of omnipotence. Bound by his law of truth and righteousness, there is nothing he will be able to do. Poor old Allah! I just love making him cry."

Hitler and his compatriots try to earn browny points, "Hail Satan! Hail the morning star! You will still have your victory!"

However, Judas was not taking part in the celebration. He was staring out of the window, his mind seemed far away. His serious expression caught the attention of Satan.

Satan faking concern, "Why, Judas, whatever could the matter be? You look worried."

Judus frowns, "I am worried. I am worried for us all."

Satan raises his eyebrows, "Worried? About Barabbas and his two earthbounds? They have already been discovered which means they have no chance of being successful. Now it's just a matter of how much I can manipulate them. We'll just take our time and play them for the suckers that they are."

Judus grows more concerned, "That's just it. I don't think we should take our time on this one. I think we should threaten them to stop, and if they don't, then we should bring it to a swift and decisive close."

Satan puzzled, "But why? I don't understand your reasoning."

Judus explains, "If their operation results in the loss of even one soul, we have defeated them, and can claim possession of all souls involved."

Satan smiles evily,"I know this, but if we give them a little rope down here, we will also quite possibly be able to capture a bundle of earthbounds as well. So why should we be in a hurry?"

Judus continues, "There is something wrong here that I can't put my finger on. I have seen the two earthbounds involved, and I was not impressed by anything that I saw or heard. One of them is a homeless veteran who is suicidal, and the other is a hopeless dreamer who is thinking of leaving his job and his wife."

"So, what's your point?" Scoffs Satan.

Judus worried, "Why would Barabbas risk his fellow zealots and himself spending an eternity in the Outer Darkness if he …"

Satan finishes his sentence for him, "If he had more time to pick two better, more stable earthbounds."

Hitler chimes in, "He must think that the Great Game is about to come to a close, and if that is the case, then his last chance to hit you with a significant blow is also our last chance to significantly hurt Yahweh and Jesus. Judas is right. We must strike quickly and without warning. We must not give this plan any chance at all for success."

Satan now looks a little concerned, "Yes, maybe your right."

Hitler continues, "We are fortunate that one of the demons under my command was involved in the temptation of one of Barabbas's earthbound zealots. He had the whole stage set for him to commit adultery, contract the AIDS virus, and commit suicide. Thinking that it was a lock, he left the earthbound unattended and that's when Gideon showed up. He watched the guardian angel warn him, and followed the earthbound to learn a little bit more about him. That's when he witnessed the meeting of Mark Pitifer and Nino Jones. This is also when he heard about the plan. We'll just take this lucky break and turn it to our advantage."

"Yes, you must go at once. Adolf, I want you to take Judas and track these guys down. Once you have discovered their whereabouts, leave two tracker soldiers with them and then report back to me for your final orders."

Satan dismissed the members of the CSL, and Judas and Adolf embarked on their journey.

> **"I saw Satan falling from Heaven as a flash of lightning! And I have given you authority over all the powers of the enemy."**
> **-JESUS OF NAZARETH (Luke 10:18 & 19) (80 AD)**

Author's Note 1: I know that many of you believe in God and the Holy Angels, but not in Satan and his demons. However, whether you recognize it or not, a titanic battle is being fought over the rights to our souls, and it behooves each and everyone of us to take an active role in this struggle. Learning from the wisdom presented in all of the Holy books will do much to protect our souls. However, we must also acknowledge the existence of our spiritual enemies. We must learn how they think, how they attack, and how they can be defeated. In order to understand Satan, we must first understand evil. And in order to understand evil and all of its subtle malignancies, we must consult the expert on this subject, Dr. M. Scott Peck. The following paragraph is a short compilation of excerpts from Dr. Peck's outstanding novel 'People of The Lie'. This is a truly holy book which I feel is divinely inspired. 'People of The Lie' provides a detailed description of how Satan systematically imprisons the human personality, and ultimately, if we let him, gains possession of our souls. It also holds in its pages the keys to mental and spiritual health. Thank you Dr. Peck for sharing your wisdom, and having the courage to buck the establishment.

"It is not their sins per se that characterize evil people, rather it is the subtlety, persistence and consistency of their sins. This is because, the central defect of those who are evil is not the sin itself, but rather their refusal to acknowledge it. In their hearts they consider themselves above reproach, so they must lash out at anyone who does reproach them. They sacrifice others to preserve their self-image of perfection. They project their own evil onto the world. They never think of themselves as evil; on the other hand, they consequently see much evil in others. The evil deny themselves the suffering of their own guilt-the painful awareness of their sin, inadequacy, and imperfection. Their omnipresent narcissism prohibits them from even acknowledging it. The evil of this world is committed by the self-righteous who think they are without sin because they are unwilling to suffer the discomfort of significant self-examination. It is out of their failure to put themselves on trial that their evil arises. The evil are the "people of the lie," deceiving others as they also build layer upon layer of self-deception. They themselves may not suffer, but those around them do. The evil create for those under their dominion a miniature sick society.
-Dr. M. Scott Peck (Excerpts from: People of The Lie)

"What do you want with me, Jesus, Son of God Most High? Please, I beg you, oh, don't torment me!" "What is your name?" Jesus asked the demon, "Legion" they replied, for the man was filled with thousands of them! (A legion consists of 6,000 troops) The demons kept begging Jesus not to order them into the bottomless Pit." They pled with Jesus to let them enter a heard of pigs instead, and Jesus, always most merciful, grants their request. Jesus said that Hell is a place where "The fire is never quenched & the worm dies not." How bad must Hell truly be, if even the demons are terrified of it?
-JESUS OF NAZARETH & The demon Legion (Mark 5:8&9)

"Hate the sin, not the sinner."
-St. Augustine (425 AD)

CHAPTER 32

▼

"Do not judge each day by the harvest you reap, but by the seeds that you plant."
-Robert Louis Stevenson

Give birth to and nourish all things without desiring to possess them. Give of yourself, without expecting something in return. Assist people, but do not attempt to control them. This is how to realize the deep virtue of the universe.
-Lao Tzu (550 BC)

Pitt and Nino are just finishing up breakfast at Mamma Mia's.

Pitt pats his belly, "Boy oh boy was that a good breakfast, Nino! That Mamma Mia sure can cook!"

Nino jokes, "If you think her cooking is good, you should see her with a feather duster."

"See what?"

Nino chukles, "It's an inside joke, only Mamma Mia would get it!"

Pitt shakes his head, "You're a nut, Nino. A total nut.... Okay, my man, where to next?"

Nino points and beckons Pitt to follow, "Right next door to Romeo's Shoe Repair. It's the best shoe shine place in the city."

Pitt faking agitation, "What? You're stopping to get your shoes shined?"

Nino looks down at his shoes and frowns, "Look it here, there is no way on God's green earth that I am going to take my last walk through this city with unshined shoes. There's nothing worse than seeing someone with dirty, scuffed up shoes. It says something about who you are."

Pitt laughs, "My father always used to say having dirty shoes is worse than having a dirty face. His shoes were always good to go."

"Your father knew what he was talking about."

"Is the guy's name really Romeo?" Pitt asks.

Nino nods, "Yup. Romeo "Bandi" Liberio. He's like a brother to me. Now come on and watch a master at work."

The two men burst into Romeo's shoe repair with Nino hollering and laughing and as usual, scaring poor Bandi half to death.

Bandi wipes imagined sweat from his forhead, "You know, one of these days you're gonna cause me to shoot your ass, Nino, and it ain't gonna be my fault!", the young man shining shoes exclaims. "You see I've got a new customer and you're probably gonna scare him off!"

Nino begins to tease Bandi, "This boy ain't here to see you. He's here to watch the real master!"

Bandi gives it right back to Nino, "Well, I'm sorry pal. My father's not in today."

Nino agrees, "Your father is very good. But I'm great!" Nino starts dancing around like a boxer and starts talking like Muhammad Ali. "I'm the greatest shoe shining man of all time!"

"Hey kid, there's only one great one in this room and the store is named after him. My name is Romeo Liberio, but my friends call me Bandi."

Pitt shakes hands with the store owner. "I'm Mark Pitifer, but my friends call me Pitt. It's a pleasure to meet you." Pitt looks around the store and smiles to himself. There is a picture of the Pope and the blessed mother, a crucifix, an Italian flag, and autographed pictures of Chazz Palminteri, Al Paccino, and Robert DeNiro, and various old fight posters Ali/Frazier, Leonard/Hearns, and **Fratto/Mosley** ... "Is Nino really as great as he says he is?"

Bandi fakes disappointment, "I hate to admit it kid, but he is the best I've ever seen."

Nino blushes, "Be quiet Bandi, now you're gonna put pressure on me. Okay, Pitt. Hop in the seat."

"Nino, I'm wearing sneakers."

"I can see that. What size foot do you have?"

Pitt frowns, "10 or 10 1/2, why?"

Nino explains, "Because you're gonna take off those sneakers and put on my size 11 boots so I can polish them."

Pitt teases Nino, "I'm not putting on your sorry boots. You probably have roaches living in them."

"You're right, Pitt" Bandi laughed. "I wouldn't put on boots where his old crusty feet have been, either!"

Nino grins, "Ha, ha, ha! Now, hop up here smart ass, and sit ringside as the greatest of all time does his dance." Nino was every bit as good as he said he was. He has the polish rag snapping like a whip, and he is as proud as a peacock about his performance.

Nino beams with pride, "Look at that! Just like looking in a mirror! Alright, chump, take my boots off. You don't deserve to wear shoes that look that good."

Pitt takes of the boots and takes a closer look, "These really are something." Pitt is impressed. "Ok, let every knee bow, and every tongue profess that Nino Jones is the undisputed King of Shine!"

Bandi must agree, "He really is the best. Even better than me, and it's how I make a living. Nino has been shining shoes in here with me on and off for years. The only problem is that once he shines someone's shoes, they don't want me to do it any more!"

Nino continues to playfully tease Bandi, "That's why you should rename the place Nino's Prime Time Shoe Shine! Then you could come be my apprentice!"

Bandi waves off Nino's suggestion, "And you can go shit in your hat! Now get out of my store, I've got shoes to repair, and we know who the real king is here!"

Nino smiles salutes his friend, "Yes we do. Have a nice day my king. I will see you on the flip side."

Bandi smiling, "Not if I see yo first. Nice meeting you, Mark."

Pitt and Nino leave Bandi's store and continue north, up Broadway.

Pitt teases Nino "Okay, partner, where do we go to next? A dry cleaner?"

Nino picks up the pace, "Nah, uptown towards 178th Street."

"178th Street? Oh, yeah, the GWB ... So, what do we do? Just walk and talk?"

Nino nods, "That's right, we walk. But as we move along, we look, we listen, we taste, we feel and we smell. We will use today's experiences, to help you paint a picture of paradise."

Pitt somewhat confused, "Paint a picture of paradise? You mean Heaven? What is it you need me to do?"

Nino explains "Okay, rookie, for example, what did we just do together?"

Pitt answers, "We ate breakfast, and you got your boots shined. But what's that got to do with our mission?"

Nino smirks, "Well, I just came down from Paradise. Wouldn't you like to know, for instance, if we eat up there?"

Pitt gets Nino's drift, "Oh, I see what you mean. Yes, I'd definitely like to know about that. Wait a minute, are you telling me there's food in Heaven?!"

Nino puts his arm around Pitt's shoulders. "My man, words cannot describe the flavors or the smells of the food that is prepared in Forever. It is absolutely extraordinary. It's kind of like walking down Mulberry Street in little Italy and going past the different restaurants…." Nino's mind floats back to Heaven, and then he continues. 'First of all in Forever, everybody can cook extremely well, and every meal always comes out perfect. The way the food looks, the way it smells, the way it feels in your mouth while you are eating, and even the sounds of it being prepared are perfect!"

Pitt can't believe it, "So what are you saying, they have restaurants in Heaven?"

Nino continues, "Are there restaurants Heaven?! You can't even begin to imagine how many restaurants there are up there! And the word restaurant doesn't seem an exquisite enough word by which to call cathedrals of cuisine. They have these beautiful magnificent mansions with fabulous views from every seat. They are always open, and you don't need any money. The meals are prepared by the greatest chefs in the universe, and their only requirement is that you enjoy the food that they prepare."

Pitt confused, "If there is no money what do they get out of it? Why do they do it?"

Nino turns somewhat serious, "Pay attention to this Pitt. Because when you understand how the restaurant business works in Forever, you will recognize this reoccurring theme for how and why everything exists in Heaven.... What's your nationality?"

"American citizen, Italian heritage."

"Did you have a grandmother that could cook?" Asks Nino.

Pitt smiles at the thought of it. "Yes. She was an artist with food."

"Did she used to cook for you?" Nino asks.

Pitt still smiling, "Yeah. She liked to cook for everybody."

Nino continues, "Did she get money from it? Did you have to pay her to do it?"

Pitt purses his lips, "No. She would just sit there and watch me eat. The more I ate, the happier she would get. If I told her I loved it, she would just gush with joy."

Nino smiles, "There you have it. In Heaven, this is why the great chefs cook. And the more you eat, the better they like it!"

Pitt soaks up the thought of it, "That sounds so wonderful. What a perfect way of doing things." Pitt thinks for a moment "Nino, speaking of eating, is it possible to be overweight up there? I mean with food that good for free, I envision a lot of fat people sitting around an all you can eat buffet."

Nino laughs at Pitt, "I know what you mean, that could get ugly. Only thing is there is nothing unbecoming in Heaven. In Forever there is no such thing as overweight or obesity. **There is no waste in pardise. Everything you eat is completely transformed into energy**, so ...."

Pitt cuts Nino off, "So, there's no going to the bathroom?"

Nino nods, "That's right. Think of all the times in your life that having to go to the bathroom has inconvenienced you, especially in this city. In Heaven the butt is just something pretty to look at. In paradise everyone has a nice butt." Pitt is laughing, as Nino continues, "It's true. Like I said everything that is taken into the body is turned into 100% power. Nothing is wasted. There is no pollution of any kind. Can you imagine going for an eternity without stepping into a pile of dog shit again?"

Pitt continues to be entertained, "Man, this is really something.... Nino you said there's no need for money?"

"None whatsoever. In Forever money is obsolete, and that makes everybody equally wealthy."

Pitt tries to imagine how a moneyless society would work, "but what if you need somebody to do something for you? How would you get them to do it?"

"What do you need them to do?" Asks Nino.

Pitt tries to think up a scenario, "What if you have a bad tooth and need a dentist, or something goes wrong with your plumbing or electricity in you mansion?"

Nino gives details, "That's not gonna happen in Forever, Pitt! There are no doctors or dentists or psychiatrists or proctologists up thers. Our heavenly bodies are perfect in every way. Nothing breaks down or wears out. There is no sickness of any kind …" Nino pauses and then continues. "There are carpenters and engineers, but they build for the same reason that the great chefs cook. Also once someone in Forever builds something, it will never need to be repaired. There are no electricians, because in Forever everything gets its power from the light of God, much like a flower gets its energy from the sun, only our petals never wilt. There are no plumbers, because there is no need for plumbing."

Pitt surprised, "Don't people have to wash? Isn't there body odor?"

Nino sighs "Every person has his or her own unique aroma that is a perfect reflection of their soul. The scent of the soul is intoxicating." Nino takes in a deep breath, and sighs as he remembers … "What beautiful fragrances. It is truly a sniffers delight! And we both know that your nose is always open. Your a sniffoholic!"

Pitt laughs, but his mind is racing and full of questions, "Is that why we like to wear perfumes and colognes down on earth?"

Nino nods, "Yes, exactly. Now, you are starting to do what I need you to do. **Everything that we do down here can be traced back to some unconscious memory we have of how things used to be back in the Kingdom. We all strive to be unique individuals in every way, but on earth this is difficult. In Heaven, it's a reality. Up their no one has to try and be unique, you are created that way.**"

Pitt tries to think of other earthly pastimes, "What about shopping? Are there stores or malls in Forever? Because I know some people that will be very disappointed if they have to go an eternity with no shopping."

Nino laughing, "I'm sorry to tell you that there are no malls in Forever. However, if you like to shop? Then Forever is you kind of place." Pitt thought for sure the answer would be no, and he is surprised to find out that he is wrong, "Really? I can't believe this place."

Nino nods, "Pitt, every community has these giant, sprawling, beautifully laid out market places. At which you can shop for anything that you can imagine, and even somethings that you can't!"

"But I thought there is no money in Heaven. How do you shop with no money?" Pitt asks.

Nino frowns, "Like I already told you there is no money in Heaven. All you need to shop is two things, a please and a thank you. These heavenly merchants are simply thrilled to have you walk away with their created goods. In a moneyless, profitless society, your pleasure comes from seeing people enjoy what you have created."

Pitt tries to imagine, "What's it like a giant farmers market?"

Nino nods, "Kind of, but much better. And you don't need giant enclosed malls because the climate is always perfect."

"What's it like a giant outdoor Wegmans?" Pitt asks.

Nino smiling, "Kind of. Those are beautiful stores. Danny Wegman is gonna love Forever.… But just imagine for one moment a wonderful setting filled with: artists, musicians, painters, tailors, gardeners, furniture makers, farmers, sculptors, woodcarvers, candy makers, pie and cookie bakers, and on and on it goes. **Pitt, if you really like to shop, you will absolutely love the Kingdom of Forever!"**

Pitt smiles, "I can't wait to get up there. Hey, Nino, shouldn't I be writing this stuff down, or recording it in some way? What if I forget?"

Nino reassures Pitt, "I told you there's no need, Pitt. Just think of Heaven. Let your imagination take over and think of all that Heaven should and shouldn't be, and you will be right on target. You can't be wrong."

Pitt remains worried."But what if I'm wrong? I've never been to Heaven. You're the one who's had the grand tour. Maybe we should steal a tiny DV Wrist Pilot or something. So that I can record some of this stuff."

Nino scoffs, "First of all, what kind of prophets would we be if one of the first things we do together is go steal something?" Nino laughs. "Secondly, Forever is the place where all of your hopes, your dreams and your longings are realized. Thirdly, and get this through that thick head of yours, they assured me that you will be able to remember all that I tell you. I also wrote down a lot of notes for you in this blue note book. So don't worry."

Pitt still concerned, "So my brain is going to work like a computer, right?"

Nino somewhat agitated. "Your brain is going to work like an unencumbered brain, not some sorry ass computer. Did you know that if they took all of the computers of the world, and networked them together so that they would work as one giant super computer, it would still not have the capacity of one healthy human brain!"

Pitt smirks "Oooh, Nino, it sounds like you got a bad attitude about computers."

Nino continues, "What I don't like is this. God made man. Man invented the computer, and the modern computers are held in greater esteem than the human brain. Hey, don't get me wrong. I acknowledge that we have been able to do some remarkable things with computers. I guess another part of my disdain for them is that I don't really understand how they work."

Pitt can relate, "I hear ya. I know a little bit about them, but the technology is moving so fast that yesterday's information is obsolete. My brother-in-law, Robert Toups, is one of the top computer minds in the country. He runs and maintains the computer systems for MTV, through the Viacom company."

Nino is impressed, "He really must know his stuff."

Pitt is proud of Robert, "He does. His new Macintosh computer has 20,000 GH quad deca-prosessors, and operates at 1,000 teraflops."

Nino mildly agitated,"Speak English! What does that mean?"

Pitt explains, "It means that his new computer can perform 500 trillion different operations per second!"

Nino shakes his head in wonder, "That is truly unbelievable." Nino thinks for a moment … "Pitt, how many people are in the world?"

"I don't know, probably about 12 or 13 billion? Why?"

Nino has an epiphany, "Did you ever wonder about how God can listen to everyone's prayers at the same time?"

"Yeah, sure, it's a mystery. Right?" Says Pitt. Nino illuminates, "Is it? We now have a man-made device that can do 500 trillion different operations per second. God's creation's, creation can perform 500 trillion different tasks per second."

Pitt smiles impressed by Nino's wit, "I see where you're going with this! **If God's creation's, creation—the computer—can handle 500 trillion different pieces of information per second, then it's not so difficult to think of the creator worrying about 9 billion different people at the same time.**"

Nino tips his cap, "Right on. Maybe I do like these computers after all. They can help us prove that God exists, and that he is omnipotent and omnipresent.... But that Internet still scares me."

"You mean the Virtunet." Says Pitt.

Nino agitated, "Yeah-Yeah whatever they call it now. The grand information highway, great for the mind, rough on the soul."

Pitt agrees. "That's right. You can't believe how many marriages have ended due to internet affairs. And not only that, the internet allows Satan to have access to his full arsenal when dealing with a soul that is online."

Nino agrees, "Whatever your weakness or obsession, Satan now has the power to dangle it in front of your eyes and ears more vividly and efficiently than he ever could before."

Pitt sighs, "That's it Nino. People are being sucked into cyberspace more and more each day. They find it harder and harder to pull away from their dark desires. They've even got those new electrode dream simulators that actually allows people to control their minds. They can now fully experience whatever they want to. People don't even leave their houses anymore. You can climb Mt. Everest from your living, or make love to you favorite movie star. They have even got people living in these new cyber villages in which they buy grocereies, go to the movies, pay bills, go to school, get a job, get married, make love, have children, and eventually die all on line! They feel as if they are self-sufficient beings. Real people and relationships are becoming obsolete!"

Nino determined, "Then you've got to help them. Express the pit falls you see, and tell them to **turn off the computer and turn on to people.** Tell them to use it as a tool, and not as a lover, a dealer, or a pimp. If you've got spare time, then play with your children, visit a friend, or read a book."

Pitt looks at Nino proudly, "See, it's a good thing I brought up computers after all!"

Nino agrees, "That's why you're the messenger." Nino forgets where he is and nearly steps in front of a speeding taxi. The driver blows his horn and tells Nino, in not such a nice way, to watch where he's going. His language brings another question to Pitt's mind.

"Nino, what do they say about swearing in Forever. Is what that taxi driver just said considered a sin?" Pitt asks.

Nino explains, "How he treated me was sinful, because I don't think he treated me the way he would want to be treated. But if you're just talking about the swearing? Using profanity around people who may be offended by its use is insensitive, and should not be done. But if you're playing basketball with a bunch of your friends and you say "fuck", to be honest with you, I don't think God really cares. Oh, I'm sure if he had his druthers he'd probably rather have you use some other superlative, but I don't think swearing is a big concern. Next time you get mad at someone try calling them a "pear pulling, apple biting, orange sniffer!" See if that works.

Pitt laughs, "Is that what you do?"

Nino smirks, "No, I like swearing to much."

Pitt still laughing but then turns serious again, "Me to ... What about taking the Lord's name in vain? That's done all the time. I'm as bad as anyone. I have a vulgar mouth when I get angry. But isn't saying God damn it, or Jesus Christ, breaking the 3rd commandment? I don't really mean what I say, but ..."

Nino interrupts, "Using the name of God, or Jesus in a negative way is showing them disrespect and should not be done for that reason. Taking the Lord's name in vain, however, has a little more to it than that. What the third commandment is referring to is when people who claim to be believers, call upon the name of God, but don't really believe that he will help them, or those they pray for. You see what I mean? They are asking for something they don't really believe God can or will do. Hollering out "God damn it "is completely disrespectful to God, and the phrase, if taken literally, is absolutely the worst thing that anyone could ever say to another person. However, taking the Lord's name in vain indicates a much more serious spiritual problem than a foul mouth."

"I think I see what you mean. It's not so much what we say, but how we truly feel about God, that could lead us to say his name in vain."

Nino nods in agreement, "That's right and only God can determine our true motives and inner feelings. Which brings me to another important point. Why do you think that cab driver got so mad at me? I mean after all he's the one who almost ran me over. I didn't do anything to him. What do you think counselor? Why did he get so upset?"

Pitt thinks for a moment, "He probably assumes that you are one of those people who think that they always have the right-of-way, like you are disrespecting him by your actions."

"So if his response is anger, he must be assuming that my motives are not only bad, but intentionally malicious, correct?"

"Yup, I can't stand people like that. They never give you the benefit of the doubt." Says Pitt.

"Pitt do you know why these people are so miserable?" Nino asks.

Pitt frowns, "I guess probably because they think everyone's out to get them in some way. I don't know."

Nino smiles, "What if I told you that the source of their misery is they are too righteous?"

Pitt is confused, "Righteous? I'm not following you. I thought being righteous is a good thing. What do you mean?"

Nino makes clear, "Pitt, if you are certain that your motives are good and righteous, and all people who slight you in some way are malicious and unrighteous, what role in life will you usually find yourself in?"

Pitt knows exactly where Nino is coming from, "The role of the victim."

"You've got it. While I was on the Grand Tour a pretty little bird named Sophia told me that this "victim" type of personality causes a lot of problems in this world."

Pitt is shocked, "A little bird told you?! You had a conversation with a bird?"

Nino chuckles because of the look on Pitt's face, "Yup, I was astonished to. And guess what else? You'll never believe this. All of the pretty song birds you see hanging around humans...." "Pretty song birds?"

"You know like chickadees, robins, cardinals, and finches." "Oh yeah, I know what your mean."

"They are all helping the Guardian Angels do their job. They are spies! They are the eyes and ears of the Angels!"

Pitt pushes Nino, "Get out of town. That's unbelievable!"

Nino grins, "I'm not kidding you. When you hear birds chirping away to one another, They aren't really singing songs, their communicating with our Angels from sun up until sun down."

Pitt laughing, "What about crows, blue jays and those other sour sounding birds?"

Nino turns serious, "I was told that if they don't have a pretty face and a sweet song, then they work for the other side."

Pitt smiles, "So when my mother used to say "a little bird told me" she wasn't lying was she?"

Nino Nods, "Nope, like I told you before Pitt, almost everything on earth originates in Heaven."

"So, did Sophia explain why these "victims" cause so many problems?" Asks Pitt.

"Yeah she did. In order to take on this victim mentality, you first must be very self-righteous, self-centered, and judgmental."

"That sounds like the product of evil." Says Pitt.

Nino continues, "It can be. These types of people go through life assuming that other people have malicious motives, when in reality most of the time these "other people" are not even thinking about them. The irony is that most of these people who become chronic victims start out as very loving and sensitive souls, who quite often are truly very righteous people."

"So what happens to them? What turns them so sour?" Asks Pitt.

Nino explains, "These sensitive souls get worn down by life quicker than other souls. They get to the point where they feel they can't take anymore, they need an escape. That's when Satan steps in and manipulates their keen sense of righteousness, along with their need for peace, and turns them into miserable judgmental humans."

"You're right Nino. These chronic victims end up becoming the grudge holders of the world. These are the souls who disown family members and friends. They negatively scrutinize everyone else's motives, and fail to see how their own self-centered, judgmental perspective is the true source of their problems in life."

Nino looks sad, "If only they could see the truth, and discover that most people are not malicious individuals who intentionally disregard our feelings. Most of the time when we offend somebody it's simply because we are preoccupied, impatient or frustrated about something totally unrelated to the person we offend. We humans have many weaknesses that cause us to appear insensitive, but the truth is that most of us do not want to intentionally hurt other people, and we feel sorry when we do."

"You're so right Nino. My good friends father eventually cut off everyone in his family, and the sad part is he felt justified in doing so. Even the people who tried to maintain a relationship with him eventually got fed up with walking-on-eggs around him."

Nino frowns, "It sounds like it was a bad scene."

Pitt looks sad, "It was. Nino, this was a real tight family that gradually just fell apart for no reason other than this victim stuff we're talking about. His friends and family were constantly being accused of some form of malice or insensitivity so they either gradually distanced themselves from him, or they snapped on him and he, being above reproach, cut them out of his life. He claimed that all he really wanted was peace, love, and loyalty and yet his love and acceptance was strictly conditional."

Nino agrees, "Which means it's not really love, and he didn't really accept them."

Pitt nods, "Exactly, Nino, I'm telling you this guy could have had the world on a string. He was smart, funny and entertaining, but he was just so very domineering and controlling that eventually no one could stand to be around him. He would constantly tell you how you let him down, ruined his day, or hurt his feelings in some way. He had an endless stream of expectations that you had to meet in order to stay in his good graces, and if you didn't, he would be right there to tell you exactly how you failed, and why you should feel guilty. It's like he became so self-righteous that everyone became estranged from him."

Nino puts his arm on Pitt's shoulders, "It sounds like you've really experienced the pain that can be caused by just one self-righteous victim. The real sad thing is when these souls get over to the other side and they finally have their eyes opened. That's when they see for the first time all the pain they caused by their self-righteous malignancy. Can you imagine finding out that you have become that which you claim to despise?"

Pitt cringes, "It must be an awful realization."

"Don't forget, counselor, Satan's ultimate goal is to get you and keep you self-centered."

"So what's the remedy?" Pitt asks.

Nino makes clear, "People should expect to get their feelings hurt in this world on a daily basis. That is the sad reality of the world in which we live. However, we must give our brothers and sisters the right to be selfish, lazy, self-centered, imperfect people. If someone hurts you, try to give them the benefit of the doubt that it was not intentional. Self-righteous people have a tendency to remember all the bad that anyone has ever done to them, and never let the person off the hook for doing so. But this is contrary to what the holy spirit of God wants from us."

Pitt laughs, "My friend Reverend Williams of Mt. Cavalry Church used to say 'Once someone sees me wrong, they can't ever see me right.'"

Nino smiles "I like that, and he is right…. Allah wants us to be happy, forgiving souls, who are not easily offended, and who can look past each others faults and become one family under God."

Pitt salutes Nino, "Ok, Nino from now on everytime I hear a taxi's horn I'll remind myself that I'm not the center of the universe, and he is probably mad at someone else."

Nino grins,"Very good my brother. They almost always are. Come on. Let's move along."

The two continued walking north on Broadway and unbeknownst to them, their fine morning together was about to come under siege.

> **"He is not a friend who always eagerly suspects a breach and looks out for our faults."**
> **-Sutta-Nipata**

A Note from my wife Leigh: If you are trying to live holy lives by walking the path of Jesus, then you must remain kind and merciful, even when the world you encounter is rude and unmerciful. Don't let the actions of people who are behaving poorly cause you to act in similar manner. In doing so you **are giving**, as Jesus said, your pearls to swine. Never take that which is **holy, and** allow it to be turned into something that is evil. We must be **the constant** guardians of our souls. Be merciful, and judge not, so **that you can escape** judgment. The standards of judgment that you apply to others, **will be the** same ones that are eventually applied to you.

"One day I hopped in a taxi and we took off for the airport. We were driving in the right lane when suddenly a car jumped out of a parking space right in front of us. My taxi driver slammed on his brakes, skidded, and missed the other car by just inches! The driver of the other car whipped his head around and started yelling at us. My taxi driver just smiled and waved at the guy. And I mean he was really friendly. So I asked, "Why did you just do that? This guy almost ruined your car and sent us to the hospital!" This is when my taxi driver taught me what I now call 'The Law of the Garbage Truck.' He explained that many people are like garbage trucks. They run around full of garbage, full of frustration, full of anger, and full of disappointment. As their garbage piles up, they need a place to dump it and sometimes they'll dump it on you. Don't take it personally. Just smile, wave, wish them well, and move on. Don't take their garbage and spread it to other people at work, at home, or on the streets. The bottom line is that successful people do not let garbage trucks take over their day. Life's too short to wake up in the morning with regrets, so... 'Love the people who treat you right. Pray for the ones who don't.'

Life is ten percent what you make it and ninety percent how you take it'
-Maryrose Melito Kemp

"Don't give holy things to depraved men. Don't give pearls to swine. They will trample the pearls and turn and attack you."
-JESUS OF NAZARETH: Matthew 7:6 (78 AD)

CHAPTER 33

▼

"If you love only those who love you, what good is that? If you are
friendly only to your friends, how are you different from anyone
else? But you are to be perfect, even as our father in Heaven is perfect. God
sends his sunlight to both evil and good, and his rain to
fall on the just and the unjust."
-JESUS OF NAZARETH: Matthew 5:45-47 (78 AD)

*"All illness comes from sin. This everyone must take, whether they
like it or not; it comes from sin—whether it be of body, mind, or of
soul. "Many times innocent people's sufferings are the results of
someone else's sins. However, there are probably a greater number
of people who suffer because of their own poor choices. Sin causes anxiety.
Anxiety weakens the immune system, and this in turn leads to illness."*
-Edgar Cayce & Mark Salvatore Pitifer

"Bad things happen when you're bad."
-Leigh Ann Pitifer

Judas and Adolf traveled back to the storefront on the corner of 77th Street
and Broadway called "Wings." This is where the prophet and his messenger were last spotted together.

Judas looks up and down the street, "The report I received said that the
two targets were last seen heading down Broadway."

"That's a big help." Adolf snaps sarcastically at Judas. "They could be
anywhere in the city by now."

Judas nods, "That's true, but we might get lucky. The homeless man,
Nino, was last seen walking south on Broadway. I say before we look any-

where else, we take a little flight downtown." Adolf agrees and the two begin their search.

Demons have the ability to remain invisible or to take on a human or animal appearance. They can also walk, run or fly. Judas and Adolf took on invisible forms and flew south on Broadway in search of Nino and Pitt. They flew in silence, but as they approached Times Square, Adolf began to speak.

Adolf smiles evilly, "I love this type of assignment. It reminds me of my days in the military. Satan will be in a good mood when we have successfully completed this mission. We should be up for some good R&R."

"If we are successful, that is." Judas interjects.

Adolf sneers. "What are you talking about? These two unstable souls are no match for the likes of us! We are mighty demonic warriors cloaked with the powers of evil. We will grind them up and sift them like wheat. I cannot wait to torture them and their conspirators when we get them back to our home sweet hell."

Judas shakes his head in disgust, "Adolf, you are one of the most miserable souls I have ever encountered in all my years of existence."

Adolf scowls, "What, you think you are better than me because I enjoy this kind of stuff? I don't know why Satan puts up with you and your "better than thou" attitude. There were many soldiers in my German army that thought it was wrong to exterminate the Jews. However, they still carried out my orders, which makes them, in some ways, worse than I was. At least I was not a hypocrite. I believed in what I was doing. Souls like you are cowards, Judas. You and and your kind are the blamers of the world. Your entire existence is a disgraceful one. We do the same work, you and I, and that makes us equal partners."

Judas frowns, "No Adolf. That's where you are wrong. I do this work to keep from going to that God-forsaken place any sooner than I have to. I may be sentenced to Hell, but I still do God's work."

Adolf smirks, "Judas! Stop deluding yourself. You are responsible for sending countless souls to Hell and the outer darkness. How can you possibly think that you are helping God in any way? You, like me, are God's enemy. He hates us, and when the Great Game is over, He will torture us for the rest of eternity. You pathetic soul. You probably think somewhere in the back of your mind that God still cares for you in some way. Why don't you wake up and smell what you've been shoveling? You look down on me, but at least I know where I stand and whom I serve. Satan used you on earth and he's still using you now. Rationalize all you will, Judas, but you are nothing more than a demon. You are an officer in Satan's Army, and sentenced to an eternity in Hell."

Judas is stung by Hitler's words, "You are right in all regards except one, Adolf, and this is the difference between you and me. You send souls to Hell because you enjoy it. You want the admiration of Satan and this is what drives you. I send souls to Hell with a heavy heart because these souls, like me, are not worthy to be citizens in the Kingdom of Forever. So, in my own way, I am helping to purify Heaven. I am helping God by preventing people who are evil from committing more and more evil. They live lifetime after lifetime and they learn nothing! 99 out of 100 times, they come back through purgatory and are worse off than they were in their previous lives, and so the final state of the soul is almost always worse. As God snatches the pure in spirit to Heaven whenever the opportunity presents itself, so too do I cast the evil in spirit to Hell so that they can no longer lead any more souls astray. I care nothing about Satan's admiration for me. I now serve God only because I know his way is good. I have no hope for salvation, but at least when I am finally cast into that miserable sea of anguish, I will know that until that time came, **I did what I could for my God and my King. Not because I was going to be rewarded, but because I know in my heart it is the right thing to do.**"

They fly for miles in silence, and then Adolf starts again.

Adolf salivates like a hungry wolf, "Look at all of those souls milling about the highways and byways of this wretched city. They look like nothing more than a large hill of ants. It disgusts me to even be around them."

Judas shakes his head in dismay, "Why do you hate them so much?"

Adolf snears, "Because they are weak, because they ..."

Judas excited, "Adolf! Look over near that church on the corner of East 10th and Broadway. Does that look like our targets?"

Adolf smiles, "Very good, Judas. Let's move in for a closer look."

As Adolf and Judas move in on their targets, Pitt and Nino sit on the steps of a church for a couple of minutes so Nino can rest his feet and take some aspirin.

"The bible says you're only supposed to hate the devil and love everyone else. My name is Ruth May and I hate the Devil."
-Barbara Kingsolver (Ruth May Posionwood Bible: for Nina)

"The path of the Godly leads to life. So why fear death?"
-Proverbs: 12:28

CHAPTER 34

▼

"For what shall it profit a man, if he shall gain the whole world,
and lose his own soul? Or what shall a man give in exchange for his soul?"
-JESUS OF NAZARETH/Mark 8:36-37 (57 AD)

"What is the use in saying that you have faith and are good Christians,
Muslims, Jews, Hindus, Buddhists, and so on, if you are not proving it by
helping others. Will that kind of faith save anyone? It isn't enough just
to have faith. You must also do good to prove that you have it. Faith that
doesn't show itself by good works is no faith at all, it is dead and useless. So
you see, a person is saved by what they do as well as what they believe."
-James 2: 12-24 (I added Muslims, Jews, Hindus, Buddhists and so on.)

"Let's sit here for a moment," Nino says, a little breathless. "My boots may
be shining, but they're still old boots and my feet are killing me. I just have
to take a couple of aspirin and I will be alright."

Pitt worried, "Are you sure you are going to be able to make it all the
way up to the George Washington Bridge?"

Nino reassures Pitt, "Oh, sure. I have to do this every day. I especially
like to stop at this church. They always have a passage from the Bible or a
thought provoking statement up on their marquee. I usually just sit here for
a couple of minutes, take my aspirin, think about what's written, and
head out again. Go on over there and read to me what it says today."

Pitt reads from the marquee, "You were gone astray like lost sheep, but
now you have returned to the Shepherd and guardian of your souls."

Nino comments, "That's pretty much speaking to what we have to do."

"What?" Asks Pitt.

Nino makes clear, "We have to paint such a beautiful picture of Heaven that people will start to be interested in getting there. Once they are interested in getting to Heaven, they will return, or find for the first time, the shepherd and guardian of their souls. Jesus showed the world the path that leads to Heaven. In the same way as a good shepherd leads his sheep to water and food, our shepherd leads us to the Kingdom of Forever."

Pitt begins to invision what he must do. "So, what I have to do is write a book, make a movie, and write music that will make people want to go to Heaven," Pitt reaffirms. In his mind, he is already picturing how he will go about this—and who will play him in the movie.

Nino nods, "That's right. If people start to think about how great our Heavenly paradise truly is, then they are going to start working harder to make sure they get there. Jesus gave us the hope and the way to get back home. When Jesus came to earth he had most of the same problems we all face. However, his primary objective was to make it back to Heaven himself, which he did."

Pitt clarifies, "The message being, that this is the way to Heaven. You must live as I have lived. God knows it's difficult, if not impossible, to live a perfect sin-free life. What I believe is most important to him is that we try. That's all I'm doing, Nino. I'm just trying to get to Heaven."

Nino agrees, "Me too. Now, let's get moving. We have to get to that bridge. I just got this feeling that if we make it to that bridge, our mission is going to be successful. I feel it in my heart and soul."

"Then why not just get on a subway right now and go straight there?"

Nino smirks, "Because, Pitt, I haven't told you and shown you all that I feel I need to. When I have, believe me, we will get on the train and speed up this trip. Don't forget, Pitt, this is my final walk through what has been my home for nearly thirty years. So, while I know that I must get to the GWB, I still want to take my time for your sake and for mine."

They continue walking north on Broadway. They pause for a moment on the corner of 12th Street and Broadway to admire the first full view of the Empire State Building.

Nino looks up, "Isn't that a powerful sight, the way that building cuts right through the sky?"

Pitt stares in awe, "It sure is. I always liked the Empire State Building. There is just something special about the way it sits in the middle of all the other buildings, yet stands out as different and distinct."

Nino agrees, "Kind of like Jesus, huh? There are a lot of other buildings in the world, just like there are lots of other religions in the world. Who dared to come up in the midst of us all and gradually rise above all others that had come before him? Pointing with his words and deeds towards Heaven, just like the Empire State Building points like an arrow to Heaven. It's compelling us to keep our heads to the sky."

Pitt wonders, "Nino, how does God feel about all the religions of the world? Does he like some better than others, or does he dislike certain ones?"

"I asked that question and I was shown a passage in the Heavenly Bible."

"The Heavenly Bible? Is that like a normal Bible?" Pitt asks,

Nino explains, "No. It is a book that contains all the truly holy and wise scriptures from every religion in the world. The existence of this Heavenly Bible is in-and-of-itself the answer to your question, in that all religions are represented. However, there was one particular passage that was pointed out to me by two delightful souls named David and Harriett. These souls were Jehovah Witnesses during the Great Game, and like all true Jehovah Witnesses they know their Bible inside and out"

Pitt agrees, "You got that right! Nobody researches the Bible as extensively as the Jehovah Witnesses. So what was this passage they showed you?"

"They turned to a portion of the book that was taken from the Bahgavad Gita and they said … Well, here let me read it to you."

Pitt laughs, "You stole a page out of the heavenly Bible?!"

Nino grins, "No they gave it to me. There is no need to steal in Forever; if you want something all you have to do is ask."

"That's awesome. Ok let me hear it."

Nino reads the verse, "**I despiseth not the worship of the humble and the simple souls, whom in their loving devotion present me with flowers, fruits, water, incense, or any gift that they think I will enjoy. I accept and enjoy all such offerings from these my children, and in the spirit of the gift do I accept it. All sacrifices accepted I them, even in the spirit of the offer-**

ing, not in the value of the gift. Therefore, whatever you do, whether it be eating, giving, sacrificing, performance of ceremonies or rites, or being kind to your neighbor do these things as an earnest offering to me. By offering up to me a life of kindness and love shalt thou be delivered, and set free from the bonds of action and consequence. I see my children of the world, and all living beings with an equal eye, and without partiality. There is no child or religion more dear to me than another. Truly I love all of my children the same. Those who worship me with devotion, truly find the path that leads to my heart, and I am in them and they are in me. Even an evil sinner who turns to me with an undivided heart shall not escape becoming virtuous, and he shall obtain the gift of peace, love, and paradise that is given to all of my loved ones. So remember, my children, this earth is nothing more than a temporary home. Control your bodily urges, which people call the avenues of the senses. Concentrate your mind upon your inner self. Know and worship me in all that you do, and realize that the life you live is your religion. Repeat in the silence of your soul the mystic syllable "Aum". Think about me, without distraction, and you shall come into my presence, yes, you will be blended into me. I will live in you, and you will live in me, and in so doing you will reach your supreme goal."

Pitt's heart is warmed, "That was beautiful. It's always how I imagined God would feel, but how am I going to remember all of that?"

"Here, take my copy. You'll need it much more than I will."

Pitt smiles,"Thank you my brother, I knew I could count on you."

They continued onward to Union Square Park. Nino takes in the views, "I always liked this little park. There is just something quaint about this part of town, something a little softer and warmer than some of the other parks in the city," Nino says as they take in the smells and sounds of the farmers' market at 14th Street.

Pitt remembers, "I was in this park once with my sister, Sharla. We went to see Molly Ringwald in a play called "How I Learned to Drive." It was cool, because she took some pictures with us and talked to us for a couple of minutes after the show. The theater is right over there on East 15th Street. It's a tiny place, but there's not a bad seat in the house. We came late and got tickets for $15. You can't beat that! That Molly is some great actress. I really enjoyed that afternoon. I especially enjoyed spending time with Sharla. I really miss her. I don't get to see her that much anymore."

"Why's that?" Asks Nino.

Pitt looks sad, "Ah, she moved here, fell in love with this guy, and then they got married and moved to Texas. My little sister …"

"Get back to Molly for a moment. What did you think of her? How did she strike you?"

Pitt smiles, "Like I said, she was friendly and nice."

Nino continues, "I understand that, but what about underneath the surface? Did you pick up on any vibes? Come on, counselor, what was your gut feeling?"

Pitt thinks for a moment and then responds, "That she was sad. I don't know why. She didn't do or say anything that would indicate that she was sad, I just remember feeling that. And it is strange that you would ask me about it.… Why did you ask me?"

Nino explains, "I just wondered, you being a counselor, if you picked up on that. It has been my experience that most of the famous people I have met have this underlying sadness that I feel when I meet them. Tell me counselor, why do you think that is?"

Pitt gives his analysis, "I think it's because they have found out what the ordinary people don't know, that being rich and famous does not take away life's problems. It actually can multiply them. Fame becomes its own little prison. The famous are all trying to get out, and the ordinary are all trying to get in, or at the very least, get a little peek."

Nino smiles, "Very insightful. Now, answer me this, why do you think there is a desire to be famous?"

Pitt looks melancholy, "I used to think it would be cool for everyone to know me and like me, but as I have gotten older, I look at things differently."

"How so?" Nino asks.

Pitt clarifies, "Well, like you were saying earlier, I don't think that the adoration of strangers is something to be sought after. I had a bit part in a Sly Stallone film one time, and I would sit off to the side and listen to the endless stream of fans and actors come to him and talk to him. They thought they knew him based on the parts he had played in his movies, but in reality, they knew nothing about him. What a sad spot to be in. He told me, when I ran into him late on the set one night, that he would rather be where I was, an unknown actor trying to climb his way to the top. He said that is where the fun was. I try to see fame for what it really is now. Nothing more than an illusion. A movie role may give you a brief escape from reality, but only a brief one. Maybe it's just sour grapes, but I don't think so."

Nino smiles with the quiet realization that his messenger has been well chosen. "It's not sour grapes my man, it's wisdom. Satan dangles fame and fortune in front of our eyes from the time we are tiny. We sit there in the movie theaters, or watching TV and he whispers in our ears that becoming a star will take away all our problems and make us truly happy. What a Crock of shit. It's like if you win an Oscar you'll never get hemorrhoids again." Nino chuckles at his own joke. "Get your name up in lights he says, and you'll be remembered forever. Big deal. First of all, it's a lie, because people can't remember what they had for dinner last week, let alone forever. Second of all, what value is it to be remembered for portraying some part or character that does not represent who you really are? Remember this Pitt: Broadway lights may glisten, but their heat won't keep you warm. Real love is the only thing that can do that. True unconditional love, in this life and the afterlife, is the only treasure worth trying to obtain. But you can only obtain love by giving love. This means that you have to go out and live in the real world. The things you do on stage or in front of a camera may get you notoriety, but you'll never be truly loved, or for that matter, truly remembered."

Pitt wonders, "Nino, speaking of being remembered, I take a lot of photographs and video tapes. Is there anything like that in Heaven? I mean, you know, like memories of our earthly lives?"

Nino nods, "Every piece of your life is recorded, every word that you speak and every deed that you do. From your first step to your last breath, not one moment is missed. Do you know what all those distant stars really are? They are the lights of our relatives' digital video disc cameras."

Pitt is totally taken in. "Really?! I can't believe it! That's amazing!" "Man, oh man, are you gullible!" Nino laughs. This is gonna be a trip."

Pitt laughs, too. "You little skunk! Hey, it sounded believable."

Nino chuckles, "Part of what I said is the truth. The stars are not the lights of video cameras, but your life, every word and every deed is recorded and stored in two forms, book and film."

Pitt excited, "So everybody's life story is secured for all time?"

Nino nods, "Not only is it secured, but you can make all the pictures you want to hang in your mansion. The pictures are absolutely beautiful, and you can really capture every special moment that you have ever experienced. You can even create your own personal highlight film."

Pitt is ecstatic, "Boy oh boy! Talk about your home movies. That is such a relief to me. I've always tried to capture life's moments, and it's very frustrating because many times I miss them, or the flash doesn't go off. You know the typical things."

Nino grins, "You know how it's kind of a joke down here when people talk about having to watch other peoples' home movies? Well, in Forever it is a very pleasant pastime. It's a big part of visiting and story telling about years gone by, and then being able to call up in a moment the very piece of life you are talking about!"

Pitt is in awe. This has truly sparked his interest. "So, if you're telling me a story about a thrilling basketball game that you won, we could sit there and kind of watch the memory together?"

Nino pulls Pitt close to him, "Not only could we watch it. We could step into the moment. You and I together could live any real life moment that we want. And when you are done you will feel like you lived it yourself. It's amazing."

Pitt is truly baffled. "What do you mean we could step into the moment?"

Nino explains, "I know it sounds strange, but those are the best words I can think of to describe the experience. Movies in Heaven are not merely watched. They are alive and they stimulate all of your senses."

As they continue walking Pitt notices one of many new gated communities that have sprung up in the city, and across the country.

Pitt point to the entrance, "Nino, what do you think about these new gated communities. They seem pretty cool don't they?"

Nino frowns, "They seem nice, but I was told that they are dangerous."

Pitt scuffs, "Dangerous? and living on a normal New York City block is safe!"

Nino clarifies, "I don't mean it like that. These gated communities seem wonderful at first glance, but some of the newer ones are going to a cashless system."

"I heard about that somewhere, what does that mean?"

Nino clarifies, "The citizens are getting a number code invisibly implanted into their hand or forehead, and a laser scanner lets them buy groceries, go to the movies, and so on."

"What's bad about that?" Asks Pitt.

Nino continues, "People who don't belong to their communities can't even get in without a code, and if they do come as a guest they won't be allowed to do any business in the community. I was told that in time these gated communities will grow in size and number until eventually they will become giant cities in this country, and around the world. Don't you see Pitt these gated, cashless cities will set the stage for the coming of the Anti-Christ. Remember what Jesus said? The number of the beast is the number of a man, and his number is 666."

Pitt catches on "The Bible also speaks about people who refuse to wear the mark of the beast on their hands or their forehead will not be allowed to by our sell goods."

Nino nods, "That's right, eventually many of these gated cities will discourage people of faith from living in them, and the people of faith will be forced to start their own communities. As the world becomes more secular and atheistic the faithful communities will lose their power and appeal. And when this happens …"

Pitt jumps in "They will have to renounce their faith, in order to by and sell in the new cashless society of the future."

Nino looks sad, "Now you see the danger. The Anti-Christ will soon rise to power, but not many will see him for what he truly is. He will be popular, handsome, and well spoken. He will appear to be a unifying leader, who wants world peace, but he is in reality the prince of all wars and strife."

Nino and Pitt walked for awhile in silence. They began talking again as they took a once-through the park heading towards East 17th Street. Nino leads Pitt to a giant Barnes and Noble book store.

"What are we going in here for?" Pitt asked, worried they may waste precious time.

Nino lets out a tired sigh."I've got to cool off a little bit, and there are some things in here that I want to show you."

Pitt smiles, "That's fine with me. This is my kind of place."

Nino and Pitt walk into the store and head to the religion section, never suspecting that Adolf and Judas are close behind.

THE JUDAISM P.O.J.
WHAT IS HURTFUL TO YOU, DO NOT TO YOUR FELLOW MAN. THIS IS THE ENTIRE LAW; ALL THE REST IS COMMENTARY.

"Beware of false teachers who come disguised as harmless sheep, but are wolves and will tear you apart. You can detect them by the way that they act, just as you can identify a tree by its fruit. You never need confuse grapevines with thorn bushes or figs with thistles. Trees that produce delicious fruit never produce an inedible kind. Don't let anyone mislead you. For there will be many false messiahs and false prophets who will do wonderful miracles that would deceive if possible, even God's own children. No one, not even the Angels in Heaven, nor I myself, knows the day or the hour that these things will happen; only God knows. Stay alert. Be on the watch for my return, and don't let me find you sleeping. If anyone tells you that they have found the Messiah pay no attentionto them. When I return you won't have to search for me. Keep a sharp eye, and you will see me coming in the clouds with great power and glory. As lighting flashes across the sky from east to west so shall my return be illuminated for all to see."

-JESUS OF NAZARETH (Matthew 7:15-20 & Mark 13) (AD 57)

CHAPTER 35

▼

*"The man who allows his mind to dwell closely on the objects of
sense, becomes so wrapped up in the objects of his contemplation
that he creates an attachment which binds him to them. From this
attachment ariseth desire, from desire springeth passion, from passion cometh folly
and recklessness, from these proceed loss of memory, and from loss of memory cometh
loss of reason, and thus he
loseth all."*
-KRISHNA/THE BHAGAVAD GITA (3,137 BC)

**"The proper Muslim attitude is neither to renounce this world,
nor to be so engrossed in it as to forget the spiritual future."
-THE HOLY QUR'AN/Surah 2, Note 224,
(ABDULLAH YUSUF ALI) (600 AD)**

Inside the bookstore, Pitt follows Nino up to the religion section. Once there, Nino pulls out a tiny paper back book called <u>Wisdom of the Desert,</u> and he and Pitt sit down at one of the reading tables.

"That a good book?" Pitt asks.

"It's a very good book. It's called <u>Wisdom of the Desert</u> it's a book written by Thomas Merton. It is a collection of stories that were told to him by Christian monks who left behind the cities of the pagan world in which they lived, and sought to become one with God."

Pitt takes the book from Nino, "I really like Thomas Merton, but I've never heard of this book."

Nino nods, "Yes, he's very good. The tiny stories in this book are very insightful and entertaining. There is one in particular that I want to share with you, because it relates to an obstacle that you must overcome."

"What's that?" Pitt asks.

Nino looks serious, "Your lust for women."

Mark's shame is apparent when he speaks. "It's true. It's one of my biggest shortcomings. But, I've never committed adultery. Shit, I never even kissed another woman since I've been married."

"I'm not saying that you did, and I'm not saying that you are any different from most healthy, heterosexual males on the planet. However, the facts are these, if that angel didn't intervene the other night at the China Club, you would have done more than just kiss that girl, and you would have ruined your life and permanently marked your soul."

Pitt tries to rationalize, "Nino, I like to walk the line, and I'll admit that I sometimes dance a little close to the flame, but that's as far as it goes."

Nino purses his lips, "That's what I'm talking about. You can't keep playing that game, because it's a dangerous one. You're messing around with one of the most powerful forces on the planet. You're like a kid playing catch with a hand grenade saying to himself, 'I know what I'm doing ... the pin won't come out.'"

Pitt looks down, "You're right. I was in a bad spot the other night. To be honest with you, I was thinking, "How much can I do, without really being guilty?""

Nino continues, "What would Jesus say to you?' Go ahead, Pitt—have some fun! As long as you don't have sex, everything is cool.'"

Pitt nods, "I know he says that if you look at a woman with lust in your eye, then you have already committed adultery with her in your heart. But I've always thought that he was just saying that because he knows how weak we are, and he is trying to prevent us from getting ourselves into trouble."

Nino somewhat angry, "So, what if he is? You think that you're so unique that the King's counsel doesn't apply to you?! ... Your pride in who you are and what you are capable of will cause you to be successful in many areas of life. But spiritual pride, the kind of pride that tells you those words apply to all other men but not to you, can bring you down." Nino's tone softens, "Hey, Pitt, I don't mean to preach to you, because you truly are one self-disciplined individual. You may have it together 99.9 percent of the time, but if you continue along this path, someday you are gonna fall, and on that day, for one torrid moment of passion, you may exchange all that you've worked so hard to accomplish in your life. You could possibly even lose your soul."

Pitt ashamed, "You are right, Nino. I've struggled with it all my life. I'm just one of those hopeless romantics. What can I say? It's in my genes."

Nino chuckles, "You are not a hopeless romantic. You are a hopeful romantic, and therein lies the problem. I want to read to you a short passage from this book. **There was a famous Christian monk who left the city and moved out into the barren lands to become one with God. The monk had been in the desert for over twenty years, and he believed he had overcome the temptations of this earth. It just so happened that one day a beautiful woman of easy virtue overheard some young men talking about how holy this monk was. As she listened to them talk, Satan influenced her to say "How much will you give me if I can seduce this famous monk of yours?" A wager was made and this very beautiful temptress went out to find the monk. She arrived at his house pretending to be lost. She told him that she had been separated from her party and she was afraid. The monk, being moved with pity and compassion, said, 'You can stay out on the porch, but you cannot come into my house.' As night fell, she knocked on the door again, this time pretending to weep. She told the monk that she was afraid that a lion would come to eat her, and she convinced him to let her in the house. As soon as she stepped into his room, Satan began to fill his heart with lust. To remove the lustful thoughts, the monk would hold his hand over the flame of his lantern. As the woman undressed and began her seduction, he had to hold his hand over the flame longer and longer. Although his skin was burning, he did not feel it. That's how strong that fire of lust burned inside of him. This went on all evening long. The woman was so taken aback by his behavior that she slipped into a state of shock. When her friends came in the morning to see if she had been successful, the monk told them what happened. 'This evil temptress has cost me all of my fingers.' And indeed, all that remained of his fingers were charred stubs....** Pitt, this monk had to burn his fingers off to keep from being seduced. That's how strong the force is. So please, don't play with the fire of lust. Don't make the Devil's job any easier than it already is."

Pitt agrees, "I won't forget this story Nino, but it's still going to be hard to kill my romantic side. I mean, I don't look at a woman and say 'hey, I'd like to have sex with her.' If a female moves me physically and mentally, then I want to connect with her. It doesn't happen to me very often, but when it does, it's a strong pull. It's like I want to let her feel what I feel. I want to make her swoon. Hey, Nino, I'll do my best, but I know it's not going to die easily."

Nino explains, "I don't think God would want you to kill it altogether. In fact, I don't think you can. The monk tried for twenty years to kill his romantic passions, and all he really did out in the desert was hide from them. At least you are honest enough with yourself to recognize who you are and what your weaknesses can be. Pitt, God is the father of love and romance. He knows what you feel, and I can tell you this, if you can refrain from lust for this short interval called life, you will drink from the cup of romance to your heart's content. Your longing for romance is natural. Love, romance and enchanted evenings are a very big part of the Kingdom of Forever. So, don't try to eliminate your romantic passion. Try instead to find ways to re-channel it. Follow me, Romeo." Nino leads Pitt through a labyrinth of books.

Pitt stops and picks up a hard cover <u>ESPN Magazine</u> that features the 2020 Olympics. "Hey Nino look at this." Pitt points excitedly to the front cover of the book and shows it to Nino. "Fiona Thompson, the pride of Geneva!"

Nino smiles. "Fiona's from your home town? Boy you folks must be proud of her. A 16 year old gold medalist and world record holder all in one! What an amazing accomplishment."

Pitt smiles, "Yeah that was awesome. Her mother Dee Dee Tuxill Thompson was a great hurdler in high school and college, Fiona just took it to the next level."

"Hey, that's the most you can hope for as a parent."

"No doubt about it…. You know, Fiona's Olympic coach Mike Canali is also from Geneva." Pitt shows Nino a picture of him from the book. "He was my high school coach. We had one of the most dominant track teams in school history. We averaged over 105 points per meet! He and his buddy Wes Kubacki were the best track coaches I've ever seen. It's really fitting that they made it all the way to the Olympics."

Nino smiles, "Well it just goes to show you Pitt, you don't have to be from Hollywood or New York City, to make it big. You just gotta have talent, heart, and faith."

"That's what I have always believed." Says Pitt.

They continue to weave through the various isles. Nino stops to comment about a poster that promotes safe sex, which makes him scowl. **"Safe sex for teenagers! What a crock of shit. That's like putting out literature on how to safely play with dynamite."**

Pitt laughs out loud. "You're right, man. It's a ridiculous concept. They should be teaching abstinence. Since nobody ever ends up marrying their middle school or high school sweethearts anyway, it doesn't make sense to let any of these relationships get to a sexually serious level. After all the kiss is the greatest of all God's inventions!"

Nino gives Pitt a high five, "You've got that right."

Pitt frowns, "Our modern generation really is missing the boat on relationships in general. Everything is just so sexually charged, their music, their movies, and especially their attitudes about the opposite sex. The other day this girl came into my office and said "I just love this new boy Tonito! He's so hot!" I said honey, I'm not picking on you but here's my problem with what you just said. You're telling me that you love someone that you don't even know, based on his looks. **I could put chocolate frosting on a card board box and it will look like a delicious cake, until you cut into it.** These young kids aren't very good about finding out what's on the inside. Out word apperence is trumping the beauty of the soul. They don't care if their personalities are compatible. All they do is go straight to the physical. I had this popular athlete tell me the other day that he very rarely kisses the girls he goes out on dates with, but, he bragged, I get all the sex I need."

Nino shakes his head in disgust, "That's sickening. All he's doing is using these girls. And the sad thing is that their letting themselves be used. It's like they've got no standards at all. As long as the guy is good looking and popular there gonna serve it up. Can you imagine losing your virginity to a creep like that? You've given this guy everything you have to give, and you're not even being kissed! The sad thing is that even the females are not valuing their virginity any more."

Pitt nods, "It's heartbreaking when you really think about it. I mean, I guess in some ways boys have always been on the prowl. But back in my day, girls would just give it away like candy on Halloween. You had to, and you wanted to, do a lot of kissing. These girls made you court them. Then after many-

many dates, they might let you get a little touch. A little sniff of the promised land. And that's all you need…. It's all you need."

Nino laughs and nods, "Your crazy, but your telling it like it is."

Pitt continues, "Hey I'm just being honest. I never have, and never will take anything that a woman wants to give me for granted. Those were real special moments to me. I was always grateful, and the girl's virtue was never compromised."

Nino agrees, "That's how it should be."

Pitt serious, "I never looked at a woman like she was just an object. My mother told me that I should always treat the girls that I dated in the same way that I would want someone to treat my sister or someday my daughter. She also told me to save myself for marriage. So I was never really looking to lose my virginity. I'd say that most of my friends felt the same way, and you know what? I don't think we missed out on anything. My father used to say, "You be careful what you're looking for out there Markie, because you might just find it." You know something else, Nino?"

"What's that?"

"I never wanted someone to be able to say they slept with me. The very thought of it made me cringe. In my opinion, virginity should be held on to for as long as you possibly can. It should be seen as a symbol of honor, and something all boys and girls should take pride in."

"Is that what you teach your students?" Nino asks.

Pitt nods, "You bet your neck I do! I tell them that is how I lived, and if I can do it, so can they."

"That's cool. But what do you say to the kid who has already lost his or her virginity?"

Pitt spreads his index and middle fingers wide and then closes them together,"I say if you've lost it then take it back."

Nino is confused by this concept. "Take it back?!"

Pitt explains, "That's right. I tell them, starting today, from now on, you go back to living like a virgin. You keep your legs crossed and your zipper up. When it comes to the opposite sex, you can share your mind, but not your behind!"

Nino laughs, "You're alright, Pitt. Speaking of talking to kids, what's your approach? Do you psychoanalyze them or what?"

Pitt clarifies, "Nah, and even if I wanted to, there's not enough time in the day. I'll let them tell their life stories for a few sessions, but I won't allow them to wallow in the past very long. My approach is **"Hey, there may have been some terrible, hurtful things that happened to you in the past, but there is nothing we can do about that.** They have to be brought to the realization that nothing we can do or say will ever change what has happened in the past. The most we can do is try and diminish the importance it currently plays in your present. **How are you allowing something that happened along time ago to continue to hurt you, and negatively effect your behavior and current relationships on a daily basis?"** I try to focus on what the person can start doing today that will make life better. They also have to learn that coming to counseling will not change some third party. **The only person you truly have the power to change is yourself.** Behavioral change, believe me, doesn't come easy even in the most motivated clients. It's a long process. We look at their current life problems and goals and determine what they have the power to do to make changes, and what they are going to have to learn to live with, at least temporarily. We come up with a plan of attack, and from that moment on I support them in their efforts. For many of my kids, I am the first stable male role model they have ever encountered. Children need to have someone to love and believe in them. They learn over time that no matter what they do, I will always be there for them. I'll stand and support them when they are right, and I'll verbally, and if necessary physically jack them up if they're wrong. However, no matter how heinous their crime, I will never reject them."

"How do the kids respond when you have to come down on them?" Nino asks.

Pitt continues, "They accept it, because I have never judged them. I give them a hundred pounds of sugar for every teaspoon of vinegar. We play games, eat lunch together, and when a problem occurs, we talk about it. I call my method **CONTACT UNTIL CRISIS (C.U.C)**. I don't believe a school counselor should get a child thinking about a home related issue, unless the child brings it up. My role is to help them if a home related problem starts to negatively affect their school day. My door is always open to them, and they all have my home phone number. The bottom line is that they know I really care about them, and they know I walk my talk."

Nino wonders, "Do you teach them about God?"

Pitt pauses for a moment. He wishes he could teach his clients about God everyday. "I work in a public school system, so I have to be careful about how I bring up issues about God. It's a shame to, because their starving for God. Many of the children I work with are very depressed. They have no hope, nothing to believe in. They come from miserable situations, and the see no light at the end of the tunnel. How is a kid gonna believe in so God that they can't, when they're own parents don't even show them unconditional love?'

Nino frowns, "I know, it is awful how our country has moved away from God. But hey, it sounds like at least your trying save them."

Pitt brightens, "It can be done, even in the public school. **The State law says as long as you don't do anything to promote or degrade a specific religion, then you can speak of God in a general sense**. I don't think that anyone in public education has the right to force their religion on their students. And I also don't believe that anyone should be allowed to talk negatively about religion. What I do is share my faith. I tell them this is what I believe and it works for me. My business card says **Believe in God, Believe in yourself, and Never give up!** I tell kids and parents that these are the rules I live by. I make it very clear that I am not saying in any way that I am an authority and that they have to accept my faith. I explain that these rules have helped me all of my life, and maybe they will help them too. A couple of weeks ago a friend of mine told me that her 9 year old daughter was starting to doubt the existence of God, and that she was asking her a lot of tough questions that she had no answers for."

Nino raises his eye brows, "So what did you tell her?"

Pitt smiles, "I said, the next time you and Phi-pha go into Wegmans, take her to the bakery and let her pick out her favorite doughnut. As soon as she bites into it, ask her if she believes if there is a baker or not. When she answers yes, point out how much more beautiful and complex a human being is compared to a doughnut. **If it takes a baker to bake, then it must take a creator to create!** How do you like that poetry. Shakespeare ain't got nothing on me!"

Nino laughs and teases Pitt, "Yeah, Shakespere Ain't got nuttin on you. That's funny." Pitt laughs at the irony of his statement, and Nino chuckles, but turns serious again, "You've got a good approach counselor. I wish there were more people like you working with our nation's children."

Pitt grins, "But not as an English teacher."

Nino laughs, "No, leave the poetery to Shakespere…. Hey speaking of great Poets." Nino walks and points. Pitt follows him back down the escalator to the poetry section of the store. He pulls out a book of poems called <u>Forbidden Fruit—Love Poems and Writings From The Garden of Marriage.</u>

Nino is pleased, "Ah yes, here it is. You are really going to relate to this, Pitt. All of the poems in this book are written by hopeless romantics, who just happen to be either married, in love with someone who is, or both."

Pitt gets a goofy smile on his face. "You read romantic poetry?"

Nino smirks, "Pitt, in my younger days—shit, in all my days, my imagination is romantically inclined. The difference between you and me is that you're married, which means you can look at all of these beautiful flowers."

Pitt laughs. "Tell me something I don't know!"

Nino hands the book to Pitt, "Most of the poems are written by an Italian poet named Johnny Theobaldi. He calls himself the gay caballero."

Pitt raises his eyebrows, "This guy is a gay poet?"

Nino smirks, "No, that's just what he calls himself. You know gay also means happy and carefree" Nino shakes his head and fakes disgust, "You'll love this stuff. Go ahead, turn to any page you want and read me the poem."

Pitt opens the book to a random page, "Here is one called The Sweetness of Slumber."

Nino recognizes the title and smiles, "Ah, yes that's a nice one. Go ahead and read it to me."

Pitt hesitates and looks around, "What if someone hears me reading you romantic poetry?"

Nino chuckles, and pushes Pitt, "Just read the poem chump."

Pitt grins and begins to read, "We tangoed upon slates of rock underneath the moon and stars. The classic music spun our souls as we ate crumbs of cake from Mars. The warm and steamy summer's air keeps all our petals warm. The innocence of youth returns, God's gift of solace from this storm. But alas I wake and reemerge from night times rosy haze. A dream of timeless moments, that I'll remember all my days…."

Nino sighs, "Isn't that nice."

Pitt agrees, "Yeah, he's good."

Nino grabs the book back from Pitt, and thumbs through the pages.

"Check this poem out. It's called Che Bellezza {The Flower of My Desire}. Here sit for a moment, and I'll read it to you:

"Che Bellezza … Grazie Dio. Serenely she …"

Pitt interrupts. "What's Kaybellerina gratzie dono mean?"

Nino can't stop laughing. "You call yourself Italian, and you don't even know the language!"

Pitt grins sheepishly, "I know how to swear in Italian and Puerto Rican, but that's it!"

Nino shakes his head faking dismay, "That's typical for your generation. Okay rookie, here you go. Che bellezza means what beauty, and grazie Dio means thank God. Sometimes when I'm walking through little Italy, I hear the old men say this when they see a beautiful girl walk by."

Pitt smiles. "Che bellezza. Grazie Dio. I like that. I'm gonna use that line. Okay, Mr. Poet, continue. No more interruptions I promise."

Nino clears his throat and starts to read, "From the very first time I saw her she has swirled in and out of my thoughts like some lovely maiden dancing through a sea of enchanted dreams. Her youthful radiance transforms my words into poetic clouds, and her voice, laughter, and scent move me to song. The moons light is magic once again, and in her presence my youth is restored. In this garden of life she is a rare, and very beautiful flower. How I long to caress her tender petals! Oh, to unhurriedly breathe in her seductive fragrance, and taste her sultry nectar … Oh, to be melted like wax and poured over the smoldering stones of her desires. But, alas, this is only a longing and a hope. For this flower is not mine to pick, nor am I hers to receive. God himself has placed a boundary between us. Forbidden fruits, it appears, still grow in the Garden of Eden. I stepped into this circle of gold on my own accord, and happy am I with the wife of my youth. And yet, why does my foolish heart at times remain troubled, and my mind confused. In my heart I truly feel content, but then why do I still on occasion walk about passion-crushed and lust-smitten as a school boy? My his starved for intimacy, and my soul longs for something much deeper than physical affection or sexual gratification. In the depth of my being I know that even if I were to drink from this forbidden cup, my heart's lips will remain parched. Oh, to discover that for which I truly thirst. I have shared my troubled heart with God, and in the midst of my passionate prayer I was raised up to the bosom of the Almighty. Can I ever truly capture the essence of my delight without eating the fruit for which I crave? Reveal to me my brother, a higher path that I may follow. Teach my soul how to truly inter mingle with that of another, without being drowned by the currant of lust, need, and possession. I hear your voice in the wind and it whispers … if you can refrain from picking that which is not yours in this life, your cup of passion will overflow in the next. In Heaven, you will be free to indulge every flower that you desire. For lust and need will be reformed into the ecstasy that comes from the well nourished soul.… I return to my real world, and contently wait for that next unexpected encounter that warms my heart, and satisfies my passions. She sails past me and the wind moves her long flowing hair across her body like waves falling on some distant romantic shore. I take in these moments, for these moments are all that I can have, and now all that I desire. I am now the grateful-giver reaching out to the thankful-receivers of the world. The hunger for the body has been replaced with the hope of touching the essence of their soul. A compliment. A smile. A dance. A nod of appreciation. I throw the bouquet, and hope that she will catch it, gracefully and gratefully. Allowing me to touch her, and love her in the only way that I am able—gently, and purely, soul to soul.

Che bellezza Grazie Dio."

Pitt smiles, "That's beautiful, Nino. He really hits the nail on the head."

Nino agrees, "Remember the wisdom of this poem. Being a married man, you have got to try to keep your relationships with other women from ever reaching a romantic plane. However, sometimes these things just happen. Feelings emerge for another person that you do not ask for. Let's face it, if the opportunity presented itself, there are many people that we could fall in love with on this planet. You just have to be smart enough to see the bigger picture."

"And that is?" Pitt asks.

Nino explains, "I know I may be repeating myself, but this is important. If you were to attempt to satisfy every romantic or sexual need that comes to your mind you would end up hurting a lot of people, including yourself. What will be possible in terms of intimate relationships in Forever, is impossible on earth. It is a thirst that can never be quenched!"

Pitt clarifies, "It's like you said before, I have to recognize that I will always have a sexual attraction for the opposite sex, but I have to learn that sex is not my ultimate desire. If I feel romantic feelings for another person, I should re-channel those feelings toward my wife."

Nino excited, "That's right! Save up that juice for her. That will keep your mojo strong, and your wife happy."

"My mojo?"

"Your sexual drive or prowess." Nino explains.

Pitt nods, "I gotcha. And then, if I still can't shake those feelings I can use what's left of my passionate energy to write a poem or a song."

Nino tips his imaginary cap, "Now your talking, just be careful about sharing that poem or song with the object of your affection."

Pitt puzzled, "Why, what harm can that do?"

Nino raises his eyebrows, "A song or a poem can warm another person's soul. Believe me when I tell you, if you romantically touch a woman's heart, you could go from the pursuer to the pursued in the blink of an eye. And if that happens, you might end up having to burn something off in order to escape, comprendi?"

Pitt laughing but turning serious, "I hear you, Nino. I guess I have to use discretion."

Nino scowls, "I'm serious Pitt. Don't be rationalizing away what I have to say to you on this matter. This is your Achilles heal, and satan will continually attack you from this angle. Never get involved with a woman who is having relationship problems. Don't flirt or anything! These souls are very needy and unstable. If you make a vulnerable woman swoon, your ass is in trouble. I'm not trying to preach to you Pitt, but if you want my advice I would avoid sharing your feelings with members of the opposite sex altogether."

Pitt hangs his head, "I'll try, but …"

Nino cuts him off, "I know what you're going to say. Easier said then done right?"

Pitt nods, "Exactly."

Nino thinks for a moment, "Ok, if you can't give it up all together at least do this. Only reach out to people that you feel are spiritually and morally on the same plain as you."

Pitt looks disappointed, "That really narrows it down, doesn't it?"

Nino continues, "That's right. I mean, if you think about it, why should it be any other way? We spiritual romantics must train ourselves to search for something deeper and more satisfying than sex. Never let your romantic energies move you to reach out to someone who is physically attractive but not spiritually on your level. This type of mistake can create a serious problem for you. You need to guard your heart. These special soul encounters, if they occur at all, should not happen very many times in your life. Don't rationalize your actions in regards to other women, analyze them. Ask your self honestly what is motivating your behavior. Is it lust? Is it alcohol induced? Do you really want to leave your wife and start a new relationship? Do you seek to possess this person? Or do you simply want to feel young again? Remember Pitt, the soul is not the body or the brain. Our souls live in these bodies for the short period called life, and the brain quite often desires things that are not in the best interest of the soul. It's your job to determine the root of your desire. Is it something that is good for the body and the soul, or is it something that is just good for the body? Sometimes you even have to trick your mind."

Pitt nods, "It think I know what you mean. Its like when I'm trying to lose weight I resort to what I call creative dieting. For example, if I'm craving pizza and wings, I will order a slice of pizza, and get an order of chicken wing sauce on the side to dip my crust in. It satisfies my craving for the wings, and I don't get any of the fat. You see, I trick my mind into thinking it really ate some wings."

Nino smiles, "That's a perfect example. However, when it comes to memebers of the opposite sex I can still forsee some problems with this approach."

Pitt smirks, "Really, like what?"

Nino raises his eyebrows, "Well for one thing I'm not sure what part of your body you'll be you calling your crust, not to mention where you dip it!"

Pitt laughs, "I hear ya … I do. But I do believe it can work. You know a dance here, a sniff there."

Nino shakes his head in fake disgust, "Pitt your to much, but here's the bottom line. **If you want to lead an extraordinary life, then do not settle for that which is ordinary, or common.** Always seek the higher path in all that you do. **Don't just play marriage, stay marriage!** Understand? Always think family first

Pitt. Always!.... Don't let anyone or anything jeopardize your family or your reputation. Do I need to speak any further on this subject, rookie?"

Pitt smiling, but serious. "Nope, you have made your point my brother. No more rationalizing my romanticizing. I see it for what is now Nino. Those countless possible relationships that Satan dangles in front of us are all just walks down different dead end streets. They lead to no where."

Nino looks worried, "Actually they do lead to somewhere Pitt, but not any place you, or I'd like to be...."

As they walked toward the front of the store, they passed by a children's book section. Pitt stops and picks up a book called **Banzi The Bravest Little Badger**, and then sets it back on the shelf."

"Nino, did you know that the Badger is the only animal the dares to stand up to the Lion? I tell my athletes that they should develop **the strength of a lion, the courage of a badger, and the heart of a champion.**"

Nino smiles and nods, "I like that. The courage of a badger."

Pitt chuckles, "You know my sister Sharla writes children's books."

"Really? Does she have any published?" Nino asks.

"No, but she is very talented. She wrote a book about my father called **Papa's Cloud.** It's a delightful book. She even did the illustrations."

Nino enthused, "Hey, maybe she will be able to help you with the book you are going to write."

Pitt agrees, "Oh, I'm sure she'll be into it. She has a very creative imagination. She acts, sings and even wrote and directed her own play called "Our Children's Children." It was awesome."

Nino is impressed, "That's great. Do you have any other talented family members?"

Pitt speaks proudly, "They are all talented. Shari is a singer and actress. She writes her own music. In fact, she just put out her first CD called 11:11. Her music is very good." Pitt starts to laugh as he thinks of Shari's CD."

"What's so funny?" Nino asks.

Pitt chuckles, "I was just thinking about Shari. I used to tease her because a lot of her songs are sad. I call her Shari Manilow!"

Nino grins, "As in Barry Manilow, yeah, he's one sad joker, isn't he?"

Pitt continues, "I give Shari a lot of credit. She was always shy, but she's really done well for herself. She always dreamed of making it on Broadway. She came to New York on her own, and she's come close to making it. She's been on a couple of soap operas and last month she almost got a part in the revival of 'Jesus Christ Super Star'. She was excited because she got to work with Keith Childs. He is one of Broadways most talented directors. Most recently, she hooked up with movie director's Steve Posen and Jim Conley who are doing an independent film on the making of her CD. It's called 11:11. She is one of the lead characters, and she even got me a bit part. Jim Conley has connections in the music business as well. He won a Grammy for his song **Have You Seen My Mother**."

"It sounds like there is a lot of talent in your family, and some connections to. Nino smiles and looks up…. So that's it? Just two sisters?"

Pitt looks sad, "Nope, there's one more. My sister Sally is married, and has three sons. She lives around the corner from me in G-Town."

"So why the sad look? What's the matter? Is there something wrong with her?"

Pitt clarifies, "Not really. It's just that she has one of the greatest female voices I have ever heard, but she doesn't have the confidence to perform in front of people. I've tried to get her to sing some of my music, but she can't do it. She won't even sing in front of me. She tries to hide behind the music stand."

"Is she just really shy?" Nino asks.

"No. She's got a real bubbly and outgoing personality." Says Pitt.

Nino frowns, "Then what's her problem?"

Pitt makes clear, "She's a perfectionist. She's so self-critical that her beautiful voice no longer flows like it used to. She's so nervous that it won't be perfect, that she'll sometimes intentionally sabotage her own performance. I don't know if you see what I am saying."

Nino understands, "I've seen it all my life. Instead of people letting it all hang out and doing their best, they are so afraid of making a mistake that they either pull themselves out of the running altogether, or they don't give it their all, so that when they lose they rationalize in the back of their minds that they could have won if they really tried. The sad thing is that they never really do their best. Perfectionists are really just cowards."

Pitt agrees, "I never thought of it like that, but you're right. They're afraid to try their best, because if they try their best and fail, they have to live with the fact that their best wasn't good enough. They truly are just people who are afraid to fail."

Nino continues, "The ironic thing is that their fear of failure ensures that they will fail in most things they attempt. They sabotage any chance they might have for being successful, by putting forth a half-hearted effort. Hey, you're her big brother, don't give up on her. Maybe you'll be able to pull her out of her shell."

Pitt gets excited, "Nino, if I can, believe me, we'll have our hit song. Sally can hit notes that are in outer space! She's really got soul, man. I mean, for an Italian girl, she has soul!"

Nino jokes, "Of course she does. Hey, there's only about ninety miles of water that separate Africa from Italy, that is why Africans and Italians have so much in common! …" Nino turns serious again, "How about your mother and father? What do they do?"

Pitt looks sad, "My father died a while ago, but he was a great performer during his life. He could play the organ, the harmonica and the accordion. He could also do a great impression of Al Jolson. He was also very interested in religion. He used to invite people from all different religions to our home and they would read the Bible and have discussions. He used to let me sit in on these meetings, and he would always let me express my feelings. He never shut me down or tried to force his religious opinions on me."

Nino shakes his head, "You were lucky to be raised by such a good man. He sounds like quite a fellow."

Mark smiles at the memory of his father. "He was quite a character. He did what he wanted to do, and he said whatever he wanted to say. There was not a politically correct bone in his body. And you talk about tempers! If he got mad, you had better run for cover! Nobody messed with my father when he was angry. One time he got this new boss who was being sarcastic and arrogant toward him. This guy's name was Elmer Patrick, and he was a giant man—about 6'6, 250 pounds. My father was only about 5'7. My dad was a meat cutter and he really took pride in his work. Well, one day my father worked really hard to get the meat case looking just right, and Elmer came in and insulted my father's work. So, my father says to him "If you don't like the case, get in there and fix it yourself!" At that, he picked up his giant boss and threw him into the meat case."

Nino hoots. "Now that's my kind of man. Yes, sir Well what happened? Did he get fired?"

"No, they became pretty good friends after that day." Mark's smile suddenly fills with melancholy. "My father was friends with everybody. If you respect him then he would respect you. He never held a grudge, or anything like that. Everyone loved Sully Pitifer, especially his wife and kids.... Man, I miss him."

Nino forgets himself for a moment. "He really misses you too, man." He blurts out, astonyshing Pitt.

Pitt shocked, "What? Have you seen my father?"

Nino tries to cover up his mistake, remembering he's not supposed to share such information. "No, I mean—he must really miss you, too. It sounds like you were real close." Pitt is obviously let down. "Jeeze, I thought for a moment—well, anyway. He was quite a man. I hope some day you get a chance to meet him."

Nino looks away. "Me too. I'd really like that.... What about your mom? Tell me about her."

Pitt smiles proudly, "My mother is very beautiful both inside and out. She probably has more brains and talent than any of us, but she is content to stay behind the scenes. It is her belief and support that has allowed all of us to make it as far as we have. My father gave us the courage to stand up to anyone or anything, and my mother gave us her faith that our dreams could come true. She also taught me how to be a counselor. She is the best you'll find at conflict resolution. She went back to college and became a nurse when she was in her forties. That really impressed me. She changed her life circumstances by taking a big risk. She could have just stayed in "Soap Opera Ville" for the rest of her life. You know, reading romance novels and thinking about what might have been. She just woke up one day and said, "I'm gonna be a nurse." Going back to school while you're trying to raise four kids is a tough thing to undertake, but she did it. She was one of the best nurses to ever nurse. She is one heck of a human being ..." Pitt pauses for a minute, his mother's love radiating toward him even now. "Me and my family really are blessed to come from such loving and faithful parents."

THE GIVING TREE

"We must all try to be like the fruit trees who give freely to whoever needs. As human beings we must share the fruits that God has provided: Time, money, food, shelter, knowledge, water, wisdom, strength, prayers, and so on... Give freely and lovingly to all who need your assistance, especially to those who are less fortunate than you. Stretch out your branches to shelter the weary, and offer your fruits to feed all who are hungry. Be peacemakers amongst all peoples, and sow seeds of love wherever you may wander."

-Salvatore Eugene Pitifer... "SULLY"

CHAPTER 36

▼

"The strongest desire of everything, and the one first implanted by
Nature, is to return to its source. And since God is the Source of
our soul and has made it like unto himself, therefore this soul
desires above all things to return to Him."
-Dante (1317 AD)

"Melchizedek's is the king of peace and justice who was honored by
Abraham (The first Jew & Muslim). Melchizedek has no father or
mother, and there is no record of any of his ancestors. He was never
born and he never died but his life is like the son of God-a priest forever.".... And Jesus replied "Truly I tell you, before Abraham ever
existed, I am!"
-Excerpts from The Book Of Hebrews (77AD) & Mark (7:1-3)

As Pitt and Nino walk past the psychology section of the bookstore, Pitt
picks up a book by Sigmund Freud. "Nino, you didn't by chance run into
old Siggy up there if Forever did you?" He asks.

Nino smirks, "You know the funny thing is I did ask about him, and
do you know what my escort told me?"

"What?"

"Old Siggy didn't make it. He went downtown baby."

Mark is stunned, to say the least. "Sigmund Freud's in Hell? Holy
mackerel, I knew he was an Atheist.... I guess you just don't expect that
someone like that is going to Hell. I mean he did do a lot of good in a way,
didn't he?"

Nino frowns, "First of all, Pitt, if he did a lot of good he wouldn't be in
Hell, and secondly, did you ever stop to think about what he actually cre-

ated? Psychiatry and Psychology have always been the champions of atheism. Freud was a staunch atheist, who was openly antireligious. He believed that if his scientific version of mental illness was to be embraced, then religion and the idea of the immortal soul must be destroyed. He taught people that religious belief should be characterized as an illusion, and that Religious faith was a social mental disorder that eventually people would grow out of. All people who held onto their faith were portrayed by Freud as neurotic. Why, do you know that I read somewhere that only 1.1% of the American Psychological Association believes in God? 1.1%! Pitt, this guy was bad news, any which way you slice it."

Pitt can't believe that his own profession stems from such a basis. "How could I have studied about him all those years of college, and not seen the obvious that you just pointed out to me?"

"That's simple, Pitt. There you are in college studying to be a counselor. You are surrounded by teachers, students, and textbooks that are all singing praises of this man. You were blinded by that liberal arts smoke screen. You probably, either consciously or unconsciously, knew that if you started ripping Freud, your professors and your peers were going to start attacking you. You would have alienated yourself in taking such a stance at that time of your life. However, the time has come to point it out, regardless of the consequences."

Mark smiles at Nino in awe. "Nino Jones, you are an ever unfolding surprise to me. You're absolutely right. That's what it was. It was fear. Fear, basically of how my professors might respond. I am ashamed of myself. I should have spoken out."

Nino puts his hand on Pitts shoulder, "Pitt, everything is timing man. You obviously were born to be a counselor. If you had come to this realization back when you were in college, it may have prevented you from achieving your goal. Or, it could have caused you to change your career. Don't be so hard on yourself. Everything happens for a reason. Those who walk with God are all taught in due time. You have to look at yourself openly and honestly. If you find that you were a coward at some point in your life, examine the reasons why you were afraid and overcome them through faith, prayer and determination. Like Winston Churchill said, **"Sometimes a battle has to be fought more than once to be won."** Just make sure you're ready the next time that type of situation presents itself. The book that you are going to have to write is probably going to offend some powerful people, but you're going to have to be brave. Psychology and Psychiatry are being manipulated and influenced by Satan. You must expose this and find a way to tie in religious faith with psychology. Then you will be on the right track."

Pitt agrees, "You know, this summer I was reading a book by a guy named Boisen. He was a fella who was once placed in a mental institution by his parents. He gradually cured himself through his belief in God. **He believed that all mental illness is the result of some unresolved psycho-spiritual conflict, and I think he is right. There is a growing amount of research that indicates a strong correlation between religious commitment and overall mental health.**"

Nino smirks at Pitt. "That's nothing new. If you stay close to God, you will remain mentally healthy.

Pitt walks over and picks up one of M. Scott Peck's books called <u>People Of The Lie.</u> "Have you ever read any of this guy's stuff?"

"Are you kidding me?" Nino laughs. "That guy is one of the greatest self-help authors of our time. As far as I'm concerned, that book you're holding is one of the best books in the whole store. Mr. Peck is a brave man. He knew he would be attacked for writing <u>The People Of The </u>Lie, but he didn't care. M. Scott Peck said "the hell with what my peers are going to say. I'm gonna write what I believe is the truth!", and that's just what you've got to do."

Pitt Smiling "You're right. He is a brave and wise man. It is people like him who make me think there is still hope for my profession."

"Speaking of wise men, we had better get moving on down the road. The great star of the north beckons us."

As they walked out of the store they passed by a table that had religious books and books of prophecy for sale. The book, <u>Life After Life </u>by Dr. Moody, catches Pitt's eye. "Have you ever read this?" He asks Nino, excitedly.

Nino thinking, "No. What is it about? Reincarnation?"

"No, this guy is an M.D. who has done extensive research on near death experiences. He has silenced a lot of skeptics who claimed that these experiences were merely hallucinations brought on by the trauma of a life threatening event."

Nino is intrigued. "How did he silence his critics?"

Pitt explains, "He interviewed thousands of people from all over the world, people of different nationalities, religions, and ages, and found remarkable similarities in the stories they recounted. Even Atheists experience the same events. All people who had a near death experience became spiritually changed individuals. They no longer feared death, and some even longed to return to what they call Heaven. Many of the interviewees also had precise knowledge of technically specific medical procedures that were performed on them while they were out of their bodies. Their brains where showing no activity and yet they were still able to remember1"

Nino smirks "So **during the time at which these peoples brains are dead, their brains are actually functioning on an even higher level then when they were alive.** That's what I call proof positive for the existence of the immortal soul."

Pitt Smiling, "There is no other explanation. Dr. Moody concluded that there is no way this type of experience is a hallucinatory response. Number one, how could a lay person be able to describe a technical medical procedure, and ..."

Nino interrupts, excitedly. "And number two, why would an Atheist have the same experience as a believer?!"

Pitt nods in agreement, "Exactly, this type of phenomenon absolutely proves the existence of the immortal soul. Earthly circumstances and beliefs may cause great differences in the physical world, but in the end we all experience the same passage."

Nino is comforted by Mark's acceptance of the immortal soul. "All paths lead to the throne of God, but only one path will allow you to return to Forever."

Pitt smiles, "The P.O.J. [The Path of Jesus]!"

"That's the one." Says Nino.

Pitt excitedly picks up a book and shows it to Nino. "Hey Nino have you ever read Lee Strobel's book, <u>The Case For Christ?</u>"

Nino rubs his chin, "No, I must have missed that one. What's it about?"

Pitt explains, "This guy was an Atheist who worked for some big Chicago news paper. He said he got tired of religious people trying to convert him, so he decided to research the life and times of Jesus for himself."

"Was he going after the unbiased reporter's perspective?" Asks Nino.

Pitt continues, "Yes, he thought he was going to come up with enough evidence to shut up his friends when they would argue with him about Jesus. However, what happened was that as he went through the process of collecting the information, he ended up converting himself! Isn't that something?"

Nino laughing "That really is. I'm going to have to remember that one. You know the other day I was reading an antique book called." Nino thinks for a moment, and then remembers, "The Divine Plan Of The Ages: The Way To Life and Happiness. It was written in 1924 by a pastor named Russell. I doubt you will ever be able to find the book, but he said some very interesting thing regarding the existence of God. He said if you want to see proof that there is a Creator simply look at the intricate construction of a flower. Pick a Lilly of the Valley for example."

Pitt smiles, "That's a perfect example. Their shape is like ornate china, and their smell is truly Heavenly. Sometimes I just close my eyes and breathe in its fragrance. It was my mothers wedding bouquet."

Nino continues, "So you know what I mean. That flower is exquisitely beautiful in form and texture. To look at it, to touch it, and to smell it, is to give the flower a voice.'

Pitt interjects, "A voice that speaks of a wisdom and skill far above that of any human invention or work of art. The flower bears witness to the existence of God."

Nino smiles proudly at Pitt's wit, "How short sighted these absurd people are, who boast of human skill and ingenuity, and then attribute to mere chance the regularity, uniformity, and harmony of nature. Not to mention the human being."

Pitt smirks, "These people are blind Nino. They acknowledge the laws of nature, but then deny that nature has an intelligent lawgiver. They recognize and reward the creators of our imperfect human endeavors, but refuse when confronted with true works of beauty and perfection, that there is a God! I don't understand their logic. The proof of God, Jesus, and the prophets is all around us, if we would just open our eyes and take in the obvious."

Nino shakes his head in agreement and discouragement. He then reaches down and picks up a book by William Barclay called The Mind Of Jesus. "Speaking of a case for Christ, have you ever read any of William Barclay's books?"

Pitt reaches for the book, "No, why? Is he a good writer?"

Nino fakes agitation, "Is he a good writer?!" Nino opens the book randomly and begins to read. "This is perfect. Listen to this. "**The victor is the man who refuses to believe that God has forgotten him even when every fiber of his being feels that he is forsaken. The victor is the man who will never let go of is faith, even when he feels its last grounds are gone. Jesus was beaten to the depths of human comprehension, he passed through the uttermost abyss, and he still he holds on to God. If we cling to God, even when there seems to be no God, desperately and invincibly clutching the remnants of our faith, quite certainly the dawn will break, and we will win through.**"

Pitt smiles and adds, "All who remain faithful until the end will be victorious."

Nino nods, "You keep that in mind, and don't forget about Sir William. This man breaks down the Path of Jesus and the scriptures better than anyone else I have ever read. You need to read some of his stuff before you write your book. He is very wise and insightful. If you can mix what I give you with his spiritual insights, believe me, you'll have a best seller."

Mark chuckles, "Alright, I'm convinced! Don't get yourself so worked up. I'll read him. I promise." Mark turns to another table full of books. "Hey Nino, what about all these different books on prophecy. Did anybody up there say anything about the apocalypse?"

Nino looks concerned, "Yes every one that I spoke to believes that we are in the end of times. In fact, Barabbas seems to think the Great Game will come to an end real soon. While I was on the tour, Barabbas introduced me to one of the royal descendents of Ireland, a very holy man named Mac Spellecy, who told me this poem. Oh, and Pitt, he wrote this poem shortly after the fall of Rome in 77 AD. When the Jews return to their homeland and silver birds fill the sky. The Holy Roman Empire rises. Then you and I must die. From the sea of politics and law he rises. Creating wars on every shore. Turning man against his brother, until God's people exist no more." Nino looks over at Mark and sees a veil of sadness over his face.

"What are you thinking Pitt?" Asks Nino.

Pitt frowns, "Law and politics should be vehicles that help bring God's peace, justice, and equality into the world. But so often they seem to do the exact opposite."

Nino nods, "I know what you mean."

Pitt angry, "Nino, I got in an argument with an attorney just last week over this kind of shit."

"What happened?" Nino asks.

Pitt gives details, "I had an 11 year old girl come to me and tell me that her stepfather raped and sexually abused her. The guy even makes a confession to the police."

"So what happened?"

Pitt grows angrier, "This guy's attorney gets him off on a technicality! And you wanna hear the kicker, this lawyer's got a daughter the same age! So I ask him. How can you feel proud about what you have done? Do you know what he tells me?"

Nino chuckles, "Yeah, that he was practicing the law, and your problem should be with the law not with him."

Pitt looks surprised, "That's right, how did you know?"

Nino smirks in disgust, "That's what they all say. It's like the Nazi war criminal saying "Your problem is with Hitler, not with me. I was just following orders." They rationalize these awful things they do. They convince themselves that they are doing what they are supposed to do, and therefore they are not guilty of any wrong doing."

Pitt wonders, "Well are they? I mean, did you talk to any lawyers in Heaven?

Nino laughs, "Yeah, but as you joked, their profession is not well represented, especially when you take into account all the lawyers who have ever lived."

Startled, "So most attorneys end up in Hell?"

Nino responds, "No, I'm not saying that, but a high percentage of them do end up in Purgatory. I talked to this guy named David Cohen during my tour. You've probably heard about his daughter Lesley Cohen Hickey."

Pitt smiles, "Oh yeah, she's that famous District Attorney from Cleveland, that just got nominated to the Supreme Court. She's something special. Her child outreach programs are some of the best in the country. I hope she gets appointed. If she does she will definitely be the prettiest supreme court justice of all time!"

Nino laughs, "That's' the one. Her father is very proud of her ... Anyway, he was a lawyer and a Judge during his time in the Great Game, and he was truly bothered to see how Satan was manipulating his noble profession. He said to remind his fellow lawyers that the law, unless they are a court appointed defense attorney, does not force them to represent every client who comes to them. He said to tell them to be more selective in who they represent, and if they find that they are representing someone who is a danger to society, they should remove themselves from the case, even if they think they can win. He said that he used to tell his children that, **if what you are doing doesn't make you feel proud, then stop doing it.**"

Pitt smiles,"I like that. This is a saying that all people in every profession should live by."

Nino nods in agreement, "Yes they should. All people in general should live by it. He also said that when you, as an attorney, take on cases that ultimately help the few, the guilty or the rich, and hurt the many, the innocent and the poor, that your actions, no matter how well they are supported by the letter of the law, help Satan's cause. What does it benefit a man to gain riches, fame, and fortune if the price at the end of it all is his soul? The law and the practice of law is not inherently bad. It is the manipulation of the law, for the sake of power and greed, that has spiritually polluted a profession that should be noble and holy."

Pitt is impressed, "He sounds like a really good man. I'm sorry if I got you side tracked. This law stuff just really irritates me."

Nino shakes his head, "No, as a matter of fact I'm glad you brought that up. Dave would have been disappointed if I had forgotten to mention it to you."

Pitt moves on, "Ok, so explain that apocalypse poem for me a little more." Nino breaks down the end of time a little more clearly for his messenger."

Nino explains, "Mark, as it was told to me, there are seven signs that must occur before the end comes. (1) Europe will be reunited; (2) the Jews will return to Israel; (3) the seasons will begin to blend together causing droughts, famines, and rising tides; (4) the armies of the world will gather to fight in the Middle East. Israel will be surrounded; (5) the eagle will unite with the bear [Russia and the United States will become allies]; (6) the

Antichrist will come into power, and will reopen the Jewish temple of worship; and finally, (7) the moon will turn the color of blood, and the rapture will take place."

Pitt looks devastated. "Most of those things you described have already happened."

Nino looks grim, "That's my point. If you read the signs of the times, the end appears to be very near."

Pitt somewhat frustrated, "But how near? One year, ten years, a hundred years? I mean what does "near" mean?" There is a sense of panic in Mark's voice. "Didn't anybody up there give you a guesstimation?"

Nino shakes his head, "No, no one knows when the end will come except God himself. Not even Jesus knows. I don't think God even knows for sure!"

Pitt surprised, "What do you mean by that?"

Nino takes a deep breath as he collects his thoughts. "Well, the way it was described to me is that **God, in his mercy, keeps on postponing the end. As long as souls with faith and hope still exist in the world the Great Game will continue.** Jesus said "when the son of man returns will he find anyone that has faith?""

Agitated woman, "Of course he won't, but it's his own fault," a woman's voice interjects. Mark and Nino turn to find a woman who has been listening to their entire conversation. She looks very frustrated. Nino sets down the book he was holding and he and Pitt turn towards her.

Nino calmly, "Excuse me ma'am, are you talking to me? I mean, I don't mind if you are; I just didn't hear exactly what you said."

The woman blushes, now wishing she had kept her mouth shut, "I'm sorry. I shouldn't have butted into your conversation, it's just that ..." She starts to cry, and Nino and Pitt move closer to her. Nino takes her hand and talks gently to her.

Nino warmly, "What's bothering you, child?"

The woman dries her eyes with a tissue she pulls from her purse and tries to compose herself. "I just couldn't help overhearing your conversation. My name is Mary Lou."

Nino smiles, "Mary Lou, my name is Nino and this is my friend Mark."

Mary Lou attempts a half smile, "It's nice to meet you Nino and Mark." She pauses briefly, gathering courage. "I used to believe in God and Jesus, but I just can't anymore."

"Why, what's caused you to stop believing?" Mark asks, concerned.

The woman's eyes well up with tears again, and she wipes them before she begins to speak. "Four years ago my 10 year old little boy died of Leukemia." She lets a few sobs escape, then recomposes herself. "I prayed and prayed for God to make him well again, but he just kept getting sicker and sicker. He was our only child. My poor little Benny. He was a beautiful boy and loving little soul. He gave my life so much meaning and joy. When he died, my faith died with him."

Heavy sobs take over again, and Nino and Pitt stand for a moment in silence. Finally, Nino's compassionate voice is heard. "You poor, dear woman, now I understand the source of your pain and why you no longer believe. I wish I had a religious explanation for why your little boy had to die. I wish …"

Mary Lou interrupts, her sadness subsiding to some sort of anger. "There is no explanation, because there is no God!" she practically shouts. Her body is shaking. "I mean, just look at our world. No, just look around this city! This open sewer. If there was a God, how could he just sit back and let so many bad things happen? Crime, sickness, starvation, exploitation. People behaving like animals toward one another. As far as I'm concerned, Darwin was right. This is a survival of the fittest world. We're the descendants of animals, not some loving, omnipotent God. We live in a random universe, on some tiny speck of a planet, on which random shit just happens all the time, wherever, whenever, and to whomever it likes. Hey, I'm sorry fellas. If you can hang onto your faith, more power to ya. I've just been let down too many times in my life. I can remember listening to the people at my son's funeral telling all these ridiculous religious clichés. You know like "Its Gods will; He's in a better place, He won't have to suffer any more. Oh and the worst one of them all "God never gives us more than we can bare!" It's such bullshit, it was more than I could bear, and their words seemed empty to me. An endless stream of humans trying to make sense out of something that is senseless! I'm just through kidding myself. Sometimes I think I should just kill myself and get the whole thing over with. I mean what's the point of all this? Live, learn, save, suffer, for what?!"

Nino remains composed, and answers the hysterical woman in a calm voice. "I once stood in a spot where you are now standing, a long time ago. You're right Mary Lou, there are a lot of messed up things that happen in this world. People do behave like animals, and evil can be found everywhere you turn. There seems to be a lot of evidence to support the nonexistence of God. But, there is one thing that puzzles me."

Mary Lou raises her eyes to meet Nino's. "What's that?"

Nino continues, "If Darwin's claims are true, and we are nothing more than evolved apes living in a survival of the fittest world, then it's not surprising that, like in the animal kingdom, there is a lot of killing, stealing, fighting, raping, and your basic overall lack of compassion."

"So you agree with me?" Mary Lou asks, confused.

Nino smiles, "If that was the limit of what I experienced in the world I would have to say yes. But, you see, we have some things that exist in our world that do not take place in the animal kingdom: love, compassion, charity, and mercy for those who are not part of our immediate family. Where there is love, mercy, compassion, and charity, there is God. If you buy into Darwin's theory, the presence of everyday self-centered driven death and destruction is understandable. The existence of love, however, is unexplainable. True compassionate love transcends the need to fit into established norms. The human side of us that can be moved to help a stranger who is down trodden, the capacity to place the needs of someone else over our own personal needs, is a phenomenon that is truly unexplainable. For you see, my sister, love, true **love, is tangible evidence that GOD IS REAL.**"

Mary Lou is spiritually moved, "I never thought about it like that before. It warms my heart to hear you speak. I actually feel your love," Mary Lou says softly, surprised by her own emotions.

Pitt smiles warmly, "Are you sure it is Nino's love you are feeling? Jesus said where two or three are gathered together in my name I ..."

Mary Lou interrupts, tears joy well up in her eyes. "I am in their midst ... It's true. Love is the proof, but what about my poor little Benny? What about him?"

Nino reaches down and picks up a book by Joseph F. Girzone called Never Alone, and holds onto it. "Bad things happen in this world, Mary Lou. Natural disasters, and the laws of nature don't know the difference between good and evil. They just randomly occur, and when they do good people are injured, and sometimes die. However, I am certain that God does not bring about the miseries of this world, and he certainly takes no delight in them. I believe that for those who have faith nothing suffered is in vain."

Pitt joins in. "Its true Mary Lou. God is always on the side of the victim. I don't believe that he ever wants any of us to suffer in any way."

Mary Lou somewhat angry, "Than why doesn't he do something about it?! After all he's supposed to be all powerful isn't he?"

Pitt continues, "I believe he is all powerful, but I also think that he is unable to intervene as much as he would like to, because to do so would probably prevent people from attaing sincere faith."

Peturbed but kind "What do you mean?"

Pitt makes clear, "Well for example, if he let everybody that believes in him live to be 100 years old, and never have anything bad happen to them, it will cause a variety of spiritual and social problems. You would have people who would start believing in God for the wrong reasons. You would also have over population, food shortages, fuel shortages, increased starvation, pollution, and so on."

Softer "I kind of see what you mean. But he's God, why can't he just step in and make everything perfect."

Nino answers "He will, and he does, but like Mark said, down here he is limited, and not just for reasons of faith and population problems. I think **God can only touch this world through the people who open their lives up to Him, and allow themselves to be his instruments of help and healing.**"

Mary Lou responds "So if more people would open themselves up to God, and have compassion for all God's children, then He would be a stronger force in our world, and in our daily lives."

Nino smiles, "Yes, the quality of our lives would improve immensely, and the suffering that occurs in this world would greatly diminish."

Mary Lou clarifies, "So the most we can do is open ourselves up to God, and hold on to the belief that in Heaven we will live the life of paradise that we long for."

Nino nods in agreement, "Mary Lou I know for certain that your little Benny has gone to Heaven. He is not dead, he was rescued from a cold cruel world, and released from a sick and painful body. His soul has returned to the place of his origin. A heavenly paradise where he now waits for the return of his mother and very best friend. The only thing is, that if you take your own life, you can't return to Heaven. You will also be hurting your son a million times more than the leukemia ever did."

Nino is also teary and Mary Lou hugs him. "You must stay strong, Mary Lou. Don't let this world wear you down and cause you to give up. Turn your pain in a positive direction. Seek out others who have suffered similar losses and help strengthen them. The road to Heaven is a hard one to follow, but it leads to paradise. Follow the simple path of Jesus, Mary Lou, and you will never stand alone."

Nino hands Mary Lou the book he is holding. "This book will help you stay on the right path. It will keep your faith strong." Nino thinks for a moment. "My good friend Samantha always used to say **"I would rather live as if there is a God and find out there isn't. Than live as if there isn't a God and find out that there is!"**

Mary Lou takes the book and hugs Nino again. A smile finally finds its place on her face. "I like that…. Thank you … Nino, is it?"

Nino tips his imaginary cap, "Yes ma'am, Nino Jones."

Mary Lou is beaming, "Thank you Nino Jones, I will never forget you. Goodbye Mark. Take care of that friend of yours. He's an angel." With that she smiled and walked away.

Despite her parting smile, sadness still lingers in the air as Nino turns to Pitt. "There are so many sad, disheartened people like Mary Lou out there in the world. They get mad at God, and then they end up rejecting him."

"And when they reject him he can't help them, so more bad things just keep happening to them," Pitt says, finishing Nino's thought.

Nino agrees, "That's right. It's a dreadful cycle to get sucked into. One time, that marquee at the church where we stopped earlier read: "Does God seem far away? Who do you think moved?"

Pitt nods, "I know. I see it all the time in my line of work. That book you gave her, Never Alone, is that written by Joseph Girzone?"

"Yeah it is. Have you read some of his stuff?"

"I think he wrote a book called Joshua. My sister gave it to me for my birthday."

"That is probably his best known book, but I think <u>Never Alone </u>is the best novel he has ever written. This guy really illuminates the Path of Jesus. He especially understands the mind of God. Listen to this dedication in his book **Never Alone**."

Nino opens the book and begins to read: <u>"I dedicate this book to my friend, who is always by my side and in my heart. Who is never far when I am lonely and confused, who always gives peace to my soul when I am troubled and frightened, and fearful of the future. I share my deepest secrets, my joy, my sorrow, my accomplishments, and my shame. He always understands. He never accuses or criticizes, but often suggests a different way of doing things. When he does he inevitably prepares the way. So it is not as impossible as I thought it might be. Over the years I have learned to trust him. It was not easy. I thought in following him I would have to give up all of the fun in my life, but I found that he is the source of all joy and adventure. And indeed he turned my life into a great adventure at a time when I thought it was about to come to an end. I would like to suggest that he could become your friend to, if you would like him to be. Do not be afraid. He will respect your freedom and your independence more than anyone you have ever met, because he created you to be free. He just wants more than anything that you accept him as your friend. If you do, I can promise you, you will never be alone."</u> "Isn't that nice?"

Pitt smiles, "Yeah, that's a beautiful way to think about God. There is this band I like called **Israel and the New Breed. On their Rejoice CD there is a song called "I Am A Friend of God"** and it conveys that feeling. It's comforting to think of a God in those terms. Like a good friend who will never reject you and always has your back. You can tell Joseph is a special soul."

Nino agrees, "Yes he is, and this is definitely another book I want you to read. But, in reading these books do not neglect the time you spend reading the Bible and the Qur'an. You, as a messenger of Jehovah, must always be arming yourself with God's words. Especially the words of Jesus."

"How much time are you talking about?" Pitt asks.

Nino scratches his head, "I guess to each his own. The important thing is not how much, but how often. It is better to read a little bit at a time at a relaxed pace. I like to read the Bible or other holy scriptures a little while before I go to bed at night, and in the morning before I start my day. I read 10 to 15 minute's tops, and that's enough for me."

Nino stops and takes one last look at the giant book store. "You know, Pitt, this book store in a lot of ways is like Heaven." "Really? How so?" Pitt asks.

Nino explains, "In Heaven there are representatives from all races and all religions. Every country, every religion, and every people is represented in the Kingdom of Forever, just as I imagine they are all represented in this book store. In Forever everything that is good about every culture still exists. The different foods, music, and dances all remain in their highest form, and there are no communication barriers. Think about all of the communication problems we are faced with in this world, and how these barriers have hindered our lives and kept us from uniting as children of the same God."

Pitt wonder, "I bet it also prevents us from solving many of the problems we are faced with in our lives. Just think if everyone could completely understand each other, if all of the great minds of the world were really united and unencumbered by language. We would probably already have a cure for cancer, AIDS, blindness, paralysis. Just think of all the remarkable things that could be accomplished."

Nino nods in agreement, "Just think about Heaven, Pitt. In Forever there are no barriers of any kind. Everyone is united, and all minds are great and unique. The splendid thing about Heaven is that there are no problems that need solving. There are only dreams to be realized. In Heaven, when a group of souls unite to work on a common goal, it is only to make paradise more pleasing in some new way so that everyone can enjoy it. In paradise the pleasure you give is the profit you receive."

Pitt somewhat excited, "That's really all Heaven is about, isn't it? Pleasure."

Nino smiles with the memory of Forever. "That's it, Pitt. Pleasure, love, peace, tranquility, humor, adventure, music, sports, art, and camaraderie. There are no more things that must be done. There are no deadlines to be met, or tests to be taken. There are only "things that you feel like doing".

"Don't we have to go to church or pray? You know, stuff like that?" Pitt asks.

Nino shakes his head, "Nope ... Well, on Christmas they have a big to-do at the temple, but it's more like a party than a ceremony. In Heaven all of that boring formality and ritual is gone away. God is no longer separated from his children, and Jesus lives amongst his siblings. When you get to Forever your mental and physical labor is truly over. Nothing more is required of you other than that you enjoy life. Come my faithful messenger, our star looms on the horizon, and we had better get a move on. We've got miles to go before we sleep."

Pitt grins, "Always the poet."

Nino laughs. "Don't you know it."

Pitt and Nino make their way out of the crowded book store and back onto the street. The laughter and conversation die as both men are lost in thoughts of their families, which seem so far away at this time.

Author's Note: It is a scientific fact that the endorphins that are released during sexual activity are the same ones that are released when one is taking Heroine (the most highly addictive substance on the planet). This means that there is something very addictive about all sexual activity. As the drug addicts continually search in vain for the ecstasy of their initial high, so to does the struggling hopeful/hopeless-romantic search for that first-time romantic feeling of their youth. Solomon in the book of Proverbs implores us not to let our desires get out of hand. If you are married and you have a person that you are attracted to Solomon says that you should not even let yourself think about them. "Don't go near them. Stay away from where they walk, lest they tempt you and seduce you." Adultery, he explains, has been the ruin of multitudes. A vast host of men and woman have been its victims. Jesus, went a step further and told us that to even think of someone in a lustful manor is to commit adultery. This is because he knows that when it comes to adulterous sexual activity, like heroine, no matter how small the dose, there is no safe amount!

<u>Author's Note #2:</u> For all of you hopeful/hopeless romantics out there, you need only read the book of Mark to realize that very soon you will have all

that you long for. In Heaven there will be no marriage, laws, guilt, limitations, or possessiveness of any kind. Behold the endless summer beckons.

"Your trouble is that you do not know the scriptures. For when we
are resurrected we will not be married, but will live like the
Angels." "Marriage is for people here on earth. Those who are
worthy of Heaven do not marry. And they never die again. In these
respects they are like Angels, and are sons of God.
-JESUS OF NAZARETH/Mark 24-25 & Luke 20:34-36

THE JAINISM P.O.J.
A PERSON SHOULD WANDER ABOUT TREATING ALL
CREATURES AS HE HIMSELF WOULD LIKE TO BE
TREATED.

CHAPTER 37

▼

"Love your enemies, do good to those who hate you, bless those who curse you, pray for those who mistreat you."
-JESUS OF NAZARETH/Luke 6:27-28 (80 AD)

"Never does hatred cease by hating; hatred ceases by love. Let people overcome anger by love; let them overcome evil by good."
-Dhammapada

"Subdue wrath by forgiveness, conquer vanity by humbleness, fraud by straightforwardness, and vanquish greed through contentment."
-Dasha-vaikalika/Jainism

Judas stayed with the two targets and sent Adolf back to discuss their plan of attack with Satan. When Adolf returned to the command center, he was told that Satan was on the roof waiting for their return. Satan liked the roof. He liked looking down at this kingdom and his potential subjects. Whenever Satan went to this lofty perch, he would get energized by taking pride in his diabolical accomplishments. So, when Adolf found him, he was in a good mood, for Satan that is.

Hitler walks up to Satan, "MS, we have found the subjects and they are traveling north on Broadway."

Satan expressionless, "What is their exact location?"

"Union Square Park. Judas is with them as we speak." Says Hitler.

Satan looks to the South east, "Union Square Park ... That's near 14th Street, right?"

Hitler nods, "Yes. They seem to be headed uptown via Broadway. The older one, Nino, seems to want to get to the George Washington Bridge. He's got this idea that if they can make it to the bridge their plan will be successful. However, there doesn't seem to be any logical reason for this assumption."

Satan grins evily, "Well, by the time we get through with them, if they do make it to the GWB, they will be ready to jump into the Hudson River and end it all."

Hitler nods, "I wouldn't be shocked! Neither of them seems very bright. However, the old man has definitely seen the other side."

This sparks Satan's curiosity, "Really? That's interesting. How could they have pulled that off? That old Barabbas is getting quite clever in his old age. So, what is their plan? Did they say?"

Hitler makes clear, "It appears that the old man is supposed to tell the younger man all that he has learned about Forever, and then the younger man, Pitt they call him, is supposed to write a book, make a movie and write some songs about Forever."

Satan snears, "That's it? That's their big plan?" Satan is pacing back and forth. "Is this Pitt fellow a rich man?"

Hitler shakes his head, "It doesn't appear so. The demon who attempted to seduce him the other night said that he is some kind of school counselor, an aspiring song writer with marriage problems."

Satan's eyes grow wide, "Wait a minute ... wait one minute! Why Barabbas, you sly old fox. I see what he's doing! He makes us think this is his A-plan, but all it really is ..."

Hitler excited, "Yes! It's a diversionary plan—a distraction."

Satan excited, "Listen, I want you to hook back up with Judas immediately. I want you to take on the identity of this Jones fellow. Find someone in the area who has sold his soul to us. Kill him, rob him, and put the wallet of the victim, and the weapon, unknowingly, into the pocket of Jones when the police come to search him."

"This plan should be no problem, MS, but can Judas do the killing?" Hitler asks.

Satan raises his eye brows, "Why, Adolf, what has gotten into you? That's usually your favorite part."

Hitler shutters, "I can't bear the thought of putting on that dirty black skin. Even if it's only for a moment. It's probably got something to do with Jesse Owens."

Satan grins, "Adolf, still prejudice after all these years? Even after finding out the truth? Your evilness sometimes rivals my own. Sure, let Judas do it. Give him a little extra irritation."

Hitler frowns, "What about the other guy? What do we do with him? Do we make him an accessory to the crime?"

Satan pulled out what looked like a small pocket sized computer and punched in the names of Nino Jones and Mark Pitifer.

Satan stares at the screen, "Let me see what the soul scanner has to say about these guys. Let's see if either of these guys has any dirt on them … No, tying him to the crime will only help the old man. It says here that Pitifer is a school counselor who has a spotless record and so does Jones. Jones is a decorated war hero with a Congressional Medal of Honor. We don't want Pitifer connected to Jones in any way. He could possibly help exonerate him. Just carry out the plan. Jones will get arrested and if things go extremely well, maybe even killed."

Hitler concerned, "But what about Pitifer? Do you think it's wise to just let him go?"

Satan unworried, "Strike the shepherd and the sheep will scatter. When Pitifer sees what happens to Jones, he'll run for the hills. But even if I'm wrong and he's braver than I think, he's got no shot at being successful. He has a wife and a job that he has to get back to, so his time here is limited. I will strike down this Nino Jones, and his scared little lamb will run back to his home. Even if he attempts to do something with the information that Jones gives him, what will the public think of a prophet who is in jail or dead because he murdered and robbed an innocent person."

Hitler understands, "I see what you mean."

"You also are forgetting one other very important thing." "What's that?" Asks Hitler.

Satan smiles broadly, "How many people get record, book, or movie deals without my assistance?"

Hitler laughs, "You are right, MS, he's got no shot!"

Satan continues, "At the very lest, we will keep his name on our hit list. We'll send some of the lesser demons after him from time to time. A little periodic torture of the body, mind and soul. Have no fear, we will gradually wear him down. We'll get him to commit adultery, ruin his family, smash his dreams, steal his hope, and chip away at his faith until eventually he takes his own life, or dies a faithless, hopeless soul. Either way, we can do more overall damage by keeping him out of it. You always have to see the big picture, Adolf."

Hitle bows to Satan, "I am humbled by the cleverness and depth of your evil, and I pledge my undying support to you and your kingdom." Adolf salutes MS—his Master Satan. Hail Satan, King of all he surveys!"

Satan warmly excepts the compliment, "Thank you, Adolf. You are like a son to me."

Hitler worried, "MS, there's one more thing."

"Yes, my son, what is it?" Satan asks.

"Do you realize how much Judas holds you in contempt? He still swears his allegiance to our sworn enemy."

Satan nods, "Of course I am aware of it, but who cares? I used Judas when he was an earthbound, and I continue to use him now. Whether he supports our cause or not, he still does my work. He can rationalize all he wants to, but he has made his choice and he is damned like all the rest of us. The main thing is that Judas is a productive gatherer of souls, regardless of what his driving motivation is. He carries out my orders well."

"Are you sure he won't turn on you someday?" Hitler asks.

Satan angry, "Turn on me? And go where? To whom? His father doesn't want him. I'm all he has and he knows that! He either does what I ask him to do, or his eternal torture begins prematurely. Don't worry about Judas, Adolf. His eternal destiny is the same as ours. He just has a hard time accepting who and what he really is. Now, you better run along. Report back to me later this evening. Right now, I have some business to attend to in North Korea and Iran. I am also going to stop in the Middle East and check points west, to put our soldiers on full alert. We have to get on this A-Plan ASAP."

Satan disappears over the horizon, and Hitler beams himself back to Judas' location, in front of the Barnes and Noble bookstore on East 17th Street across from Union Square Park. As he approaches Judas, Hitler decides not to tell him that Satan believes this is just a diversionary plan.

"Where are they now?" Hitler asks.

"In the bookstore."

"Okay, Judas, here's the plan. You are going to take on the identity of Jones. We will then find a target that we already have possession of, kill him, and rob him."

Judas annoyed, "Why do I have to do it? Why can't you?"

Hitler cringes, "The very thought of being black, even to do something evil, makes my skin crawl. So, you'll have to do it. It's Satan's command."

Judas reluctant and angry "Alright, you go find a target, and I'll stick close to these two. Hey, what about Pitifer? What's he gonna be, an accessory to the crime?"

Hitler somewhat annlyed, "No. MS decided he can do us more good by keeping him out of it. He is confident that if we take Jones out, Pitifer's interest will fade fast. He'll go back to his ordinary life and we'll just keep him on the hit list. You know, wear him down over time, and gradually change him from apostle to demon. Remind you of anyone we know?"

Judus frowns and pushes Hitler, "Get away from me you disgusting waste of a soul."

Hitler just grins, "Oh, I'm sorry Judas, did I offend you?"

Judas flips Hitler the bird.

Hitler fakes disappointment, "Oh, dear, obscene finger gestures from a former apostle! Whatever is the world coming to?"

Judas snaps, "I' m still an apostle. You snake!"

Hitler smirks, "You wish, Judas. You had your chance to help the King of Kings, and you sold him to his enemies for, what was it? 30 pieces of silver? Oh, I'm sure he looks down on you from Paradise with such admiration. At least Satan appreciates what you've done with your life."

Judas is red faced with anger, "It's a lie! I never took any money. They used me! I was set up!"

Hitler fakes compassion, "Poor, poor Judas. It's tough being a victim, isn't' it?"

Judas steams as Adolf flies off to find a suitable target. Judas has no more than turned his back towards the park when suddenly, Adolf is pulling at his sleeve.

"What is it now, Adolf?" Judas says still burning with anger.

Hitler smiles, "We're in luck. We have a target. He has just sat down to eat his lunch. He's on the third bench in, over in Union Square Park. You can't miss him. He's got that beautiful black aura around him. The eye is the window to the soul, you know…. Wait until these guys start moving again, and then go do what you have been ordered to do, Judas."

Judas disgusted, "Get out of here, you twisted little beast. I don't need any advice from you. I'll wait until they are a block or two away, and then I'll do it. You just make sure you stay with them."

Judas goes back to the Park to find the target and Adolf stays out in front of the store, waiting for Nino and Pitt.

"These two won't get far," Hitler says to himself. "I've just got to watch Judas kill this guy. I know how much he hates to do it. At least I'll be able to have some fun this morning." With that, he turns away from his assignment and sneaks into the Park to watch Judas.

THE BUDDHISM P.O.J.
HURT NOT OTHERS IN WAYS THAT YOU YOURSELF
WOULD FIND HURTFUL.

CHAPTER 38

▼

"In order to be truly brave, you must first be truly frightened."
-Mark Salvatore Pitifer

"The Lord is my light and my Saviour; whom shall I fear? The Lord is the defender of my life; of whom shall I be afraid."
-Psalms 26:1 (King David 1,100 BC)

"The Lord may not come when you want him, but he's always going to be there on time."
-Lou Gossett Jr.

Nino and Pitt stop in front of the store on their way out. "I really do love these Barnes and Noble bookstores."

"Me too. This is one of my favorite hangouts." Oh, Pitt, wait till you see the libraries in Heaven."

"Are they cool?"

Nino excited, "Pitt, they're awesome! You can read at any pace you want. If you want to simply touch the book and completely retain all of its information and substance. You can become a character in the book and step into the story. If you only want to live a certain part of the book, you can, and you can even change the ending if you choose to."

Pitt wonders, "When you step into these stories, do you realize it is make believe?"

Nino explains, "If that is what you want to experience. You can also bring friends along with you. The options are endless. Pitt, I can't explain to you the endless adventures that await you in Forever. Come on now. We better move along."

As they head toward 20th Street, Nino's head snaps back toward the park. He hears what he immediately recognizes as gunshots. He sees an elderly black man run past him and disappear on one of the side streets. Men and women are hollering for help, and some seem to be chasing the man. A few people look very suspiciously at Nino. He hears one man say to another that he thinks Nino was the gunman. Pitt grabs Nino by the shoulder.

"Nino, let's go see what just happened."

Nino worried, "No, we have to get outta here now. Something is wrong Pitt. I'm not sure what, but I can feel it in my gut. Come on, let's get to the subway."

As they approach the Flat Iron Building on 23rd Street, a yellow cab screeches to a halt right in front of Nino and Pitt, nearly hitting them. The driver has a familiar Jamaican accent and begins speaking to Nino.

Martin smiling, "Nino, my brother, hop in mon and I'll give you and your friend a ride. I am on my way uptown to pick up a regular fare in Times Square, so I hope that will do."

Nino tries to catch his breath, "Times Square will be fine."

Nino hops in the back seat that already had some bags in it so Pitt had to sit in the front next to the driver, Martin.

Nino starts to breath easier, "Martin, this is my friend, Pitt."

Martin tips his cap, "Nice to meet you, Pitt. You been in the city long?"

"No, in fact, Nino is just giving me a tour." Says Pitt.

Martin acts like a tour guide, "Well, if you look behind you, you will see the Flat Iron Building, and this area here is known as 23 Skidoo. Have you ever heard that expression, mon?"

Pitt Chuckles, "Yeah, sure."

Martin explains, "This is where it originated. With so many streets going in so many different directions, it is easy to get away with 23 Skidoo. You blink your eyes and the person has vanished, in which direction, you'll never know."

Pitt smiles, "That's a cool, man … I like it."

Martin grabs Pitt's shoulder and points, "Keep your eyes and ears open and you will learn lots of things riding in old Martin's cab, right Nino?"

Nino looks troubled and doesn't answer Martin.

Martin concerned, "Nino, what's troubling you mon? Is there some thing wrong?"

Nino frowns, "I heard some gunshots coming from Union Square Park, and something told me that we were in danger. I don't know why, but I just felt strongly that we had to get out of there."

Martin nods, "My momma told me that if I ever felt that strong feeling move my mind, that it was an angel talking to my soul, and I had better listen to it. Don't you agree, counselor?"

Nino raised his eyes at Martin. He hadn't told him that Pitt was a counselor.

Pitt surprised, "How did you know that I am a counselor?"

Martin winks, "Maybe I'm an angel sent from God to help you. Maybe I know everything about you from when you were a little boy."

"Oh my God, is it true?" Says Pitt.

Martin chuckles, "Or maybe your business card fell out of your pocket when you got in my cab. I assumed that Pitt is short for Pitifer. The Counselor. That's catchy. Who do you counsel?"

"Little kids, 3rd through 8th grade."

"Do you like your job?" Asks Martin.

Pitt smiles, "Yeah, I have a rewarding job, and I get paid to do something I really enjoy."

"So, what do you do, psychotherapy on third graders? Do you prescribe pills and all that jazz?" Martin asks.

Pitt frowns, "No. They don't need psychotherapy or medicine. All most of them need is someone to love them, someone to give them hope. They need mothers and fathers that stay married and let them have a childhood."

Martin agrees, "That's the main problem, aye? Divorce. It is like Satan's cancer. You don't see the effects it has on society until it is too late."

Pitt purses his lips and shakes his head, "The children don't have anything to believe in. It's hard for them to imagine a loving God who loves them unconditionally, and cares about them, when they don't believe their own parents do."

Martin grins, "Well, at least they have you. I wish there were more people who think as you think. Are you married?"

"Yeah."

"Do you have any kids?" Martin asks.

Pitt looks down, "Not yet."

Martin surprised, "Why not? You would make a good father."

Pitt looks sad, "I was busy trying to write music and become a star. I kept making my wife wait and now that we are trying, well, maybe I made Leigh wait too long. We've been trying to get pregnant for over a year now and we haven't had any luck."

Martin excited, "You want luck? I'll give you some luck. You see what street we are passing?" Martin points. "You see Macy's?"

"Yeah."

Martin chuckles, "This is a magical street, not only because its numbers add up to seven but because this is where the miracle took place Mon."

Pitt knows he's being teased, "What miracle?"

Martin straight faced, "The miracle on 34th Street. Didn't you ever see the movie?"

Pitt laughs, "Are you kidding me, that's one of my favorite films."

"So, it'll give you some luck, okay mon?"

Pitt giggles, "Okay, Mon."

"So, how many kids do you want?" Asks Martin.

Pitt thinks for a moment, "I guess three … Maybe four."

Martin smiles broadly, "Good. Good. You see, 34 comes up again. Alright, you will have three or four kids, now just do me this one favor."

"What's that, name one of them Martin?" Jokes Pitt.

Martin shakes his head, "Nah, I don't like that name much. Name one of them Noah."

Pitt raisies his eyebrows, "Noah? Why Noah?"

Martin grins, "Because I think by the time your son is grown, this world may need another Noah."

Nino and Pitt are both laughing.

"And Pitt," Martin continues. "You will write a book, and it will be a great book that will help many people, especially God's young people. You must write something that will give people hope, especially the children who have no faith. Teach them how to live right. Illuminate the path of Jesus. Yes, this is what you will do. I see it all clearly, mon."

"What are you, a psychic?" Pitt asks.

Martin makes clear, "No mon, just Martin the spiritual seed planter. **Judging each day's work not by the harvest, but by the number of seeds I have planted.** Now, as for your music, you must first form a band. This band will be called … ALL GOD'S CHILDREN!"

Pitt smiles, "All God's Children. I like that. It's a catchy name."

Martin raises his eyebrows, "You see, I'm no ordinary cab driver."

Nino laughs, "You can say that again!"

Martin pulls the cab up to the curb, "Well, here we are boys, 42nd Street and Broadway. Welcome to Times Square."

Nino extends his hand, "Thanks a lot Martin. Pitt and I will be seeing you around soon, I hope."

Martin squeezes Nino's hand, "Don't worry, Nino. You just keep listening to those voices, and everything will turn out all right."

Pitt also shakes Martin's hand, "Take care Martin, I hope your spiritual seeds grow."

Martin beaming, "Oh, they will grow, Mon. Believe me they will grow. Oh yeah, one last thing. I want you to write a song for me named Heaventown. You got it? Heaventown. Ok mon, God bless."

Pitt waves goodbye, "God bless you, Martin. Keep planting those seeds … Heaventown, hah, I like that. Heaven-Town. That Martin is quite a character. What a loving soul."

Nino agrees, "Yeah, in a lot of ways, Martin is just like that little cheesecake shop we went into. He's a little more than you'd expect just based on the package he's wrapped in."

"You've got that right, Nino.…" Pitt takes in the sights and sounds, "Boy oh boy, don't you just love Times Square?"

"Yes sir buddy, There's no place like it in the whole world. I've spent many an afternoon sitting on this hydrant right here, just watching the world go by. Say rookie, you got our lunch?"

Pitt pats the bag, "Yup, it's right here. Why, is it lunch time?"

Nino rubs his stomach with both hands, "Yes sir, it's twelve noon, right on the dot. We can sit right here and eat our lunch.… Nope, I take that back, first we've got to do something more important."

Pitt frowns, "What's that? Pray?"

Nino smirks, "No, no … go to the bathroom!"

Pitt chuckles, "That's one thing about New York. For a society as big and smart as it is, it's pretty hard to find a decent bathroom."

Nino points "Not for me. My bathroom is right over there, the biggest and best bathroom in Times Square.' Nino changes to an engish accent. "For the next 10 minutes, you and I will be guests at the beautiful Times Square Marriott." They walk over to the Marriott Hotel on 46th and Broadway. They take the glass elevator to the restaurant level and help themselves to the facilities.

Author's Note: Deepak Chopra is a fellow seeker of wisdom and truth. He to looks for the common thread of wisdom that weaves through all of the love based religions. In his book called <u>Life After Death</u> he makes the following observations. 'The spiritually mature person pursues a mean-ingful life through the following:

<u>SELF-WORTH:</u> I matter in the divine plan and I am unique in the universe.

<u>LOVE:</u> I am deeply cared for and care for others deeply.

<u>TRUTH:</u> I can see past illusions and distractions.

<u>APPRECIATION & GRATITUDE:</u> I cherish the gift of creation.

<u>REVERENCE:</u> I can feel & see the sacred.

<u>NONVIOLENCE:</u> I respect life in all its forms.

"To live outside these values is painful in this world and the next. In fact the pain could be so intense that it puts a person in Hell."—Deepak Chopra

THE WICCAN P.O.J.
IN THAT IT HARMS NONE, DO AS YE WILL.

CHAPTER 39

▼

"Blessed are those who hunger and thirst for righteousness, for
they will be filled."
-JESUS OF NAZARETH/Matthew 5:6

When you stand praying if you hold anything against anyone, forgive him,
so that your Father in Heaven may forgive you your sins.
-JESUS OF NAZARETH/Mark 11:25

"It isn't your sacrifices and your gifts I want. I want you to be
MERCIFUL!"
-JESUS OF NAZARETH/9:13

Union Square Park is still buzzing with news of the recent murder. Judas and
Adolf are arguing about Adolf"s negligence and letting the targets get away.

Hitler red faced with embarrassment, "I tell you I just turned around for
a second and they were gone. They gave me the old 23 skidoo."

Judas smirks in disgust, "Adolf, don't lie. I know you followed me into
the park to watch me. My God, you act just like a little kid sometimes."

Hitler scowls, "Don't make it out to be such a big deal. They said they
are going to the GWB. And Broadway is the straightest path there. I'm sure
we'll have no trouble finding them and when we do, we will lead the police
right to them. It's that old police hunch thing. We convince the people to
commit the crimes, and then we help the police catch them."

Judas still steaming, "Oh, just shut up for a minute and let me think.
You're probably right about Broadway, but if they hopped on a subway
they could already be there. Here's what we'll do. You take the subway and

I'll stay above ground. We'll just keep going up and back between here and the GWB until we find them."

Hitler tries to brighten the situation, "Another thing in our favor is that the police have a good composite drawing of Jones, so they will be looking for him all over town."

Judas looks worried, "Wait a minute. I've just thought of something."

"What's that?" Asks Hitler.

Judas explains, "We can't have Jones get arrested without us being there to plant the evidence on him. Here's what we have to do. You stay in this area between Chinatown and 23rd Street. I know you don't like to be black, but if you don't do this, I'm going to tell Satan how you messed things up, and if the other side is successful, it will be you he blames. Your hero MS can be awfully unmerciful, can't he?"

Judas' words sting Hitler, "All right! I know what you want me to do."

"Tell me."

Hitler sighs, "I have to get the police to think that I am in this area so they are not looking for him in other parts of the city until you find him."

Judas nods in agreement, "Very good, Adolf. And while you are doing that, I'll keep making loops above ground and below until I find them. I will send for you by tracer beam as soon as I do. Agreed?"

Hitler raises his eyebrows, "Um, don't I need a gun?"

Judas shakes his head, "No. I'll keep it with me for now. There is no need for any more murders. It will bring too many police into the area. Just rob people for right now. But don't over do it."

Hitler disappointed, "No killing, just robbing, how about a rape or two?"

Judas scowls, "You are a disgusting, depraved soul. Do whatever you must, just don't make anymore mistakes, and like I said, don't' be too busy. Space out your crimes."

Hitler offers a mock salute, "Aye-Aye, Sir."

Judas needles Hitler, "Have a nice afternoon, Jesse."

"Jesse?" Hitler asks.

Judas grins, "I just can't help noticing how much you look like Jesse Owens in that body!"

Adolf hisses in disgust and slithers away to start his crime spree. As Judas makes his way up Broadway above ground, he isn't flying as fast as normal because he doesn't want to miss Pitt and Nino. He passes through Times Square and up toward 50th street, just missing his targets as they duck into the Marriott Hotel. Judas keeps flying north as Nino and Pitt return to sit on the hydrants by one of the theaters and enjoy their lunch.

THE ISLAM P.O.J.
NO ONE OF YOU IS A BELIEVER UNTIL HE DESIRES FOR HIS BROTHER THAT WHICH HE DESIRES FOR HIMSELF.

"Jesus set the book of nature before me and I saw that all the flowers he has created are lovely. The splendor of the rose and the whiteness of the lily do not rob the little violet of its scent nor the daisy of its simple charm. I realized that if every tiny flower wanted to be a rose, spring would lose its loveliness and there would be no wildflowers to make the meadows gay. It is just the same in the world of souls—which is the Garden of God. He has created the great saints who are like the lilies and the roses, but he has also created much lesser saints and they must be content to be the daisies or the violets which rejoice his eyes whenever he glances down. Perfection consists in doing his will, in being that which he wants us to be. God does not look at the greatness of our actions, nor even at their difficulty, but at the love with which we do them. He has no need of our works, but only our love.

-Saint Therese of Lisieux, from Story of a Soul.

CHAPTER 40

▼

"Millions of spiritual creatures walk the earth unseen, both when we wake, and when we sleep."
-John Milton

"The intoxication of life and its pleasures and occupations veils the truth from our eyes.
-Jalalu'd-Din Rumi

"Where can I find a man governed by reason instead of habits and urges?"
-Kahlil Gibran

Nino and Pitt finish lunch and continue walking around their favorite part of town.

"Boy, that lunch you bought was really delicious, Nino. You sure know your way around this town."

Nino takes a small bow, "Why thank you, sir. Hey look at that." Nino smiles and points to a movie theatre that is playing Mel Gibson's Movie The Passion of The Christ. "Pitt. It's been almost 20 years since that movie was released, and it still makes the rounds."

Pitt smiles, "I know, I love that movie. It is a work of art. The reason I think it still makes money in the theatres is because of how much more dramatic it is on the large screen. You don't get the same impact on the smaller TV screens."

Nino agrees, "Yeah, that's probably it. Here's something that will surprise you though. This film is considered a modern day miracle by the citizens of Forever."

"Really, why's that?" Pitt asks.

Nino makes clear, "Who would have ever imagined that during the pinnacle of Satan's power and influence, a movie like "The Passion of The Christ" would be made? The fact that a big star from Hollywood, of all places, would put up 25 million dollars of his own money to show the world what Jesus truly went through is, as I said, a miracle."

"Are you telling me that Mel Gibson is a saint?" Asks Pitt.

Nino shakes his head. "I'm not saying he's a saint. But from what I was told, his movie made Jesus cry tears of joy. Barabbas told me that Jesus said that when he went through the actual passion all those years ago, he never imagined that 2,000 years later one of his brothers would show the whole world a portion of what he really went through. Don't you see Pitt? Mel Gibson gave the passion to the world in a way that it had never been done before. He was as brave as any apostle, and his film was divinely inspired. Do you hear what I'm saying? God gave him a gift and he shared it with the world! He didn't hide his light under a basket, or allow the Hollywood elite to bully him."

Pitt raises his eyebrows, "Isn't that something? Saint Mel Gibson. He really is a Braveheart isn't he?"

Nino nods, "Yes he is Pitt. Oh, yes he is."

Pitt puts his arm around Nino, "Nino I could listen to your stories forever."

Nino smiles but turns sad. "And I wish I could share them all with you." Nino sighs, "If only we were going to have more time together."

Pitt somewhat agitated, "Nino, I don't understand something. Why does it all have to happen so fast? Why is time such a factor?"

Nino shrugs his shoulder, "I don't have the answer to that question. All I know is that the shooting back at the Park had something to do with us."

Pitt grows more annoyed, "What are you talking about? We didn't even go back and see what happened. How can you be so sure?"

Nino makes clear, "Because Barabbas told me that whenever I got a strong feeling that something was either very wrong or absolutely right, that I should believe it. He told me that once my mission began, he would have to communicate with me like all of the other guardian angels and nothing more. If he materializes, Satan can cry foul. Believe me, Pitt, that was Barabbas back at the park, talking to my soul."

Pitt jokes, "Maybe it wasn't Barabbas. Maybe it was just a little indigestion."

Nino becomes angry. "Pitt, this isn't just some game we are playing here. I don't want to scare you, but I feel it."

"Feel what?"

Nino's expression turns grim, "Evil, I feel Satan and his demons on our trail, and I am certain that our time together is growing short. You already know most of what I need to tell you. You hold on tight to that notebook I gave you, remember the things we've talked about, and no matter what happens you be brave."

Pitt looks worried, "Nino, you're talking like you are going to die or something. Come on, think positive. We're going to get to the GWB and you're gonna keep right on walking and living."

Nino looks doubtful, "I hope you're right, Mark, but I just don't feel it. I'll tell you one thing, though, by hook or by crook, I am going to make it to that bridge. They'll have to kill me in order to stop me."

Pitt grabs Ninos hand, "And if they kill you, then they are going to have to kill me, too."

Nino pushes his hand away, "No! You can't think like that! My job is to deliver the message so that you can share it with the world. If you die trying to save me, who is that going to help? God or Satan?"

Pitt looks down at his shoes, "I see what you are saying. It's not really going to help God, but if we both die trying, Satan won't be able to claim victory, either."

Nino remains adamant, "But, if that happens, what have we accomplished?! A tie? This isn't just about you and me. There are very brave souls in Heaven who are counting on us so much that they are willing to risk their eternal fates. There are also countless souls down here that desperately need our help. This mission, to me, is like being in a championship prizefight. We're fighting in the other guy's hometown so we have to go for the knockout. To die during the fight, or to earn a draw, just won't do. This is our chance, Pitt, to stand up and do something that really matters. The stage is set. The curtain is drawn, and the spotlight is on us. Let's not spend the rest of our eternities thinking in hindsight about all of the different ways we could have been successful. I have to try with all my might to give you everything I have until it is my time to go."

Pitt tries interject, "But—"

Nino Angry, "But nothing! Pitt, my time, any which way you slice it, is short. When we get to that bridge, if there is a demon on our trail, I want him to follow me, not you. I'm like the bright father bird who captures the enemy's attention and draws away from what is really important. My eggs. My notes and my words have to grow into birds and fly all around this world through your productions!"

Pitt starts to understand, "It's just like Jesus in the Garden of Gethsemane. He was more worried about the safety of the apostles than he was about himself. He sacrificed himself so that his apostles could live. Thereby, he protected his word."

Nino softens his tone, "That's right. He knew that he had given them all they needed to be successful by then, and that now their survival was what was ultimately important. Do you understand now? Once I have given you my message, you have to faithfully deliver it. You must survive, or my death will be in vain, and the hopes and dreams of our very brave brothers in Forever will be laid waste. Pitt, I need you to promise me, give me your word of honor, that you will not put your life in jeopardy trying to save me."

Pitt hesitates, "I don't know if I can promise that, Nino."

Nino starts to walk away, "Do it, or we separate right now. Better for you to be alive with three quarters of the message than to be dead with the whole thing. So, what's it gonna be?

Pitt gives in, "You have my word, Nino."

Nino brightens "Pinky swear?"

Pitt smirks, "Pinky swear?"

Nino chuckles, "That's right. Cross your heart, too."

Pitt laughing, "Nino, you're crazy!"

Nino laughing, "Come on, now."

Pitt complies, "Alright, alright. Pinky swear and cross my heart, you have my word."

Nino looks releaved, "Good. Now, once our walk is over and we say goodbye, your guardian angel will return to you. As long as you stay on the path, Satan and his demons will not be able to harm you. They will try to scare you. They can tempt you, and believe me, they will come at you hard, but they won't be able to hurt you in any way. They can't harm one hair on your head."

"How come I don't have my guardian angel with me right now?" Pitt asks.

Nino explains, "We're both out here on our own, Pitt. That's the way it has to be. No other prophets ever stood in such a precarious spot. Oh, don't get me wrong, I'm not putting them down. Their lives were in danger just as ours are. The big difference with our mission is that our eternities are hanging in the balance. The other prophets, never had to risk their eternity."

Pitt looks a little pale, "When you put it like that, it's very scary."

Nino pats him on the shoulder, "I know, my man, but just be brave. I've got this strong feeling that God is with us, and that everything will work out if we just have faith and remain courageous. Now, be strong and let's continue our journey."

They turn their attention to Times Square and continue making their way uptown along Broadway.

Pitt frowns, "Nino, I remember for a while they were trying to clean this place up, but everything has gone back to the way it used to be."

Nino nods, "The way it used to be? Shit, this place is a hundred times worse than it's ever been."

"What happened? Why did things go backwards?" Pitt asks.

Nino searches for an analogy, "It's like bombing for cockroaches in an apartment building. The most you can hope for is that they will stay away for a little while, but they always come back. And more often than not, the situation is worse than it was before you bombed. But, we're not dealing with roaches here. No sir, what you are dealing with here is demons, dope and an endless stream of temptation."

"Demons and dope?" Pitt asks.

Nino nods, "Hey, I was shocked too, but it's true Pitt. Believe me when I tell you, the demons are everywhere."

Pitt tries to envision demons flying around, "This is crazy."

Nino speculates, "I'd have to guess that at least half of the people out here right now are possessed by demons, and the other half are being tempted by demons, as we speak."

Pitt can't believe what he is hearing, "Possessed by demons? Fifty percent? Are you kidding me?"

Nino explains, "No sir, I'm not. In our modern society, even those who consider themselves religious, for the most part do not believe in demons or the existence of the Devil. Nor do they recognize that it is the demon possession and influence that causes almost all of the mental, physical, spiritual and social problems that wreck havoc on the human condition. Think of Jesus' ministry for a moment. What did he do to prove he was the Messiah? Here, rookie, open up the book to Matthew. Chapter 10 ought to do the trick."

Nino hands Pitt a tattered minature Gideon Bible and Pitt pushes it away.

Pitt faking agitation, "I don't need that! What kind of a messenger do you think you have here?"

Nino smiles, "Okay, alright … let's hear it."

"Alright, he umm … cured people who were sick or crippled. He miraculously fed thousands of people. He turned water into wine. He raised the dead."

"And?"

Pitt stares out at the huddled masses, "And he expelled demons … My God, Nino, I've read the Bible hundreds of times and it never hit me."

"What never hit you?" Nino asks.

"What you are saying about the demons. If they were so prevalent in Jesus' time, why should they be any less prevalent in our days?"

Nino nods, "Now you are starting to get the picture. The demons didn't go away. Their numbers have grown as steadily as the world's population since the beginning of the Great Game. There are more demons now than ever before. Why, If I could let you see for a moment what they showed me from Heaven, you would die. Demons are swarming around people, like bees around a hive. They are tireless, and they are looking for any opening they can find."

Pitt wonders, "But, shouldn't the number of fallen angels have remained the same as when they were first cast down?"

Nino raises his eyebrows, "You are sharp, but you are missing something. You are forgetting about the souls of the damned. Satan's army receives hundreds of thousands of new recruits every day to avoid being sent to the abyss. They are given some of the same powers as the fallen angels to possess and influence souls. It is important when you write your book to spend some time talking about Satan's soldiers."

Pitt stops walking for a moment and stares out at the people, trying to envision the air filled with demons.

"Nino, it's so strange to try to visualize that demons are swarming all around us."

Nino agrees, "At night it's even worse."

"Why's that?"

Nino clarifies, "Satan is not omnipotent and all powerful like Allah. His sources are limited. He can do more damage at night because there are less people awake. The demons leave their sleeping host souls unattended and go searching for new victims to lead astray. The demon to soul ratio is in Satan's favor after midnight, and it reaches its pinnacle at 3:05 am. This is when the forces of evil are the strongest. It is also the exact opposite time of when Jesus was killed. Think about it for a moment. When do most of the bad things happen in this world?"

Pitt thinks for a moment, "You're right. Most crimes do take place during the night and early hours before dawn."

Nino looks worried, "If I could describe to you the spiritual and physical danger you are in when you are out and about after that 'witching hour' of midnight, you would never leave the house after dark again. Watch any little child after the sun goes down. Their spiritual instinct compels them to fear the night. It is natural to be afraid of the dark, because this is when the prince of darkness and all his allies are at their strongest. This is when they do the most harm."

Pitt chuckles nervously, "So, after all these years the truth is finally out, there really is a boogie man, isn't there?"

Nino looks scared, "Oh, yes there is Pitt, and he's after each and every one of us."

"It is just so hard to imagine. I mean, exactly what are the demons after? Our souls?" Pitt asks.

"Think of the predicament of a demon for a moment. If you were sentenced to an eternity in Hell, with no chance of parole, wouldn't you try to have as much pleasure as possible until then?"

Pitt tries to empathize with the demons plight, "Yeah, I see what you mean, but what pleasure do they get out of pulling other souls down with them?"

Nino explains, "If they don't do Satan's work, they are sent back to the abyss. A demon can only experience pleasure vicariously through the souls that they possess. They take delight in controlling even the tiniest portion of your personality. They look for your weak spot and then they try to exploit it. The demons' ultimate goal is to gradually enslave the soul until eventually it has almost complete control of the person's mind, or personality. The demon will weigh you down systematically with seemingly harmless little addictions that gradually destroy the soul's hope, faith, and quality of life. They get souls hooked on dope, and then the soul is in trouble. The most precious commodity on earth is time, and stealing time is what Satan does best."

Pitt confused, "What do you mean, they get us hooked on dope? Are you telling me that all these people are secretly using crack and heroin?"

Nino shakes his head, "The demon's dope is anything and everything they can use to steal your time."

"What do you mean?" Pitt asks.

"You've got to remember something, the immortal soul temporarily imprisoned in a mortal body, under the very best of circumstances, is at least moderately depressed. The precariousness of life's existence, our aging bodies and the knowledge of our inevitable death weigh heavy on our minds. What did Psalm 119:37 say: **Turn my eyes away from worthless things; renew my life according to your word.** In order to push these bad thoughts out of our conscience, we turn to dope."

Pitt somewhat agitated, "What are you talking about? I never used drugs in my life. Even when I was pledging the Kappa Sigma fraternity at Hobart College, I didn't take a sip of alcohol … Well maybe a sip." Pitt grins.

Nino continues, "Pitt, follow my logic now. Dope is anything that wastes your time, TV, music, sports, beauty, anything in excess is a dope. It numbs you and makes room for the demons to do their work."

"So, you are saying it's all dope, and everyone is hooked in some way?"

Nino nods, "That's right. Just look around you. Open your eyes. The dope is everywhere."

"Nino, I kind of understand what you are saying, but what am I supposed to see?" Pitt asks.

Nino points, "Well, let's start with the obvious first. Do you see that man in the cowboy hat going into that store across the street?"

"Yeah."

Nino opens Pitts eyes, "Well, he's not going in there to buy bread. That's a whore house and his dope is sex. He goes there at least five to ten times a week to purchase all types of various sexual favors. He has no savings. He spends every extra cent he can gather on prostitutes. And speaking of prostitutes, all the call girls who work in that cat house are hooked on at least two controlled substances. They are totally addicted and simply live from fix to fix. They turn their tricks to get that fix. Oooh—check me out I'm rapping! … See the man standing near the three card monte dealer?"

Pitt smirks, "Yeah, you can't beat those guys. Believe me, I know."

Nino chuckles, "They got you, huh? Well, you know what they say—there's a sucker born every minute!"

"How was I supposed to know that I was set up by a whole group of people?"

"So, now you understand the game, right?"

"Right, it's purely a sucker's game." Says Pitt.

Nino agrees, "That's right, but not for that man over there. He is the bankroll for that group of three-card-monte, hide-the—pea playing jokers. He's not gambling, he wins every time a sucker loses his money. His mistake is what he does with the money he earns. He takes his cut of the winnings every day and goes to visit my man, Zipp."

"Zipp?"

Nino nods, "That's right, Zipp. Thomas Anthony Mazzocchi. My friend Zipp and his partners Joey-B & Johnny-Q run one of the most lucrative gambling joints in all of NYC."

Pitt wonders, "Is gambling a sin?"

"Let me put it to you like this, if you are a dishonest lawyer or a car salesman you can stay in business for years, but if you are a dishonest bookie, you won't last one weekend. The way I see it, gambling isn't a sin, unless it becomes excessive."

"Excessive in what way?" Asks Pitt.

Nino puts into simple words, "How often do you gamble? How much do you gamble? How much does it control your life? Is it something you do from time to time because it gives you a rush, or is it something you feel compelled to do every day? Is it something you have to do or else you feel bad? Have you lost so much money over the years that you will never even come close to breaking even? Or even worse, are you indebted to a bookie or a loan shark? It is hard for me to say what is or isn't a sin, all I know is that when something starts to take control of your life, no matter what it is, you are in danger of being possessed. Your behaviors are controlled by an unnatural need."

Pitt can relate, "You know, a couple of years ago I started going out without my wife. I started hanging around with a younger crowd, going to parties and wild clubs. I didn't realize it at the time, but I was developing some bad habits that had more of a hold on me than I would like to admit. Before I knew it, all I could think about was when I would go to the club again, or when the next party was. I was on a evil road, and I didn't even see it coming. I was rationalizing, trying to justify my bad behavior. I was even trying to convince my wife that there was nothing wrong with going to a striptease club."

Nino smiles, "How did you fare, counselor?"

Pitt chuckles, "Not very well. She and her sister ganged up on me, and made me promise that I would never have another lap dance again. I woke up in the middle of the night in a cold sweat. The thought of not being able to feed that part of me woke me out of a sound sleep, and that's when I realized that there was something bad about the whole scene. I had been trying to partially quench which is in reality an unquenchable thirst. I now see the downward spiral I was in. The cycle of sin is never ending, and increasingly more controlling. I was becoming a slave and didn't even realize it."

"You were hooked on pornography." Says Nino.

Pitt somewhat irritated, "I wasn't hooked on pornography. I was spending time with other women, and thinking lustful thoughts, but that's it … One time a friend and I went to a gentlemen's club called the Musky Fig. That was the first time I ever went into to a place like that, and I really liked it. I figured hey, if I do this once in a while, it was kind of like getting the excitement of being single again, but not hurting anybody. New girls to spend time with, a little dancing, a little touching, but no strings attached. Over time, I got to know some of the girls, and I liked the attention they gave me. However, it gradually started to become a preoccupation. I was being pulled out onto a dangerous sea. So I just stopped going—cold turkey. I still feel the urge to go in sometimes…." Pitt sighs at the thought of it. "I really did like that scene."

Nino smirks, "And I'll bet you liked that dress code too, didn't you? Don't you see, Pitt, even though you were not sucked all the way into the world of pornography, you were on the road. Exotic massage, lap dances, prostitution, extramarital affairs, divorce, remarriage, and a continuing cycle. You were a druggy and strange-pussy was your dope."

Pitt blushes at Nino's bluntness, "You're right. I know. I see it more clearly now. It also caused an emotional wedge to form between me and my wife. I tried to tell her that my behavior had nothing to do with being dissatisfied with her, and that this was just a "man thing", but you could see how the stress of it was taking its toll on her."

Nino frowns, "Hey, Pitt, you can't lay that "just a man thing" on a woman and expect her to buy into it. When you do that, you are no different than any other chump who's trying to get his wife to say that she understands his needs and that it's okay for him to satisfy his sexual appetite by being with other women. Shit, even if a woman is convinced that she understands, it won't ever be alright. If she really loves you that is. All that will happen is that you'll both end up growing further and further apart. Nothing good will come of it believe me.

Your feelings for your wife may not change because you will be doing anything you want, but her feelings for you will eventually grow cold, or even worse, numb. She will begin to snub your sexual advances. You will grow angry. The arguments will increase. In time you will leave her, and in your blindness, you will think that it is her fault. That's the road you were on, Pitt. The road to adultery is the road that leads to death, purgatory, and ultimately, Hell. Only the truly loving, unselfish souls will be allowed to enter the Kingdom of Forever."

Pitt tips his imaginary cap, "Thank you, Nino, for counseling the counselor. I see the dope side of it now."

They cross Broadway and walk by some of the grand old theaters. Nino pats Mark on the shoulder, a sudden thought occurring to him. "Hey Pitt, you're old enough to remember Wilt Chamberlain, aren't you? He used to be the center for the LA Lakers back in the seventies."

"Yeah sure, why?"

"He once claimed to have had sex with 20,000 different women. Wilt was a real egomaniac, and I was always a loyal Knick fan so I never really liked him to begin with. But I heard him give an interview a year or so before he died. He said the wisdom he gained from having had sex with so many different women was that he felt he would have had a richer more fulfilling life if he had sex with just one woman who really loved him 20,000 different times. You hang on to what you have Pitt, and God will bless you with a rich and fulfilled life."

Pitt contemplates this bit of information for a second. "He was the ultimate bachelor, wasn't he? Big Wilt seemed like he had an envious life, a pro basketball player, all the ladies he wanted. And yet it sounds like he died sad and lonely. The man who slept with 20,000 of the world's most beautiful women and scored 100 points in a single game, died disillusioned. Poor Wilt."

Nino laughs. "Poor Wilt nothing, he made it back to Forever, where he is more famous for sharing that last bit of wisdom then he is for scoring 100 points. You also need to mention some of the less obvious forms of dope."

"Like what?" Asks Pitt.

Nino"For example, see those guys in the $2,000 suits? Those are my friends Nick Ferreri & Gary Teague. They're both self made millionaires. They started the Truck Town/Laid Law empire, but they had to work over ninety hours a week for much of their youth. Their dope is work and money.

Oh, and Pitt, try to remember their names. Those guys are two of the most generous people in the city, and they have reputations for helping under-dogs get started. Nick was quite a basketball player in his day to. Back in the early 70's he was the starting point guard for the Florida Gators!".

Pitt laughs. "Wow that's big time basketball.... Pitt writes down his name. "Ok Nino, I'll remember him. That could be helpful down the road. Man, you sure do know a lot of people."

Nino agrees,"That's because I talk to everyone, and usually I listen more than I speak."

Pitt smiles "You've got that counselor blood."

Nino smiles and continues walking. He points to Bobby Didsbury's pala-tial 5 Star Sports Club. "Check out that fine looking brunette on the tread-mill, her name is Tiffany Sculli. She's one of the best personal trainers in the city. She also teaches aerobics and yoga classes 6 days a week! But she still has to work out at least an extra hour every day or she feels anxious and unproductive."

"So her dope is exercise?"

Nino nods, "That's right."

"I never thought of exercise as being a dope. But I see what you mean." Says Pitt.

Nino points across the street and waves, "See those three guys getting on the subway with their golf clubs? That's Timmy Northrup, Joe Sposato, and Mike Ferrara. There real nice fellas, but they have to play golf almost every day of the summer. They also gamble everytime they play so theirs is a double dope."

"But who are those people hurting?" Pitt asks.

"Themselves. God wants us to be self disciplined. He wants us to have control over our lives and our behaviors. Jesus fasted in order to control his bodily urges."

Pitt nods, "I see what you mean. So when Satan tempted the very hun-gry Jesus to turn stones into loaves of bread, Jesus had the internal power to turn him down."

Nino perks up, "That's right. The more self disciplined we become, the harder it is for Satan to ensnare us. You also have to remember that one of Satan's greatest tactics against us is to preoccupy us with activities that will cause us to spend our time on something other than gaining wisdom, connecting with people, and doing God's work."

Pitt interjects, "So, if a father is out playing golf, then he's not home doing doing something his wife and children, or reading one of the holy books."

Nino agrees, "That's right. **There is only so much time in a day, Pitt. And there are only so many days in a life.** If people only knew what was really important in the infinite scheme of things, they really would change their lives. Look at our modern society. People would rather sit in front of a TV or a computer screen than visit with other people."

"But, Nino, what is specifically negative about watching TV?" Pitt Asks.

"TV keeps you from thinking."

Pitt disagrees, "What do you mean? I think all the time in front of the TV."

Nino explains, "Sure, but not in the same way as when you are reading a book, or talking to another person. The thinking that goes on in front of the TV is an extremely controlled form of thinking. You are not free to pause and ponder the way you can when you are reading a book or talking with a person, because the movie or TV show is continually moving forward, taking your thoughts where it ultimately wants you to go. It's mind control and nothing less. The human mind wants what it sees and hears about. It goes where it is led. Human beings really are a lot like sheep in that we are easily led. Think about what the movies and the music of our society make us long for, sex, drugs, money, power, food, and so on."

"So, Satan is really using mind control?" Pitt asks.

"It's not like Satan is a movie producer or a TV program controller. However, it is obvious that the majority of the people in that line of business are very secular in their way of thinking. Their actions usually are not influenced by thoughts of what God would want them to do, or what's best for children, the family, or society. They have no moral compass. All they care about is whatever will get them the best ratings, or sell the most tickets."

Pitt tries to understand, "So, it isn't like these people actually know what God would want and are consciously going against God."

Nino shakes his head, "Probably not. Most of those people simply do not possess God's wisdom. In many ways, they are symbolic of the society they represent. Amoral, rather than immoral."

"Amoral?" Questions Pitt.

Nino explains, "Amoral means that they fail to see that certain behaviors are actually wrong. For example, they may think that a man cheating on his wife is normal human behavior. They don't see it as right or wrong. To the blind observer, that's just the way things are. It is only when you clearly know that something is wrong in God's eyes, and you do it anyway, that you are guilty of acting immorally."

Pitt is filled with shame. "Now I know what Paul meant when he said, "Why is it the good I want to do I don't do, and the bad I don't want to do, I do?" Hearing you speak the truth simply woke me up to what I already knew and could feel in my heart."

"You're right Pitt, the apostle Paul summed us up well didn't he? But, God our father understands our weaknesses. He knows how Satan is trying to trip us up. All he wants you to do is to keep on trying. If you stay close to God, hopefully you will in time be able to outgrow these potentially dangerous desires. Just always keep trying to be a better person, and always remember that God truly does help those who help themselves."

Pitt discouraged, "Everytime I think I've over come a certain temptation and reached a new spiritual level, I am always disappointed. It's like thinking you've finally mastered the game of golf because you shoot one great round. I'm starting to realize that we merely experience temporary moments of spiritual strength, but the battle will never be won completely until the game is finally over."

Nino can relate, "I know what you mean. It's like my suicidal thoughts. I'll go through periods of my life when everything is going well, and I'll think, wow, I'm finally past it. But the depression and the thoughts always return."

"That's just it. Satan never gives up, and we have to understand that. He knows our weaknesses and he will gradually try to wear us down. Our occasional spiritual victories do not discourage our great adversary."

Nino continues, "Just remember, TV and movies are a very big part of Satan's plan of attack. He isolates individuals little by little. He gradually cuts people off from the very souls that could help them become better human beings. He is using technology to break up families, friendships, and communities. He is also using it to prevent new relationships from ever blossoming. Satan has learned that the isolated soul is easier to control."

Pitt's eyes have been opened, "It's so obvious when it's pointed out to me. How can we all be so blind? Even when I'm home with Leigh, we usually just watch TV together. We don't really talk that much, unless we're in an argument."

Nino nods, "The sad thing is that you wouldn't be getting into so many arguments if you would talk more. Share your feelings with one another and let her know she is an important part of your life. You modern married couples don't share your lives. You cohabitate, but most of you don't even know each other."

Pitt agitated,"What do you mean, we don't know each other. I've known Leigh for over twenty years!"

Nino makes clear, "Pitt, it takes a lifetime to really get to know someone, and it doesn't happen by watching TV together. You kids nowadays are something else. You want everything yesterday. Every one of you are just in one big a hurry. You go steady too soon, you have sex too soon. You get married too soon, you have kids to soon, you get divorced too soon, and before you know it, you die too soon. Most of you end up no wiser than you were at sweet 16! There are to many people living these lives of perpetual adolescence, allowing themselves to be controlled by hormonal urges, and making the same mistakes over and over again, this is not truly living. When a soul sees its life and all that it could have been, it is a very disheartening experience. If people would just take the time to love others and enjoy them, their lives would be so much more rewarding. The Devil steals our time by driving us to excess. He fills our day with so many distractions, preoccupations, addictions and obsessions, that gradually and eventually he takes control of our minds and possesses our souls. Once that happens—"

Pitt finishes Ninos thought "He becomes our God ... My father was talking about this before he died, and I didn't really grasp what he was saying until just now. Your God is that which influences or affects how you choose to behave in your life. So if all you can think about is how to make more money, then money is your God."

Nino agrees, "And since money is not a being, then to serve money or be controlled by money is to serve the being who created money."

Pitt shakes his head in dismay, "Bad old Satan—the father of money, greed, adultery, pornography, gossip, envy, murder, hatred, perversion, prejudice, violence, and the list goes on and on …"

Nino excited, "We must warn the people Mark, before it's too late. Every soul must start examining their lives and asking themselves, 'Why am I driven to do such and such? What is the origin of this urge, and who will benefit from my behavior?' People must to start examining what their true motivation really is. Who is really pulling their strings, God or Satan?"

Nino notices some young men dressed in suits preaching to people on the street corner.

Nino points at the young men, "We also must learn to be happy about anyone who is trying to do God's work. Jehovah's Witnesses and Mormons are laughed at and scorned by many people because they go door to door with their message. But, they are modern day apostles in Yahweh's eyes, and they should be supported."

Pitt agrees, "I hate to admit it, but I used to get irritated when they would show up at my door. However, as the years have gone by I have come to enjoy their visits. I just let them no right up front that I am not a potential convert."

Nino claps his hands, "That's what you should do. I encourage them to try and make converts of those who have no faith, and to respect those who do. Sometimes they are over zealous, but most of them mean well. They just need to realize that a religion serves its purpose if it helps to keep you on the Path of Jesus. We all need to except that God loves and works through all sincere religions whose mantle is love."

Pitt smiles, "I agree with you Nino. There is holiness in all of the love based religions. I live near the Mormon's holy mountain, Hill Cumorah. This is the spot where an Angel gave Joseph Smith the holy book of Mormon. I like to go up there and meditate sometimes. It's cool to think that an Angel once stood there, and that people from all over the world consider it their holy land. Even though I am not a Mormon, I still feel very serene when sit on that holy hill. I actually feel the Holy Spirit, which to me is further proof that God is with the Mormons, The Jehovah's Witnesses, … he's with us all.…"

As Nino is about to respond, A New York City patrol car slowly passes by on the other side of Broadway. Nino sees a thick white hairy arm hanging out of the window. He feels as if the police officer is staring at him and as he makes eye contact with him, the officer guns the engine, flicks his lights on, and attempts to make a u-turn. Nino grabs Pitt's arm and pulls him through the ocean of people trying to get lost in the crowd. The police car is trapped in a bottle neck caused by a broken-down cab. The cop jumps out of the car, yelling for Nino to stop, but he cannot leave his car unattended in the middle of the road. Nino and Pitt bolt into the subway station and make their way up town, toward the GWB.

THE AFRICAN P.O.J.
BEFORE TAKING A POINTED STICK TO PINCH A BABY BIRD, YOU SHOULD TRY IT ON YOURSELF TO FEEL HOW IT HURTS.

"When Life hits you with one of its devastating blows. And you don't feel like you can take even one more step, drop to your knees and crawl!"
-Mark Salvatore Pitifer (Ryan Parry & The Miracle Mile.)

CHAPTER 41

▼

"The good Shepard is always in search of the lost sheep."
-Bishop Fulton J. Sheen

"Be selfless, and love all life."
-*Siddhartha Gautama* BUDDHA (563 BC)

"He who has found the way has many helpers."
-Mencius

Millions of miles away from New York City, Jimmy Natelli the heavenly accountant is not having a very good day. He is fuming as he paces back and forth, shouting at Peter.

Natelli fuming, "Peter! The numbers just don't add up. Do you realize what this means?"

Peter remains calm, "Nitt, it means the numbers don't add up."

Natelli shakes his head, "Oh, that's right! Make light of the situation. Things have been a mad house around here since September 13th. Inexperienced Guardian Angels are jumping the gun and not waiting for the outcome. New arrivals are coming in from all over the planet. Do you realize how hard it is to keep all those numbers straight? And now, on top of everything else, I've got a missing soul that we can't account for."

Peter puts his arm around Nitts shoulders, "Nitt, I was swamped too. Maybe I missed somebody in the confusion. Maybe the number I sent you is wrong. I doubt it is a missing soul, it hardly ever is."

Nitts mood lightens a bit, "But what if you are wrong this time. I wish it was just as simple as taking your word for it, but Jesus wouldn't like it very much if we were wrong. You know what this means, don't you?"

Now Peter looks worried, "Oh, no, not a heavenly audit."

"What other choice do we have?" Asks Nitt

In Heaven, as strange as it may sound, the comings and goings of all souls are meticulously recorded by hand.

"Peter get your crew to do a search of all the records from September 13th and 14th. If we don't find a name without a number, then all is well. However, if you do find a name without a number, contact the soul's guardian angel right away. Have them first conduct a search of Forever and then, God forbid, an earthly search. Let's try to keep the whole thing hush-hush. We don't need to unnecessarily upset the King."

Peter confident, "Nitt, don't worry. I'm certain it's just a normal oversight."

Nitt grows irritated again, "Peter, oversights aren't normal. They only happen once in a great while, and everytime they do, it worries the day-lights out of me."

Peter remains positive, "Well, what I mean is, think of the times we usually do have oversights. It's on days like September 13th and 14th. And it always checks out. So, listen, no matter what happens, in less than two hours, we will deliver you either the number or the soul. Now relax old buddy. St. Peter is on the job."

Nitt Runs his fingers throw his hair, "Alright. Okay. I know you'll take care of this. You always do. I'm just such a worrier. It's times like these that I wish I still smoked!"

Peter puts his arm around Natelli and squeezes him tightly before they go their separate ways.

The Yogi's P.O.J.

In happiness and suffering, in joy and grief, we should regard all creatures as we regard our own self, and should therefore refrain from inflicting upon others such injury as would appear undesirable to us if inflicted upon ourselves.

CHAPTER 42

▼

"If thou chance to be slain in the battle, the warrior's Heaven wilt be thy reward. If victorious, and thou emergeth from the fray, the joys of earth await thee."
-KRISHNA/THE BHAGAVAD GITA (3,137 BC)

"Old age is not venerable because of time, nor counted by the number of years one lives, but the understanding of a person is grey hairs, and a spotless life is old age. There was a man who pleased God, and was loved by him, and while living among sinners he was taken from the earth. He was taken away lest wickedness alter his understanding, or deceit beguile his soul. *For fascination of vanity obscures good things, and roving desire perverts the innocent mind.* His soul pleased God, so he was removed from the midst of iniquities. Being made perfect in a short space, he fulfilled long years. Fore the Grace of God and his mercy are with his saints, and he guards his elect."
-KING SOLOMON/Book of Wisdom 3&4 (950 BC)

Meanwhile back on earth, Nino and Pitt jump onto an overstuffed number nine train, headed uptown to the George Washington Bridge. Nino is visibly shaken and badly winded. Pitt is upset and looking around to see who or what they had been running from. As the train pulls away from the station, Nino tries to catch his breath.

Pitt anxious, "Nino, are you okay?"

Nino breathing heavily, "Yeah, I'm alright. Boy, oh boy, that's a lot faster than I'm used to moving."

Pitt concerned, "Nino, what the hell is going on here? Why are we being chased by the cops?"

Nino irritated, "How should I know? Just keep your voice down. We don't need everybody on this train knowing our business. Just sit tight and let me think."

Nino takes some deep breaths and tries to relax. As they sit on the train, all is quiet except for the sound of a small radio being listened to by an old man seated across the aisle. The old man is sound asleep, and he has his radio duct taped to the side of his body. As the train comes to a stop at 59th Street, a newsflash comes across the airways. Nino freezes as he listens to the news.

The radio buzzes, and New York's top news man John Thomas speaks to the city: "It appears that the man who was killed earlier today in Union Square Park is the victim of a robbery. Eye witnesses say an elderly black man killed the victim in cold blood while several bystanders looked on in horror. Witnesses say that the assailant was last seen fleeing the park. Other witnesses say they saw the older man getting into a cab near 19th or 20th Street. Some park regulars said that the suspect resembled a homeless man who often visits the area. It appears that the suspect was able to pull the old 23 skidoo on New York's finest. A citywide search is still underway. It has been said that the suspect has continued his crime spree along the Broadway line. There were two more armed robberies and one rape. The suspect is considered armed, and extremely dangerous, so please do not try to intervene on your own."

Pitt whispers to Nino, barely audible as the train passengers chatter about the news. "Nino, that cop thought you were the killer."

Nino looks nervously around the train, "For all intents and purposes, I probably am the killer."

"What are you talking about?" Pitt asks.

Nino keeps his voice low, "Don't you see? Satan and his boys are trying to frame me. They are probably hoping that I'll end up in jail or dead, and that you'll skidaddle to save your own hide."

"Well, if that's what they think, they are in for a surprise. I'm not going anywhere."

Nino grabs Pitt's arm, "Pitt, listen to me. If I do get arrested, you've got to walk away like you don't even know me. We can't have you connected to a criminal."

Pitt protests, "But you aren't a criminal."

Nino continues, "Pitt, we're not dealing with some juvenile delinquent here. We're dealing with Satan, and I'm not sure how much he can do, short of having me killed. But, I don't think he's gonna have a hard time framing a crazy black homeless man, who lives in a pipe for murder."

Pitt agrees, "You're right, of course, that's just what he's going to do. But they haven't got you yet, and that means we still have a chance to get to the bridge."

Nino mood lightens, "That's right. But first I've got to do something very important. Stand up—we're getting off at the next stop."

Pitt confused, "But this is 72nd Street. Why are we getting off here? Let's just go straight to the bridge."

Nino explains, "Mark, first of all, we missed our transfer when that damn newsflash came on back at 59th Street. We've got to go back down to 59th to catch the A train to the GWB. More importantly, our tour in NYC is not over just yet. It can be nothing but divine intervention that caused us to miss our stop and end up here."

"What's here?"

Nino's smiles, "Why, only one of New York City's finest pleasures. Grays Papaya—the best and cheapest hot dogs in the world!"

Pitt is shocked, "Gray's Papaya! Nino? We're being chased by the police, not to mention the demons. Our eternities hand in the balance, and you want to stop and get a hot dog?"

Nino undaunted, "Hey messenger, don't forget who's in charge here. I could be in jail or dead any moment now, and if I get a little bit of an opportunity to grab me one last Grays Papaya, I'm damn sure gonna do it!"

Pitt shrugs his shoulders, "Ok, go get your dog. I'm gonna call my sister Shari. She lives right up the street on 79th and Amsterdam. I want her to meet you. We can walk up there while you eat your dog, and then we'll catch that train."

Nino walks toward the stand, "Sounds like a plan to me. We should be pretty safe walking up Amsterdam."

While Nino orders his hot dog, Pitt calls his sister on a nearby pay phone.

"Hello?"

"Shari? It's Mark."

Shari worried, "Mark? Where are you?"

"I'm in a phone booth near Grays Papaya on 72nd."

Shari somewhat irritated, "What are you doing there? Why don't you just come up to the apartment?"

Pitt frowns, "We are going to be walking up Amsterdam but we really don't' have time to come upstairs."

"Why not?" Shari asks.

"Shari, I don't have time to give you the whole story right now, but I do want you to meet Nino. So meet us out in front of your apartment in about five minutes. Oh, and could you bring about twenty or thirty dollars? I'm good for it."

Shari frustrated, "Oh, shut up. I'll see you in five minutes."

As they walk up Amsterdam toward 79th Street, they pass by a used book store called the Book Nook, and Nino can't resist browsing through the sale cart. He's like a kid in a candy store.

Pitt smiling. "Find anything good?"

Nino is beaming and holding a book. "Yes, this is a must read. It is a book by Harold S. Kushner, called **How Good Do We Have To Be?**"

Pitt takes the book in his hand. "Harold Kushner? He's a Rabbi, isn't he? Didn't he write **When Bad Things Happen To Good People?**"

Nino smiles, "Yes, very good counselor."

Pitt is smiling "That was a good book."

"Well this is a better one. It is his masterpiece. He paints a warm and accurate picture of God. He has a very positive and forgiving view of human nature, and his strategies for living a healthy & holy life are wonderful. Here, let me buy it for you. It's only a dollar."

Nino reaches into his pocket and then realizes he doesn't have any money left. As Pitt and Nino laugh over their poverty, the owner of the store, Beverly Sears, comes out to say hello to her friend Nino.

Beverly laughs, "Well you guys are just having way too much fun out here."

Nino is smiling at the sight of his friend. "Beverly, how are you dear?"

"I'm splendid Nino, and you?"

Nino looks inside the store, "I can't kick. Bev. Is my friend Sheila Kelly working today?"

"Nope she is out shopping for toys at FAO Schwarze with her grand-children Ethan and Caitlin, and then she's going to take a tango class at the Valhalla Dance Studio down in the village. You've seen the advertise-ments on some of the metro Busses. Mickey Donnelly King of the Valhalla Shuffle."

"Oh, yeah I've seen him around. He's a cool dude." Says Nino.

"Well anyway, she'll be sorry she missed you."

Nino focuses on Pitt, "Bev, I'd like you to meet my friend Pitt."

Smiling "Nice to meet you Pitt."

Pitt shakes hands, "Same here."

Beverly notices the book in Nino's hand. "Isn't that a great book?" Nino frowns, "Yeah, I was going to buy it for my friend here, but I'll have to come back another time. I'm a little short on funds at the moment."

Smiling warmly. "Nonsense, you take that book as a gift from me, Pitt. I hope you enjoy it."

Pitt blushes with gratitude, "That's awful nice of you."

Nino grows serious. "I'll stop by and pay you for it next week some time."

Beverly winks at Nino "Nino your money's no good here; Pitt is going to have to pay me for this book."

Pitt laughing, "I'd like to Beverly, but I'm afraid I would have to pay you some other time as well."

Beverly laughing "Pay me you will, but not with money. Just pass this book and its message on freely to another person when you're through with it, and consider your account paid in full."

Nino smiling "That's my Beverly. She's always making God Smile." Pitt extends his hand towards Beverly. "Thanks Bev, you have my word. I won't let you down."

"Ok Pitt, come by any time. That goes for you too Nino. You know Nino, Amsterdam is just as nice as Broadway." Beverly chuckles.

Nino laughing. "Alright, alright … I get your point."

Nino notices that the window decoration is featuring a model of Noah and his ark. "Hey counselor, look at Bev's art work." Pitt takes a closer look, "That's nice, man. Did you do the art work your self?"

"To be honest with you, my friends Kirstin and Hal Burrall did most of it, but I helped them. Their children Mallory, Mitchell, Abby, and Penn made the little hand prints on the window. Aren't they cute?"

Nino remembers, "Yes very cute. I know the Burralls. There good people. I used to sweep the sidewalk infront of their bike shop over on 69th street once in a while…. So what's that book you're featuring? The one in Noah's hands?"

Beverly excited, "That's a real interesting book called **The Coming Global Superstorm**. It's written by Art Bell and Whitley Strieter." "What's it about, Noah's flood?"

Beverly thinks for a moment, "Kind of, it talks about Noah's flood, global warming, the Ice age, mysteries of the world, and astrology. I found it to be a very religious book."

Nino responds with curiosity. "Really, how so?"

Beverly explains, "Well some of my Atheist friends who have read the book said that many of the questions that this book raised and the scientific facts it provided, made them rethink their stance on creationism. The funny thing is, I don't think that is authors' objective. But hey, if it works, it works."

Nino raises his eyebrows, "Alright Pitt that's another must-read to add to your list."

Pitt laughing, "By the time I read all these books you want me to read, I'll be too old to write a book, you know. Like somebody your age."

Beverly and Nino are laughing. Nino responds. "See what I have to put up with Bev? Come on Pitt, we've got to get stepping. Good bye Bev, I'll see you soon."

Pitt also waves, and Bev responds. "Goodbye boys, have a nice day."

Pitt walks away from the Book Nook and takes one last look at the Noah's Ark display that's in the window.

"Hey, Nino, did anybody on your tour ever mention the story of Noah or any of other Old Testament stories?"

Nino nods, "Oh, yeah, sure. Most of the Biblical stories happened pretty close to the way they are described. I heard an especially cool story about Noah that you won't find in any of the holy books."

"Let's hear it."

Nino clears his throat, "Well, when God told Noah to go and collect two of every kind of animal, Noah was a little down trodden, enough so that God noticed that something was bothering poor Noah. So, God asked Noah, 'Noah, my son, why do you look so discouraged? You have built a fine ship and your work is almost through. Why then are you not pleased?" Noah looked up toward Heaven and answered, "Father, I am pleased, and I am humbled that you selected me out of all of your creation to start your world over again. It's just that I am very tired from having built this very large boat, and the thought of having to go out and collect all of those animals is just weighing heavy on my mind." Well, Noah's honesty tickled our Heavenly Father, and he was moved by his compassion and love to help his son. As Noah heard this Heavenly laughter, he knew not what to make of it. Then suddenly, in his hands there appeared a drum with two solid gold drum sticks. Noah looked up to the Heavens again and he said, "God, what is this present that you have given me?" And God answered, "Noah, this is a special drum. Now when you are ready to call the animals to the ark, all you need to do is beat on this drum, and the animals will come calmly and orderly into your sacred vessel."

Pitt impressed, "So, that's how he did it? I always wondered how he got all those wild animals to come aboard!"

Nino perks up, "That's not all, Pitt. While I was in Forever, I stopped at a celebration and there was this fantastic band playing. Moses was playing the bass, Mary, Muhammad and some of the other prophets were singing. And Jesus was playing lead guitar."

Pitt is laughing, "Get out of town."

Nino starts lauging to, "And Noah was playing the drums."

Pitt playfully pushes Nino, "Nino, are you shittin' me?"

Nino chuckles, "Pitt, it was unbelievable. The whole experience was just unreal. I can't describe how remarkable it feels to be completely loved and genuinely respected by everyone you meet. Everybody you meet makes you feel like a king."

Pitt excited, "What is it like, one big party up there?"

Nino scratches his head, "A big party? No, that really doesn't do it justice. Jesus described it as the wedding feast of the lamb. That's because, back in his day, there was no event that was more festive than a wedding."

Pitt playfully pleads with Nino, "Come on, Nino just try and describe Forever to me. Do your best."

Nino gives it a shot, "Alright, my friend, I'll try to do it justice. Every moment of every day, in every way, is filled with everything and anything that you want it to be filled with. Forever and ever, every morning there is a beautiful sunrise, and every evening a stunning sunset. As the sun goes down, a beautiful harvest moon the size of Jupiter rises. Forever is a gigantic kingdom, tens of thousands of times larger than the earth. Oh, Pitt, I wish I could show you. I wish you could feel what I feel and see what I have seen. I can't put it into words."

Pitt smiles, "Yes, Nino, your words and the light of your eyes are doing just fine. Keep going."

Nino continues, "Well, in Forever, we'll be together. The sunny days shine on, and God's love takes away all pain…. You will never cry again. In Forever, there's endless pleasure. Each moment brings a new adventure. And fairy tales, like souls, are real and live on forevermore."

Pitt smiles, "That was beautiful, Nino. You're such a poet. Some day I will take your words and write a special song for you. I'll call it "Nino's Song.""

Nino grins, "Thanks, Pitt. I know it will be a good one…. It's funny but since I've returned from Heaven, thes poems just flow out of me."

As they walk a little further, a group of people in white robes come by singing songs of praise to Jesus and claiming to be sanctified.

Nino stares at the group of singers, "You know, when you choose to align yourself with God, that's when you really get Satan's attention. Once you decide to follow the path of Jesus, that's like climbing into the ring with Satan."

Pitt agrees. "Climbing into a ring with Satan is a dangerous thing to do. An opponent that hates you will not stop fighting until you either give up or win."

"And in God's eyes, all that is important is that we never give up, and that we never lose our faith in him." Says Nino.

Pitt pulls out a business card, "That's what I have on my business card. 'Believe in God. Believe in yourself. Never give up.'"

Nino grabs the card and looks at it, "You've summed it up. All who remain faithful until the end will be victorious."

Pitt clarifies his position, "God's not saying that we have to live a sinless life, he just wants us to try our hardest and to learn from our mistakes, right?"

Nino nods, "Pitt, your main job is to expose how Satan attacks our souls. He preoccupies us with all sorts of obsessions. You know the drugs we spoke about—he compels us to chase this endless stream of desires. He is the quintessential monopolizer of our time. If you're in New York City dancing with another woman, then you are not home with your wife, enjoying her qualities and keeping your marriage strong. If he can keep you up late with TV, movies, or surfing the virunet, then he can keep you from interacting with people, or from reading holy words in the Bible, the Qur'an, or any other holy book."

Pitt shakes his head in dismay, "That's all it is, isn't it? He monopolizes our time with activities that gradually either weaken us spiritually by causing us to sin, or keep us from spending more time praying, reading the holy books, and spiritually meditating about our lives."

Nino agrees, "Exactly. Like the Buddha, we have to avoid excess in everything. By living moderately in all areas, we weaken the Devil's ability to attack and control us."

"The importance of fasting and self-deprivation is that they make us spiritually stronger beings, capable of eventually standing toe to toe with Satan, and rejecting all that he has to offer."

Nino smiles and nods his head. "Just like our big brother, Jesus did. We have the ability to take control of our minds and bodies, and to reject Satan. The problem is that most earthbound adults are already enslaved to at least some level or degree. The first thing that has to happen is that people have to honestly look at their lives and perform a time audit."

"A time audit?" Asks Pitt.

"That's right, a time audit. How do we spend our time? Get people to keep a journal for one month and see how they are spending their days.

Once this is done, they need to examine the data to see where they are spending the most excessive amounts of time."

Pitt clarifies, "Like, how much time do I spend at work, how much time to I spend reading the Bible, watching TV, surfing the Virtunet, going to bars, gambling and so on?"

Nino continues, "Right on. Get people to really examine their daily lives, and once they have done this, have them re-budget their time, so that there is no longer any area of excess. Their goal must be to allot a balanced amount of time in all areas: spiritual, physical, mental, and social. For example, you may find that you're spending ten hours a week watching TV or Surfing the Net, and only sixty minutes a week reading the Bible or the Quran, then some changes have to be made."

Pitt feels guilty, "That's probably about what my ratio would be."

"Hey, at least you are being honest." Says Nino.

Pitt cogitates for a moment, "I guess those areas are some of the dopes that I use. It's funny I always thought that they were just harmless ways to pass the time. You know, not really bad for me in any way. My father use to call the TV "The Curse!" If company would come over he would say "Turn that curse off." Pitt laughs at the memory.

Nino chuckles, "Hey your father was a head of his time ... Remember, Pitt, there's only a few good drugs and Satan wants to keep you from taking it."

Pitt frowns, "What, going to church?"

Nino smirks, "Nope, self-reflection, prayer, connecting with people, and most especially reading the holy books."

"Really?"

Nino nods, "That's right. Those books have a mystical property about them. They are different from all other books in that the more you read, the more you have revealed to you by the power of God's Holy Spirit. However, if you stay away from them for extended periods of time, the wisdom that you have obtained is taken away from you."

Pitt excited, "It's true! The longer you stay away from the Bible, the more you forget. The Bible's not a book you can read once and retain forever."

Nino agrees, "You're not kidding. I used to underline significant parts of the Bible as I read it, and then each time I would read it again, I would underline some more. I finally realized that if I kept on reading and re-reading, I would have eventually underlined the entire book."

Pitt chuckles, "My Bible is the same way. The bottom line is that people must realize how important it is to read the holy books on a daily basis, so that their wisdom stays fresh on their minds."

"Reading the holy books gives us the strength that we need to meet and defeat Satan and all of his legions of demons. Think about how Jesus defeated the demons and the Pharisees. It was by his knowledge of the holy scriptures."

"You're right, Nino. That's how he did it. When I read the Bible on a regular basis, the words are present in my mind, and if I am tempted, the scriptures I need pop into my mind. I also believe that reading these holy books brings us closer to God, and makes us more spiritually powerful."

Nino agrees. "That's right. Read, read and read again, each time digging up a new piece of gold. By reading daily, we will be keeping, as Jesus said, the oil in our lamps full. I was shown in Heaven that there will come a time when you will long for the opportunity to gain more wisdom and do good works, but you will not be able to."

Pitt remembers, "There is a passage from Isaiah that I memorized that says **"Seek the Lord while he may be found; call on him while he is near … turn to the Lord, and he will have mercy … and to our God, for he will freely pardon."** He seems to be saying the same thing you are."

Nino shakes his head, "That's exactly what he's talking about. Your time will run out, and those who have obtained wisdom will not have the time to give it to those who have not kept their lamps full of oil."

"Oil in our lamps? Are you talking about the parable of the virgins waiting for the groom to come?" Pitt asks.

Nino teases Pitt, "Ooh, Pitt, you nasty man!"

Pitt laughs, "Oh, come on, you know what I mean."

Nino grabs Pitt playfully and then releases him, "Yeah, sure counselor. Your mind is always in the gutter! I'm just teasing you. Listen, it all comes down to this. How much wisdom have you acquired? How strong is your faith? How many righteous and charitable acts have you done in your life? Remember what Jesus said, **"Your love for one another will prove that you are my disciples."** A loving merciful heart and a life filled with good works, this is your oil. When Jesus returns, the time to gather this holy oil is over. Once you see Jesus with your own eyes the faithful garden in which all righteousness grows, will be no more."

Pitt concerned, "We won't even be able to save others with the oil that we have acquired, because this is something that each soul most do on its own."

"Those poor souls who do not have the oil they need will miss out on what is called the Rapture."

"So the Rapture really is going to happen?" Pitt asks.

"Yes, during the end of times, on a day not yet determined, a large number of souls who follow the POJ, will be taken to Heaven instantaneously. Those left behind will live in a world greatly devoid of faith and wisdom. The holy books will be systematically destroyed, and those who claim to have faith in God will be tortured and killed all over the world."

Pitt shakes his head sadly. "People must have got to come to realize that we are indeed living in the end of times."

Nino nods. "You're correct, but don't get hung up on the doom and gloom part of what's going to happen. What is more important is that people believe that there is a place called Forever, a Heavenly paradise that awaits all of God's children. Excite people about Heaven! Get people to start hoping for God's kingdom to come, and once their hopes rest in Heaven, they will be more concerned with doing what is necessary to return home. God is not looking for us to be saints. He just wants us to do our best. He wants us to connect with all of our brothers and sisters, and stop passing judgment on one another. He also wants us to make sure that we are not responsible for putting any stumbling blocks or obstacles in our neighbor's spiritual paths."

"You mean like convincing someone to do something that might be bad for them, or setting a bad example by our own behavior?" Pitt asks.

"That's it."

"So what impresses God most is the effort we put forth trying to get to Heaven, and the ways in which we help our neighbors to do the same."

Nino agrees, "That's all I'm doing man. I'm just trying to get to Heaven. Just trying to make it home, and helping whoever I can along the way. That's the message, Pitt."

Pitt sneezes really loud.

"God bless you!"

"My allergies are killing me." Says Pitt.

Nino remembers, "Hey, that's another thing you won't have to worry about in Forever. There is no coughing, sneezing, sniffling or wheezing."

Pitt sighs, "Oh, man, I can't wait! I have sneezed every day of my life."

Nino relishes the memory, "You can't imagine how enjoyable life is without all of these little ailments that torture us daily on earth. You simply feel fantastic. I wish I could find words to describe what it feels like to have a perfect body, a perfect mind, and boundless strength and energy. We are absolutely tireless. In Forever, we rest simply to enjoy the stillness of being, not because we need sleep."

"We're never tired?" Pitt asks.

"We rest for the pleasure of resting. **Oh, the joy of the needless nap!**"

Pitt tries to imagine. "We rest for the pleasure of resting; we eat for the joy of eating. We dance for the love of dancing. So in Heaven everything we do is pleasing in some way."

Nino nods, "Actually everything we do is pleasing in all ways. Every activity is done simply for the joy that it brings. That's why Jesus called it Paradise. It is completely set up and designed for the happiness, joy, and pleasure of its inhabitants."

Pitt wonders, "Nino, when you went up to Forever, how did it happen? Did you just open your eyes and you were there?"

Nino rubs his chin, "It's just like you hear about in those near death experiences. First I felt my body go limp, then I began to hear an uncomfortable noise—a loud ringing or buzzing which seemed to vibrate through my whole body. The onset of the uncomfortable noise was followed almost instantaneously by the feeling that I was moving very rapidly through a long, dark tunnel. After this, I suddenly found myself outside my physical body, but I was still present. I could see my own body from a distance. I could also see Papino sleeping, and I could hear the radio announcer speaking about some sort of weather disaster that had occurred during the night. At first I thought I was just dreaming, but after a while I realized that I was not. I gradually became accustomed to my odd condition. I noticed that I still had a "body", but one of a very different nature and with very different capabilities from the physical body I had left behind. The next thing I knew, I started to catch glimpses of friends and relatives who I knew had already died. Then a spirit approached me, and took my hand. It was Pilate. He didn't speak to me at first, but when I looked at him I knew I was safe."

Pitt is surprised, "Pontius Pilate?"

Nino nods, "Yep. Then, in the twinkling of an eye, I'm talking to Barabbas, in Forever."

"So, you really did die? ... It doesn't sound like dying is a bad experience."

Nino grunts, "Shit, dying ain't nothing compared to being born and living. This is the hard part!"

Pitt chuckles, "It's kind of funny how everybody is so scared of dying. But ironically, that's when everything gets easy."

"That's right. You know why babies are crying when they are born?" Nino asks.

"They're scared?"

Nino frowns, "You're damn right they're scared! That's the soul's first encounter with the hostile cold atmosphere of the earth. The baby doesn't settle down until its mother holds it close to her breast. That's the feeling."

"What's the feeling?" Pitt asks.

Nino gets a serene look on his face, "How it feels to be standing in the Kingdom of Forever. Try to remember a time when your mother or father held you close to their bosom and touched your face and said everything will be alright."

Pitt smiles and goes back in time, "I remember. You would feel so comforted, because you believed their words with every once of your being."

Nino agrees, "Exactly, and that's what it feels like to be surrounded by the spirit of God, total peace, happiness, and security. The loving light of God replenishes the soul in all ways. Like a soft summer rain falling on a parched desert flower."

Pitt smiles warmly, "That's a cool description. I'll remember that. Hey, Shari lives right up here around the corner. She should be waiting out in front of her building. I really want her to meet you."

Nino is taken aback, "Her name's Shari? You know just ..."

Nino is interrupted by a young police officer, Mario Fratto, who grabs him and puts him into handcuffs. The police officer then pushes Nino up against the front of a drug store that is next door to Shari's building. Just as he begins to frisk Nino, Sgt. Hank comes upon the scene.

Hank puts his hand on Mario's shoulder, "Hold on there, Mario, what are you doing with this man?"

Mario shakes away from Hanks grip, "He fits the description of the guy wanted for the murder in Union Square. There were tons of eye witnesses. So you can just back off."

Sgt. Hank becomes angry, "You've got the wrong man here, Fratto. Now turn him loose."

"Look sergeant, I think we should at least take him in for questioning."

Sgt. Hank points to his arm, "Hey, do you see these stripes on my arm? Nobody gave me those stripes boy, I earned them. Now, let Mr. Jones and his friend go at once, and don't make me have to say it again."

Mario flushed with anger, "This isn't over, not by a long shot."

The young officer removes the cuffs and storms off toward his police car. Sgt. Hank turns to Nino and Pitt.

Sgt. Hank sympathetically, "Sorry about that, Nino. He's just a tad bit overzealous sometimes. He'll learn."

Nino holding no grudge, "It's okay, Sgt. Hank. Hey, maybe I did fit the description. I'm just glad you came along when you did."

Sgt. Hank looks around, "Well, still and all, you better get out of this neighborhood for the time being."

Nino concerned, "Why? What's the matter?"

Sgt. Hank sighs in dismay, "If I know Mario, he's on the radio right now calling his hot shot brothers, Rocky and Frankie, who unfortunately are my bosses. If they come down here, you can count on one miserable ordeal. They'll haul you downtown for questioning, and probably keep you there at least overnight, or longer. If you know what I mean."

Nino nods understandingly, "I get the picture, Sarg. If they find out that I'm just a homeless veteran who's not connected to anyone, and the real killer isn't found, then it's so long, Nino."

Sgt. Hank looks down is shame, "I hate to think it could go that way, Nino, but why take any chances. You come back in a couple of days, and he'll have forgotten all about you."

Nino pats Sgt. Hank on the shoulder, "Don't feel bad, Sgt. You did the most you could for me under the circumstances, and I won't forget it. You take care now."

Nino waves goodbye to Sgt. Hank and then turns and grabs Pitt's arm leading him back towards Broadway.

"Where we going?"

Nino with a sense of urgency in his voice, "We've gotta get out of here and fast."

Pitt scurrying along after Nino, "Gee whiz, I wanted you to meet Shari, she should have been down here waiting." Pitt yells to Rino Minetti, the doorman, as he walks by. "Hey, Rino, have you seen my sister? She was supposed to meet me out here."

Rino in a heavy Italian accent, "Eh, there's a problem with our elevators that happens every once in a while. They get stuck between floors. You want me to buzz her room?"

Pitt shakes his head, "No, Rino, just tell her that I came by and couldn't wait. Tell her I'm taking the subway up Broadway to the George Washington Bridge, and I'll see her in a little while."

Rino reminds Pitt, "Oh, Pitt, hey don't forget you can't go straight up Broadway to get to GWB, you gotta ..."

Pitt remembers, "I know, I know, I gotta take the 1 train to 59th Street and the A-train to 175th Street."

Rino is impressed, "Hey, not bad for a country boy!"

Pitt fakes agitation, "Who you calling a country boy, you sorry joker! I'll take care of you when I get back! And don't flirt with my sister, either, or else ..." Pitt balls up his fist, bites his bottom lip and makes a mean face at Rino. Rino cracks up.

Rino laughs, "Okay, alright, relax! It's gonna be a nice day."

Nino tugs at Pitt's arm impatiently. Nino worried, "Come on, Pitt, we don't have time for this shit. A little voice just told me we have to go catch a train!"

"Alright, let's go."

As Pitt and Nino cross Broadway and head for the train, Judas crosses their path and follows them into the subway. Judas is relieved to find them, but decides to wait a while longer before telling Adolf. He knows how much it bothers Adolf to have to stay in a black body. He also has the evidence, so he can plant it at any time. There really is no need to worry now that he is reunited with his targets.

THE ZORASTRIANISM P.O.J.
THAT NATURE ALONE IS GOOD WHICH REFRAINS FROM DOING UNTO ANOTHER WHATSOEVER IS NOT GOOD FOR ITSELF.

CHAPTER 43

▼

"Greater love has no man than this, that a man gives up his life for
his friends."
-JESUS OF NAZARETH/John 15:13 (92 AD)

"The reputation of a thousand years may be determined by the
conduct of a single hour!"
-Tadashi Maharah Japanese Proverb

"Remember, too that knowing what is right to do and then not
doing it is sin."
-James 4:17 (70 AD)

"So shines a good deed in a weary world."
-Willy Wonka (Charlie and The Chocholate Factory)

As Nino and Pitt disappear with Judas hot on their trail, a NYC police car
screeches to a stop in front of Shari's apartment building on the corner of
West 79th Street and Amsterdam. Police officer Mario Fratto was back with his
brothers Frankie and Ralph, and special intestigator Kipp Goodman. All four
of them appeared to be angry, and they were in hot pursuit of Nino. Rino
noticed the commotion and offered to be of some assistance.

"Is there a problem, officers?" Rino asks.

Mario irritated, "Yeah, did you happen to see an elderly black man walking
past here with a younger, maybe thirty-something white guy?"

Rino is puzzled, "Yeah sure, but what's the problem officer? They're both
good people."

Kipp interested, "You know those guys?"

Rino nods, "Well, if we're talking about the same guys, yeah, I do. But I doubt we're talking about the same guys."

"Why's that?" Kipp asks.

Rino makes clear, "Well, the old guy's name is Nino, and he never bothers anybody. In fact, he's helpful to everyone he meets. The younger guy is a real nice fella who's just up here visiting his sister. His name is Mark Pitifer."

Frankie chimes in, "You know the guy's sister?"

Rino points to the building, "Yeah, she lives in the …"

Shari comes out of the building just as Rino is talking.

"What a coincidence, here she comes now. Shari, this cop would like to ask you a couple of questions about your brother."

Shari hysterical, "What happened to him? Where is he? Oh my God, oh my God!" Shari begins to sob and Rino holds onto her, as officer Fratto continues his questions.

Kipp puts his hand on Shari's shoulder, "Miss, calm down. Nothing has happened to your brother. We just want to ask him a few questions. Why are you so upset?"

Shari trying to catch her breath, "Well, it's just that he never came home last night, and he's been acting really strange. He told me he was going to meet me here in front of the building, but I got stuck in our elevator. Why do you want to question my Mark? What's going on?"

Ralph answers, "Your brother was seen leaving this area with a man who fits the description of a murder suspect."

Shari is shocked, "What? You've got to find him! Please! You've got to go help him."

Kipp grabs Shari's hands and tries to comfort her, "Miss, you've got to try to stay calm. That is exactly what we are going to do."

Rino also tries to calm Shari down, "Shari, Mark left here with that nice old man Nino. I think they've got the wrong guy. You know who I'm talking about, right?"

Shari's mind is spinning trying to put the pieces together, "Nino. Nino Jones?! How did he get hooked up with him? My God! What is going on here? Officer, Nino wouldn't hurt a-"

Mario detects that something has frightened Shari, "What's wrong, Miss?"

Shari remembers, "Well, the other day, Nino helped me out when this very rude businessman knocked me down."

Kipp puzzled, "So, what's wrong with that?"

Shari worried, "Oh, nothing. It's just that he does have a very bad temper. What if he's got a split personality or something? I mean, come on, he's a homeless street person, we don't know that much about him."

Ralphie nods in agreement, "The lady's right. Miss, did your brother say anything about why he was with this guy, or where they were going?"

Rino jumps in again. "I know where he's going. He's going to the George Washington Bridge. He was on his way downtown to switch trains."

Mario nods to the other officers. "Come on, boys. Let's merc." Shari can't compose herself. "Please, take me with you!"

Kipp still consoling, "No, ma'am. You stay here and we'll be right back to let you know what happens."

Shari screaming and crying, "Don't you let anything happen to my brother!" Shari tries to run toward the police car but Rino grabs her as the police car zooms away. She is crying and yelling."Let me go! Let me go!"

Rino hugs Shari, "Shari, Shari…. Try to relax and let them do their job. Please, stay here with me. Come in and sit down and I'll wait with you."

Shari is trembling and sobbing, "Rino, if something happens to him …"

Rino gets tears in his eyes, but turns away so Shari can't see that he to is now worried, "I know, I know. Now just try to relax. We'll say a little prayer and everything will be alright."

Rino tries his best to calm Shari, but the situation on the subway is anything but calm. Judas has taken on the appearance of an old black man wearing a tattered green trench coat over some baggy jean overalls, and a gray hooded sweat shirt. Nino and Pitt are waiting on the platform at 59th Street for the A-train that would take them up to the bridge. As they wait, a beautiful little girl with red curly hair and sparkling blue eyes, starts singing 'When you wish upon a Star', and then without skipping a beat goes into a beautiful rendition of 'Somewhere over the Rainbow'. Although the platform is crowded, she seems to be looking and singing in the direction of Nino and Pitt. When the song is over, Nino walks up and speaks to the little girl.

Nino's eyes are twinkling, "That was beautiful, young lady. Those are two of my most favorite songs in the whole world. I can't tell you how nice it was to hear them today, of all days."

The little girl blushes, "Thank you very much. What's so special about today? Is it your birthday?"

Nino smiles, "Oh, no, I'm just happy to be showing my friend around the greatest city in the world."

Nino looks at Pitt, "Well, is he a good tour guide?"

Pitt smiles, "Honey, he's the best I've ever seen! And, by the way, I really enjoyed your singing too. Your father and mother must just melt when they hear you sing."

The singer's expression melted into a sad frown, and Pitt could sense he had said something wrong.

Pitt places his hand on her elbow, "I'm sorry honey. I didn't mean to make you feel bad."

The singer wipes tears from her eyes. "Oh, that's ok. How could you know that I live in an orphanage? I never had a mother or father, but I always wished I did. I guess that's why those are my favorite songs, too."

Nino teary eyed, "I know what you mean honey. I'm an orphan, too. My name is Nino."

Nina chuckles, "That's funny, I'm Nina. Nina Bova. It's nice to meet you fine gentlemen."

There is something about the girl that makes Nino's heart feel full and warm. He feels connected to this child, like he had known her all of his life, but how could that be? And then it struck him, could this be the little girl from the Royal Playground? Of course it was her. He was certain, but held his tongue.

"Hi, Nina, my name is Mark, but my friends call me Pitt." Nina smiles warmly, "Nice to meet you, Pitt."

Pitt smiles, "You know, Nina, it's surprising that in such a hard and tough city every once in a while I run into an angel like you."

Nina blushes, "What a nice thing to say. Are you married?"

Pitt blushes, "Why do you ask?"

Nina stares into Pitts eyes, "I was just wondering if you had any children. You seem to have a lot of love in you. I think you would make a real nice daddy."

Nino just listened to the conversation, not saying anything as tears of joy welled up in his eyes. He turned his back as Nina and Pitt continued their conversation.

Pitt gets a lump in his throat, "Well, I'm not a daddy yet, but maybe someday I'll be able to have a little girl as nice and talented as you are."

As the train pulled up to the platform, Nina hugged Pitt with all of her might and kissed him on the cheek. She also hugged and kissed Nino, and then she vanished into the crowd. Nino thought he heard her whisper to be brave, but the roar of the train drowned out her voice. Nino and Pitt sat next to each other on one side of the train, and, unbeknownst to them, Judas has positioned himself directly across from them.

Pitt still thinking about Nina, "What a delightful soul that child was. I really felt love for her, and I'm actually sad now to be apart from her. Isn't that strange? How could I feel such a strong bond to someone I just met? Hey, Nino, maybe she was an angel?"

Nino raises his eyebrows, "You know what the good book says. **In being kind to strangers, many people have entertained angels unknowingly.**"

Pitt excited, "You really think she was an angel?"

Nino shrugs, "Pitt, you never know."

Nino begins to daydream about his time in Forever with the little girl named Nina, and without thinking what he was doing, he said her name out loud.

Nino sighs, "Nina."

Pitt laughs, "Ha! She's even got you thinking about her. Nina. What a nice, little girl.... What a pretty name."

Nino agrees, "Yes, very nice. Her name fits her."

"Maybe I'll see her again some day."

Nino chuckles, "Yeah, you can have a subway reunion...." Nino thinks of Forever. "Pitt speaking of reunions, you should see the great reunions that take place in Forever. It's like a giant family reunion filled with delicious foods, music, and wonderful stories from across the ages. You are once again surrounded by all of those firmiliar faces from your past. Your family tree unfolds and is perfectly revealed branch by branch and leaf by leaf. All that you hoped and longed for is realized in thetwinkling of an eye. The peace, the beauty, the honor, the glory, the health, the love, all things are fulfilled and all souls are reunited. Mothers, fathers, friends, relatives and pets come to greet you as you walk through the jewel covered streets of paradise. It's like a giant parade that is given in your honor. And you will never feel even the slightest bit of earthly pain ever, ever again."

"I'll bet you see a lot of tears of joy?" Says Pitt.

Nino wipes his eyes and chuckles, "You think?"

Pitt grins, "It sounds so unbelievable, but I'm kind of surprised that there is still crying in paradise?"

Nino explains, "In the Kingdom of Forever there is still crying because the Great Game is still being played. However, in the New Jerusalem, there will be no tears of any kind. Tears of joy occur because we know in the bottom of our hearts that even though we are experiencing a poignant or significant moment in our life, that the moment is fleeting. Such will not be the case in the New Jerusalem. Everything will be savored as long as you want it to be, and all that is past can be present at your command. There is nothing lost that cannot be found again. There is no goal which cannot be achieved, no dream that cannot become a reality. Oh death where is your sting?! **There is no sadness in goodbye, or lost love to make you cry.** We will live like gods. Every day will be filled with adventure and gratification. Love, peace and prosperity will abound forever more. Everyone's cup will be filled to the brim, and everyone's garden will give forth the fruits of plenty."

"Nino, these Zealots that we are working with, what are they really hoping to accomplish?" Pitt asks.

Nino explains, "They want to shed some unexpected light on the prince of darkness. These are his days. He and his army are the strongest they have ever been since the beginning of the Great Game. These are the end of times, and Satan is not expecting to find any formidable foe. The souls that we are working with are very brave, unselfish beings. They look down from Heaven at all the lost souls and it breaks their hearts to think that during the course of their lives, they could have done so much more to help Jehovah's cause. They are especially troubled over the holy souls that Satan has been able to capture over the years. Whenever they speak of Judas, they all sound broken hearted."

Pitt raises his eyebrows, "So, Judas really wasn't so bad after all?"

Nino shakes his head, "Judas was merely a product of what he was raised in. He was an educated man, and wise in the ways of the law and politics. He sincerely felt that he would ultimately be helping Jesus by what he did. However, he was manipulated by Satan and used by the Scribes and Pharisees. They lied to him, and labeled him as a traitor—someone so shallow that he would betray his master for thirty pieces of silver."

Nino's words confirm what Pitt has always felt in his heart, "I always had a good feeling about Judas. I mean, if he really was just a traitor, and his ultimate goal was to betray his master for a fee, then he should have been happy that Jesus was sentenced to death, not suicidal."

Nino agrees, "That's right. I was told that when he realized it was a set up, he went into a rage. He even jacked up one of the Pharisees, but they just laughed at him. As the events began to unfold, Judas realized that the blame was being cast onto him not only by the religious leaders, but by the apostles as well, he was devastated. He knew that this story that was being spun from all sides had sentenced him to death as well. Judas fled from Jerusalem a brokenhearted, hunted man, and he killed himself out of despair and horror. It is such a tragedy that he ended up in hell."

Pitt wonders, "So was suicide the main reason that he ended up in hell?"

Nino continues, "He ended up in the outer darkness because he killed himself. When you commit suicide, and you are not mentally ill, you are dying with a sin stained soul. However, while he was in the outer darkness, Satan convinced him that his betrayal of the Messiah had single-handedly ruined God's plan to save the world, and that he would never be forgiven, and that he would be infamous and hated by the people he cared about most, for all eternity. Satan convinced him to reign in Hell where at least he was appreciated…. Poor old Judas, If only we could do something to help him. At the very least I wish he could know how much he is truly loved, cared for, and forgiven."

Upon hearing Nino's words, Judas is overwhelmed with feelings of that he thought had died in him a long time ago. Learning that he wasn't perceived by the citizens of Forever the way Satan said he was, that he wasn't scorned or despised by God, Jesus or any of the Heavenly souls, and that he was loved and truly missed almost took his breath away. The truth was finally revealed! Judas clasps his hands together as if praying. If only he had not acted so impetuously. If only he had hung onto his faith even though he was walking through the valley of the shadow of death. If only there was something he could do to change his wretched past and his miserable future.

Judas sat with a head full of thoughts, "How could I have been such a fool!" He thought to himself. "How could I have let that snake devour my soul? If only I had remained faithful to God, he would have welcomed me back like the prodigal son. Oh, father, please help me change that which cannot be changed. Please forgive me for doubting how much you really do love me!" Judas broke down in sobs to the point that his shoulders were heaving. He knew that he was forever cut off from God, and that his prayers would go unheard.

As the train pulled into another station, Nino and Pitt were just getting out of their seats when all of a sudden Police Officers Kipp Goodman, Mario, Frank, and Rocky Fratto Jr. burst into their car with their guns drawn and pointed directly at them.

Mario points his gun at Nino and Pitt, "Hold it right there, fellas, and don't move a muscle or this subway car will be getting a fesh paint job."

As Nino and Pitt stood terrified, Judas too was caught off guard by the sudden commotion. Yet, in the midst of this siege and confusion, Judas has a moment of clarity. He springs to his feet and pulls out the gun that was used in the park, shooting and charging in the direction of the policemen. As the policemen open fire on Judas, the body that he uses is mortally wounded, and falls to the ground dead. The police inspect the body and find the wallet of the murdered victim. Mario Fratto has found his killer, and Judas has sacrificed what was left of his freedom from Hell to unselfishly help his brothers. It is the ultimate act of love and bravery. His motives are pure in that no one will ever know what he has done to help the prophet of faith in his most desperate hour.

As Nino and Pitt climbed off the floor, they were approached by Officer Fratto.

Mario reaches down to help up Nino, "Are you two alright?"

Pitt looks around visibly shaken, "I' m okay. Are you okay, Nino?"

Nino puzzled, "Yeah, I'm ok. Is that the guy you were looking for?"

Mario shakes his head, "Yeah, he's our man. I'm sorry I had to put you through that, boys. I was just trying to do my job."

Nino pats Mario on the shoulder, "And you did it quite well, rookie."

Nino stops and looks down at the body. "Actually, you know, there is some resemblance. He looks about my age, too, poor troubled soul. It's a shame to see someone die in that frame of mind. Don't worry, Mario, I'll give Sgt. Hank the blow by blow when I see him. You done good, rookie. I'm sure I'll see you around the neighborhood."

Mario, feeling a sense of shame, "You sure are quite a fella. Anybody else would be madder than a hornet. Now I understand why Sgt. Hank was so sure I had the wrong guy. My name is Mario. Mario Fratto. I am very happy to meet you sir."

Nino extends his hand, "No sir the pleasure is mine."

"And mine," Pitt interjects. "I'm glad you came along when you did. He must have heard that little voice, right Nino?"

Nino grins, "No doubt about it."

"Little voice?" Mario asks, confused.

Pitt slaps Mario on the back, "It's an inside joke."

Mario remembers, "Hey, I told your sister Shari I'd bring you back with me. She was very upset when I left."

Pitt moves closer to Mario, "Mario, do me a favor. Tell her that everything is alright, and that there is nothing to worry about, not with Mario Fratto walking the beat! Tell her that I'll be home soon."

Mario smiles broadly, "You've got it Pitt! Take care guys. And, once again, I'm sorry."

Nino pats him on the shoulder, "No problem, Mario. You take it easy man."

As Nino and Pitt wave goodbye to officers Mario, Frankie, Rocky, and Kipp, another train is just pulling in. The police paramedics arrive to remove the body and check out the policemen for injuries.

Nino grabs Pitts arm and pulls him onto the train, "Come on, Pitt, let's get out of here."

Nino and Pitt board the A-train and head toward the George Washington bridge once again. As they settle into their seats, Nino begins to speak.

"Pitt, something very strange happened here, and I just can't figure it out."

Pitt agrees, "I know. I mean, I figured Satan was trying to have you framed for that Union Square murder. That made sense. And I wasn't even surprised to have the police chasing us, but …"

Nino finishes Pitts sentence, "But why, or how did it happen that the real killer just happened to be sitting across from us on this particular train?"

Pitt nods, "Right. If he didn't wig out and start shooting, you and I would be sitting in a jail cell right now. Do you think it was somebody from the other side that came down to help us?"

Nino shrugs, "It could have been, maybe. Yeah, it must have been. But if it was one of our boys, how is it that he was in possession of the murder weapon?"

"And the victim's wallet, right?" Says Pitt.

Nino frowns, "Exactly. It doesn't make sense. If it was one of our guys, it means that they killed someone in Union Square Park."

"And how does killing that man help us in any way?"

"I just don't know. But I have a feeling that his death did help us in some way. I'm sure we'll find out soon enough." Nino looks towards Heaven.

Pitt looks up to, "Just make sure you let me know when you do."

Nino smiles, "Okay, man, it's a deal."

The subway conductor announced that they were pulling into the 125th Street stop.

"Nino, what stop do we get off at? 175th Street?"

Nino nods, "If I thought we had a lot more time, I would get off here and show you a little bit of Harlem."

Pitt tugs at Nino's sleeve, "Why don't we get off and walk the rest of the way? The danger's probably gone now."

"There are three reasons why we can't walk the rest of he way. First of all, we don't know for sure that the danger is gone. Second, as soon as the Heavenly accountant discovers that I am missing, I will be immediately recalled."

"Recalled?" Asks Pitt.

"Times up. The game's over. In other words, I die."

Pitt concerned, "Just like that? You won't ascend to Heaven?"

Nino chuckles, "That would be nice, but don't forget you have to have faith. Me ascending to Heaven would kind of take away that need, wouldn't it?"

"I see what you're saying. So, what's the third reason?"

Nino laughs, "Oh, yeah, the most important reason, my feet are killing me!"

Pitt sympathizes with his older friend, "I guess we have been walking quite a bit today, haven't we?"

Nino nods, "You aren't kidding' we did, but your right. I have a few more things to mention before we go our separate ways. We'll get off at 169ᵗʰ Street and walk the final nine blocks. Now, do me a favor and let me take a little cat nap until we get there, ok? I feel like I haven't slept in days. You know what? I haven't slept in days! But don't you fall asleep. I don't want to miss our stop."

Pitt smiles "Okay, my man. You take a little rest and I'll keep a look out for our stop."

Nino slouches over and closes his eyes as the train resumes full speed. Pitt just sits there staring out into the blackness. He can see their reflections in the windows across from him. Who is this man sitting next to him? How could a simple evening out on the town have turned into such a crazy adventure? Pitt just smiles and shakes his head as he tries to digest the day's events.

Meanwhile, Judas sends a tracer beam that leads him to Chinatown, where Adolf is waiting impatiently.

THE TAOISM P.O.J.
REGARD YOUR NEIGHBOR'S GAIN AS YOUR OWN GAIN, AND YOUR NEIGHBOR'S LOSS AS YOUR OWN LOSS.

Author's Note: Read all of William Barclay's writings. He is an astute historian, an expert on religion, and a true friend of Gods.
"The Lord who cannot wrong me nor mine, but hath made goodness and mercy follow us all the days of our lives. If we can call God father, everything becomes bearable. Fore the father's hand will never cause his child a needless tear. This is what Jesus knew. That is why he could go on, and it can be so with us."
-William Barclay

Author's Note: Taoism teaches that today more than ever before people need to learn to give up our body/ego driven attachments and experience our divinity within. Pain is a natural occurrence in this world, but suffering is a choice. Believe it or not we choose to be sick by the thoughts that we entertain. Our egos cause us to pursue things that are no good for our souls and we consequently become ill. Sickness implies that something in the body or the mind is out of balance with our source (The Tao or Holy Spirit) which is pure love, Kindness, patience, mercy, and contentment. This unbalance occurs when negative (ego driven) thinking causes us to feel afraid, anxious, angry, hateful, vindictive, and inpatient. The stress induced by these negative thoughts causes us to experience physical manifestations in the form of symptoms such as: fever, aches, pains, headaches, breathing problems, flu, cancer, heart problems, etc...Therefore we must prevent ourselves from thinking in ways that bring these symptoms about. Mental and physical illnesses are merely the physical manifestations of non-Tao thinking, and if we can stay centered in the natural well being of the Tao (Pure Love), we will live in perfect health.

CHAPTER 44

▼

*"To feel forgiven is to feel free to step into the future uncontaminated by the mistakes of the past, encouraged by the knowledge that
we can grow and change and need not repeat the same mistakes again."*
-Rabbi Harold S. Kushner (How Good Do We Have To Be?)

"A student shares his teacher's fate. A servant shares his master's"
-JESUS OF NAZARETH/John 11:11

"Blessed are the merciful, for they will be shown mercy."
-JESUS OF NAZARETH/Matthew 5:7

Judas, arrives on the corner of Canal Street and Broadway.

Adolf snaps, "What took you so long? Do you know how repulsive I find it to be cloaked in this dark skin?"

Judas smirks, "Quit complaining. You had the easy job."

Adolf smiles evilly, "Easy? Yes, it was, now that you mention it. Nothing better than an afternoon of killing, robbing and raping."

Judas sneers, "You're a sick individual, Adolf. It makes me nauseous just to be in your presence."

Adolf retorts, "You do Satan's work the same as I do, Judas. The only difference is that I enjoy it and you don't. You're the hypocrite, Judas. Not me."

Judas agrees, "You're right, I was a hypocrite. But not anymore."

Adolf frowns, "What do you mean, not any more? You're damned forever just like the rest of us. You either do your job, or go prematurely to the abyss. And speaking of doing your job, where are the targets? And what are you doing down here in Chinatown? Didn't they say they were going to the George Washington Bridge?"

Judas tries to further protect the prophets by making up a story.

"The old man is senile. He kept changing his mind. He really meant the Brooklyn Bridge. He wanted to find the old site of the Brooklyn Dodgers Stadium so that he could be near his hero Jackie Robinson for inspiration."

Adolf annoyed, "So, where are they now?"

Judas nonchalant, "Somewhere in Brooklyn, how should I know?"

Adolf fumes, "What do you mean, how should you know? Come on, we must go at once to find them."

Judas shakes his head, "I'm not helping you do anything ever again."

Adolf grabs ahold of Judas' arm, "Judas! We'll just have to see what Satan says about that. He gave you a direct order that must be carried out. To refuse to do so will result in immediate exile to the abyss."

Judas snatches his arm back, "Satan will never give me an order again."

Adolf grins, "Then you've sentenced yourself to Hell, Judas."

Judas turns from Adolf and begins to fly away.

Adolf chuckles to himself, "Go ahead and fly away, Judas. You can't stay hidden from Satan. We'll find you in no time at all. I will lead the hunt myself. My hell hounds will love tracking you down. You pathetic, misguided soul. I can't wait to see your torture begin. You have always been a disgrace to Satan's army. The only reason he put up with you is because you once were one of the great Jew boy's apostles. Satan should have banished you years ago!"

Judas feels content for the first time in many years, but turns angry when he thinks of satan, "Adolf, your hatred for me only confirms that I really never belonged with all of you, at least, not in spirit. And as for running away, I'm not going to hide from Satan. I'm going to find that snake myself, and tell him exactly what I did. If only I had the power to kill that beast I would, with my bare hands! I would choke the evil one to death. You might as well come along. He'll be sending for you and your goons shortly, anyway." Adolf hissed with pleasure. His demonic laugh is so loud and deep that some passers by looked to the sky as if they had heard a clap of thunder. The two of them fly back to the law offices of Christian, Schrouder and Li on 76th Street. When they arrive, Satan is pacing back and forth on the roof. He is eager to hear how the plan had been carried out. He is also troubled that he had not yet discovered the A-plan. With his usual smug arrogance, Satan approaches his two missionaries. "Well, what's the good news? Mission accomplished? Things went just the way I said they would, right?"

Before Judas could speak, Adolf jumps into the conversation. Adolf sounds like a little kid running to tattle on his brother, "MS, this Judas, true to form, once again betrayed his master. He intentionally let the targets get away!"

Satan seethes with anger. Smoke and fire came from his nostrils and flames of fire shoot out of the top of his head. His eyes are filled with rage and anger. Then suddenly, just as abruptly, he composes himself.

Satan walks over to Judas, "Well, Judas, what do you have to say for yourself, still pledging your allegiance to a God who has sentenced you to Hell? You sniveling, disgusting soul. Once again, you have betrayed your master."

Judas using a tone of voice in which satan is used to being addressed, "I have never served you, Satan. In my heart and in my mind, I have always been loyal to my God and my King. I reject you and all that you stand for. Your soul and your existence are a disgrace for all eternity, and though we share a common destiny, I am proud that my last act has secured my brothers' places in Forever. Now, do what you must."

Satan snorts, "Secured your brothers' places in Heaven? How? By helping those two wanna be prophets? Didn't Adolf tell you? Oh, poor Judas. Once again you have acted impetuously without knowing all the facts. Isn't it something how a soul will just keep making the same mistake over and over? No matter how many lifetimes they live?"

Judas looking somewhat concerned, "What are you talking about? What didn't Adolf tell me?"

Satan makes clear, "We have decided that their mission was nothing more than a diversionary plan. There is no way Barabbas would place his eternity in the hands of these two misguided souls. The whole thing was a set up to keep us from discovering their real plan, their A-plan. I'm disgusted that we bought into it at all. I could have done a lot more evil through that business man that you killed, but some good has come from your act of betrayal.

You have not hurt me. You have helped me. I will make them think that we failed in our attempt to stop their plan. I will lead them to believe that we are preoccupied with trying to bring down all that these two prophets try to achieve. When in reality, my legions of doom and I will be scanning the globe searching for their soon to be doomed A-plan. They will have a false sense of security, and then suddenly, without warning, unexpected as a thief in the night, we will lay them to waste. When God sees all the damage we are able to accomplish by twisting and corrupting their good and noble cause, he will be forced by his own decree to banish them to the outer darkness for an eternity. Can you imagine how pleasurable it will be for me to see those holy rollers thrown out of paradise?" Satan lets out an evil laugh. "It will be orgasmic!"

Judas is buying what Satans selling, "Satan, you are a liar. You are the father of all lies. I didn't expect you to tell me how much I really hurt you by what I did, but you already showed me your true feelings before you composed yourself. Your little temper tantrum was the only revelation I need. For the ruler of the world, you are not very complex or sophisticated in the way that you behave. You're comparable to an intelligent, manipulative, narcissistic adolescent, a spoiled brat who is so self-serving and self-absorbed that all you care about is yourself. You never admit when you are wrong. You have excuses when you lose, and you brag when you win. You are the most pathetic being I have ever encountered, and you deserve the punishment you will receive."

Satan claps his hand in a mock tribute, "Bravo, Judas. Bravo. What a speech. You still think you are better than I, don't you? Even now, moments away from being sent to the abyss, I am amazed that you still fail to realize who your true father really is. It is I, so you might as well accept it. Now curse me one last time, and be removed from my sight by the demons you despise. Wait until they get their hands on you."

Adolf smiles at his master. "Shall I summon the ghouls of Hell?"

Satan holds up a finger, "Any last words, Judas? Come on, curse me out one last time. Hit me with your best shot. I can take it."

Judas saddened the scene, "I will not curse you, or condemn you. If I could, I would pray for you. Pray that you would see the error of your ways, and give up this fruitless fight. You do not have my anger, you have my sympathy. I look at you with regret, like a brother who has chosen a destructive life of crime, you are someone to be pitied, and I do pity you. For you cannot love, nor will you ever be loved by anyone, except he whom you betrayed. I know that he still loves you and is saddened about how your existence turned out."

Satan somewhat annoyed, "Oh, enough! Enough! You have gone mad, Judas. You speak like someone who is insane! The thoughts of the abyss have shaken your faculties. But I will give you one last chance to restore your mind and your position. Right now, standing on the edge of the abyss, if you will once and for all renounce your allegiance to God and hail me as your ruler supreme, I will restore you to an even higher office than you formerly held."

Adolf doesn't like what he is hearing, and his smile turns into a look of disbelief. As Judas steps toward Satan, he kneels at his feet.

Judas speaks with pride, "Hail the Lord Jehovah, Guardian of all creation, he who raises the dead, the sustainer of all life, the ever present. Moses, Muhammad, and Paul are his prophets, and Jesus of Nazareth is his son, the world's messiah, the King of Forever."

Satan is out of his mind with anger. "Adolf! Remove this lost soul from my presence! Summon the ghouls and let his torture begin. We'll see how brave you are now, Judas. We'll see."

Adolf rings a giant black gong in the shape of a demon's head. The black shadows of demonic ghouls come immediately to the roof like a herd of wild bulls, and carry Judas off to the bottomless pit. Down to the lake of fire and sulfur, a place where the worm dies not and the fire is never quenched, the isle of eternal damnation. As Satan and Adolf waited to hear cries of terror and calls for mercy, they hear nothing. Judas opens not his mouth. He goes silently, like a sheep being led to its slaughter.

THE CONFUCIANISM P.O.J.
DO NOT UNTO OTHERS WHAT YOU WOULD NOT HAVE THEM DO UNTO YOU.

CHAPTER 45

▼

"It is good to have an end to journey towards; but it is the journey that matters in the end."
-Le Guin

"Believe in yourself! Have faith in your abilities! Fore without a humble but reasonable confidence in your own powers you cannot be successful or happy. You can achieve any goal if you think you can. Just remember, it's always too early to quit! Work and pray, think and believe!"
<u>**Norman Vincent Peale**</u>

I the Lord search the heart and examine the mind, to reward a man according to his conduct, according to what his deeds deserve."
-Jeremiah 17:10 (587 BC)

Nino and Pitt get off of the train at 169th Street, about 6 city blocks to go to the GWB. As they walk along upper Broadway, Pitt has the feeling that he is in a foreign country. He is definitely a minority as far as the color of his skin and his native language are concerned.

"Nino, it seems like we're not in the United States anymore." Says Pitt.

"On our walk today, I'll bet we passed at least one person from every country in the world. I had an old friend named Peter Burke. He was a tough old son of a gun, a merchant marine who used to hang out down on the Bowery. He had sailed around the world several times in his life, and I told him once that if I was younger, I would like to sail around the world with him. You know what he told me?"

"What?"

Nino points down Broadway, "You can go around the world in a single day without ever crossing the water. Just take a walk from one end of Manhattan to the other, and you will have traveled around the world. And he was right! It's all right here, the people, the different cultures, customs, languages, and, most importantly, the food!"

Pitt laughs, "That's my man, always thinking about his stomach. I'm the same way, though. When I was little, my buddy Gino Yannotti used to say that I was the hungriest kid he'd ever seen. I have a friend named Joe who you would really like. You can ask him directions to any place in the world, and he'll always give them to you in terms of where the nearest Perkins Restaurant is. He loves his eating out."

Nino chuckles, "He sounds like my kind of man! You know, I think one of the reasons they picked me is because I like food so much."

"Why do you say that?" Asks Pitt.

Nino sighs with pleasure, "Like I told you earlier, for those of us who enjoy good food and good drink, especially wines and champagnes, there is no place in all existence that compares to what is served up in Forever."

Pitt wonders, "I know you said they have wine, but what about other types of liquors. You know like tequila, whiskey, vodka?'

Nino chuckles, "I know your not much of a drinker, but let me tell you something. In Heaven everybody is a drinker."

Pitt laughs and pushes Nino, "Get out of here."

Nino grins, "I'm not kid you. Heres how it goes. If Forever there are always parties going on, and at these parties there are all sorts of drinks that are served. Each drink causes its own special unique buzz.'"

Pitt interested, but concerned, "That sounds cool. So what do you have a bunch of drunks up their staggering around?"

Nino explains, "No it's not like that at all. In Heaven you are always sharp. Nobody staggers about, or gets sick. What happens is that if you drink a glass of wine, you will get a nice wine pleasure buzz. If you drink another glass of wine the buzz increases. If you switch to another type of liqur you will switch to another type of buzz. If you want to combine the buzzes you can choose to do that as well.'

Pitt laughs, "That sounds like a blast!"

Nino gets goosebumps thinking about it, "Pitt, you can not imagine the fun these souls have. They party like no one you have ever seen. The food, the music, … the girls … It goes on and on because nobody gets tired, and the atmoshphere is amazing. I went to a party that actually had Elvis Presley and Ray Charles providing the entertainment! What a blast. I danced with Marylin Monroe, a slow one to, and I even smoked a joint with Ray Charles! And no I'm not shitting ya."

Pitt shocked, "What?! You telling me that they have reefer, and stuff like that in Heaven?'

Nino raises his eyebrows smirks, "They have it all, and most of the stuff you have never heard of. The same liquor formula applies. Change the drug, and you change the type of "high" that you experience.

Pitt frowns, "I can't believe they would have stuff like that in Heaven.'

Nino frowns, "If you ask me I think alcohol is much worse than marijuana in a lot of ways."

Pitt nods, "I agree with you. I mean most of the kids that I hung around with that smoked pot, were just a bunch of laid back, happy and hungry jokers. However, **the most insidious part about marijuana is that it steals your youth from you.**"

Nino curious, "How so?"

Pitt explains, "If you give a normally inquisitive rat THC (Marijuana), it will just sit in its cage and stare into space. It loses its natural curiosity about life and its surroundings. You're only young once. Most people don't realize it at the time, but that period of life between the ages of 15 and 25, when you have boundless energy, creativity, and ambition, is fleeting. The opportunities that come your way during these precious ten years will never come again. And once there gone, they never return. Kids who smoke marijuana progressively develop that pervasive "whatever" attitude. I've seen the pattern over and over. First they lose interest in school and sports. Then they lose interest in people who don't smoke. They smoke when ever they can. The play endless video games, watch movies, and surf the web. Eventually they quit school, and most of the time they begin selling dope on the side. The jails, prisons, and welfare rolls are full of these types of individuals. Hey like my friend Chazz Palminteri says "The saddest thing in life is wasted talent! And **that's what marijuana ultimately does. It causes all who use it to waste their God given gifts.**"

Nino understands, "I know where you're coming from, and I agree with you one hundred percent. **Marijuana is the father of the "Whatever Generation".** But think about it for a minute. Once all of the negative side effects are removed from these agents, there is nothing bad that can happen to you. Ther is no addiction, no waisted potential, no rebound effect or hangovers. Dope is apart of every party that is thrown in Forever. These Heavenly pharmacologists travel to all ends of the kingdom to find exotic herbs. Then they mix them together and try to come up with the newest "high". It is all good fun."

Pitt smirks, "So that's why we have so many people down here who abuse drugs and alcohol. Always searching for that new high."

Nino nods, "That's righ. It's all connected. And the souls. These wonderful loving beings. Everywhere you turn, someone is offering you something delicious to eat, drink or smoke. And the smells, all those wonderful smells." Nino starts to sing. "Baby I got my nose open, this time its for real." Nino pauses for a moment to remember, "What really blew my mind is that you never feel hungry, but it is always a joy to eat. You know how down here every once in awhile you have the perfect meal and you say to yourself, "Now that hit the spot."

Pitt mouths the words along with Nino, "So we eat simply for the joy of eating?"

Nino glowing, "That's right. In Forever, everything is done simply for the joy that comes along with doing it. There are no rules to follow, and there are no needs to drive you. In Heaven, you are completely content and free to live and express yourself in any way that you choose, for ever and ever. Forever is the land of our origin, and this is why the earth and all that it has to offer comes up short. We really are strangers in a strange land. Souls set adrift upon a sea far, far from home. And all we learn, is so we can return, each lesson, brings us closer to the shore. How's that? Good song material?"

Pitt laughs, "Nino you are a serious poet. You should stay down here and right the songs with me! We'll be the next Simon and Garfunkle!"

Nino slaps Pitt five, "I wish I could brother. But, speaking of poetry and song, why do you think most people find these appealing?"

Pitt speculates, "Because, I imagine they speak to us, or touch us, on a deeper level than just ordinary conversation." Nino impressed, "You are as sharp as a tack, counselor! One of the problems which we all face on earth is lack of meaningful communication. This is why we delight in poetic speech or beautiful music. It touches our souls, and it stirs our inner feelings. One of the amazing things in Forever is that we all speak the same language."

"Is it like no one really says any words and you just communicate mind to mind?" Pitt asks.

Nino teases, "You've been watching too many of those sci-fi flicks! I'm just kidding. No, it's not like that. Don't get me wrong in Heaven everybody has psycic powers, but it's much more fun talking. The cultural differences in Forever, are a million times more vast than those that exist on earth. The different regions of Forever, each have their own beautiful cultures, customs, music, art and food. However, as I said there is only one language in Heaven. In Forever there is this mind to mind connection, but it's more like a complete understanding before the words are even spoken."

Pitt somewhat puzzled, "What do you mean?"

Nino makes clear, "Everybody knows where you are coming from and where you are going before you even begin to speak. There is a complete understanding, and the beautiful thing is, and this is kind of hard to describe, but I'll try, when someone speaks to you they have such a command of their mind and their language that the very conversation comes across as poetry. The coolest part is that all words are accompanied by music. Dramatic, inspiring, yet ever so subtle, music colors every conversation."

Pitt has a hard time grasping the scene, "Wouldn't that be distracting with all those different songs going on at the same time?"

Nino continues, "You only hear the words and music of the person you are focusing your attention on. In Forever, you have the ability to give your complete, undivided attention. It is so satisfying, Pitt. Can you imagine talking to someone who understands you completely? Someone who loves you unconditionally, and has no hidden agendas or emotional axes to grind? In Forever, we simply communicate for the joy of communication. This is simply another way in which souls touch."

Pitt grins, "I guess in Heaven everyone is a counselor."

Nino laughs, "Yeah, but nobody needs one! I guess that puts you out of work!"

Pitt laughs, "That's fine with me.... So, what do people talk about?"

"They tell fascinating and inspirational stories of their days on earth, tales of adventures in Forever and interesting souls they have met, meals they have eaten, games they have played, romantic evenings they have spent with other souls, and distant lands they have traveled to. They talk about projects they are working on and plans for the future. It is a wonderful conversation to have. There is no complaining, just positive reflections and thoughts. In Forever, everybody is good at busting chops, too. Heaven is a boundless sea of humor, and everybody is a practicle joker. It's like sitting around the family dinner table!"

Nino's expression changes, "You ok man? You look a little sad."

Nino shakes his head, "I just get touched thinking about how peaceful and beautiful it is. Nothing is hurried or rushed, and no one is preoccupied with their own thoughts as they listen to yours. Everybody loves you and can't wait to meet you. There are billions and billions of souls to meet and interact with, and the number gets bigger every day. There is always someone new and exciting to meet and spend time with. There's always a new adventure waiting for you around every turn."

Pitt beams with excitement, "I can't wait to meet with you up in Heaven. We're going to have a lot of fun, you and me."

Nino puts his hand around the back of Pitts neck, "Pitt, were you ever a hero, even for a moment? Did you ever win a big game or do something that everybody around you was proud of?"

Pitt nods, "Yeah, it is an awesome feeling."

Nino is about to burst with excitement, "If you and I are successful, we'll get the grand prize. We'll be heroes in Forever. They'll sing songs about us. There will be movies and books about our lives. They'll have parades in our honor, and we will be treated extra special for all time by everyone we meet."

Pitt slaps Nino five. "That's an exciting thought, man. We'll be like Michael Jordan, Muhammad Ali or the Beatles!"

Nino smirks, "Pitt, if we're successful, Michael Jordan and Muhammad Ali will be just as excited to meet you as you are to meet them."

They passed a beautiful old building on West 165th Street. It has a grand bust of Saint Nicholas on it.

Pitt points at the store, "Nino, we must be passing by the north pole, because there's Santa Claus."

"You know, in Forever, there really is a Santa Claus."

"Really?"

Nino smiles, "God himself comes once a year while the souls of Forever are at rest, and gives each of his children a special gift made just for them."

Pitt stares at Nino like a little child, "I always hoped there really was a Santa Claus." ... As they continue walking Pitt notices a sign that states that Coney Island is America's first amusement park, and he points it out to Nino."

Jokingly "Hey Nino, are their any amusement parks in Heaven?"

Nino happy and excited, "Pitt I'm so happy that you brought this up. You can not begin to imagine the indescribable thrills that you will experience in these Heavenly Amusement Parks."

Skeptical "You're kidding me again right?"

Nino straight faced, "Pitt, I'm not kidding you. Why do you think so many of us love going to amusement parks, fairs, and carnivals? It's because in Heaven these are places of great joy. Fantastic roller coasters that defy gravity."

Happy and excited "I love rollercoaster's!"

"Pitt these places make Disney Land look like a slob fair. You can't imagine all the different rides and shows. The haunted houses, the fun houses, the magicians, the animal shows, all the different foods, the candies and carnival games. Oh and the water rides and slides will blow your mind. The whole experience is a pure blast."

"Do you have to wait in line?" Pitt asks.

"Never, ever. Pitt you will never have to wait in line for anything ever again. Just that fact alone is worth the price of admission."

Pitt happy but puzzled, "No more waiting in line. Now that is Heaven. I can't stand waiting in lines. But how does he do it? How can you have all of these people trying to ride the same ride, and have no lines?"

Nino explains, "I don't know all of the details, but in Heaven they do things on a lot of different dimensions. If a ride in one dimension is full you just step right into the next dimension without missing a beat. Believe me when I tell you Pitt, your childhood dreams come to life in ways that you could never imagine possible."

Pitt beams, "Man Nino, it seems like our God really has the heart of a child."

"He truly does. What a remarkable soul."

"Did you see him? Did you see God?" Pitt asks.

"Yes, and Pitt, when you see him, you will know without question that he is God."

"What did he look like?"

Nino gives details, "God has the face of a man, but unlike any you've ever seen on earth. It is the most handsome, beautiful face, surrounded by wind-blown, multi-hued hair. He is gigantic compared to other souls. He lives on a holy mountain in the recesses of the Northern part of Forever. The mountain is so high that there is no place in Forever from which you cannot see it. It is the true holy temple. The tabernacle of God is housed on that mountain. He is power and light. Magnificent colors shine forth from all parts of his being. The light that shines forth from his soul is the light of pure love. His spirit fills the entire kingdom with light and love. He is truly all merciful and all compassionate, the sustainer of life, and the guardian of all existence."

Pitt wonders, "What does he do for fun? Does he just sit there on a throne for all eternity?"

"He has no need to move, although he obviously can. His spirit lives in each soul, so when we move, he is moving. When we are happy, he is happy. He is a part of everything that goes on in Heaven. Nothing happens that he does not feel. He is all, and He is in all. All in all, he is the immovable mover of souls, the ever present one."

Pitt worried, "If that is true, how can he not know about what we are doing?"

Nino explains, "Oh, he knows, Pitt. But in our case, since we are doing this on our own, he must sit back and watch. Our particular circumstances and the rules that govern the Great Game prevent him from even sending others to help us."

"What about the others in Forever?" Pitt asks.

Nino confident, "As I said, he must sit back and silently watch how this all unfolds. I'm sure he is watching over us like a worried parent."

Pitt tries to relate, "It's kind of like my Mom and Dad watching me play in a big game. They want me to do well, and they are squeezing for me, but they can't really join in the game and help me, or the other team will cry foul and then my team would be disqualified."

Nino nods, "That's it exactly. God wants us to win, but he wants us to win on our own, so that Satan cannot protest."

"Did you ask anyone where God comes from?"

Nino frowns faking agitation, "Of course I did, and do you know what they told me?"

"What?"

Nino smiles, "We know, but we can't tell you. When you come to Forever, you will be brought before the power of God, and Jesus will escort you before his holy throne. You will then see all of the significant moments of your entire life flash before your eyes. Your own conscience will either validate you or rebuke you. If you are found unworthy, you are immediately sent to the outer darkness, to consider your future options."

Pitt worried, "Is God or Jesus mean or mad when they send us away?"

Nino chokes up when he recalls the mercy of God, "No. There is no anger. There is only deep compassionate sadness, hope, and love. Allah fills you with his holy spirit so that you can feel the true depth of his love, and Jesus hugs you and tells you how sorry he is that you are unworthy to return home. He tells you that he will continue to help you and pray for you no matter what you decide to do, and then he warns you that your time to earn admittance to Forever grows short. And that's it."

"You still didn't answer my question." Says Pitt.

Nino touches his forehead with his pointer finger, "Oh, yeah, I'm sorry. Well, if you are admitted, then God takes you with his mighty hands and holds you close to his bosom. Your soul then touches the soul of God, and he reveals all the mysteries of faith and his life. No one can reveal this to you but God … It is a rule that cannot be broken."

Pitt disappointed, "Aw, man. Well, at least we know we're going to find out eventually."

Nino moves closer to Pitt, "I can tell you this though, when I did ask this question, the other souls smiled and said, wait until you find out the whole story. You're going to be very happy and amazed. Once you are found worthy to enter Forever, Jehovah allows you to touch souls with him. This is the final piece of the puzzle. Hey I feel honored thatI got to see a little bit more of God than Moses did. Remember when Moses asked to see him?"

Pitt nods, "Yeah, God told Moses to wait until he passed by, and then he could look at his train! I always wondered what that was."

"I know. I was told that once you see and fully experience the living God there will be no further need of having or obtaining faith. Allah is so awesome that once he is fully revealed you will become one with the almighty. And in the twinkling of an eye, you will know the answers to the questions that have puzzled man since the beginning of the Great Game. The experience will be mind altering in a positive way, but you will lose none of your individuality. The origin of God is truly a wonderful mystery, but one that I was assured has a truly happy ending."

Pitt tries to imaginne, "So, we're going to be happy and surprised, huh?"

Nino grins, hinting that he knows more than he is saying, "That's what I was told."

Pitt smiles,"Man oh man, I wonder what it could mean."

Nino jokes, "God only knows."

Pitt laughs, "You got that right!"

As they walk on they hear a loud roar of a cheering crowd. Nino smiles "The Yankees must be winning."

Pitt smiles "That's right the World Series is going on. **Mitchell "The Stitchell" Calabrese** must have just blasted one out of the park." Nino smiles proudly "Boy he's something else isn't he?"

Pitt nods, "Yeah, he just crushed the single season homerun record. 107 homeruns! Do you know how he got the nickname stitchel?"

"No, how?" Nino asks.

Pitt gives details, "They say on more than one occasion he has hit the ball so hard that the stitches popped open."

Nino's eyes pop, "Now that's a strong joker. I'm glad he's wearing pin-stripes! It sure is nice to see the Yankees doing well again. There new manager Chris D'Ercola has really done a fine job."

Pitt agrees, "He's from the old school man. He expects all of his players to be good role models on and off the field. I really like how he encourages the Yankees and the other New York teams to reach out to the fans, especially the kids."

"I really like that too." Says Nino.

Pitt remembers, "When I was a little boy my father took me to see a World Series game between Baltimore and Cincinnati. We went to Memorial stadium in Baltimore really early, and stood at the back gate where the players entered the stadium. And do you know that without exception, every player stopped and shook hands with me and my father. Many of them even talked to us for a little while, and this was before the 5th game of the World Series! Brooks Robinson, Boog Powell, Frank Robinson, **Richie Siclair**, and Scott Bartucca, were all coming up to me and patting me on the head. The Cincinnati manager Sparky Lyle even threw me a ball. It was such a thrill for me. I'll never forget that."

Nino serious "That's the way it should be. Making little kids pay for your autograph is awful. It's the little kids who idolize these guys and make them stars. This new generation of pro athletes could learn a lot from the conduct of those old timers. Those guys truly cared about and appreciated their fans. Although I do have to say that last week I saw the heavyweight champion of the world Derick Gramling, playing basketball with some kids at Thomas "Red" Myers" memorial park, over on 125th Street. There were no cameras or reporters. He was just privately giving something back to his community. He even brought his cousins WBA middle weight contender James Singleton, and the Olympic Heavyweight gold medalist Aleem "Hammer" Whitfield along for the ride. It was really touching to see. Those kids were on cloud nine. That Hammer Whitfield is a unique soul, and a fantastic boxer. He reminds me of Muhamad Ali when he fought Cleveland Williams. He's got all of the tools, and a wonderful personality."

Pitt remembers "That was Ali at his finest moment. The pinnacle of his greatness. Nobody has ever done it better than he did that night. However, Gramling is a real good champion. I'll tell you one thing, those kids will remember that day for the rest of their lives. I wonder sometimes if the Pro athletes, the movie stars, and the musicians truly realize how much they are looked up to by the children of this world?"

Nino nods, "I know. They have the power to do so much good in the world. One kind gesture, like what Derick did, could be a life changing experience for some of those kids. You would think they would be some of the happiest people in the world. They get paid all that money for playing the game they love. Man I would love to do that."

Pitt agrees, "You know back in 2008 I took my nephew Frankie to an NBA finals game at the Boston Garden. It was game 2 versus the Lakers. The Garden was packed, and the fans were going crazy. They even sang "beat LA" songs for an hour before we went into the arena. After the game was over we went from bar to bar celebrating with the Boston faithful, and that's when it hit me.

Nino confused, "What hit you?"

Pitt explains, "Why the pros are so sad and miserable. Here they play this great game that millions of people see from all over the world. They are the cause of this wonderful celebration, they are the heroes of the city, and yet all they get to do is either go back to the club house with the other players, or go home. Now what kind of reward is that?! Do you know what I think they should do?"

"No, what?" Nino asks.

Pitt smiles, "If I was Paul Pierce or Kevin Garnett? After the game was over I would dance on the floor with the fans and cheerleaders, and I would stay in the arena and greet as many people as I could. Then after I showered I would walk across the street and join my fans in celebration. I would become friends with my fans. Now that would be a happy life!"

Nino smiles, "Pitt, all I can say is that you are going to love playing basketball in Heaven. What you just described is a common occurrence. And you're right, if they did that their lives would be a lot more satisfying."

They walked a little further before Nino stopped next to a tiny cemetery to tie his shoe.

Nino points at the grave stones, "No cemeteries in Heaven, Pitt."

Pitt frowns at the site of it, "Good, I don't like cemeteries. My mother and sister go to visit my father's grave, but I don't like to. The only memories that his grave stone bring back to me are of his death and burial. I don't think of my father as being in the cemetery." Nino speaks with confidence, "He's not. Nobody is. When Jesus died, that was the resurrection. Death had been conquered and the gates of Heaven were opened forevermore."

"Nino, what do the angels do? Are we all the same when we return to Forever? Are we all angels?" Pitt asks.

Nino has to think for a moment, "That's a big question, and I wrote a lot about it in the note book I gave you. Angels are God's heavenly priests. All of the Angels were given the option after the Heavenly revolution to become humans and enter the Great Game. All those who are now angels have decided that they would rather serve God for eternity than take the risk of falling short during the Great Game. It is truly the most noble and holy of all callings. These angels do so much to help all of the souls. When you get to look back on your life, and see all of the times when you were helped or warned, you will be very humbled, and eternally grateful. Without their help, we might all fail."

"God bless the angels." Says Pitt.

Nino nods, "Yes, and pray for them often. Ask God to help and bless the Angels in all that they do. Whenever I see that the time is 11:11, I say a special prayer for the angels."

"Why 11:11?" Asks Pitt.

Nino explains, "I read somewhere that 11:11 is when the angels pass closest to the earth. Even though I now know that they are always here. I still do it. It's a nice habit. I ask God to bless them in all ways that they can be blessed. To please them in all way that that like to be pleased. To strengthen them in all ways that they need to be strengthened. To ease their pain and answer their prayers."

Nino stops again to buy a couple of bananas at a corner store. Nino shakes his head, "I just had a deja vu."

Pitt "I have those all the time."

Nino leans towards Pitt, "Do you know why we have those experiences? Every soul, before they are sent to the earth, is shown a film that has many of the probabilities and possibilities that can happen in their life. The memory of this film is also the foundation of what is called intuition, which is also tied into the formation of our conscience."

Pitt interested, "So, when we get a bad feeling about something, it is because we have this faint memory that, to go that way or do that thing, could lead to something bad."

Nino agrees, "You must get people to listen more closely to their consciences. Get them to trust their intuition. That gut feeling that something is very right or awfully wrong. Tell people to quit consulting the so-called experts, and start beliving in them selves. Encourage people to gain as much wisdom as they can by reading the holy books, praying, meditating, and having conversations with souls who are older and wiser.'

"So, the holy writings, and not our earthly guru's hold the solutions to our problems." Asks Pitt.

Nino nods, "Exactly, you have child rearing experts who never even raised a single child, marriage and family counselors, who have never been married (or who are unable to stay married), and sexual experts who have probably never had sex! The psychics and astrologers who try to read the stars and predict the future … You name it, it's all related to the same problem. Earthbound souls truly are very similar to sheep. Most people are starved for direction, and have not the courage to forge their own path. It is their hunger for a shepherd usually leads them astray. If only we would take the time to develop a relationship with God and Jesus, we would remain sheep, for that is our nature, but we would no longer hunger for a shepherd to lead us. The good shepherd, once invited, will live in us and guide us safely throughout the Great Game."

"I know you said you wrote about Hell in your notebook, but just quickly tell me, is it a disgusting place?"

Nino face pales as he remembers the atrocities of Hell, "Pitt, it is the most horrible place you could ever imagine. If I could thoroughly convey to you how absolutely horrible that place is, if you could see and smell and feel what it is like to stand in Hell, you may never have a decent night's sleep again."

Pitt swallows hard, "How do these souls end up in Hell? Why aren't they in purgatory?"

Nino points to the blue note book, "You already hold the answers to these questions in the notebook. These souls have either gone too long without producing good fruit, or they have sold their soul to the Devil."

Pitt is surprised, "Does that really happen?"

Nino's expression turns serious, "You bet your ass it does. I watched and listened as Satan himself talked to one of the souls that had recently arrived in Hell. He was speaking to a man who had done much evil for the cause of Satan while he was alive. He was so evil that Satan gave him many special powers. He even promised the man that when he died, he would share his kingdom with him. Howver, when the man reminded Satan about his promise, Satan laughed in his face and said, 'What makes you think I would really share my kingdom with you? I share my wealth with no one! Then he sent this screaming, crying soul away to be tortured. Satan will become a part of your life if you ask him to. He will grant you special powers. He will help you obtain fame and fortune, but the price is your soul. Make sure you especially warn the children."

Pitt nods, "I will, Nino. Don't worry. I see how Satan makes himself attractive to the kids I work with. Middle school and Adolescence is a tough period of life to go through. It is a period of independence and rebellion. Even in the best of homes, it brings about hard times and struggles. The children who have no God in their lives, and no strong parents to lead them often become easy prey for that snake. He speaks to their needs. He tells them to be free and do what they want to do. He makes them think its okay to have sex, take drugs, get drunk, and leave school. He makes them believe they don't need brains, just muscle or weapons. Might is right, fight the establishment, argue with and manipulate your parents. Satan is the father of Anarchy. "Let nobody rule you" he whispers to your soul, especially some distant uncaring God, who is just waiting for you to mess up so he can punish you. Satan says 'Come and join me and I will accept you as you are. I am your liberator. I am a humanist. Follow me and I will never judge or reject you. Come, Cum and be free.'

Nino impressed, "You know your enemy quite well, counselor. And this is a plus. We must do something to save the children. Coal is the cheapest of all minerals, yet when it is squeezed and compressed for thousands of years by the earth, it becomes a diamond."

"The most precious of all stones." Says Pitt.

Nino points to some little children bouncing on a trampoline in the window of Leigh-Leighs Toddleraerobics, "Yes. Children come into this world as God's diamonds. His most precious thing, but as they go through this world, and are squeezed by life's troubles and are tempted by its evils, they become, over time, darker and darker. Evil deeds appear as dark spots on these diamonds. Eventually, the diamonds can get so dark, that they fail to give off any light. The only way to remove the stain of sin is to sincerely ask forgiveness for your sins in the name of Jesus Christ."

Pitt worried, "What about the good people who don't believe in Jesus."

Nino explains, "Jesus is a free gift for all who accept him. He will not force himself on anyone. Those whom you call good, who cannot accept him by word because of their religious beliefs or lack there of, must still accept him by deed. Their lives must show that they followed his path, or they cannot be admitted into the kingdom of Forever. **MERCY IS THE HEART OF JEHOVAH'S LAWS. Jesus said that God requires mercy, not sacrifice. Remember this Pitt; all who are truly merciful will receive mercy. If you can refrain from judgment and truly be merciful and compassionate, in the end God's mercy will win out over his judgment against you.**"

Pitt wonders, "Is the path that leads to Forever narrow like the Bible says?"

Nino nods, "**It is a narrow path, but it is a simple path, and that's what makes it narrow. Love God, and love your neighbor as yourself. This is what Jesus gave us. This is the only path that leads to Heaven. There is no other way home.**"

Pitt wonders, "So, if a Jew, a Muslim, or a Hindu for example, asks God directly to forgive him for his sins, does his sin still remain?"

Nino frowns, "Yes, the part of sin that must be atoned for remains. The body and blood of Jesus is now the only sacrifice that atones for sin. It is the only acceptable offering."

Pitt tries to understand, "But, if he followed, or attempted to follow, the path of Jesus in deed, he can still get into Heaven, correct?"

Nino agrees, "Yes, as I said, all who are merciful will obtain mercy. The opposite of your example is also true. There may be a Christian who asks Allah to forgive her in the name of Jesus Christ, even though she does not walk the path of Jesus. These judgmental, unmerciful, hypocrites will not gain admittance into Forever."

Pitt clarifies, "So, in order to get into Forever we must walk the path of Jesus, and be merciful to those who trespass against us. **The path of love & kindness is the path the leads to Heaven.**"

Nino smiles proudly, "There you have it, counselor. You have listened well, and you have taught as well as listened. This also strengthens my hope and faith in you. I am confident that you will make our mission successful. Your music, your books and your movies will save millions of souls. You will illuminate the path of Jesus and the joyous paradise to which it leads. You will become a great teacher, a great husband, a great father and someday maybe even the leader of this once great nation." Nino looks out at the horizon. 'Our time together has come to an end my friend. Fore look, the George Washington Bridge looms large against the western sky. My soul is beckoned, and I must not tarry moment longer." Pitt and Nino stare in awe at the George Washington Bridge as they stop on the corner of 178th street and Broadway.

"Those who bring sunshine into the lives of others cannot keep it from themselves."
-James M. Barrie/For Nancy Birdsong

CHAPTER 46

▼

"I have fought the good fight, I have finished the race, I have kept the faith. Now there is in store for me the crown of righteousness."
-2 Timothy 4:7-8

"Choice, not chance, determines destiny."
-Ellie Crystal

"A wounded Dear—Leaps highest."
-Emily Dickenson

Nino stands close to Pitt and stares at him proudly, "We have done what I have set out to accomplish. We have completed our tour together, and I have nothing more to give. Farewell, my brother, my son, and my friend. You will be in my thoughts and prayers today and always. This is your time Pitt. It is what you were born to do."

It is a tearful parting as Pitt hugs Nino close to his heart, resting his head on the old man's shoulder.

Pitt dries his eyes, "Can't I at least walk across the bridge with you?"

Nino begins walking away, "Nope, no sir. That's not the way the story goes. For years, I have been afraid of this bridge. It has called out to me in my dreams and during my waking hours. Now, for the first time in my life, I will walk across this bridge on my own, knowing in my heart that God has forgiven me for any wrong that I have done in my life, and knowing that my life is more precious to God than I could have ever imagined. I am a child again. Fore I have remembered that I am fully and completely loved by our God."

Pitt stares at the bridge, "I understand why you have to walk it alone. Nino Jones, the Prophet of faith must over come this final hurdle. The only way you ever really overcome your fears is by being brave, and standing up to them all by yourself."

Nino agrees, "It is only those who don't have God involved in their lives who need to be afraid, Pitt. We are the Lions Abijah, the lions whose father is God. You must walk through this world as fearless and as bravely as a lion walks through his pride lands. However, if you ever do feel afraid, remember this final prayer. **Dear father in Heaven, as we walk through the valley of the shadow of death, please send your rod and your staff to protect us so that we may fear no evil. Send your Angels to guard our every step. Let your Holy Spirit and wisdom dwell in us, and let your holy power flow through us, so that we may continue walking bravely along the Path of Jesus, back to the land of our origin. For we are the Lions Abijah.** Remember this prayer, Pitt, and say it from time to time as a reminder of who you really are."

They were standing on the corner of 178th street. Nino gave Pitt one last hug, and then he stepped back and gave him an iron grip handshake.

Pitt salutes his friend, "Goodbye, Nino Jones. I'll never forget you or anything you have said to me. Here." He hands Nino his card. "Here take my card and call me if you need anything, or even just to say hello."

Nino grabs the card, "I'll take it, but I won't be calling any time soon. I just got another one of those feelings, Pitt. I'll be going home soon. And I'm alright with that. Now is the time that you have to have faith. You don't need me to lean on, and you don't need me to prove that your story is true." Nino looks down at the card Mark has handed him. "What it says here, **BELIEVE IN GOD, BELIEVE IN YOURSELF, and NEVER GIVE UP!** Those are the very rules you must live by, Pitt. Stick to the path, and stay close to Allah and Jesus, and we will see each other again. I'll look a lot better, too. I can't wait to meet up with you on that great basketball court in the sky. My sweet jumper is going to be falling on you like rain baby!"

Pitt chuckles, "We'll see who takes who to the hole. Goodbye, my friend."

Nino waves, "Goodbye, Pitt."

With that, he turned and walked west down 178th Street, toward the ramp that would lead him across the bridge. He got halfway down the hill and then he stopped and turned around again. Pitt calls after him.

Pitt smiles, "What did you forget?"

Nino approaches Pitt, "I have a message for you. A message from your father."

Pitts jaw drops, "My father?! Why did you wait so long to tell me?"

Nino explains with tears welling up in his eyes, "I didn't feel that I should tell you earlier, because you had to come to have faith in me on your own, and now you do. So, now your father's words to you will be my final words, Be brave, be a good boy, and I love you very much! Marks the father now."

Nino turns and walks away, and Pitt cries tears of joy as he hears what he knows were his father's last words, spoken once again. The words had been in the back of his mind since June 11, 2017—just two days before he said goodbye to his dear father. Nino turned again and yelled from the bottom of the hill.

Nino smiling, "And Pitt! Your dad wants some grandchildren!"

Pitt smiles and waves, "Tell him I'll get right to it!"

"I bet you will." Nino laughs.

Pitt raises his fist in the air and hollers, "Bravo, Nino Jones. Farewell my friend! God Bless you, Nino Jones. Prophet of faith!"

Nino raised his fist in the air triumphantly, but does not turn back around. Pitt watches Nino slowly climb up the passage way and onto the pedestrian entrance of the George Washington Bridge, and then he turns away from Nino and walks towards a phone booth located on the corner of 178th and Broadway. Just as he is stepping into the booth, he sees two cop cars flip on their lights and take off towards the bridge. At first he thinks nothing of it, and then he sees a man jump off his stoop and start running toward the bridge with a portable scanner in his hands. Pitt stops the man and asks him what was going on.

Street person hollering as he is running, "There is some nut up on the bridge with a gun, and he's holding some people hostage."

Pitt is panic stricken, "What?!" Pitt can't listen to any more as he sprints down the hill west on 178th Street to the pedestrian bridge entrance. He hears the sounds of gun shots coming from the bridge, and he feels his heart beating in his chest. There is a young cop blocking the path so no one can get onto the bridge, but Pitt lowers his shoulder and knocks the cop out of his way. The cop shouts after Pitt in a frenzy.

The police officer is angry, but concerned, "Come back here, you crazy bastard! There's a guy shooting people up there!"

The chaos on the bridge surrounds a man standing on the south river side rail. His arm is looped through one of the cables. He has a gun in one hand, and with his other he is hanging on to an attractive Asian woman with long black hair. He hangs on to her long hair, and her two young children cling to her legs crying hesterically. The man has already shot and killed one passerby who tried to convince him to let the woman go. The man is enraged and he is pointing the gun at everyone who walks by, and shooting random shots into the air. As Nino approaches the man, he can't believe what he sees. As he stares at the scene the gunman threatens him.

The gun man sneers, "You better just keep walking, Nigger, or I'll kill you, too. Just one less nigger in the world, who cares right?"

Nino glares at the man, but the gunman keeps right on talking.

The Gunman hollers at Nino, "Don't you even look at me nigger. You look down at your shoes when you walk past me, boy."

As Nino walks slowly by, he looks out of the corner of his eye, checks out the scene. His heart aches for the mother and her two children. His heart is breaking for them, and he feels the fire of rage begin to burn in his heart. His unexpectedly flashes back just for a brief moment to that terrible moment in Vietnam. Then it strikes him, maybe he was always supposed to die on this bridge, but not in disgrace, not the suicidal death of a coward. Maybe he was supposed to die in honor, righting an old wrong. Suddenly, Nino remembers Pitt's father's words. "Don't be afraid to hit the shot at the buzzer." Nino in a moment of clarity, sizes up the situation and figures that if he can get close enough, he could lunge at the man and push him over the side. Nino stops walking across the bridge and turns back towards the crazed man. The man begins to scream and curse at Nino. But as the man turns to fire at him, Pitt makes it to the top of the bridge walkway and screams out.

Pitt enraged, "Leave him alone you bastard! Nino, No! Stop!"

Temporarily distracted, the man turns his attention to Pitt and Nino seizes the opportunity. He runs straight at him like he is possessed. Nino springs into the air like a panther and with every last bit of energy his old body can muster, he grabs the man and attempts to push him off of his perch. As the man starts to fall, he lets go of the woman and shoots Nino three times in the left shoulder. The pain is excruciating and blood flowing heavily from the wound. Nino grabs the man's arm with his right hand, and squeezing with all of his iron might, he tries to make him drop the gun. The gunman swears and spits at Nino as loses his balance and topples over the rail. As the man falls, Nino tries to break free, but he is able to grab Nino's coat and the two of them plunge helplessly into the Hudson River.

As the police, including officer Hank who just happened to be on his way home to Dumont, New Jersey, converge on the scene to comfort the woman and her children, Pitt is leaning over the rail of the bridge screaming down at the water, hoping and praying that Nino will come to the surface.

Pitt hysterical, "Come on Nino! Come on man! You can do it, Nino!"

As the people line up along the rail, scanning the water to see if someone will surface, Pitt becomes more and more desperate with each passing moment. He climbs up on the rail to jump and try to save his friend, but just as he is about to jump, Sgt. Hank grabs him from behind and pulls him to safety.

"Let me go!" Pitt shouts angrily.

Sgt Hank with tears welling up in his eyes talks softly, "He's dead, son … Ninos gone. Falling from this height into the river is just like hitting concrete. You would just end up dying, too."

Sgt. Hank put his arm around Pitt's shoulders as they looked out at the water, flowing against the New York skyline. The woman and children whom Nino saved see Pitt looking over the edge and crying, and she approaches him and puts her hands on his shoulders.

The asian mother looks down at the water, "Was he a friend of yours?" she asks in a sad voice.

Pitt dries his eyes"Yes mame, a very dear friend."

"What was his name?" The mother asks.

"Nino … Nino Jones."

The mother speaks with pride, "Nino Jones will be remembered by me, my children, and my children's children as a hero. His name will be passed on from generation to generation as a name of honor in my family tree." The woman pauses for a moment and looks out over the water. "God bless you, Nino Jones." She turns back to Pitt and offers her condolences."I'm so sorry you lost your friend. He was so brave."

The little children come and hug Pitt and say they are sorry, too. Pitt stays and stares into the water for a long time. Although he had spent less than a day with Nino Jones, it feels like it has been a lifetime. The sun hangs low in the sky, as Pitt turns and slowly walks east, back toward Broadway and the lights of the city.

"Today you will be with me in paradise. This is my Solemn promise."
-Jesus of Nazereth (Luke 23:43)

THE HIPPOCRATIC P.O.J
FIRST, DO NO HARM.

CHAPTER 47

▼

"Dare to live the life you have dreamed for yourself. Go forward with courage and faith, and make your dreams come true."
-Ralph Waldo Emerson

"I used to be The Greatest of all time! Now, I'm just trying to get to Heaven."
-Muhammad Ali

"A one in a million, chance of a lifetime, a life so compassioned, it sent to me a stroke of luck called you, a one in a million you."
-Sam Dees (sung by Larry Graham) for Leigh.

Pitt stops and visits with Shari just long enough to eat some dinner at Coppala's Italian Restaurant, and then catch the next bus home. He doesn't feel like he can spend another night in the City. He decides to go to Port Authority and take an all-night bus ride home. He wakes up to the familiar voices of Geneva's long time WGVA radio personalities Jerry Sherwin, Ted Baker, & Mike Rusinko. As the approach the city limits he sees a sign that says Welcome to Geneva the Lake Trout Capital of the world, and home of the Geneva High Panthers New York State Football and Softball Champions. His bus arrives at Geneva's famous Victor Nelson Ramada at 7:07 a.m., a good omen, he thought to himself. One of the first people Pitt sees when he gets off of the bus is an old veteran named Albert Elderkin. Albert is truly a character. Upon recognizing Pitt he brakes into a verse of "I'm Looking Over a Four Leaf Clover." Pitt promptly joins in with him as he always does, and then gives Albert a dollar, to which Albert says "Why thank you. I'll do something nice for you sometime." Pitt laughs and makes his way uptown. He walks throughout the quiet city streets of Geneva, south down Exchange Street past L&R Restaurant, Baroody's Book Store, Styles Plus, Al's Inn, Mother Earths Health Foods, and the Crisanti family's fabulous Cam's Pizzeria. He smiles as he passes Chuck & Mary's book store, and Gilbert's Jewelry. He taps on the window in front of Radical Dans and waves to his friends Danny Lynch and Marc Melito. Seeing Marc in reminds him of when he first moved to Geneva. Pitt used to get bullied and shook down for money, until Marc taught him how to box and stand up for himself. His mind goes back in time and he can actually hear Marc's words ... "You don't have to win a fight to get a bully to leave you alone, all you have got to do is make a stand. The next time someone puts their hands on you, I want to let him have it! I mean you hit this joker like Marciano hit Wolcott, and I promise you this bully will never bother you again, and neither will anyone else who is watching. In this world you have got to stand up for yourself if you want to get respect!" Pitt smiles and says in his heart "Your so right. Thanks Marc, I'll never forget you...." He then turns west on Seneca Street and walks past the credit union (Geneva's version of the Bailey Building and Loan from the Movie It's A Wonderful Life). As he walks the quiet streets Pitt actually feels a little bit like George Bailey running home to 320 Sycamore Street. Saved by an Angel named Nino Jones, he too left his bridge wanting to live again. His faith in life has been restored. His purpose is now clear, and his appreciation for his family, his friends, his job, and his dear little city of Geneva has never been deeper. Although he has only been gone a couple of days, it suddenly feels like he has been away for a very long time. He continues on past Wylie J's Bar, and thinks of his friend and long time rival JJ, Smaldone. He would always Call JJ "Frazier" [as in Joe Frazier], because Pitt is Muhammad Ali. As he walks past Don's Own Florist he steals a rose from his friend and owner Joey Cohen Davids.

Startled at first but then smiling when she sees who it is she hollers in fake agitation. "Hey, you gotta pay for that rose you crook!"

Pitt laughs, "Crime don't pay Joey you know that. Anyway it's for Leigh, and I'm broke." He says smiling.

Joey laughing and smiling "Your always broke ... Well, as long as its for Leigh.... You're probably so deep in the dog house this time one rose isn't goanna help you anyway. You might as well give it back." Joey teases.

Pitt laughing "You got that right. Ill see ya.".

He continues up the street and waves to his friends Joey, Cork, and Tammy who were up early at Super Casuals clothing store. They to are laughing at his interaction with Joey. He tips his hat to Mr. and Mrs. Guard, and his friend Hal at Burrall Insurance. As he goes past Area Records and Martins Music he wonders if they will someday soon be selling one of his CD's. The prestigious Smith Opera House brings back warm memories of his father and sisters performing in West Side Story, The Wizard of Oz, Joseph and His Amazing Technicolored Dream Coat, Our Children's Children, Jesus Christ Super Star, and last but not least, Fiddler On The Roof. His father had been the Rabbi. A fitting last performance on the same stage that he had brought the house down as a child, singing Al Jolson's "Swanny, as his buddy Sonny Alvaro played the piano." He continued on past Heavy's, Parker's and Sonny's. He laughed thinking about the surprise birthday party Leigh had thrown for him. As he made his way past Melissa's Barber Shop, and Mark's Pizza to Main Street, he turns onto Pulteney Park Circle and walks along a beautiful brick circle. He is like Dorothy returning from OZ, but it's not Aunty Em who is on his mind. He follows his own yellow brick road past the Presbyterian Church. He smiles as he reads the marquee which has a quote from Gandhi **"Be the wholeness you seek. Be the change you want to see.** Pitt chuckles as he reads the sermon of the week: "Jesus Sleeps Here." Indeed he does Pitt thinks to himself. As he glances out at the beautiful fountain which overlooks Seneca Lake, he is reminded of the reverends Jim Gerling and Nancy Birdsong (The world famous painter). How fitting, he thinks to himself, that these two holy souls, and their special little church seem to be guarding the entrance of his neighborhood. He stops outside the church for a moment and as he does Jim and Nancy's words flow out onto the street: Nancy begins, **"Dear Lord, we pray for peace and prosperity for our country and all nations who are at war. Please heal the sick and injured, comfort the families of those who have died, and watch over all of the soldiers until you can bring them safely home. Help us to find the important things in life. Teach us not to obsess over the small trivial things, but instead to focus on the more important issues in life and in our religion. Keep our families and friends safe and healthy and lead them so that they may lead us. Help mothers and fathers and husbands** and wives to stay together in marriage, and fill our children with wisdom and obedience from the womb." Then Jim continues, "Dear God, guide us to choose to do good things despite the difficulties of the task. Give us the patience, strength and courage to fulfill our obligations when the way seems blocked by obstacles that slow us down, or keep us from walking with you. Help us to stick up for other people and inspire them through our words and deeds. Forgiving God, We know we are not perfect, please forgive us for any mistakes we have made and give us the strength and wisdom to do your will. Help us to remember that Jesus said to Love our enemies, bless those that curse us, do good to those who hate and despise us, and pray for those who despitefully use and persecute us and our loved ones. Judge not, and you will not be judged. For mercy triumphs over judgment! In the name of our savior, Jesus Christ. Amen … Now go out into the world and live as free people. Hold fast to what is good. Render no one evil for …" Pitt moves on and Jim's words fade like a summer breeze into the mist of the morning. As he turns west onto Washington Street all he can think about is his pretty wife Leigh. He realizes once again the she is truly the first and only love of his life, and definitely, as Nino said, the best cheese cake in town! He knows someone in almost every house he walks by. Judge Tim Buckley, and the fabulously wealthy Professor Marvin Bram, each doorway an entrance to a part of his life, a connection to his past and future. As he walks by the great Jim Henderson's home, he is filled with gratitude for all this man has done for him in his life. Jim had taught Pitt how to become a student at Hobart College, and how to become a respected man on and off the basketball court. One block from home, on South Morrell, he pauses at the corner to remember his father's family, Grandma and Grandpa Pitifer, Uncle Junior and Aunt Diane, and Aunt Lucille and Uncle Charlie, and his cousins Charlie, Debbie, and especially Greg. He passes by Mike Connell's & Bob Verdehem's shared driveway that was once a basketball court. It is no longer a court, and it seemed so much narrower than he remembered. He stops for a moment and thinks of all the great neighborhood games he played as a child. He chuckles thinking about some of the characters that used to play their. We even had our own language "Couooomon! I'll drill ya! I tell ya." Pitt chuckles thinking of Hal Gordan, the founder of the court slang. It is also where he met his best friends Zip & Wils. He shakes his head and thinks to himself, "What a band of characters." He smiles thinking that he and his mother's shared patch of asphalt is now the neighborhood court. He continues walking west on Washington Street, then turning right, he walks north on Nagel Place. He grins for a moment thinking that if he switches the N and the A, Nagel place would become Angel Place. Pitt smiles "Maybe this really is Angel Place!" He stops at the big red house, number 33. He didn't expect his wife Leigh to be up and about at this early hour, but there she is. She runs out on to the porch and jumps into his arms, nearly knocking him to the ground. He kisses her all over, taking her face into his hands and looking at her like he hadn't seen her in years. Pitt stares deep into her eyes, "Let me look at you." He says as he continues to kiss her. "Oh Leigh, I love you so much." Pitt returns home with a new appreciation for his sweet little wife, and he is now thankful for all that he has. They sit for a long time, just swinging on the hammock while Pitt tells her the tales of his incredible adventure with Nino Jones. When Pitt is through telling his story, he sits in silence for a moment trying to digest the story for himself. He stares up at the giant pine tree behind the LaRocca home and remembers how as a boy he would climb to the top to see if he could see all the way to New York City. Maybe he always knew it was supposed to be a part of his destiny. After his short day dream, he turns back towards Leigh, who is smiling. She is so happy and pretty that she actually seems to be glowing.

Leigh Chuckles, "Well, Mr. Messenger, that was quite a story." She said lovingly.

"What are you smiling like that for?" Pitt asks her, a little suspicious of her wide-eyed grin.

Leigh gets up and strolls around the porch, "Well, because it's not the whole story. You see, that prophet friend of yours, Nino, must have some real connections all the way up to the top."

Pitt excited, "Why do you say that? Did he appear to you? What happened?! Did you get a sign, have a dream or something?"

"Mark," Leigh started in a calm voice. She stared directly into his eyes and then said the words he never expected to hear. "I'm pregnant."

Pitt grabs his wife with such jubilation it takes her breath away. He hollers for his mother so loudly that he wakes the whole street from their early morning slumber. Neighbors run to their porches to see what is going on, and to offer their congratulations. Pitt and Leigh welcome the hugs, kisses and kind words from their neighbors, and they embrace the peace that has re-entered their lives.

The morning is now a rosy haze, and a gentle zephyr tickles the wind chimes. Pitt and Leigh, whose head rests upon Mark's chest, swing in their hammock and watch a little finch fly back and forth feathering its nest. If Mark and Leigh felt like they were being watched over this morning, they couldn't have been more right. Fore all of Forever was celebrating their happy reunion.

THE HINDUISM P.O.J.
THIS IS THE SUM DUTY; DO NOT UNTO OTHERS WHICH WOULD CAUSE YOU PAIN IF DONE TO YOU.

"Now go out into the world in peace, and live as free people. Hold fast to what is good. Render no one evil for evil. Support the weak and faint hearted. Love and serve the Lord always in the power of the Holy Spirit."
-REVEREND JIM GERLING

CHAPTER 48

▼

"Suddenly, the glory of the God of Israel appeared from the east.
The sound of his coming was like the roar of rushing waters, and
the whole landscape shown with his glory."
-Ezekiel 43:2

"The righteous will shine like the sun in the kingdom of their
father."
-JESUS OF NAZARETH/Matthew 13:43

"Above all else, love one another dearly. For love covers up a multitude of
sins."
-1 Peter 4:8

Sully is playing the accordion, and the Zealots and their friends and family
are so busy celebrating that they fail to notice that Jesus, the King himself,
has shown up at the party. Nino and the rest of the Zealots, except for
Barabbas, are all nervously surprised to see Jesus walking toward Nino, and
the crowd becomes quiet.

Jesus hugs Nino warmly, and kisses him on the cheek, "Hello, my
brother." He says, embracing Nino.

Nino is overwhelmed with emotion, "Hello, my King." Nino says nervously, as he looks worriedly at his fellow zealots. "I didn't expect to see you
so soon. I thought we'd have to wait to see if our plan worked or not."

Jesus with tears welling up in his eyes, "Nino Jones, do you know how
much it means to my father and me that someone at this late stage of the
Game would have faith and love as strong as yours? The fact that you are
here, safe and warm means more than whether or not your plan is a success.

In fact, I salute all of you very brave and courageous souls for the part you played in this noble cause." Jesus and the rest of the crowd give a thunderous round of applause.

Nino looks confused at Barabbas. All of the other Zealots also looked worried, until Barabbas comes forward and puts his arms around Nino and Jesus.

Barabbas speaks with passion and pride, "Nino, my fellow Zealots, You'll be very surprised and relieved that Jesus and I came up with this idea a long-long time ago. It is a plan that will save many souls to be sure. It has already saved Nino, and his friend Pitt seems like he is now on a good and righteous path. However, it was also designed to give some of my very dear friends a chance to right some old wrongs. I always knew that your eternities were never really in jeopardy, but that doesn't take away from what any of you have done. In your minds you thought you were risking your souls, so in God's eyes you did … And now, as Paul Harvey would say, you can find out the rest of the story." Barabbas steps back and allows Jesus to finish the tale.

Jesus smiles, "Nino, a good friend of mine was captured by Satan many years ago, and based on the rules of the Great Game, I was powerless to do anything about that."

Barabbas is chokes with emotion, but composes himself.

Tears well up in Jesus' eyes "That is until now. Jesus and I have waited patiently for over two thousand years for this one moment in time." Barabbas turns to Nino, "Do you remember when you were on that subway train, and the police had their guns pointed at you?"

Nino chuckles nervously, "I sure do. I don't think I'll ever forget that!"

Jesus pats Nino's shoulder, "Well, I don't imagine you will. As you already know, the reason why you were not arrested was because that guy jumped up and attacked the police officers. However, what you don't know is that this fellow who saved you was no ordinary man."

Nino taken aback, "Oh my gosh, was that you?"

Jesus looks out at the Zealots to see their response, "No. It was our lost brother.… Judas."

The Zealots begin to smile and cheer, sensing what is about to be said., and Barabbas raises his fist to the crowd. Nino shakes his head in disbelief and wonderment, "Judas? Judas Iscariot?" He asks.

Jesus smiles proudly, "That's right, Nino. Judas. He sacrificed his soul for the sake of a noble cause. He knew that there was no way he would benefit from helping you, and that it would most certainly send him prematurely to the bottomless pit. The lowest level of Hell, where Satan and his demons will torture him unmercifully throughout eternity. He allowed himself to be nailed to the cross by Satan, and he accepted his lot with love, bravery and dignity."

Nino can't believe what he was hearing. "He acted out of pure love with no thought of his own suffering."

Jesus visibly choked up, "And in so doing, our lost brother is saved."

Thomas runs toward Jesus with tears in his eyes. "Jesus, does this mean?"

Jesus walks into the crowd with Nino and Barabbas, "Yes, my brothers. Judas is coming home." Jesus is embraced by the cheering Zealots. Barabbas smiles and holds his glass of wine in front of him. "A toast to the glory of our God, the eternal reign of our King, to All God's Children, the Heavenly Zealots, the Lions Abijah, to Nino Jones, the Prophet of Faith, his messenger Mark Salvatore Pitifer, and last but not least, to our brother Judas, for whom our plan was designed, and who has finally found his way home."

The glasses are raised when Jesus interrupts the toast. "Barabbas, aren't you forgetting something?" He winks at Barabbas, who thinks for a moment and then sees little Noah, Markie and Nina in the corner of the room. He looks towards the holy mountain of God and adds a prayer of thanks.

Barabbas bows his head, "I thank you, Father, for blessing our plan. You have given us all that we have prayed for and more. Our cups, as you promised, overfloweth with joy." Barabbas pauses again, smiling at the three little ones. "Markie, Noah and Nina, can you come up here please?" The three little souls bounce cheerfully up to Barabbas and perch themselves on his lap. "My dear little souls, this is a very special day for you. It is an unexpected surprise even to me." Barabbas gets a lump in his throat, "Nina, Noah, ane Markie, this is Nino Jones" The little ones run excitedly over to Nino, and Nina is the first to speak.

Nina anxiously reaches out to her old friend. "Hello, Nino. I am so happy you made it back safe and sound. Incredible things can happen when you wish upon a star." She winks at Nino.

Nino overjoyed, "Or go somewhere over the rainbow," he winks back at her. They embrace in a hug full of happiness. "I had a feeling that was you, you dear little lamb."

Noah is tapping his foot and staring at Barabbas impatiently. And Barabbas chuckles, "Okay, Noah, you can bring them out now."

Noah marches forth proudly, escorting two loving souls named Albertina and Charles. Sully drops his accordion and runs to greet his parents. "Mama? Daddy? What are you doing here? Were you a part of this plan, too?"

Sully's mother smiles upon him. "It appears that we were Sully, and we didn't even know it!"

Sully looks to his father, "What do you mean? Daddy? How can this be?"

Charles gives details, "Sully, when you were a very young boy, your mother lost a child at birth. His name was Francis. As Francis' angel was escorting him back to Heaven, Barabbas instructed him to send the soul of this child to a young mother who was about to give birth to a child in a New York City hospital. The woman's name was Estella Jones. She delivered your brother's soul as it united with the physical babe she bore. The young woman died of complications shortly after the child was born. She had no known relatives, so the baby was sent to an orphanage. Where he lived there until the age of 18, and then joined the army."

Nino's jaw drops as he listens to the story. Sully is yet to catch on, and stares confusedly at his father as the story continues."

Charles looks at Nino, "My son Francis' soul lived on in the body of this brave and noble soldier, and his soul stayed strong until something terrible happened during the Vietnam War. This soldier returned to America and withdrew from the mainstream of society. He started a new life of humble goodness and kindness, waiting unknowingly for the day he would hero-ically fulfill his destiny." Charles takes a deep breath before approaching the newfound prophet. "Nino Jones, Prophet of Faith, come here and give your daddy a hug."

Nino runs to Albertina and Charles and hugs them tightly. Sully finally puts two and two together, and tugs at Nino's sleeve. "Hey! Don't forget your big brother!"

Nino, with tears of joy streaming down his face, grabbed Sully in a giant bear hug. "I hit the buzzer shot, Sully! We did it man! We did it!" Sully smiles proudly, "Nino, that was a faaaannn-tas-tic shot!"

Nino crying tears of joy, "I can't believe it. I have a family. And, hey, that means Pitt, he's my nephew? Wow, Pitt's my nephew."

Noah wound his way to the center of the group grinning from ear to ear. "Barabbas, did I do a good job?"

Barabbas pats Noah on the head, "Yes, Noah. You three little chickadees have made us all very proud. Nino, this is Noah. He is the little rascal who helped us find your family." Nino hears Barabbas call Noah by his name and remembers that Martin had asked Pitt to name a son Noah.

Nino stares at Noah in awe, "Noah, are you really the one who found my family?"

Noah beams, "Yes! Me and my friends Nina and Markie all helped you Nino." Nino and Nina smile as Noah tells his story, but Markie is looking down at the ground with a sad look on his face. Nino, notices his sad expression, and walkes over to little Markie. He takes Markies face in one of his big strong hands and gently tilts his chin up. As he looks into Markie's eyes he can see that the boy was crying.

Nino sadly, "You're little Markie, aren't you?" Nino asks softly.

Markie shakes his head yes, and then gathers the courage to speak through his sniffles.

Mark wipes his eyes and sniffs, "Did I give you good notes, Nino?"

Nino bits his lip, "Yes, Markie. Your notes helped me very much."

Markie somewhat ashamed to be feeling sorry for himself under the circumstance, "I'm really happy that we were able to help you find your family, Nino. I am just sad because we still don't have a mommy and daddy. I asked you to help us, but I know you probably didn't have time to read all that I wrote to you."

"Markie, I did read your little note, and the prayer at the end of your writings. It meant a lot to me and I kept it with me throughout my adventure. But, to be honest with you, I didn't know how I could possibly help you find a mommy and daddy."

Nino stopped and notices his words had chased the smiles off of all of the children's faces. "I didn't know how I could possibly find a mommy and daddy for you, until now." The smiles returned, and God's light shines through the anxious eyes of the little souls. Nino walkes over to Jesus and grabbes his hand.

Nino bows his head in humility, "Jesus, my brother and King, I have a wish. And it would mean so much to me if you would grant it."

Jesus gently picks up Nino's chin so that he can look into his eyes, "Nino, there is no need for formality in Forever. This is the land where all wishes are granted, and all dreams come true for my Angels and the souls who have survived the Great Game. Ask, my brother, ask and you will receive whatever you wish for. Unto the half of my kingdom!"

Nino explains, "Jesus, my messenger Mark Pitifer and his wife Leigh are very good people, and they really would like to have a family."

Jesus smiled at Nino and said, "That's no problem. I'll check and see who is next in line to enter the Great Game, and send our heavenly stork to their house as soon as possible." Nino lookes down at the ground, and Jesus notices his disappointment. "Why, Nino, whatever is the matter? Isn't that what you want?"

Nino worried, "Yes, Jesus, but, forgive me. I don't mean to be ungrateful but,"

"But what?"

Nino points to the little ones, "Well, I was hoping you could possibly send Nina, Noah and Markie to be Pitt's kids."

Nina, Noah and Markie try hard to hold back their joy and anticipation. Jesus hesitates for a moment with false apprehension. "You want me to send three friends from the Royal Playground all to the same home?!"

Nino now more worried then ever, and stammering, "I don't know how things work up here, Jesus. I'm sorry if I asked you to do something that can't be done."

Jesus smiles warmly, not wishing to tease him any longer, "Nino, it really isn't the way things are normally done, but after all, I am King." Jesus turns calmly to Sully and calls him over. "Sully, come over here, will you?" He then turns to the children and calls them over as well. "Nina, Noah and Markie come to Jesus and he takes them all in his arms, and caresses them, kissing them gently on their heads, and stroking their angelic faces. "My children, I want you to meet your Papa. He is the father of the man who is soon to be your daddy."

Sully is crying tears of joy as the children jump into his arms. All of the great crowd which had gathered begins to cheer. Sully picks up his accordion again, and began to play. Nina, Noah, Markie and Nino are now singing and dancing with the other Zealots. As the celebration gets into full swing, Barabbas, Jesus and Chebar walked off to a quiet spot.

Chebar is scratching his head, still bewildered by the unexpected celebration. "I still can't believe that you knew exactly who was going to be the prophet of faith all along, and didn't tell me. Do you realize you two have pulled off the greatest sting of all time? My brothers, you have stung the Devil, himself! Wait until Newman and Redford hear about this one!"

Barabbas and Chebar embrace, "Well, I didn't know for sure, but I was hoping. And Chebar, you watch too many movies!" Barabbas laughs a hearty laugh and grabs his old friend by the neck. Jesus smiles proudly at his loving brothers.

Jesus puts a hand on each of their shoulders, "You have done well, my brothers. When Barabbas came to me all those years ago with this plan to rescue Judas from the bottomless pit, I never could have envisioned that so much good would come from it. It just goes to show you that when your heart is in the right place, our heavenly father will be on your side. Now go, my brothers, and spread the good news for all to hear. Pour the wine and line up the entertainment. Prepare the fatted calf, for our brother who was dead, is alive! He who was lost is found. He who was held captive is now rescued. Thank you, Barabbas and Chebar. Thank you from the bottom of my heart. Finally, after all these years, my family will also be reunited. Go, my brothers, Go and prepare the grand feast! For behold, the prodigal son returns!"

As Barabbas gives the Heavenly Zealots their final orders, they all cheer and dance about. They are hugging and giving each other high fives and Sully breaks into a new song as the fantastic celebration continues. The Zealots scatter throughout the kingdom like fireflies on a warm summer's night to spread the good news, as Nina, Noah and Markie dance on and on with their Papa.

Eons away from the happiness, the torrid blackness of Hell is swelling with the tormented cries of its wretched souls. Then suddenly a light breaks through the darkness, and the demons and fallen angels fall silent at his sight. Jesus has once again entered Hell. Even Satan hides behind his throne and peeks out like a timid child. Now there is a great cry coming forth from all of the suffering souls, pleading with Jesus to free them. They scream and cry in heartbreaking sobs, "Save us Jesus! Please, take us home! Please don't leave us! Jesus reacts to their voices as if being whipped with a thousand lashes. He is greatly pained by the fact that he cannot help them, and his sacred heart is breaking. He speaks to the hoards of Hell in a voice that booms through the hollow cavern.

Jesus wiping the tears from his eyes, "Please, dear children. Please be still. You have my peace and love, and that is all I can give." In a single moment, Hell had once again fallen completely silent, and Jesus continued to address the masses.

Jesus looks out into the bottomless pit and cries out in a mighty voice, "Judas … Judas my dear brother, come forth from this pit of evil and inequity. For in your unselfish deed, you have atoned for your many sins. By banishing yourself to the bottomless pit, in order to help God and hurt Satan, you have righted many wrongs. With no chance for reward other than the knowledge that you were doing what was righteous and good, you have saved your soul, and the souls of many others will profit from your kind deed. Judas, your time has come to Return … to … Forever!"

As Judas began walking toward Jesus, all of a sudden many of the tortured souls began to stand and cheer for their brother who was being released. A joyful noise was ringing through the hallways of Hell, and the demons and fallen angels trembled with fear, hiding under rocks and in caves. As the regretful damned shared a brief moment of celebration, Satan boils with anger and screeches out at the cheering souls. He was black with rage.

"Silence! Anyone of you who continues to stand and cheer for this traitor will be tortured and suffer like never before. Your fate will be a thousand times worse than any soul has ever seen. Judas may have escaped me! But you fools will feel my wrath! We'll see how happy you are when Jesus turns to leave again."

Some of the souls stopped cheering out of fear, and others who had not cheered scorned those who did in an attempt to win points with the Prince of Darkness. The uncheering souls were jealous of Judas. Even after years of torture and reflection on their evil ways, these souls remained selfish and self-serving. They were incapable, or at least, unwilling to feel for anyone other than themselves.

As Judas comes forth he nearly falls into Jesus' arms out of exhaustion. Jesus helps Judas to his feet. He hugs and kisses Judas, and then He and Judas look back at the hundreds of thousands of souls who not only continue to cheer, but cheer even louder than they had before Satan's retort.

Judas looks at his kind and loving brother. "These poor, poor souls. He is going to torture them as if they were me. He will pour out every ounce of his wrath on them, and yet they continue to cheer. God, I wish there was something I could do for them."

Jesus has tears streaming down his face, "I know, Judas. My heart also weeps for them. If only they could have learned how to love when they were on earth. If only ..."

Jesus looks toward the Heavens and seems to be praying. A mighty wind is followed by seven tremendous claps of thunder. This is no ordinary wind, but the Holy Spirit of God. The spirit rushes through the caverns of Hell like a great flowing river of multicolored visual wind. It swirls about each of the cheering souls, spinning each one in what looks like a miniature tornado. It spins the souls, including Judas, and as it does, they are transformed. Their once broken bodies are replenished, and their tattered garments are swirled into the dazzling multi-colored robes. As Jesus stand dumbfounded, Jehovah's great voice is heard like the rumbling surf of a thousand oceans.

Jehovah speaks majestically, and the power of his voice actually makes the ground rumble, "GOODNESS BEGETS GOODNESS, AND LOVE BEGETS LOVE. JUDAS, MY SON, THE UNSELFISH LOVING DEED YOU HAVE PERFORMED HAS DONE MORE THAN YOU OR EVEN JESUS COULD HAVE EVER IMAGINED. THE FAR REACHING RIPPLE EFFECT FROM YOUR ONE ACT OF LOVE HAS REACHED THE PITS

IN THE DEEPEST DEPTHS OF HELL. THESE ETERNALLY HOPELESS SOULS HAVE BEEN GIVEN ONE LAST OPPORTUNITY TO PROVE THAT THEY ARE CAPABLE OF LOVE—TO SHOW THAT THEY COULD TAKE HAPPINESS AND PRIDE IN THE GOOD FORTUNE OF ANOTHER—IS THE ULTIMATE PROOF OF LOVE.…" There is a moment of pause and anticipation, and then Allah continues, "JESUS, MY BELOVED SON, YOUR PRAYER IS ACCEPTED. THE SACRIFICE YOU HAVE OFFERED IS SUFFICIENT AND YOUR REQUEST IS GRANTED. NOW ALL OF MY POOR, SAD AND BRAVE CHILDREN WHO REFUSED TO STOP CHEERING DESPITE SATAN'S WORDS OF WARNING, ARE NOW FREE TO RETURN TO THE LAND OF YOUR ORIGIN! WELCOME HOME MY DEAR SWEET CHILDREN. WELCOME HOME.

The fires of Hell are almost extinguished by the joyful tears that poured from the saved souls' eyes. They leap and run from their pits toward Jesus and Judas, like children released on the last day of school. They hoist Jesus and Judas onto their shoulders and in one voice sing songs of praise to their merciful and compassionate father. Jesus and Judas, smiling and laughing, join hands and raised them in victory, as the roaring crowd carries them on their mighty shoulders. Fists are raised high in honor as they march out of the bottomless pit, toward the light of Paradise. Judas and all the saved souls are finally, as God commanded, RETURNING TO FOREVER!!!!!!

"I will send out the angels to gather together my chosen ones from all over the world-from the farthest bounds of Earth and Heaven."
-JESUS OF NAZARETH/Mark: 13: 26-2

Post Script

▼

"I see skies of blue, and clouds of white. The bright blessed day, and the dark sacred night. And I think to myself ... what a wonderful world."
-Louis Armstrong

Leigh awakens Pitt in the middle of a cold winter's night. It was time. He checks the calendar on his way out the door to the hospital and chuckles to himself. "January 13th, (1-13) ... Nino's winning Quick Draw numbers." That day after such a long wait, Pitt and Leigh were finally blessed with a beautiful baby girl, who was healthy in every way. Pitt was going to name his child Nino if it was a boy, but when he found out he had a daughter, he asked Leigh to pick the name. And she chose the name ... Nina. Leigh said she had always liked that name. Pitt was warmed by the name as well. And as he looked down at his little girl for the first time, he is unexpectedly reminded of the little girl from the subway who had sung so sweetly for him and Nino. He pictured her long red spiral curls and her big blue eyes that sparkled as she sang "Over the Rainbow". Pitt cradles his little lamb close to his bosom and his heart is warmed in a way he could never have imagined. He rocks her ever so gently and softly sings the first song Nina will ever hear ... **"When you wish upon a star. Makes no difference where you are. Anything your heart desires will come to you...."** As Nino requested, Pitt and Leigh were blessed with two more beautiful children. Noah arrived two years later on May 2nd, and Markie two years after Noah on June 22nd. The little family is now complete. And The Lions Abijah, as their daddy calls them (the Lions whose father is God), are all living happily ever after!

TETELESTAI!
"This is my victorious proclamation. I have completed my task. I have won through the struggle. I have come out of the darkness into the glory of God's light, and I now grasp my crown."
Jesus' Final words from The Cross at Golgotha 3:05 P.M.
-Interpreted by William Barclay

"Thus I am born ... for the establishment of righteousness."
-KRISHNA/THE BHAGAVAD-GITA

Authors Note: This book was started on June 13th, 1992 and completed on July 23, 2005 (My father's 77th birthday) ... As you go through this life always remember that the earth is not our real home. We must all try to become like little children once again. Let your imaginations reblossom, and dare to dream about the wonderful paradise that awaits All of God's Children. Yes, it is true! The Kingdom of Forever exists! And love is the only path that will lead us home ... Share your faith and compassion with all people, and all nature. Open up your heart to God so that he can touch the world through your deeds. Be charitable so that you will store up riches in Heaven. Be Merciful so that you may receive mercy. Let your daily lives be your religion, and be brave so that your wisdom will bare much fruit. Try with all your might to Return To Forever. Live life to the fullest, and share your love in all ways. BELIEVE IN GOD, BELIEVE IN YOURSELF, AND NEVER GIVE UP! Always remember that all who remain faithful until the end will be victorious! May God, Jesus, and all of the Angels bless, and protect you always. God's Peace, Blessings, and Best of Life.
-Mark Salvatore Pitifer "Pitt"

"Was it I who spoke? Was I not also a listener?"
-Kahill Gibran

IN LOVING MEMORY & CELEBRATION
TO THE LIVES OF
SULLY & ANN MARIE PITIFER

One year before my father died we threw a surprise 35th anniversary party for my parents. One of the keynote speakers was my father's good friend Sal Chiolo, from Cherry Hill, New Jersey. I thought it would be fitting to use some of Sal's words, because I think his first impression and eventual love for my father was a universal experience for everyone who ever met and became friends with Sully Pitifer.

"Did you know that God intended Sully to be six feet four inches tall? When I first met Sully he was wearing a black shirt, black trousers with a black belt, black shoes and socks, and a black banded wrist watch. He looked like he belonged to one of those motorcycle gangs! Little did I know on that day that we would develop such a tremendously great friendship. I have no words to describe how deeply I care for him, but true friends don't need words ...—Salvatore "Sal" Chiolo

The Daffodils of Spring Time is a song that I wrote for our mother to express our love for her. Daffodils in bloom embody my mother's love, smile, beauty and laughter.

"When I was a baby all the love that you gave me is the strength that sustains me now that I'm on my own. In the cold lonely winter I become the pretender, and I dream you are with me, and not so far-far away. I know you walk beside me, like an Angel you guide me and as long as you're with me, I can face any storm. It's a long way to Heaven, but I know the direction. In the life that you lived I found a path that leads me home. I see you in spring's blossoms as they fall on me like snow. And in the wind I hear your voice sing lullabies from long ago. But oh my joy when the daffodils of spring time, like your lovely smile return to warm my days. I'm a child each time the daffodils of springtime ... Bring you home."—Mark Salvatore Pitifer

Life and death are one, even as the river and the sea are one. In the depth of your hopes and desires lies your silent knowledge of the beyond; And like seeds dreaming beneath the snow your heart dreams of spring. Trust the dreams, for in them is hidden the gate to eternity. For what is it to die but to stand naked in the wind and to melt into the sun? And what is to cease breathing, but to free the breath from its restless tides, that it may rise and expand and seek God unencumbered? Behold I have found that which is greater than wisdom. It is aflame spirit in you ever gathering more of itself. It is life in quest of life in bodies that fear the grave. There are no graves here. These mountains and plains are a cradle and a stepping-stone. Whenever you pass by the field where you have laid your ancestors look well thereupon, and you shall see yourselves and your children dancing hand in hand. Only when you drink from the river of silence shall you indeed sing. And when you have reached the mountain top, then you shall begin to climb. And when the earth shall claim your limbs, then shall you truly dance
-Kahill Gibran (The Prophet)

Mom and dad you will always be apart of our lives, and you will be loved forever.

-Mark, Sally, Shari, and Sharla & all of The Lions Abijah.

THE PITIFER FAMILY'S MUSIC IS NOW AVAILABLE!
ALL GOD'S CHILDREN

Featuring: Mark-Sally-Shari-Sharla & Nina Pitifer

Well Pitt took Martin's advice and started a band called ALL GOD'S CHILDREN. He also produced a CD called HEAVENTOWN, which is one of the featured songs. If you would like to purchase a copy of our CD you can send a check or money order of $15.00 (This includes shipping & handling) to: Mark Salvatore Pitifer, 33 Nagel Place, Geneva, New York 14456. You can also go to heaventown.net to order by VISA or MASTERCARD.

Our CD can also be ordered by phone through the Hobart & William Smith College Store (315)-781-3449, or the Book Nook 781-6665 (VISA or MASTER-CARD). You can also fax in your order at (315)-781-3450, or heaventown.net.

If you live in the Geneva area you can also purchase our CD at Area Records & Music (Mike George), or Martin Music (Joanie & Tom Martin), The Book Nook (Chuck & Mary Bakogiannis), and Irene's Coffee & Jazz House (Bobby Greco).

We sincerely appreciate your support.

God's Peace & Best of Life

Mark Salvatore Pitifer & The AGC Family

THANK YOU KYLE BAILEY!

I have always loved the songs of Earth-Wind & Fire. The words and music of Maurice White and Philip Bailey move me body and soul. Although my family and I have now released several CD's, for along time I was afraid to produce my music, because I knew it would never be as good as theirs. However, the message I have learned in my musical pilgrimage is that our songs don't have to be as good as EWF. Like the book Return To Forever, our music is a gift from God, that we are privileged to share with the world. Allah inspires us, and we in turn share the gift, and hopefully inspire you. As I was finishing this last bit of writing, a serendipitous moment occurred. A little boy named Kyle Bailey came to my door. He was holding our <u>All God's Children</u> CD in his hand. "Mr. Pitifer" he said. "I just want you to know that I listen to your CD all the time. It really makes me feel good. My favorite song is Heaventown. Will you listen to it with me?" "Yes Kyle, I will." Thank you God, and thank you Kyle for blessing me with such beautiful gifts.

"You're a shinning star no matter who you are. So plant a pretty flower each day, be ever wonderful, and don't let the world change your mind. Fore, in the land called fantasy, you will never be alone. The reasons, true love is written in the stone."
-Maurice White/Phil Bailey & Earth-Wind & Fire

FOOT PRINTS IN THE SAND

One night a woman had a dream. She dreamed she was walking along the beach with the Lord. Across the sky flashed scenes from her life. For each scene, she noticed two sets of footprints in the sand: one belonging to her, and the other to the Lord.

When the last scene of her life flashed before her, she looked back at the footprints in the sand. She noticed that many times along the path of her life there was only one set of footprints. She also noticed that it happened at the very lowest and saddest times in her life.

"Lord, you said that once I decided to follow you, you'd walk with me all the way, but I have noticed that during the most troublesome times in my life, there is only one set of footprints. I don't understand why when I needed you most you would leave me?"

The Lord replied, "My daughter. My precious child, I love you and I would never leave you. During your times of trial and suffering, when you see only one set of footprints, it was then that I carried you.

-Mr. Melchi Zedek

"Through the wind and the rain she stands hard as a stone in a world that she can't rise above. But *her dreams give her wings and she flies to a place where she's loved….*"

-Martina McBride (Concrete Angels)

Author's Note For My Students: Never, ever, ever, ever, under any circumstances, give up. As Martina McBride suggests "Let your dreams give you wings." Live a life that is filled with mercy, love, compassion, hope and wonder, and together we will fly to that place where we are loved … I'll see you in Forever.

THE HELL APPENDIX 666

"The devil took Jesus to a very high mountain and showed him all the kingdoms of the world and their glory. And he said to him "All these I will give you, if you will fall down and workship me." Then Jesus said "Be gone, Satan! For it is written, You shall worship the Lord your God and him only shall you serve. Then the devil left him, and behold, Angels came and were ministering to him."
-Matthew 4:8-11 (New Testament)

"That evening they brought to Jesus many who were possessed by demons, and he cast out the spirits with a word and healed all who were sick."
-Matthew 8:16 (New Testament)

"What have you to do with us, Jesus of Nazareth? Have you come to destroy us? I know who you are, the Holy One of God."
-Mark 1:23-26 (New Testament)

"In order to truly defeat your enemy, you must first get to know him well enough to have compassion for him!"
-MARK SALVATORE PITIFER

"As I stood in Heaven, I was shown a vision of Great pageantry. A woman clothed with the sun, with the moon beneath her feet, gave birth to a son. This son was destined to rule all nations. However, the Great Dragon, the ancient serpent called the devil or Satan, tried to kill the child. Henceforth, there was a war in Heaven; Michael and the Angels under his command fought Satan and his host of fallen angels (Nearly 1/3 of all the angels in Heaven joined Satan's army). The devil lost the battle and was forced from Heaven. Satan and his demons were thrown down to earth, where they are now attempting to deceive the whole world ... Yes woe to the people of the world, for the devil has come down to you in great anger, knowing he has little time. Satan is furious at all of God's Children who try and keep his commandments, and who love one another. He is also filled with hate and rage, because he knows that very soon he and his demons will be thrown into hell. The bottomless pit. The lake of fire burning with sulphur, were they will be tormented day and night forever and ever."

-Excerpts form The Book Of Revelation

Authors Note: As I did my final read through of <u>Return ToForever</u>, I felt compelled to give you an extra dose of M.S.Peck's Master piece <u>People Of The Lie</u>. Dr. Peck attended actual exorcisms and discovered that Satan truly does exist. However, these writings are just the tip of the ice berg. I strongly encourage you read this book.

<u>SATAN IS A REALITY</u>

"Before witnessing my first exorcism I read Malachi Martin's book <u>Hostage To The Devil</u>. I had always believed that there was some relationship between Satanic activity and human behavior. I was intrigued, but hardly convinced of the devils reality. However, it was another matter after I had personally met Satan face-to-face. An expression appeared on the client's face that could only be described as Satanic. It was an incredibly contemptuous grin of utter hostile malevolence. In another exorcism the person's expression was even more ghastly. He suddenly resembled a writhing snake of great strength, and it was viciously trying to bite us. More frightening than the body was the face. The eyes were hooded in a reptilian torpor, and when it would attack its eyes would open wide with blazing hatred. What upset me the most though, was the extraordinary sense of a fifty-million year old heaviness that filled the room. I felt that I was in the presence of something alien and inhuman. The spirit I witnessed at each exorcism was clearly, utterly, and totally dedicated to opposing human life and growth.

I know no more accurate epithet for Satan than the Father of Lies. Throughout both exorcisms it lied continually. Even when it revealed itself, it did so with half-truths. It was revealed to be the Anti-Christ when it said, "We do not hate Jesus, we just test him." But the reality is that it does hate Jesus."

"The list of lies it spoke was endless-sometimes boring litany. The major ones I remember were: humans must defend themselves in order to survive and cannot rely on anything other than themselves in defense; everything is explainable in terms of negative and positive energy (which balance out to be zero), and there is no mystery in the world; love is a thought and has no objective reality; science is whatever one chooses to call science; death is the absolute end to life-there is no more; Kill yourself, there is no reason to suffer; all humans are motivated primarily by money, and if this appears not to be the case, it is only because they are hypocrites; to compete for money, therefore, is the only intelligent way to live.

"Satan can use any human sin or weakness to attack you-greed and pride, for instance. It will use any available tactic: seduction, cajolery, flattery, & intellectual argument. But its principal weapon is fear. And in the post-exorcism period, after the lies had been exposed, it was reduced to haunting the patients with dully repetitive threats: "We will kill you. We will get you. We will torture you. We will Kill you." Although Satan repeatedly threatened to kill the patients and the exorcists. Its threats were empty. Satan's threats are always empty. They are all lies. The only power that Satan has is through human belief in its lies. He also has no power except in a human body."

Note: <u>Exorcism "The Ritulae Romanum" is neither a religious ceremony nor a sacrament. It is rite in which the priests confront the demon in the afflicted's body and demand that it show itself. Once the demon is revealed, the priests attempt to use their own faith to drive it out of the innocent. An exorcism team consisting of two priests, a medical doctor, and members of the afflicted's family. Through the repetition of a set group of prayers: The Litanies of the Saints, Pater Noster, The 23rd Psalm, the Gloria Patri, Anima Criste, and the Salve Regina. The exorcism is can last days or even weeks. It is a mentally and physically exhausting trial in which they attempt to expel the demon.</u>

My Franciscan friends Brother Gregory & Brother Benedict (St. Anthony of Padua 1967-1970) explained to me that when a priest asks God publicly and with authority, in the name of Jesus Christ, that a person, place, or thing be protected against the power of Satan, and withdrawn from his dominion, this is called an exorcism. Exorcists often have what they call protectors in their chambers such as crucifixes, pictures of the Virgin Mary, St. Michael, Gabriel, and Raphael the Archangels, religious statues of the Madonna, Jesus, saints, former popes, especially John Paul II, Holy water, Holy oil, Rosary Beads that have been blessed, and the signs of the new covenant (Communion: Bread and Wine that have been transformed through the Catholic mass into the Body and Blood of Jesus Christ). The various types of demonic influence and manifestation that catholic priests are often called to remove are the following:

-Infestation: The priest is asked to bless a place, anmimal, or object to remove the evil spirit.
-Vexation: The priest is asked to pray for a person who has suffered from long term bad luck in work, health, love, etc …
-Obsession: The priest is asked pray for the removal of unconrotllable evil thoughts, that are so pervasive, the prevent the person from enjoying life.
-Possession: In these more uncommon forms of demonic manifestations, The priest is asked to perform an exorcism. In these cases Satan actually takes possession of a person, and controls their behavior and personality. The following signs and/or symptoms distinguish possession from other types of demonic influence, mental and physical disorders:

1. The person developes the ability to speak in languages that were previously unknown to them.

2. The are given knowledge about future or past events that the victim did not know prior to the possession.

3. The person develops periods in which they display super human strength.

4. The person goes through periods of blassphemic rage and violence.

5. The person displays violent aversion to priests, holy sacraments, and Christian symbols.

6. The person is deeply melancholy.

7. The person sometimes calls for the Devils help.

8. The person vomits bizarre objects, like knives, pieces of glass, or small relgious objects.

9. Change in vocal patterns: hoarse, young, old, deeply masculine, unearthly screaches.

10. The person swears and uses profanity that is uncharacteristic of their normal way of speaking.

-Willful Subjugation to Satan: In these cases the person actually seeks out the devil or demons. These people mock the traditional Italian masses with what are called "Black Masses". During these masses they perform rituals that are designed to worship Satan, and mock God, Jesus, and all that is holy or sacred. These types of people very rarely seek help from a priest.

Special Note: The tormented soul should prepare for an exorcism by praying, communion, confession, and fasting.

"GESU CRISTO!" (JESUS CHRIST) PRAY FOR US.
"AVE MARIA, FULL OF GRACE. THE HOLY MOTHER OF THE MESSIAH, PRAY FOR US SINNERS NOW AND AT THE HOUR OF OUR DEATH.
ST. MICHAEL THE ARCHANGEL PROTECT US.

PRAYERS OF THE EXORCIST:

-THE OUR FATHER: "Padre nostro, che sei nei cieli, sia santificato il tuo nome. (Our father, who art in Heaven, hallowed be thy name ...) Our father, who art in Heaven, Holy is your name. May your kingdom come soon. May your will be done on earth as it is in Heaven. Please

give us this day all that we will need for the day, and help us to be generous with what though hast given. Forgive us our trespasses as we forgive
those who trespass against us, and our debts as we forgive those endebted
to us. Lead us not into temptation, but deliver us from the evil one.
Expose the devil and his demons to us so that we may turn against them
always. For thine is the is the kingdom, and the power, and the glory for
ever and ever. Amen.

-THE HAIL MARY: "Hail Mary, full of grace. The Lord is with thee.
Blessed are you among women, and blessed is the fruit of thy womb
Jesus. Holy Mary, Mother of the Messiah pray for us sinners now and at
the hour of our death. Amen.

-St. Michael the Archangel, defend us in battle, be our protector against
the wickedness and snares of Satan; may God rebuke him, we humbly
pray; and do thou, O Prince of the heavenly host, by the power of God,
thrust into hell Satan and all the evil spirits who wander through the
world for the ruination of souls. Amen.

"The prayers of each exorcism are for God and Christ to come to the rescue, and each time I had a sense that God did just that. *A confirmed atheist who took part in the exorcisms had found there was much about them
that he could not explain.* For me, however, the power of God on these
occasions was palpable. In the end it is God who does the exorcising!"
                                              -Dr. M.Scott Peck

Authors Note: I feel compelled to share some research I did on the movie
The Exorcism of Emily Rose. This movie is based on a true story! Further
more I believe that this child died so that Satan could be exposed to millions of viewers. I think she will one day be recognized as a martyr and
a saint. Her story is further proof that Satan is a real being. I also added
some additional writings about the anti-christ and the end of times that
I thought you would find interesting.

FURTHER PROOF!
The Exorcism of Emily Rose

The Exorcism of Emily Rose (Co written by Paul Harris Boardam and director Scott Derrickson): is a movie based on the REAL-STORY of a Bavarian girl named Anneliese Michel, who was born in the early 1950's. She was a German college student and a devout catholic who died during an exorcism in 1976. Doctors speculated that her seizures and demonic visions were caused by epilepsy. Her family and their bishop believed that it was demon possession, and follow up interviews confirmed that all of the people who witnessed the events surrounding Anneliesse's exorcism had know doubt that she was possessed by demons. However, the German officials responded by prosecuting the parents and the priest for criminal negligent homicide. Although they were all found guilty, they were all given suspended sentences!

At the age of 16 she began seeing what she described as demons, violent terrible creatures that would haunt her day and night. Indeed she displayed all of the signs of possession: Abnormal strength, paranormal powers such as levitation or telekinesis, and the knowledge of a language they've never studied. Anneliese displayed all of the symptoms. She was eventually diagnosed with Epilepsy. However, the demonic attacks only grew worse. The demons began giving her orders. They told her to beat and insult people. They would not allow her to eat normal food. She would often eat bugs and spiders. She would drink her own urine. She would sleep on the floor and slip into fits of rage and screaming in which she would break religious artifacts such as family crucifixes and rosaries. She would often mutilate herself. She would tear off her clothes and urinate on the floor. In 1974 the family contacted Pastor Ernst Alt to examine the child, and came to the conclusion that Anneliese was truly possessed and in danger from these demons. Even Scott Derrickson (co-writer & director) said that the research phase of this story was one of the most horrible things he has ever experienced. The evidence he collected troubled his mind and his heart, and he would never do it again. The factual evidence that he discovered during the course of his investigation made him realize that this story would be more for education & illumination, and not merely entertainment.

During the final exorcism Anneliesse refused to eat for several weeks. Though she grew emaciated she still exhibited unbelievable strength. She would spit at, curse, and bite those around her. She would often have to be held down by 3 full size men! She would speak in the voices of the native tongues of the demons who claimed to inhabit her body including: Judas Iscariot, Cain, Hitler, a disgraced priest from the 16th century, a host of damned souls (Legion), and even Lucifer himself. Anneliesse said that the Virgin Mary, appeared to her and told her that she could come to Heaven immediately and end her suffering, or she can stay and be used to turn people to Mary and to God. As she says in a note to her exorcists "People think that God is dead. But how can they believe that if I show them the Devil?!" I am certain that this poor child is a martyr who suffered so that the world could entertain the possibility of Satan. She saw and experienced the reality of Satan and his demons, and she suffered and died so that we might believe. Let not her death be in vain.

"Beg for absolution."
-St. Anneliesse's last words

"PEOPLE THINK THAT GOD IS DEAD. HOW CAN THEY BELIEVE THAT IF I SHOW THEM THE DEVIL?!"
-Anneliese Michel/Paul Harris/Scott Derrickson

Author's Note: Theologians and historians have tried for years to solve the 666 riddle. There are many different theories and formulas that have pointed to such figures as Hitler, Nero, Stalin, and many more. One need only examine their lives to see that these people were extremely evil souls. However, the Antichrist will not come at you as he really is. He will probably be a handsome, well spoken person, who promotes world peace, global environmental issues, starvation, and the equal rights of all people. However, this is nothing more than a set up, by the worlds greatest conman. We must all keep our eyes and ears open. If a leader comes along with these traits, examine all of his deeds over an extended period of time. The tree will be known by its fruit. You will never see a truly compassionate person be unmerciful. Just as you will never see a man of peace instigate war after war. Therefore remain ever vigilant, and you won't need a formula to find the antichrist. The subtle yet persistent contradictions of his character over time will ultimately expose the evil within.

666 THE MARK OF THE BEAST

Here is wisdom. Let those who have understanding count the number of the beast: for it is the number of a man; and his number is Six hundred threescore and six (666). And he will causeth that everyone, both small and great, rich and poor, free and slave, to receive a mark in their right hand, or in their foreheads: And no one will be able to buy or sell unless they have the mark, or the name of the beast, or the number of his name.

-The Book of Revelation: 13:16-18

Antichrist Anagram Code?

A=100	J=109	S=118	H=117
B=101	K=110	T=119	I=108
C=102	L=111	U=120	T=119
D=103	M=112	V=121	L=111
E=104	N=113	W=122	E=105
F=105	O=114	X=123	R=117
G=106	P=115	Y=124	666 (THREESCORE AND SIX)
H=107	Q=116	Z=125	
I=108	R=117		

*Note: Some manuscripts read 616.

Obviously Hitler is dead, but it is interesting that his name can be converted into the number of the beast. No human to ever exist was more demonic than Hitler. However, since Hitler appears to be a precursor to the antichrist, let us assume that these letters (IHRTLE) may be an anagram. Rearrange the letters to form a new name I.e.: Relith, Lehtir,

Helrit, Thelir, etc … I think it is important to try and solve this evil riddle, but you must exercise caution in doing so.

I believe that the antichrist may have been born on June 6, 2006 at 3:05 A.M. (The opposite time of when Jesus was Crucified). However, there is no way to be sure. We must also consider that the numeric value could be based on letters as they occur in another language such as Greek or Hebrew. Just be ever watchful, and remember that "The tree is known by its fruit."

Author's Note: In the 1997 Movie THE DEVIL'S ADVOCATE starring Al Pacino and Keanue Reeves you get a very accurate description of how I believe satan functions in the modern world.

THE DEVILS ADVOCATE 1997
(How Satan views modern humans)

How Satan & the anti-christ look at Humans: Satan smugly: "These people … it's no mystery where they come from. You sharpen the human appetite … to the point where it can split atoms with its desire. You build egos the size of cathedrals. Fiber-optically connect the world to every eager impulse. Grease even the dullest dreams with these dollar-green … gold-plated fantasies until every human becomes an aspiring emperor … becomes his own god. Where can you go from there? As we're scrambling … from one deal to the next … who's got his eye on the planet? As the air thickens, the water sours … even the bees' honey takes on the metallic taste of radioactivity … and it just keeps coming, faster and faster. There's no chance to think, to prepare. It's buy futures, sell futures … when there is no future. We got a runaway train … You're all alone, baby. You're God's special little creature. Maybe it's true. Maybe God threw the dice once too often. Maybe He let us all down."

-John Milton/Satan (The Devils Advocate) JONATHAN LEMKIN & WGA, NOVEL: ANDEREW NEIDERMAN

"Underneath the rumbling yellow stone … lies a hidden piece of Satan's thrown. A molten sea not yet full grown. Will show its might at an hour

unknown, and destroy the final Babylon.... Beware the sunrise! And
those who talk with fluttering eyes."
-Mark Salvatore Pitifer

THE SIGNS OF THE END TIMES

1. Anarchy-War & Terrorism will be wide spread all over the world.

2. Prices will be inflated to the point where a loaf of bread will cost
    $20.00. Flour & Barley will be expensive commodities. Wine & olive
    oil will be hard to find, and bottled water will cost more than milk!

3. ¼ of the earth will be killed by war, disease, and wild animals.

4. There will be a terrible earth quake, which will be so devastating that
    it will blot out the sun's light. Every mountain and island will shake
    and shift. The moon will turn blood-red. The stars will appear to be
    falling to the earth.

5. Hail and fire mixed with blood will fall from Heaven, and it will burn
    1/3 of all of the trees, and grass.

6. Terrible volcano's will erupt that will cause burning mountains to fall
    into the sea. The ocean will turn the color of blood. 1/3 of all of the
    ships will be destroyed, and 1/3 of all the fish will die.

7. An asteroid will fall upon the rivers and streams, and will poison 1/3
    of all the fresh water of the world. The asteroids name will be called
    wormwood or bitterness.

8. Terrible locusts will be released from the bottomless pit. The will have
    what looks like golden crowns on their heads. Their faces will look
    human. The will have long hair, and the teeth of lions. They will have
    what appear to be iron breast plates, their wings will make a roaring
    sound, and they will be given the power to sting like scorpions.

9. A general leading a 200 million man army will kill 1/3 of all mankind. (China has a 200 million man army!)

10. People will be perplexed by the rising tides, strange weather patterns, and fierce storms.

11. The final prophets will come to the holy city and preach for 1,260 days (3 ½ years). They will have the power to stop the rain, and send forth terrible plagues. In time they will be killed in the spot which Jesus was crucified, and the world will rejoice. But they will rise again 3 ½ days later.

12. The United States of America (The first world Empire founded upon the JudeoChristian Doctrine) will remove God and any reference to him from their government, their classrooms, their money, and their public pledges & creeds. The will also ban religious music, books, and holidays.

"Satans in the classroom moving seat to seat. His words are a distraction. His evils so discrete. He stalks you through the hallways. Yes even in your home. He's crumbled every empire from Babylon to Rome.... We won't fall!"

-MARK SALVATORE PITIFER "AGC-WE WON'T FALL"

"Stop crying, for look! The Lion of the tribe of Judah, the Root of David, has conquered, and I have proven myself worthy. Now to everyone who keeps doing things that please our God-I will give power over the nations. Every one who is victorious shall eat of the hidden manna, the secret nourishment from Heaven; I will give each of you a white stone, and on this stone will be engraved a new name that no one else knows except the one receiving it. I will not erase your name from the book of life, but I will announce before my Father and his Angels the you are mine. See I am coming soon, and my reward is with me, to repay everyone according to the deeds he has done. I am the A and the Z, the Beginning and the

End, The first and the Last. I am both David's root and his Descendant. I am the bright Morning Star. Blessed forever are all who are washing their robes, to have the right to enter through the gates of the city, and to eat the fruit from the tree of Life."
-Excerpts form The Book Of Revelation

"The power of Satan is, nonetheless, not infinite. He is only a creature, powerful from the fact that he is pure spirit, but still a creature. He cannot prevent the building up of God's reign. Although Satan may act in the world out of hatred for God, and his kingdom in Jesus Christ, and although his action may cause grave injuries, of a spiritual nature and, indirectly, even of a physical nature, to each man and to society, the action is permitted by divine providence which with strength and gentleness guides human cosmic history. It is a great mystery that providence that providence should permit diabolical activity, but "We know that in everything God works for good with those who love him"—(Tracy Wilkinson & Romans 8:28)

"The Battle against the devil…. is still being fought today, because the devil is still alive and active in the world. The evil that surrounds us today, the disorders that plague our society, man's in consistency and brokenness, are not only the results of original sin, but also the result of Satan's pervasive and dark action."—Pope John Paul II

"Awaken! We stand at the threshold of the Great Games final Quarter! All those who remain faithful until the end will be victorious!"
—Nino Jones

THE HEAVEN APPENDIX 777

I watched as thrones were put into place and the Ancient of Days, the Almighty God, sat down to judge. His clothing was as white as snow, his hair like the whitest wool. He sat upon a fiery throne brought in on flaming wheels, and a river of fire flowed from before him. Millions of angels ministered to him and hundreds of millions of people stood before him, waiting to be judged. Then the court began its session and the Books were opened.... Next I saw the arrival of a Man, or he seemed to be, brought there on the clouds of Heaven; he approached the Ancient of Days and was presented to him. He was given the ruling power and glory over all the nations of the world, so that all people of every language must obey him. His power is eternal, it will never end. His government will never fail.

The Prophet Daniel 7:9-14 (550 BC)

And instantly I was in Heaven and saw-oh, the glory of it!-A throne and someone sitting on it! Great bursts of light flashed forth from him as from a glittering diamond, or from a shining ruby, and a rainbow glowing like an emerald encircled his throne. I watched that wondrous city, the holy Jerusalem, descending out of the skies from God. It was filled with the glory of God, and flashed and glowed like a precious gem. The City of Heaven was pure transparent gold, like glass. The wall was jasper, and was built on twelve layers of foundation stones inlaid with gems. The first layer with Jasper; The second with sapphire; The third with chalcedony; The fourth with emerald, The fifth with sardonyx, The sixth with layer with sardus; The seventh with chrysolite; The eighth with beryl; The ninth with topaz; The tenth with chrysoprasel The eleventh with jacinth, and The twelfth with amethyst. The twelve gates were made of pearls-each gate from a single pearl! The streets were made of pure, transparent gold. Its gates never close. A river of pure Water of life flows from the throne of Allah, and the Messiah. It flows down the center of main street. On each side of the river grows the

Trees of Life, which bare new fruit once a month, and whose leaves are
used to heal the nations.
-Excerpts form The Book Of Revelation

Praise the Lord God of Israel, for he has come to visit his children and
has redeemed them. He has sent us a mighty Savior from the royal line
of David, just has he promised through the prophets long ago. He is
merciful to our ancestors and Abraham himself, because he remembered his sacred promise. Heavens dawn is about to break upon us. Our
Messiah will show us how to find salvation through the forgiveness of
sins. He will give light to those who sit in spiritual darkness and deaths
shadow, and guide us to the path of peace. God, with the tender mercy
of a loving parent, has given us a chance to fearlessly serve him, by making us holy and acceptable, ready to stand in his presence forever.

Excerpts form The Book Of Luke 1:68-79 (Zacharias')

THE FIRST AMMENDMENT
CONGRESS SHALL MAKE NO LAW RESPECTING AN
ESTABLISHMENT OF RELIGION, OR PROHIBITING THE
FREE EXERCISE THEREOF; OR ABRIDGING THE FREEDOM
OF SPEECH, OR OF THE PRESS; OR THE RIGHT OF THE
PEOPLE PEACEABLY TO ASSEMBLE, AND TO PETITION THE
GOVERNMENT FOR A REDRESS OF GRIEVANCES.
The Bill of Rights to the U.S. Constitution was ratified on December
15, 1791

Author's Note: The logical simple reason that our countries founding
leaders decided to write the first amendment was to ensure that our government would never have the power to control or influence our religious
beliefs or lack thereof. They would have never wanted the separation of
church and state that the ACLU desires. As you can see in the following
table (A SNAP SHOT OF OUR MODERN WORLD DURING THE
END TIMES) 77 percent of this world's population believes in some
form of God. That percentage is even higher for our country, and yet we

allow the few lead the many. We must stop being afraid to stand up for what we believe in. We must not sit idly by as our beloved United States of America, is stripped of all the religious qualities and traditions that made this the greatest country in the world. We have the power as a people to save our beloved USA from becoming the final Babylon. Awaken, fore these truly are the end times! READ-THINK-VOTE-WRITE & SPEAK OUT! This is our country, and if it falls the fault is ours.

A SNAP SHOT OF OUR MODERN WORLD

If you could fit the entire population of the world into a village consisting of 100 people, maintaining the proportions of all the people living on the Earth, that village would consist of:

57 Asians
21 Europeans
14 Americans
8 Africans
There would be:
52 Women and 48 Men
30 Caucasians and 70 non-caucasians
30 Christians and 70 non-Christians
89 heterosexuals and 11 homosexuals
6 people would possess 59% of the wealth and they would all come from the USA.
80 would live in poverty
70 would be illiterate
50 would suffer from hunger and malnutrition
77 would believe in God & Heaven
1 would be dying
1 would be being born
1 would own a computer
1 would have a university degree

Author's Note: Since the Pledge of Allegiance and the Lord's Prayer are not allowed in most public schools anymore, because the word "God" is mentioned, a 15 year old student from Arizona wrote this new school prayer.

"Now I sit me down in school, where praying is against the rule. For this great nation under God finds mention of him very odd. If scripture now the class recites, it violates the Bill of Rights. And anytime my head I bow, becomes a federal matter now. Our hair can be purple, orange, or green, that's no offense; it's a freedom scene. The law is specific, the law is precise. Prayers spoken aloud are a serious vice. For praying in a public hall might offend someone with no faith at all. In silence alone we must meditate, God's name is prohibited by the state. We're allowed to cuss and dress like freaks, and pierce our noses, tongues, and cheeks. They've outlawed guns, but first the Bible. To quote the good book makes me liable. We can elect a pregnant Senior Queen, and the unwed daddy can be her king. It's inappropriate to teach right from wrong. We're taught that such judgments do not belong. We can get our condoms and birth controls. Study witchcraft, vampires, and totem poles. But the Ten Commandments are not allowed, no words of God must reach this crowd. It's scary here I must confess, when chaos reigns the school's a mess. So, Lord, this silent plea I make: Should I be shot; my soul please take! Amen."
-15 year old student from Arizona

"As the family goes, so goes the nation and so goes the whole world in which we live."
Pope John Paul II

LEIGH ANN PRINCIPIO

"I know I'll always love you, as long as there are stars above you. You
never need to doubt it. I'll make you so sure about it....
God only knows what I'd be without you."

-The Beach Boys

It is only fitting that the last words of this book are dedicated to my loving wife & best Friend Leigh Ann. No words can express how grateful I
am to you. In my eyes you are peerless, and in my heart you are my one
and only true love....

MY ONE IN A MILLION YOU!

Love Always & Forever

Mark

"The kiss is the greatest of all God's inventions."
-M.S.Pitt

PS-And nobdy does it better than you!

NINO'S BOOK LIST

▼

The Living Bible/Complete Catholic Edition, (Tyndale 1978)

THE HOLY QUR'AN/Text, Translation, & Commentary: Abdullah Yusuf Ali (Amana Corp 1409 A.H./1989 A.C.)

The BHAGAVAD GITA by YOGI RAMACHARAKA (The Yogi Publication Society, Chicago, ILL. U.S.A 1907)

Harold S. Kushner, How Good Do We Have To Be (Little, Brown, and Company, 1996)

William Barcaly, The Mind Of Jesus (Harper San Fransisco 1976)

M.Sott Peck, People Of The Lie & The Road Less Travaled (Simon & Schuster Publishing Group, 1997 & 1978)

Thomas Merton, Wisdom Of The Desert (New Directions Publishing Corp. 1972)

Art Bell, & Whitley Strieter, The Coming Global Superstorm (Simon & Schuster Publishing Group, 2000)

Lee Strobel, The Case For Christ (Zondervan, 1998)

Kahill Gibran, The Prophet (Alfred A. Knops Inc. 1976)

Dr. Wayne Dyer, Change Your Thoughts-Change Your Life. (Hay House, 2008)

Joseph F. Grizone, Never Alone (Doubleday & Company Inc. 1995)

Dr. Raymond A. Moody, Life After Life (Harper San Fransisco, 2001)

Maxwell Staniforth/Translator, <u>Marcus Aurelius Meditations,</u> (Barnes & Noble Books, 1996)

Shared Visions In World Religions/Audio Book, (Theosophical Publishinghouse, 1988)

Bill O'Rielly, <u>Who's Looking Out For You,</u> (Broadway Books, 2003)

Anton T. Boisen, <u>The Exploration of The Inner World</u> (Wilett, Clark & Company, 1936)

Russell H. Conwell, <u>Acres of Diamonds,</u> (Jove Inspiration, 1978)

Ken Mc Farland, <u>The Lucifer Files,</u> (Pacific Press Publishing Association 1988)

Dr. Helen Caldicott, <u>Nuclear Madness,</u> (Bantam Books, 1978)

Marion Blumenthal Lazan & Lila Perl, <u>Four Perfect Pebbles,</u> (HaperCollins, New York, N.Y. 1996)

Peter R. Breggin M.D., <u>Toxic Psychiatry,</u> (St. Martins Press, 1936)

Bernard Goldberg, <u>BIAS (Regnery Publishing)</u>

Charles Pellegrino, <u>Return To Sodom and Gomorrah,</u> (Avon Books, 1994)

Viktor E. Frankl, <u>Man's Search For Meaning,</u> (Washington Square Press, 1961)

J.B. Phillips, <u>Your God Is Too Small,</u> (The Macmillan Company, 1955)

Elisabeth Kubler-Ross, <u>On Life After Death,</u> (Celestial Arts PO Box 7123, Berkeley, California, 1991)

Bill Bryson, <u>A Short History of Nearly Everything</u>, (Random House 2003)

Deepak Chopra, <u>Life After Death</u>, (Crown Publishing Group 2006)

Tracy Wilkinson, The Vatican's Exorcists: Driving out the Devil in the 21st Century, (Warner Books, 2007)

Louie Quethera, <u>The Duplicity Factor: An American Story</u>, (Heaventown RTF/AGC Publishing Inc., Geneva, New York 2007)

Printed in the United States
130901LV00003B/1-42/P